MEMORY

By K. J. Parker

MEMORY

The Scavenger Trilogy
Book Three

K. J. PARKER

www.orbitbooks.co.uk

An *Orbit* Book

First published in Great Britain by Orbit 2003

Copyright © 2003 by K. J. Parker

The moral right of the author has been asserted.

A CIP catalogue record for this book
is available from the British Library.

ISBN 1 84149 171 3

Typeset in Horley
by Palimpsest Book Production Limited,
Polmont, Stirlingshire
Printed and bound in Great Britain
by Clays Ltd, St Ives plc

Orbit
An imprint of
Time Warner Books UK
Brettenham House
Lancaster Place
London WC2E 7EN

Chapter One

Precepts of religion. Every victory is a defeat. Every cut made is a wound received. Every strength is a weakness. Every time you kill, you die.

In which case, he thought, clawing briars away from in front of his face as he ran, the enemy must be taking a right pounding, the poor buggers. A dry branch snapped under his foot, startling him and throwing him off balance for a split second. Slow down, he urged himself; haste breeds delay. Another of those wonderful precepts.

Behind him, he could hear them, a confused noise, like a huge blind animal crashing through the brittle dead trees. Not a good place for a battle; not a good place for anything much, but certainly not for a battle, where you need to be able to see what's happening. Only the idiot son of a congenital idiot would pick a fight in a wood – can't see, can't move, can't hold the line, can't communicate, can't swing, can't do any bloody thing. Slow *down*, before you fall over and do yourself an injury.

Precepts of religion, he thought. Every strength is a weakness; well, quite, and by the same token every bloody stupid idea is a stroke of genius. Such as attacking a larger, better armed, better led enemy in the heart of a dark, boggy, overgrown forest – dumbest idea in the history of mankind; stroke of genius.

Twenty-five yards; that far he could see, at best, and no further (all these goddamned *trees* in the way), so he didn't have a clue what was going on, other than that he and what was left of his command were doing their best to run away from the enemy, last seen over there somewhere, unless (as he secretly suspected) they'd mislaid their sense of direction along with their courage and their brains, and were going round in circles – in which case, any moment now, they were due to crash into the back end of the enemy line. Fat lot of good it'd do them, heavy infantry in dense scrub. The finest spearmen in the Empire, trained to the utmost pitch of perfection to fight shoulder to shoulder (each man sheltered by his neighbour's shield, each man's shield sheltering his neighbour; what more perfect metaphor could there be?) – only that was precisely what they couldn't do, not with all this fucking lumber in the way. So instead they were puffing and stumbling from briar-tangle to sog-pit, either chasing or being chased, and a thousand years hence historians would pinpoint this moment as the decisive battle that changed the world for ever, and it'd *all be his fault*—

He saw them in the shadows, the debatable shades of grey between the black and green stripes, and for an agonised moment he couldn't make up his mind: our men or theirs? Then a little logical voice chimed in somewhere at the back of his mind: axes, they've got axes, none of our lot have got axes, they've got to be the enemy. He swung round, to see how many of his men were still at least vaguely with him, then wheeled back, waved with his sword and yelled, '*Charge!*' Probably not a good thing to do, since they were already running as fast as they could go (under the misapprehension that they were running away; easy mistake to make); but they were broad-minded, they forgave him and carried on running, and a few seconds later he could hear shouts and the clatter of ironmongery as battle was joined. Great, he thought, I love it when things work out; and then he noticed that he was right up where the fighting was, and the man in front of him wasn't on his side. The last thought that crossed his mind before he diverted all his attention to not being killed was, *Hang on, though, what about the Seventh Light Infantry? They're on our side and they've got axes.* Every careless mistake is in fact the right answer. Precepts of fucking religion.

The man in front of him was just a man. A big, long, skinny bastard with a turkey neck, huge nose and knuckles, slashing at his head double-handed with an axe; he sidestepped, only to find there was a tree standing where a lifetime of diligent study and training dictated he ought to be, and he couldn't go there. So he ducked behind the tree instead. It did just as well as the low backhand parry in the fourth degree; in fact considerably better, since the skinny bastard's axe lodged itself in the soft, rotten wood and stayed there, defying the skinny bastard's best efforts to get it free. Nothing simpler, meanwhile, than to nip out round the other side of the tree and stick him under the armpit – not a true lunge from the middle ward, nothing like it at all, but it got the job done, and the poor dead bastard slid obligingly off the sword blade and flopped in a heap on the soft ground.

If that was supposed to prove a point or something, he thought, I'm far from convinced. He looked round, both ways and then behind, but for the moment at least he was mercifully alone. Remarkably so, in fact. Last time he'd looked there had been people everywhere, but now there wasn't a living soul (important distinction) to be seen. The battle, presumably, had got tired of waiting for him and gone on without him. Annoying, to say the least, since he had no way of knowing whether it was a winning battle going away in front of him, or a losing one that had swept past him while his attention was engaged elsewhere. I hate forests, he thought.

Precepts of religion, he muttered to himself; but just for once, there wasn't one that seemed even remotely relevant, so he pressed on forward to see what would happen. Silly, to be chasing after the war – *his* war – panting and yelling 'Wait for me!' like a fat man after the carrier's cart. Luckily, it hadn't got far. The battle was still there, just over a little stony hump and through a clump of holly bushes; it had contrived to get itself caught up in a tangle of brambles, like an old unshorn ewe.

Which wasn't how the historians would describe it, a thousand years hence. They would feel obliged to mention the wide, black, boggy rhine lurking under the mess of waist-high brambles (like it was somehow intentional, a clever idea on somebody's part) into which the enemy, retreating, had obligingly stumbled and got hopelessly stuck. And there they were, poor unfortunate bastards, mired in the smelly, wet black shit up to their thighs; it'd take a lot of clever men a long time and probably a couple of miles of rope to get them out of there, but that wasn't the job that needed doing. If only. But no, instead of that comparatively simple task, he had to do something really clever. He had to kill them.

By some miracle, his men hadn't charged down on them screaming battle-cries and got hopelessly stuck as well. They'd held back on the top of the rise – not common sense, he'd never accuse them of that, it was probably just that they were too pernickety to push through the briars and risk a scratch or two – and were waiting for someone to tell them what to do. Someone; anyone; him.

On the other side of the rhine (it was an old drain, he

observed; dug a hundred years ago in a vain attempt to draw off the surface water from the hillside, but all it had done was silt up and make things infinitely worse) he could see a dozen or so of the enemy, also standing about listlessly, also trying to figure out what they were supposed to be doing. Best guess was, they'd somehow managed to scramble through the mud, maybe treading on their comrades' shoulders to get across, and now they were thinking that maybe it was their duty to go back and try and help get them out, except that then they'd get stuck too, and *everybody* would end up dead. Safe to ignore them, he thought, they'll get scared and bugger off as soon as I've thought up a way of slaughtering their friends. Meanwhile the main part of the enemy forces (as the historians will describe them) were still floundering in the stinking mud, every frantic effort to get loose pulling them in deeper.

It crossed his mind that if only he waited a little longer, they'd all go in over their heads and be swallowed up, and he wouldn't have to do anything at all. But apparently not; the slough was waist-deep but no more, and there they all were, hundreds of them, enemy soldiers from the waist up, conscientiously clutching their axes and spears and halberds as though there was still a battle, as opposed to a horrendous disaster resulting from a confluence of bad luck and stupidity. Problem, he thought. Going in after them was clearly out of the question. Standing here watching wasn't going to help, either. The obvious thing would be to call up three companies of archers and shoot the bastards down where they stood, but he didn't have any archers with him, only the finest spearmen in the Empire.

Then he started to grin. Precepts of religion, he thought: the best course of action is no action. They weren't going anywhere in a hurry. There was, of course, the problem of the others, the dozen or so on the other side, but he couldn't help that. If he was lucky, really lucky, the poor fools would go down into the bog to try and fish out their mates, and get stuck too. There was, after all, nothing they could do without rope (which they hadn't got), or at least if there was, then the finest military mind in the Empire was buggered if he could figure out what it was. At least some of them would try it, however; and eventually there would come a point when there weren't enough of them left unmired to get out those who were helplessly stuck, and then it'd all be over.

He frowned, doing mental arithmetic. Suppose the survivors went for help; nearest place would be the village on the far western edge of the forest, and the very earliest they could get there and get back (assuming the villagers downed tools, left their dinners on the table and ran straight out to help as soon as they arrived) was five days, more likely six. But it wasn't as straightforward as that; in order to do any good they'd need to bring tools and ropes and poles and planks, that'd mean carts or packhorses at the very least. Six days or more likely seven.

Fine, thought Feron Amathy. No further action required. Time to go home.

'Battle Slough, it's called,' said the old man, 'on account of there was a battle here once.'

Poldarn nodded. The logic was impeccable.

'Hell of a battle too, it was,' the old man said. 'One lot, they chased the other lot into the slough, they got stuck – midwinter it was, slough's mortal sticky in winter, and that's nowadays, with all the drains they dug over Winterhay taking off the worse of it – and the first lot, they just walked away and left 'em there. You can still find bones, if you look.'

Poldarn looked at him. 'What happened?' he said.

The old man shrugged. 'Oh, they all died,' he said. 'Stuck in the mud, couldn't get out. Nothing their mates could do for 'em. Oh, they went for help, but by the time they came back, they'd all died. Just stood there – well, not standing, they were all slumped over like stooks of reed, strangest thing you ever saw in your life. Makes you wonder, though, what it must've been like.'

Poldarn decided he'd like to change the subject. 'It's mostly oak here, then.'

The old man nodded. 'Some oak,' he said, 'some chestnut, but mostly oak. Damn good charcoal wood, oak. There's some as prefers beech, but it's too hot for our line of work. Oak holds the fire longer, see.'

'Seems a waste, though,' Poldarn said, without thinking. Back home (of course, he'd never once thought of it as that while he'd been there) he'd seen maybe half a dozen oak trees, no more; and even the spruces and firs were precious, as he'd found out to his cost. Curious; he'd had to leave the islands because he'd accidentally burned down a small stand of immature firs, and now here he was on his way to a charcoal camp, where on average they burned a dozen fully grown oaks a day.

The old man was looking at him. 'Why?' he asked.

'Oh, nothing,' Poldarn answered awkwardly. 'But aren't you worried you'll run out, the rate you're felling at?'

This time the old man stared at him for a moment before laughing. 'I keep forgetting,' he said, 'you're not from round here. Odd, though, you sound like you're a local boy. Leastways, most of the time you do – and I can tell an off-comer soon as he opens his mouth,' he added, with pride. Poldarn had worked out that 'offcomer' (which was probably the most offensive term in the old man's vocabulary) meant someone born out of earshot of where they were standing. 'Plenty more where these came from,' the old man went on, 'plenty more. I been felling in these woods since I was a kid, and we ain't hardly started yet.'

He made it sound like he was a man with a mission, to

rid the world of the lurking threat of deciduous timber once and for all. Good luck to him, Poldarn thought, though he couldn't really bring himself to share the old fool's passion. Chopping down very big trees was too much like hard work, in his opinion. 'Well, that's all right, then,' he said. 'Is it much further? Only—'

'Nearly there,' said the old man. 'Just up over the steep and down along through.'

Poldarn nodded, wishing he hadn't asked; the old man had given him exactly the same answer a good hour ago, and his left heel was beginning to blister. 'Are there many of you up at the camp?' he asked, by way of making conversation.

'Dozen,' the old man said vaguely, 'couple of dozen. Folks come and go, see. Some of 'em stay a couple weeks or a month, some of 'em's been there twenty years, and nothing to say they won't be up and gone come the morning. Always work in the burning for them as wants it, but some folks can't settle to it, and then they move on.' The old man shook his head sadly, as if to say that humankind was a sadly unsatisfactory breed. That at least was something Poldarn could agree with, though he'd probably arrived at that conclusion by a different route.

No way in a forest of knowing how long they stumbled on for; no way of seeing the sun, to gauge the passage of time. It felt like hours and hours and hours, probably because they were mostly going uphill, and where it wasn't boggy and wet, the way ahead was blocked with curtains of brambles and low branches. Poldarn had already learned to walk bent over like an elderly cripple, his left hand pushed out in front to ward off flailing twigs and briars. He had, of course, not the faintest idea of where he was or which direction he'd come from. If there was a path, he couldn't see it, and all the trees looked identical.

Then, without warning, he shouldered through a screen

of holly leaves and found himself on top of a steep rise, looking down into a clearing. For maybe five hundred yards in front, there were no trees, only stumps. In roughly the middle of the cleared space stood four huge round domes. How they'd been made and what they'd been made from he couldn't tell at this distance; in fact, they hardly looked artificial at all, and if the old man had told him they were some kind of massive woodland fungus he'd probably have believed him.

'Here we are,' the old man said.

As they climbed down the slope, Poldarn got a better look at the domes; in particular, the furthest dome away on his left, which was only half-built. Fifteen yards across and five yards high; inside, it was composed of stacks of neatly split logs about four feet long, stood on end like books on a shelf; these, the old man told him, were the shanklings, whatever that signified. Covering the wood was a six-inch layer of bracken, straw and dry leaves, which in turn was covered with a skin of fine soil. ('We call that the sammel', the old man told Poldarn, who nodded seriously, as though he could care less.) Here and there, men were fooling about with rakes, hooks and odd-looking arched ladders. They were moving slowly, as though they'd been doing this job for a hundred years and had another hundred still to go.

'Got to be careful, see,' the old man was saying. 'Hearth's got to be dead flat, and you've got to be careful there's no stones or anything. Leave a stone and like as not it'll shatter in the burn and poke a bloody hole out the sammel, and then you'd be buggered.'

Poldarn learned a great deal more about the art and science of burning charcoal before they reached the bottom of the slope. He learned that the slabs of turf that the slow little men were fitting carefully round the apex of the dome made up the cope; that the thick log stuck in the very centre was called the mote peg; that the gap between the bottom skirt of the sammel and the ground was the flipe. He heard about how the rate at which the fire burned was governed by the amount of air it drew in through the flipe, and how the burn was controlled by packing sand round the base, and how the sand had to be dug out and moved each time the wind changed direction, to make sure the burn was even all the way through. There was something about the old man's voice, probably its pitch, that made it impossible to ignore, no matter how hard Poldarn tried.

'To start the burn off,' the old fool was saying, 'you pull out the mote peg and drop in a bucket of hot coals, then fill up flush with clean charcoal – lumps, mind, not fines or dust; then you cap off with fresh turf and there you go. To start with you get a lot of white smoke and steam, that's the roast drawing the wet out, see. Then it goes blue, and you know it's time to shut down the burn. That's when it gets tricky, mind.'

'I see,' Poldarn lied. 'It's obviously a very skilled trade. I never knew there was so much to it.'

The old man grinned. 'Oh, that's not the half of it,' he said. Poldarn was sure he was right, at that; fortunately, before the old man could educate him further, Poldarn caught sight of a familiar face – Basano, the man they'd done the deal with, back in the relative sophistication of the stable yard of the Virtue Triumphant in Scieza.

He waved hard, and Basano waved back, slowly. Poldarn frowned. Back in Scieza, Basano had come across as almost normal, apart from the length of his beard and the powerful stench of smoke that clung to everything he wore. At any rate, Poldarn hadn't noticed any particular sloth about the way the man moved. Here in the woods, though, he seemed to have slowed down like everyone else; he was trudging up the rise to meet them as though he was one of the unfortunate soldiers trapped in the mud of Battle

Slough, all those years ago. Maybe it was something to do with prolonged exposure to extreme heat roasting the nerve endings; or perhaps it was what happened to you if you breathed in too much smoke.

'You got here all right, then,' Basano said. Poldarn nodded, figuring a little white lie was permissible in the circumstances. 'Olvo's been looking after you, I hope.'

'Oh yes,' Poldarn said, with a nice smile. 'He's been telling me all about how you do things.'

'Splendid,' Basano replied. 'Actually, you couldn't have come at a better time. We'll be lighting up number four later on this evening, so you'll be able to watch.'

'Wonderful,' Poldarn muttered. 'I'll look forward to that.'

After the lighting ceremony, which turned out to be almost exactly the way Poldarn had imagined it would be, the small crowd of charcoal burners ('only be sure to call them colliers,' Basano told him in a loud whisper, 'it's very important to get it right') quickly thinned out and drifted away, leaving Poldarn and Basano alone in front of the newly lit dome, which was gushing out fat plumes of white smoke from top and sides. The colliers mostly lived in tiny low hutches the size of an army tent, built of slabs of turf laid on rickety frames of green sticks. As burn-master, however, Basano enjoyed the privilege of sleeping in the watchman's lodge, which proved to be a slightly bigger version of the same thing. Once Poldarn had got used to the thin light of the single oil lamp, and the rather unnerving sight of wriggling worms poking out through the ceiling, he found it wasn't too bad, if you didn't mind damp and smoke.

'Hungry?' Basano asked; and before Poldarn could answer, he'd pulled the lid off a large stone crock and fished out an elderly loaf and a slab of pale, glazed-looking cheese.

'There's beer in the jug,' he added, pointing at what Poldarn had taken to be the jerry. The taste of its contents didn't do much to persuade him that he hadn't been right all along. 'We're a bit rough and ready,' Basano added, as Poldarn's teeth grated on the crust of the cheese, 'but we do all right for ourselves.'

'So I see,' Poldarn said, spitting out a small piece of grit, or tooth enamel. 'How's business?'

'Bloody wonderful,' Basano replied. 'Can't make enough of the stuff. They're desperate for it in the towns, like it's gold dust or something.'

'That's good,' Poldarn said. 'But you reckon you can guarantee us a regular supply?'

'Oh, that won't be a problem,' Basano said decisively. 'You just tell me how much you people need, and we'll see you get it.'

'Fine,' Poldarn said. Something dropped from the turf roof onto his head and squirmed. 'And there won't be any difficulty about the grade? The sort of work we're doing, we have to be sure the fuel's consistent to get exactly the right temperature. If it burns too hot or too cool, it can screw a job up completely. You get cracked moulds, cold shuts, air bubbles—'

Basano shook his head. 'Don't worry about it,' he said. 'I'll pick your supplies out myself. First-grade lump, from the top centre of the stack, where it gets raked off first. That way there's no danger of it getting overcooked, or coming up brown in the middle. You can bet your life on that.'

Poldarn wasn't sure he was prepared to go that far; but Basano seemed confident enough, and in spite of the old man's intensive coaching Poldarn didn't know enough about the trade to contradict him. 'In that case,' he said, 'that ought to suit us just fine.'

Basano nodded and poured out more beer; and that, apparently, was all there was to it. So simple; a pity, Poldarn couldn't help thinking, it couldn't all have been settled back at the Virtue Triumphant, where the beds were dry and you couldn't stand a spoon upright in the beer. On the other hand, if he'd done the deal in Scieza, he'd have missed a two-day trudge through the woods and all that fascinating stuff about mote-pegs and flipes. He drank some of the beer. It tasted disgusting. He drank a little more, nevertheless.

'Nice drop of beer, though I say it myself,' Basano said. 'It's a traditional colliers' recipe,' he added, with more than a hint of pride. 'Bracken instead of hops, gives it that sort of nutty tang.'

For a moment, Poldarn hoped he was kidding. 'Distinctive,' he said. 'So, you do your own brewing here?'

'And baking,' Basano replied. (Well, that accounted for the bread.) 'Not that we can't afford stuff from town; like I told you, business is damn good. But it helps pass the time, you know?'

'I'm sure,' Poldarn replied.

Basano drained his cup and poured out some more. 'Essential supplies,' he said. 'Dry work, see, and then there's all the sitting around. Got to stay close to the fire all the time, see, keep an eye on it in case the wind changes. A good burn'll take you, what, sixteen, seventeen days till the core's cooled down and you can rake out. Doesn't seem nearly so long if you've got a drop to drink.'

Poldarn smiled thinly. 'I'll bet,' he said.

'Mind you.' Basano pulled a face, then blew his nose loudly into the palm of his hand. 'There's some up north as prefers cider. Well, they burn a lot of fruitwood, and apple's as good as any,' he added, with the air of someone making a flimsy excuse for an unspeakable perversion. 'You like cider?'

'No.'

'Nor me.' Basano belched suddenly. 'Gives me wind, cider. Want some more cheese?'

'No, thanks. I'm fine.'

'Have some more beer.'

'Thanks.'

Basano passed the jug, and Poldarn filled his cup. It was still horrible, but there were worse things in life than the taste of dead yeast and stale eggs. 'So,' Basano went on, 'you been in the foundry business long?'

Poldarn thought for a moment. Absolutely no reason why he should share his life story with a stranger; lots of excellent reasons why he shouldn't. Nevertheless. 'Just over two years,' he said. 'Really?' Basano squinted at him, as if the hut was full of smoke. 'No offence, but you're a bit old to go taking up a new trade.'

'Long story.'

Basano grinned. 'Best kind, hanging round a charcoal camp.'

'I guess so,' Poldarn said.

Short pause. 'So,' Basano said, 'you from round here?'

Poldarn shook his head. 'I don't think so.'

'You aren't sure?'

'That's right.' Poldarn could feel cramp coming on in his left leg. He tried to stretch out, but there wasn't room. 'Truth is,' he said, 'I don't really know much about myself.'

Basano looked at him.

'Really,' Poldarn felt compelled to add. 'Actually, the first thing I can remember, apart from a few little scrappy bits, is waking up lying in the mud beside a river; and that was just under four years ago.'

'Get away.'

'Honestly.' Poldarn swallowed a yawn, and went on: 'I guess I must've had – well, an accident or something, because I woke up and suddenly I realised I couldn't remember anything. Not my name, or where I was from, or what I did for a living, whether I had any family, nothing at all.'

'Fuck,' Basano said, with feeling. 'So how long did that last?'

Poldarn smiled weakly. 'It's still lasting,' he said, tilting the jug over his cup and handing it back. 'To start with, I kept expecting it all to come back to me, but it didn't, or at least it hasn't yet. Anyhow, while I still thought there'd be a chance of remembering, or running into somebody who could tell me who I was, I just sort of wandered about, not settling to anything – well, where'd be the point, if at any moment I'd be going home? But time went on, and nothing came back to me, so I thought, screw this, I'd better get on and make a new life for myself.'

'So you joined up at the foundry?'

Poldarn hesitated. There'd been a lot more to it than that, of course, but he was damned if he was going to tell anybody about it, even if the beer was starting to taste almost palatable. 'That's right,' he said.

Basano's face crumpled into a thoughtful scowl. 'Yes,' he said, 'but surely there's some thing you've been able to figure out. Like, your accent, the way you talk. That ought to place you pretty well. I mean, round here they can tell which village you were born in just from the way you fart.'

'Not in my case,' Poldarn said. 'At least, nobody I've met so far's recognised my accent and said, "Ah, you're from such and such a place." Actually, I don't even know how many languages I can speak. It's half a dozen at least, maybe more.'

'Bloody hell,' Basano said, clearly impressed.

Poldarn shook his head. The hut wobbled a little. 'Oh, it's not like it's anything clever,' he said. 'Don't even know I'm doing it half the time. Sometimes I'll be talking to someone and they'll start looking at me all funny, and it's because I've suddenly switched to a different language without realising it. I just hear my own voice in my head, you see.'

'Oh. And what about when other people talk to you?'

'Same thing. I just hear what they're saying, not the words they use. I think—' He checked himself. He'd been about to say that it could be something to do with his people back home on the islands in the western sea being natural telepaths; but if he said that, Basano would only stare at him even more fiercely, since nobody in the Empire knew that the western islands existed, let alone that their inhabitants were the merciless, invincible raiders who'd burned so many cities and done so much damage over the years. Saying something that'd identify him with them probably wasn't a good idea. 'I think I must be from the capital or something, where there's people from all over the Empire. You'd probably pick up several languages if you lived somewhere like that, maybe even get so used to switching from one to the other without thinking that you wouldn't notice.'

'Or maybe you were in the army,' Basano said. 'Been posted all over the place, learned a bit of this and that every place you've spent time in. I knew a man once, he'd been in the services, and he could do that. Knew twenty-six different words for beer.'

'Useful,' Poldarn said with a grin, whereupon Basano passed the jug. Nothing would ever make him like the stuff, of course, but he was feeling rather dry, he couldn't help noticing. The heat, or something to do with the hut being built of turf. Something like that, anyhow.

'Still,' Basano was saying, 'must be bloody odd. I mean, the thought that once you had a completely different life, and any minute it could all come back, like a roof falling in. I mean, any second now, maybe you're going to turn to me and say, "Bloody hell, I just remembered, I used to be a rich merchant," or "My dad used to run the biggest brewery in Tulice."' He shook his head. 'That'd get to me, the thought that I could be, you know, really stinking rich or a nobleman or something, and yet here you are wasting your life pounding sand in the foundry. All that money just waiting for you to come back home and spend it. Or women, maybe. Or you could be the son and heir of a district magistrate, even.'

Poldarn looked away. 'Sure,' he said. 'Or maybe I was something really horrible, like a day labourer in a tannery. Or an escaped convict, maybe, or like you said, I was in the army and I deserted. That's why I stopped trying to find out, actually, for fear that I wouldn't like what I discovered. Think about it: what if I turned out to be somebody really evil and disgusting, someone that everybody hates?'

Basano thought for a moment. 'Well, if everybody hated you, surely you'd have been recognised before now. And if you were on the run from the gallows or the stone-yards, they'd have been looking for you and someone would've caught you. And if you were like a dangerous nutcase or whatever, sooner or later you'd murder someone or set fire to a temple or whatever it might be, and then you'd know that way. And if you found out you'd only ever been a milkman, or the bloke who cleans the blood off the slaughterhouse floor, well, that'd be all right, you wouldn't have to go back to your rotten old life if you didn't want to, and that way at least you'd know—'

Poldarn pulled a face. Partly it was the foul taste of the beer. 'There's other bad things it could be,' he said. 'Like, suppose I was married and there was trouble at home, something like that. My theory is, you see, that deep down I don't want to remember, which is why my memory hasn't come back long since. I reckon you'd have to be stupid to take a risk like that.'

Basano pursed his lips. 'I guess so,' he said. 'It'd depend on how good life was where I am now. I mean, do you really, really like working in the foundry?'

Poldarn shrugged. 'It's all right, I suppose.'

'You're settled in just the way you like it? Got yourself a really tasty bird, nice house, all that stuff?'

'Well, no.' Poldarn frowned. 'But that sort of thing comes with time. I mean, you find somewhere you want to be and settle down, and happiness just sort of grows on you, like moss on rocks.'

Basano nodded. 'And you don't think any happiness had grown on you before you had your accident and forgot it all? I mean, a man of your age, you'd expect to be settled and doing well. So maybe you were.'

'Like you are, you mean?'

'Oh, I'm not doing so bad,' Basano answered, wriggling sideways as a handful of dirt dropped from the roof onto his head. 'I told you, we're doing a hell of a trade, I'm putting a lot of good money by. Another ten years or so, I'll be able to retire, buy a place, spend the rest of my life playing at being a gentleman.' He grinned. 'I got it all worked out, don't you worry. See, I know where I'm from, so I can make up my mind where it is I want to go. You don't, so you can't. See what I'm getting at?'

'Sort of.'

'Well, there you go.' Basano suddenly froze, and said, 'Shit.'

'What's the matter?'

'Beer jug's empty. Excuse me, I have to go to the out-house and fill it up again.'

That, Poldarn felt, was open to misinterpretation; but when Basano came back and refilled both their cups, the beer tasted no worse than before. 'I was thinking,' Basano said.

'Hm?'

'About what you were saying. You not wanting to know, in case you turned out to be the nastiest man in the world. Well, you can set your mind at rest there.'

'Can I? Oh, good.'

'Sure.' Basano grabbed two handfuls of wood and threw them on the fire. 'It's like this. You go anywhere, ask anybody you like who's the nastiest man in the world, they'll all give you the same answer. Well,' he added, after a pause for thought, 'maybe not, because we've just had the taxes round here, so a lot of folks would say the Emperor. Bastard,' he added, with feeling.

'He's not popular?'

'You can say that again.'

Poldarn nodded. 'I don't even know who the Emperor is,' he confessed.

'Really? Well, we had a change recently, just over a year ago. The old Emperor died. Throat cut. Terrible business, even if he was a complete arsehole.'

'I'm sure. So who's Emperor now?'

Basano yawned. 'A man called Tazencius,' he replied. 'Cousin or second cousin of the last bloke.'

'And he cut the last man's throat, did he?'

Basano shook his head. 'No,' he said. 'In fact, he was hundreds of miles away when it happened. Oh, he was in on the plot all right, he just wasn't around for the actual killing. Anyhow, everybody was mighty pleased when the old bastard got cut up, but by all accounts, this Tazencius is even worse. Well, that goes without saying: taxes up by a fifth. And what's worse, they actually collect them, even out here.'

'That's unusual, is it?'

'Too right. First tax collector some of the younger blokes had ever seen, caused quite a stir. Anyhow, we cracked him over the head and stuck his body in number three, and reckoned that ought to be the end of it.'

'And was it?'

'No way.' Basano pulled a wry face. 'Couple of months later, a whole army shows up. Well, several dozen, anyhow, all in armour and stuff, asking had we seen this man, because he'd gone missing, and he'd been headed out our way. So we said, no, we'd never set eyes on anybody like that; and of course they couldn't prove anything. But they made us hand over the money. Two thousand gross-quarters. Worse than robbery, if you ask me, because with robbers at least you can fight back. But if you scrag two dozen soldiers, all that happens is that next time they send two hundred, and then you're screwed.'

Poldarn dipped his head by way of acknowledgement. 'Well,' he said, 'I'm definitely not the Emperor Tazencius,' he said. No earthly point in mentioning that he had good reason to believe that Tazencius, assuming they were talking about the same man, had at one stage been his father-in-law. 'How about the second nastiest?'

Basano grinned. 'If you ask me, Tazencius is a pussycat compared to five or six other people. No, if you'd asked the question any time when we hadn't just had the taxes, what everybody'd have said was Feron Amathy. General Feron Amathy, he is now, or probably Marshal or Protector, because it's practically a known fact that it was him as had the old Emperor killed. Pretty much running things, especially since he married Tazencius's daughter. Makes him next in line to the throne, see, if anything happens to Tazencius. Which it will,' Basano added, 'or I'm an earwig.'

Poldarn dipped his head again. 'So that's two nasty men I'm definitely not,' he said.

'Three,' Basano said, pouring beer and getting a respectable proportion of it into the cup. 'Third nastiest by anybody's reckoning is this priest bastard, the one who's running around with all the sword-monks and that sort.'

'Sword-monks,' Poldarn repeated. 'Weren't they all killed by the raiders?'

'Most of them,' Basano confirmed. 'But not nearly enough. Actually, that made things a whole lot worse;

because before the raiders burned down the monks' castle, place called Deymeson, the monks mostly stayed home and didn't bother anybody, apart from princes and rich merchants and the like. But now they've got no home, so they're just sort of wandering about the place, stealing and killing anything that moves. And a lot of other scumbags have joined up with them. Supposed to be all about religion – the end of the world is nigh and all that shit – but if you ask me it's just an excuse for riding round the home provinces in this huge caravan of carts and slaughtering people. Anyhow, their boss is some ex-monk who goes by the name of Monach – which is just some foreign word for "monk", so nobody knows what his real name is. Could care less; he's just some evil shit who likes killing people. Wouldn't be you, though, since he only started off doing it a couple of years ago, and only last month he was in Iapetta.'

'I see,' Poldarn said. 'Well, that's a great comfort, I must say.'

'And then there's number four,' Basano continued. 'General Muno Silsny, there's another really unpleasant man for you.' He frowned. 'Not in the same league as Feron Amathy or this Monach character, and of course he's not the Emperor, but you'd have to be a total arsehole to be anything like as nasty as he is. And he only popped up a few years back. Hell of a taleteller, Silsny; that's how he's got on so fast. Came out of nowhere; he started off as nothing but a poxy little captain in some outfit of second-rate horsefuckers, but then there was this battle and he got his leg broke, and he went around telling everybody he was snatched out of the jaws of death by the divine Poldarn himself, no less. For some crazy reason folks believed him, and since then he's every place you look. Fought alongside General Cronan, rest his soul, when he beat the raiders; then he was off fighting the rebels, really making a name for himself. But he must be smart, because he changed sides at just the right time, joined up with the Amathy lot right after he'd kicked shit out of them in some battle, and now he's commander-in-chief of the home provinces, no less. And you can't be him, either.'

Poldarn's smile had glazed over, like a properly fired pot. Muno Silsny was the name of the wounded soldier he'd saved from being murdered by looters after some battle in a river; he'd practically tripped over the man, and for some reason had wasted time and effort getting him back to his camp instead of leaving him to die.

'Number five, now,' Basano was saying. 'Now that's a dead cert, no way you could be the fifth evilest bastard in the Empire, because she's a woman, and you're not.'

Poldarn had an uncomfortable feeling that he knew who Basano was talking about. 'Who's number five?' he asked.

Basano grinned. 'Good question,' he said. 'Nobody knows shit about her. Her regular name's supposed to be something in one of those crackjaw southern languages, Xipho Dornosomething, and what she calls herself is the Holy Mother of Death or some such shit, but everybody knows her as Copis the Whore. On account of she used to be one, so people tell me. Anyway, she's with this Monach character, rattling round with him in the steel-plated carts. Religious nut, apparently; telling everybody she screwed the divine Poldarn and had his kid. I don't understand religion much, but by all accounts this gives her the right to go around burning down villages.' He sighed. 'I liked it better when religion was about not coveting your neighbour's ox, and whether true angels have wings. Anyhow,' Basano said, 'there's five really, really nasty people for you, and you aren't any of them, so what are you worried about?'

The next morning, Poldarn had a headache, probably due to the smoke or the smell of rotten leaf-mould. Basano woke him to say that breakfast was ready, but Poldarn wasn't hungry. 'I think I ought to be getting back,' he said. 'They'll be wanting to know about the charcoal.'

But Basano shook his head. 'Can't spare anybody to go with you, sorry,' he said, 'not with number four starting to burn through, and the wind being about to change any bloody minute. You can head off on your own if you like, but I wouldn't recommend it.'

Poldarn thought about Battle Slough, and decided he didn't like the idea of wandering into it because he'd lost his way in the woods. 'How soon do you think you can spare someone?' he asked.

'Difficult to say,' Basano replied. 'Four should be burnt out to blue in four or five days' time, but by then we'll have fired up two again, unless it rains, in which case we'll need all hands to rake out four before the whole lot spoils; and three'll be ready for sifting and bagging up some time in the next week.'

'Oh,' Poldarn said. 'No offence, but you make it sound like I'm going to be here for the rest of my life.'

Basano frowned at him. 'Don't talk soft,' he said. 'For a start, we'll be sending three wagons down the road before the end of the month. You could hitch a ride with them, then get the post back to Scieza, it's only a couple of days.' He looked up, sniffed, and disappeared back into the lodge, emerging a moment later with a frying pan in his hand. 'Sure you don't want some?' he said. 'Fried oatcakes and wood mushrooms. Speciality of the camp.'

Poldarn was about to ask what wood mushrooms were; but then he caught sight of the strange black objects in the pan, carbonised versions of the repulsive-looking growths he'd seen on the boles of rotten ash trees. 'Really,' he said. 'I don't usually eat breakfast. Indigestion.'

'Ah,' Basano replied. 'Know what you mean.' He stabbed one of the charred fungi with the point of his rusty

knife, and Poldarn looked away. 'Alternatively,' Basano
continued, 'you could stay here till the new moon and catch
the Chestnut Day party. Well worth hanging on for, that
is.'

'Oh? What's Chestnut Day?'

Basano shrugged. 'Once a year, we all give each other a
bag of chestnuts. It's a tradition,' he explained, 'very old,
very important in the collier community. Actually, it's just
an excuse for a really good piss-up. And at midnight, we
roast the chestnuts in the embers of Number Two and sing
songs and stuff.'

Poldarn invented a smile from somewhere. 'Sounds
really good,' he said. 'But I really had better be getting
back, or else they'll start getting antsy and sign up for their
charcoal with someone else.'

Basano pulled a face. 'Impatient lot, you are,' he said.
'Well, in that case you'd better go off with the wagons.' He
paused, as if he'd just remembered something. 'Or,' he said,
'tell you what. It'd be quicker, if you don't mind roughing
it a bit.'

Roughing it a bit, Poldarn repeated to himself, looking
at the contents of the frying pan. No, I don't think I'd mind
that terribly much. 'No problem,' he said.

'Well, in that case,' Basano said with his mouth full,
'Corvolo – you know, the old geezer you came in with –
he's going up to collect the mail; straight over the top, mind,
it's a pig of a walk, but you'll come out on the road halfway
between Iacchosia and Velny, and you can hitch a ride with
the mail right into Scieza. How'd that be?'

Poldarn nodded enthusiastically. 'Sounds good to me,'
he said. 'When's he leaving?'

Basano thought for a moment. 'Now, probably,' he said,
'or else he's already gone. Come on, we'll see if he's still
here.'

* * *

It turned out that Poldarn wasn't the only one going with Corvolo to get the mail; they were joined at the last moment by a tall, thin young man with short, spiky hair and an enormous burn scar on the left side of his face. He hadn't said why he was coming with them, and Corvolo hadn't asked. The young man hardly said a word all the way, though it could have been the steepness of the climb, which didn't leave much spare breath for talking, or the difficulty of getting a word in edgeways. (Shortness of breath didn't seem to be a problem with Corvolo, unfortunately.) It was only when they'd cleared the top of the hills and come to the edge of the tree line, with the road clearly visible a mile or so below them, that the young man said anything.

'You,' he said suddenly, stopping and looking Poldarn straight in the eye. 'I know you from somewhere, don't I?'

Poldarn nodded. 'Quite possibly,' he said. 'I don't know you, though.'

The young man frowned. 'Well, that's as may be. Were you ever in Torcea?'

'I don't know.'

'What d'you mean? If you'd ever been there, you'd know about it.'

Poldarn shook his head. 'Long story,' he said. 'But yes, I may have been to Torcea, and no, I wouldn't expect to remember if I had. Also,' he went on, 'I wouldn't want to remember. No offence,' he added. 'It's a personal thing.'

The young man looked mildly startled. 'Oh, right,' he said. 'Only, I'm sure I saw you once, long time ago. You were in a procession or a parade or something.'

'Really.' Poldarn shrugged. 'Thanks, but I'd rather you didn't tell me any more.'

The young man started walking again. 'Be like that,' he said. 'No skin off my nose. Only, I'm sure I remember you, because you were riding along down the street on a great big white horse, and people were cheering like you were somebody important.'

Poldarn grinned. 'Do I look important?'

'No,' the young man said. 'But neither do a lot of important people.'

'There you go, then,' Poldarn said. 'If you really did see me and I looked important, then obviously I wasn't, by your own admission. Glad to have cleared that up for you,' he added kindly.

The young man didn't seem to know what to make of that, but at least it shut him up for the rest of the journey.

They reached the road just before sunset. According to Corvolo, the mail coach would pass the two hundred and seventh milestone ('That big lump of rock you're sat on,' he explained) three hours after sunrise the next morning; meanwhile, they could camp out by the road and be sure of catching the coach, or they could kip down for the night in a spinney two hundred yards down the slope, and hope they woke up in time. Poldarn said that where they were would do him just fine, and the young man didn't seem to have an opinion on the matter, so they unrolled their blankets and built a fire, using some of the charcoal samples Basano had given Poldarn to take back with him. It was good charcoal, no doubt about it, but he didn't say anything for fear of another lecture from Corvolo. Nobody seemed to have brought along anything to eat, but Corvolo had a leather bottle full of beer. If anything, it tasted worse than the stuff Basano had given him; it also gave him heartburn, which kept him awake long after the other two had dropped off and begun to snore.

Poldarn lay on his back and thought about names: Tazencius, Copis, Monach, Muno Silsny, Feron Amathy. The last time he'd seen Copis, she'd tried to kill him and he'd had to hit her, so hard that he'd broken her jaw. He still wasn't clear in his mind about why she'd picked him up in her cart the day he'd woken up and found his memory gone. From what he'd been able to gather – she hadn't told him, of course, that'd have been too simple – the sword-monks of Deymeson had ordered her to accompany him, as a spy or a bodyguard, or just possibly because he was really the Divine Poldarn returned to earth to bring about the end of the world, and Poldarn needed to have a priestess with him in order to make the prophecies come out right. At one time he'd imagined he loved her – no, not quite that, but they'd been close enough that she'd apparently been carrying his child – when she'd pulled a sword on him in the ruins of Deymeson, at which point he was back with his grandfather's people, the raiders, burning the place and slaughtering the monks. He thought about that. For a man who never deliberately did any harm, who had no reason to hurt anybody in the world, fire and death did tend to cling to him rather, like the smell on a pig farmer's boots. Then he thought about the reason why he'd left the islands in the far west: because he'd started a bloody feud, mur-dered a man called Cary in cold blood, burned his best friend to death in his own house – and there had been good reasons for all of that, anybody else would've done exactly the same in his place, probably.

Precepts of religion, he thought (and his eyes closed, and he drifted towards sleep like a carelessly moored boat); the guilty are innocent, only the innocent can commit crimes. The god in the cart is foretold, preordained, inevitable, and therefore not to be blamed for what he does. The only crime is to try and interfere with the working out of the pattern. But that—

A man was speaking; a big, fine-looking man with a bushy black beard, standing in a pulpit at the front of a huge, high-roofed stone building full of people. But that, he was saying, conflicts with another essential precept, whereby Poldarn returns in wrath to punish the evildoers and avenge the sins of men. Think (said the big, fine man, whose name was Cleapho) about the logic behind that. Poldarn's coming is foretold, inevitable, it must happen; yet it is the deadly consequence of free choice, the choice on the part of the people to commit sins. See the fallacy. If the people's choice was free, then Poldarn is not inevitable; the people might decide not to sin, and the punishment might not be incurred. But if Poldarn is inevitable, then the choice cannot be free, the people are doomed to sin, whether they want to or not – and if they don't want to sin, how can they be wicked enough to merit punishment, since it is not the act alone that makes a crime, but the evil intention as well. Accordingly (said the big man, and Poldarn wondered where he, Poldarn, was all this time: in the audience, listening, or in the pulpit, preaching?) religion has another precept to cover the discrepancy. Only the innocent are punished.

Something settled on Poldarn's nose, making him jump up; a moth, or possibly a big mosquito. The sky was lighter now. Time had passed, so presumably he'd fallen asleep after all. He discovered that he'd been lying on his left arm, and his hand was cramped up and painful. If that was dawn coming up in the corner of the sky, the coach would be here in three hours – reasonable enough, if it stopped overnight in Iacchosia and started out again at first light. He could remember Iacchosia quite clearly, having been through there a couple of months previously. A poxy little town, no big deal, entirely unmemorable. He propped himself up on his right elbow and looked round. The old man, Corvolo, was still fast asleep. There was no sign of the young man.

He woke Corvolo up and told him. Corvolo offered no explanation, but didn't seem unduly concerned. Colliers were like that, he said, especially the young ones; suddenly they'd take it into their heads to move on, and off they'd go, without collecting their stuff, as often as not, or even their pay. Probably he'd decided to try his luck at one of the other camps further down the line – not that it'd do him any good, all the camps were pretty much alike, but that was colliers for you. Why, when he'd been a kid . . .

The mail coach arrived before Corvolo had a chance to tell Poldarn the complete history of his life, which was probably just as well. Corvolo had an amazing memory and could recall trivial conversations from thirty years ago, apparently word for word. If the coach had been even a quarter of an hour late, Poldarn was sure he'd have murdered the old man.

The coach only stopped for a few moments; just long enough for the postillion to hurl a cloth bag off the box, and for Poldarn to grab the running-rail and hoist himself aboard. As for it being a coach, that was an exaggeration; it was nothing but an ordinary cart, slightly longer and broader than the basic farm or carrier's pattern but just as bare and uncomfortable. Apparently, the Empire didn't believe in wasting good hardening steel on cart springs, Poldarn concluded, when it could be used for making spear blades; there were two soldiers to guard the mail, just in case.

'In case of what?' Poldarn asked the driver, who appeared not to hear him this time.

Fine, Poldarn thought. Not so long ago, he'd had a short but exciting career as a courier, working for the Falx house back in the Bohec valley. Two trips; and on both occasions he'd made it back alive but the driver hadn't. He gave up trying to make conversation with the mail driver. If past experience was anything to go by, there wouldn't be much point trying to get to know him.

Instead, he exchanged a few words with the other passengers. One of them was just a crazy old woman; she was dressed in a man's shabby coat several sizes too big for her, and her lanky grey hair was mostly crammed under a cracked old leather travelling hat. On her lap she nursed a small wicker basket as if it was a newborn baby. She started to tell Poldarn a very involved-sounding story about her younger son's progress in the district excise office in Falcata, but fortunately she fell asleep in the middle of a sentence.

The other passenger was a man. He was wrapped up in more coat than the slightly chilly air called for, with the collar drawn tight round his chin and the hood down over his eyes. This gave him an almost comically furtive look, like a caricature of a spy, or of the young prince in exile on the run from the usurper's guards. When Poldarn asked him who he was, however, he replied that he was a travelling salesman on his way to Scieza. His particular line of business, he added, was dental prosthetics.

'What?'

The salesman grinned under his hood. 'False teeth,' he said.

Poldarn frowned, puzzled. 'How do you mean, false?' he asked.

For a moment the salesman wilted, as if the thought of explaining it all *again* was too much for him. But he pulled himself together and launched into what was clearly a well-worn sales pitch. Are you missing a tooth or two? he asked dramatically. Are you one ivory chorister short of a full choir? Do you find excuses not to smile, because of the ugly secret your lips protect? If so, help is at hand, because—

'No, actually,' Poldarn said. 'I've got pretty good teeth, as it happens. Look.' And he smiled.

'Fine,' said the salesman tetchily. 'Good for you. Now, if it so happened that you weren't so almighty fortunate in that respect, our company would undoubtedly be able to help you out and improve your quality of life to a degree

you wouldn't have thought possible. Our individually
made, twenty-four-carat fine replacement gold teeth can
be fitted painlessly in minutes, and are guaranteed to last
you a lifetime of normal and reasonable use. For only
thirty-five quarters, we undertake to replace any standard-
size front or back tooth—'

'Oh,' Poldarn said, 'I see. Hang on, though – thirty-five
quarters for a little stub of gold? That's a lot of money.'

The salesman scowled at him. 'Cheap at half the price,'
he grunted. 'I mean, twice. Well, anyway, there's no point
telling you any more because, like you said, you don't need
one. Though,' he added half-heartedly, 'that's no reason
why you shouldn't join the long list of satisfied customers
who've discovered that a Collendis Brothers gold tooth is
an outstandingly impressive fashion statement.' He
stopped, and leaned forward a little in his seat. 'I know you
from somewhere, don't I?'

This time, it was Poldarn's turn to feel weary. 'Maybe,'
he said. 'I don't recognise you, but that's nothing to go by.'

'Oh?'

Poldarn shook his head. 'I have a truly appalling memory,'
he said. 'Straight up, I do. Basically, I can't remember anything that's happened to me since about three years ago.'

Instead of pulling a sceptical face at him, the salesman
nodded. 'Accident, was it? Bump on the head, something
like that?'

'More or less,' said Poldarn, mildly impressed.

'Same thing happened to a cousin of mine,' the salesman
said. 'Got kicked in the head by an ox. This was before I
was born, mind,' he added, as if to assure Poldarn that he
had an alibi. 'Anyhow, he couldn't remember spit, not even
his name or where he lived, and then quite suddenly, twenty
years later, he was walking up the street in the village where
he used to live, and someone bumped into him and without
thinking he said, "Mind where you're going, can't you,

Blepsio, you idiot" – something like that, anyway, I'm making the name up, of course – and then, wham! It all came back to him in a flood.'

'Really,' Poldarn said. 'That's encouraging.'

The salesman grinned. 'You'd think so,' he replied. 'But my cousin wasn't too pleased. He rushed home, found his wife had declared him legally dead, married someone else, and the new bloke had mortgaged the farm fifteen ways to buggery and then run off to Torcea with the money. Still hadn't sorted out all the legal bullshit when he died. Whereas before he started remembering stuff, he was nicely settled as a wheelwright and was doing quite well.'

Poldarn looked away. 'Funny you should say that,' he said. 'You see, it's crossed my mind that maybe, if I did get my memory back, I'd find out that my old life wasn't really worth going back to; and, like your cousin, I'm just starting to get settled, I'm quite happy as I am. So—'

The salesman nodded. 'So if I suddenly remember where I've seen you before, and tell you who you used to be, you'd rather I kept my gob shut and didn't tell you.' He pulled a face. 'Just goes to show, really, what you'd assume people want and what they really want aren't necessarily the same. Actually,' he added, looking sideways at Poldarn under his hood. 'I seem to recall there's a precept of religion that says the same thing, only neater.'

Poldarn nodded. 'Kindness is for enemies,' he said; and then looked up sharply. 'Precepts of religion,' he repeated.

The salesman was still looking at him. 'Proverbs,' he said. 'Little snippets of popular wisdom, made up by the monks for the most part, like the maxims of defence and stuff like that, only they're usually even more useless than the maxims. Don't worry,' he added, 'loads of people beside the sword-monks know them, so you haven't inadvertently tripped over a slice of your past. It doesn't prove you were once a monk, or anything like that.'

Poldarn looked away. 'That's all right, then,' he said. 'Just out of interest, have you figured out where you know me from?'

'No,' the salesman replied.

'Good.' Poldarn looked up as the salesman rolled back his hood to reveal a round, clean-shaven face with cropped black hair. 'Did you say you were headed for Scieza?' he asked.

'That's right,' the salesman replied. 'Actually, just for once I'm not really going there on business. That is, if I can possibly get a few orders along the way, so much the better, though to be honest there's a fat chance of that out here in the sticks. But mostly I'm going there for – well, personal reasons, if you follow me.'

'Of course. None of my business, in other words.'

The salesman grinned. 'Precisely,' he said. 'So, what line of work are you in? Haven't been to Scieza before, but isn't it all metalworking down that way?'

'That's right,' Poldarn said. 'Biggest foundry in the district, which is where I work.'

'Got you,' the salesman said. 'The bell-foundry at Dui Chirra, right? Well, maybe that's how I know you, then. Before I got into this gold-tooth lark, I was a pattern-maker. Well, I say that; mostly I just sanded and painted. Very boring, so I packed it in. So, what do you make at this foundry? Just general casting, or do you specialise?'

Poldarn smiled. 'We make bells,' he said.

'Bells.' The salesman looked slightly bewildered, as if he'd always assumed they grew on tall brass trees. 'Well, that's probably a good line to be in – must be a fair old demand, and I've never heard of anywhere else that makes them.' He shrugged, dismissing the topic like a wet dog shaking itself. 'My name's Gain Aciava, by the way.'

Poldarn smiled. 'Pleased to meet you,' he said. 'I'd tell you my name if I knew what it was – well, that's another long story – but recently I've been answering to Poldarn. Like the god in the cart,' he added before Aciava could say anything, 'I know; but I sort of picked it up before I knew any better.'

Aciava looked at him for a moment. 'Fair enough,' he said. 'Anyhow, pleased to meet you too. Welcome to Tulice.'

'Thank you,' Poldarn replied solemnly. 'Just out of interest,' he went on, lowering his voice a little, 'what're they in aid of?'

'What, the soldiers?' Aciava looked grave. 'You haven't been in these parts long, then, or else you've been out of the flow. Bandits.'

'Oh,' Poldarn said.

Aciava grinned ruefully. 'They call them that,' he said, 'because it doesn't sound so bad. You know, bandits, sort of thing that can happen anywhere. Actually, they're nothing of the sort. Civil war's more like it, only it's not as simple as that. All you need to know really is, don't bother them and they probably won't bother you. Unless you're a bandit, of course.'

A slight sideways glance came with that last remark. Poldarn ignored it. As far as he could tell, Master Aciava just enjoyed making himself seem mysterious to strangers met on the road. No harm in that, coming from a gold-tooth salesman. 'Thanks,' he said, and changed the subject to the merits of the inns along the road between Falcata and the coast, on which topic Aciava proved to be erudite, passionate and fairly amusing. He was in the middle of a tirade against the Light In Darkness at Galbetta Cross when Poldarn looked up and realised that he knew where he was. 'Scieza,' he said.

'Ah,' said Aciava, 'here we are, then. Just as well, I've never been here before, and they don't always call out the names of the stops.'

The wagon rolled to a halt outside the Virtue Triumphant (which had received a vote of qualified approval in Aciava's catalogue, its effect slightly tarnished by the assessor's admission that he'd never been there). Poldarn jumped down while Aciava started unloading his baggage, of which there seemed to be an unexpectedly large amount.

'Right,' Aciava said, straightening his back and grimacing. 'Are you staying here overnight or heading straight back home? Only, if you're stopping, I think I owe you a drink and a meal for keeping me entertained on the road.'

Strange way of putting it, Poldarn thought; but it was almost dark, and he didn't fancy three hours' stumbling on the boggy, rutted track to the foundry. 'Go on, then,' he said. 'After all, I'm on expenses.'

Aciava smiled. 'In that case,' he said, 'you can buy the drinks.'

'No,' Poldarn replied, and led the way to the taproom.

Like most of the inns on the coast road, the Virtue had originally been built as a religious structure, complete with dorters, refectory, great house, library, chapter house and several small chapels. The stables and kitchens were a hundred yards away from the main buildings, tucked out of sight among the barns and stores. With the decline of public religion, the great house had evolved into the taproom and common room; the crypt was now full of barrels rather than desiccated monks, and the potmen scampered to and from the transept carrying sticky jugs full of beer. To get something to eat, you had to traipse through the cloisters and climb the refectory stairs; or you could make do with bread and cheese from the baskets in the nave, all you could eat for two quarters; or, for six quarters, you could have the roast brought to you in the Lady chapel, with enough beer to poison a garrison town. Aciava, who was on expenses too, opted for the Lady chapel. This surprised Poldarn slightly, since he couldn't imagine that the tooth merchant wanted *that* much more of his exclusive company after a day on the road; then again, perhaps Aciava simply wanted to finish his witty remarks about the cockroaches in the Light In Darkness. Since Poldarn stood to get a hot meal out of it, without costing the foundry anything, he didn't mind particularly.

'Well,' Aciava said, while they were waiting for the food to arrive, 'here I am. It's been a long trip, but I'm hoping it'll turn out to have been worth it.'

Poldarn sipped his beer. It was considerably better than Basano's home-brew. The same could have been said about sea water. 'You said you'd come here to meet someone,' he said politely.

'That's right.' Aciava steepled his fingers over his nose. 'An old friend, actually. Someone I haven't seen in years. Come to think of it, not since we were at school together.'

Poldarn stifled a yawn. 'Really?'

'Yes.' Aciava tilted the jug over his cup. 'Took me a while to find him, but I got there eventually.'

'I don't know many people in these parts,' Poldarn said, 'apart from the guys at the foundry, of course, so I don't suppose I know who you mean.'

Aciava was looking at him. 'Oh, I expect you do,' he said.

'Oh? Who is it, then?'

'You.'

Chapter Two

Poldarn put his mug down slowly. 'Look,' he said.

Aciava laughed. 'It's just struck me,' he said. 'In context, that sounded like a pick-up line. No, absolutely not. The truth is, I know who you are. And I've come a very long way to find you.'

That was, of course, the moment when the door swung open and a sutler backed into the chapel, holding a large tray full of plates of food. Smoked lamb, Poldarn noticed, with cabbage, artichokes and creamed leeks Tulice style. Not bad for six quarters.

The sutler put the tray down. 'Ready for more beer?' he asked.

'We will be,' Aciava said, his eyes fixed on Poldarn's face, 'by the time you get around to fetching it.'

'Fine,' the sutler replied, and left.

'What did you say?' Poldarn said.

Aciava sighed, and pulled one of the plates towards him. 'You're probably asking yourself,' he said, 'why I made up all that garbage on the coach; like I didn't know you, and so forth. Actually, it's very simple. I already knew you'd lost your memory, and that the chances were you wouldn't recognise me. I'd also figured that if you'd gone this long without remembering anything, it was a fair bet it's because you don't really want to. Of course, I didn't know how much you'd found out about yourself since; partly, that's what the charade was in aid of. Luckily, I've always been easy to talk to. I do this boisterous, likeable idiot thing very well, and there's nothing like a long wagon ride for striking up conversations, often about things we wouldn't normally discuss with strangers.' He speared a slice of lamb with the point of his knife. 'So, how much have you found out? I know you went home for a year.'

Poldarn stared. 'How the hell do you know about that?'

'Good question,' Aciava said with his mouth full. 'How many people in the Empire even know about the islands in the far west, where the raiders come from? I can't be sure about this, but my guess is, three. Two of whom,' he added, 'are drinking beer from the same jug. Refill?'

Poldarn shook his head. 'How could you possibly know?' he said. 'Who in God's name are you, anyway?'

But Aciava only smiled. 'Now that's interesting,' he said. 'Anybody else in the world, in your shoes, his first question would've been, *Who in God's name am I?* But you're more concerned with me. Haven't you been listening? I can tell you who you are. Your name.'

Poldarn kicked his chair back and stood up. 'I asked you a question,' he said.

Aciava scowled. 'Sit down, for heaven's sake. Eat your dinner before it goes cold. This is going to be hard enough as it is without melodrama.'

So Poldarn sat down. 'You're lying,' he said. 'This is what you do for a living. You get talking to people on coaches. They tell you something, like me telling you about losing my memory; then you think up some scam—'

'Fair assumption,' Aciava replied. 'And your scepticism

does you credit. But it seems to me you're trying suspiciously hard to make excuses for not asking me the sort of thing you should be wanting to know. Who am I? What did I do for a living? Where do I live?'

'I told you,' Poldarn said hesitantly, 'I'm not sure I want—'

Aciava put his knife down on his plate. 'Your real name,' he said, 'is, of course, Ciartan. Your father's name was Tursten, but he died before you were born. You were brought up by your grandfather, at Haldersness. You had to leave home because of some trouble over someone else's wife, which is why you came to the Empire in the first place.' He frowned. 'Look, if you're going to hit me with something, please don't let it be the beer jug; that's solid earthenware, you could do me an injury.'

Poldarn sat back and stared at him.

'That's better. Now,' Aciava went on, 'I don't actually know if any of that stuff is true, because it's only what you told me, many years ago, in an out-of-bounds wine shop in Deymeson. But it ought to knock the itinerant con artist theory on the head, don't you think?'

Poldarn nodded without speaking.

'By the way,' Aciava went on, 'if you think this is easy for me, just because I'm being all laid back and relaxed about it, think again. This is just my defences, like all the wards and guards we learned back in the second year. We had to pretend it was someone else in the ring sparring with sharp blades, not us, or we'd have died of fright. Remember? No, of course you don't. You still don't know me from a hole in the ground, do you? That's – well, that's rather hard for me. But we won't worry about it now. Have some spring cabbage, it's not half bad.'

Poldarn didn't move. There was a precept of religion about why that was advisable, tactically, but he couldn't remember the exact words offhand.

'Anyhow,' Aciava went on, 'when you were telling me, in the cart, about not having remembered anything because, basically, you don't want to – I can tell you, that actually makes a whole lot of sense. At any rate, it puts me in a dilemma. If you believe that I'm your friend, at least that I used to be the friend of the man I used to know – you appreciate the distinction, I'm sure – then you'll understand why I'm doing all this faffing about, instead of spitting it straight out and telling you, whether you like it or not. Truth is, I don't know you any more; I don't know who you've become. And I can imagine how some of the stuff I could tell you might do you a lot of damage. Hence – well, I suppose it's a sort of test, or what the government clerks call an assessment. Only way I can find out what you'd really like to know is to ask you; only I can't ask you straight out without risking doing the damage. Like, if I said, "Do you want me to tell you about that time in the Poverty and Prudence, with the violin-maker's daughter and the six goats?" – well, you get the idea, I'm sure.'

While Aciava had been saying all this, Poldarn hadn't moved. For some reason, he was acutely aware of every detail of his surroundings – the hiss of slightly damp logs on the fire, the smell of the onion sauce on the smoked lamb, the pecking of light rain on the chapel slates. He realised that he'd breathed out some time ago and hadn't breathed in again.

'Who are you?' he said.

Aciava sighed. 'Now that,' he said, 'is what Father Tutor used to call a very intelligent question. Well, for a start, my name really is Gain Aciava. I was born in Paraon in eastern Tulice thirty-nine years ago; my father was a retired cavalry officer who got a sinecure in the governor's office when he left the service, and my mother was his CO's younger daughter. When I was twelve they decided that since both my elder brothers had gone into the army, it'd be sensible to diversify a bit and send me into religion; so they packed me off to Deymeson as a junior novice. I did my time there, and eventually I was ordained. As luck would have it, I got a transfer away from Deymeson the year before you and your relations trashed the place; I joined Cleapho's office in Torcea as a junior chaplain. When the order abruptly ceased to exist and Cleapho formally rescinded its charter I found myself out of a job, and since sword-monks were distinctly out of favour by then, I hunted round for someone who'd pay me a wage, with indifferent success, until I sort of stumbled into this false-teeth lark. Amazingly, it's turned out to be a good living, totally undemanding, quite relaxing in fact, and I'm enjoying it rather more than eight hours perched on a high stool in an office followed by six hours' sword-drawing practice and sleeping on a plank bed in a small stone cell. And that, give or take an unimportant detail or two, is basically all there is to know.'

But Poldarn shook his head. 'That may be the truth,' he said, 'but it sure as hell isn't the whole truth. How do you know all that stuff about me, and why did you go to all the trouble of finding me?'

Aciava grinned offensively. 'I could give you an answer, only it's not allowed. If you want to know why you're worth busting my arse to find—'

'All right,' Poldarn conceded, 'you've made your point.' He stood up. There wasn't really enough room in the chapel for pacing up and down, at least not without making himself look ridiculous; but he felt uncomfortable staying still. 'Perhaps it'd be better if I just left.'

'For you, maybe,' Aciava said. 'But don't I get a say in the matter? Come on, give me a chance. I've been rattling about in mail-coaches for a week, and that's not taking account of three years of painstaking, dreary investigation. Surely I deserve some consideration.'

'Why? I never asked you to—'

'How,' Aciava interrupted calmly, 'do you know that? I mean,' he went on, 'for all you know, there was an evening many years ago when you took me on one side, confessed that your biggest fear in all the world was losing your memory, and made me swear on my mother's life that if it ever happened to you, I'd find you and tell you who you are.'

Poldarn looked at him. 'And did I?'

'No. But there could be all sorts of reasons. Maybe there are people who need you. Have you ever once considered that?'

'Yes,' Poldarn said, without much confidence. 'But – well, I may not remember further back than three years, but I learned a few things about myself back in the old country – not things I did, things I am. I reckon anybody who knew me before is probably better off without me.'

'Oh, sure,' Aciava said, pulling a face. 'You're a sadistic wife-beater and you carry thirteen infectious diseases. While sleepwalking, you set fire to hospitals and orphanages. You are, in fact, the god who brings the end of the world. But apart from that—'

'Fine.' Poldarn sat down. 'Just tell me, why was finding me so important?'

Aciava hesitated, then grinned sheepishly. 'I missed you,' he said.

Poldarn stared. 'You what?'

'Straight up. I'd better explain. At Deymeson – you do know, don't you, you were at Deymeson?'

Poldarn nodded.

'Well, that's something. You were a novice there. You joined in second year of the third grade; you were eighteen months older than the rest of us, but Father Tutor reckoned you had to stay down, because you were so far behind. Anyhow, that's beside the point. There were six of us. No, that's misleading, because there were twenty of us in the class; but there were six of us who always went round together. Bestest friends, that sort of thing. There was you, and me; and Elaos Tanwar – he's dead now – and the only girl in our year, Xipho Dorunoxy—'

Poldarn felt as if he'd just been slammed back in his chair by a kick in the stomach. 'Copis.'

'That's right, Copis. That makes five. And one more. Cordomine was what we knew him as, but he's better known these days as Chaplain Cleapho.'

There was a long silence. 'I don't believe you,' Poldarn said eventually.

'Oh.' Aciava frowned. 'What a shame, because it's true. I can prove it, you know.'

'I don't want you to prove it,' Poldarn shouted; then he took a deep breath. 'No matter what you say,' he said, 'I'm not going to believe you. See, I've been through this before; I was at Deymeson – before the raiders burned it down – and they told me all sorts of stuff, all perfectly plausible, about who I was. And I believed them; but then I found out they were lying, using me, it was something to do with the war and some general called Cronan—'

Aciava nodded. 'I know about that,' he said. 'Hardly surprising, you weren't very popular with the sword-monks after you left. Anyway, that was when Copis told you she'd been – well, looking after you, bad choice of words, on their instructions, and then she pulled a sword on you. No wonder you're suspicious when I tell you I used to be a monk too. And you don't believe she was one of them, because you were in love with her at the time. Sort of.'

'No,' Poldarn said.

Aciava shook his head. 'Trust me,' he said, 'you were. You were in love with her back in fifth grade – sorry, I'm not allowed to tell you that, am I? But she wouldn't have anything to do with you, so it's probably all right.' He smiled. 'Actually, it's bitterly unfair, because when you did finally get her in the sack, you weren't to know that you were finally achieving a lifetime ambition.' He leaned back in his chair and folded his hands in his lap. As he did so, a fold of his coat fell away, revealing the hilt of a short sword tucked into his sash. Poldarn wondered if it was deliberate. 'Now do you want me to piss off and leave you in peace? If you do, I will.'

Poldarn closed his eyes. 'No,' he said.

Then the door opened, and the sutler came in with a big jug of beer. 'Here you go,' he said. 'You haven't finished the first one.'

'Leave it,' Aciava said, 'we've got a use for it.'

The sutler went away again. 'Sorry,' Aciava said, 'I've lost my thread. Did you just agree that you do want me to tell you?'

Poldarn sighed. 'I'm not sure,' he said.

'Progress,' Aciava said brightly. 'A few moments ago, you were absolutely dead set against it.'

'That was before—'

'Would you rather I hadn't told you? About Xipho – sorry, Copis?'

'That's academic, isn't it? You've told me now.' He slumped forward onto his elbows. 'I guess you'd better tell me the rest.'

But Aciava shook his head. 'Not so fast,' he said. 'I've still got your best interests at heart, remember. I'll tell you some things, but only what's good for you. All right?'

'I'm not in the mood for games.'

'Ah.' Aciava grinned. 'I've heard you say *that* before. You always were an impatient sort – you know, always reading ahead, wanting to learn lesson five before you'd properly got the hang of lesson three. I can still just get up and leave, and I will if you don't behave. Understood?'

'Fuck you,' Poldarn said. But he stayed where he was. 'Go on, then.'

'Thank you so much.' Aciava settled himself in his chair and picked up a slice of smoked lamb in his fingers. 'Now,' he said, 'one step at a time. Do you want me to tell you your name – not Ciartan, the name you had in the order? Or not; it's up to you.'

'Yes.'

'Splendid. You were called Poldarn.' Aciava smiled. 'No, I'm not kidding you, it was the name Father Tutor chose for you, since he refused to call you Ciartan, he said there was no such name; and it's quite usual for novices to take a name-in-religion. Signifies a complete severance of ties with the outside world, or some such shit. Anyhow, that's what we all knew you as.' He breathed in deeply, like a man of sensibility smelling a rare flower. 'My guess is, Xipho was playing a game with you. Probably, being told to look after you put the idea of the god-in-the-cart stunt into her mind. Also, it'd be easier for her, so there wouldn't be any risk that she'd suddenly call you Poldarn by mistake, out of habit, and then you'd get suspicious. Either that, or it was just her idea of a joke. You see, it was always a source of extreme merriment and wit in our gang, Father Tutor giving you such a wonderfully apt name.' He paused. 'You do know why it's apt, don't you?'

'Enlighten me.'

Aciava sighed. 'Well, Poldarn's the god of fire and the forge, and before you joined up, you were working in a blacksmith's shop. You learned the trade back in Haldersness, and when you wound up over here and needed to start earning a living, it was the only useful thing you knew how to do.'

'I see,' Poldarn said. 'That explains – no, forget it. None of your business.'

'Suit yourself.' Aciava shrugged. 'So that's your name,'

he said. 'I reckoned there couldn't be any harm in telling you, since that's what you've been calling yourself anyway. And of course, it's not your *actual* name, because really you're Ciartan. Bit of a non-issue, really.'

'I've had enough of this,' Poldarn said, jumping up again. 'I think I was right to start with. I don't want to know any more, it's just making me angry—'

Aciava nodded gravely. 'Because you're finding out you've been made a fool of. Same old Poldarn, always was scared to death of being made to look stupid in front of the class.'

If he'd had a sword, Poldarn would probably have drawn it; he could feel the intrusion into his circle, like a splinter in the joint of a finger. 'Maybe,' he said. 'But you've told me now, and I don't want to know any more, thanks all the same. You can piss off now.'

'Fine.' Aciava held his hands up. 'Whatever you like. But a moment ago you were dead set on knowing why I'd come looking for you. Obviously you've changed your mind.'

Poldarn closed his eyes. 'You said you missed me.'

'Oh, I did.' Aciava laughed. 'But I miss loads of people. Hardly a day goes by when I don't ask myself what happened to old so-and-so. But I don't go hunting them down across half the Empire. There's a reason why I'm here, something that affects your present and your future, not just your past. You can ignore it if you like.'

'Thank you,' Poldarn said, and left.

Three hours' walk, down a muddy, rutted lane in the dark, when he could probably have had a good night's sleep on a soft mattress in the Virtue Triumphant, at the gold-tooth people's expense. He cursed himself as he walked; never did know a good thing when he saw it. It was hard to imagine a sensible person in his situation walking out on a good offer like that. All that had been expected of him in return was sitting still and listening to some stuff about some people he used to know, one of them being himself. He carried on, feeling the mud slopping under his boots. It was a long nine miles, and his own stupidity went with him all the way.

The tragedy of my life, he thought; wherever I go, I take myself with me. And I expect my mother warned me about getting into bad company.

Copis, he thought (and at that moment, the low branch across the road that he knew was around there somewhere smacked him across the face; it probably laughed at him too, behind his back). Why the hell should the worst thing, the most important thing, be that she made a fool of me? All that time, on the road, in that bloody cart; she knew and I didn't. At Deymeson she said she was quietly hating me all the way, under her breath, because she knew who I was and what I'd done. Our kid'll be – what, two, nearly three by now, assuming she didn't strangle it as soon as it was born.

It'd be so much simpler, so much better, if Aciava (his real name? God knows) was lying. Sure, he knew all that stuff about the old country, but maybe a whole lot of people knew that once, in which case he could've found it out easily enough. Poldarn stopped, one foot in a puddle; just because he knows who I am doesn't necessarily mean he's telling me the truth. Think of what the sword-monks did to me, and he even says he's one of them. Probably *I* was one of them – it'd explain this knack of being able to pull out a sword and kill people. And Aciava said it himself, they had some reason to hate me. So I'd have to be crazy to believe them, wouldn't I?

He remembered an old joke: *I wouldn't believe you if you told me my own name.*

He shook his head, like a carthorse bothered by flies. It all came down to whether he wanted to know. What could there be in the past that he could conceivably want back? Like the old character-assessment question, what one thing would you save if your house was on fire? It stood to reason, he'd been three years away from his past and there hadn't been any one thing he'd felt the lack of. He could sleep in ditches and eat stale bread and raw meat; the state of his clothes or his boots didn't seem to bother him; luxury and comfort and pleasure weren't worth going back for, he could manage without them just fine. Company, now; in the past three years he'd had two lovers and a friend. Hadn't worked out too well; the lovers he'd lost to the past, but the friend— He remembered what it had felt like, that very short time when he'd been able to do what everybody else back in the old country could do: hear other people's thoughts. It had been while he stood outside the house at Ciartanstead, while Eyvind, his friend, was burning to death inside.

I killed him; and that wasn't the past's fault. That was just some quarrel over some trees.

Indeed; that had been a bad business, and in consequence he'd left the old country and come back here, so as to transfer Eyvind's murder from his present to his past, like a banker moving money from current account to deposit. The past would be useful if you could use it like that, as a place where you could bury dead bodies, shovelling this convenient loss of memory into the grave to cover up their faces. That's not what the past was for, though. It was where the present went to rot down, so you could use it to grow the future.

He smiled; nice piece of imagery, but it was too glib to fool anyone.

What harm could it do? After all, just because I know about the past doesn't mean I've got to go back there. And besides, it'll make it easier to avoid the bad stuff if I know what I'm avoiding.

That made Poldarn wonder if there was a little tiny lawyer lurking maggot-like deep inside his brain. It was a specious argument, designed to lure him into a trap. Yes, but.

Yes, but if I'd known then what I know now, Copis couldn't have played that dirty trick on me. And what about the sword-monks at Deymeson? If I find out about my past, they won't find it so easy the next time.

Assuming *this* isn't the next time.

Big assumption, given that the source of the information appeared to be a sword-monk. If he was going to believe anything one of them told him ever again, he might as well go the whole hog, shave his scalp and have the word IDIOT tattooed on it in bright purple letters. Except, of course – what if they were the only people who knew the truth and could tell him? In that case, better not to know?

Clearly, he told himself, there are arguments on both sides, like an ambush in a narrow pass. Now, if he wanted something really scary to occupy his mind with, how about the ease with which this joker had found him? He hadn't come to this godforsaken place because he liked mud and fog, or because he'd always wanted to be a bell-founder when he grew up. If someone could find him here—

Assuming anybody wanted to; anybody else, apart from the incredibly annoying man who claimed his name was Aciava; who apparently wanted him for something, and had been prepared to tell him what it was (assuming he hadn't been lying)—

Fine. Poldarn's head was spinning, and he hadn't even stopped long enough to drink much of the free beer. Which was another way of saying the same thing. He was going to be miserable anyway, so why not have something tangible to be miserable about?

Stupid line of reasoning; stupid, like the very rich merchants in Falcata, who took crucial business decisions on the basis of the phases of the moon, and whether Saturn was in the fifth house. Stupid; but the answers thereby derived must've been right, or the merchants wouldn't have ended up very rich.

Did it really matter that Copis had made a fool of him, after all? Arguably, he'd had the last laugh, if the man had been telling the truth; he'd got her into bed in the end, hadn't he, just like he'd always wanted. No wonder she'd wanted to kill him, come to think of it.

(It was all a bit like his name, assuming it was his name. First he'd been a god. Then he was called after a roof-tile. Then it turned out the roof-tile was named after the god. And now it turned out it really was his name – called after the god, who'd probably been called after the roof-tile in the first place. Is that where gods come from, he wondered?)

Or he could carry on as he was (assuming they didn't burst in and drag him away if he wouldn't come quietly). He could stay here, in flat, wet, foggy, horrible Tulice, living in a turf house and working in the foundry. A lot of people lived in Tulice, in turf houses, working in foundries; and as far as he could tell, most of them seemed to get away with it, without ever being recognised or discovered or ambushed by their past lives. It couldn't be *difficult*, if they could manage it. Old joke: if a Tulicer can do it, so can a small rock. So, if they could do it, so could he.

Or maybe the bastard was lying to him. Ready-made pasts had to be on the list of things you weren't supposed to accept from strangers. Not without—

Ah, Poldan thought (and there was a faint, thin yellow light in the distance, the lantern burning outside the foundry gates), that's the word I've been searching for. Not without *proof*.

(—Assuming Aciava has any, and that he hasn't been so offended that he gets on the dawn mail-coach and buggers off back where he came from before I can ask him. Assuming I'm going to ask him. Come to think of it, the whole of our world is made up of assumings, like chalk is the bones of billions of small dead fish.)

At least the turf houses at the foundry were better than the horrible little dirt dog-kennels at the charcoal-burners' camp. The foundry had been in business for over a century, and the workers' houses had to be at least forty years old, if not older; long enough for the turf to put down roots and knit together nicely. The foundrymen were almost proud of them, in a way. It wasn't everybody, they said, who lives in a living house, with walls and a roof that grow, even if it is a bit like living in your own grave.

Poldarn was shaken out of a dream about something or other he couldn't remember by Banspati the foreman. 'You're back, then,' he said, looming over Poldarn like an overhanging cliff.

'Looks like it,' Poldarn mumbled. 'What's the time?'

Banspati grunted. 'Some of us've been up for hours,' he said. 'So, how did you get on?'

The question puzzled Poldarn for a moment; then he remembered. The charcoal. He tried to recall how all that had turned out. 'It's all right,' he said. 'We did the deal.'

'Fine,' Banspati said. 'What deal?'

Pulling the details out of his memory was like levering an awkward stone out of a post-hole. 'They can let us have all we need,' he said, 'two quarters a bushel on the road, tenth off for cash on delivery, half a quarter a bushel penalty for failure to deliver. The quality's good,' he added, 'I think. Looked all right to me, anyhow.'

Banspati nodded slowly. 'That's more or less what we decided on,' he said. 'Dunno why you had to go all that way when we'd already settled it here. Still, that's that sorted.'

Poldarn wanted to point out that the trip hadn't been his idea, but he couldn't face the effort of putting it into words. 'Yes,' he said. 'First load should be with us by the end of next month. The bloke said they're rushed off their feet, but he was lying. I think they were glad of the business.'

'You bet. Who wants charcoal round here, except us? Probably we could've got it cheaper if you'd sweated 'em a bit, but it's all settled now, so never mind. Good trip?'

'No.'

'Get yourself together, and get down to the shop. The Vestoer job's all done, bar scouring and polishing, so you'd better get a move on.'

Poldarn nodded, and reached for his boots. His head hurt, but there wasn't any point in mentioning that.

Besides lifting things and hauling on ropes and shovelling wet clay into buckets when the need arose, Poldarn's main job at the bell foundry was the forge work, making brackets and mountings and clappers; none of which could be made and fitted until everything else had been done, by which time the job was usually a month or so late. Somehow matters had so resolved themselves that every late delivery was officially his fault, and he didn't mind that particularly, nor the fact that he was always having to do difficult and delicate work in a hurry. Just this once, however, he'd have preferred it otherwise. He wasn't really in the right frame of mind for concentrating on precision work. But he hauled himself to his feet nevertheless. There was some bread in the crock, but it had gone a funny shade of green, and the water in the jug had flies and stuff floating in it. Skip breakfast, he thought, and I can wash my face in the slack tub when I get there. He tied on his leather apron and shoved through the door into the yard.

As usual, the yard gave no indication that thirty or so men worked there, or that there was anybody around the place at all. To Poldarn's left and in front of him were the abnormally tall timber-framed sheds, with high lintels and curved doors, where the carpenters made patterns and jigs, and where the half-finished bells were ground, polished and accoutered; away to the right was the muddy wilderness of casting pits and furnace cupolas. He was halfway across before anybody else appeared: an old man and three boys, hauling sand up from the river in wheelbarrows. He didn't recognise them, and if they knew him they didn't show it. He reached the forge, unlatched the heavy door and went inside.

It was, of course, dark in the forge; shutters closed and bolted, no light other than the splinter of sun from the doorway. On his way he grabbed a sack of charcoal, which he heaped around the little pile of kindling he'd left there a few days ago. For once, the tinderbox was where he'd left it, and the kindling caught quite easily. He hadn't had much trouble getting a fire started, not since the night at Ciartanstead when he'd murdered Eyvind.

As Poldarn drew in the coals with the rake, he tried to clear his mind of all extraneous concerns. Making the clapper for a bell involved careful thought. Both the length and the weight had to be exactly right, or the note would be false. He could either draw the thing down in one piece from a thick bar and swage the round bulb that actually made contact with the bell, or else he could use thinner stock and forge-weld bands around it to form the bulb. Quicker the second way, less heavy work, but considerably trickier, because of the weld. Because he was always in a hurry, he always ended up doing it the second way, and this time looked like no exception. A pity, but there it was.

If only Halder could see me now, he thought; his grandfather had kept on at him to learn the trade (relearn it, rather, since he'd been taught it as a boy and since forgotten it, until after the burning at Ciartanstead, by which point Halder was dead and Poldarn no longer needed the skill). Or Asburn, the real smith at Haldersness, who'd tried to teach him and failed; Asburn could've done four awkward welds one after the other without turning a hair. But Asburn wasn't here, and if he was they'd cut his head off for being a raider. Poldarn took the lid off the flux jar. Just about enough, if he was sparing with it (and that was the wrong approach).

In spite of the lack of flux, the welds took, rather to his surprise. Oddly enough, it seemed as though he was starting to get good at this, now that he was just an employee of the foundry rather than the master of Haldersness and Ciartanstead. Another slight miscalculation with past and present; story of his life, apparently.

Once he'd made the basic shape, he stopped. No point going any further until he'd measured up the bell and spoken to Malla Ancola, the chief founder, who'd have worked out how long and heavy the clapper had to be. Annoying; should have done that before he started, because now he'd have to let his fire burn out. Waste of time and good charcoal, and that was what came of not giving your full attention to the job in hand. Never mind the past, or the future; you had to concentrate on the present, and on the work you were supposed to be doing.

Malla didn't look like a foundryman; he should have been either a prince or a poet, ideally both. He was tall and slim, with long, delicate hands, a smooth round face and, most of the time, a profoundly gormless expression, as if he'd just been interrupted in the middle of composing an ode by a courtier needing something signed.

'You're back, then,' he said, as Poldarn edged his way past the grinding-house door, which had stuck at slightly ajar since the accession of the dynasty before last. 'Any luck with the charcoal people?'

(Malla even sounded like a poet; low-voiced, quiet,

droopy. The accent wasn't necessarily a problem. Even Tulicers wrote poetry sometimes.)

'All settled,' Poldarn replied briskly. He knew from experience that getting into any kind of conversation with Malla was a fatal mistake if you ever wanted to get some work done. Malla could talk about anything, indefinitely. 'I'm just doing the clapper now, so I need some measurements.'

'Ah,' Malla replied. 'Right. She's over here. We'll be making a start on grinding her directly.' Poldarn sighed. Making a start meant that Malla was just beginning to think about it; like a god at the creation of the world, he was opening his mind to the vague, inchoate possibility of the existence of shapes and forms. In other words, he hadn't got round to figuring out the measurements yet. Before he did that, he'd need to prune away the rough, gritty skin of casting waste, which might be anything up to an eighth of an inch deep. Until he knew precisely how thick the walls of the bell would eventually be, he couldn't calculate anything. If this world was going to take a week to create, Malla was still in the mid-afternoon of the second day, turning over in his mind what colour the sky should be.

'Right,' Poldarn said. 'Well, not to worry. I'll go back and rough out the brackets.'

Malla shrugged. 'Yes,' he said. 'That'll be all right.'

'See you later, then.'

'See you later.'

Poldarn had managed to get one arm of the bracket drawn down and was making good progress with bending up the scrollwork when Aciava finally showed up. Poldarn had been expecting him all day, and now it was almost noon. There could be some deep significance to that, but it was rather more likely that he'd had a lie-in.

'Hello there.' He heard Aciava's voice coming from the junction of light and darkness just by the door. 'So this is where you work. Nice set-up you people have got here.'

Poldarn didn't turn round or look up; he was watching the steel in the fire, waiting for the right colour. He wished the steel was ready and he could start hammering it, so he'd have an excuse for drowning out whatever Aciava said. 'It's all right,' he replied.

'I should say so.' The voice was getting nearer. 'Biggest foundry this side of the mountains, and the only bell factory in Tulice. Founded, no pun intended, over a century ago, the secret of its success is the unique composition of the mud and sand deposits found in the nearby Green River, which are ideally suited to the extremely specialised business of large-scale deep-core cupola founding.' He stopped, and in spite of the heat of the fire Poldarn could almost feel the glow of his grin. 'I read up on this outfit before I left,' he said. 'Rule number one in the gold-tooth racket: always do your homework before you set out.'

Poldarn nodded. 'I'd sort of got the impression you like knowing more than everybody else,' he said. 'Gives you the edge, I suppose.'

'Of course.' Aciava chuckled. 'Going in somewhere without knowing all about it'd be like walking into a pitch-dark room where there's an enemy waiting for you.'

Poldarn was, of course, standing next to the fire, plainly visible. 'Well,' he said, 'this is it. But I don't suppose you're here to order a bell.'

'Nice idea. Out of my price range, though. Talking of which, did you know the bell in the cloister tower at Deymeson originally came from here?'

Disconcerting. The man sounded like a tour guide. 'Really,' Poldarn said. 'Sorry, don't remember it.'

'Don't you? We all cursed it often enough for dragging us out of bed in the wee small hours. Anyway, here's where it was made. Clapper forged on that very anvil, I dare say. It's a small world, isn't it?'

'So you say,' Poldarn answered. 'Only got your word for that, though.'

'Ah.' Aciava sounded pleased. 'So you've had enough of bland assertions, and want some hard evidence. I think we can manage that.'

Frowning, Poldarn laid down his hammer. The work would go cold and the fire would probably go out, but he wasn't too bothered about that. 'Go on, then,' he said.

'Fine.' Aciava took a step forward, and broke into the circle of firelight. As if to greet him, the fire flared up (or else it was just poor-quality charcoal). Poldarn felt a sharp tug in the tendons of his right arm. 'Let's see,' he said. 'What would you like me to prove first?'

Put like that – good question; and he hadn't given it any thought. 'My name,' he said. 'Prove to me that I used to be called Poldarn.'

'All right.' First, Aciava held up his hands, like a conjuror demonstrating that he had nothing palmed or up his sleeve. Then he drew his coat open and reached for his sash. As he did so, he took a step forward. Maybe it was the way Aciava did it, or else at the back of his mind Poldarn was thinking about the sword he'd seen there the previous evening; he skipped back two steps, and seized the hammer. At once, Aciava raised his hands again.

'Reflex,' he said. 'Something you'll never be rid of, no matter how hard you try. You were trained to do that from third grade onwards. I made it look like I was drawing my sword, so you took two steps back, left leg first, and grabbed for the nearest weapon. Conclusion: you used to be a sword-monk.'

'Maybe,' Poldarn conceded. 'But I'd sort of figured that out before you showed up. And if you do that again, don't blame me if I bash your head in.'

Aciava grinned. 'You can try,' he said. 'Actually, that's just the first stage of the proof, to establish that you were

once a member of the order. Now, take a look at this.'
Very slowly, he dipped his fingers into an inside pocket
and fished out a scrap of paper. 'Nothing very exciting,'
he said, 'just a twenty-year-old class timetable. See for
yourself.'

He looked round, picked up a fairly clean piece of rag
from the floor, and spread it rather ostentatiously on the
anvil; then he put the paper on it and stood back.

It was just a list of names; twenty of them, divided into
four unequal groups. One of them read;

Elaos Tanwar
Xipho Dorunoxy
Monachus Ciartan
Monachus Cordomine
Gain Aciava
Monachus Poldarn

Poldarn took a closer look, trying to force himself to be
calm, analytical. The paper could easily have been twenty
years old; it was yellow and frayed across two folds, and
the ink was greyish-brown. The letters – well, he could read
them without thinking, but it wasn't the same alphabet that
they used in Tulice. There weren't any names in the other
groups that he recognised, though several of them started
with *Monachus*; he remembered what Aciava had said the
previous evening, and guessed that those were names-in-
religion. There were four little pinholes, one in each corner,
as you'd expect on a notice put up on a door or a notice-
board.

'That's not proof,' he said. 'The most it could mean is
that there was once a class with people with those names
in it. Or this could just be something you wrote yourself,
and dipped in vegetable stock to make it turn yellow.'

'Very good,' Aciava said. 'And if I showed you my business seal, with Gain Aciava engraved on it, you'd tell me I murdered someone with that name and took his seal before I wrote the paper. Fair enough. I said I'd show you some evidence. I didn't say it was irrefutable. But now you've got to tell me why I'd go to so much trouble.'

It was Poldarn's turn to grin. 'I can't,' he said. 'Not without knowing who you really are, and what you're really up to.'

'Quite.' Aciava dipped his head to acknowledge the point. 'As I recall, you weren't at all bad at analytical reasoning when we did it in fifth grade. Better than me, anyhow. Mind you, I did miss a lot of classes, because of them clashing with archery practice. I was on the archery team, you see.'

'I'm impressed,' Poldarn yawned. 'So this is your proof, is it? Just this little bit of old paper.'

'*Allegedly* old paper – you missed an opportunity. Come on, it was twenty years ago, what do you expect? I was damned lucky to have found that; I mean, who keeps old school notices?'

'Good question, who does? Why would you hang on to something like that?'

'Look on the back,' Aciava replied. Poldarn did so. He saw a sketch: a diagram of an eight-pointed figure, drawn in charcoal, and below it a childish doodle of a vaguely heraldic-looking crow.

'The diagram,' Aciava said, 'is the eight principal wards. Lecture notes. The crow was just me being bored during lessons, though I probably chose to draw it because the crow was our team mascot. I was never very imaginative, even then. Innovation's always struck me as being somehow disrespectful. Result of a religious upbringing, I suppose, the tendency to couple together the words *original* and *sin*. Anyhow, to answer your question: I kept the paper for the sketch, and it was sheer accident, coming across it the other day. I'd used it to mark the place in an old textbook. Satisfied?'

Poldarn shook his head. 'No,' he said. 'There's still nothing linking that name on that bit of paper to me. If you can do that—'

'Can't, sorry.' Aciava scratched his ear. 'And I haven't brought anything else with me, because – well, to be honest, I wasn't expecting this kind of attitude, all this suspicion and hostility. I thought that maybe you'd be in two minds about whether you'd want me to tell you about the past and all, but I didn't anticipate that you wouldn't believe me. It's like I'd given you a cute little carved ivory box for your birthday and you're demanding to see a receipt.'

'Really?' Poldarn raised an eyebrow. 'You told me you knew about what happened when I went to Deymeson. Didn't it occur to you that after that I wasn't likely to be in a hurry to believe anything a sword-monk tells me?'

'Now you put it like that,' Aciava conceded, 'I can see your point, sort of. But all right, then. You tell me what'd make you believe, and I'll see what I can do.'

Poldarn turned away and started raking out the hearth. 'Why should I?' he said. 'If you're lying, I'd be telling you how to deceive me.'

'Fine.' Was there just a hint of impatience in Aciava's voice? Or was that just play-acting too?

'I'll tell you what I think, shall I? I think you still don't want to know the truth about yourself, and not believing me's the only way you can do it. If you can persuade yourself I'm lying, you can chicken out of learning who you used to be. Am I getting warm?'

Poldan frowned; any warmer, and he wouldn't have to bother lighting the fire. 'You can think what you like,' he said. 'But maybe you should go and do it somewhere else. This is tricky work, and I need to concentrate.'

Aciava yawned. 'Not all that tricky,' he said. 'You've

done the drawing down, so now all you need to do is bend
the angles on a bick stake and punch the holes. Like I said,'
he added cheerfully, 'I do my homework.'

That, or he can read minds. 'If you're so smart, you do
it.'

'Not likely. I'd get my hands dirty. Besides, my idea of
research is looking stuff up in books. Except for sword drill,
I'm what you might call physically inept. And I'm not here
to do your work for you. I don't think your outfit could
afford me, for one thing.'

Maybe it was the residue of a religious upbringing,
Poldarn thought; this compulsion to fence, shadow-box,
score points, even at the risk of seriously pissing off the
person you were talking to. If so, it was the most convincing
thing about Aciava. Unless it too was fake (homework, and
attention to detail). 'I see,' he said. 'So, what are you here
for? We've established that it's not just for a class reunion.'

Aciava sighed. 'Not just that, no. I need your help. Or—
' He hesitated, as if he was trying to figure out how to put
it tactfully. 'I thought I could use your help. Now, no
offence, but I'm not so sure. You've changed, you know.
Hardly surprising, after all these years, and the stuff you've
been through. I suppose I have, too. But you're—'

'I'm what?'

'Smaller.' There was a faint, sad smile on Aciava's face.
'You've lost something, you know? That hardened edge,
that touch of devilment—' He walked past Poldarn and sat
on the small anvil. 'It's only a slight change, but it makes
all the difference. Pity.'

If Aciava was trying to be annoying, he certainly had
the knack for it. 'I've got no idea what you mean,' Poldarn
said.

'Don't suppose you have.' Aciava pulled a stick of dried
meat out of his pocket, bit off the end and started to chew.
'It's all part of the tragedy, I guess. Not only have you lost

that extra something that made you special, you don't know you ever had it. Now that's sad.'

Lying. Of course. But—

'Explain,' Poldarn said.

'All right, then,' Aciava replied, spitting something out. 'Here's a little story for you. Back in fourth grade – I think; not totally sure. Anyhow, it was our first lesson in full-contact sparring. Wooden swords, no worries. Anyhow, Father Tutor calls for a volunteer. All the volunteer's got to do is knock the sword out of Father Tutor's hand, and he'll be let off the ten-mile cross-country run scheduled for that evening. Now you never could abide running, you'd rather stand and fight a herd of stampeding cattle. So up you go; you both stand on the mat, bow and draw, Father Tutor swats the wooden sword out of your hand and cracks you across the cheekbone, hard enough to draw blood. You take a step back, ask – well, demand's more like it, you demand to be given another shot at it. So you try again, same result, only he bloodies your other cheek. Never mind, he says, you've shown character and there was no way you'd ever have been able to win, you're let off the run. But no, you say, give me another chance. Father Tutor grins, and this time, instead of bashing you, he kicks your knee out from under you before you've even reached for the hilt. You go down on your bum, everybody laughs like mad, Father Tutor says, right, back to your place. But you won't go. You're hopping mad, and you demand another try. No, says Father Tutor, now sit down. But you won't sit down. You shout; one more try, just one. Now, instead of punishing you, like we all thought he would, for not showing respect and doing as you're told, Father Tutor nods and says, all right, but if you fail this time, you run fifteen miles, carrying a sack of stones. Fine, you say, and you both stand on the mat; but before he can go for his sword, you drop down on one knee, grab the edge of the mat and give it an almighty tug. Polished floor, of course; you pull the mat out from under him and Father Tutor goes down flat on his back. He's up again like a flash, into position, hand on sash ready for the draw, but you look him in the eye and just stand there. Draw, he says. No, you say, and you fold your arms and grin. I said draw, he says; but you shake your head again and say, No, I won't; precepts of religion – like you've scored a point or something. And he scowls at you and says, What do you mean, precepts of religion? And that's when you grab an inkwell off the lectern and throw it in his face. He's not expecting that; and while he's staggering back with ink in his eyes, you reach forward, cool as ice, pull the wooden sword out of his sash and throw it across the room. Never heard such silence in all my life. We were sure he was going to kill you, or at least kick your arse clean over to Torcea; but all he does is stand there, dripping ink, and finally he says, Yes, I see what you mean, well done. And then he lets you off the run, class dismissed, and we're all out in the fresh air half an hour early.'

Poldarn waited to see if there was any more, but apparently not. 'I don't understand,' he said.

'Oh.' Aciava looked disappointed. 'Precepts of religion,' he said. 'The best fight is not to fight. And you didn't – fight him, I mean. Beating you wasn't enough for him, he wanted a proper drawing match, to prove his point. He wanted to fight. You didn't. All you wanted to do was win. Your best fight was not to fight at all. So you won.'

Poldarn thought about that for a little while. It sounded too romantic to be true; it sounded like something you'd be taught in school, as an example. 'That doesn't sound like me,' he said.

'Of course not.' Aciava stood up. 'You'd never do anything like that now – proves my point. You've changed.

Back then, you cared about winning. Now, you don't care about anything.' He took a couple of steps toward the door, then turned round. 'If you want to me to go away and never come back, just say so. I can still help you, but you're no earthly good to me any more. It's like with you and Xipho. You finally got her, but it doesn't count, because it wasn't really you. The real you just wasn't there.'

'Fine,' Poldarn said. 'The real me sounds like a menace.'

Aciava looked at him. 'What do you want?' he said. 'Most of all, in all the world?'

Poldarn thought. 'I don't know,' he said.

'There, you see. The real Poldarn wouldn't even have had to think; there'd have been something he wanted, and he'd have answered, just like that. Victory, revenge, to be the Emperor, to know the truth, there'd have been *something*. Something worth coming back for. But you.' He shook his head. 'You're just a waste of space.'

Poldarn turned his back. The fire was almost out, but not quite. With the rake, he flicked a handful of unburnt charcoal onto the glowing embers, and pulled down hard on the bellows handle. The red heart of the fire glowed immediately. *He'd have answered, just like that.* No need to ask fire what it wants; it wants to burn. No such thing as a fire without purpose.

'Goodbye,' Poldarn said. 'I'm sorry I couldn't help you.'

'Doesn't matter. Sweet dreams.'

Poldarn turned to face Aciava. 'What's that supposed to mean?' he asked.

Aciava grinned. 'I shared a dormitory with you all those years,' he said. 'You get strange dreams, where you live bits of other people's lives. True stuff, things you couldn't possibly know about, but in your dreams you're there, like you'd found your way into the other guy's memory. Do you still get them?'

'I'm not sure,' Poldarn said. 'I know I get dreams, and

they're incredibly vivid, and all sorts of things happen. Sometimes, I think, I even die. But when I wake up, they're all gone, about a second after I open my eyes. All that's left is, I remember that, for that one second, I *knew*—'

Aciava nodded. 'Sounds right enough. We used to think it was because you were one of them, the island people from across the ocean. They can read minds, for want of a better way of putting it, and we reckoned you saw bits of memories in other people's minds, and explored them in your sleep. To begin with, it was just like you're describing now; you knew there'd been something, but as soon as you woke up, it went away again. Then Tanwar and Xipho found something in a book in the library, about how to make it so you could remember your dreams when you woke up. You tried it, and it worked.'

Poldarn looked at him doubtfully. 'Did it?'

'So you told us,' Aciava replied. 'We only had your word for it, of course. But we trusted you. Anyhow, I suppose you must've forgotten how to do it, along with everything else. It's very simple,' he went on. 'You just think of something, deliberately, when you're awake – a white cat, for instance, or a carthorse, or an old blind man selling buttons. Come to think of it, you decided on a crow, because of it being our group mascot. Anyway, next time you had a dream, there was a crow in it somewhere; and you knew, deep down inside you somewhere, even while the dream was going on, that you were just dreaming and that the crow was you. And ever since then, you could always remember the dream when you woke up. You couldn't help it,' he added, 'after that it always just happened. All your dreams had a crow or two in them, and they didn't melt away as soon as you opened your eyes.'

Poldarn stared at him. 'And these dreams,' he said, 'they were other people's memories?'

'Mostly,' Aciava replied. 'Just occasionally, you told us

you saw glimpses of the future. But we were almost sure you were lying.'

A strange chill spread up from Poldarn's fingertips. 'I think,' he said, 'that if you're right—'

'Proof?' Aciava grinned lopsidedly. 'If you find yourself remembering your dreams from now on, you'll know I've been telling the truth? Oh, come *on*.' He yawned. 'See you around,' he said. 'You *have* changed, you know – rather a lot. For one thing, the man I used to know – he was a lot of things, but he wasn't a coward.'

Poldarn frowned. 'Should I be mortally offended by that? I'm not.'

'You've changed. And now, if you'll excuse me, I have to go and poke about in rich people's mouths.'

Aciava was almost through the door when Poldarn spoke to him. 'Hey,' he said. 'Have you changed too?'

'Me?' Aciava hesitated, as though it was something he hadn't previously considered. 'Oh, sure. Ever such a lot. Take care of yourself. Don't cast any square bells.'

Of course, the fire had gone out. Poldarn prodded it a few times to make sure, then took the rake to it. There was a fist-sized chunk of clinker jammed in the flue. After he'd dragged that out, he had no trouble getting it lit.

Chapter Three

Behind him, the sea was just a huge grey shape; he wasn't concerned with it any more. He trudged across the beach, worried about turning his ankle over in the deep shingle. Well, he thought, here I am. Directly ahead, a seagull got up and dragged itself into the air, shrieking resentfully at him. At some point in its ascent, it turned into a very large, very black crow.

(*Like burning wood, only in reverse; white ash to black charcoal. Which means this fire is burning backwards. Which is fine; now I know where I am.*)

The contact was waiting for him on the edge of the shingle; a woman, young, not pretty. 'You're him, then,' she said.

He wasn't in the mood for cryptic stuff. 'Depends,' he yawned.

'The spy.'

'Ah yes.' He grinned. 'That'll be me.'

'You're to follow me up to the farm,' she said. She turned and started to walk. He shrugged, and did as he'd been told.

It was a long way, all uphill, and he hadn't had much exercise on the long sea journey. 'Hold on,' he said breathlessly. 'You're going too fast.'

'No,' she replied. 'You're dawdling.'

'Ah. Thanks for explaining.'

It didn't look like a farm, when at last they got there. He knew what farms looked like; this was just a shack, like a storage shed or a small barn. Also, it was made of piled-up stones, not wood. He thought of how much work there'd be, building something out of stones. Didn't they have trees in this rotten country?

'We're here,' she said, unnecessarily. 'You wait here, I'll fetch my dad.'

'Here' was a small cobbled yard. In one corner stood a mounting-block: red sandstone, overgrown with moss and a busy green-leafed weed he hadn't seen before. Opposite was a midden, of great size and antiquity, newly garnished with leek stalks, turnip-tops and half a dozen fresh turds. Behind that was the plank wall of a small lean-to; the timbers were grey, and about a hundred years ago someone had nailed up two stags' heads to cure. For some reason or other they'd never come back for them, and now the bone was smudged with green. Directly in front of him was the house. There was a doorway, but apparently no door. Through it, he could see a stone-flagged floor, and a chicken wandering aimlessly about, pecking.

Charming place, he thought. And this is probably the garden spot of the whole Empire.

A man appeared in the doorway and stared at him. He stared back. It was pretty obvious that neither of them had ever seen a foreigner before.

'You,' said the man. 'You speak—?'

He'd said a word that made no sense; the name of the language, presumably. 'Yes,' Ciartan replied.

'Oh, right. Didn't know if you did or not.'

'Learned it on the boat,' Ciartan lied. 'So you're our contact, then.'

The man shook his head. 'I just do as I'm told,' he said. 'Bloke you want, he's due in the morning. Meanwhile, you're to wait here. There's dinner, if you want any.'

'Thank you,' Ciartan said politely. 'Do I come in, or what?'

The man nodded gloomily, and stood back to let him pass. Inside, the house was even stranger than on the outside. Ciartan found himself in a tiny little room, no more than ten feet square. It was empty, apart from a few pairs of muddy boots and a rusty scythe, and there didn't seem to be any point to it. The man went through a doorway in the far wall; Ciartan followed, and found himself in another small room. This one had a table and six chairs in it. Bizarre, Ciartan thought. Do people really live like this?

'What is this place?' he asked.

'What?'

'This – building,' Ciartan replied. 'Is it some sort of lodge or guest house or something?'

The man looked at him as though he'd just said something offensive. 'It's my house,' he said.

'Oh.' Well, no reason why the man should be lying. 'Isn't it a bit cramped, then?'

'No.' Ciartan got the impression that the man didn't like him much. 'It's plenty big.'

'I see. How many of you live here, then?'

The man gave him a none-of-your-business-but look. 'There's six of us, seven if you count the nipper. Me, the wife, our eldest – Jarla, you met her just now – and the three boys, and Mito, that's the babe.'

'Oh.' Just seven of them; no wonder the house was so tiny. 'It's different, where I come from,' he said, and hoped that'd do for an explanation. The man either accepted it or didn't care. 'You can sit down if you like,' he said.

'Thanks.' The chair was small, too, and thin, made out of little twiggy bits of wood. No arms. Pathetic bloody excuse for a chair, really.

'The wife'll get you your dinner,' the man said. 'I got work to do.'

Ciartan looked up. For a moment he felt confused; he had been made aware that there was work to be done, but he didn't know what it was, and therefore couldn't figure out what part of it he should be doing. He expected the man to tell him, in default of normal methods of communication, but he just walked away.

Unimpressive, Ciartan decided. You'd have thought that, if these people really couldn't hear each others' minds and had to rely on spoken words to talk to each other, they'd have been rather better at it than either this man or his daughter appeared to be. Apparently not. Already, he was starting to feel vaguely panicky. He hadn't really given much thought to the implications of what he'd been told; that these people couldn't hear minds, didn't even know it was possible, and that their minds couldn't be heard by normal people. In fact, it was downright frightening. For one thing, how on earth were you supposed to know if they were telling the truth or not?

My mother was one of this lot, he remembered uneasily. The idea was disconcerting, as if he ought to be on his guard, in case half of his body turned out to be on their side.

He realised that he was uncomfortably cold, and that the fire in the hearth (one small fireplace, and stuck in the *wall*, not the middle of the room; now that was just plain perverse) had gone out. The urge to get up and light it was almost overpowering – you see that a fire's gone out, you light it, that's what people *do*; but since everything else was arse-backwards here, maybe he'd be better off leaving it alone. He had an idea he'd already made enough trouble for himself as it was.

He kept himself amused for a while by looking at the battery of strange metal gadgets in the fireplace, trying to figure out what they were for. The poker and tongs were easy enough, though they were ever such a funny shape; but the thing with the long iron spikes – clearly it revolved around its axis, but why? For a long time he couldn't think what it could be used for, except as a particularly unpleasant instrument of torture. Then inspiration struck; maybe they used it for cooking. You could stick a lump of meat on the spikes – it'd have to be a really big lump, you could practically get a whole sheep on there – and then somehow the thing with the chains and weights would turn the whole thing round, so that the meat would get warmed up evenly all over – yes, and that huge iron dish underneath was to catch the juices and the dripping as they drained off. Ingenious, in a cockamamy sort of a way.

A woman came in, carrying a small wooden plate. She was short, and looked as though all the features of her face had been worn away by rain and wind, or by over-vigorous polishing. On the plate were a few slices of hard grey bread, some indeterminate vegetable matter, and what Ciartan devoutly hoped was a sausage. The woman looked away as soon as she could, as if he was somehow obscene, and scuttled back the way she'd come.

The food was, of course, disgusting.

Nobody else came anywhere near him, though from time to time he could hear voices in the yard outside. There were young kids screaming; the man shouting at someone; a female, probably the daughter rather than the wife, singing as she went about some chore or other. He saw the red light of sunset through the doorway, and then it was suddenly dark. It was also getting even colder, all the time. He hoped, and prayed earnestly to the non-existent gods, that this house was just a crummy little peasant shack and not anything bigger or better. If this place was the sort of house the local gentry lived in, then screw spying and screw being in disgrace, he was going home.

Only he couldn't, of course.

No way home, unless he fancied swimming. No ships; and even if there were any, none of them would be going where he wanted to go, for the simple reason that nobody on this side of the water suspected that his homeland even existed. Stranded, he told himself. Marooned. Stuck.

Or, looked at from a different perspective, a brand new start, a new life in a new country; rebirth. Here, he didn't have to be Ciartan from Haldersness any more, with all the trouble and unpleasantness that that implied; he could be any damned thing he liked. The question was whether there was anything in this miserable place worth being.

But there. Here I go, he thought, judging an egg by its shell. Bloody stupid proverb. He'd almost made up his mind to light the fire and the hell with the lot of them, when the man came back, carrying a very small pottery lamp.

'I'll show you where you're sleeping,' he said.

'Thank you,' Ciartan heard himself reply, and he wondered if he'd have his very own pile of damp straw or whether he'd be mucking in with the pigs. Instead, he found himself following the man up a flight of narrow stairs into what was presumably the roof space: big beams and joists, and a triangular ceiling. But the room was huge; ten feet square, at least, and in the middle was a large wooden thing, with something that looked like a flat square bag on top, and another smaller bag up against the wall. 'What's that?' he couldn't help asking.

'What?'

'That thing there.'

'It's a bed,' the man told him, and Ciartan, whose best guess so far had been some kind of cider press, was too astonished to say anything. A bed. Well, bugger me. I wonder how it works.

The man put the lamp down on a stool and went away again, and Ciartan walked over and examined the large wooden contraption. Hell of a lot of trouble to go to just for sleeping, he thought; hell, even Grandad dosses down on a pile of old fleeces, and his room's half the size of this. Do they all use these extraordinary sleeping machines, or is this just for princes of the whole blood and other hon- oured guests?

He tried hard to pluck up the courage to get up on it, but couldn't quite manage it. For one thing, it had to be the best part of three feet off the floor; what was there to stop you rolling off it in your sleep and crashing to the ground? You could break your arm. Instead, he nervously tugged off a blanket, wrapped himself in it (no fire in the fireplace) and shivered himself to sleep. Perhaps it was the strange- ness of his surroundings, or maybe it was just the horrible, indigestible food, but he found himself dreaming, and even by his standards, it was a very strange dream. There were crows in it, of course, and—

Poldarn woke up.

The familiar feeling, of the dream slithering away; but then he reached out and caught it, and it stayed trapped in his mind, like a lobster in a basket.

Memory, he thought. And the man in the dream was called Ciartan. That was me.

(A fire burning backwards; unconsuming what had once been destroyed and gone for ever. Crows that brought carrion, instead of taking it away.)

Time to get up. Get out of bed. Wash. Eat something. Go to work. He yawned.

Outside, in the hazy sunlight, something had begun without him. As he stood in the doorway of his cabin and watched the foundrymen hurrying backwards and for- wards across the yard, he couldn't help being reminded of

Haldersness, where everybody knew what they had to do without being told. There was a difference, but he couldn't quite figure out what it was.

'There you are,' said a voice on the edge of his vision. 'Been looking for you.'

Bergis, the head mud wrangler. Too late now to dart back inside; so he smiled feebly and asked how he could help.

'We're starting on the ward-tower bell for Falcata guild lodge,' Bergis replied. 'When you've pulled yourself together, I'll see you down at the cutting.'

Poldarn managed not to groan until Bergis was out of earshot. Marvellous. The cutting was what the foundrymen called the thick seam of grey muddy clay, which was the main reason why the foundry had been built here in the first place. Mixed with straw and lots and lots of cowshit, the cutting clay was perfect for building moulds and lining furnaces, being capable of soaking up vast amounts of heat and retaining it without cracking. It was also very sticky and slimy, and it didn't smell very nice, either. Bergis's job was to pounce on anybody who didn't see him coming and march him off to the cutting to dig and pack the revolting stuff. A job this size would probably call for at least five tons.

Oh well, Poldarn thought, never mind. He picked up a long-handled shovel from the tool store, and drifted slowly across the yard and down the slope through the scraggy wasteland the foundrymen referred to, rather bizarrely, as the orchard.

They'd already filled one cart by the time he got there. As usual, they'd piled so much into the cart that it was far too heavy to move, even with a team of mules pulling and the digging crew pushing; the more they heaved and struggled, the more bogged down the cart became, its wheels digging wide, soft ruts in the grey sludge. Eventually, someone would break down and fetch a few barrowloads of straw to pack under the wheels; until then, they'd wear themselves out and get spattered in mud up to their eyebrows trying to shift it by brute force. Hell of a way to run a commercial enterprise, but it wasn't Poldarn's place to make suggestions; particularly blindingly obvious ones.

It was too early in the morning for mud-wrestling and pulled muscles, so Poldarn gave the cart a wide berth and headed for the digging pit. The drill was to fill the wicker baskets with mud; when they were full and each one weighed slightly more than a farrier's small anvil, they had to be manhandled up off the ground and onto the bed of the cart. Grabbing the nearest empty basket, Poldarn walked up to the glistening grey face of the pit and started carving his way into it, like a cook slicing a hefty joint of meat. There was, of course, a knack to it, a matter of angles, leverage, mechanical advantage, which Poldarn mostly understood but couldn't quite get right.

Well now, he thought, as he stamped the shovel into the clay with his heel. The man – Gain Aciava, though that remains to be proved conclusively – was right about the dreams; so, either he's a shrewd guesser who knows how dreams work, or he was telling the truth. As for the dream itself: entirely plausible, but it didn't really show me anything I hadn't already conjectured for myself, so it could just've been me reconstructing my first hours on this continent, like a scholar speculating about things that happened a thousand years ago. Nothing decided either way; but do I *believe*? It's like asking me, do I believe in gods?

Do I believe?

Yes, Poldarn discovered, apparently I do. I think that's how it was when I first came here: the plain girl and her annoying father, and everything seeming strange, and the revolting food. Question is: am I remembering what happened, or has somebody told me the truth about some-thing I've forgotten, like the scholar suddenly discovering an ancient manuscript? Does it matter?

He considered the point; yes, it probably mattered a hell of a lot, because if he believed the dream, he probably couldn't avoid believing Aciava as well. Now that could be awkward.

(But here I am anyway, in a filthy mess, digging clay out of a stinking hole in the ground in return for a few ladles of grey soup and the privilege of sleeping in a turf hut. The question can therefore only be: is it worth risking all this for the sake of finding out who I used to be? And the answer can only be: no, it isn't.)

The blade of Poldarn's shovel hit a stone, and the shock jarred his wrists and elbows. He winced; for some time he'd had an idea that he'd done something to damage the joints or tendons of his arms. Maybe it was the forge work, or perhaps it was an old injury, the result of drawing a sword and slashing empty air a thousand times a day for years on end. Pretty metaphor – no idea where the damage came from or how far back it went, dimly aware that it could have a harmful effect on his future, too stupid to care. His elbow was aching, as if he'd just banged his funny bone. Not a good sign, but here he was anyway; and the mud wasn't going to prise itself out of the bank and climb into the basket.

Only an idiot ignores the past and takes risks with his future; but Nature relies on idiots, or nothing would ever work properly. If it wasn't for the stupidity of all rabbits, hawks and foxes would starve to death; if cows and chickens stopped for a moment to consider that maybe something was wrong, there'd be no milk and eggs on the table. If the god in the cart happened to look over his shoulder and notice the trail of ruined cities and burning farms stretched out behind him, the prophecies would never be fulfilled and the world could never end. And then where would we all be?

But here he was anyway, digging clay when maybe he should be a Father Tutor, with purple slippers and a personal chaplain to open his letters for him. He thought about that; a sword-monk with a trick elbow was about as much use as a blind helmsman, and just as liable to die young. By the same token, there's not much call for a smith who can't swing a hammer, or a foundryman who can't dig. Once the injury's there, and that joint or tendon has acquired its small, crippling piece of history, the damage is done; and the glorious irony is that it's the craftsman's history of practising his craft that makes him unable to practise it further in the future – you can lose the memory, but still the pattern bleeds through the bandage. *I am what I was, I will be what I am, the mechanism of history is a circular movement with a repeating escapement, like a trip-hammer.* Poldarn clenched his left hand. His elbow still ached, and the tips of his fingers had gone numb. (And if my arm is my life, the damaged tendon connects the pain and the loss of memory.) 'Bugger,' he said, and leaned the shovel against the side of the pit. What he needed, even more than the exquisite symmetry of it all, was some nice hot water to soak his arm in. Well, at least he was in a foundry, where hot water was never a problem.

'Here,' Bergis shouted as he hauled himself out of the cutting. 'Where do you think you're sloping off to?'

'Furnace,' Poldarn replied. 'Done my wrist in.'

Bergis pulled a face; either sympathy or annoyance at lost production. Knowing Bergis, probably lots of both. 'Don't take all day,' he said.

Number five furnace was a baked-clay beehive, suitable for bees the size of vultures. As Poldarn approached, lugging a large copper pan full of water in his good hand, the two firekeepers looked up from their game of knuckle-bones and grinned at him. 'Hurt your arm?' said one of them.

Poldarn nodded. 'Hit a stone.'

The firekeeper nodded. 'Watch you don't splash the clay,' he said. 'It's getting pretty warm in there.'

Fair point; a stray drop of water on the hot clay could make it crack or even shatter, and that'd be a week's work spoilt. He set the pan down very carefully, then sat on a spare stool. 'Room for one more?' he asked, though he wasn't all that wild about knuckle-bones; as a game, it was too random to be interesting, and besides, he was a pretty hopeless gambler.

'Sure,' the other firekeeper said 'Basic rules: five and seven wild, three means roll again, and twelve pays the banker. Two quarters buys you in, half-quarter to raise and quit. All right?'

Poldarn nodded. 'I'll have to owe you,' he said. 'Left my money in my other coat.'

'You haven't got another coat.'

'True,' Poldarn admitted, and dug out a handful of coins, which went in the pot. True to form, he lost on the first four games.

'Don't worry,' said the firekeeper, raking the coins over to his side of the playing area. 'Your luck's about to change, I can feel it.'

'That's what I'm afraid of,' Poldarn replied gloomily.

He won the next game, lost the next two, won the fourth. By then, his pan of water had warmed through. The fire-keepers helped him lift it off, and he sat out the next five games, his arm sunk in the hot water. He had three quarters left to his name, having lost a total of nine.

'You *used* to have another coat, though,' the firekeeper suddenly remembered. 'What happened to it?'

'Lost it playing knuckle-bones,' Poldarn replied. 'Go on, I can throw right-handed if I've got to.'

The firekeeper pursed his lips. 'Dead unlucky, that.'

Poldarn grinned. 'Ah yes,' he said, 'but my luck's about to change. Your half-quarter and raise you a quarter.'

'Can if you like.' The firekeeper shook the bones in his cupped hands, blew on them for luck and threw. 'Three,' he announced. 'Roll again. Bugger.'

'Twelve,' said his friend. 'Twelves pay the bank. Who's the bank?'

They counted back through the previous games, and it turned out to be Poldarn's go. Including the three quarters he'd just paid in, the pot came to exactly twelve, which was what he'd started with. 'That'll do me,' he announced cheerfully and stood up, ignoring the protests of the fire-keepers. 'My arm's much better now, so I think I'll go and do some work. Thanks for the game.'

'Welcome,' grunted one of the firekeepers, his eyes fixed on the bones and his small pile of coins. Poldarn waved to his turned back, and walked slowly across the yard toward the cutting. Someone else had appropriated his shovel and bucket, not that he minded. 'About bloody time,' Bergis grumbled, as he came back with replacements. 'What took you so long?'

'Won twelve quarters in the dice game.'

(Which was true, he reflected, as he stamped in the shovel blade; at least, it was true in the present, though the past made it a lie. He wondered if the same applied to what Aciava had told him. That'd be a laugh, if no matter how long he played for, he always ended up with exactly what he'd started out with. Forever going round in circles, like the miller's donkey.)

'Is it just me,' Spenno the pattern-maker complained to nobody in particular, 'or doesn't anybody care whether we make this fucking bell or not?'

Nobody said anything. In all the time he'd been at the foundry, Poldarn couldn't recall a single instance of anybody answering one of Spenno's questions. He seemed to exist in a bubble floating on the crest of ordinary communication, up where everybody could see him but no one could make out what he was saying.

Under other circumstances, Poldarn might have found Spenno's patterns of behaviour disconcerting or even alarming, but he'd come to the conclusion that they were just another aspect of the different rules that applied to everything concerned with casting bronze. In this instance, it was a positive comfort to hear Spenno yelling into space, since he only ever seemed to get this frantic when everything was going perfectly according to plan. As soon as an unforeseen difficulty arose, Spenno would stop ranting and prancing; instead, he'd scuttle purposefully about the yard as quickly and deftly as a mouse, muttering, 'It'll be fine now' or 'That's got that sorted' under his breath. In the face of disaster and catastrophe, he'd pull out an ancient folding chair, park it in the middle of the yard, prop his feet up on a pile of scrap metal or cordwood, and spend a relaxing hour or so turning the pages of a battered and incredibly ancient-looking book with the intriguing title *Concerning Various Matters*, which he carried with him at all times, stuffed down inside his shirt. Whether the book really did contain the answers to all conceivable problems, as Spenno claimed, or whether he used it as an aid to relaxation and concentration, and thought the solutions up out of his own head, nobody knew or greatly cared.

Today, however, Spenno was yelling and waving his arms about, so it was safe to assume that all was well. The pattern itself was already well under way. Spenno had started at crack of dawn with a stout oak pole, which he'd planed down to a taper. He'd worked with drawknives and spokeshaves and planes and scrapers, hurling each tool over his shoulder when he'd finished with it and yelling for someone to pick it up and hand it to him when he needed it again.

Once he'd finished it and walked round it several times, squinting along it from various angles, shaking his head and swearing fluently, he fitted a cranked handle at the top end and slotted a thick oak plank over each end, so that the pole spun freely when the crank was turned. Now he was building the mould itself around this spindle, smacking and punching handfuls of clay onto the gradually forming core, while two bored-looking men slowly turned the handle. Every so often he'd stop, run his clay-caked hands through his hair and shriek abuse at his handiwork, before plunging his fingers into a basin of water. Apart from Poldarn, nobody seemed to be paying any attention to this performance; and Poldarn, who'd seen it all before, was only watching because he had nothing in particular to do.

'You there.' Poldarn, who'd slipped into a sort of gentle trance, looked up. 'Yes, you, miserable gloomy bastard with the big nose. Get up here and do *exactly* what I tell you.'

Poldarn sighed and stood up. He knew what Spenno would want him to do, because he'd watched him the previous evening, cutting a bell-shaped template out of pine board with a large fretsaw. It wasn't the template itself that was needed at this point in the operation; rather, Spenno would use one side of the leftover plank, which had a perfect silhouette of half a bell cut out of it. Poldarn's job would be to shove this against the clay core as the crank-operators turned it, to shear off the excess clay and leave the exact profile behind, smooth and regular. Marvellously clever, Poldarn reckoned; pity it was such a filthy job.

How long it took, he couldn't say; it seemed like a very long time, and since all he had to do was stand still and lean on the plank, he allowed his mind to wander. Spenno's constant stream of rage and despair soon began to have a pleasantly soporific effect, like rain on thatch, or the chatter of a shallow rill tumbling down through rocks. In the distance, forming a kind of counterpoint, he could hear the heavy clang of sledgehammers on thick bronze plate, where a working party was smashing up an old, flawed bell for scrap. More pleasant symmetry, Poldarn thought; and everywhere he turned there was symmetry, from the relentless cycle of scrap and melt to the clay core being turned to shape next to him. A man could be fooled, if he let his guard down. He could allow himself to be persuaded that symmetry was his friend, instead of the main component of the trap he should be avoiding. Maybe, he speculated, that was why Spenno ranted against it, when everything seemed to be going so well; no doubt about it, Spenno was a clever sod, a genius in his own way, so it wasn't inconceivable that he'd noticed something that had managed to escape everyone else's attention. Symmetry, pattern, shapes being formed; perhaps that was the secret wisdom known only to pattern-makers – eccentrics like Spenno, and himself.

'Bloody fucking *thing*,' Spenno said; and that was apparently the accepted word of command to stop turning the crank. The core stopped dead, making Poldarn lurch forward and drop his plank scraper. 'Right, you lot bugger off, and for crying out loud none of you touch it, it's *wet*, it hasn't *dried yet*. Understood?'

The crank-winders shrugged and walked away. Now the core had to be left to dry, while Spenno scampered away to the middle shed, to heat up a large cauldron full of tallow. Once it was hot and soft, he'd start kneading it in his hands into long, flabby strips, to be pressed onto the clay core until he'd built up a layer of tallow as thick as the bell walls. The tallow would be left to set, until it was hard enough to be cut with knives and chisels; then the carvers and lettermen would get to work, gouging out the relief decoration – flowers, birds, scenes from myth and religion, the letters of the dedicatory inscription and so on – before a further thick skin of clay was plastered on top and left to dry. Once the tapered spindle had been carefully withdrawn, the mould would be ready for hauling down to the casting pit, where the tallow would be melted out of the middle, leaving a perfect bell-shaped cavity between the core and the upper clay coating, into which molten bronze could be poured. All very simple, when you stopped and considered it objectively. As with most things, the further away you got, the clearer it became. It was only up close, with splodges of wet clay flying in all directions and Spenno shrieking abuse, that you could be forgiven for wondering what it was all in aid of.

Tallow-warming and tallow-fondling could be relied on to take two or three hours at least; five, if something cocked up and Spenno was driven to the pages of *Concerning Various Matters* for guidance. This made it a good time for avoiding the open yard. With Spenno safely out of the way for a while, the other gang masters (who were all scared stiff of Spenno, though they'd none of them admit it) were liable to come out prowling for anybody with nothing to do and march them off to dig clay or smash up scrap or load charcoal. Having been caught this way on a number of occasions, Poldarn knew the drill: find a safe place to hide, and stay there until Spenno started cursing again.

In Poldarn's case, the forge was as close as he was likely to get to absolute sanctuary; since, if anybody came round with a press-gang, he could always pretend to be busy forging clappers or brackets or hinges or staples; and since nobody else understood forge-work, there was no one to contradict him. He dragged the outer door to, closed up the shutters, raked out the hearth and laid in a fresh bed of charcoal. A good fire always came in handy sooner or later.

Paradox: having fled in here to escape from doing work, Poldarn was now bored and looking round for something to do. The part-finished bell-fittings still lay on the anvil, lightly covered with a thin dew of blotchy red rust, but he couldn't do anything more with them until the bell itself was finished and the final dimensions established. What else? Nothing in particular needed about the place, apart from the insatiable demand for nails. He wasn't in the mood for drawing down nails; it was tedious and fiddly work, and it reminded him of Haldersness.

In search of inspiration, he turned over the outskirts of the scrap pile, in case some interesting-shaped hunk of metal he'd previously overlooked snagged his attention. Since he'd done this dozens of times before it was a fairly vain hope, except that just occasionally he'd catch sight of a width or a profile or a taper he hadn't properly appreciated before, and he'd get an idea. A twisted length of wheel tyre would suddenly look like the leg of a trivet, or a gate-hinge would blossom unexpectedly out of a discarded attempt at a bell-bracket. Well, it was better than spooning clay out of a hole in the ground. Most things were.

This time, something did catch his eye. He had no idea what it had been in its previous life, before it failed at its unknown purpose and got dumped in the scrap; but it was square-section, as long as his arm, tapered up and down from a bulge about two-thirds down its length, and if he was any judge, it was good hardening steel, not soft iron. Just for devilment's sake he picked it out, took it over to the grindstone and touched it lightly against the spinning edge. A shower of small, fat yellow sparks scattered around his hands like falling blossom, telling him everything he needed to know.

Still entirely for devilment, Poldarn pumped the bellows until the fire roared, then poked the sharp point of the bar into the heart of the coals. A dozen or so pulls on the bellows handle: when he drew the bar out, the tip was yellow, sparkling where the steel was burning. Hardening steel all right; he let it cool to bright orange, then dipped it in the slack tub. A small, round cloud of steam drifted up into his face. He clamped the bar in the leg-vice and tested the hardened end with a file, which skated off it like a careless footstep on sheet ice. No cracks that he could see – prime hardening steel, the very best. Far too good to waste. Now all he had to do was think of something to make it into.

Square-section, tapered, as long as his arm. There was really only one use it could be put to, unless he was prepared to sin against serendipity and waste this fine material on a billhook or a crowbar. Then, just as he'd made up his mind what he was going to make out of it, he suddenly realised what it had previously been – a monster bell-clapper, partly drawn down and then abandoned before swaging, probably because the steel had proved too dense and chewy to work comfortably. He smiled, for some reason. Maybe it was because the memory in the steel was an unhappy one, failure and rejection, and he was about to set all that right.

He paused before starting the job. Time. If Spenno didn't run into any snags with his tallow-wrangling, that meant Poldarn would have three hours or thereabouts to work on his pet project today. Without a striker to swing the hammer for him, he'd be hard put to it just to flatten and peen out a thick bar like this one in three hours. That was fine; since it was just a whim, there was no hurry, no schedule to meet. If he didn't manage to get it flattened before he had to go back to work, so what? At least he could make a start. He dug the bar into the coals, drew more charcoal over the top with the rake, and reached up for the bellows handle.

Five or so hours later, Poldarn paused, drew the piece of steel out of the fire and let it rest on the iron surround of the hearth to cool. Definitely getting there; although right now, to anybody but himself, it looked like nothing on earth. He'd drawn it down into the shape of a grotesquely elongated diamond, or a snake that had just swallowed a field mouse; then he'd bent it right round, like a horseshoe. In his mind, the final profile was clearly visible, as if he was able to see into the future; but first he had to forge in the bevel. That would force the tight curve outwards into a gentle concave arc, with the bevel on the inside, and that'd be the easy part done. The pause broke the trance he'd fallen into, hypnotised by the repeating pattern – heat, hammer, heat – and he felt as if he'd just woken up out of a prophetic dream, only part of which he could remember. At any rate, he was getting there; at any rate, he hadn't screwed it up *yet*. Then he remembered about the bell. Oughtn't Spenno to have finished kneading the tallow by now? He glanced down at his piece of work; the next stage would need concentration – if he had to quit halfway through he might easily lose sight of the thread, the tentative insight into his own future where he pulled the finished article out of the quench and held it admiringly up to the light, to check for consistency and straightness. Without that thread, it was still just a piece of scrap from the pile. Best to leave off starting the bevel until another day.

That being so, it'd only be polite to take a stroll out to the yard, just in case they'd begun the laying-on of the tallow without him. It was always a good idea to take a break from what you were doing, once in a while, and spend ten minutes or so on the job you were actually being paid for.

It was still daylight outside. A large group of men were standing or sitting about, mostly in silence, with gloomy, resigned expressions on their faces. As Poldarn got closer to the mould, he could see a glistening skin covering most of the clay; and Spenno, lounging at ease in a rickety wooden chair, reading a book.

Shit, he thought, as bad as that. He'd have turned right round and sneaked back to the forge, except that a dozen or so of the sad loafers had seen him now, and it was never wise to be too obvious when you were skiving. So instead, he amused himself by trying to figure out how far the job had advanced, and what the problem was.

The tallow layer was about half-done, as far as he could judge. A cursory inspection made the nature of the disaster only too obvious: the clay of the core hadn't dried through properly when Spenno had started applying the tallow, and a large chunk the size and shape of a horse's head had broken away and fallen off. In order to put it back they'd have to strip off the tallow that had already been put on; but any attempt at doing that would probably damage the core further. Besides, if the core was breaking up, it was probably riddled with little cracks and flaws, so that when the melted bronze was poured in, there was every chance it'd disintegrate, and the yard would be flooded with very hot runny metal, as quick and antisocial as molten lava from a volcano.

Wonderful. Unless there was something in the book that Spenno was reading, Poldarn couldn't see any way of salvaging the core; all they could do would be to cut their losses by junking the whole thing and beginning again with a new oak pole and a mountain of fresh clay. Patching up a dodgy mould was never worth the risk. Poldarn squatted down on a small pile of logs and cupped his chin in his hands. No wonder everybody looked so miserable. Three days' hard work, all wasted.

The crack that disrupted his train of thought proved to be Spenno closing the book with a snap. 'All right,' he called out, in a voice from which all anger had been leached out, 'tear the bloody thing down, we'll start again in the morning.' Sighs, some muttering, and half a dozen men got to their feet, fetched sledgehammers, and started working out their feelings on the failed core. For flawed, shaken, half-dry clay it took a lot of breaking up. That wasn't helping anything.

Move along, Poldarn thought, nothing to see here. Since there wasn't really anywhere else to go, he wandered back to his horrible little turf-walled shack and lay down on the pile of blankets. Quite out of the blue, he realised how tired he was and closed his eyes.

'So that's why they call your lot blacksmiths,' a voice said.

He sat up and opened his eyes. He must have been asleep for a while, because it was now pitch dark outside. 'Really?' he said groping in the dark for his hand-axe. 'Why's that, then?'

'You obviously haven't seen your reflection,' said the voice. 'Your hands and face. Black as a crow. Are you really going to go to sleep like that, without washing?'

He found the axe and closed his fingers round the shaft. 'Who the hell are you, and what are you doing in my house?' he demanded.

'House.' Clearly he'd said something amusing. 'I like that. I've seen snugger field latrines. Come on, don't you recognise me?'

Now that he mentioned it, yes. 'Aciava,' he said.

'Thought you'd get there in the end. Well,' Aciava went on, 'a right cow you people've made of our bell. Just as well for us there's a penalty clause in the contract to cover late delivery. We can sue you, it'll be something to do while we're waiting.'

Poldarn blinked in surprise. '*Your* bell?' he asked.

'That's right. Quarter paid in advance, too.'

'I thought you worked for a false-tooth outfit.'

Aciava clicked his tongue. 'Dental engineers, please,' he said. 'And no, that's not who I meant. I was talking in my capacity as chief lay deacon for the united congregations of Falcata. We're going to be bitterly disappointed, of course.'

Poldarn thought for a moment. 'This congregation of

yours,' he said. 'Whose idea was it to order a bell in the first place?'

'Mine.' Poldarn could practically hear the grin on Aciava's face. 'There's nothing quite so classy as the mellow sound of a good bell, summoning the faithful to prayer on a warm summer evening. Of course, I spend most of my time on the road so I wouldn't be there to hear it very often, but it'd be wonderful just knowing it was there.'

'You ordered it,' Poldarn said. 'You only did it because you knew I work here.'

Aciava sighed. 'I guess I've been found out,' he said. 'And there I was, preferring to do good by stealth. It was the least I could do for an old pal, I reckoned, to make sure there'd be work in hand so they'd be able to keep paying you, even if you do spend most of your time on projects of your own. Besides, it's the congregation's money, not mine.'

Poldarn could feel the anger; it was almost objective, as though he was watching it build up from a distance. 'Like hell you were,' he said. 'It's some stupid game of yours, so you can make me do what you want. In fact, you probably did something to bugger up the mould, so we'd be late and you can sue us and put us out of business.'

'Hardly.' Aciava sounded highly amused. 'Even if I was that warped, how do you suggest I managed to persuade your pattern-maker friend – you know, the nutcase who yells all the time – to start putting the wax on before the clay was dry? No, that was just an unfortunate bonus.'

'Really.'

'Yes, really.' The voice was extremely close; if only Poldarn could pin it down exactly. But he suspected that Aciava was moving quietly about. 'You know the rule: never assume malice when the facts are consistent with mere stupidity. The nutcase was in too much of a rush, and he got it wrong. I didn't have to do a thing.'

Over there, close by the door. Poldarn was almost ready

to risk lashing out into the darkness; a few more words, and he'd be practically certain. 'Look,' he said, 'just exactly why are you doing this? What're you up to?'

No answer. Poldarn breathed out and listened. Experience and intuition told him there was nobody there. Aciava must've sneaked out through the doorway. Sensible behaviour on his part, Poldarn decided, since otherwise (he realised with a certain degree of horror) he'd have taken a swing at him with the axe. Not good; Aciava's prudent retreat suggested that he knew more about the way Poldarn's mind worked than he did himself. The implications of that weren't pleasant at all.

'Maybe I just dreamed all that,' he said aloud. (But he didn't believe it. No crow. Or had there been a crow, but it'd been too dark to see it? Query: does a crow in a dream count if it's not visible?)

In Spenno's personal opinion, it was the clay. According to Bergis, it was all Spenno's fault for not letting the core dry properly. Banspati the foreman reckoned it had to be the damp weather, while Malla Ancola blamed the sap in the green pole Spenno had used as a pivot for the pattern. Several dozen other explanations were available, if you didn't get out of the way quickly enough. For his own part, Poldarn couldn't make up his mind between sabotage and plain ordinary bad luck.

Not that he cared all that much. Aciava's threats (if he hadn't dreamed them) of penalty clauses and lawsuits were all very well, but the fact was that they still had two weeks before the delivery date stipulated in the contract, so that was all right. As for wasted materials, there was only the clay, which hadn't actually cost them anything. A day's lost production was neither here nor there in an outfit as thoroughly disorganised as this. If pressed, he'd have opted for bad luck: always plenty of it about, and much easier to believe in. Belief is everything in such matters.

It meant, of course, another long day digging clay, followed by an even longer day ignoring Spenno's hysterical outbursts – except that they were comforting, since they implied that, this time, everything was going perfectly. That evening, Spenno melted out the tallow and declared the mould fit for use. They'd melt the metal overnight and be ready to pour shortly before dawn.

Attitudes differed where the night before a pour was concerned. Some of the foundry crew reckoned it was unlucky to go to bed, and preferred to sit up and watch the melt; others tried to get some sleep, though the raucous noises from the general direction of the furnace meant that this was a fairly vain hope. Usually Poldarn belonged to the trying-to-get-some-sleep faction, but this time, for some reason, he decided to head over to the fire for an hour or so.

The furnace crew had been there for quite some time when he got there, and the cider jug had passed round the circle once or twice, with the result that there were more people sleeping by the fire than in the camp. The dozen or so who were still awake were mostly chatting amiably while some old bloke who Poldarn recognised but couldn't quite place droned methodically through a limited repertoire of popular ballads. Most of them were concerned with the activities of sword-monks and innkeepers' daughters and he'd heard all of them before; mixed in with these in a fairly indiscriminate fashion were a few old hymns, and at least three versions of Poldarn's personal favourite, *Old crow sitting in a tall thin tree*. Since several of the tunes were practically interchangeable, the old man occasionally lost track of what he was singing, so that something that started out as a hymn ended up with the unexpected return of the innkeeper, and vice versa. The result could be disconcerting if you were only giving the performance part of your attention, but Poldarn felt that several items from both genres were, like fortified wine, significantly improved by the blending.

'If you ask me,' said the man on his left (Poldarn hadn't), 'this whole country's going to hell in a handcart. I mean, Tazencius, who the fuck is he, anyhow? Never even heard of him a few years ago, and now he's running the whole bloody Empire. And if they think we've seen the last of them raiders, they're kidding themselves. You hear them talk, you'd think we'd killed off the whole bloody lot of 'em, instead of just a couple hundred or so. I mean, what's that? Drop in the ocean. Plenty more where they came from. Thousands. Millions, even. And we still don't know bugger-all about them. Course, what they *should* be doing—'

'Actually,' Poldarn lied, 'there's something I've been meaning to ask you.' It was really just a way of shutting him up, easier and less open to misconstruction than cutting his throat and pitching his body into the fire. 'Someone was telling me the other day that Feron Amathy—'

'That bastard. Someone ought to fix him good, one of these days.'

'Damn straight,' Poldarn said, nodding emphatically. 'But this bloke was telling me, years ago when he was a kid, he trained with the sword-monks. Is that right, do you know?'

'Oh, everybody knows that,' his neighbour grunted. 'Taught him everything he knows, they reckon, which is another good reason they had it coming, the bastards. Best thing Cronan ever did was kicking shit out of that bunch of arseholes.'

Poldarn frowned, because of course it was the raiders who'd destroyed Deymeson, not General Cronan, even though the monks had sent men to murder him. Still, it made a better story that way, since Cronan was one of the good guys, and the raiders were unmitigated evil. It was good to know that memory could be melted down and recast if it came out flawed the first time around, just like a bell. 'The same bloke was telling me,' Poldarn went on, 'that when Feron Amathy was with the monks, he was in the same year as this mad woman who's going round saying she's the priestess for the god in the cart – you know, the one who makes the world end, or whatever. Is there any truth in that, or—?'

The other man shook his head. 'Can't be right,' he said. 'Their ages are all wrong for that. Far as I can remember, Feron Amathy's been in business for years and years – that's right, because wasn't it him who screwed over General Allectus, way back? That mad woman – Xipho something, she's called – she'd be about your age, from what I've heard tell. So she'd still have been a little girl when Allectus got done; and Feron bloody Amathy started up years before Allectus's bit of bother. He must be getting on a bit by now, Feron Amathy; sixties, maybe even early seventies. Wish the bastard'd retire,' he added. 'Then we could all get some peace.'

'Ah,' Poldarn said, 'thanks. Tell me, have you ever heard of someone called Gain Aciava?'

'Gain what?'

'Aciava.'

The man shook his head. 'Don't think so,' he said. 'Why, what's he done?'

'Just someone this bloke was talking about,' Poldarn replied. 'He reckoned this Aciava was at Deymeson along with Feron Amathy and the mad woman. But if Feron Amathy's as old as you say, maybe the bloke was wrong about Aciava too.'

The other man shrugged. 'Never heard of anybody call that,' he said. 'Doesn't mean there wasn't a sword-mo with that name. All sorts of bloody odd names, th bastards had, and I wouldn't trust any of 'em further than I could spit.'

Just then, the cider jug intervened, and Poldarn took the opportunity to start talking to the man on his other side, who'd just woken up. He turned out not to have anything much to say, so Poldarn sat back and tried to listen to whatever it was the old fool was singing.

At first, he couldn't quite make out if it was another hymn or one of the smutty ballads. There was a man and a woman in it, which suggested the latter, but they didn't seem to be doing anything much apart from talking, and the absence of lewd puns tended to favour the hymn theory. The woman seemed to be telling the man his fortune, and he didn't seem particularly happy about it – understandably enough, since most of what the man was destined to do was profoundly unpleasant, a list of close family members he was scheduled to betray, rape or murder when he wasn't busy burning down cities and plundering houses of religion. Poldarn didn't need to be in holy orders to figure out that this was something to do with the god in the cart, his namesake. On balance, he decided, he'd rather talk to the man on his right, or even the man on his left. Or he could drink some of the disgusting cider. Worth a try, he decided; but by then the jug had passed on round. He closed his eyes and tried not to listen to the old fool singing; not that it mattered, since shortly afterwards, the god-in-the-cart song mutated seamlessly into further adventures of the sword-monk and the innkeeper's daughter, whose brief union had apparently been blessed with issue. Poldarn sighed, and closed his eyes—

Discomfort. He identified the source; a toecap nudging his ribs. 'You going to lie there all day?' growled a voice he recognised. He opened his eyes and looked up. Banspati the foreman was looming over him like an eviction order.

No crows anywhere to be seen, so it wasn't merely a bad dream. Pity.

'Now what?' he heard himself say, and he wondered why he'd said it.

'Get up,' Banspati replied, 'and get your idle bum down to the cutting. We need more clay.'

Hold on, Poldarn thought, we're ready to pour, what do we want more clay for? 'Problem?' he asked.

Ugly smile on the foreman's face. 'You could fucking well put it like that, yes. Bloody mould cracked in the night, way past fixing. So, we're starting again.' He sighed, shook his large, round head. 'You know what?' he said. 'This job's starting to get to me. Any more of it and I'll end up crazy as Spenno. I mean, two fuck-ups in a row. That's not good, really.'

He means it, too, Poldarn realised. It wasn't so much that he was worried – Banspati was the foreman, being worried defined him absolutely – as the unusual look of bewilderment in his eyes, as though he'd just been badly let down by the one person in the world he was sure he could trust. No anger, just a total inability to understand why this was happening. Not good; not good at all. 'Right,' Poldarn said quietly, 'I'd better get down to the cutting, then.'

Banspati looked at him, then nodded and said, 'Thanks'. And that was way, way past disturbing, out the other side into very scary indeed. Poldarn quickly broke eye contact, and fled.

Chapter Four

'What the hell sort of a sword do you call that, then?' the wheelwright said, with a mixture of apprehension and scorn in his voice. 'Looks more like an overgrown beanhook to me.'

Several of the men behind him laughed, but mostly out of loyalty. Ciartan grinned.

'You never seen one of these before?' he asked.

The wheelwright shook his head. Ciartan shrugged, as he surreptitiously looked round for something he knew was missing. Clear skies behind the bleak, bare winter branches of the trees, not a crow to be seen anywhere. Just as he was starting to worry, he caught sight of the inn sign, and nearly laughed out loud: a single crow on a light blue background, though it looked rather more like a sooty chicken with a broken neck. Anyhow, that was all right.

'Seen plenty of swords,' the wheelwright was saying. 'My dad was in the free companies all his life, got his old sword up in the rafters somewhere. Never seen anything like that.'

The inn was called the Redemption & Retribution; it was the first inn Ciartan had ever seen, though he'd learned all about them, naturally. Inns, they'd told him were where members of the local community gathered to relax, exchange news and discuss current events while drinking beer and playing games of skill and chance: ideal places to gather intelligence unobtrusively and assess the mood of the country. He could see what they'd been getting at, but he reckoned they hadn't expressed themselves very well.

'Here,' Ciartan said, backflipping the sword a couple of times (this impressed the crowd no end) and presenting it to the wheelwright hilt first, horns upwards. 'See what you make of it.'

The wheelwright took it as if he was shaking hands with his dead grandmother. 'Not bad,' he admitted. 'Lighter than it looks, too. Where did you say it comes from?'

They really should have warned him about the beer. Sure, it tasted like last month's rainwater, but apparently it was quite strong, enough to get you into conversations you'd have preferred to avoid. 'That I don't know,' Ciartan said. 'I bought it off a bloke in an inn; he said it was from up north somewhere. Beyond that, your guess is as good as mine.'

Maybe he'd said that in time, maybe not; at least one of the other men seemed to be able to recognise a raider backsabre when he saw one. As for his explanation, his advisers had made a point of telling him that 'bought it off a bloke in an inn' was a credible provenance for nearly anything, no matter how sinister its associations. With luck, the men in the crowd would assume it was a battlefield pick-up, or something of the sort. If not – well, he'd just have to kill them all, that was all. Serve him right for being indiscreet.

'Nice,' the wheelwright grunted, handing the sword back to him. 'But I wouldn't reckon it for actually using, not with that weird shape. I mean, you couldn't get that out the scabbard in a hurry, for a start. Not without slicing off your own fingers.'

'Really?' Even as he said the word, Ciartan was begging himself not to show off. Unfortunately, he couldn't have been listening. He sheathed the backsabre and let his hands fall down by his sides; then, without any conscious decision, he drew. Logic dictated that there had to have been a moment between sheathed and drawn, but if there was one, Ciartan wasn't aware of it. The point, he realised, was resting on the side of the wheelwright's neck, with precisely the amount of pressure that wouldn't quite cut the skin. He grinned, double-backflipped and slid the sword back into its scabbard.

'Fucking hell,' someone said. The wheelwright just stared at him.

'It's a knack, really,' Ciartan heard himself say, but all his attention was on plotting the best way out of the situation, the most direct route to the tethering post where his horse was waiting, without turning his back on them or breaking eye contact. 'You've got to do a sort of wiggle to get the curved bit past the bend in the scabbard. Once you've mastered that, it's a doddle.'

Nobody said anything. Gather intelligence unobtrusively, they'd said. Well, unobtrusive was a joke, and by the looks of it he still needed to get a whole bunch of intelligence from somewhere if he was planning to be alive come summer. Laying off the beer wouldn't hurt, either.

'Well,' he said, 'I'd better be getting along. Thanks for the drinks and all.'

He made it to his horse, jumped up and didn't look back to see if he was being followed. Chances were that he wasn't; they were farmers and craftsmen, not soldiers, so they were under no obligation to go picking a fight with a retreating hostile. They'd undoubtedly mention his performance to the first patrol or convoy they met, however, so he was a very long way from being clear. Best thing would be to put as much road between the Redemption & Retribution and himself as he could manage in the time available.

Three miles later, Ciartan stopped and looked down the valley, back towards the village. On the positive side, he couldn't see any dust clouds betokening squadrons of pursuing cavalry. On the other hand, here he was, miles out in the bush, no food, no blanket, and the only inn for miles around definitely out of bounds for the foreseeable future. Also, the beer was catching up with him. Things to do: throw up, lie down, find a cave or something before it started pissing down with rain.

He slid off his horse, knelt down and waited. Up there on the horse, he'd been certain he was about to be sick; down here, it was no more than a distinct possibility. He swallowed a couple of times and closed his eyes. All in all, he wished he'd never left Haldersness—

'You,' said a voice behind him.

Instinct took over, but various things got in the way; his balance was shot and his physical control was way below par, so that when he tried to draw, he forgot or overdid the scabbard-clearing wiggle and tried to pull the sword out through the neck of its scabbard. The blade was as sharp as a good blade ought to be and did its best; it sliced through the wood and leather and bit into the fingers of his left hand. He winced, swore and let go. The voice behind him (he'd forgotten all about him, just for the moment) was laughing.

Try again. He made himself relax; draw the sword *slowly*, he ordered himself, there's no need to rush it. This time he managed it and stood up, trying hard not to stagger. He'd screwed up badly but he was still alive, so things weren't too bad, after all.

The voice belonged to a young man about his own age, who was sitting on a small-looking mule ten yards or so away. Black hooded cloak, good quality, but you'd expect someone who could afford fine cloth to go for something rather less plain and drab. A uniform, maybe; or, more likely, religious garb of some kind. The man's face was bright and pink, and his hair was short, standing on end as if he'd just taken off his hat. Ciartan had seen more menacing objects floating in his milk; but then the kid drew back the hem of his cloak – a rather melodramatic gesture – to reveal the hilt of a sword.

Ah, Ciartan thought, I'm supposed to be scared. Well, why not? I'm not bothered either way, and it doesn't look like anybody wants a fight. 'Hello,' he said.

'You cut your hand.'

'Yes,' Ciartan replied. 'Clumsy. You startled me,' he added, as an afterthought.

'I was watching you,' the kid said, 'back at the inn there. I was wondering what the hell you thought you were playing at.'

'Me too,' Ciartan admitted. 'It was that filthy disgusting beer. Back on the farm, we stuck to water and ewes' milk.'

'Ah,' the kid said, nodding gravely. 'You're not from round here, then.'

'No.' Always tell the truth if it's not absolutely inconvenient. 'Passing through.'

'Thought so. On your way to Deymeson.'

'Where?'

The kid didn't believe him. 'Deymeson,' he repeated. 'On your way to join the order. Start of the new academic year. You're obviously new, because I haven't seen you there and believe me,' he added with a grin, 'I'd remember you if I had. My name's Gain, by the way. Gain Aciava.' Ciartan nodded politely. 'Pleased to meet you,' he said. 'Just a moment,' he added, and threw up, only just missing the toes of his boots. 'Sorry, yes. I'm Ciartan Torstenson.'

'Honoured,' the kid replied, with just the right degree of well-bred disdain. 'What's the matter?' he went on. 'Something you ate?'

'Yes,' Ciartan said.

'Ah. So you can draw that weird gadget pretty good, and yet you're not on your way to Deymeson. Curious.'

'Never heard of it till you mentioned it just now,' Ciartan said truthfully. 'What happens there, then?'

'It's a house of religion,' Aciava told him. 'Correction; it's *the* house of religion. Holiest place in the Empire. Headquarters of the order.'

'Fine,' Ciartan said. 'I'm not religious.'

That seemed to puzzle the kid. 'You think so?'

'Well, yes.'

The kid shrugged. 'Well, it's your business. You looked pretty damned good at it back there at the inn, but what the hell, I'm no expert. Maybe it was just a trick of the light or something.'

Not for the first time, Ciartan wished his head was just a little bit clearer. 'What's what happened back at the inn got to do with religion?' he asked.

'When you drew your sword—' The kid frowned. 'Hang on,' he said. 'You don't know, do you?'

This was starting to get on Ciartan's nerves. 'Don't know what?'

'Religion,' Aciava said patiently. 'The sacrament of the sword. It's only the most profound concept in the whole of orthodox doctrine.' He was hesitating, Ciartan could tell; something had struck him as not quite right, but he couldn't figure out what it was. 'You don't know about—'

'What you said, yes. Never heard of it.' True, it was a risk; it made him seem odd, conspicuous. On the other hand, pretending he knew would be an even bigger risk, liable to betray him as a spy or impostor, which of course he was. 'So, what's it all about, then?'

The kid's eyebrows shot up. 'Well,' he said, 'it's hard to explain, really. The idea is that – oh shit, I never was any good at this stuff, I'm more the practical sort myself. Faith through works, all that kind of nonsense. Anyhow, the deal is, religion – or let's call it the presence of the divine, all right? Wherever you have an instance of perfection, the divine is present. I mean, that much stands to reason, surely, because if the divine wasn't present, it couldn't be perfect, could it? Anyway, that's by the way. Religion – and now I'm talking about your formal, organised religion, the stuff that people do in order to sort of cultivate the presence of the divine within themselves – religion is trying to create instances of perfection by, well, doing things perfectly. You know; light in me the fire that makes all things fine, and all that crap.'

Ciartan assumed that that was a quotation, something so well known that even he ought to be able to recognise it.

'Well, anyhow,' Aciava went on, 'you know what it's like, there just aren't that many things in life that can be done perfectly; not *perfectly*, like in you simply can't imagine them being better. Most stuff in life just isn't like that. So the monks – they're the people who do religion all the time – they looked around for something that they could learn to do perfectly, and that's how they came to study swordsmanship; to be precise, the art of drawing your sword and chopping the other bloke so quick, it's all over before he can even move. It's perfection, see? You eliminate the moment between the sword being in the belt and the sword being wedged in the other poor bugger's head, and that's perfect. It's an act of the gods, quite literally; because an ordinary man could never manage to do it, he can draw a sword pretty bloody quick but there'll always be a moment in between. But the gods, the divine, they can sort of snip out that moment so it's just not there, and that's perfection. Religion, in fact. And that's what they do at Deymeson.'

Ciartan wasn't sure he quite followed. 'They kill each other?'

'No, no, they practise with wooden swords, it's all perfectly civilised. They practise, and they train, and there're these old, really holy monks who've been training since before they could walk, practically, who teach you all about it. Plus you do a lot of meditating, and you've got to learn the theory, of course, and a whole lot of mysticism and stuff which apparently you've got to know or else you're wasting your time. And in the end, if you work really hard at it and you understand all the theory and you're very lucky, you get to achieve religion and get a piece of the divine actually inside you—'

'Like a tapeworm?'

The kid scowled. 'Yes, I know, it all sounds a bit dumb. But that's just because I'm not explaining it right – you need one of them to explain it. And the point is, if you can do the sword-drawing stuff that well without being trained at all, then it sort of stands to reason that you're halfway there already; maybe you've even got a little tiny bit of the divine in you that's been there ever since you were born. I mean, that'd practically make you a god, even though you don't seem to be aware of it.'

Ciartan thought for a moment. 'So you're saying you think I should go to this Deymeson place and join up. It can't be as simple as that, though. I mean, presumably there's a test before they'll let you join up. And what about board and lodging, and paying for the teaching, and things like that? I haven't got any money—'

'They have,' Aciava said. 'They're incredibly rich. You see, people give them money, and leave them money and land and stuff when they die, so the monks will pray for their souls. And they get money from tithes and local taxes and customs and tolls and all sorts of things. They're major landowners, particularly up north – which is why some people send their sons to join, so they'll work their way up the ladder and become abbots and whatever, as an alternative to going in the army or to Court. The point being, if they want you, they'll pay for your keep and all your tuition and everything, for the rest of your life. I mean, for poor families it's a wonderful deal.'

'I can see that,' Ciartan said. 'So, what do you have to do to get in? Do you just have to draw a sword very quickly, or is there other stuff as well?'

The kid shook his head. 'It's not like that,' he said. 'When I joined, I was shown into this long, dark room, and half a dozen of the senior tutors and so on looked at me for a while, and they asked me a question or two, which didn't seem to make much sense but I'd been expecting that so it didn't bother me; then I had to show them a few draws; and then the Father Tutor, that's the senior monk in charge of training, told me I'd passed and where to go to get my clothes and stuff, and that was it, I started straight away; in classes the next day. Mind you, our family's been sending its younger sons to Deymeson for six hundred years. But what I'm trying to say is, if they think you've got what it takes, they'll take you in and train you, even if you're – well, *nobody*. It's like they say: it's not who you are or who you used to be, it's who you're going to be that's important.'

Ciartan thought about it for a moment or so. The whole thing sounded pretty bizarre to him, especially the vague bits about perfection. On the other hand he had to face facts; when his people had brought him here, obviously they'd only had a very sketchy idea about how the Empire worked. They'd imagined it was more like back home, where there was a place for everyone and everyone found his place. Instead, it had turned out to be all loose and ragged and disorganised; everyone telling everyone else what to do, nobody actually doing anything. In consequence, he'd had to think about all sorts of things that really ought to have taken care of themselves, such as food and clothes and places to sleep. What was more, providing for even such basic things as these was hardly easy or straight-forward. In fact, it was absurdly hard to make a living here, unless you owned land (now there was a strange notion; it was like the ox owning the plough) or your family had taught you a trade, or there was some other pre-existing pattern you could fit into. In a way it was like being an offcomer back home, except that here everybody was an offcomer, and nobody knew where they ought to be. By comparison, the order sounded almost normal. And further, Ciartan considered, if the order was rich and powerful like the kid said, what better way to gather useful intelligence and so on than to get in with the upper crust? Put like that—

'You really think I'd be able to get in?'

'Of course.' Aciava smiled. He seemed pleased, as though he'd just found a big clump of mushrooms. 'Trust me. Come along with me, and everything'll be just fine.'

Ciartan took a step back. 'I know it's silly,' he said, 'but every time someone says *Trust me*, I get suspicious. What's it to you whether I join this order of yours or not?'

'What on earth do you mean?' The kid looked suddenly hurt and angry, as if Ciartan had just spat in his face. 'I'm just trying to be helpful, that's all. And doing my bit for religion, like we're supposed to. Why? What other reason could there be?'

Offhand, Ciartan couldn't think of one; nor could he figure out why the two crows that were circling overhead were in any way relevant. But they were, because—

(Because he remembered: he'd had a dream once, when he'd been just a child, back at Haldersness. He could remember the dream, because it had had crows in it, and that meant the dream didn't just evaporate as soon as he woke up. In that dream he'd been here, exactly this place, talking to this rather annoying young man. In fact, he'd had this same dream several times and, on each occasion, as soon as the kid asked him *What other reason could there be?* he'd woken up.)

Aciava was staring at him. He didn't look happy. 'Well?'

'Well what?'

'Well, have you come up with a reason why I should want you to come to Deymeson, apart from trying to help you and help the order? I think you'd better think of one, because otherwise I'm going to have to take that as an insult.'

(Every time, Ciartan remembered, except once; and on that occasion, the dream had been slightly different, because part of the way through – at this exact point, in fact – everything had changed suddenly. Both he and the kid were somehow much older, and the kid wasn't asking him to come to Deymeson. He was asking him to join up with some other venture, which apparently involved people they both knew, old classmates, something like that. For some reason, he'd told the kid no, and things had started going wrong after that; cracks in the clay, lies, mistaken identities, (Clay? What clay?) deception and murder and coincidences and just plain rotten luck. And for some reason, it had been very important – he'd made a point of telling himself he had to remember this when he woke up – that the pattern that recreates the lost shape (where the tallow is burnt out in the middle) is in fact an empty hole, a gap waiting to be filled, like a blank memory.)

Deep breath. 'I'm sorry,' Ciartan said, and Aciava relaxed – it occurred to Ciartan that if he hadn't apologised the kid would've felt obliged to fight him or something like that, and the thought of fighting him was scaring the kid half to death. 'I didn't mean to insult you,' Ciartan went on. 'It was just me thinking aloud. I guess I'm not used to people being nice for no reason.'

'Well,' the kid replied, 'I guess that's fair enough. Only, it's not for no reason. Religion's a reason, and after all, I'm training to be a monk, hopefully an ordained priest further along the line. Got to start somewhere, you know. And it'll do me no harm at all with Father Tutor if I bring along a good new recruit for the start of the new term.'

Was that just a little bit glib, a tad too reasonable? No, Ciartan decided, it could have been, but this time it wasn't. 'That's all right, then,' he said. 'I guess that makes it mutual benefit.'

'Exactly.' Aciava smiled. 'The only way to receive is to give,' he added portentously, 'and that's a genuine five-quarter precept of religion.'

A what? Ciartan wanted to ask; but instead he woke up, because some bastard was prodding him in the shoulder with a stick.

'Piss off,' Poldarn muttered.

'I said, wake up,' Banspati replied. 'Bloody hell, you're harder to wake up than a dead tree.'

Poldarn opened his eyes. 'What do you want?' he grumbled.

'You missed the meeting.'

'What meeting?'

'The one you missed. It was important. We had a vote and everything.'

Poldarn remembered. *That* meeting. To decide whether, in view of the fact that they'd spent the last four weeks trying to cast the Falcata guild bell and every time the mould had failed, they should close the works down or keep trying. And he'd missed it. Buggery.

'Oh, right,' he said, sitting up. 'So, what was the result?'

Banspati sighed. 'Bloody disaster,' he said mournfully. 'You know, there's times when I wonder why the hell I bother. I mean, it's an uphill struggle every bloody step of the way, and at my time of life I just don't need this kind of—'

'The vote,' Poldarn interrupted. 'Yes or no?'

Banspati pulled a face. 'Yes and no,' he said. 'What they all reckoned was – and since when does voting for something make it true even if it isn't? Supposed to be *craftsmen*, but I didn't see any bloody sign of it. Anyhow, what they reckon is, the only way we're going to get this fucking bell made is if we let the core dry out thoroughly – I mean, really dry out, like three weeks before we even put on the tallow. What difference that's supposed to make I really don't know, but hey, I'm just the bloody foreman.'

'Three weeks,' Poldarn repeated.

'That's right. We make a core, leave it three weeks, then we carry on. In the meantime, I'm afraid I'm having to lay the lot of you off. Don't want to, can't afford not to. We've got this fucking penalty clause hanging over us, and there just isn't the money for wages until we know how much we're going to be made to pay.'

Poldarn scowled at him. 'Wonderful,' he said. 'And what're we supposed to live on in the meantime?'

Banspati shrugged. 'That's your business,' he said. 'If I was you, I'd start looking round for a job somewhere, just to tide you over. After all, you've got to eat, and we can't pay you.'

Poldarn stood up. 'What do you mean, get a job? A job doing what? This isn't the city, you know, I can't just go to the hiring fair or stand about outside the corn exchange till somebody hires me. We're in the middle of nowhere—'

'Well, the others are in the same boat too,' Banspati replied. 'It's not just you, you know. And don't pull faces at me like it's all my fault. I didn't vote for this bloody stupid idea, so you can't go blaming me.'

Poldarn never did find out for certain whose idea it had been or whose fault it was. Nobody at all seemed happy about it, even though the vote in support of the motion had apparently been unanimous (though everybody he asked

said they'd voted against, which was odd). More important, nobody seemed to have given any thought as to how
they were going to earn a living while the works were shut
down.

Poldarn had been exaggerating slightly when he'd said
they were in the middle of nowhere. Falcata was only a few
days away, and there were half a dozen small villages that
could be reached in a day or so of hard walking. But the
chances of finding any work at that time of year were slim
to non-existent. Any day now, the rains would start; the
flat plain that began at Ilno and stretched over as far as the
lower slopes of the Sourwater Hills would soon be flooded,
with only the villages and the embanked roads above water.
Good for the reed-beds and the osier gardens; good for the
market gardeners in the fat strip between Falcata and the
Green River, since the alluvial silt that the flood water
washed down off Sourhead was just the job for beans and
cabbages. For everyone else on the levels, it was simply a
fact of life; six weeks every year when you stayed home and
found something to do indoors. It had never been a fact of
life that bothered the foundry crew, since the flood water
had never come far enough up the vale to affect them, and
if they had finished work to deliver, there were always
barges and rafts – easier, in fact, to float a bell than lug it
about on a cart. So long as everybody stayed where they
were meant to be, in fact, the wet season was nothing to
worry about, and who'd be stupid enough to go wandering
about in those conditions?

Someone or other, possibly Malla Ancola but probably
not, made vague noises about sticking together and taking
the road up the vale into the hills, through the big woods
and out the other side, heading for Balehut or even the
coast. That idea was so impractical that nobody could be
bothered to point out the problems; but someone else suggested spending the forced holiday in the woods, burning

their own supply of charcoal, which (if they got it right) could save them enough money to cover what they stood to lose on the penalty clause, in the long term; and as for the short term, everybody knew how easy it was to live off the land in a forest, hunting and gathering all those deer and birds and wild pigs and nuts and roots and berries, not to mention wild mushrooms and truffles. In fact, the argument ran, the only real danger was that they'd get so used to the carefree life of the forester and the collier that they'd never want to go back to rotten old foundry work.

This proposal went the rounds all the next day and halfway through the night, and then died, as quickly and suddenly as it had arisen; at which point people started to drift away, most of them aiming without much hope to reach Falcata before the rain started. The group Poldarn joined up with, however, declared that they were headed the other way. Burning their own coals, they acknowledged, was obviously not a realistic proposition (why this was so, nobody bothered to say; presumably because it was obvious and they didn't want to look ignorant); but hadn't Poldarn said they were always on the lookout for casual labour at the burning camps, to replace the ones who suddenly took it into their heads to drift away and do something else? It was worth a try; and even if there wasn't any food, from what Poldarn had told them there was no shortage of free beer for anybody who was too slow to get out of the way in time.

Poldarn wasn't entirely sure that that was what he'd said; but it couldn't be denied that his memory wasn't the best in the world, so maybe they were right, at that. At any rate, since this expedition appeared in some way to have been his idea, he felt more or less obliged to tag along with it; also, he could see the sense in setting off *up* the hill if the plains were about to flood. As far as his companions in the venture were concerned, they all seemed like honest, decent, good-natured people, and it'd only be for a few weeks, until the core dried out.

'There's been a change of plan,' Chiruwa said casually, as they reached the edge of the forest.

'Oh?' Poldarn shrugged. The afternoon sun was pleasantly warm, and his mind had been elsewhere. He hadn't actually been paying much attention to what the others had been saying; least of all Chiruwa, who had a tendency to chatter away as though he was trying to use up a stockpile of words before they went stale. 'Fair enough. What's changed?'

Chiruwa avoided his gaze. 'We talked it over, the rest of the guys and me, and we reckoned looking for work round the charcoal camps probably wasn't such a good idea after all. Like, it's the wet season coming on, they won't be shipping much charcoal till the roads are clear again, most like they'll be slowing down production, having a rest, that sort of thing. Probably not much work going.'

That seemed reasonable, now that Chiruwa mentioned it. Pity nobody had thought of it before. If they couldn't get casual jobs around the burning camps, the prospects weren't wonderful. Apart from the colliers, nobody much lived in the big woods; apart from the two or three inns along the road that catered to travellers, there weren't any houses or settlements till you reached the Stonebick river. 'So what did you have in mind?' Poldarn asked. 'Do we turn round and go back, or what?'

Chiruwa pulled a face. 'We did consider that,' he said. 'Only we probably don't have enough in the way of supplies to get as far as Falcata; and the smaller places might not have anything to spare. So we thought we'd carry on along the road for a bit.'

Poldarn looked at him. 'Why?'

'Well.' Chiruwa, the foundry's chief polisher, was a short

man, very broad and wide, with an honest face partly shrouded by a big black moustache. You'd have felt fairly confident about paying him in advance for a large order of dried beans. 'What we thought we'd do, we thought we could make a quarter or two in these parts. Not right here, of course. More where the road goes through the edge of the wood.'

'Doing what?'

'Well.' Chiruwa said again and breathed in through his nose. 'There's quite a bit of traffic on the road this time of year, people coming up from the plains before the rain starts. Also merchants and freight on the way to Ridgetop and Spadea – there's big fairs there in a couple of weeks.'

Poldarn didn't say anything, but that contradicted what Chiruwa had implied a moment or so before, about the colliers not being able to ship any charcoal because of the roads being impassable. Or maybe he'd just misunderstood, or didn't know enough about the local geography. 'Right,' he said. 'So, what about it? Are you planning on setting up an inn or something, because—'

'Not really,' Chiruwa replied. 'What we had in mind was more like robbing them. Happens a lot around here,' he went on quickly, in an it's-all-right-really tone of voice. 'And the weather'd be on our side, because we wouldn't have to worry about the soldiers – once the rain starts they won't be able to get up the road from Falcata. By the time the roads south are open again, we'll have finished and be long gone. It'd be safe as houses, really.'

'Robbing them?' Poldarn reckoned he must have heard him wrong, or misunderstood what he'd been trying to say. 'You mean, like – well, highwaymen, bandits, that sort of thing?'

'Sort of,' Chiruwa replied.

'Sort of?'

But Chiruwa didn't seem inclined to explain any further. 'So,' he said, 'are you in with us, or aren't you?'

Didn't look like he had very much choice in the matter. 'Yes, all right, then,' Poldarn said; then he hesitated. 'I'm not killing anybody, mind. That's—'

'Oh, don't worry about that,' Chiruwa assured him quickly. 'You don't get big escorts, or soldiers or anything, it'll just be one or two people on their own. It's not like we'll be ambushing supply columns or anything like that. Besides, if they look like they'd be trouble, we just stay back and let them go on through. Goes without saying, really.'

For a moment, Poldarn wondered if he ought to be keeping an eye out for crows, in case this was a bad dream or a memory. (And what ought he to think if he did see one? Just the place for them, after all, this close to the edge of the big wood; in fact, he was surprised there weren't any. Or was it the case that crows really only existed in dreams? He doubted that.) 'You know,' he said, 'I'm not sure. Maybe we really ought to at least try the charcoal outfits, just in case they're hiring. After all, it couldn't do any harm just asking, could it?'

'Well, actually,' Chiruwa replied awkwardly, 'the others've more or less made their minds up about it, so I don't suppose there'd be any point. I mean, you can suggest it if you like, but I don't imagine they'll listen to you.'

Poldarn figured he knew why. They'd never had any intention of going to the colliers' camps looking for work. This had been the plan all along. Odd that he hadn't figured it out for himself. 'Is this what you usually do, then?' he asked. 'Whenever there's a lay-off at the foundry, or when you feel like a change of pace?'

'Oh no. Well, not me personally; this'll be, what, my third or fourth time. Some of the guys come up this way quite often, that's how they know there won't be any soldiers or armed escorts. We know what we're doing, if that's what's bothering you.'

It'd be a good idea, Poldarn decided, to pretend that it was. 'Well, if you're sure,' he said.

'Quite sure,' said Chiruwa. 'It'll be like hop-picking, you take my word for it.' (Well, Poldarn thought, Chiruwa did have an honest face.) 'We'll get all the food and supplies we need, and a bit of spending money as well; and long before they can send anybody out after us we'll be back home down on the plain, with no one any the wiser. I mean, if you're wandering about in a godforsaken place like this, you're practically asking to be robbed, people expect it. Far as they're concerned, it's just bad luck, like breaking an axle.'

At that, Poldarn nodded and changed the subject. He was wondering whether it'd be possible to slip away before they reached the woods and maybe head for the charcoal camps. The man he'd stayed with, Basano, would probably find him a job, or maybe just let him hang about for a few weeks – he hadn't seemed to mind the prospect of Poldarn waiting there until the wagons left, time didn't seem to matter much to the colliers. Come to that, maybe he'd be better off staying there for good; if he sloped off from the robbing party, it was possible they wouldn't be too pleased to see him when he got back to the foundry when work resumed there, particularly if something went wrong with their plans, such as an unexpected column of soldiers – they'd assume he'd betrayed them or something. Or maybe it'd be better to stay with the party and keep his head down. He didn't like the prospect of cold-blooded robbery, but there were worse things, and he had a bad feeling he'd done most of them. It was, after all, a matter of survival in a hard country in a bad season. And the world was full of predators: eagles and lions and bears, all of them doing nothing worse than making a living.

(He couldn't believe he'd thought that; hearing himself suggest such a line of argument was the most worrying aspect of the whole business. It had come quite naturally, like reaching out in the dark for something he knew was there. Even so; even so. If he went to the colliers' camp and told them he needed work or a place to hang out while the foundry was closed down, it'd be as good as betraying the others; because the colliers would know that men from the foundry had been in those parts, and when news of the robberies filtered through to them, they'd have to be stupid not to draw the obvious conclusions. It *would* be betrayal; and which was worse – to betray his friends and colleagues, or to persuade a few wealthy merchants to share their good fortune with others less favoured than themselves? And of course the people they'd be robbing would be the rich, because the poor don't have anything to steal . . . Even so. Even so.)

'I guess you're right,' Poldarn said. 'And we'd only be taking what we need, wouldn't we?'

Chiruwa nodded enthusiastically. 'It's a way of life in these parts, really,' he said. 'I mean, if this was a civilised place, with towns and places where you could find work, there wouldn't be any need. But we've all got a right to live, is what I say. Isn't that right? I mean, one man's as good as another, there's no reason we should starve when there's people who've got more than they need. You'll see, usually they're quite good-natured about the whole thing.'

He'll be telling me they enjoy the thrill of the chase next. 'It's all right,' Poldarn said, 'I'm not bothered about it, so long as nobody gets hurt. That's the main thing, isn't it?'

(And he thought: it *is* all right, because I know what I'm doing; and besides, I've done worse. I was happy enough swindling peasants, when I was being the god in the cart. I've killed soldiers for getting in my way, I've killed sword-monks just to please my distant cousins, I killed my best friend for stealing back his own horses. Compared to what I've done when I was sure I was doing the right thing, stealing a few quarters beside the road is practically an act of charity and conscience. I have nothing to prove to anybody. I am who I am, and that's fine.)

Two days in the highway-robbery business were enough to convince Poldarn that he'd been worrying unnecessarily.

Their first victims looked a likely enough prospect; a man and a woman, elderly and mildly shrivelled, driving a large covered cart slowly along one of the main droves leading up to the forest roadways. Anybody with eyes in his head could see they were farmers, and since they were going up the hill, it stood to reason that they were taking their surplus produce to the colliers' camps, undoubtedly (this was Poldarn's private assumption) to sell them to a captive market at grossly inflated prices.

Once they'd stopped the cart, however, and managed to get across to the old man (who was deaf) and the old woman (who appeared to speak no known language and at least three unknown ones) that this was a *robbery*, not a request for directions, they were surprised and extremely annoyed to find nothing in the back of the cart except empty sacks. Eventually, the old woman contrived to explain that they were on their way to pick up their village's quarter-year supply of charcoal, which had already been paid for. Since vigorous searching failed to produce a single coin, Chiruwa had no choice but to take their word for it and send them on their way, with a rather sad request that they shouldn't tell anybody about the incident.

The next cart they stopped wasn't empty. On the contrary; once they'd peeled back the thick covering of hides tied down tight with about a mile of best jute rope, they found it was piled high with exceptionally rich and pungent goat manure. For some reason the carter didn't mention this until it was too late; then he explained that he was taking the stuff to the government supply depot at Tin

Chirra, where the superintendent was reportedly stock-piling dung of every type and description for eventual onward shipment to the foundry at Dui Chirra . . .

Before anybody could stop him, Chiruwa pointed out that he and his party had just come from the Dui Chirra foundry, which was deep enough in shit already without needing any more. It was only later, when the cart had continued on its way and Chiruwa was asking why everybody was scowling at him like that, that someone explained to him exactly why telling their victims where they'd just come from was a bad idea. The point wasn't wasted on Chiruwa, who was all in favour of chasing after the dung-wagon and killing the carter to keep his mouth shut. Nobody else seemed to think that way, however, and the matter was eventually allowed to drop.

('Though what they want with all that stuff over to Tin, God only knows,' someone pointed out. 'It's not like they grow any crops there, and what in buggery else can you use it for?')

Somewhat disillusioned and extremely hungry, the robber band was just trying to make up its group mind whether to stop where they were and try and snare a rabbit or two, or whether to carry on down the road for an hour or so to the trout-haunted Star river, when a horseman galloped up the drove and right through the middle of them. There was no way they could have stopped him, but fortuitously his horse caught sight of Rusty Dancuta's nasty little dog, which he'd insisted on bringing with him. Why a large horse was so mortally afraid of such a small, ratlike dog nobody knew; but it bucked, reared and hurled its rider off into a clump of wild honeysuckle before leaving the road and darting off among the trees, where it was quickly lost to sight.

On examining the rider, who'd clumped his head and fallen fast asleep, Chiruwa and his desperadoes discovered that he was carrying a large, fat linen bag, stuffed full to bursting with coins. That was more like it, even though the coins proved to be small green coppers rather than the smart Imperial gold grossquarters they'd been hoping for.

'What do you think you're doing?' the rider asked, sitting up and staring at them while they counted the take.

Chiruwa laughed theatrically and told him they'd stolen his money and were counting it. Fine, the rider said, you crack on and help yourselves; because even if the money was still legal tender, instead of obsolete issues now being called in to be taken to Tin Chirra and melted down, there'd be maybe just enough to buy each member of the robbing party half a small loaf each for a day. Alternatively, he went on, if they cared to catch up with his horse and fetch it back, in the saddlebags they'd find a good heavy stash of government biscuits, the sort the soldiers took with them on long route marches. He'd packed them for his own use just in case the Hope & Endurance had shut down for the wet season before he reached it; but as things had turned out, the inn (famous for its smoked lamb and pickled black cabbage) had still been open, and he'd pigged out to such an extent while he'd been there that he wouldn't be able to face another mouthful till he reached Tin Chirra.

'Tin Chirra?' someone asked. 'What's there?'

'Government supply depot,' the rider said. 'I'm the new supply and requisitions clerk. Who're you, then?'

They found the horse eventually; and government biscuit turned out to be just about edible, smashed and ground into dust and mixed with water to make porridge. After they'd parted from the clerk it started to rain.

Next day was no better. First catch of the day was someone Poldarn had met before—

'Hello,' she said, peering down at him through the mail-coach window. 'I know you, I'm sure I do. You were going to Scieza—'

She was still dressed in a man's shabby coat several sizes too big for her, and the same cracked old leather travelling hat. She was also still nursing the wicker basket. The smell hadn't got any better, either.

'Hello yourself,' Poldarn muttered. 'You said you were on your way to Falcata. To see your son,' he remembered, God only knew why.

'I was,' she replied solemnly. 'But unfortunately there was some dreadful mistake about money – they said I hadn't paid my fare, and I had, I remember it distinctly; and they made it sound like I was deliberately trying to deceive them, and I couldn't do something like that, really I couldn't, and they put me off the mail at Cardea, and there I was, stuck, because of course I'd spent all my money on the fare, because of course my son will be meeting me at Falcata, so I didn't need any for the journey. Anyway, it was quite dreadful, and I don't know what I'd have done if a kind gentleman hadn't given me nine quarters at Cardea lodge, which meant I could catch this coach, but it's only going as far as Chacquemar, and what I'll do then I have no idea—'

Poldarn could only think of two ways of shutting her up; and, since he'd resolved that he wasn't going to kill anybody, no matter how annoying they were, he had no option but to go with the other alternative. He stuck his hand in his pocket and brought out two of his four remaining gross-quarters. 'Here,' he said, 'this ought to get you from Chacquemar to the city.'

'Oh.' The old bat looked quite startled, even shocked. 'But no, that's far too generous, I couldn't possibly. And besides, I'd worry so much till I'd paid you back. Of course,' she added quickly, 'my son will be delighted to send you the money as soon as I reach Falcata, if you'll give me your address.'

Clearly she hadn't quite grasped the fact that Poldarn

and his friends were highway robbers. True, there wasn't much about the way they'd gone about handling this hold-up to suggest it. 'Forget about it, please,' Poldarn said. 'In fact, here's another,' he added, sticking a third coin in her hand. 'You'll need to get something to eat – it's a long road.'

She smiled at him. 'Oh, I hardly eat anything any more,' she replied. 'It's one of the best things about getting old, if you ask me. But thank you ever so much, and would you mind awfully if I bought some millet and corn and seed for Slowly and Surely – my little darlings,' she added, pointing to the wicker basket. 'They're fast asleep at the moment, bless them, or I'd open their basket and you could say hello to them. They haven't had anything but horrid old crusts and breadcrumbs since we left Aleomacta.'

Poldarn closed his eyes just for a moment. 'Fine,' he said. 'As far as I'm concerned you can treat them to haddock roe and smoked eels, just so long—'

'Oh, they wouldn't like that. They don't eat fish.'

'Really. Well, have a safe trip.'

'Are you sure you don't want my son to send you the money? I really do feel—'

'Goodbye,' Poldarn said, and he stepped back, slapping the lead horse hard on the rump. It started and broke into a trot. Poldarn turned, pulled his axe out of his belt and faced the rest of the desperadoes.

'Not one word,' he said.

After that it rained heavily for the rest of the morning and all afternoon. A lumber cart and a small chaise went by, but the desperadoes couldn't be bothered to leave the shelter of the trees. Besides, as Chiruwa pointed out to nobody in particular, where was the point, it'd only end up costing them money . . .

Just before sunset the rain stopped, and the robbers debated what they should do next. A significant faction were in favour of calling it quits and making for the colliers'

camp, where at least they'd be sure of finding a nice warm
fire, even if they struck out where food and beer were concerned. A slender majority, however, held out for staying
put and waiting to see what the morning would bring;
Poldarn's being the deciding vote. Mostly, he guessed, it
was the shame of having been seen in the act of gratuitous
charity; partly, though, he was concerned that the colliers
might have heard rumours about the spate of robberies on
the road. Crimes were still crimes, and ludicrous inepti-
tude was no defence. Besides, it was quite possible that one
or other of their victims, in telling the tale of his adventures, might have altered the facts slightly, preferring to
attribute his escape to cunning or valour rather than the
fecklessness of his assailants. Accordingly, the gang held
their position and huddled down in what little shelter they
could find. It rained hard all night, needless to say.

Poldarn was sure he'd only just closed his eyes after many
hours of wet, sleepless misery when someone grabbed him
by the shoulder and hissed at him to wake up.

'Coach,' Chiruwa was whispering. 'Come on, get up.'

Poldarn yawned and stumbled to his feet. The coach,
which he could see quite clearly through the dripping
branches, had slowed down to ford a shallow stream that
crossed the road. It was rather a splendid affair; painted
blue and yellow, with a fine canopy of waxed brown leather,
and drawn by four good-looking horses. The driver perched
on the box was wearing a fine grey cloak and a new-looking
black felt hat.

'Money,' someone murmured. 'I mean, just look at the
buggers.'

Poldarn could see his point; after all, how could it be fair
for rich bastards to bounce happily up and down the roads
in well-fed, dry comfort, while poor starving thieves had
to sleep out in sodden rags? They'd see about that.

It wasn't till the coach was right up close that it occurred

to the gang that this was their first serious attempt at practising their craft. Nobody really knew what to do. Even if
they all jumped out in front of the coach there was no guarantee it'd stop, and they could get hurt that way. What they
should've done, Poldarn realised, was block the road ahead
with a fallen tree, then take the coach from the rear as soon
as it stopped. No time for that now. It was jumping out in
front, or nothing.

'On three,' Chiruwa said, but nobody heard him; they
were already on their feet and scampering out onto the road,
waving their arms and shouting. It turned out to be a good
manoeuvre; the driver must have assumed they were
warning him about some hazard ahead on the road, because
he pulled up as they approached, and asked them what the
matter was. Then Chiruwa yelled out, 'Shut your face, this
is a hold-up,' and things started to go rather badly.

The driver was pushed abruptly aside and men started
crawling out from under the canopy onto the box, and
jumping down. There proved to be eight of them, big men
with swords and matching helmets. It was at this point that
the desperadoes began to wonder whether they were ade-
quately equipped for the job in hand.

True, they all had something that'd pass for a weapon:
some had hammers, Chiruwa had a knife with a blade a
foot long, and Poldarn had his short axe, the one he'd found
in the ditch where he'd killed the crows. They also outnumbered the coach escort, eleven to eight. In theory, they
had the advantage. It just didn't feel that way at the time.

The hell with it, Poldarn told himself; suddenly, the picture was starting to look depressingly familiar, the pattern
emerging. He should, of course, never have tagged along
in the first place. Now it was time to leave, as quickly as
possible, before he got hurt or killed anybody. He turned
and ran back into the wood, as fast as he could go without
crashing into a tree or tripping on a fallen branch.

After a while, he stopped, leaning forward, hands on knees, catching his breath and listening. Nothing to suggest he'd been followed (and why should they go haring off into the trees when they were already outnumbered?) He'd got away, free and clear. No harm done.

Even so.

Even so, it hadn't been the right thing to do. Chiruwa and the rest were criminal idiots, but unfortunately he was on their side. The coach guards had looked as though they'd make short work of the foundrymen, assuming they hadn't done so already. But there could be survivors – or prisoners, which was worse still. With a sigh Poldarn turned round and headed back toward the road.

It hadn't gone well, for his side at least. As he approached the edge of the wood, he could see two of them quite clearly. One was lying on his face, his arms under him, both feet pointing to the left. The other one lay on his back, and he'd been cut almost in two. One of the guards was sitting with his back against a tree, unarmed and helmetless; the dark pool surrounding him implied that he'd bled to death. There didn't seem to be anybody else about.

Shouldn't have come back, Poldarn decided; there was nothing he could do for the two dead foundrymen and his sense of duty stopped short of searching for the others with an unspecified number of enemies close at hand. Everything had changed, of course. The highway-robbery project was over now, for good. Assuming he managed to get clear of the scene, he had grave reservations about going back to the foundry when it started up again after the lay-off, since some of the others might have made it back, and he'd been the first to run. The colliers' camp was probably out, too. In spite of everything he couldn't help grinning; here he was again, alone except for dead bodies at the scene of a fight he'd missed out on. The pattern emerging, as the tallow burns out, leaving a gap – but this time he had a memory of sorts; and this time, no options at all that he could think of.

'You,' someone yelled behind him. 'Turn and fight, you thieving bastard.'

Not the sort of voice he'd have expected: high, slightly shrill, a deep-voiced woman or a boy. No point speculating in ignorance; he turned round and saw a boy, maybe fourteen years old and tall for his age. He was wearing a mail shirt – fine quality, junior size, what the well-dressed nobleman's son was wearing to the wars these days – and a gilded helmet with enamel and niello decoration, all in excellent taste. And he was holding a sword – short-bladed, regulation length for concealed carry for a sword-monk, just the right size for a kid's two-hander. The boy was standing in a second-position upper-back guard straight out of the coaching manual, and scowling at him horribly.

Poldarn relaxed. 'Piss off,' he said.

The boy seemed shocked by the bad language, but not deterred from his grim purpose. 'I said stand and fight,' he piped, 'or I'll cut you down like a dog.'

It was the first good laugh Poldarn had had in a while, and he indulged himself. That didn't please the boy at all. 'Right,' he said, 'I warned you'. He took a big stride forward, sweeping the sword up and round his head in the approved circular movement.

It was at this point that Poldarn thought about something Gain Aciava had said; about being young sword-monks, and training at fencing since they were kids. The boy, he suddenly realised, seemed to know exactly what he was doing; and there Poldarn was, a nice large target for cutting practice, armed with nothing but a hatchet.

He jumped sideways in time, but only just; the sword blade sliced the air where he'd been just a moment ago, and if he'd still been there, it would have severed his leg artery. I wonder, Poldarn thought, as he danced out of the way of another pretty respectable cut, I wonder if I was this good when I was his age? No, because I was still at Haldersness. Aciava, maybe? Assuming he was telling the truth—

An inch-and-degree-perfect sixth-grade rising cut next, and Poldarn made a mess of the avoid. There was just time to block it with the handle of the axe (but clumsy and shameful; the block is the last resort, the admission of failure) and take a standing jump backwards without time to see what he was likely to be landing on. Unfortunate, since he pitched on a large chunk of flint, jarring his ankle and losing his balance; the boy was at him with a good clean middle cut and he had to block again, this time with the poll of the hatchet. He could feel the sword's edge cut the soft iron of the poll, and recognised that he'd been lucky not to have the axe knocked out of his hand.

Bastard, he thought. Go pick on someone your own size.

He could see the boy earnestly concentrating, as if the youngster was playing a difficult new flute piece for his proud mother and father. As Poldarn stumbled backwards, feeling his crocked ankle unreliable under his weight, he tried to remember; if he'd been a sword-monk he must have taken the same classes, learned the same drills, memorised the same precepts of religion, which set down in firm, definitive terms the infallible techniques for dealing with such a situation without killing or being killed. Defence is no defence; strength is weakness; resistance is surrender. He could almost hear the words, though where they were coming from was another matter entirely. Thought is confusion; the winning fight is no fight; wisdom is an empty mind. Wonderful stuff, but what the hell did it all *mean*?

The boy swung at him again, and Poldarn could see two circles in the air, his own and the boy's, about to collide. He scrambled backwards but his ankle gave way; as he slumped to the ground he instinctively put out his right hand to steady himself, and as his wrist took his weight he

felt something give in his forearm, just above the elbow.
At some point he must have shifted the axe into his left
hand, because there it was; and there was a fine killing shot,
a peck to the right temple, avoiding the space that the sword
blade would be occupying, blocking the boy's right arm
with his left elbow, he could see it as plain as a sketch in
the manual of arms; but he couldn't do that, kill a thirteen-
year-old kid just because of his own clumsiness in ricking
his ankle on a stone. There had to be a non-lethal defence,
he knew there was one but he couldn't, at that precise
moment, recall what it was. I wish, he thought, I wish I
had my memory back—

The boy cut him. For a thin sliver of time Poldarn panicked, but the moment didn't last. It was just a nick, the
very tip of the blade tracing the skin over his cheekbone,
a trivial scratch. Another hop-and-skip backwards, disen-
tangling the circles; step back into safety, keep away, keep
the danger out of his circle – and he could hear that same
voice in his mind: safety is danger, danger is safety; if he
can reach you, you can reach him. Let live and die; kill and
live. Precepts of religion. There was an empty space in his
mind, where the tallow had been melted out, but its shape
defined all the other shapes around him, just as the past
shapes the present and the present shapes the future.

The past shapes the future; action is self-betrayal. Poldarn
stepped back once more, feeling the slimy mud of the
stream under his heel, and at that moment he saw the boy
shuffle forwards and sideways, toe leading, heel dragging;
and at the same moment that he saw the lad lift his arms, he
saw the cut as well, as though it had already happened;
he saw the answer to the question at the same moment as
the question itself, as if he'd broken into Father Tutor's
study and peeked at the next day's test paper. The answer
was one step forward, right into the middle of the opposing
circle – safe as safe could be, because he could see the boy's

sword coming down even as he was lifting it, and all he needed to do was edge out of its way, and—

In religion there is no in between; only the sword before and the sword after.

Poldarn hadn't known the answer, because the question and the answer were simultaneous; he made the move before he knew what it was, because in religion there is no moment in between knowledge and action. As the axe blade, sliding through the gap in the boy's guard, sliced through the youth's jugular vein on the push-stroke, the answer became apparent. Strength is weakness – Poldarn hadn't fought back, because he was older and stronger than the boy. Let live and die; kill and live.

It was a messy answer. Poldarn felt the heat of the blood as it splashed across his face like a duellist's glove. The light went out in the boy's eyes, and he stopped, like a mistake abruptly corrected; then he dropped straight down into the mud beside the stream, an untidy pile of joined-together limbs.

Shit, Poldarn thought. Made a right hash of that.

Not the first time, either.

He stepped back, felt his ankle fade and give way, and ended up sprawled on his backside, spine painfully jarred, a mess. Not the first time; I've done this before. Years ago, I killed a kid the same age as this one, in the same way exactly. That's how I knew what he was about to do before he did it; because I was remembering the last time. Precisely the same: the absolute precision of the drill hall (a floor divided into a grid by scored lines deeply engraved in the slate flagstones, each square and each junction lettered and numbered; Father Tutor calling out coordinates and the designation of each stance, ward, cut, move, his eyes shut, the whole duel worked out beforehand for both sides, so that in effect it had already happened before it began—)

(Suppose there's no such thing as learning, or intuition, or skill, or thought. Suppose instead that it's all just memory; suppose that every cut and counter-cut and parry and block is just recollection of the same fight fought out a lifetime ago. Suppose the draw is religion, the sword before and the sword after, because when the hand closes around the hilt, the sword has already been drawn and swung, and the skin cut open. Suppose that nothing is learned – languages, names, skills, facts – only remembered from the last time round, which was nothing more than a memory of the time before that, the same sequence of moves repeated over and over at the instructor's word of command until they're perfect, and that's religion.)

'Bloody *hell*.' Chiruwa's voice came from directly behind him. 'What did you want to go and do that for?'

Poldarn stood up, pulled his heel out of the squelching mud, and wobbled as though he was drunk.

'Fuck off,' he said. 'He nearly killed me.'

'Nearly killed you? For God's sake, he's just a *kid*. We're going to be in so much shit—'

'He nearly killed me,' Poldarn repeated. 'Stupid bloody rich bastard, he'd been trained, knew all the moves, straight out of the book. And I did my ankle.'

'You did your ankle? So bloody what? You're a *grown-up*.'

Poldarn shook his head. He couldn't care less what Chiruwa thought, anyway. 'Sword-monk training,' he said. 'You *have* heard of the sword-monks, haven't you? If it'd been you instead of me, he'd have paunched you like a rabbit.'

'Listen.' Chiruwa was shouting, the clown. 'You don't go killing bloody *kids*. Not noblemen's sons, anyhow. They'll send soldiers and start burning down villages till they find out who did it. You know how bad this is? We're dead already, that's how bad. Well, don't just stand there, let's get out of here—'

'Just a moment,' Poldarn said. 'The others. Where'd they get to?'

Chiruwa didn't answer; he just shook his head. For a moment Poldarn didn't understand; then he said, 'What, all of them?'

'Except you and me. You ran, you bastard.' Chiruwa suddenly remembered. 'You fucked off and left us, and now they're all dead except you and me.'

Poldarn shrugged. 'I came back, though, didn't I? So what about the soldiers? Where'd they go?'

'Same place as the lads. Fucking hell, this is a shambles. Doing the soldiers was bad enough – you wait till they find out we killed a nobleman's kid. Trust me, you'll wish you'd let the little shit kill you.'

'Maybe I do already,' Poldarn replied. 'But that won't change anything. Do you have any idea who this lot are?'

Chiruwa shook his head. 'Don't want to know, either. The less we know, the less chance there is of giving something away. Not that it matters worth shit; they'll figure out it was us and then they'll hunt us down and kill us slowly. You ever see a man vivisected to death?'

All this negativity was starting to get on Poldarn's nerves. 'Be quiet,' he said, 'and let me think. Now then; if it wasn't us, who was it?'

'But it *was* us. It was *you*, you bloodthirsty northern bastard.'

Poldarn managed a smile. 'No, it wasn't,' he said. 'We were never here. But of course they won't believe that, so it'd better have been someone else. Do you understand that?'

Chiruwa nodded sullenly.

'Fine. So who'd do a thing like this? Massacre a whole half-platoon of soldiers, *and* a dozen harmless foundrymen who just happened to blunder across them at the wrong moment? Suggestions?'

'Well.' Chiruwa was frowning. 'It'd have to be someone really sick and vicious. Feron Amathy?'

Poldarn grinned. 'What about the raiders?' he said. 'Think about it. For all we know, Feron Amathy spent all day today playing pegball with the Emperor – we can't pin it on him unless we know for sure he could've done it. No,' he went on, 'we'll make it the raiders. Everybody knows, they appear out of nowhere and just vanish when they've done. And it's completely their style, killing without reason.'

'Right. So you're an expert on the raiders now, are you?'

Poldarn shook his head. 'I never could understand them, not one little bit. Fortunately, neither does anybody else. All right, how about this? We got separated from our mates here, and when we caught up to them, this is what we found. Dead bodies everywhere, including the kid.' He frowned, then glanced round. 'Tell me something,' he said. 'What does your average raider look like?'

Chiruwa stared at him. 'God knows. Nobody's ever seen one and lived, remember?'

Not entirely true; but that was what people believed, so close enough. 'Precisely,' Poldarn said. 'Now, who around here don't we care about?'

After a short interlude of indecision, Poldarn chose a dead foundryman by the name of Dancuta, mostly because he'd never liked him much. He dragged the body across to the coach and found the cause of death: a simple stab wound, entering under the left armpit, straight to the heart. Fine. Chiruwa held the body still, propped up against the coach wheel, while Poldarn took careful aim and, using the dead kid's very fine and fancy sword, slashed down the dead man's face, slicing off the nose and cutting away the lips and the point of the chin. Nice job, no denying it; the mutilation could easily have been the result of a wild or lucky cut, and those parts of Dancuta's face that had made it possible to tell him apart from a million other tall, fat men were lying in the leaf mould. Next step was to strip off his coat, which was too obviously a cheapie from Falcata market, and his boots. (Ex-army; old, but well looked after. Luckily, they were just Poldarn's size.) The last and most important touch was the best part of all – because Chiruwa was wrong: some things *were* known about the raiders in the Empire. Shortly before Poldarn had left and gone across the sea to the islands where the raiders lived, the late General Cronan had inflicted on them the only defeat they'd ever suffered. It went without saying that government officers had been over the dead bodies left behind after the disaster, searching them diligently for any sort of clue that might cast light on the mystery of who they were and where they came from; and it was virtually certain, Poldarn was sure, that at least half of those dead bodies would've been wearing the distinctive thick-soled ankle-length horse-hide boots that the raiders brought from home, though Imperial footwear was better, no doubt about it – so much better, in fact, that Poldarn had often thought about getting himself a pair of decent Tulice shoes to replace the boots he'd made for himself at Polden's Forge, back in the old country, and worn ever since.

Trading shoes with a dead man wasn't easy, and it took Poldarn an age to get his old boots onto Dancuta's feet. He managed it in the end, however, and dumped the body face down in the stream. He wiped his hands on a clump of grass before standing up.

'What the fuck do you think you're playing at?' Chiruwa said.

'Needed a new pair of shoes,' Poldarn replied. 'Waste not, want not, after all. Right, that's that. Time to go.'

Chiruwa was delighted to leave, and they walked quickly in silence until they were deep in the wood, well clear of the road. On the way, Poldarn checked the details in his mind. Because of the kid, it wouldn't be just the local garrison commander investigating. They'd send to the fort at Falcata, or maybe even to Tarwar, and the colonel would send his own men to figure out what had happened; they'd be smart enough and well enough informed to notice that one tiny elusive clue – raider boots on one of the dead men – and they'd report back with smug grins on their faces, having been clever enough to solve the mystery. The raiders would be blamed; and, since they were effectively an act of the gods, the whole affair would in real terms be nobody's fault, which meant it could be dropped and forgotten about. And not only that; Poldarn was better off by a pair of good-quality army boots, on which he could walk back to Dui Chirra as soon as the foundry started up again. No real harm done, and nearly everybody off the hook and happy—

(A dead body with no face, no identity, lying in the mud beside a shallow stream, surrounded by dead bodies. No face, no identity, all the memory leached out of it, except for a pair of horse-hide boots representing an elaborate deception. Had Aciava been lying too, or had he been telling the truth?)

—And behind them, two fat, scraggy old crows, floating down through the trees. A better class of scavenger, more efficient; not concerned with boots, only the very essence of the waste they feed on.

Chapter Five

'Are you kidding?' Chiruwa said. 'I'm telling you, if we'd known there were raiders on the loose in the woods, we'd have been out of there so fast—'

The foundrymen nodded sympathetically. The story had grown a little each time it had been told, like a tree growing in rings. At the centre, the original lie, and radiating out from it the layers of embellishment. Pretty soon, Chiruwa would start believing it himself.

For his part, Poldarn was overjoyed to be back at Dui Chirra, standing in the cutting, grey sticky mud plastered up his legs. It was almost disturbing how relieved he'd been to come home. Things had started going well in his absence. The clay had dried without even a trace of a crack, and while Spenno smeared the tallow over the core, cursing fluently and reassuringly as his hands moulded the shape that would soon be the gap into which the metal would eventually flow, Poldarn and the rest of the courtyard hands were digging out material for the outer layer and the furnace itself. Good honest, useful work. If he wasn't careful, a man could kid himself into believing that this was what life is all about.

It would have been stretching the truth a little to say that everything was back to normal. For a start, ten of the court-yard crew had gone away and not come back. Presumably the government had buried their bodies, or nine of them at least, once they'd finished poring and scrabbling over the scene of the fight. But replacing them hadn't been dif-ficult. There were always a certain number of displaced men wandering about during the rainy season, only too glad to dig clay or do anything they were told in return for shelter, a cooked meal and a bit of money.

'So what were you and your mates doing in the woods anyhow?' the investigating officer had asked them. He'd shown up at Dui Chirra two days after they'd got back; it was worrying that he'd found them so quickly.

'We were on our way to the colliers' camp,' Chiruwa had replied, innocent as a snowdrop. 'We reckoned we might find work there, to tide us over till this place got going again.'

The investigating officer had thought about that. 'Taking your time, weren't you?' he'd asked. 'I mean, it's not a long way to the camp from your place, and there's more direct routes.'

Chiruwa had nodded sadly; the weight of guilt on his shoulders would've crushed a roof. 'I know,' he'd replied. 'My fault, basically. I'd been on at them about keeping going, maybe as far as Tarwar or someplace like that; but then we heard there were bandits on the road, and I got scared, made us all turn back and head for the camp – and that's how come we walked straight into that party of raiders at just the wrong moment. If I hadn't got panicky about the bandits, the lads'd all still be alive—'

'Ah yes,' the officer had interrupted, 'those bandits. Didn't run into them by any chance, did you?'

'Us? No.'

'Interesting,' the officer had continued, 'because we've got witnesses who reckon there were twelve of them – the bandits, that is – and that just happens to be how many there were in your party. Still,' he'd gone on, ignoring Chiruwa's attempts to speak, 'that's really none of my business, I wasn't sent here to look into any alleged bandits. Now, how many raiders did you say you saw?'

As to who the boy in the coach had been, nobody seemed to know anything. The investigating officer had more or less confirmed that he'd been the son of someone very important indeed, but that was as far as he was prepared to be drawn. On the other hand, there hadn't been any wholesale reprisals, no villages burned or mass executions – which, in the view of the foundry crew, meant the kid couldn't have been anybody special. Raiders or no raiders, the consensus was, if he'd mattered a damn to anybody the government would've had to do something, even if it was nothing more than sending out a squadron of cavalry to lop off a few heads along the Falcata road. People had a right to know that their taxes are being used productively, after all.

'To understand the act of drawing the sword,' said the skinny old crow, 'it is first necessary to understand the nature of time.'

Ciartan, who'd been dozing (and in his doze he'd been dreaming about a place where a stream crossed a road in a forest, where a boy and a man were fighting, and both of them had been him) sat up and opened his eyes. He still hadn't got the hang of lectures; back home, where hardly anything needed to be said aloud, *Oh look, the crocuses are out* or *It's your turn to feed the chickens* counted as interminable speeches. Sitting still while someone talked at you for a whole turn of the water-clock didn't come easily.

'Time,' continued the skinny old crow (and Father Tutor

did look exactly like a crow sometimes, in his long black robes, with his little spindly legs sticking out underneath) 'is all too often compared to a river; so often, in fact, that our minds skip off the comparison like a file drawn along a hard edge, and we no longer bother with it. But if we pause for a while and put aside our contemptuous familiarity, we may find the similarities illuminating.'

Next to him on the floor, Gain Aciava shuffled and stifled a yawn. Gain had problems keeping still in lectures, too; he couldn't be doing with theory at any price, reckoning that no amount of half-baked mysticism was going to help him get his sword out of the scabbard and into the bad guys any quicker. Actually, Ciartan didn't agree. He had an idea that at least a tenth of what the old fool told them in lectures might actually be helpful, if only he could figure out what it meant. He looked off to one side and as he did so caught sight of Xipho Dorunoxy; she'd been watching him, and quickly turned away. Now that was interesting—

'A river is substantial,' said Father Tutor, 'and yet its components have no substance. You can't hold on to water in your hands, just as you can't seize hold of time. A river is always there, and yet the water in it is never the same. A river is not an object so much as a process confined inside a shape; and the same, of course, is true of time. When, therefore, we come to consider the draw,' he continued; paused, sneezed, wiped his nose on his sleeve and went on: 'When we consider the draw, the relevance should be obvious. The draw is an exercise in time; in the broadest possible terms, the draw is an attempt to eliminate time, because we all want to do it as quickly as possible. But before we can eliminate a thing, first we must properly understand what it is.'

Carefully, just in case Xipho was watching, Ciartan looked sideways. She was sitting with her hands folded in her lap, looking straight ahead – not at the old fool, but at a space on the wall slightly above and to the right of his head. She'd been taking notes, because the lid was off her inkwell and she was holding her rather fine ivory-handled pen; but now the nib was dry. He realised he'd been watching her rather longer than was safe, and turned away before anybody noticed what he was doing.

'Time in the draw,' said the old fool, absent-mindedly picking at a tiny scab on the back of his left hand, 'is what separates the decision to act from the act itself. Let us call the decision to act, the past – because the decision arises out of things that have happened to us, a perceived danger, orders from an officer in battle, an insult or an incentive; therefore the decision is the past, and in our river analogy is represented by the source of the river. The act itself is the present, because it is substantive, positive; it consti-tutes the latest turn of events, until it is in turn superseded by another act. Accordingly, it represents the river lapping at our feet. The consequences of the act lie in the future – consequences that will, in due course, motivate further decisions and further acts, just as the present cools into the past, and the rain falls on the mountains. The draw, then: the draw is only the gap between the past and the present, and as such – logically speaking – it cannot and does not exist. Between the decision to cut and the cut there can be no interval of delay – logically speaking.'

Ciartan yawned. Drivel time, he thought. Pity; up till then, the old fool had sounded like he was about to make some kind of sense.

'We are faced, then,' said Father Tutor, 'with a gap; a hole in nature. We confront something that isn't there, because it can't be there, but which we know is there, because we experience it every time we lay hand to hilt. To understand this paradox, let us consider the act of casting a statue in bronze. An image is carved out of wax or tallow and packed in clay or sand. Then the mould is heated, the wax melts and pours out through a drain hole, and leaves behind a gap, an absence. It has no substance, this gap or void; it can't be touched or held, it is merely a shape confined between two definitions. And yet, when the molten bronze is poured in, it takes on the shape left behind by the melted wax, imposing its will on the substantial material, even though itself it has no form. In other words, it's a process; a process confined between parameters, just like time, or the river; or, of course, the draw. In the act of casting, the gap, the process, is memory. In the river, the gap is water. In the draw – as should now be obvious, if you've been following at all – the gap is religion. If we could pour molten bronze into the gap between the decision to draw and the cutting of the flesh, we could cast for ourselves a perfect image of a deity – or, as the proponents of the Morevish heresy would assert, of Poldarn the Destroyer.'

Ciartan gave up. He'd tried resisting. He'd tried rubbing his eyes, kicking his own ankle, digging his nails into the palm of his hand. He'd done his best, but it was no bloody good. He apologised to the old fool under his breath, and closed his eyes.

'The Morevish heresy,' the skinny old crow repeated. (Was he still the old fool, or was he really a crow now? In which case this was just a dream.) 'We call it that, and certainly it has no place in the orthodoxy, rightly so given that its very premisses are idolatry. But we should consider it with an open mind, just as we looked more closely at the trite metaphor of the river. In the Morevish heresy, Poldarn the Destroyer visits our mortal world shortly before the destruction of all things; he comes from outside time, being an immortal god, and he comes on behalf of the past, since the destruction he brings is punishment for the wickedness of mankind – our sins being the source of the river, rising in the bad acts we have committed. But he has no memory of who he is or why he's here among us, or what he's come to do; past, present, future are all missing, and all that remains in their place is a gap, an empty space confined between parameters. Poldarn, in other words, represents the process. Poldarn is the draw – according, that is, to the people of Morevich. And here is a significant point; because, according to tradition, in the distant past when Poldarn first left this world, boarding the ship that would carry him away to the timeless islands in the far West – at that time, long ago, the people of Morevich didn't communicate one with another as we do, speaking out loud and listening to what we hear. Instead, they communicated directly, mind to mind, hearing each other's thoughts inside their heads, so that words were largely unnecessary. Which is how, it goes without saying, they were able to form the concept of Poldarn – because speech is also an intangible, a process confined between parameters, an empty gap that shapes matter. But the men of Morevich did what we claim is impossible: they eliminated the non-existent gap we call speech, and so could proceed directly, thought to thought. In Morevich, therefore, the draw is also possible . . .'

At precisely the moment when Ciartan fell asleep, Poldarn woke up—

—Because someone was shaking him by the shoulder and yelling in his ear, 'Get up, you idle bastard, or Banspati'll do his block.'

Poldarn crawled out through the wreckage of his dream like a man escaping from an overturned cart; all around him, in his mind, were splintered fragments of truth, like the flotsam from a shipwreck. Gain Aciava, younger but still basically the same – he'd looked older than his age as a boy, younger than he really was twenty years on. And Copis, Xipho Dorunoxy. He'd been in love with her then, that thunderstruck passion, that religion that strikes only when we're too young to know any better. And who else, who else had been in the classroom with them? Twenty or so students, but he'd not been paying attention. He *had* been paying attention, in a way, to the skinny old crow part of the time, and to the slender, bony, long-limbed girl, but apart from that he hadn't allowed his concentration to wander, and so he hadn't studied the other faces in the room, and so he'd missed the whole point of the lesson. Typical.

'What?' he mumbled.

'Meeting,' snarled the voice – some man he only knew by sight and didn't much like anyway. 'In the coalhouse, compulsory or else. They're all waiting for you. *Move!*'

Just as well I was so tired I fell asleep in my clothes, with my boots on, Poldarn thought.

On the way to the long, dark coalhouse Poldarn and his escort passed the casting yard where the mould stood, shrouded under a thick swathe of tanned hides to keep out the damp. He remembered: today was the day, everything was ready for the pour. After the final frantic preparations, he'd scuttled away to get a few hours' sleep while the scrap bronze was packed into the cupola and melted; four hours, maybe five. What time was it? And why the hell have a compulsory meeting? Either the metal was ready to pour, or it wasn't. Nothing to have a meeting about.

As Poldarn shuffled into the coalhouse, a hundred heads turned and scowled at him. Just what he needed.

'Right.' Banspati's voice, clearly at the very furthest reach of his rope. 'That's the lot, we're all here. Now listen up, all of you, this is really important.'

Nobody heckled, joked, or said a word. Why? Because they're frightened, Poldarn realised with a jolt of panic. Terrified. For the gods' sakes; I close my eyes for five minutes and suddenly the world's all different.

Banspati – standing on an upturned crate – was about to say something else, but he stopped and jumped down quickly, a man anxious to get out of the way. His place was taken by a short, stocky man with white hair and a big nose. Friendly sort of face, bright blue eyes. For some reason, Poldarn knew before the short man said a word that he was an army officer.

'My name,' the man said, 'is Brigadier Muno Tesny.' Pause. 'If my name sounds familiar, it's because you've almost certainly heard of my nephew, General Muno Silsny, commander-in-chief of land forces. I've come here today to brief you on a very important commission which you're about to undertake on behalf of the general staff and, ultimately, the Emperor himself.'

In the privacy of the coalhouse's darkness, Poldarn frowned. So the Emperor wants a new doorbell. For that they send a brigadier, and I get jerked out of my pit at crack of dawn on a pour day. Well, quite possibly yes; it's just what you'd expect from an emperor, these exaggerated notions of his own importance.

'I've spoken with your foreman—' Nod to Banspati hunched in the front row; Banspati winced back, as if trying to disclaim all complicity. 'And I've informed him that this commission will, of course, take priority over all other com-mitments, effective immediately. Accordingly, the project you've been working on has been cancelled, and the treasury department will indemnify you against any finan-cial losses you may incur as a result. From now on, until further notice, you'll be working for me, full time and exclusively, until this commission has been completed. Is that clear?'

If the brigadier had been expecting questions, he didn't get any. No wonder; they were all scared rigid.

'The next point I have to impress on you,' the army man went on, 'is the need for absolute security and discretion.

It is essential' (he made the word weigh a ton) 'that nobody outside this building gets to know anything about the nature of the work you'll be doing. To this end, it's my duty to inform you that any act or omission on your part tending towards a breach of security will be considered an act of treason and punished accordingly.'

Oh well, Poldarn thought; presumably the old bastard didn't come here to make friends, so he wasn't going to be heartbroken about failing in that regard. So—

'Now,' the brigadier said, 'we come to the nature of the commission.' He paused, for effect as much as for breath. One thing was certain, he had their undivided attention. 'Some of you may be familiar with a type of conjuring trick commonly known as Morevich Thunder; another name for it, so I'm told, is Poldarn's Fire. The trick consists of a standard baked-clay pot, into which a mixture of charcoal, sulphur and ordinary tanner's curing salts is packed; a lamp wick is inserted, and the pot is then sealed with soft, cold wax. When the wick is lit, the mixture catches fire and erupts into flame, rather like a volcano, making a sound like thunder. In Morevich these devices are used as part of religious ceremonies, parades and general festivities; they've always been regarded as a curiosity, mildly amusing but highly dangerous if carelessly handled or abused.'

Copis, Poldarn thought: she'd had a boxful of the things, used them as part of the god-in-the-cart routine. That they were also known as Poldarn's Fire didn't surprise him in the least.

The army man cleared his throat and went on. 'Armourers working directly for the general staff,' he said, 'have made a careful study of these devices, and have concluded that in these toys may lie the answer to the threat posed to the whole empire by the foreign pirates generally known as the raiders. It is the view of our best armoury officers that if the Morevich Thunder mixture is packed into a stout bronze tube sealed at one end, the force of the eruption will be sufficient to hurl a stone or an iron ball with enough force to do tremendous damage. Given a large enough stone, it might be possible to break down a wall, or –' theatrical pause '– or to sink a ship. As you all know, it has in the past proved beyond our ability to contain the raiders' forces once they land. Neither do we possess sufficient naval strength – or, quite frankly, skill – to engage them by sea. If, however, we could contrive to sink their ships while they were still at sea, by means of weapons operating from shore batteries, we believe that the devastating and intolerable attacks that the Empire has suffered over the last eighty years could be discouraged and ultimately brought to an end. In other words, the Morevich Thunder project could mean an end to the raiders, and thereby, without exaggeration, the salvation of the Empire.'

Total silence. It was obvious that nobody had the faintest idea what the old bastard was talking about, but that wasn't stopping them hanging on his every word. Of course he hadn't mentioned money yet; but the salvation of the Empire . . . It had to be worth more than making a few lousy bells, surely—

'Your task,' the army man continued, 'will be to cast the bronze tubes. Since this is an entirely new field, it necessarily follows that any designs or specifications our people have to offer you will be mere theoretical conjecture. You have been chosen because your foundry has a reputation for casting the very finest bells in the Empire; also, your secluded location will make the job of enforcing security that much easier—'

(He had to go and spoil it, Poldarn thought. Even so.)

'To be brutally frank,' the brigadier went on, 'we chose a bell foundry because the nearest thing to one of these tubes that anybody could envisage was a bell; a bell is, after all, a bronze tube, open at one end. That is more or less as far as we can take you; the rest is up to you, your skill, experience and ingenuity. You will, of course, receive all possible support in terms of resources, equipment, specialist supplies, additional manpower—'

And money; please don't forget the money . . .

(Making a weapon that'd be used to kill his own people – Asburn, at the forge, and Cetil, who'd shown him how to prune fruit trees, and Raffen, and Lothbrook who was so handy at mending furniture, and Carey – no, wait, he'd killed Carey with his own hands, for what had seemed like a very good reason at the time. Even so . . . But the army man's bronze-tube thing wasn't going to work, not in a thousand years, so there'd be no actual harm done.)

'—And in return, we will expect nothing less than your very best efforts and your complete devotion to the success of the project. It's nothing less than the truth to say that the eyes of the general staff, the court, the palace itself are currently fixed on Tin Chirra—'

(Idiot, Poldarn muttered to himself. This is *Dui* Chirra. Tin Chirra's ten miles up the valley)

'I myself,' said the army man, rather grimly, 'will be stationed here with my staff to supervise progress and liaise with the general staff on your behalf. A team of our best men from Torcea arsenal will shortly be arriving to brief you on the technical side; they'll demonstrate the Morevich compound and give you the preliminary designs for the first experimental prototypes. I have to inform you that from this moment, nobody is allowed to leave the foundry premises for any reason whatsoever without written permission from myself. If this is inconvenient for any of you, I can only apologise; I hope I've said enough to prove to you that such precautions are justified and essential where a project of this importance is concerned. If you have any specific questions, please see me privately after the meeting. Thank you for your attention.'

The brigadier, with Banspati in tow, left the shed in dead silence, which lasted for maybe half a minute after the doors had shut behind him. Then everybody started talking at once.

Over the next couple of days, during which time nothing at all happened (they could have cast the Falcata guild bell and done most of the grinding, but the army man had said abandon the job, so they'd abandoned it) opinion among the foundrymen polarised into two extremes. The lesser faction, led by Malla Ancona and tentatively supported by half the pattern shop (though with numerous reservations), held that nothing good could come of a project that nobody seemed to know anything about, which entailed backing out of a contract – didn't matter that the government were buying them out of it, assuming they'd be as good as their word (hardly a certainly where government was concerned); what was important was the damage they'd do to their good name for reliability in the trade, which was where they'd be spending the rest of their working lives once this daft caper was over and done with. The majority view, however, was that nothing on earth beat government work, which was basically a golden opportunity to overcharge, pad invoices, fiddle supply requisitions and pass off shoddy work as first-class trade practice. Better still in this instance: because nobody had a clue how to make the bronze tubes, or had any reason to believe they'd do what they were supposed to even if they were built a hundred and ten per cent according to spec, it was going to be the next best thing to impossible to define failure. So when the tubes shattered into bits every time they were tested, it wouldn't be anybody's fault, and so there'd be no need to bother or make any kind of effort; just put in an appearance around the yard, look busy when anyone in uniform was watching, and draw wages at the first and last of the month. Every craftsman's dream,

working for the State. Wasn't there a saying, 'Good enough
for government work'? Meaning a three-eighths pin
peened over to snag-fit in a seven-sixteenths hole, or
cracked woodwork pinned back together and bodged over
with sawdust and glue?

(A third faction, consisting solely of Spenno the pattern-
master, spent both days locked away in the boiler-shed loft
with half a Tulice red cheese, a quarter-barrel of death's-
head cider, and his precious copy of *Concerning Various
Matters*. As far as this faction was concerned, the project
posed a fascinating technical challenge of the kind that
crops up only once in a lifetime. Anybody other than
Spenno would've been dunked in the river for such a disgusting display of keenness; but since it was him, nobody
took any notice.)

'I mean, yes,' a melt hand called Chainbura explained
to the two dozen or so men who'd gathered from force of
habit round the curing fire in the south corner of the yard,
'the whole idea's bloody ridiculous, just like you'd expect
from a bunch of army blokes who wouldn't know hot metal
if you poured it down the back of their trousers. So bloody
what, so long as we get paid. And since it's not like we got
any choice in the matter, I can't say as I can see what you
buggers're cribbing about. Quit whining and let's get on
with it, I say. I mean, it's got to be better than work.'

'Missing the point's what you're doing,' someone
objected at the back, 'which is about right for you front-
yard buggers. We aren't working for the government,
we're working for the fucking *army*; and that's a completely different kettle of fish, you hear what I'm saying?
Army's all bull and procedure and chits for every bloody
thing you use and checks every five minutes to see if
you're doing it right – and if they don't know bugger-all
either, they just make it up as they go along, anything so's
they can give you a bollocking. I was in the army nine

years, I know all about it, and I'm telling you—'

Poldarn had tried to take an interest, just to be sociable, but he found he couldn't even muster a convincing pretence. One significant difference between the others and himself was that he'd actually seen a Morevich Thunderpot in action, and the more he thought about it, the more convinced he became that the army's wild scheme might turn out to be feasible after all. The implications of that weren't appealing, given who was likely to be underneath the flying stones if ever they got launched in anger. Needless to say, this wasn't a concern he could share with anybody. Neither was the matter that occupied far more of his attention than the new project.

He hadn't had any dreams (that he could remember) since the one about the lecture, when he'd been staring at Xipho Dorunoxy when she wasn't looking. Probably just as well; there'd been enough solid material needing to be digested in that dream to last him a month. And the unavoidable conclusion, which he'd tried to dodge and fence away from but which kept coming back at him like two crows mobbing a hawk, was that Gain Aciava had been telling the truth, or a part of it, at any rate.

What about that?

Poldarn thought about it for a while, as the foundrymen argued the toss and grew steadily more angry with each other. In the end he came to the conclusion that it was like being chased by his own shadow; it could never actually catch him, but it'd never give up trying.

On the third day, Spenno the pattern-master came down from his loft like some ascetic prophet from a mountain top, with three days' stubble on his usually butter-soft chin, and a huge grin. He'd got it figured out, he announced; basically, it was the same as founding a bell, only—

At that point, somebody cleared his throat and invited Spenno to meet the armoury men.

There were four of them: a bearded man, very short, with arms as thick as an ordinary man's legs, and three long, thin clerks, spindly like unthinned trees in an unmanaged forest. The short man smiled, stepped forward on recognising his opposite number, and identified himself as Galand Dev, chief pattern-maker to the royal arsenal at Torcea. He'd been looking forward to meeting Spenno, he went on, because he'd heard a great deal about his innovative work in hinged cupola casting, and the initial designs he'd come up with depended heavily on the use of a cupola furnace. Spenno glared at him for a few long moments, then pretended he wasn't there; looked past him, and carried on with his announcement where he'd left off. He'd finally cracked it, he declared; basically the same as casting a bell, only—

'Excuse me,' Galand Dev interrupted quietly (far more effective than shouting), 'but there seems to be some confusion here. I'm sorry, somebody should have told you. I'm in charge of the design work—'

Spenno stared at him, as though the short man had just materialised out of thin air. 'Who the fucking hell are you?' he asked politely.

'Galand Dev,' the short man repeated, in a soft, reasonable voice. 'Chief pattern-master at the Arsenal. I designed the tubes. And what I've been meaning to ask you is, do you think your local greensand has enough body to hold a simple wired core, or—'

'Piss off,' said Spenno.

One of the clerks tried to punch Spenno in the mouth. A huge foundryman by the name of Salyan grabbed the clerk's fist in mid-air and yanked his arm behind his back. With a mild sigh, the short man took a step forward, kicked Salyan in the groin so hard that the crack echoed off the barn roof, and finished the job with a short, horrible punch to the side of the head. Salyan rolled sideways and lay still. Nobody moved.

'He'll be all right,' the short man sighed. 'Now, please, if we could all get back to the job in hand. This greensand of yours—'

Poldarn left them to get on with it. He remembered that he had a little job of his own to finish, and chances were that once Spenno and the government man had sorted out their professional differences, there wouldn't be much spare time to waste on personal projects. He wandered across to the forge and got a fire in.

He'd left it about half done; the shape was more or less there, but so vague that only he could see it, because he knew what he was looking for. He forged in the bevels, trapping the inside edge of the flat tapered bar between the anvil's horn and the hammer; it was slow, patient work, only a few hard, careful hammer-blows each time before the steel had to go back in the fire and take on more heat. The profile and geometry of the bevels had to be perfect, since each hammer-fall squeezed a dab of orange steel up into the body of the work, subtly twisting and distorting the shape, which meant that for every strike he made on the edge, he needed four on the flat and the spine to maintain the lines he'd drawn in his mind. Every so often he had to spend a whole heat renewing the angle of the back curve, either hammering over the horn or fixing the work in the vice and twisting it with a long rod with a U-bend on the end. It took him the rest of the day to get the bevels done, and he decided to leave it at that. No point starting on the fullers and having to abandon the job part-way through. And he was still on the easy bit.

After what passed for dinner (the rains were still up on the road, though the level was perceptibly dropping, half an inch a day; fairly soon it'd reach the point where the drainage rhines began drawing again, the level would drop by a foot overnight and the food wagons from Tin Chirra could get through again) Poldarn drifted over to one of the watchfires to toast a slice of cheese onto a slab of stale grey bread. Nobody looked up as he joined the ring round the fire; theirs was a circle that could be broken into without risking bloodshed.

'That woman they got with them,' someone was saying, 'the crazy bitch who's into all that religious stuff. They reckon she's the worst of the lot.'

'Worse than the Mad Monk?' Someone on the other side of the circle wasn't convinced. 'Don't believe it. Women aren't like that.'

That amused someone else. 'You never met my old lady,' he said. General laughter. 'No, I mean it,' whoever it was went on. 'I remember one time – she'd been on the cider, mind, and I'd done something or other, never did find out what; anyhow, she got really mad at me, came and stood over me while I was eating my dinner, yelling and carrying on, scaring the kids to death. Well, I wasn't in the mood for a fight just then, I'd had a long day and you've got to feel right for a really good row, so I just got up and walked out, didn't say a word or anything. So what does she do? She follows me, still yelling her daft head off; so I go through the house into the barn, and she comes after me, still yelling and screaming, not getting the point at all – but they're like that, aren't they? So I push on through the barn to the outhouse, nip in, shut the door and put the latch across. She's hammering on the door, I'm shouting at her, fuck off, you stupid cow, I'm having a piss – which was true, as it happens. And next thing I know, she's fetched the axe out of the barn and she's smashing up the outhouse door – and I'm in there, for crying out loud, and I can see the axe blade coming in through the wood. Scared? I'm telling you, I was in the right place, or else I'd have pissed myself. If she hadn't swung wild with the axe and bust the head off the shaft, Poldarn only knows what'd have happened. Anyhow, she went inside, I waited till I thought it was safe and buggered off over the hill into town. Three days before I reckoned it was all right to come home, and then only because she sent the boy over to say that maybe she'd gone a bit too far. A bit too far – those were the exact words. Women? I promise you, when they lose it, they really lose it bad. And I guess this Dorun-whatsername's like that, only she hasn't calmed down yet.'

Poldarn couldn't help remembering the burning of Deymeson, and Copis with a sword in her hands, straightening up into the front guard. So maybe it had just been something he'd said—

'She's a nutcase, all right,' someone else said, 'but it's the Mad Monk who's the really dangerous one; because he's mad, sure enough, but not rolling-on-the-floor mad, that's not really a problem so long as you stay clear. He's more the ninety-per-cent sane type. They're the ones you got to look out for, because one minute you're standing there talking to them all nice and pleasant about the weather or the war or something, and next minute they'll pull out a knife and try and chop your bollocks off. Never know where you are with them, see.'

Nobody seemed inclined to comment on that for a while. Then someone else (Sineysri, from the mould-scraping crew) coughed nervously and said that the Mad Monk and the crazy bitch were one thing, but at least they weren't anything like as bad as Feron Amathy. 'And if you ask me,' he went on, 'absolutely the worst bloody thing they could do now is what they're planning to do, by all accounts: give Feron Amathy the job of sorting those two out.'

General mutter of agreement. 'Total disaster,' someone said. 'Those religious nutters prowling about up one end of the country, the Amathy house on the loose down the other, and us poor buggers caught in the middle. All it'd take would be for the raiders to show up, and it'd be damn well near the end of the world.'

'That's right.' Someone Poldarn knew, but couldn't put a name to: thin voice, slight speech impediment. 'If you ask me, old Tazencius has got the right idea for once with these tube things.'

'Sure,' someone interrupted. 'If only we can make bastards work.'

Muted laughter. 'That's right,' Thin-voice went on, 'and that'll only be when that little short bugger pushes off and lets Spenno alone to figure it out for them. But if it all works out, I reckon it's not the raiders they'll be wanting to point the tubes at, it's the Amathy house, followed by the Mad Monk. Then we might be getting somewhere at last.'

'You say that,' growled a deep voice from the dark edge, where Poldarn couldn't see. 'But you know exactly what'll happen, soon as they hand those tubes over to some general or other – assuming they do what they reckon they'll do, and don't just go off *phut* like a old ewe farting. They'll hand them over to some general and tell him, go fight the raiders or Feron Amathy or whatever; and he'll turn right round and stick 'em up Tazencius's arse, and next day we'll have a new emperor. And so on, over and over. Truth is, there's nobody in this empire you'd trust as far as you could sneeze 'em, not since Cronan died. No, the simple fact is, it's time for us here in Tulice to say enough's enough, boot the garrisons out of Falcata and Torneviz, and get on with it ourselves. Same for the folks in Morevich, and the Two Rivers country. Let those arseholes in Torcea play their games in their own back yard, and see how they like it.'

The discussion got lively after that, and Poldarn decided that it might be sensible to take his toasted cheese and eat it somewhere else, just in case Brigadier Muno or one of his staff were hanging about somewhere in the shadows, learning a few illuminating facts about the loyalties of some of the workers engaged on his last-best-hope project.

Brigadier Muno: if he'd got it straight (he sat down under a cart, one of the monsters they used for hauling the finished bells – huge wheels, plenty of room under them to sit upright, and the dropped sides kept out the night breeze), then this Brigadier Muno was the uncle of the sad young cavalry officer he'd saved from looters and scavengers in the aftermath of some damn-fool battle or other, when he'd come across him lying all bloody beside a river, surrounded by dead men. Whether that memory was an asset or a liability he wasn't entirely sure. The officer he'd carried on his back as far as the man's unit's camp had been properly grateful at the time; but now he was a very grand general, and his attitude to previous benefactors might have warped a little, like sawn planks left lying in the wet. A lot would depend, for a start, on whether Muno Silsny recognised him if and when he saw him again; if not, and if the story of the river rescue was tolerably well known, Poldarn could turn up at the great man's tent only to find he was the fifteenth person that week to have come forward claiming to be the general's personal angel of mercy. That could be enough to embarrass a man to death.

And, since it appeared that he was in a contemplative mood and thinking about old times: what if Gain Aciava had been telling the truth . . .?

That old question again. It was beginning to lose its meaning, like a word endlessly repeated until it became a mere sound. Besides, Poldarn knew the answer, and entirely unhelpful it was, too: *Some of what Gain Aciava told me was almost certainly true.*

But that was only a starting point. A better question was: *What did Gain Aciava want from me?* It had to be something to do with Copis; because she was a celebrity now, a household name – the mad woman, the crazy bitch. (And how had she got that way?) But he couldn't bring himself to believe in any of that. Not her style, madness; she'd stood and watched him kill people – soldiers, two successive gods-in-the-cart – and the only aspect of it that had seemed to bother her was the inconvenience, the interference with her plans. He'd seen her angry, but that was something else entirely. Even at Deymeson, she'd been entirely rational when she'd tried to kill him.

If their child was still alive, he'd be about three years old now. He or she.

So what use would Poldarn be to Gain Aciava in some matter relating to Copis? To use against her, presumably, since she was a public enemy and therefore liable to be worth money, or money's worth. But in what way? She felt quite strongly about him, for sure, but Aciava seemed to know all about the terms on which they'd parted, so it wasn't likely that his role was bait for a trap (unless she hated him enough to take foolish risks to get at him, which he doubted). It'd help, of course, if he knew what she was really playing at.

Then again, it was possible that the fall of Deymeson and the ruin of the order had unhinged Copis's mind. She must have believed in it, loved it, to do what she'd done with him, to him, on its behalf. He could almost believe that, until he remembered her eyes. (Cold, bright, always full of life, always devoid of feeling; he couldn't see her going mad for the fall of the order, just as he couldn't see her dying for it. Living for it, yes, even if her life had become an intolerable burden. But Copis wasn't the dying sort.)

A dog was peering at Poldarn through the spokes of the cartwheel, as if he was some strange new animal never hitherto seen in those parts. He reached about for a stone to throw at it, but couldn't find one.

The sensible thing, of course, would be to find Gain

Aciava and ask him. Quite likely he'd only get lies or evasions, but any kind of data was better than none at all. But that was out of the question – all leave cancelled, nobody to leave the premises without written permission, deserters hunted down without mercy. Maybe Poldarn could have written Aciava a letter, if he had any idea where to send it and some way of getting it out past the brigadier's soldiers. Instead, all he could do was wait and see what snippets of information he could scrounge out of his own dreams. Hardly scientific. Poldarn stretched out his legs as far as they'd go, closed his eyes and drifted off to sleep; and – to his intense disgust upon waking – dreamed an entirely unhelpful dream about haymaking at Haldersness when he'd been seven.

The technical debate between the armoury man, Galand Dev, and Spenno the pattern-maker was rapidly evolving into a full-scale religious war. The point of dogma at issue was whether the tubes should be cast pointing up or down. Not surprisingly, Spenno espoused the orthodox view. He declared that the tubes should be cast just like a bell, with the open end pointing downwards. Galand Dev maintained that the solid core of the mould, which would create the hollow inside the tube, should hang from the top of the mould rather than stand up inside it, which meant casting the tubes with the open end pointing upwards; he reckoned that if they used the traditional method of melting out tallow to leave a gap for the bronze to flow into, the core might shift position during the burn-out, which would result in a tube whose hole wasn't straight down the middle. His version did away with tallow altogether, and relied on four pins to hold the core suspended ('dangling,' Spenno declared scathingly, 'like an old man's balls') in the exact centre of a hollow clay tube.

As clashes of conflicting faiths went, it was rather more

logical and comprehensible than, say, the cause of the devastating schism that had torn the Empire apart during the
reign of Nikaa the Third. That conflict had stemmed from
the refusal of the Congregationalists to admit that two hundred years earlier a monk had miscalculated the date of a
minor irregular festival, in spite of the claims of the
Revisionists that a divine messenger with the wings of an
eagle and the head of a lion had appeared to their leader in
a vision and told him the shelf and docket number in the
archives of the file in which the incriminating documents
were stored.

What the core debate lacked in picturesque embellishment, however, it amply made up for in passion and
intractability. Spenno immediately retaliated with a whole
decalogue of concerns about porosity, stress fractures and
crystalline structure, all supported by citations from
Concerning Various Matters. When Galand Dev refused to
accept the infallibility of Spenno's adored book, the
pattern-maker flew into such a terrible rage that only
Galand Dev's extraordinary reflexes saved him from being
stabbed with the sharp ends of a pair of heavy brass calipers.
Thereafter, the two opposing factions communicated
strictly in writing, with two teams of messengers being kept
busy carrying furiously scribbled notes backwards and forwards between Galand Dev in the pattern office and
Spenno's headquarters in the boiler-shed loft. Whether
either Galand or Spenno managed to spare time from
writing their own notes to read each other's was a moot
point; unless they could read and write at the same time,
it was hard to see how it could have been done.

('Plain fact is,' Banspati muttered gloomily, as the
foundrymen crowded round the yard fire on the third
evening of the debate, 'neither of them's got a fucking clue.
You go trying to cast a tube that thick with a hole down
the middle, you'll get the metal at the edges cooling faster'n

the metal in the middle, and the whole bloody lot'll crack
like ice at midday. If you ask me, it just can't be done and
that's that; which means the best thing to do is cast one
arse-up and one arse-down; and when they both fall to bits
soon as look at 'em, maybe all the government bastards'll
piss off back to Torcea and let us get on with some work.')

When the argument had been raging for five days and
still showed no sign of calming down, almost the entire
foundry crew had divided, in roughly equal proportions,
into factions supporting one or other of the two rival doc-
trines. In most cases, adherence to a faction had precious
little to do with the merits of arse-up or arse-down, and
was rather more closely concerned with whether the man
in question hated the government more than he hated
Spenno. Poldarn, who had mixed feelings about both sides,
did his best to steer clear of the subject every time it came
up in conversation; but since there was nothing for the men
to do all day except talk and nothing else that anyone
wanted to talk about, he didn't really have any choice.
Rather than make the effort to follow technical arguments
he couldn't really understand, he fell into the habit of
agreeing with whoever he was talking to and hoped nobody
would notice how quickly his loyalties tended to change.

In the event, Galand Dev won the argument – up to a
point – by adopting a wider fame of reference, or cheating.
When Brigadier Muno complained to him that time was
getting on with nothing he could put in his dispatches that
the people back in Torcea would want to read, Dev replied
that there really wasn't anything to argue about – he was
right and Spenno was wrong – but that the workers weren't
prepared to believe him without a compelling reason to do
so. Muno nodded, and said that compelling reasons were
easy. Then he sent for Banspati and told him that, for security reasons, he was putting the Virtue Triumphant out of
bounds; at least, he added meaningfully, until such time as

Spenno and Galand Dev could agree on how they were going to do the job, and something was actually achieved.

Banspati didn't like that one bit. True, the Virtue had officially been off limits from the start, but nobody had taken the prohibition seriously, figuring that nobody, not even a government administrator, could be that cruel and unfeeling. Quite apart from the beer, the Virtue housed a dozen or so tired-looking, sad-eyed women whose job was to part the foundrymen from their money on a regular basis. As the foundrymen themselves used to say, they weren't much but they were a damn sight better than nothing, and therefore essential to the smooth running of the foundry. Muno's prohibition, Banspati knew without having to be told, was likely to prove considerably more explosive than anything the alchemists of Morevich ever brewed up in one of their little clay pots. After a stunned silence, therefore, he promised Muno that he'd talk to Spenno right away and see if there wasn't some middle ground that might be acceptable to both parties.

Whatever he said to Spenno, for three quarters of an hour up in the boiler-house loft while the foundry crew milled about angrily in the yard below, it probably didn't have much to do with porosity, stress fractures or crystalline structure, but it did the trick. Spenno, looking suitably chastened and watched in furious silence by his assembled colleagues, scuttled down from his loft and across the yard towards Galand Dev's command post in the drawing office. Ten minutes later, the two men appeared at the door and announced that they'd got it all figured out, and work on the first prototype would start at dawn the next day. Meanwhile, anybody who cared to celebrate the reconciliation with a brief visit to the Virtue was free to do so, provided that they were in a fit state for work come morning.

Very soon afterwards, the yard was deserted. Poldarn,

for his part, couldn't be bothered to go; instead, he crossed over to the forge and spent the rest of the day by the fire, drawing down, splitting, shaping and jumping up. By evening, his strip of odd-looking steel had taken on a definite and unique shape; like a leaping dolphin with a broad, splayed tail (where the upper and lower horns of the handguard arched round until they almost touched). He hardened and tempered the steel with an unexpected degree of trepidation; but for once, everything went right, and the piece that emerged from the barrel of burning olive oil was unmistakably a Raider backsabre. It wasn't, Poldarn suspected, entirely perfect, but that was only to be expected of his first attempt at making such a thing, done entirely from memory. As he took a break from drawfiling out the hammer marks and speckles of forged-in firescale, it occurred to him to wonder, for the first time, what he'd actually made the thing for. If he needed to chop kindling he already had a perfectly good hand-axe. And he wasn't about to kill anybody – was he?

Chapter Six

They faced each other down a thin steel road; two circles, separated by the smallest possible distance. The draw had been inconclusive; there hadn't been the smallest fraction of a second between them, because both of them had eliminated time in the moment (which doesn't exist in religion) between the impulse and the result; and all that had come of it was an awkward collision of flats, nothing achieved either way. From there they'd both immediately fallen back into their own circles, swords in the first guard, their minds in their eyes, as the precept of religion puts it, both waiting for the other to move first. And since they were identical in every respect (having attained religion, at least as far as the third grade, and thereby eliminated themselves except as copies, cast from the same pattern in the same mould) there was no way that either of them was going to make that first move, in the same way that a shadow can't pre-empt the body that casts it.

Father Tutor was drumming his fingers on the desk, trying to annoy them (one or both, didn't matter), break their concentration, needle them into making a mistake. Behind him, the rest of the class sat completely still – it was perfectly legitimate for Father Tutor to distract the candidates, but God help a student who sneezed or scratched an itch while the bout was in progress. Quite right, too; in the school at Deymeson, it was traditional that exactly half of the students in each grade after Grade Three moved up a class at the end of the year. The other half, those students who failed the practical, were buried in the yard behind the junior refectory, unless their families were prepared to pay the cost of shipping them home—

He caught his breath; was that a movement, or the different kind of stillness that comes before movement (as waves ripple out in all directions when a stone falls in water, so a movement ripples backwards and forwards in time, the perceived outcome and the perceived anticipation) or was he just imagining things? The other face, his mirror image, was watching him in exactly the same way as he was watching the other face. Had his equal-and-opposite imagined that he'd seen the anticipation of movement too? That'd be right. Combat is a mirror (precept for the day, a couple of terms back); also, combat in religion is a battle between two shadows (presumably meaning roughly the same thing, but with added mysticism).

—Which was why friendships were rare among the students at Deymeson; difficult to get attached to someone when it was quite possible – probable, even, given Father Tutor's macabre sense of humour – that you'd wind up meeting your best friend on the thin steel road, knowing that one of you wouldn't be back after the summer recess. Unfortunate; but here they both were, the very best of friends, so close it was hard to tell them apart, so close that even the draw had failed to separate them. There hadn't been time to apologise, to say *No hard feelings, if somebody's got to get through over my dead body I'd rather it was you.* That shouldn't have needed saying, of course, not between friends; but apparently it did, and it hadn't been.

Father Tutor yawned loudly; and that wasn't a legitimate examination tactic, that was just plain rude. Something as out of the ordinary as this, a year-end practical that lasted longer than a sneeze, you'd have thought he'd be pleased, not bored.

Maybe he'll stop the fight. No way of proving it, but he was sure the idea had crossed both their minds simultaneously; followed immediately by *Maybe we can stop the fight; if we both sheaths our swords together, now—*

He felt the impulse tug at his wrists, but he defied it. Yes, he knew his friend, he knew his friend wanted to end the fight more than anything in the world. But he knew also that his friend was thinking exactly the same thing as he was: *Bloody stupid I'd look, if I put up and he doesn't;* and then I'd be dead, and *that bastard,* that traitor who said he was my friend, he'd still be alive and through to next grade, and that'd make him better than me—

In religion, there is no time, there is no space, because the sword doesn't move from scabbard to flesh and it takes no time getting there. Between the impulse and the result no time, no space, therefore in religion nobody and nothing can exist.

'Very good,' Father Tutor called out, in a voice that suggested he didn't think it was very good at all. 'On the count of three, you will both step back three paces and put up your swords; and then we'd better start again from the beginning, see if we can't do better next time. One, two . . .'

(And both of them thought: on three the practical will be over, and we'll have to do it again; another draw, as bad as having to die twice. That gives us this little bit of time, between two and three, to get this mess cleared up.)

Just before Father Tutor could say the word, both of

them moved. Both stepped forward, two circles intersecting (like the ripples from two stones thrown simultaneously into water) and once again the swords met in mid-air, at the point where the shadow joins the body, and so nothing was achieved, nothing happened—

'Three,' Father Tutor said. 'Well,' he added, as they stepped back and sheathed their swords with a click, 'that was a bit of a shambles, wasn't it?'

He couldn't help it, he was shaking all over. Partly it was simply fear, the reaction to the extremes of danger and concentration. Partly though it was shame, and abhorrence; because at this moment in time there was only enough room in the world for one of them, and yet both of them were still there, illegally sharing it, like a shadow or a mirror-image being soaked up into the body that cast it. Two circles superimposed, becoming one.

That's not supposed to happen. And if it does – Not quite sure about the details, but isn't that supposed to mean something really bad is on the way, like the end of the world, Poldarn's second coming, something like that?

Maybe the same thought had just occurred to Father Tutor, because he was looking very grave all of a sudden, with possibly just a hint of why-did-it-have-to-happen-in-my-class.

'Match drawn,' said Father Tutor quietly. 'Both pass. Both through to the next grade.'

A moment when nothing happened (religion); then everybody in the building started talking at once—

'You,' said a voice in his ear. 'Wake up, now.'

Bloody hell, Poldarn thought, not again. Why can't I ever get a full night's sleep?

'Fuck you,' he muttered, and opened his eyes. Banspati – no, not this time. Banspati was there, but he was standing back looking very worried and unhappy (rather like Father

Tutor in the dream). The man who'd woken him up was that soldier, Brigadier Muno. A pity, Poldarn reflected bitterly, that *I just told him to fuck himself.*

'On your feet,' Brigadier Muno growled at him, and his big cheerful face wasn't quite as friendly as usual. 'Get your boots on and follow me.'

Not good; not good at all. Poldarn didn't know all that much about the Imperial regular army, but he had an idea he'd read or heard somewhere that the top brass don't usually come round waking you up and bringing you breakfast in bed. In the background, Banspati was glowering at him with a mixture of hatred and sympathy; *you're for it this time, and thanks to you, so am I . . .*

Typical: when you're flustered and in a hurry, your feet won't fit in your boots. Poldarn managed to get them on somehow, though they really didn't want to go; also he had pins and needles in his left foot, which really didn't help matters. Was it worth telling the brigadier he was sorry for saying 'Fuck you'; or would that only make it worse? Probably best not to say anything, he decided, knowing that whatever he did, he'd be bound to get it wrong.

Across the yard a lot of people were milling around, even though the angle of the sun told him it was ridiculously early for the day shift to be up and about, unless something was seriously wrong and he was the only man in the camp who didn't know about it. (That'd be right.) Outside the drawing office, which was apparently where they were headed, he noticed a bunch of riding horses tied up to the tethering post; unusual sight, since nobody in the foundry had a horse – even the brigadier and his staff had come by coach as far as the Virtue and footslogged the rest of the way. One very fancy horse; white, nervous, thoroughbred, with a gilded red leather saddle, worth a lot of money. *Looks like we're entertaining the quality. Is that good?*

Poldarn reflected on the sort of person who seemed to make good in the Empire – Tazencius, Feron Amathy – and decided no, probably not.

'In there,' said the brigadier.

Usually the drawing office was crowded – people working, people watching other people work – but not today; there was just one man, sitting on the corner of the long, broad table that Spenno and Malla Ancola used for drawing out designs. He lifted his head as Poldarn walked in, and at once Poldarn knew who he was. The last time he'd seen him had been at some army camp in the Bohec valley, where he'd had to trick and threaten a sentry into taking responsibility for the cavalry captain he'd rescued from two murderous old women who'd been looting the dead. He remembered carrying the cavalryman all the way up from the river – he'd been trampled by his own troop's horses, and both the man's legs had been broken; it had been an ordeal for both of them, but the cavalryman had been rather more stoical about it. He remembered how the poor bastard had made a point of telling him his name. Muno Silsny.

And here he was. As soon as he caught sight of Poldarn, he jumped to his feet; staggered, caught his balance and started to hurry towards him. Seated, he'd been like something off one of the grand triumphal arches in Falcata market square: pale, cold and handsome, as if his head had been cut off his head and replaced with a marble portrait bust of himself. But when he moved, Poldarn noticed, he waddled like a duck—

Two broken legs, badly set by an overworked, apathetic surgeon; it was a miracle Muno Silsny could walk at all, all things considered. Even so; the second most important man in the Empire, bouncing along like an oversized toddler. Not something you expect to see.

Just before breaking into Poldarn's circle, Silsny stopped.

His mouth was open, and his coin-portrait face wore a sort of idiotic, stunned expression. 'It's you,' he said; then, as if he'd suddenly caught sight of himself in a mirror and remembered with a start that he was a general, 'Here, you lot; Gianovar, Catny, Uncle – it's him. The man who saved my life.'

For a split second Poldarn was left wondering: yes, but is he pleased to see me or not? Then the stunned look melted into a huge boyish grin, and the general (crimson gold-trimmed cloak, best-quality gilded parade armour) took a long waddle forward and, quick as a sword-monk's draw, reached out and hugged him so hard that the air was squeezed out of his lungs.

'You've got no idea,' Muno Silsny was saying, 'how much I've looked forward to this. Damn it, what happened to you? I can remember you carrying me, and then I must've zonked out, and next thing I knew I was lying on the floor with my legs splinted, and my useless nephew Bel was leaning over me saying it was all right, I was safe, and you'd gone—'

'That's right,' Poldarn said, with the little breath he had left. 'I traded you for a horse. Your nephew got me one; I think he stole it from somebody.'

Muno Silsny laughed and said, 'He did indeed. A major from the general staff – he was absolutely livid about it. But anyhow: you left, and I never had a chance to say thank you.'

Poldarn shrugged awkwardly. 'Oh, it was no big deal,' he said.

'No big deal.' Muno Silsny shook his head. 'Well, I think it was a hell of a big deal, thanks all the same. Those ghastly old women, hovering over me like carrion crows, just about to murder me for my socks. I still get nightmares some-times, you know.'

This is getting embarrassing, Poldarn decided. 'Well,

I'm glad you made it in one piece,' he said. 'And you don't seem to have done too badly for yourself since.'

Behind him, he could feel the expressions on their faces: Banspati, looking like he'd just been stuffed with bread-crumbs; Uncle Muno probably scowling and shaking his head, everybody else staring and thinking, so what's in it for us? But as far as Poldarn was concerned, he'd rather have been somewhere else. He trusted the past – and any-body who came from there – about as much as he trusted Gain Aciava (who apparently had been telling the truth, at least some of the time).

'Oh, things have been going really well for me, yes,' Muno Silsny was saying. 'Damned if I know why, it's not like I'm anybody special; I mean, I never did anything brave and unselfish like you did. Makes you wonder, really, what the hell makes this world tick. But at least I've found you again. It's time we settled up, you know. It's been preying on my mind.'

Poldarn grinned feebly. 'Don't worry about it,' he said. 'No charge.'

Muno Silsny laughed, as if he'd just said something funny. 'This is absolutely amazing,' he said. 'I really don't know what to say. And to think, all this time you've been here, just quietly getting on with it, like nothing had ever happened. Why the hell didn't you come and see me, once I'd started getting famous and everything?'

'Oh, well,' Poldarn said. 'I had things I had to do, you know how it is.'

Muno Silsny was looking at him as though he'd just remembered something. 'You told me,' he said, 'that day by the river, you told me you'd lost your memory. That's right, you said you'd lost your memory and you couldn't even remember your name or anything about who you were. I remember thinking at the time, bloody hell, that must be about as bad as it can get, worse than broken legs or even getting killed. I mean, in a way it's a sort of death, because everything you were, which is everything you are, when you come to think about it – all gone, lost, and all you're left with is the clothes you stand up in. Certainly as bad as being robbed, or burnt out of your house, because you don't even know what you've lost. So,' he added brightly, 'that's all sorted out now, is it? Everything back to normal, and here you are home again. I'm so glad about that.'

Well, why not? Poldarn thought; and he nodded.

'Wonderful,' Muno Silsny said, slapping Poldarn hard on the shoulder. 'So, how long was it before it all came flooding back? Days? Weeks? As long as a month? I've heard it can take that long, in extreme cases.'

'Something like that,' Poldarn said.

'That's awful.' Muno Silsny shook his head sympathetically. 'It's terrifying, really, when you think how fragile memory can be. It's like when someone dies, and nobody knows where he left his will or the deeds to the farm or the keys to the strongbox. All that absolutely essential stuff that only exists inside our heads, and one little tap on the head's all it takes to lose it for ever and ever. I think I'd go mad if it happened to me. It'd be like being struck blind and deaf and dumb, all at the same time. Listen to me,' he added, 'I'm prattling on like a lunatic. I think it's just because I'm so very pleased to see you again. I mean to say, it's not every day you meet someone you owe your life to, and you'd started believing you'd maybe never see him again.'

Thank you, and can I go now? Poldarn wanted to say. Sure, he knew that by rights this was an amazing stroke of luck, almost as good as finding the genie in the bottle, like in the old stories. Somehow, though, he felt sure that it wasn't good luck at all, probably quite the reverse. Absolutely no idea why, of course.

In the event, it took him a very long time to escape from
Muno Silsny. Over lunch (in the drawing office; some weird
and wonderful picnic of Torcean haute cuisine that Silsny
had brought with him – obscure parts of rare animals
drowned in thick, spicy butter sauces) he heard how Uncle
had happened to mention in one of his letters that they had
a chap in the camp who'd lost his memory once, just like
Silsny's bloke; and as soon as he'd read that he wrote back
asking for a detailed description, and of course he knew
straight away that it was the same man, so he dropped
everything, cancelled dinner with the Emperor, and
hopped straight on the first boat he could find; and how it
had been a pig of a crossing, freak winds in the Bay, had
to put in thirty miles south of where he'd been intending
to land, and then all the problems of getting here, with the
floods and all. Over dinner (at the Virtue Triumphant; same
room as the night he'd dined with Gain Aciava) he heard
all about Muno Silsny's meteoric and totally unexpected
rise to power; how General Cronan had died at just the
right time, though of course it was a tragedy, the best man
in the Empire and that was including Tazencius, though of
course nobody had heard him say that; and how at every
step up the ladder he'd told himself, well, now at least I'll
be in a position to say thank you properly to the guy who
saved my life that time, if ever I can find him—

'So,' Muno Silsny said at last, with a big silver goblet of
wine in one hand and a pheasant drumstick in the other,
'here we are. And the question is, what can I do for you?
Anything you like – *really* anything, so long as I can do it
or get it for you; and if I can't, it won't be for want of doing
my absolute damnedest. You just name it, it's yours. Well?'

Well, Poldarn thought.

Well, what I really want, what I want most of all in all
the world, is for Gain Aciava to have been lying. Do you
think you can fix that for me, General Muno?

'Well,' Poldarn said. 'Nothing, really.'

Muno Silsny looked at him. 'No, seriously,' he said.

'Seriously.' I can't believe I just said that. Even so. 'I honestly can't think of anything I want, thanks all the same.'

'But—' Muno Silsny looked like a small boy who's just been told as he's pulling his boots on that they aren't going to the fair after all. 'Oh, come on,' he said. 'Money. A country estate, big house and loads of land. Are you married? No? Look, if you wanted me to, I might even be able to get you Tazencius's daughter. Seriously.'

No, thanks, Poldarn thought. I make it a rule not to marry the same woman twice if I can help it. 'How about the woman with the cart?' he said. 'The one who goes around with the Mad Monk. Could you get me her?'

A look of horror crossed Muno Silsny's face; but he removed it immediately and said, 'Well, I can try, certainly.'

'Only joking,' Poldarn said. 'Look, it's incredibly generous of you, but really, I can't think of a single thing I want that I haven't got right here.'

'You can't mean that.'

Yes, I can, Poldarn thought; because what I've got here is nothing at all, and that's just the way I want it to be. A big house and loads of land – I had that, at Haldersness and Ciartansdale, and I was glad to leave it behind. And the emperor's daughter, too—

(He hadn't forgotten the terms on which he'd parted from Tazencius the last time they'd met; Tazencius had called him 'my punishment', among other things, and had made a number of threats which hadn't meant anything to him at the time and still didn't. Far better to keep it that way.)

So he leaned forward (a gross intrusion into Muno Silsny's circle, but he didn't even seem to realise that) and said quietly: 'Can I talk to you in private, just for a moment or so? Won't take a minute, and then you'll understand.'

Muno Silsny looked up at him with surprise all over his face, like froth in a drinker's beard; but he nodded, got up and led the way out of the inn into the stable yard. It had started to rain, and he started to take off his cloak, to offer it to Poldarn who refused it with a slight shake of his head.

'Listen,' Poldarn said, before Silsny could say anything. 'It's very kind of you and all, and I appreciate it, but could you please leave me alone?'

The look in the general's eyes was heartbreaking; kicked dogs and slapped children weren't even in the running. 'I'm sorry,' he said. 'But after what you did—'

'Fine.' For some reason, Poldarn could feel himself getting angry. He made an effort to resist the impulse. 'It's that old gag about no good deed going unpunished. Do you know why I'm here?'

It was clear that Silsny hadn't given that any thought. 'I assumed this is – well, where you come from. What you do.'

Poldarn shook his head. 'This is where I am now,' he said. 'And yes, this is what I do, at the moment, for as long as I can. It suits me just fine. I like sleeping in a rabbit hutch and digging clay all day in the pouring rain. I like it better than being a farmer, or a blacksmith, or a courier for the Falx house; and it beats being a god into a cocked hat.' Silsny looked at him, but Poldarn went on: 'You're under the impression that I've got my memory back. I haven't. I still don't know who I am. The only thing that's changed is, I've reached the conclusion that I don't want to know. And that means I want to stay clear of anybody who might tell me. Does that make any sense at all to you?'

Silsny frowned, but nodded. 'I guess so,' he said. 'But all I wanted to do was – well, make things better for you.'

Poldarn smiled. 'I had a go at that, too – making things

better for people, I mean. Some of them are dead now, and
the rest won't forget me in a hurry. The point is,' he went
on, before Silsny could interrupt, 'sometimes it feels like
I'm walking blindfold in a small room stuffed full of fragile
things, and any moment now I'm going to bump into something and break it. Everything I do, there's a risk I'll meet
someone who knows me or I'll jog someone's memory and
they'll think, who does he remind me of? Oh, there's a few
things I've remembered, or found out about myself. For
instance, it seems pretty likely that I did something – well,
very bad to Prince Tazencius, many years ago; I ran into
him a while back, and he didn't seem very well disposed
toward me. At the moment, I think he believes I'm either
dead or a long way away. I'd rather he carried on believing
that. And anybody you do a favour for – particularly if it
means dashing away from Court, galloping a hundred miles
over bad roads, a man in your position – it does rather tend
to draw attention to the object of your bounty. Do you see
what I'm getting at?'

'I suppose so,' Silsny replied, rather grudgingly. 'I hadn't
really thought about it. I'm sorry.'

Poldarn shrugged. 'Don't worry about it. Does you
credit, I'm sure. Only, now I'm going to have to leave here.
I guess that's something you can do for me; I'm not allowed
to leave without permission, because of this special project.'

'Leave?' Silsny looked shocked. 'Why do you have to do
that? You just said that you like it here.'

'I do,' Poldarn replied. 'It's great, I'm just an extra pair
of hands around here, it's all I could possibly wish for. But
now we've had all this excitement, and the special presentation ceremony and everything—'

'You don't have to leave,' Silsny said firmly. 'You leave
it to me, I'll make everything all right. And truly, I'm sorry.
I had no idea I'd be making things hard for you. After all,
I owe you my life—'

'Not any more,' Poldarn said. 'Forget about it, like it never happened. Make that my special favour.'

'All right.' Silsny pulled a wry face. 'If that's what you want. But here.' Impulsively, he pulled a heavy gold ring off his finger. 'I don't know how much this is worth, but I'd guess it'd buy a house and enough land to keep someone comfortable. And nobody needs to know you've got it, or where it came from. Please, take it. It's not enough, but at least it's something.'

It matters to him, Poldarn thought; it matters enough that he probably won't go away unless I accept. 'Thanks,' he said. 'That makes us square.'

'Almost.' Silsny smiled. 'Personally, though, I'd value my life at slightly more than that. I mean, if I was killed on the road by robbers and all they stole was that ring, I'd figure it was rotten value for money. So I want you to take this, as well.'

Poldarn looked at the object he was being offered. He felt he ought to recognise it, but he didn't; some kind of small badge or brooch, with a pin and a keeper on the back. 'What's that?' he said.

Silsny nodded. 'Army stuff,' he said with a grin. 'Basically, it's a combination safe passage and get-out-of-trouble token; show it to a watch sergeant or a guard commander and unless he's got specific orders to the contrary from the Emperor or myself, he'll say sorry for troubling you and forget he ever saw you. Or if you need to get someone's attention in a hurry, something of that sort, it's good for that, too.' His grin spread a little. 'They tell me that the going rate for these things among the gang bosses in Torcea is up around the five thousand mark; not that I'd want to put ideas in your head, of course.'

'Of course.' Poldarn thought for a moment, then took the badge and pinned it to the inside of his collar, out of sight. 'Reminds me of a story I must've heard once, about a hat or a cloak or something that made you invisible.'

'I know the one you mean,' Silsny said. 'Poldarn's hood, from the time when he defeated the spirit of the fire-mountain. I always wanted one of them for my birthday when I was a kid, but all I ever got was socks.'

It didn't take long to clear up the misunderstanding. Somehow, a rumour had got about that General Muno Silsny, commander-in-chief of the Imperial forces, had come all the way to Dui Chirra (breaking off from a crowded schedule and riding through the night along flooded roads) to visit with an old friend or something of the sort. Not so. General Silsny had, in fact, come to the foundry to make a personal inspection of the Poldarn's Tube project – prompted, it had to be said, by the alarming lack of progress that his uncle had felt obliged to report directly to him. What more telling indication could there be of the importance that Torcea placed on the project than an impromptu inspection by the second most powerful man in the Empire (and so on). Silsny left the next day, having put the fear of several pantheons of gods into Spenno and Galand Dev. (He'd smiled at them, been extremely polite, and assured them that he didn't blame either of them *personally*: rumour had it that Galand Dev didn't stop quivering until late the next morning.) Assurances had been made by everybody concerned that work – actual sawing of wood and pounding of metal – would start the very next day, or the day after that at the very latest.

As far as Poldarn was concerned he was delighted to see the back of Silsny, even though he was the first person Poldarn could remember who actually had cause to be grateful for having met him; perhaps for that reason. For the next few days he had to put up with an insufferable amount of curiosity from everybody he met – what had all that been in aid of, had he really saved the general's life or was it mistaken identity, and what exactly had he said to the great man, all alone out there in the yard with nobody listening – which he dealt with by pretending to be deaf. Fortunately, there were plenty of other issues to occupy people's minds, and so the matter drifted and faded, with no worse effects for Poldarn himself than a useful reputation for being a miserable bastard.

The tremendous distraction was the sudden and unexpected announcement by Spenno and Galand Dev of their startling new plan of campaign. Since nothing could induce them to agree on which way up the core was to be, they'd decided to do without a core altogether. Instead, they declared, they were going to cast the tubes as solid bronze cylinders, and make the holes down the middle by drilling.

This was, of course, insane; and the foundrymen lost no time in pointing it out. In order to drill a hole down a solid lump of bronze that size, they said, you'd need to build a special lathe. Not just an ordinary lathe: it'd need to be the biggest, strongest, most precise lathe ever built. And then there were the cranes, gantries, steadies – in fact, you'd need to build a special shop for the bloody thing if you were going to do it properly; and even if it could be done at all, which was pretty unlikely, you'd be asking a hell of lot to have it up and running within a year, more like eighteen months. The headstock alone—

Spenno and Galand Dev replied that they'd thought of that. Furthermore, there were plans and detailed directions for building just such a lathe in Spenno's estimable book, *Concerning Various Matters*, which, if followed to the letter, would answer their needs perfectly. Brigadier Muno (they went on) had already sent to Torcea for specialist engineers who'd do the skilled work; while they were waiting for them to arrive, the foundry crew could get on with building the shed which, as they'd correctly assumed, would be needed to house the new machinery. By the time the engineers reached Dui Chirra, the Imperial lumber-yards at Sirupat should already have provided the necessary raw materials, including the enormous blocks of the very finest seasoned oak from which the headstock, tailstock and ways were to be fashioned. Nor, they added, would the blacksmith's shop be idle during this time: plans and sketches for the racks, pinions, cranks, spindles, bearings, lead screws and other necessary hardware would be ready in the morning, by which time bloom iron and steel billets would be at hand from Falcata. The time allocated for getting the lathe built and functional (Galand Dev added, with a broad grin) was thirty days.

Did anybody have a problem with that?

In the event, Galand Dev's time estimate proved to be hopelessly inaccurate. Instead of thirty days, the job was done in two weeks. It wasn't a pleasant time at Dui Chirra. Four overlapping shifts worked day and night, so arranged that there was no down time at all – when it was your turn to go to bed, you passed your hammer or your plane to the man standing waiting behind you, who carried on without missing a stroke. The specialist engineers turned out to be foreigners from Morevich; they were being paid for the job rather than by the day or the week, and they were clearly in a hurry to get finished and away from the filthy cold and wet as quickly as they possibly could. Most of the major components had been partly shaped in Sirupat, where they had huge water-powered sawmills that could cut a ten-foot length of thirty-by-forty heart of oak to within the thickness of a scribed line. Inside every shed and house in the compound, the air was thick and brown with sawdust – apart from in the forge, where the dust was black instead of brown and where Poldarn slept on the floor when he wasn't working, so tired that even the crashing of the three hundredweight trip-hammer that Galand Dev had had sent down from the Torcea arsenal wasn't enough to keep him awake. (It took twelve men to work the windlass, and when it dropped they could feel the ground shake right across the yard; it'd had to come in through the smithy wall since the doors were far too narrow, and there hadn't been time to make good or even rig a canvas sheet over the hole. But the extra ventilation turned out to be a life-saver, when the wind changed and blew the smoke from the enormous fire back into the shop.)

There came a moment when the trip-hammer fell and nobody winched it up again; when the fire was allowed to die down and go out. There was still work to be done – bolts to shank, a long thread to recut so it would turn freely, a cracked brace to weld – but it could wait, because the job was very nearly finished. (No job is ever finished; see the precept of religion that states that there is no end and no beginning, only the time that separates them.) The lathe was as nearly ready as it'd ever be, but nobody quite had the courage to throw the brake and set it running.

Poldarn celebrated the sudden outbreak of silence in the forge by sitting down hard against the wall, closing his eyes and going straight to sleep. When he woke up an unspecified time later, the building at first seemed empty; but then he heard what sounded like a soft, expressionless chanting, like some religious ceremony: an early-morning litany performed by sleepy monks. But it couldn't be that, so he climbed to his feet (pins and needles in his feet and hands) and staggered in the direction the noise was coming from.

The source of the chanting turned out to be Spenno. He was sitting on the big anvil with his precious book open on his knees, swearing in his sleep. Poldarn remembered what that meant, and grinned; if Spenno was cursing a blue streak, all was right with the world. The complex mechanism that moved the stars and the planets about their axis was balanced, oiled and running true; soon the pinions would engage with their ratchets and rotate the dial on which day was painted light blue with a golden sun, night dark blue with silver stars (cut out of sheet iron with heavy shears and riveted in place). The entire movement and escapement of the world was in order, and therefore Spenno could afford to sleep, still mumbling his mechanical obscenities (like charms to scare away evil spirits). Poldarn grinned – and then he caught sight of the book, open and unguarded.

If, as alleged, Galand Dev had been allowed to study the lathe plans set out in *Concerning Various Matters*, he was the only mortal in living memory apart from Spenno himself who'd seen inside the book and lived to tell the tale. As far as Spenno was concerned, the matter was perfectly simple. If anybody even tried to sneak a look at the book without his permission (which would never be granted), he'd kill them. He'd told the foundrymen so on many occasions, and they believed him.

And here it was, the repository of all known wisdom – one or two sceptics had cast doubts on its infallibility in the past, but not any more, not after the matter of the lathe plans – left negligently open for anybody to see, while its custodian nodded, snored and swore into space. It was tempting; very tempting indeed. Just a quick glance, not even a whole page, just to get a taste of it. Couldn't do any harm, and Spenno'd never know. The words would still be there on the page, undamaged by the intrusion.

Poldarn crept forward, then hesitated; and as he paused, Spenno opened both eyes, stared at him for a moment, mumbled 'Fucking arseholes', closed his eyes and snorted like a pig. Dead to the world.

Even so. The plain fact was, Spenno was a brilliant but completely unstable individual, who happened to be obsessive about this book of his; if he did wake up for real while

Poldarn was violating its pages, there'd be trouble for sure, quite possibly violence. Just for a sneaked glimpse of some mouldy old book, more than likely written in a language he didn't even understand. Not worth it.

But by this time Poldarn was so close that he could feel the soft draught from Spenno's foul-mouthed mumblings – too late to be sensible, he told himself cheerfully, what a pity, never mind. He craned his neck, and saw—

—*If any kind of glass vessel gets broken, this is how to mend it. Take ashes, carefully sifted, and soak them in water. Fill the broken vessel with them, and place in the sun to dry. Fit the broken bits together, keeping the join clean of dirt and grit. Then take some blue glass, the kind that melts easily—*

Ultimate wisdom, Poldarn thought. Fine. Handy to know, of course, but hardly worth risking a jawful of broken teeth for. Did ultimate wisdom really cater for cheapskates, the sort of miserable tight buggers who'd bother patching up a broken bottle rather than buying a new one? Even if the gods were omniscient, could they be bothered to remember something like that?

He frowned. Maybe it was just a book, after all, and maybe Spenno was so uptight about it because he was afraid that if other people read all the smart stuff in it, he wouldn't be the cleverest any more. Rather more likely (just as it was rather more likely that rain was moisture sucked up into the sky by the heat of the sun and then precipitated by mountains, rather than being the gods pissing through colanders; but if you have faith, you know better than to be fooled by the speciously probable). Even so.

Even so, Poldarn realised; the pins and needles in his feet were now so bad that he wasn't going anywhere for several minutes at least. In which case, if Spenno woke up he was going to be in deep trouble anyway, caught standing over the sleeping pattern-maker with his nose inches from the holy pages, whether he was actually reading the confounded thing or not. In which case, there was no point in not reading it, surely?

All very true; but Poldarn didn't really want to know how to mend broken bottles, so he cautiously reached out a forefinger and slid his fingernail under the edge of the page, lifting it until it turned and fell. At that Spenno squirmed in his seat and muttered something extremely vulgar, even by his standards; a scary moment, but he didn't wake up. Still safe, then, so far.

To make a Poldarn's Flute, such as the Rai and Chinly people of Morevich used to employ in war, first cast a solid round bar of good-quality bronze, of the sort used in bell-founding (see below, under bells). Mount the bar in a Morevish lathe (see below, under lathes) and bore out the hole while simultaneously turning down the exterior until it's smooth and even. To make the pins around which the flute pivots, to enable it to be aimed accurately, take a thick wheel tyre and swage the pins by folding a hand's breadth of the tyre into a cylinder on each side; then heat the tyre, slide it over the tube, and shrink it in place firmly by cooling.

And that, as Asburn used to say, is all there is to it. Now that sounded rather more like a god talking, because to a god, it'd be as simple as that – cast a thick bar, drill a hole in it, job done. He wasn't in the least surprised to learn that all this had been done before (in Morevich, where his people originally came from; where else?) because if he'd learned anything over the last year or so, it was that nothing was ever invented or discovered, only remembered – by men or gods who'd had the misfortune to lose their memories for a time. And if that wasn't a precept of religion, it damn well ought to have been.

Then he wondered: had that page been there in the book a month ago, or this time last year? Or had it grown somehow, like the new season's leaves, once the book had realised that the information would be required at some point? He considered the book: big, fat thing, nobody could possibly have read it from cover to cover, not in a single lifetime. So nobody could know for sure whether those pages had always been there (like his own memories, grudgingly spoon-fed him in dreams; had they always been there in his mind, or was someone writing them in from scratch while he was asleep? And had Gain Aciava been telling the truth, really?)

'Bastards,' Spenno grunted. Poldarn had to concede that he might have a point there.

Well: if the book (standing, of course, for his own lost memories – even Poldarn could understand symbolism when it was stuffed remorselessly down his throat) kept making up new stuff as it went along – and the new stuff was *true*, as true as anything else – then it simply wasn't fair. There was no point running away from memory, if it wasn't just behind you but quite possibly all around you and in front of you as well. You could run as hard as you could manage and not be running away at all; you could be heading straight for it, and never know until it was too late.

That wasn't a pleasant thought, and Poldarn was tempted to dismiss it as unproven or wildly unlikely (but no more unlikely than Spenno's bloody book just happening to contain a full set of detailed instructions for building these Poldarn Tubes that Muno Silsny and his clever engineers in Torcea had only just invented). The only thing he could think of doing was to have another look at the book and see what else it chose to show him. Either he'd catch it out in the act of being written, or he could forget all about this nonsense and get some more sleep before they finally plucked their courage up and tried out the lathe.

Just as tentatively as the last time, he toppled over a page. He saw—

To divert the course of a lava flow from an active volcano, first procure a number of steel-tipped drills, at least ten feet long and two inches in diameter—

Poldarn scowled. The bloody thing was playing games with him. He tried another page.

The flight of the stones thrown from a Poldarn's Flute can be controlled by raising or lowering the mouth of the flute, causing the stone to fly high or low; the higher it's thrown, within certain limits, the further it will travel—

Skip a paragraph or so and continue—

An alternative is to substitute for the stone a stoutly made leather bag filled with small rocks, metal scrap, potsherds &c. When discharged at short range, the bag will burst almost immediately on leaving the tube, scattering its contents over a wide area at tremendous speed. Each flying stone, potsherd or metal fragment will become a lethal weapon, making this technique especially suitable for use against closely packed enemy infantry.

Nasty little book, Poldarn decided. He skipped a dozen or so pages, and read—

This effect draws its name from an incident in the myth of Poldarn, patron god of Morevich. According to legend, after playing his pipes which bring death to all who hear them, Poldarn will—

'Shit,' grumbled Spenno amiably, stretching his arms and legs and rubbing his eyes with his knuckles. 'Shit, fuck and piss in a bucket. Fuck—'

This time he was waking up, for sure. Pins and needles or no pins and needles, Poldarn hopped backwards five paces in a straight line, bumped into the small two-horned anvil, sat down on it and pretended to be trying to tease a splinter out of the ball of his thumb. Just in time—

'Oh,' Spenno said, opening his eyes. 'Good heavens. Don't tell me I fell asleep.'

He shifted, and the book slid off his lap and onto the

floor, closing itself and losing its place. (Which was very considerate of it, Poldarn thought, to wipe out all memory of his intrusion, though arguably rather disloyal to its master.) 'Where is everybody?' Spenno asked.

'Resting,' Poldarn replied. 'Lathe's almost finished, apparently. In fact, you'd better be getting over there right now, or you'll miss the first try-out.'

Spenno made a loud squawking noise, scrabbled on the floor for his book, jumped up and ran. Poldarn counted to ten, to give him time to get clear, then followed, limping.

The sun had come out while he'd been stuck in the forge. (How long had it been since he'd left the building? He couldn't remember. The pools of water that had stood in the yard since the rains began had dwindled into small reservations of black mud. Soon it'd be high Tulice summer (to which, the old lags assured him, the rainy season was vastly preferable): ground-splitting, skin-peeling heat, just the weather for tending the hellburning furnaces they were planning on building to melt the enormous quantities of bronze they'd be needing for the tubes. Under normal circumstances, they'd shut the works down for a month at midsummer. Just my luck, Poldarn thought.

Nobody about; he guessed that everybody was snatching a little sleep before the next phase began. From what he could remember of Galand Dev's briefing, this would consist of building a set of giant trestles fitted with spindles on which the wood and clay patterns would be turned. (More lathes, in other words; at least Galand Dev had had the tact not to call them that.) The idea was basically a variation on the standard method of making bell patterns: a pole, rotating on trestles, around which they'd build up a full-size clay model of the tube; then slap a thick layer of tallow on top of the clay, then more clay on top of that; melt out the tallow to free the core, and you had your mould. All there was to it.

Poldarn yawned, wondering what to do next. He could limp back to his little mud hut, or he could try and find something to eat (fat chance); or he could be really sybaritic and decadent, and have a wash. Not just a splash of black, gritty water out of the slack tub on his face and hands, but a genuine, no-holds-barred, wet-all-over *bath*, the kind that normal people had once a day. He knew just the place; where the river tripped and stumbled down a heap of rock slabs into a deep round pool, curtained with ferns and flag iris. It couldn't have been better suited for the purpose if some duke or king had commissioned an architect to build him an alfresco bathhouse. Of course, nobody ever went there, except in late autumn, when there were rumoured to be fair-sized salmon in the deepest corner.

After Poldarn had scoured off the worst of the grime with handfuls of dry moss, he lay floating on his back in the water, staring up at the blue sky. Suppose, he thought, that the blue sky is a mirror in the same way as the blue water; suppose the sky could show you your reflection, not in space but time. Interesting concept, but false; nothing to be seen except the sun, a few fluffy white clouds, the silhouettes of a few crows – scouts for the big mob that hung around the back of the sheds, robbing the feed bins where the fodder for the treadmill and windlass mules was stored. Suppose, he said to himself (he knew that he was starting to get drowsy) that there are crows in the afternoon sky like there are stars at night: small twinkling spots of black, as opposed to silver. Could you learn to steer a ship by them, or tell your own fortune?

'There you are.' The voice came from behind the screen of flag irises. 'Why am I not surprised? You always were a luxurious bastard.'

For a few drowsy moments he tried to convince himself he was dreaming; but the crows were too high up and far away. The voice belonged in his dreams, but also in the real world. 'Gain Aciava,' he said.

'Hello, Ciartan.' Gain Aciava pushed through the reeds and stood at the edge of the pool, his reflection torn up and shattered by slight ripples in the water. 'Father Tutor once said you were an otter pretending to be a monk.'

'What the hell are you doing here?'

'Same as you.' Aciava grinned. 'Wonderful thing, administration. They keep a big list somewhere in Torcea, of people with valuable specialist skills. Then, when the government suddenly needs us – die-founders, fettlers, people with relevant experience in advanced foundry work – they know where to look. And here I am. Some people might consider it an unpardonable intrusion, but the way I look at it, it's got to be better than peddling false teeth for a living. What's the water like?'

'Overlooked,' Poldarn replied. 'You know about foundry work?'

'Practically wrote the book.' Aciava yawned. 'Not that there really is a book, unless you count that musty old doorstop your pattern-maker lugs round with him. Spenno, is that right?'

Poldarn nodded. 'Is there really a register?'

'Oh yes. You're on it, of course, only not under your current name. And half the people on it are dead, or far too old to work. What's the matter? Aren't you pleased to see me?'

'I don't know,' Poldarn replied. 'Depends. Were you telling the truth, last time?'

'I always tell the truth.' Aciava's grin was full of teeth. 'It's a habit I got into when I was a kid, and I stuck like it. My old mother did warn me; I guess the wind changed when I wasn't looking. Come on,' he added, 'don't you remember the class motto when we were in fifth grade?'

'No.'

'Ah well.' Aciava sat down on a rock. 'So how's the big secret project coming along? Did Galand Dev get his monster lathe built? Must say, I had my doubts when I heard about it. Seems a bloody strange way to go about making a tube. Me, I'd have tried casting it with a core, and the hell with what the book says.'

For some reason, Poldarn's flesh began to crawl. 'What book?' he asked.

'*The* book, stupid.' Aciava reached inside his coat and pulled out a small book, bound in white vellum. 'Next you'll be telling me you've lost your copy. You haven't, have you?'

'What book?'

'Here.' He tossed the book in the air. Poldarn stood up and just managed to catch it before it fell in the water. On the spine, in long, spindly writing: *Concerning Various Matters*.

'Where that idiot Spenno got hold of a copy, God only knows,' Aciava was saying. 'Different edition, obviously; probably an earlier one, not quite up to date. You can keep that one,' he added, 'I've got a spare. Look inside and you'll see that it's not mine anyway.'

Poldarn opened the book at the flyleaf. Written in the top left-hand corner: *If this book should chance to roam, Box its ears and send it home. Xipho Dorunoxy, Grade II.* 'Where did you get this?' he asked.

'Ah,' Aciava replied with a smirk, 'that'd be telling. Are you going to stay in there all day, or are you going to show me where they keep the food? It's been a long day, and you owe me dinner.'

Poldarn waded ashore and put his clothes on; they felt clammy and foul against his clean, wet skin. 'Why are you here?' he asked. 'I don't believe there's any register. I'd have heard about it before now if there was.'

Aciava sighed. 'There is too a register,' he said. 'And my

name's on it. So's yours. But those clowns in Torcea have either lost it or forgotten about it, or else it got burned when your horrible relatives crisped Deymeson. Offhand, I can't recall if there was more than one copy. Like I told you,' he added, 'I always tell the truth.'

'Why are you here?'

'Let's say I came early for the class reunion. What's the grub like on this project? I heard the idea was nothing but the best for our brave lads. But they say that in every war, and it always ends up being porridge and salt bacon. Remember the bean stew at Deymeson? Sometimes I can still taste it, in nightmares.'

'Are you really an expert in foundry work?'

'Of course.' Big grin. 'You don't think they only taught religion and swordfighting at school, do you? I've forgotten more about pouring hot metal than your friend Spenno'll ever know. They were lucky to get me, I'm telling you.'

'Are you here for the project, or just to annoy me?'

'That's not a very nice thing to say to an old friend.'

Poldarn shrugged. 'I'll show you the canteen,' he said. 'Does anybody else know you're here?'

'I reported to the brigadier as soon as I arrived,' Aciava replied. 'I'm glad he's in charge here. He's a good man, and I always did get on well with him.'

The cookhouse was shutting up shop when they got there; they were just about to pour away the last of the soup and put out the fire. Once they'd finished their shift, nothing would ever induce the cooks to issue so much as an apple core – it was an inviolable rule of the foundry.

'Never mind,' Aciava said. 'I'll just have to make do with the last of the stuff I brought with me for the road. Join me?'

Poldarn remembered that he hadn't had anything to eat for a long time. 'No, thanks,' he said.

'Let's see,' Aciava said, as if he hadn't heard. 'I've got

salt beef from Sirupat, you know, with the peppercorns on the outside, and some of that black rye bread, and Torcea biscuits, and there's a chunk of that red Falcata cheese left. And I've got a couple of bottles of Cymari that I was going to take back home with me, but what the hell. They say it keeps, but I've never been able to restrain myself long enough to find out. Oh yes, and some apples. What I always say is, even if you do spend all your time on the road, there's no reason to rough it if you don't have to.'

'No, thanks,' Poldarn repeated, and walked away. Somehow he got the impression that Aciava hadn't expected him to do that; as though the list of fare had been carefully compiled to include all his pet favourites. (What in any god's name was a Torcea biscuit, anyway?) Instead, he gnawed at the stub end of a stale corn cake and washed it down with needled beer. Wonderful thing, integrity, but it tastes horrible.

He'd just managed to drift off to sleep when somebody prodded him awake. Not again, he thought, and propped himself up on one elbow. 'Now what?'

This time it was Chiruwa, which made a change, though not a particularly welcome one. 'Get up,' he was saying. 'Something's happening.'

Poldarn scowled and sighed. 'Chir, you bastard, there's always something happening. Can't you piss off and let me go back to sleep?'

Apparently not. He slouched across the yard and joined a mob of foundrymen, mixed up with offcomers (soldiers, the Torcea engineers, a few nonentities from the brigadier's staff; no sign of Gain Aciava, so maybe he'd dreamt him after all). They seemed excited or upset about something, and the way they were milling about round the drawing-office door suggested that they were expecting someone to come out and announce something.

Maybe it'd be worth missing sleep for, after all. 'What's

going on, Chir?' he asked again, but the other man just shrugged. 'Search me,' he said. 'Malla met me a short while ago, told me something was on and they'd be issuing a statement any minute now. That's all I know.'

'Fine,' Poldarn said. 'So why'd you come and wake me up?'

Chiruwa looked surprised, even rather hurt. 'You're my friend,' he said, 'I thought you wouldn't want to miss it.'

'Oh,' Poldarn said. No, he hadn't been expecting that.

A few moments later, the door opened and Galand Dev came out. He was frowning, as though considering some technical matter that should've been straightforward but that was proving unexpectedly difficult. He looked round, then held up his hand for silence, which he got.

'Brigadier Muno's asked me to make an announcement,' he said. 'We've just had word that on his way back to Torcea, General Muno Silsny and his escort were attacked. We don't have any details as yet, but I'm sorry to say that the main point has been confirmed, direct from Torcea. General Muno Silsny is dead.'

Chapter Seven

Monach woke up out of a strange dream to find that someone was touching him. Immediately, he pushed back the instinctive response. Curious: he'd spent so many years training himself to react instantly to any intrusion into his circle, and now he was having to learn not to.

'You were shouting,' she said.

'Was I?' He grinned feebly. 'Sorry about that.'

She shrugged. 'That's all right,' she said. 'It's nearly dawn, anyhow. Was it the same dream, or a different one?'

'Different,' he replied. 'And, I don't know, more sort of odd than horrible, if you see what I mean. Did I wake up Ciartan?'

She shook her head. 'He's dead to the world,' she told him. 'Just as well,' she added. 'You know it upsets him when you get bad dreams. Also, he's teething.'

'Again?' He grinned. 'That kid's going to have more teeth than a polecat, the way he's going on.'

'He can't help it,' she said defensively. 'And he hates it when they hurt.'

'You fuss too much,' he replied, knowing it'd annoy her. 'Suppose I'd better be getting up now. We're supposed to be making an early start, aren't we?'

She shook her head. 'It's pissing it down,' she said. 'There's no point, we'd only get the wagons stuck.'

'That's all right, then.' He lay back, staring at the barn rafters. 'We'll wait for it to stop and try and make up time when we hit the military road. Does it always rain like this in this horrible country?'

'Yes,' she said. 'This time of year, anyway.'

'Bloody hell. It's a miracle anybody manages to live here.'

'They're used to it.' She pulled a blanket round her shoulders and looked at him. 'You'd better tell me about it,' she said.

'Tell you about what?'

'The dream,' she said. 'It's making you act all nasty, so it must be bothering you.'

He nodded. 'Like I said,' he told her, 'it wasn't so much bad as strange. Bad dreams I can handle,' he added with a faint smile.

'Go on,' she said.

'Well.' He thought for a moment. 'We were back at Deymeson, all of us – you, me, Gain, Elaos, Cordo, Ciartan – and it was just after first lesson. We were in third grade, I think, but you know how you can never tell how old you are in dreams. Anyway, the lesson had been metalwork, we'd been doing casting in bronze—'

'That's odd,' she interrupted.

'Well, of course it is, that's the point. We never did that, any of us.'

She frowned. 'Hold on,' she said. 'Didn't Gain take foundry as an option in fifth grade?'

He thought about that. 'You know,' he said, 'I think you're right. Ciartan and Cordo took forgework, you and

I did precious metals, Elaos – what did Elaos do? I can't remember.'

'Engraving.'

'So he did, you're right. God only knows how you remember all this stuff.'

'Practice,' she said. 'So, we were all coming out of class. Then what?'

'We were moaning,' he continued, 'about the assignment we'd just been set. We had to cast a flute—'

'You don't cast flutes. You—'

'I know that, thank you. But in the dream, we had to cast a flute, in bronze, and we weren't allowed to use a core.'

She looked blank. 'Is that good or bad?' she asked. 'I don't know anything about casting.'

'Well, I don't know a hell of a lot,' he admitted. 'But in the dream it was pretty serious, because we were all arguing like mad about it. And then Ciartan lost his temper—'

'What's odd about that?' she interrupted, smiling. 'Sounds just like real life to me.'

'Ciartan lost his temper,' he repeated, 'and one of the other kids – I'm blowed if I can remember his name, but he had straight black hair, small nose, played the flute—'

'Torcuat.'

'That's right,' he said, surprised. 'Now there's a name I haven't heard in a while. Torcuat. Anyhow, they got into a fight; and you remember how Ciartan went through that phase of carrying a knife all the time. Stuffed down inside the leg of his boot, the stupid clown, I'm amazed he never cut his shin open. Anyway, he got this knife out and he was waving it around, and Torcuat was yelling bloody murder at him, and we were all worried Father Tutor'd hear the racket and come and see what was going on. So you jumped in and took the knife off him – only for some reason it wasn't a knife any more, it was a little axe, sort of a hatchet.

But you got it away from him, and he'd gone all dumb and ashamed, because you'd told him he was an arsehole. Then the door opened and Father Tutor came in, but he didn't seem to have heard the noise, or maybe he was preoccupied and wasn't bothered about it; he had this really serious look on his face, and we all knew there was something badly wrong. And here's where it gets a bit surreal, because suddenly we were all sitting in his study—'

'All of us? There wouldn't be room.'

'All of us,' he repeated. 'And in front of him, right in the middle of his desk, was this sort of stump thing, and on it there was this statue of a crow; only it wasn't a statue, because suddenly it spread its wings and said "Caw" or whatever crows say—'

'A crow,' she said. 'Interesting.'

'Well, quite. Sort of like what my old mother used to tell me: don't play with that, dear, you don't know where it's been.'

She frowned. 'Well,' she said, 'we've both known him a very long time, and remember what he told us, about the people where he came from, so maybe it's not so surprising after all. Go on.'

'It gets weirder,' he said. 'Father Tutor calls Ciartan up to the front, tells him there's this really bad news from home; his grandfather's died, and left him the farm – so, I was thinking, not such bad news after all; and his best friend's been burned to death in a fire, and his daughter's expecting a baby.' He paused, and she got the impression he'd missed something out at this point; nothing he felt was important, but something that she wouldn't like. 'And then he went on, Father Tutor, that is; he said that the volcano had erupted and buried his house and all the farmland under molten lava, so he couldn't ever go back home again – and I was thinking, bloody hell, even though it's him, you can't help feeling a bit sorry for the bastard, all that dreadful stuff happening all at once.'

'How very sweet,' she said.

'Well,' he replied, 'you were sobbing your little heart out, so you can't talk. And he was just stood there, grinning like an idiot; and the crow was cackling away like it was laughing, and then he sort of reached out – I tell you, he never moved that fast in real life – and he grabbed the crow round the neck and squashed it, literally *squashed* it down into the fireplace and held it there till it was all burned up. And Father Tutor just sat there, like he didn't mind a bit; and then he said to Ciartan to cheer up, because as a sort of consolation prize he was being given the hand of the Emperor's daughter in marriage, and if that all went all right – like it was a test or probation or something – if that all went all right, he'd be allowed to kill his son, make the flute and take his rightful place as king of the gods once term was finished. And I was sitting there thinking, that's a bit rich, this is bloody Ciartan we're talking about; then he leans across to me and says, yes, fine, but—' He paused, an embarrassed look on his face.

'But,' she said. 'Go on. It's about me, isn't it?'

'Well, yes. Basically, he was saying it was all very well getting all that nice stuff Father Tutor had just said, but it didn't count worth spit because I'd – well, you and me . . .'

She was grinning. 'You've gone all pink,' she said.

'Yes, well. I used to be a *monk*, remember? Anyway, the gist of it was that all the goodies didn't matter if, well, if it was going to be me getting the girl and not him; only that wasn't going to happen, since he'd kill me first, and all sorts of charming stuff like that.'

'Sounds pretty much like Ciartan to me.'

'Quite. Anyway, then he got his hands round my throat, and I was struggling and yelling, "No, stop—"'

'I know. I heard you.'

'And then,' he concluded, 'I woke up.' He shook his head sadly. 'Bloody hell, Xipho, I've got to admit, I've had about as much of him as I can take.'

'*You* have.'

'Well,' he said, embarrassed, 'anyhow. But it's getting beyond a joke.' He looked at her. 'You don't – well, you don't actually think there really is anything to it, do you? Seriously, I mean.'

It took her a moment to figure out what he was talking about. 'What, you mean about him? Being the god in— Being *Poldarn?*' She stared, then giggled. 'You idiot,' she said.

'Yes, all right. But I can't help it, really, wondering sometimes. Like when I found out you'd been doing that bloody stupid scam thing, with him pretending to be— And there I was, stupid bloody clown, galloping all round the countryside following you two about, and all the time it was *you*. And him,' he added. 'Which Father fucking Tutor never saw fit to mention—'

She shook her head, as if forbidding him to take the subject further. 'He must've had a good reason,' she said. 'He always had a good reason.'

'Yes, but then he went and *died*, thoughtless bloody bastard; and here's me left behind trying to figure out what in any God's name his ever-such-a-good bloody reason might've been.' He stood up and shivered in the cold. 'I mean, I ask you; he sends you trailing after him. Then he loses his mind, or his memory, whatever; so Father Tutor sends me off to trail after the two of you, but for some fucking reason neglects to mention to me that the god in the cart and his beautiful lady assistant are two of my old classmates. Yes, I know Father Tutor could be pretty bloody deep sometimes, but that's just—'

'Just bad luck that he died when he did,' she said calmly. 'Or maybe even good luck, I really don't know.'

'Good luck?' He sounded shocked. 'Like, you think the old fool somehow *decided* to die at that precise moment? You mean, as part of the grand design? Come off it, Xipho, that's just silly.'

But she shrugged. 'All I'm saying is,' she said, 'I don't know what he had in mind. But I trusted him and I still do. I have—' She smiled. 'I have *faith*. You remember faith, don't you? We did it in first grade; or were you away that week?'

He wasn't happy, though. 'And now all this stuff,' he said. 'General Muno Silsny. I mean to say, we hadn't even heard of him back when the old man died, so how could he possibly have intended that as part of his grand and wonderful plan?'

'It was logical,' she said. 'General Cronan, General Muno. General Allectus before that. Tazencius becoming Emperor. That was right at the heart of it—'

'It was?' He stared at her. 'Tazencius? That *moron*?' He looked as though he was in physical pain. 'You mean Father Tutor wanted me to scrag Cronan – General Cronan who was the only man ever who beat the raiders – just so all-dick-and-no-brains *Tazencius* could get to be Emperor? Oh for crying out loud, Xipho. It doesn't want faith, it wants brain damage.'

She was starting to get annoyed with him, but he couldn't help that. 'You don't know,' she repeated. 'You haven't got the faintest idea, really, what his plan was.' She drew in a deep breath. They'd been taught to do that, in second grade, as a way of keeping their tempers, but it'd never worked for him. 'Look at it this way. Suppose you came from a place where they didn't have doctors, all right? And suppose you saw a surgeon, a real top-notch Guild surgeon from Boc or some place like that; and he's got his patient on his back on the table, and they've stuffed rag in his mouth and they're holding him down with ropes while the doctor grabs a scalpel and starts cutting him open. And you're thinking to yourself, they must be crazy. This guy's sick enough already, and sticking a knife in his guts is supposed to make him *better*?' He was pulling a face. 'All right,' she said, 'it's a corny example. But for all we know, he wanted Tazencius to get the throne so's the provinces would rebel and overthrow the Empire and restore the Republic. It could be as big as that. We just don't know. The thing is, if we don't do exactly what we're told, we're liable to screw it all up and everything'll go wrong. You do see that, don't you?'

He yawned and shook his head. There was a leak in the roof, he noticed; every so often, a big fat drop of water would fall from the thatch and land, plop, on the rotten place in the fifth floorboard in from the wall. 'Yes, I guess so,' he said. 'Only, Father Tutor's dead, we don't know what the rest of the plan was going to be; so it's probably pretty safe to say that the plan's gone wrong already. To take your example,' he added (she was beginning to fidget; extended discussions and debates weren't her style), 'suppose I'm this guy from far away who's never seen a doctor; and I see this surgeon of yours, and I think, great; all I've got to do to cure someone if he's sick is take a damn great knife and carve him open. You and I may think we know what the old fool had in mind, or we can guess, or maybe reconstruct, whatever; but, like you keep saying, we don't *know*. So maybe we should just leave well alone, right?'

'Oh yes?' Now she was starting to get angry. 'Fine. The patient's lying on the table with his guts hanging out, you're saying, we don't know what to do, let's just walk away and leave him there. That's so intelligent, Mon.'

He could see the fallacies in her reasoning, but even he had the common sense not to point them out. 'Screw it, Xipho, it's got me so messed up I don't know anything any more.' Suddenly he laughed. 'You know what?' he said.

'You and me, we're in pretty much the same god-awful fix as Ciartan. He's lost his memory, we've lost Father Tutor and the rest of the plan; we're stuck midway across the river, with the current dragging us away, and we don't know what the fuck's going on or what we're supposed to do. Only,' he added with a scowl, 'Ciartan might get his memory back. Gods forbid, but he might. Father bloody Tutor's going to stay dead, no matter what.'

She was smiling; bad temper averted, apparently. Wise tactic on his part, to show a little weakness to defuse the situation. And he'd worked it all out for himself, too; they hadn't offered Understanding Women at Deymeson. 'You never know,' she was saying. 'Maybe he wrote it all down somewhere, and tomorrow or the next day someone'll find the bit of paper and suddenly we'll all know. Yes,' she said, forestalling him, 'I know, totally unlikely. But it might happen.'

He grinned. 'Faith.'

She grinned back. 'Moves mountains.'

'I thought that was extreme volcanic activity.'

'That too. But faith doesn't spit them up in the air and dump them on your head.'

Thinking about that, he wasn't so sure; but it was a good place to leave the argument. They had a long way to go today in terrible conditions; it'd probably be as well if the joint commanders of the enterprise were on speaking terms. He pulled on his boots (sad excuses for boots; and not so many years ago, footwear was like the rising of the sun, he never had to worry about it, it was simply there . . .) and squelched outside to see to rescheduling their departure.

Being a warlord, Monach had learned the hard way, was about three per cent fire and the sword, the rest incessant pettifogging administration. Regular armies, he supposed, were like rich men's sons, never having to worry about where the next supply train or six hundred pairs of thick leather gaiters were coming from; they had indulgent parents at the capital who sent them what they needed, and were always there to fall back on when weevils got in the cornmeal or twelve wagonloads of tents got swept away crossing a flooded river. Warlords, by contrast, are the sturdy peasant farmers of warfare, forced to rely on their own sweat and initiative or else do without. Right now he needed fifty sets of chains for cartwheels, if he was to have any hope of getting his sad convoy up the river of mud that passed for a highway as far as the luxuriously metalled military road. No wheel chains to be had for love, money or the fear of death this side of the Bay, so they were going to have to think of something else. Relays of men carrying armfuls of brush to lay down in front of the wheels – no, that'd be ridiculous, all that'd happen would be that half his army would get filthy dirty and bad-tempered, and they'd maybe cover two miles a day before getting hopelessly and irreversibly stuck in some bog. A regular general could simply write a friendly letter to Divisional HQ and be sent sappers, engineers, cartloads of fascines and portable roadway, those great big rolled-up carpets of birch twigs tied together with cord. Spoiled rotten; and could they hold together five minutes against the raiders? Could they hell.

The only other option was to dump the carts, load the supplies onto the men's backs, and porter the whole lot as far as the hard surface; the carts could then follow on as and when the roads were passable again. Or mules; mules were the ideal solution, except that he hadn't got any. Any fuzzy-chinned clown of a hereditary colonel could have all the mules he wanted just by handing a note to his junior equerry, but a hard-working warlord was going to have to break it to the lads that each of them would be lugging a hundredweight of junk on his back all the way to Falcata—

—Unless there was a river. Boats, barges, rafts. All this

disgusting water everywhere – there had to be a river going in vaguely the right direction. Then he remembered: they were going *up* the hill to the military road. Even if there was a navigable river, it'd be bugger-all use to him.

(And she wasn't helping, he thought, unfairly. Why the hell didn't she ever stir herself and deal with something; something important, like bacon or socks or duty rosters, instead of all that religious garbage? He knew perfectly well why; because he was in command, and the men wouldn't take orders from her. But he carried on resenting for a minute or so anyway.)

On his way to the staff meeting in the derelict linhay, he shared his concerns with one of the line captains, an ex-monk by the name of Trecian. 'It's only a dozen miles to the military road,' he said wretchedly, 'and it might as well be in Morevich for all the good—'

'Why don't you take the short cut?' Trecian interrupted.

Monach stopped and looked at him. 'What short cut?'

Trecian grinned foolishly. 'Actually,' he said, 'it's not a short cut, because it's actually six miles further; but we call it the short cut, because this time of year it cuts half a day off the trip.'

Monach understood. 'You're from round here, then.'

'That's right. Born just down the road, in fact, place called Ang Chirra. Poxy little village, really, haven't been back there since I was fifteen. But I expect the short cut's still there. Don't suppose they could manage without it, this time of year.'

'What's so good about this short cut of yours?' Monach demanded. 'We'll just get the carts stuck, same as if we went the other way.'

Trecian shook his head. 'No fear,' he said. 'Good hard going all the way. People hereabouts reckon it must've been a government road once, years ago; probably from before Tulice was part of the Empire. True, you'll find about half the paving slabs mortared into farmhouse walls and gateposts from here to Danchout. But the other half are still there, and there's a good eighteen inches of compacted rubble and gravel under that. Whoever built it sure knew how to lay a good road.'

'Wonderful,' Monach said, rather bewildered at this amazing slice of luck. 'So how come it's not on any of the maps?'

Trecian laughed. 'People round here've always had a funny attitude toward telling the government about things. I think the argument was, if the government knew about the road, they'd decide it was worth fixing it up, and we'd be stuck with the bill. Or maybe when the surveyors came out here they pissed off the locals, so they kept quiet about it just for spite. That's Tulice for you. We may look to the outside world like a bunch of inbred hillbillies, but there's less to us than meets the eye.'

It occurred to Monach to ask why nobody'd seen fit to mention this secret road to him earlier. But he reflected on what Trecian had told him about the Tulice mentality, and concluded that he'd be happier not knowing.

The Sticklepath (as the short cut was apparently known) obviously wasn't used much, even in the wet season. In fact, if Trecian hadn't told him where it was Monach could easily have gone past it without realising. A deep carpet of pale yellow flowers covered it; Trecian told him what they were called, something really uninspiring, like gravelwort. But it suited the carts just fine, and when they camped for the night on a spur overlooking the dense, sprawling Cherva forest, they'd already covered just over half the distance to the military road. Monach gave orders for setting watches, organised the duty rosters for the morning, the sort of things he now did without having to think or remember; they came as naturally as drawing a sword.

He was thinking hopefully of getting to bed before

midnight for a change when someone behind him called out his name – not Monach; his old name, the one he hadn't heard or thought about for over twenty years.

He turned round slowly. It was fully dark now, and he wasn't even sure of the direction the voice had come from. Instinctively, he lifted his right hand to his sash, until the knuckles brushed the hilt of his sword. 'Hello?' he said.

'Over here.' The voice was familiar, sort of; something like a voice he'd once known, except that it had changed, as voices will over time. 'Keep quiet – pretend you're taking a leak or something.'

At least religion trained a man to do what he was told. Monach advanced on where he thought the voice was coming from, stopped in front of a large oak tree, planted his feet a shoulder's width apart and pretended to loosen his trousers. Bloody ridiculous, he thought; but who on earth who's still alive knows me by *that* name?

'Hello,' the voice said, this time so close that Monach jumped and took a step back. As his heel touched the ground, he remembered whose voice it was. Absolutely no doubt in his mind at all, in spite of the fact that its owner had been dead at least twenty years.

'Hello, Cordo,' he replied slowly. 'Why aren't you dead?'

A hand closed around his right wrist, twisting it behind his back. It never occurred to him to resist. 'Cordo?' he asked. 'What're you doing? What's the matter?'

'Sorry.' The apology was sincere enough; as if Cordo had just trodden on his foot or spilt his beer. 'You haven't seen Gain lately, have you?'

For a moment, it was as though they were back at Deymeson. It took a conscious effort for Monach to remember where, and when, he was. 'No,' he answered, 'not for years – well, not since we left. I don't even know if he's still alive. Why?'

The voice – it *was* Cordo – tutted, as if to say it was a nuisance he'd missed him, but not to worry, he'd be bound to run into him later, after lunch. 'What about Ciartan? Seen anything of him recently?'

'No. Look—' Monach was cut short by the extreme pain in his arm, as Cordo twisted it savagely.

'Sorry,' Cordo repeated, same tone of voice. 'You wouldn't happen to know where either of them are, do you?'

'Yes. Look, Cordo, would you mind fucking well letting go of my arm? There's no need, I'm not going to attack you or anything. And you're hurting me,' he added, hearing the surprise in his own voice.

'Sorry,' Cordo said again, and the pressure relaxed, slightly. 'Where? And which one?'

'Ciartan,' Monach said. 'He's not far from here, in fact. Dui Chirra, the foundry. He's working there.'

'The Poldarn's Flute project?'

'That's right. Cordo, will you please tell me what's going on? I *saw* you, you were dead. Bloody hell, I *cried*—'

'Did you?' Genuine surprise. 'You soft bugger. No, I'm still alive, more or less. How long's he been there, do you know?'

'A fair while; a year, eighteen months.'

'Only,' Cordo went on, 'I heard he'd gone away. Back to where he came from; you know, originally.'

'That's right,' Monach said. 'But there was some trouble.'

'That I can believe,' Cordo said. (It was one of his turns of phrase.) 'Any idea what the trouble was? And how do you know this?'

'No idea,' Monach said. 'No idea on both counts, come to think of it,' he realised.

'What d'you mean?'

'I mean I know he's back,' Monach said, 'but the bit about the trouble, over there – offhand, can't say where I heard that. Actually,' he admitted, 'I can: it was in a dream. So it may not be true at all.'

'It's true,' Cordo said. 'Funny you mentioning dreams, though. Where's Xipho?'

'In the lead cart, probably, she was dog tired last time I saw her.'

'Fine. Listen, I'd rather you didn't mention anything to her about me being – well, back. So you'll keep it to yourself, right? For old time's sake?'

'Will I hell as like,' Monach replied angrily. 'She's got a right to know. We were *friends*, damn it.'

A chuckle. 'Did she cry too?'

'Yes.'

'No kidding? That's – well, there you go. Now, you're sure you haven't seen Gain, or heard anything about him, where he might be or what he might be up to? Sure?'

'Bloody positive. For God's sake, Cordo, you can tell me. What's going on?'

'Tell you later. Sorry,' Cordo said a fourth time; and then Monach's senses overloaded in a very brief instant of extreme pain, centred around the back of his head.

He couldn't have been out of it for long. When he came to, the darkness was still full and thick, no diluting strains of light to suggest the closeness of dawn. He was lying on his back, looking up into the face of Runting the quartermaster-sergeant, backlit by torchlight. 'Can you hear me?' he was saying, and the worried frown on his face was almost comical.

'Cordo,' Monach said; then, 'Yes, I can hear you just fine, stop yelling in my face.' He stopped, and winced; his head was splitting.

There were other faces looking down at him beside Runting's. 'What happened to you, then?' the quartermaster was saying.

'Don't know,' Monach replied. 'I guess I must've slipped and bashed my head or something.' He remembered Cordo's question: where was Xipho? He repeated it.

'I sent one of my lads to fetch her,' Runting said. Then he frowned. 'That was a while back,' he added. 'She should be here by now. Here, you.' He turned to the man beside him. 'Go and find out what's keeping her.'

A face withdrew from the circle. Monach tried to sit up, but that made him feel horribly dizzy. He could feel panic, very close: Xipho not there, and his body not working properly. 'Find her, quick,' he heard himself say; he sounded worried, frightened. But that was silly; Cordo wouldn't hurt Xipho, they were friends.

Cordo wouldn't hurt him either, for the same reason.

He made another attempt at sitting up; this time, it was like he'd always imagined drowning must feel, a total failure of the most basic systems. There was nothing he could do, about anything.

When Monach came round again, he was lying in one of the carts. Runting was there, and Trecian, and all the other necessary officers. They looked unhappy about something. 'How are you feeling now?' one of them asked.

He found it very hard indeed to speak. 'Xipho?' he said.

The man, whoever he was, Monach couldn't remember his name, looked at someone else before answering. 'We can't find her,' he said. 'We've looked all over.'

Monach opened his mouth, but words had failed too.

'There don't seem to be any signs of a struggle or a fight,' someone was saying. 'No blood or anything like that. And some of her stuff's gone, clothes. Not her sword, though.'

At that moment, Monach hated his body for failing him when he needed it. He made a tremendous effort; he could feel the harm it was doing him, as if it was tearing flesh. 'Someone was here,' he said. 'He knocked me down. He may have been—' He could feel the words draining away, as if there was a leak in his head and they were gushing out, going to waste. It occurred to him to wonder if he was dying, or just very badly concussed; but that was a side issue, and he couldn't afford to let his attention wander. 'Look for signs,' he said, 'footprints, whatever. He may have taken her—' And then he knew he couldn't say any more, not now or not ever, unclear which. He hoped he wasn't dying; it'd be pathetic to die at a time like this.

He could see, but couldn't remember opening his eyes. It was logical to suppose, therefore, that he was dreaming.

(*Funny you mentioning dreams*, Cordo had said.)

In fact, it was fairly certain he was dreaming, because he was standing up and his head wasn't hurting; also, in real life you can't understand what crows are saying.

This crow was perched on a stone window ledge, the only window in the small round room; and it was telling him something. 'They're coming,' it said. Fat lot of use that was; so he waved his arms and said, 'Shoo, get out of it,' and the crow spread its wings and flapped reproachfully away. Crows, he thought. Marvellous. Then he turned round. He hadn't noticed that there were people in the room; people he knew.

Ciartan: older, naturally, and gaunt-looking, scruffy (and him always so picky about his appearance, like a girl). And a big, broad man, short black beard, stub nose, huge round brown eyes. Someone Monach had known years ago, but he'd changed a lot since then. That was how it went. Some people kept on looking the same, others you'd hardly recognise.

'You're a bloody fool,' the big man was saying, to Ciartan. 'What the hell was all that about?'

Ciartan just seemed confused; he opened his mouth but didn't say anything. The other man went on, 'I know it's all part of the mystique, this deliberately walking round in plain sight because you're so cool and daring, but next time please leave me out of it. Dear gods—'

The crow was back. They couldn't see it, because they were facing the other way. Monach went to shoo it away again, but it winked at him.

'He doesn't know,' the crow said. 'Hasn't figured it out yet.'

Monach frowned. 'Who doesn't know what?'

'Him.' Bloody unhelpful bird. 'He doesn't know Poldarn's lost his memory, that's why he's getting so upset. He thinks he's just doing it to be annoying, showing off. Tragic misunderstandings like this shape history, you know.'

It's only a dream. You can't throttle birds in dreams, even when they're really aggravating. 'Like what?'

'Like this. Because of this, thousands of people will die. Cities burned down. Emperors overthrown. War, plague, death. Everything so fragile, so *messy*.'

Monach shouted: 'Because of what?' But it was as if the crow couldn't hear him. Meanwhile, the man he couldn't recognise was saying, 'Let's get down to brass tacks. This business up the road—'

'What business?' Monach asked imploringly, but the stupid fucking crow had gone again.

'Tazencius and his people aren't ready,' the man was saying. 'He hasn't even started recruiting openly yet – dammit, he hasn't had anything to recruit *for*, that's my point, there's been no build-up, just this, suddenly, wham—'

Monach felt something tickle his ear. 'Timing,' the crow was saying, 'very unfortunate timing. Disaster for all concerned. He was supposed to bring them there, you see, and then betray them so the prince had a glorious victory. But it all went horribly wrong. Horribly.'

('The supply of large cities in these parts is somewhat

limited,' the man was saying. 'We can't go torching one a week till Tazencius gets his act together.')

'Ciartan's not got much to say for himself, has he?' Monach said.

'Ah.' The crow sighed mournfully. 'He doesn't realise. He doesn't know. Ignorance, folly, madness, death. The soldiers are coming.'

'What soldiers?' Monach asked, but the crow didn't answer; it had gone again, or forgotten how to speak, or maybe Ciartan had killed it with a stone. Then the man with the beard and the stub nose swung round to face the door, as a soldier appeared and said something; and the angle of his chin, the way his eyes narrowed before he spoke – I know you, Monach thought.

Cordo? Why aren't you dead?

'Why isn't he dead?' someone was saying. 'Damn well ought to be, bash on the head like that. He must have a skull like a barn wall.'

So I'm not dead, then, Monach thought, looking up at the circle of faces above him. Either that, or I died and I must've been a very bad man indeed, to get sent to an after-life with this lot in it.

'He's woken up – look.' A face came closer. 'You all right, chief?' it said. 'How're you feeling now?'

'Like a mountain fell on me,' Monach replied. 'Where is she? Have you found her?'

Nobody answered, which in itself was an answer.

'In that case,' Monach said, 'we're going to Dui Chirra.'

And a miserable journey it was, too. The quickest route to Dui Chirra meant leaving the military road at Sarcqui and splashing through runny mud for two days down a miserable sunken lane with high hedges on either side; both boring and nerve-racking at the same time, since there was no way of knowing what was lying in wait for them around every corner. Ideal setting for an ambush; fell a substantial tree across the track, and you'd have the whole army bottled up. If the reports were accurate, Brigadier Muno was in charge at the foundry; a difficult man at the best of times, and it was unlikely that the untimely death of his nephew would have done much to improve his temper. He was just the sort to have a brigade or so of regular heavy infantry on hand to guard his precious compound, and an opportunity like a sunken lane would be something he'd be sure to make the most of. The idea of fighting a desperate defensive action in a cramped space, mud underfoot, against a horribly competent enemy didn't appeal to Monach in the least; and God knew, they wouldn't exactly be difficult to detect. If Muno was doing his job properly, he'd have picked them up already and either be on his way or already in position. Unfortunately, there was no other way of getting to Dui Chirra, apart from a week-long detour that'd take them through every sad excuse for a town between Falcata and the sea. Ignorance, folly, madness and death, just like the crow had warned him. It was a pity he didn't have any choice in the matter.

Even so, it shouldn't have been a problem. He was, after all, a brother of the order of Deymeson, trained to cope with problems of every kind. But in order to deal with the situation, he needed a clear head, the ability to concentrate, and that was proving to be beyond his abilities. Xipho; Xipho missing, Cordo alive and suddenly turned hostile. No matter how hard he tried to concoct some feasible alternative explanation, he had to face the virtual certainty that Cordomine, his old college friend, habitually top of the class in strategy and tactics, diplomacy and the huge variety of antisocial and unethical activities which the Deymeson syllabus lumped together under the heading of Acts of Expediency, was alive, and he'd either taken Xipho with him by force or tricked her into going with him – or she'd gone of her own accord, gladly, or possibly even by previous arrangement. That thought was terrifying, far more so than the prospect of Brigadier Muno's infantry suddenly pouncing on him from some gap in the carelessly-laid hedges of the Sarcqui to Dui Chirra road. Was it possible, he asked himself over and over again, that all this time she'd been playing him along, as she'd been playing Ciartan, not so long ago; following orders, furthering the Grand Plan by every means in her power. The loathsome symmetry of that possibility wasn't lost on him. Suppose that's what was really going on; now why hadn't Father Tutor and the rest of the faculty ever bothered to cover that aspect of the trade in their third grade Expediencies coursework? What to do when you find out your lover is really your enemy; a dozen lectures, six tutorials, a written paper and a practical.

(It's a tragedy, he told himself bitterly, that I can only kill Ciartan once.)

—And Cordo; Cordo alive, even though he'd seen him dead, once in the butchered flesh, and two or three times a week in bad dreams since. Cordo, who'd hit him hard enough to kill (but he'd said he was sorry in advance.) As the carts lurched and wobbled through the mud and jolted over the stones washed out by the rain, he tried to understand exactly what that was supposed to mean.

There had been six of them; the Crow's Head Gang, named after the crumbled, slapdash carved stone corbel that looked down over their stall in the chapter house at Deymeson, where they'd stood patiently shivering and bored through countless assemblies, chapters, lectures, liturgies. Elaos Tanwar, born leader, prime mover, inspiration and guiding spirit, long since incontrovertibly dead, for what little that seemed to be worth nowadays. Xipho Dorunoxy, born second-in-command, always the cleverest, always the most sensible, the most patient, the one who

stopped the rest of them fighting among themselves, the
one who'd somehow got it into her head that the Gang
mattered, that it was about something other than breaking
rules and relieving boredom. Ciartan – always had been a
nasty piece of work, but he'd had other qualities then: a
narrow and rigid loyalty, courage, a reckless disregard for
risk and danger, an evil bastard but *their* evil bastard, even
more terrifying to outsiders than he was to the other members of the Gang. Cordomine: always there, never left out,
never missed a council of war or a staff meeting, always
knew what was going on, what the opposition was up to
(the faculty, the groundsmen and domestics, the other
gangs; how he knew they never found out, never asked);
always thinking long thoughts, cherishing grudges,
exploiting little cracks and rifts, always listening, never a
wasted word; always top at Expediences, and Doctrine too,
for some bizarre reason. Gain Aciava, Cordomine's self-
appointed henchman: at times no more than an associate
member, and then suddenly he'd be in the thick of it, master
of alternatives, the eternal custodian of Plan B; always
talking, never saying anything unless he wanted to – and
in the end he'd proved to be something rather more than
Cordomine's shadow, an extension of his friend's mind;
more and worse; and of course, it was Gain who brought
Ciartan to Deymeson, having found him wandering in the
wilderness, like some prophet in scripture. It'd be nice,
Monach thought, if he'd seen the last of Gain Aciava, but
he wasn't at all sure about that. Himself the seventh; and
of all seven, the one he knew least about and had the most
trouble labelling and pigeonholing. At the time he'd have
said: always the most reasonable, always the most boringly
sincere, the one whose homework the others copied, not
because he was the best but because he always did the work.
The most stolid, reliable, prosaic; Father Tutor's pet, the
one who wanted to do well at lessons, the one who actually

cared about religion and stuff. That had been then, of course; and it was notoriously hard to form a clear view of history while it was actually going on. To the above, he could also add, always the most marginal, the least important, the least valued, always the one picked last for the team, always the one they had to remember not to leave out. Since then he'd always believed: the last one left, the only survivor – until Xipho had turned up, popping up out of the ruins of Deymeson and shattering what little peace of mind he had left by announcing that she'd been the priestess of the god in the cart he'd been vainly chasing after, while the world had been getting ready to end all around him. Then, in the same breath, bloody Ciartan; he was still around, and worse still, at some point in the intervening years he'd somehow become the most important (Ciartan, always the least likely to succeed), until suddenly he'd lost it all in the muddy fringes of some river, surrounded by dead bodies and crows—

(He remembered; it was Ciartan, of course, who'd come up with the gang's name. Who else?)

And now Cordo, materialising out of the darkness like a fairytale goblin, bashing heads and abducting princesses (unless she'd gone willingly; unless she'd been waiting for him; maybe she'd been the one who hit him, not Cordo –); and he'd asked after Gain, implying that he was still out there somewhere, still hovering and listening and cooking up little plots. Still the same old gang, out to cause mischief, insisting that he join in but not bothering to tell him what it was all about— And his one triumph, his late achievement; it had almost made up for the trashing of Deymeson and the death of the order. Finally, at the end, it'd been him, the runt of the litter, who'd scooped the pool (by right of survivorship only, he'd freely admitted that) and got what the other five never managed: he'd got Xipho. Sure, she'd been with Ciartan, she'd had his child, even named the little brat after him, but that had all been in the line of duty, yet another intolerable burden she'd borne for the sake of the order; but (she'd told him, beetroot red with embarrassment and shame) actually, always, it had been him she'd loved, right from the start, only she'd never given in to it for the sake of the gang, knowing that if she did it'd be the end of them, splitting them up, driving them apart (as if that'd have mattered; after all, it was only an informal student's club, a trivial thing . . .) Until at the end, in the ashes and rubble—

Had she told Ciartan the same sort of lies? No, of course not, because he'd lost his memory; she'd have had to think up some different lies for him. So, what about Cordo? Had she loved him and him only, all along, too?

As if it mattered, Monach told himself. Far more important issues to be dealt with here – an army to command, lives at stake, all these poor fools depending on him, following him to the ends of the earth, his people. (And you could ask two dozen of them exactly why were they following him, to achieve what ultimate purpose, and get maybe one sensible answer – if you were lucky.)

And then it got worse.

The fact that he'd been expecting it didn't help terribly much. All the way up that terrifying chimney of hedges and high banks he'd been waiting for the moment when armed men would start pouring down on him, like burning lava from a volcano. Of course, it happened only when he'd eventually stopped watching the sides of the road and allowed his attention to wander. Worse still, they attacked when the army was at its most vulnerable, straddled across a deep, fast ford.

It began with rocks and stones; then a fat old chestnut tree yawned and flopped across the track, so closely following Monach's worst-case scenario that for a moment he almost believed he was remembering something that had already happened. The attackers gushed out of the dense cover behind and on both flanks like sea water flooding a holed ship.

No room, Monach acknowledged hopelessly; no room to turn the carts to form defensible redoubts, which was about the only worthwhile trick he and his officers knew. Without that slim advantage, Monach's army quickly resolved itself into what it had really been all along: a loose and unreliable confederation of poorly motivated individuals. As if that wasn't bad enough, he realised that he hadn't got a clue who these predictable but horribly efficient enemies were. Not regular army, not raiders, not rustic levies. Amathy house? Didn't matter. No time to bother with trivia, such as who precisely was killing his people, let alone why.

Clarity; give me clarity, or else let me die quickly and avoid the shame. Training told; he snapped into focus, assessed the situation, calculated the inevitable outcome. Unfortunately it wasn't good. Whoever these people were, they had ambushes and surprise attacks polished up as sharp as a needle. No point looking for mistakes, they wouldn't have made any. Simple as that.

Precepts of religion, Monach thought wildly as the man standing next to him was pulled down off the cart by his ankles. Strength is weakness; and the precepts are never wrong, it's just that occasionally humans are too obtuse to grasp the subtleties. Strength is weakness; their strengths were surprise, speed and efficiency. All right then, bugger precepts of religion. We're just going to have to slog it out and see what happens.

Once he'd reached that conclusion, it was easier for him; he was excused strategy and tactics for the duration of the battle, and was free to indulge himself in the one thing he was actually rather good at. He'd never enjoyed killing, for the same reason he'd never enjoyed breathing – it was too reflexive to be capable of being enjoyed. (How can you relish a moment that doesn't exist?) But at least it gave him something to do and took his mind off the miserable shambles all around him. He jumped down from the cart, identified a target and dealt with it. His sword was shaken free of blood and back in the scabbard before he had time to think about what he was proposing to do; the best way, he'd always found.

Monach wasn't aware of a precept that said: *When all else fails, lead by example.* But maybe he'd been off sick that day. It proved to be a valid approach; whoever these people were, they didn't seem to be prepared to cope with calm, unruffled-looking men who treated a battle like a stroll through long grass, leaving a trail of sliced tendons and arteries behind them. If Monach had been the only sword-monk in the army, maybe they'd have coped, but he wasn't; simply getting out of his way wasn't enough. Nevertheless, it came as something of a surprise to him when the enemy ran away, as if it hadn't occurred to him that a fight could end without one side wiping out the other. Naturally, mass combat and wholesale slaughter hadn't been on the syllabus at Deymeson; and he'd never actually participated in a regular battle before. But for one party simply to turn round and leave struck him as vaguely unfair, cheating; because they'd have another chance some other day, and they hadn't earned it. He felt a simmering sense of injustice, as if someone had made a fool of him.

'What the hell was all that about?' someone asked him, some captain or other. 'Who were they, anyhow?'

Monach shrugged. He was standing beside the ford, looking down at dead men lying face down in the mud, thinking, *So that's what Ciartan would've seen when he woke up with his mind suddenly empty: horrible.* He tried to imagine how he'd have reacted under those circumstances, but it was impossible. 'No idea,' he replied. 'Could have been the Amathy house, I suppose, only I don't remember ever doing anything to set them against us. Still, I don't suppose they need a reason.'

'Could be.' The captain crouched down on his heels to turn a dead body on its back. Neck cut to the bone; the mud was bright red all round it. 'They aren't regular army, but they're not different enough to be raiders.'

'Local militia, then,' he suggested, though he'd already dismissed that possibility.

'Too professional for that,' the captain replied. 'Militia would've just run away, for one thing, not retire in good order like this lot did.'

'Amathy house, then,' Monach said. He tried to think of the implications of that: what exactly did the Amathy house *want*? Hitherto he'd always tended to think of them as little more than a superior class of bandits, descending without warning on remote settlements to rob, burn and kill. But bandits wouldn't pick a fight with an army for no reason. Their actions, specially battles, would have to be cost-effective, a solid and guaranteed financial return for every life lost. Businessmen – the same, he realised with a shudder, as us; and we wouldn't have attacked them without provocation. We haven't got anything worth stealing, so it must have been our lives they were after, rather than property. Taking out a potential rival? Maybe. Perhaps they were planning to raid the Dui Chirra foundry, with its substantial stock of valuable metal (scrap bronze is something tangible and valuable, worth shedding blood for), reckoned we must have the same idea and wanted to forestall us. It still seemed far-fetched. If the wealth of Dui Chirra was the motive, then at the very least it'd have made sense to attack us *after* we'd looted the foundry. Two crows with one stone – get the bronze and dispose of us, save themselves a job.

It had to be that, though; or else they'd decided to appoint themselves as guardians of the Empire, Tazencius's loyal and trusted supporters—

—Or maybe there's some reason why they don't want the foundry destroyed; not yet. Poldarn's Flute, for instance. That made a whole lot of sense; basically the same motive as driving the crows off your growing corn until you're ready to cut it. Dear God, Monach thought in high disgust, does *everybody* in the Empire know about the wretched things? They're supposed to be a deadly secret.

Well; in that case he quite understood, couldn't blame them in the least. It also meant they'd definitely be back, better prepared and organised. Not a cheerful thought, almost as disturbing as the suspicion forming in his mind about the timing of Cordo's visit and Xipho's disappearance.

'So,' the captain was saying, 'now what? I don't know the proper procedure after a battle. Like, are we supposed to bury the bodies, or do we just leave them lying about?'

'Hadn't given it any thought,' Monach answered. 'Though it's academic, really – we haven't got time. I guess we leave them for the crows, right thing to do or not.' A thought struck him. 'Any idea how many of ours didn't make it?' he asked, trying not to sound horribly callous but not making a very good fist of it.

The captain shook his head. 'Could've been worse is probably the most you can say for it,' he replied. 'We got more of them than they got of us, if that's any good to you.'

Monach shook his head. 'No,' he said. 'Not really.'

The next day brought them to the military road, where the captain whose name Monach couldn't remember had an answer to his question; at least, they saw an example of how the regular army dealt with the problem.

The crows were visible from a long way off, swirling

their sloppy, asymmetrical helix in the middle sky. Why do they do that, Monach asked himself. Waste of time and energy, surely. But birds and animals don't do anything without a very good reason, so presumably there was some advantage to be gained from it – an efficient formation for maximum all-round observation, or something like that. When Monach's column broke the skyline they cleared off, with much resentful shrieking, apart from one or two defiant individuals who refused to leave the banquet until they were walked off, like the last few resilient drunks at closing time.

They looked at the sight in silence for quite some time; then someone or other, some company commander, shook his head and said: 'All in all, not a good week for the Amathy boys.'

Assuming, Monach thought, that's who they were. It'd have been nice if just one of them could have been bothered to stay alive a few hours longer, so he could have asked him who he belonged to. But no, they'd all died and taken the information with them, memories all wiped clean, nothing now but cold meat and scrap metal.

The approved procedure, apparently, was for the regular army to bury its own dead in a single long trench, the sort you dig to plant vines in, and leave the enemy for the scavengers. Judging by the size of the newly made earthwork, the regulars hadn't had it all their own way, but they'd definitely had the better of it. As he picked his way between the flat, dirty bodies, Monach recognised a face, one of the men he'd seen during his own battle. On that occasion, he'd seen this man (memorable for his long, rather concave face: stub nose, recurved chin) looking at him from about five yards away; he remembered watching as the man frowned, pursed his lips slightly (like a doubtful buyer in a market) and then turned his back and walked briskly away. Now he was on his back, both feet pointing left, arms flopped by his sides, head twisted round and back by the force of the cut that had severed his neck into but not through the bone. His eyes were wide open, and the eyeballs were filthy with dust and mud.

'Serves them right,' someone else said. Nobody replied. By the looks of it, all of those who'd withdrawn from the battle in the sunken lane had fallen here; if this was an example of Brigadier Muno's work, he was good at what he did. A professional soldier, of course, would have other agendas beside simply staying alive and holding the field. In this instance, there must have been some advantage to be gained from wiping the enemy out practically to the last man – sending a message to the Amathy house, raising the morale of his own troops, letting off steam after the murder of the brigadier's nephew. Or maybe they'd just needed the boots.

The hell with sightseeing, Monach thought; time we were getting on. He gave the order to fall in. It was reluctantly obeyed (can't blame them, he thought; naturally they don't want to carry on in this direction, with the risk of running into the people who did this – not a nice neighbourhood) and they began the last leg of the journey to Dui Chirra; a pleasant, comfortable stroll down this excellently maintained government road.

An hour or so along the way, they were met by a single man on a rather fine black horse. Soldier; staff rather than front line, judging by his clean boots and crisp riding-cloak. He sat on his horse in the middle of the road like a sheriff's officer, as if Monach had got behind on the payments for the army and he'd come to repossess it. Whoever he was, he either had strong nerves or no imagination. In any event, Monach decided, that sort of confidence deserved a little respect, so he rode out ahead to meet him.

'Hello there,' the man said; calm, slightly cocky even. 'I'm Captain Olens, Imperial staff. Who the hell are you?'

Monach nodded politely. 'Pilgrims,' he said.

Captain Olens thought about that for a moment. 'Rather a lot of you for that,' he said.

'Safety in numbers,' Monach replied. 'I get the impression that the roads around here aren't as safe as they might be, no disrespect intended. Gangs of bandits and the gods know what else roaming around all over the place. After what happened to the prince the other day, it's like nobody's safe any more.'

'Quite so,' Captain Olens said. 'So, if you're pilgrims, where are you headed for? I never knew there was anything particularly holy around here.'

Monach raised his eyebrows. 'You surprise me,' he said. 'You mean, you haven't heard about the miracle?'

'Miracle,' Olens said. 'No, can't say I have.'

'Good heavens,' Monach said. 'Everybody's talking about it back home. Manifestation of the Divine Poldarn; quite possibly the Second Coming and the end of the world. Right here,' he added, 'at Dui Chirra.'

Olens looked at him. 'Are you sure you've got the right place?' he said. 'There's nothing at Dui Chirra except a rather scruffy inn and a run-down old foundry.'

'Poldarn in his aspect of the god of fire and rebirth,' Monach said. 'Where else would you look except a foundry?'

Olens shook his head. 'Sorry,' he said. 'but I think you boys have had a wasted trip. Nothing miraculous going on there, just a bunch of layabouts messing about in a clay pit. If you're looking for miracles, you might try heading south. I did hear they've got a two-headed calf out at Chosiva.'

'Two-headed calves aren't anything special,' Monach said, shifting his reins into his left hand. 'Once you've seen one, you've seen them all.' He nudged his horse with his heels, and as they moved forward he laid the back of his right hand on the hilt of his sword, snuggled in his sash like a baby. Captain Olens must have seen him, or else he was properly aware of his circle; he pulled his horse's head around and kicked savagely. Monach's draw cut the air he'd just left.

No point chasing after him; a fine government horse like that could outrun Monach's old bag of bones any day, and even if he did catch up with him, there was nothing to be gained from killing one staff officer in the middle of nowhere. *I wonder if he had a similar conversation with the commander of those poor bastards we left at the cross-roads,* Monach thought.

'What was all that about?' someone asked him, when he'd rejoined the column.

Monach shrugged. 'Far as I could make out, I think the government doesn't want us to go to Dui Chirra. I get the impression it's not open to the public these days.'

'Fine,' somebody said. 'So what do we do now?'

'What we're told, of course,' Monach replied. 'Unless you like the idea of a meeting with the outfit that did over the Amathy house; in which case, you carry on. Personally, I'm going the other way.'

Silence; but Monach didn't care. He was, of course, going to go to Dui Chirra, because it was the only place he could think of where Xipho might sooner or later turn up. Taking this collection of misfits with him was clearly out of the question, but it had never been anything more than a means to an end, an instrument to be used. If he'd wanted to be a soldier, he'd have joined the army.

Chapter Eight

'It was desperate,' someone said. He recognised the voice, couldn't quite put a name to it. *Desperate* had been the in word in fourth grade, enjoying a brief vogue in between *howling* and *essential*. 'I thought the old bastard was going to have a fit and drop dead on the spot. Boy, he was absolutely frothing.'

Frothing helped narrow down the time-span even further; it had been Cordomine's pet word for the first half of Hilary term in fourth grade, and they'd reluctantly adopted it for a week or so, until the sixth-graders started saying *steaming*, setting a trend that nobody dared flout. So, he asked himself, what happened in the fourth, fifth and sixth weeks of Hilary term in fourth grade? He had an idea he ought to know, but he couldn't quite remember. Meanwhile, the old stone crow carried on leering at him from its place on top of the pillar (he could feel it, even with his eyes shut) which could only mean they were in the chapter house at Deymeson, waiting in their appointed places for Father Abbot to lead in the faculty for the start of Traditional Prayers; in which case, it had to be fifth week, because—

'So,' someone else interrupted, 'did you see them? What do they look like? Any good?'

The first speaker paused to consider. 'The middle one's a solid seven,' he said. 'The eldest – she's the one who's married, to that captain in the guards – she's just a milky old doe. The youngest, though—' Words apparently failed the speaker at this point.

'Hot?' The other voice prompted.

'As a stove-pipe,' the first voice confirmed. 'Like, so hot you could fry eggs.'

Ah, Ciartan thought, now we know where we are. Of course, there was no excuse for not remembering this day of all days. He opened his eyes and looked round.

The first speaker, as he should have known all along, was Elaos Tanwar; the second voice, Gain Aciava. Beside him, looking distinctly frosty, was Xipho Dorunoxy – she always wore that pained, constipated expression when the boys were discussing girls, particularly when they started using the scale of one to ten. Without looking round, she said, 'You'd better not let Turvo hear you talking about his sisters like that.'

Elaos grinned. 'You're just jealous,' he said; and ducked, just in time, as Xipho tried to reach round the back of Gain's head to stick a finger in his eye. Sword-monk reflexes.

'Do you bloody well mind?' Gain snapped; then he too had to dodge out of the way as Xipho tried again. Elaos, of course, was grinning like a monkey.

'I can't believe it,' he heard himself say, 'Turvo having sisters who're half decent-looking. It's hard to imagine a female version of Turvo. Just as well,' he added, 'I missed breakfast.'

'Cordo says they take after their mother's side,' Gain replied. ''Course, he knows the family. His lot know everybody, bloody social climbers.'

'Where is Cordo, anyhow?' the Earwig asked, from his

place next to Xipho, on the left. (What was the Earwig's regular name? Couldn't remember; he'd been the Earwig since before Ciartan had come to Deymeson. Even the faculty called him that, so rumour had it.)

'Infirmary,' Elaos replied, his tone of voice suggesting that he believed Cordo's illness was wholly tactical. 'Anybody want to bet me he'll make a miraculous recovery shortly after Third Bell, so's he can go prowling round the Sty just when Turvo's giving them the guided tour?'

Xipho sniffed her disapproval. 'Trust Cordo to find a way of skiving off double Theory,' she said scornfully. 'I know for a fact he hasn't done the practicals, because he was creeping round me last night after Seventh Bell asking for the answers.'

'Which you refused to give him, of course,' Gain said dangerously.

'Of course I didn't,' Xipho replied. 'I'm amazed he had the nerve to ask.'

Something in Gain's grin suggested that he believed that Cordo had had certain motives beside attempted cheating for lurking round the girls' common room after dark. Fortunately, Xipho was looking the other way and didn't see him.

'It really shouldn't be allowed,' Xipho was saying. 'It says explicitly, in the rules, that visits from family aren't allowed in term-time except at Commemoration and Intercessions, or during Elections with special permission. It's only because Turvo's dad is some kind of minor royal. I thought we were above that sort of thing here, but apparently not.'

Elaos made that funny snorting noise of his. 'Tazencius is more than some kind of minor royal,' he said scathingly. 'He's, what, ninth in succession? Or is it tenth? Can't remember. Anyhow, he's quite a nob. We should be honoured. And I expect Father Abbot and the candlewobblers'll be after him with the begging bowl.'

Xipho sniffed again. For a girl who'd never had a cold in her life, she could sniff quite majestically. 'It's disgusting what the faculty'll do for money,' she said, and then glowered angrily as the boys (the Earwig excepted, of course) started sniggering. 'Well, it is,' she went on. 'And they shouldn't have to. If the government saw to it that our tithes were paid in full, we'd have more than enough funding—'

The last thing the boys wanted to talk about, needless to say, was tithes and indulgence of clergy; not with three new girls in town (or two, discounting the milky old doe). Of all of them, leaving the no-hoper Earwig out of the reckoning, Ciartan was probably the least interested. Unlike them, he hadn't been a monk since puberty, and therefore the subject wasn't as mysteriously fascinating to him as it was to them. Generally speaking, in the interests of not making himself irredeemably unpopular, he tended to shut up and let them get on with their highly theoretical speculations. Even so: a visit by three half-princesses of the blood was distinctly out of the ordinary, and he couldn't help being just a little curious. And if Elaos was right, and the youngest really was hotter than a stove-pipe, it couldn't hurt just to take a very brief look, if by chance he just happened to be passing—

By the same time next day, Ciartan was about ready to give up. Turvo's sisters had proved to be harder to reach than a mountain top. Father Tutor's apoplexy, which Elaos hadn't exaggerated at all, wasn't enough to stop him devising security measures that'd have done credit to the Imperial Guard, all designed to make sure that nobody just happened to be passing any place where Turvo and his sisters (and, infuriatingly, Cordo, who'd contrived to attach himself to the party as visitor-liaison officer, on the strength of the old family friendship) could see them, even to the extent of a distant glimpse. Throughout the long,

hot day an endless stream of students was evicted from
every hiding place on the premises by grim-faced prefects,
temporarily enjoying powers of extreme violence over their
fellows. Not for nothing, on the other hand, did the
Deymeson syllabus cover persistence, endurance and dia-
bolical ingenuity, to the point where the challenge pre-
sented by the faculty's efforts at security outweighed the
attraction of three pretty girls (or two pretty girls and one
milky old doe.) A cynic would've been forgiven for
assuming that Father Tutor had set the whole situation up
as an Expediencies practical; if so, he should have been
proud. Deymeson rose to the challenge and excelled itself.

Faced with such a level of competition, Ciartan decided
he couldn't really be bothered. Once you've seen one pretty
girl, he told himself, you've seen them all, and the best of
them wasn't worth the risk of getting on the wrong side of
the prefects. There was also a very palpable fringe benefit
to be considered—

'Hello,' Xipho said. 'What're you doing here?'

'Me?' Ciartan shrugged. They were the only two living
souls in the library, usually crowded at this time of day.
'Reading up for the Theory presentation, of course.'

She looked at him. 'Oh,' she said.

He yawned. 'Where is everybody, anyway?'

'Them.' A look of contempt crossed her face. 'Buzzing
round the honeypot, of course, trying to get a look at
Turvo's stupid sisters. Why aren't you out there with
them?'

Ciartan shrugged. 'Can't be bothered,' he said. 'Can't
see what all the fuss is about, really.'

Xipho didn't comment on that, but he could sense a
slight relaxation of her legendary guard. 'Really,' she said.
'How many fingers am I holding up?'

He sighed. 'No, I haven't gone blind. And yes,' he added
with a very mild leer, 'I do like girls. But—' He judged the

hesitation nicely; that hint of a busy, mysterious past, enough to intrigue without involving him in telling outright lies or, even worse, the truth. 'Well, I've been around a little bit, and you know what? Half the human race is girls; so if I don't see these particular specimens, chances are I'll run into some others before I die. You never know.'

Maybe he'd overdone it, he thought, because Xipho was frowning slightly. Nevertheless. There was an old saying back home, about the fox knowing many tricks whereas the hedgehog knows one bloody good one. His bloody good trick was dropping veiled hints about his past, but never actually letting slip anything outright, concrete. He knew perfectly well that if he told them he'd grown up on a big farm in a valley but had had to leave in a hurry because of trouble over another man's wife, he'd have committed his reserve and be left with nothing in hand except the rather inadequate resources that made up his personality. Leading them to believe that his history was as rich, dark and exotic as the Empire's was a game he could play easily, and although he was sure they'd figured out by now that there was considerably less to him than met the eye, they still couldn't quite resist the lure, like cats who know it's just the end of a piece of string but can't help lunging after it when it twitches. How long he could keep up this man-of-mystery pose he had no idea, but while it lasted he was determined to make the most of it.

'Well,' Xipho said eventually, 'maybe you're not as shallow as a pauper's grave after all. Did you come here to do some work, or just to be annoying?'

He smiled on the inside. A compliment, even a backhanded one, from Xipho Dorunoxy happened about as often as a dry summer in Tulice; and although it was murderously difficult to impress her, once you'd managed it she generally stayed impressed. On balance, therefore, well worth the effort. (Besides, if Turvo's sisters were anything

like their brother, you'd pay an extortionate price in excruciating boredom for their good looks. Also, Turvo loved
garlic; if he'd picked up the taste for it at home, Ciartan
was in no hurry to meet other members of his family.)

He spent a couple of hours reading Zephanes on
Deception (he was actually enjoying Expediencies this
term) while basking in the unshared proximity of Xipho –
the line of her neck and shoulders silhouetted against the
high west window was enough to boil your brain out
through your ears, but he'd just about mastered the art of
ignoring it. Then she closed her book with a snap, called
out, 'See you tomorrow, then,' as she stood up to leave, and
actually smiled. It was faster than the draw, one of those
moments-in-religion that are over so quick that they never
actually happened; but if you're lucky enough to survive
them, you carry the scars for life.

Fuck, he said to himself, just when I thought I was being
so cool and smart; but there it is, it's happened and I can't
ignore it, any more than I could ignore nine inches of steel
poked in my ear. I really am in love with her; not just a
fancy or the intellectual interest of long-term flirtation, not
just the fascinating challenge of the vain quest to get into
her pants. That flash of the eyes, too quick for me; past my
guard like it wasn't there, sidestepping my wards, a
moment of true religion. And he thought, so it does exist
after all, that moment (he'd never stumbled across it in the
draw, though he was faster than any of those who reckoned
they'd found it there), that less-than-a-heartbeat that
changes everything, because suddenly between you and the
other there's a third presence, that of the divine. He'd never
been there before, but he'd seen the place from a distance;
years ago, in a muddy ditch beside a stream, where he'd
crouched waiting for the crows to pitch and then found
himself ducking down again, with the memory of a stone
in his hand and a death in mid-air. On that occasion he'd

fancied he'd talked with a stranger for a minute or so, an older man who reminded him of himself, but with someone else forge-welded into him, layer and fold and layer, fire and hammer; and he'd wondered, in his immature faith, whether he'd possibly had a vision of the great god of his people, the divine Poldarn, who lived under the hot springs on the high slopes of the mountain.

And this was the divine, the moment of religion, which he'd found in Xipho's tense little smile. He compared the two, and found the similarities were too many and too great to be mere coincidence; in which case, he decided, he must have seen the god of the forge there that day, when he slaughtered the crows over the spring peas. Somehow, that was a comforting thought (because he'd always worried about it, at the back of his mind; if it hadn't been the god, was there something wrong with him, because normal adolescents don't chat with imaginary friends?); in a way, oddly enough, it felt like coming home.

He reproached himself for thinking that way. Being in love with Xipho wasn't something to be pleased or happy about. Rather, it was as good a definition of being in deep, deep trouble as any conscientious lexicographer could ever hope to find. Being in love with the only girl in a class of nineteen monks – He wondered if there was still time to drop by the Infirmary and have his head pumped out, but probably not. Too late. He was stuck with it.

Pity about that: it complicated things horribly. For one thing (he realised, as he put Zephanes back on his proper shelf, and headed for the door) there was the small matter of end-of-grade tests. Deymeson didn't encourage friendships among the students; love was out of the question, when you had no way of knowing who you'd be facing down the narrow steel road, which led half of the class to the next grade and the other half to the closely planted plot of ground outside the back gates. Of course, love wouldn't get in Xipho's way, even if she was capable of it, which everybody was inclined to doubt: she'd cut her lover down for religion's sake as cheerfully as slicing through the neck of a rose. But if he, on the other hand, ended up facing her at year's end, he'd be dead. Consideration; was Deymeson the only place on earth where the lover's traditional promise to love until death was a practical proposition? Discuss, with examples.

Yes, but it wouldn't come to that; and she could kill whoever she liked out of the others and bloody good luck to her. But what if she didn't make it to fifth grade; suppose someone else got put up instead of her, and—? That wasn't going to happen either, he reassured himself. In sparring, the only ones who'd ever outdrawn her were himself and the absurd Earwig, who'd had a crush on her long before his voice broke. Pointless worrying about that.

Pointless, all of it; pointless as a man with no hands buying nail scissors. Nothing good could come of being in love with Xipho Dorunoxy; even a sublimely gifted chancer like himself didn't have a hope. It was just bad luck: infuriating, meanly capricious on the part of Destiny, who could so easily have paired him off with somebody else – Turvo's kid sister, for example, hotter than a stove-pipe and rich as egg soup into the bargain. (What an amazing career move that'd be, though, a real coup for an ambitious young man of the cloth. They reckoned that Tazencius was a man to watch, that his son-in-law was practically guaranteed a top-drawer chaplaincy, and after that, the gods only knew. And if anything – heaven forbid – ever happened to good solid old Turvo, such as coming second out of two at year's end—)

He strolled across the yard, nothing to hurry for, his mind bent on long, improbable thoughts; accordingly, he was almost back at the entrance to Morevich House when a voice called out to him.

He looked round.

Now, for some reason, he had no idea what it could be, Turvo (Depater Turvonianus, only son and heir of Depater Tazencius, prince and hereditary marshal of all sorts of obscure places) had taken a liking to Ciartan the outlander, farm boy and general outcast. The liking wasn't reciprocated. On the rare occasions when Turvo wasn't painfully boring, it was because he was being objectionable enough to court serious injury. But the fact remained: Turvo was always pleased to see Ciartan whenever Ciartan hadn't seen him first.

'There you are,' the idiot was saying. 'Come over here a minute. I'd like you to meet my sisters.'

Not now, Turvo, you arsehole; not *now*. If you make me do this, then so help me but I'll find some way to rig the ballot for who fights who at year's end. 'Actually—' he started to say; but what excuse could he possibly make for ducking out of what the whole Upper School had been desperately trying to achieve all day? I've got an essay to finish, I have to go and polish my boots. Whatever he said, it'd be perceived as a mortal insult, not just to the moron Turvo but to his great and influential family.

Praying to the god (if any) who lived under the hot springs of Poldarn's Forge that Xipho wouldn't choose this particular moment to stick her head out of a window and see him, he crossed the yard—

He was woken up by a scream.

Not often you hear a man screaming, Poldarn thought, as he opened his eyes. Extreme pain will do it sometimes, but usually only when there's extreme terror as well. He stuffed his feet into his boots and stumbled out through the door.

It was as dark as fifty feet down a well outside, but he could see fast-moving lights, which he assumed were lamps and torches in the hands of running men. There hadn't been a second scream; bad for somebody. The lights were all headed in the same direction. He consulted his mental plan of the foundry: the casting yard. Hellfire, he thought (and he was surprised at his own reaction). The thought-less bastards have started the pour without me, and some careless bugger's got himself burned.

Not that he cared an offcomer's damn about the Poldarn's Flute project; it was all a load of nonsense and nothing was going to come of it, that was an article of faith among the entire foundry crew. But not to be there when they did the first pour – he remembered the scream, which meant somebody badly hurt, probably dead, and felt ashamed of himself.

'Who the hell's making that bloody awful noise?' someone shouted. Nobody answered. People were gath-ering from all over the site, some running, some walking at the weary, reluctant pace of men going to a funeral. They were lighting the big lanterns in the casting yard, the ones that gave enough light to work by. One or two of the hands were running up with ropes, ladders, poles, then suddenly stopping, not doing anything – implying that there was nothing they *could* do.

The scene reminded Poldarn of something. It didn't take much imagination to figure out what had happened. On Galand Dev's orders, and flying in the face of the very clear instructions set out in *Concerning Various Matters*, the cupola furnace had been built on top of a mound of earth and clay, to provide the necessary height above the mould to allow the molten bronze to flow easily. What they should have done was dig a deep pit for the moulds, and run the melt down a channel from a furnace built at ground level; but Galand Dev had reckoned to save two or three days by having the mould on the surface and elevating the furnace, with the fire chamber directly underneath it. But the heat

of the fire had dried out the mound, shrinking the platform on which the furnace rested. Result: the crucible,
holding three hundredweight of very hot molten metal, had
leant sideways, to the point where it had tipped over,
pouring the melt down on the poor fools who'd been
scraping the dried clay of the model off the inner wall of
the mould. It must've happened quite suddenly, but it
appeared as though there'd been a second or so for the men
to get clear, because nearly all of them had made it. All, in
fact, save one.

And even he'd been lucky, in a sense. Because the crucible had toppled before the molten bronze had reached
flowing heat, the melt hadn't been hot enough to pour like
water. When the mound collapsed and one of the heavy
props had toppled over, pinning the unfortunate mould-
fettler by the knee, the escaped melt had flooded out down
the mound slope straight at him; but before it could actually reach him and reduce him to cinders, it'd cooled down
enough to stop moving. This was good, up to a point. True,
the wedged man wasn't going to be burnt to death by a
lava flow from the crucible; but the metal was still hot
enough to strip skin and muscle down to bone on contact,
and if the mound dried out and shifted any more, as it was
almost certain to do, a hundredweight blob of searingly hot
bronze flash would go slithering down the slope directly
on top of him; and by the time it had cooled enough for
anybody to go in close, there wouldn't be enough remaining
of the trapped fettler to be worth burying. Of course, only
a lunatic would risk getting in close enough to pull him
out, when the slightest movement could disturb the mound
enough to get the hot flash moving.

The man pinned under the prop was Gain Aciava.

Even so, Poldarn told himself firmly; even so. This was
the man who claimed to have all Poldarn's lost memories
packed and slotted away in his own memory, like tools in

a cabinetmaker's chest. If he died, all that would be lost (because heat draws the temper, relaxes memory; the symbolism was right bang on the nail, but Poldarn wasn't in the mood) and quite possibly he'd never know—

He was shocked.

Ordinary fear he could've forgiven himself for; and anybody with enough sense to breathe would have every right to be scared out of his wits at the mere thought of trying to get down there, heave a huge log out of the way, drag a helpless man up a muddy, slippery slope with that enormous glowing chunk of death poised to slither down on top of him; and all of it to be done in the face of excruciating heat. Perfectly valid reason, perfectly acceptable excuse for not getting involved, even if the man being cooked alive down there was an old, old friend (and he only had Gain Aciava's word for that, and maybe he hadn't been telling the truth). But that wasn't what was keeping him back; because wasn't he the man who'd tricked and beaten the fire-stream on the slopes of Poldarn's Forge, duping, conning the mountain into vomiting its burning puke on his best friend's house instead of his own? He knew fire, he had its number and its measure; fire was his pet, it gambolled alongside him like a big, happy dog being taken for a walk. He'd thrown sticks for it to fetch, sent it running down the mountainside onto Eyvind's wood, set it on Eyvind's roof and walls and doors. He was its master, made it work for him, softening steel, obliterating memory in the wrought object, wiping out past deeds and making new ones—

—And if he let it, fire was here now, ready to do his a favour by crisping another old friend, leaching out more memory, dissolving the past and all the horrors that might be trapped there, like flies in amber. If he let Gain Aciava die, he might never know who he'd been.

Fire, crouching in the cherry-red glow of the flash

bronze, grinned at him, wagged its tail. *Let him burn*, it urged him, *just like Eyvind, just like the men you fed me on the mountainside, Scerry and Hending and Barn; just like the crow you burned on the forge in Asburn's smithy. Burn the crow, burn the memory, and be free of them all for ever.*

'Shit,' Poldarn muttered, and looked round for the men he'd seen earlier, the ones who'd brought rope. It took a while for him to explain what he wanted, longer to persuade them to cooperate (but Gain was still there, and the glowing hot metal, waiting for him; it'd have been too easy if the mud had given way while he'd been talking); and then he was gingerly picking his way down the face of the slope, edging by the heat – he could smell his own hair singeing as he passed it – digging his heels in to stop himself slipping forwards or losing his footing and sliding the rest of the way on his bum. I must be crazy, he told himself a dozen times, but he knew it wasn't true; I must be out of my tiny mind, all this to rescue some chancer who's probably just trying to use me in some godawful plot or scheme.

'Gain,' he heard himself whisper (as if he was worried he'd wake the fire; stupid). 'You all right?'

'Get this fucking log off me,' Gain Aciava replied graciously. 'And watch out, for crying out loud, you'll have the whole lot down on us.'

There's gratitude, Poldarn thought, loosening the rope tied round his waist and looping it round and under the log. No way he could lift the bloody thing on his own; an excellent chance that when the men up on top started hauling on the rope, the bank would shift, dislodge the hot bronze, and that'd be an end of it – the last thing he'd hear would probably be Gain Aciava screaming abuse at him: 'You careless, clumsy fucking idiot—'

He raised his hand to signal to the rope men to take the strain. With his other hand he tried to guide, calm, control the log – deluding himself, thinking that'd do any good, because either the bank would come down or it wouldn't. Who did he think he was, some god almighty? As the log shifted, Gain yelled and cursed at him, which suggested that the procedure was causing him pain. Tough. Pain was beside the point, very low priority. After all, Poldarn could feel the skin roasting off his face and hands, and he wasn't making a fuss.

(Eyvind, he thought, in the burning house. And the crow. And rescuing Muno Silsny, whose legs had been broken, but who never cried out once.)

And the log moved slowly away, each bump and knot rasping Gain's broken bone, like a man roughing out a shape in wood. 'You bastard,' Gain was howling at him, 'you're fucking doing this on purpose – I'll kill you. This is just because she chose me, isn't it? It is, you know it is.' And eventually the log slid off his leg with a bump – a moment of sheer terror, because the jolt dislodged a double handful of burnt mud; Poldarn watched it tumble down the slope, observing every detail of its descent. But no more came after, or at least not yet.

'Gain,' he said, 'shut up.' He edged closer, a quarter step and then another, like a shy crab. 'Can you sit up? Can you move at all?' Gain shook his head. Lazy bugger, he's not even trying, expects me to carry him all the way up the bastard slope like a babe in arms. Well, he can forget that. 'Grab my hand,' Poldarn said, reaching out, 'I can't get in close, I'll have to drag you out.'

'Fuck you,' Gain replied.

So Poldarn went in a little closer, and then a little more, until he could get his hand under Gain's armpit and lift— He could feel muscles and tendons coming to grief in his shoulder and back, because that was no way to go lifting heavy weights, any bloody fool knew that. But he carried on with it anyway, and—

'Gain,' he said, 'what did you mean by that? Who chose you instead of me?'

'For fuck's sake,' Gain yelled at him. 'Concentrate on what you're bloody doing.'

'Who was it?' he repeated, because even Gain Aciava (assuming he was a liar) wouldn't tell lies at a moment like this. 'Was it true, what you told me? Was all of it true, or just some of it?'

'You *bastard*, Ciartan. Watch out, you nearly dropped me then.'

Poldarn stopped. If he let him go now, if Gain's intolerable weight slipped through his grip and slumped back into the powder-baked mud, the whole terrible lot would come thundering down on both of them, and somehow that made it fair. 'Tell me the truth, Gain,' he said. 'Were you lying, or not?'

'Of course I wasn't lying, you shit,' Gain said. 'For God's sake, Ciartan, *please*—'

Oh well, Poldarn thought; and with his left hand he snatched at the rope tied round the log. 'Pull,' he shouted, and for a moment he was afraid they couldn't hear him or something; and then the log began to move, pitifully slowly, like an hourly-paid snail. More dirt tumbled down in his face; damn, he thought; never mind, it was worth a try, but then the log gathered pace as the men on the other end hauled and grunted, dragging Poldarn and his vituperative burden through the filthy dirt, across the face of the slope and up—

The bank did give way after all, and the massive blob of heat did go thundering down. But by then, Poldarn was being helped off his knees by the rope-pullers, people were running up, shouting, calling for stuff. Their hands on his skin were sheer torture and he swore at them to leave him alone. Stupid clumsy fucking bastards, they were only trying to help—

'Tell Galand Dev,' Poldarn heard himself say; and he wondered, tell Galand Dev what? What dark and amazing secret had he noticed while he was down there? 'Tell Galand Dev he's an arsehole,' he heard himself say. 'And next time, to dig a bloody pit—'

Later, they told him he was a hero, but he wasn't inclined to believe them.

Much later still, he woke up out of a confused dream that slipped away before he was finished with it, and deduced from memory and the look of the rafters overhead that he was probably in the charcoal store.

Industrial humour, maybe: where else would you put a partially burned foundryman? Or maybe it was the nearest convenient place for a makeshift hospital. He tried to move his head for a more informative scan, but the pain persuaded him to stay where he was and make do with the view of half a dozen dusty rafters.

'Ciartan.' He knew the voice; then realised he knew it from recently: Gain Aciava, the unreliable witness. 'Ciartan, are you awake?'

'Probably. Dreams don't hurt as much. That you, Gain?'

'Yes. Ciartan, what the hell did you go and do that for? Could've killed us both.'

Bastard, Poldarn thought. 'I saved your stupid life, Gain. Or had you forgotten?'

'I hadn't forgotten. Are you all right?'

'I don't know,' Poldarn admitted. 'Am I?'

'I think you got burned up pretty bad,' Gain replied. 'I know I did, and my leg's busted where that prop fell on it. Hauling it across me didn't help much, but I suppose you had to do that. But they've sent for a doctor, from Falcata. He'll be here in a day or so, if the rain holds off.'

'Won't hold my breath, then,' Poldarn replied.

Silence for a while. Then Gain said, 'Ciartan, why did you ask me if I'd been telling the truth? Didn't you believe me?'

'I wasn't sure,' Poldarn replied. 'I mean, I don't know you from a hole in the ground.'

'Fine. Well, in that case, you risked your life for a stranger. I'm impressed.'

For a stranger, Poldarn reflected, I wouldn't have thought twice. 'You make it sound like it was out of character,' he said. 'Was it?'

'Yes,' Gain replied. 'Seems you've changed since Deymeson.'

'Good or bad?'

'Good. Mind you, any change'd have been for the better.' Pause. 'Last time, back at the inn, and afterwards, I got the impression you didn't want me to tell you; you know, stuff about the past. I probably should tell you; in your shoes, I'd rather not know either. Though of course, I wouldn't know that I wouldn't want to know, if you follow me.'

'Sort of,' Poldarn said. 'So in other words I was an evil bastard back then.'

'At Deymeson?' Strange question to ask, Poldarn thought. 'Well, you weren't the most popular boy in the school.'

'Fine,' Poldarn said. 'Who was?'

'No one,' Gain replied. 'It wasn't that kind of set-up. Friendships weren't encouraged, let's say.'

Poldarn wondered, but let it pass. 'Who was it chose you over me?' he asked. 'Was it Copis? Xipho,' he amended.

'Yes. Though that's not strictly true either; I mean, she turned you down flat, but I never got anyplace with her either. Really I only said it to be nasty.'

'Water off a duck's back,' Poldarn replied. 'I can't remember, remember?'

Gain laughed; the sound was familiar, not from recently. From a dream, maybe? 'You can't expect me to think of the finer points when I'm burning to death under a bloody great log,' he said. 'And I don't know why I said it. Just plain terrified, I guess, and lashing out because you were the closest. I do that,' he added.

'Human nature,' Poldarn said. 'So it really was all true, then? I've been wondering. Actually, I've been thinking about it a lot. I thought it might start the ball rolling, so to speak, and then I'd begin remembering things.'

'Did it?'

'Not sure,' Poldarn told him. 'You see, I took your advice, about how to remember my dreams when I wake up.'

'You put crows in them, right?'

Poldarn shrugged. 'Actually,' he said, 'I think the crows were there already; they've always been there in my dreams, since I was a kid. Probably because of all the time I spent trying to keep the horrible things off the growing crops, hence the deep-rooted symbolism or whatever.' He took a deep breath, though it was painful. He'd been burned before, in the forge or getting too close to the hearth, but never like this. He thought about Eyvind, and the crow at Haldersness. 'Back at the inn that time,' he said, 'you seemed to know a lot about me. At least, more than I do. And there's a lot you couldn't possibly know, unless I told you, or I talk in my sleep.'

'You do, actually,' Gain interrupted. 'At least, you always used to, don't know about nowadays. But we could never make out a word of it. Foreign language, or just plain gibberish. We reckoned it must be what they speak over where you came from.'

Poldarn thought about that. 'Figures,' he said. 'All right,' he went on, 'so here we are. Looks like we're going to be here some time.'

'Unless the Falcata doctor kills us,' Gain said. 'I've heard it said that folks over that way are so damned tight that they only go to the doctor when they can't stand the pain any more. So all the doctors have to take other work, to tide them over between terminal cases. Some of them are clerks, some of them run stills or make perfume, some of them are carpenters and joiners – handy with a saw, I guess. Butchers, too, and there's one who's supposed to make a good living in the glue trade, boiling down bones and hides. Doesn't exactly inspire confidence.'

Poldarn hoped that in this instance Gain was lying. 'Hope it rains a lot, then,' he said. 'Meanwhile, we're stuck here, just you and me. I guess you'd better tell me all about it.'

'About what?'

'My life,' Poldarn said. 'I get the feeling it's about time I knew.'

Silence. Then: 'Are you sure?'

'No,' Poldarn confessed. 'But I do know that for the next week or so I'm not going anywhere, so I can't suddenly lose my nerve and run away. Can't even move my hands to cover my ears. I figure it's the only time I'm liable to hold still long enough to hear you out, if I haven't got any choice in the matter.'

'That's not a very good reason.' Gain sounded doubtful.

'Fine. What else are we going to talk about? It'd be crazy to survive all that just to die of boredom.'

Gain laughed. 'You were always a kidder, Ciartan. Nobody laughed much, though, except the Earwig. He thought you were a scream. Must've shared a sense of humour that the rest of us didn't get.'

'Tell me,' Poldarn said.

He counted up to fifteen while he was waiting for Gain to answer. 'All right. But if you want me to stop, just say stop.'

* * *

I first met you (Gain said) on the day before term started, third grade. I'd been back home to see my family, special compassionate leave because my sister was getting married. I ran into you on the road; long story, can't be bothered with it now. But I told you about Deymeson, suggested you might like to come along, see if they'd take you. Actually, I didn't think they would. For one thing, you were too old – you're two years older than me and the rest of us, so at the time you were, what, eighteen, we were sixteen. But either you were young for your age or the other way about; once you'd been there a month or so you'd never have guessed we weren't all the same age.

Well, they started you off in third grade. You had to cram all of grades one and two, it was a hell of a scramble, but you managed it all right. This probably sounds like I'm trying to be funny, but back then you had the most amazing memory; you only had to hear something once and it was in there for good. We all reckoned it was to do with your people all being these thought-readers. That really freaked us out when you told us, by the way, we were all convinced you could see inside our heads, what we were thinking. But you told us you couldn't, and we decided to believe you. Well, it was that or kill you and stash the corpse under the groundsman's shed, and we were only third-graders.

Anyhow, you picked it all up pretty damn quick; the theory side of it, I mean, the bookwork. The practical stuff, drawing and fencing and all, you were a complete natural; I think that's why they gave you a place. Essential religion, see? Someone who can draw that quick by light of nature must be a hundred miles closer to religion than someone who's had to learn it all painfully slow in a drill hall. Anyway, after a few sessions of private coaching you were a match for any of us. You weren't quite the model student, you made mistakes and there was a lot of stuff we all took for granted that you simply didn't know, stuff about the

Empire, how things work here. But you were always a length or two ahead of the rest of us – Xipho excluded, of course. She was top in every damn thing; worked all the time, nose stuck in a book or extra sessions in Hall, hours and hours of practising draws and cuts. Because she was the only girl, you see; not in the whole of Deymeson, but in our class. Put her under pressure to be the best, I assume.

That's beside the point. You were good. You got on well, but truth is, the faculty didn't like you much. Basic stuff, really quite silly. Like, when you first came you had this weird accent you could have spread on new bread, and they didn't like that. Couldn't place it, for one thing, which drove them nuts. Being you, of course, you got rid of the accent in about two weeks; but they remembered even after you'd learned to talk normally. There were other things too. Attitude was a big one. There again, you were pretty quick to learn how not to get people's backs up, but even so they remembered you as the snotty kid, the one who always knew best and answered back. And I think how fast you picked things up spooked them a bit. I remember eaves-dropping when Father Tutor was talking about you to one of the others; he said it wasn't like you were learning at all, more like you knew it all already and it'd temporarily slipped your mind, and all they were doing was jogging your memory.

Yes, straight up, that's what he said – maybe not word for word, but the general idea, anyway. And now you mention it, the other one, I think it was one of the research fellows; anyhow, when Father Tutor said that, he went a funny colour and changed the subject double quick. That's stuck in my mind, because he took it so big.

So anyway, that's how you were in those days. Smart, no two ways about it, but not the teacher's pet, and not Mister Popularity. Don't get the wrong idea, the rest of us didn't hate you or anything. But it was a strange set-up at

Deymeson, because of the year-ends. You know about them, don't you?

Well, it's very simple. At the end of each year there were tests: loads of written and oral tests on theory, but what really mattered was the practical, because that was when we all lined up in Hall and Father Tutor announced who was paired with who. And we were all holding our breath, because the test was drawing and cutting, sharps not foils. If you were still alive at the end, you went up a grade. Coming second earned you a rectangular hole and a wooden box.

You bet it was a crazy system, and the gods only know what prompted people to send their kids there. I mean to say, how could you do that, pack your own kid off at the start of the year knowing he only had a fifty-fifty chance of coming back? And to keep on doing that, every year for six years. But my parents, the gods forgive them, they were up for it; in fact, my dad sold a third of the fields and half the herd to keep me there, and he was so proud, the day they wrote to say I'd got a place. I can't understand people.

So anyway, that's why friendship was something of a vexed issue. We never used to talk about it; it was understood, somehow. It's amazing how quickly kids can get a handle on difficult stuff like that, where grown-ups would talk and talk for years and never get close to coming to terms with it. Mostly we put it at the back of our minds; like, we never forgot about it entirely, but we found a way of living in spite of it. You can't stop kids making friends, like you can't stop beans climbing beanpoles. But all the other kids in the world, they've got friends and they've got a best friend. Not at Deymeson. Instead there were gangs, I suppose you could call them that, or clubs, or whatever. Ours was the Crow's Head Gang; you chose the name, after a carving on top of a pillar we always stood under in Chapter. You always did have this thing about crows. Point is, it wasn't like other kids' gangs, where A is best friends with B, good friends with C and D, gets on all right with E,F,G and H, doesn't really like I and J much but puts up with them because J's best friends with C – well, you get the idea. In the Crow's Head, we were all friends with each other equally, or at least that was the theory. That way, come year-end, it wouldn't be so hard . . .

What screwed that up, of course, was having Xipho in the class. There were, what, a couple of dozen girls in the grades at Deymeson, compared with a couple of hundred boys. Bad news. I swear, I'm sure they only arranged it that way to cause trouble, because anything that made life more difficult was good for our education. And, inevitably, at any given time out of those two dozen you'd get ten sluts, ten ice maidens, a couple who didn't like boys, if you get my meaning, and two who somehow managed to stay just about normal. Looking back, I feel sorry for them. It must've been hell on earth for a girl at Deymeson.

Xipho – well, she was the iciest of them all. God help you if you tried it on with her; and you did and so did I, and so did every poor fool, and all of us thinking at the back of his mind about year-end, and getting the brush-off, reckoning, well, probably for the best. Except you; maybe because you were from outside, you hadn't had time to think about it like we had, or – well, you were always different anyhow. But you kept on and on at her, it was quite embarrassing at times; and Xipho – Xipho didn't like you at all. I mean, no one ever knew what she was thinking, so when she told someone to get lost, they'd be thinking, Maybe she really likes me a lot, but she can't handle the thought of year-end, so that's why. But not in your case. Even if everything had been normal, like on the outside, she'd never have touched you with a ten-foot pole, unless maybe it had a sharp point on the end. And you could never see that. Strange, for someone who could read minds. Or maybe you just liked really, really difficult challenges.

About year-ends. First year you were there, they put you up against a kid from Thurm who lasted what we called a moment-in-religion, which means no time at all. That was all right, because he wasn't one of us, and nobody much liked him anyway. The next year was very strange. Father Tutor – he was a mean old bastard, no two ways about that, and he'd noticed that the Earwig was a special pal of yours. That's not quite right; he liked you, but you didn't like him or dislike him, he was just one of the crowd as far as you were concerned. Anyway, it was an interesting match, because you two and Xipho were far and away the quickest in the whole grade. Honest, I never saw the like. Year-end practicals usually lasted about as long as a sneeze, but you two were hacking and bashing away for several minutes before Father Tutor called it off and said you'd both passed. He was really pissed off, by the way, but he didn't have a choice. Maybe it was because he was so upset about it; anyhow, the year after that, he matched you with Turvo, Prince Tazencius's only son, and that had to be sheer spite, since you'd just got engaged to Turvo's kid sister.

'What happened?' Poldarn asked.

Gain laughed. 'I'm telling you, if you pissed off Father Tutor the previous year, it was nothing compared with that time. Bloody impressive show, though; got to hand it to you for that.'

Poldarn's throat was dry. 'What happened?' he repeated. 'Did I kill him?'

'Did you hell as like. At the moment of the draw, you did this little shuffle – quick as lightning, it was too fast for me to follow, but apparently as you drew, you also side-stepped through about sixty degrees, so Turvo's draw just cut air, and instead of yours slicing through his neck, all you did was cut him to the bone. Didn't even cut through an artery, though whether that was skill or luck I don't know and you presumably can't remember. Saved his life, though; poor bugger lost the use of his right hand, but neither of you got killed. Even the prince had to admit you'd done really well by him and his son. Lysalis – that's Turvo's sister, your girlfriend – she was all over you, reckoned you were fantastic risking your neck to protect her brother. Old Turvo wasn't exactly thrilled about it, him being left a cripple and made a fool out of, but that didn't matter in the long run.'

Poldarn frowned. 'What's that supposed to mean?'

'Oh, he died anyway,' Gain replied. 'But that's another story – remind me to tell you about it sometime. Anyway, that's the epic tale of you and Turvo, and how you outsmarted Father Tutor two years in a row. We were all dead impressed, except we reckoned you were probably too clever to live. Xipho was hopping mad, though. She'd been hoping Turvo'd do you.'

Poldarn couldn't help shuddering a little. He thought of her in the ruins of Deymeson, when she'd drawn a sword on him and he'd batted it away. Of course, he hadn't known at the time that she was one of the three best fencers in their year—

'Was there another year after that?' he asked quietly.

'Of course. And typical, you saved the best till last. But we're skipping ahead; unless you don't want to hear the bits in between.'

Like I just told you (Gain went on) you hadn't exactly endeared yourself to Father Tutor, what with one thing or another. We all reckoned he'd either get you killed or he was training you specially for some very exalted and important job, probably a suicide mission. He had this thing about suicide missions, Father Tutor, seemed to feel they were a very useful and efficient way of getting things done.

You, on the other hand – well, you rather got it up your nose after the Turvo thing, reckoned you were very much the gods' gift to applied religion. Maybe you were trying to impress Xipho; I've got to say, getting engaged to Turvo's sister didn't seem to have any effect on you as far as besieging her citadel was concerned, and we couldn't make that out at all; because Xipho was, frankly, nice-enough-looking in her way but a bit on the stringy side even then, while Lysalis was an absolute honeypot, and talk about besotted— None of us could figure why you didn't pack in religion as soon as the two of you got engaged. After all, you'd only joined up because you had nothing better to do, it wasn't like you had faith or any of that crap; and there was Tazencius, practically begging to be allowed to set you up in a nice little command or governorship somewhere, no work, palace, posh clothes, nice food, no more fleas in the blankets. But no, you were dead set on finishing the course; and that made no sense, because naturally there's no such thing as a married monk, so you couldn't have made a career in the Order. We all reckoned it was because of Xipho: you weren't going to quit until you'd settled your score with her. I have no idea if that's how it was, and you can't tell me, needless to say. Pity, really, I'd love to know what was going on there.

And now I guess I'd better tell you about Elaos Tanwar. You may not like this bit. If you want me to stop, just say.

No? Fine. Elaos Tanwar – well, you've probably gathered by now we were an odd lot, all of us, and the Crow's Headers more than most. But Elaos – he was as near normal, I guess you could call it, as anybody could be at Deymeson. He was mostly straight down the middle, reliable, loyal, said what he thought, tried to be nice whenever he could; if he was on your side you were glad of it. We all liked him. I don't mean we were all his friends, because we were all each others' friends. I mean we actually liked him,

thought he was a good sort. He had his faults, but not that
many and not that bad. At Deymeson, that practically
made him a saint.

One day in sixth grade, Elaos was sitting in the common
room just after chapter. We had a study period, no lectures;
Xipho was fooling about reading up for some tutorial or
other, the rest of us were just hanging around, like you do.
You weren't there. But Elaos was just sitting on his own,
didn't want to talk, face like a failed harvest; and that wasn't
like him. His face was his title-page, like we used to say;
his expression told you exactly what was going on inside
his head, no messing, and on this occasion he looked
depressed and worried, which was very rare with him – he
was usually a fairly cheerful type. So, naturally, we all clus-
tered round and asked him what the matter was.

First off he just told us to go away, leave him be; but we
weren't having that, goes without saying. So eventually we
forced it out of him. He'd heard something that had got
him puzzled and worried and upset, and he didn't know
what to do for the best. And he hadn't said anything to us,
he went on, because it was something to do with one of
us. In short, you.

Elaos came from some little place in the Bohec valley;
nowhere you'd have heard of, I can't remember the name.
His dad was what passed for a big-time merchant in those
parts, pretty small fry by Torcea standards but a slice above
clod-busting. Well, you must know by now that the Bohec
valley was where the raiders had been very busy for many
years, to the point where it was getting completely out of
hand – cities burned down, people slaughtered wholesale,
Imperial armies wiped out, all that. Over the last couple of
years, though, it'd all got a whole lot worse, and people
were starting to wonder if the raiders hadn't somehow got
themselves a new source of information; because whereas
before they'd mostly just blundered about, hacking down

anybody who was dumb enough not to have got out of the way in time, now they seemed to know all the useful stuff well in advance, they were going straight to where the pickings were best, sidestepping Imperial forces, suddenly appearing out of nowhere, using roads that weren't on maps, that only the locals knew about. But the objection to that was, what kind of maniac would collaborate with *them*, for the gods' sakes; and even if there was someone sick enough to be prepared to do it, how was it physically possible, since nobody knew a damn thing about them, knew where they came from, spoke their language, even. It'd be impossible, like a human being collaborating with locusts or crows.

But Elaos reckoned there was a traitor, and what's more, he knew who it was. Not to put too fine a point on it, you.

'Me?'

Short pause, silence; except that outside somewhere, someone was driving posts into the ground with a post-rammer – slow, regular thumps like a heartbeat.

'We were pretty taken aback too,' Gain said at last. 'You can tell how knocked sideways we were by the fact that nobody screamed and shouted or told Elaos he was crazy or anything like that. Just stood there gawping, while he started to point out the evidence: you came from a strange place far away that none of us even knew existed; in your sleep you spoke in a weird language none of us recognised; you'd said yourself that, as far as you knew, you were the only person from your country in the whole Empire. As for practicalities – all the big attacks were in the Bohec and Mahec valleys, and Deymeson's right in the middle of the area where the attacks were taking place; the Order had the best information-gathering resources in the Empire, all you'd have to do would be to sneak up to the Map Gallery at night, pick the lock and look around, and you'd see at a glance where all the Imperial troops were stationed, which ones were out in the field, exactly where they were at and where they were headed. Nobody outside the order or the military could find out that kind of stuff – and even inside the service, only the top brass on the general staff had access to it. So you see, you had the means; and if, as we guessed, your mysterious people were the raiders, you surely had a motive. As for opportunity – well, there's messengers leaving Deymeson and going in all directions every day, nothing easier than to slip in a note of your own, tell the rider it's a message to your girl back home who the cruel faculty wouldn't let you write to. Or maybe one of their people came round the back door pretending to be a bum begging scraps. Don't ask me; but you were always the smart, imaginative one, really hot at Expediencies. You'd have found a way—'

'But hold on,' Poldarn interrupted. 'This stuff is all – what's the word? – circumstantial. I thought you meant there were witnesses or something.'

'Just let me tell the story, all right?' Gain complained. 'But you're right, and that on its own wouldn't have set Elaos thinking, because he wasn't that sort, seeing plots and conspiracies everywhere. And there was something else, too,' Gain went on. 'You and Lysatis, not killing Turvo, all that. Elaos asked us, he said how come a scruff like you – offcomer, no family, no money – how come a prince of the blood like Tazencius was letting you marry his daughter. Never mind giving his consent; you'd have thought he'd have had you strung up from a tree just for looking at her. But no, you asked for her and you got her – and then, instead of the big wedding the very next day, before he's had a chance to change his mind, you're still here, still training to be a monk, still drooling round after Xipho.'

'All right,' Poldarn said. 'So what's your point?'

'Not mine,' Gain said. 'Elaos's point. He said, what if

Tazencius is in league with the raiders, and you're the link, the contact man? And before you ask, we asked it too – why the hell would Tazencius do that? But Elaos had an answer to that; he said, suppose Tazencius is ambitious, wants to be Emperor; but he's too far down the list to get his chance – unless something happens. Like maybe the raiders become a major threat, and Tazencius defeats them, becomes the popular hero with an army devoted to him, prepared to follow him if he marches on Torcea? Or maybe he's planning to use the raiders to take Torcea for him. Or there's his feud with General Cronan; was that genuine or just a blind? Was he in with Cronan – he supplies the big threat, then sets the scene for Cronan to win a big victory, and Cronan takes over, instals Tazencius as Emperor, they share the cake between them? There were any number of possible reasons, he said.'

'Speculation,' Poldarn broke in. 'Drivel. No evidence—'

'Let me finish, for the gods' sakes,' Gain said. 'Actually, Elaos said exactly the same thing when we all started raising the same objections. He'd told us all that, he said, just so we'd take him seriously when he spoke about what he'd seen and heard; otherwise we'd all think he was nuts, seeing things, or making it up out of spite.'

They'd stopped driving posts, at any rate. The only sound apart from Gain's voice was rain on the roof. They won't be able to pour in the rain, Poldarn thought absently. Water dropping on molten bronze is very bad news indeed. 'Go on,' he said.

'Here's what Elaos told us,' Gain continued. 'He said that one morning, early, before Prime, he'd got up because of a stomach bug, couldn't get back to sleep; so he walked down as far as the sally-port in the back eastern wall. He was sitting in the crook of the old fallen-down watchtower there – you could lurk up there and have a grand view over the wall, be able to hear someone talking through the sally-port, and they'd never guess there was anybody there. Anyhow, he said that he heard you, talking to someone; so he scriggled round until he could see. There you were. The sally-port gate was half open; outside there were a man and a woman sitting in a cart, with their hoods drawn right down over their faces, and that's who you were talking to. And there in the cart, at the man's feet, he could distinctly see a raider backsabre.'

Rain on the roof; no chance of the doctor coming out from Falcata while it was raining, the roads'd be a quagmire.

'Well,' Gain was saying. 'Everybody knows, the only people who carry those things are raiders; apart from them, nobody's got one. People said that there were only maybe a dozen in the whole Empire, and they were all in Torcea, at the palace or GHQ. Peasants in carts didn't carry them around for splitting firewood. Also, Elaos said, you were talking to these two in that strange weird language you used when you talked in your sleep, and they were using it too. Inference: the couple in the cart were scouts from a raider army, and you were briefing them. Not much on its own, maybe; but put it together with all that circumstantial stuff— He wasn't saying it was proof, he added, or anything like it; but it raised a question, was all, and until he got an answer that convinced him there was an innocent explanation, he was worried. Like, should he tell Father Tutor about it?'

'So,' Poldarn said. 'What did you all decide?'

'We didn't,' Gain said. 'Like I told you, it was way too much for us all to take on board. We couldn't actually bring ourselves to believe it, but we couldn't disprove it. Upshot was, we decided we'd all think it over, and have a meeting in a week's time, reach a decision then.'

'Fine,' Poldarn said, more than a little angry. 'And what did you decide at your grand meeting?'

'Never happened,' Gain said. 'Because the very next day, Elaos was found up in the same place, the old tower by the sally-port, with his neck sliced open.'

Oh, Poldarn thought. So did Gain trace me here to kill me? 'Was that me?' he asked. 'Did I do it?'

Pause. 'And a couple of hours later,' Gain went on, in a completely neutral voice, 'Father Abbot called a special emergency chapter, told everybody what'd happened, and said that the murderer had been caught and the matter was closed.'

'Not me, then?'

'You were at chapter with the rest of us,' Gain said.

'And did he explain what'd happened, why Elaos was killed?'

'No.' Gain's voice had become slightly brittle. 'The matter was closed, that's all he said. And we all wanted to believe him, of course. We wanted it to be outsiders – robbers or some wandering lunatic, someone who was nothing to do with us. It was very strange,' Gain went on. 'Elaos getting killed – well, if he'd died at year-end, that wouldn't have been a problem, we'd just have put him out of our minds, pretended he'd never existed. We'd learned how to handle that sort of thing, goes without saying. You had to, at Deymeson, or the place wouldn't have been able to keep going. But there's a huge difference between – well, failing an exam, and being murdered. That's the difference malice makes, malice or desperation or just sheer indifference, like where someone's murdered simply because he's inconvenient, in the way of some grand plan. Indifference is the scariest of the lot, believe me.'

Poldarn was silent for a moment. 'You didn't answer my question,' he said. 'Was it me? Did I kill him?'

'I don't know,' Gain replied without emotion. 'It's possible. Or else someone else killed him to protect you – and if so, you may have known about it in advance, or not. We didn't know; what's more, we didn't want to. Really didn't want to. You of all people can understand that, can't you?' Gain sighed. 'I'm sorry,' he said, 'but I'm feeling really tired now. I've got to get some sleep. I'll tell you the rest some other time.'

Poldarn lay awake long after Gain's breathing had fallen into the long, slow rhythm of sleep. As if in a court of law, he tried arguing a wide range of defences, each one of them further or in the alternative: Gain was lying; Gain was only telling part of the truth; Gain was lying about the murder; Gain was telling the truth about the murder but lying about betraying the cities to the raiders; Gain was telling the truth about betraying the cities (and it wasn't betraying, because they weren't Poldarn's people; the raiders were. You can't be a traitor if you betray the enemy – can you?) but lying about the murder. Elaos Tanwar had been murdered, but not Poldarn; or not for that reason. It was self-defence; or Tanwar had made up the story about him betraying the cities, and killing him was justified revenge. Or he'd done it, but only on the orders of Father Abbot, or Father Tutor, because Elaos Tanwar was the real traitor. So many possibilities, plausible alternatives; wasn't it perverse instinctively to believe in the one that showed himself up in the worst light? Besides; he'd taken a lot of lives, to his certain, recent knowledge. He'd killed soldiers, civilians, enemies, friends; just recently, he'd killed a kid less than half his age, in self-defence, there being no other way. He'd killed Eyvind's friend, that first time they'd met, on the road; he'd killed Eyvind. So what was one more death at his hands more or less? Might as well blame the scythe for chopping the necks of corn.

Eventually he drifted into sleep; and there was a crow—

There was a crow looking down at him from the top of a pillar; but it was only a carving, a mason's memory of a crow trapped in stone, like a fly in amber.

He was in the chapter house, but he was alone, just him and the crow. He was waiting for someone. The someone was late, maybe not coming at all. He wasn't pleased about that. It hadn't been easy getting there without being seen, and any minute the doors might open, someone else might come in, see him there, ask what he thought he was doing. He had no right to be there, it was against the rules—

As if that mattered; as if losing ten house points or getting detention mattered when blood had been shed (and all his fault, if he cared to look at it from that perspective). He didn't even have to stay here any longer; any day now, and he'd be out—

She came in through the small low door from the vestry, not the main doors as he'd been expecting. Typical Xipho, planning every entrance, figuring out the optimum strategic advantage, balanced against the acceptable and unacceptable risks. She treated life as extra tuition for core syllabus subjects.

She looked at him sourly. 'Melodrama,' she said. 'With you, everything's got to be a bloody performance. So, what do you want?'

'I needed to talk,' he said.

'Fine. Go ahead.'

'Xipho.' He felt like he wanted to be sick. 'I didn't kill him. Elaos. It wasn't me.'

'Well, of course it wasn't,' she replied. 'Father Abbot said so. Matter closed.'

'Yes,' he insisted, 'but is that what you believe?'

She looked into his eyes before answering. 'I don't have an opinion on the subject,' she said.

That made him angry. 'Of course you do,' he said. 'You've got an opinion on everything.'

'If you say so.'

Precepts of religion; the best fight is not to fight. 'Please,

Xipho,' he heard himself say. 'Even if you think I did it, that'd be better than this.'

'Are you saying you did it?'

'No.'

'All right, then,' she said. 'Matter closed. Was that it, or did you want me for anything else?'

He shook his head. 'You don't believe me,' he said. 'You wouldn't be acting like this if you believed me.'

'I told you,' she said, 'I haven't got an opinion, and I don't believe anything. That's why we have doctrine, so we don't have to believe in every single bloody thing. Father Abbot says the matter's closed, which means that even if you confessed, even if you showed me a sword with blood on it, I wouldn't have an opinion. Do you understand that, or have you completely wasted the time you've spent here?'

He looked at her for a moment. 'You think I killed him,' he said. 'You think I killed him and Father Abbot either approved or he's got some reason for not doing anything about it. Bloody hell, Xipho, he was our *friend*.'

'No friends in religion,' Xipho replied. 'Against the rules.'

There was something about the way she'd said it. 'If I didn't kill him,' he said quietly, 'maybe I've got an idea who did.'

'That's an interesting choice of words,' Xipho said. 'Look, I'm sorry but I've got work to do. I thought you wanted to see me about something *urgent*. Not something that no longer exists.'

She walked out, not looking back. He sat staring at the door she'd gone through for a while, as if it was somehow to blame for the use it had been put to; then he stood up and followed. Instead of taking the north cloister, however, he turned east, past the stairs that led to the tower where Elaos Tanwar had died, until he came to a small door. He wasn't supposed to know what was behind it, and he wasn't supposed to be able to get through it. But a small piece of wire passed through a crack where one of the panels had shrunk with age was enough to lift the latch on the other side. He pushed it open and shut it quickly behind him.

He'd known about this place for some time, ever since he'd overheard a conversation in the porter's lodge between the senior porter and a large, round, well-dressed man who'd arrived on the box of a large cart. The round man's name, he'd learned as he eavesdropped, pretending to check his pigeonhole for messages, was Potto Ulrec, a button merchant from Sansory, and he'd come to collect something: a large, bulky consignment that was going to prove awkward to shift and load, especially with Potto's trick shoulder playing him up again. The senior porter had taken pity on him or was more than usually anxious to rid his lodge of unseemliness, so he'd sent one of the junior porters to help Potto with whatever it was he was collecting. For some reason, Ciartan had been intrigued enough to follow unobtrusively. On the way, the junior porter had made a detour to the small yard behind the tool store at the back of the east quadrangle, and had picked up a fair-sized wheelbarrow. He had trouble keeping up with Potto Ulrec, who was clearly in a hurry.

And so they'd come to this door. The junior porter had been entrusted with the key, a huge lump of iron on a long loop of string, which he'd hung round his neck. He unlocked the door, but then stood back, as though unwilling to enter. Potto gave him a mildly scornful look and went past him through the doorway. A few moments later he came out again, his arms laden with a substantial heap of bones.

Leg bones mostly; some arms. He stacked them neatly in the wheelbarrow, the way Ciartan used to pile lopped branchwood back home, so as not to waste space in the bed of the barrow. When he went back in, the porter looked away with a nauseated expression on his face. It took Potto four trips to fill the barrow; once or twice he'd stop, go back, pick out a leg or an arm that somehow wasn't suitable and take it back in with him. Ciartan remembered wondering what on earth he wanted with a load of old bones, and where they'd all come from. When the barrow was full – overfilled by the look of it, with femurs and tibiae balanced on top of the load, wobbling ominously as the porter lifted the handles – Potto pushed the door to and followed the porter back in the direction of the lodge.

Deductions: well, for one thing Potto was buying these bones by the barrowload, hence his anxiety to cram in as much as possible; and of course they made bottons out of bone, and Potto was a button-maker. Beyond that, however, it was a mystery; and it stayed that way for a long time, until one day Elaos and Cordo had been talking about something, while they were all hanging about in Hall waiting for a class to begin, and somehow the conversation had come round to how the Order disposed of the remains of students who'd failed their year-end practicals. Cordo was saying how he'd sneaked out to look at the graveyard out back, and how he'd done a few sums, and there simply wasn't room in the burial plot for more than five or six years' worth of dead novices; and Elaos had replied, well, of course not; they only leave them in there for a few years, long enough to compost down nicely, and then they dig them up again, bleach the bones and store them in the ossiary—

Memories of memories, recalled in dreams; and here he was (in the place where novices weren't supposed to go but where most of them ended up anyhow). A large place, like a vault, with a high roof, plain, the air musty, the smell not very nice. Very much like a woodshed, with the bones all carefully stacked to make the best use of the space available: against one wall a tall heap of legs; on the other side, arms, ribcages, pelvises; in the middle a pyramid of skulls, all facing the same way, like a good display of turnips in the grocery market down in the lower town; fat oak-staved barrels full of finger and toe joints. The most efficient way to break down and store what remained of the human body after everything that could be stripped out was gone; no way to tell one person's bones apart from another's or figure out which arm had gone in which socket, which skull had once fitted on which spine. All memory purged; nothing left but basics, components, scrap, the raw materials for the celebrated Potto range of buttons for all occasions.

(He wondered: if I was a god, do you think I could piece all these bits back together again, bodge up a new race of men and women to populate some derelict world somewhere? Like a faker, a dishonest tradesman; sling them back together again any old how, smear on a bit of flesh and a coat of skin, hair, eyes, pass them off as genuine human beings? What would come of that, he wondered: a head from one life grafted onto a neck from another, a farmer's hands on a blacksmith's arms slotted into a monk's shoulders, capped off with the head of a soldier and the legs of a charcoal-burner. Poor bloody fool wouldn't know what day of the week it was—)

And here he was again. He stood for a while looking at the racks and rows and stacks, then knelt down and picked something up off the floor: a sword, a raider backsabre, its blade crusted with rust and dried blood. He gave it a cursory examination, then slipped off his cloak, wrapped the sword up in a bundle, tucked it under his arm—

He woke up abruptly. 'Gain?' he called out. No reply. Well, Aciava was probably asleep. 'Gain? Wake up, will you, I need to ask you something.'

Still no reply; but he heard a door creak open, then shut. 'What're you making that racket for?'

He recognised the voice but couldn't put a name to it (a
stack of voices on one side of the room, names on the other).
Some foundryman.

'Sorry,' he said. 'Is he asleep?'

'Is who asleep?'

'Gain. The other bloke, in the other bed there.'

The stranger laughed. 'He's gone, mate. No, not dead,'
he added. 'He's been moved out – orders. Cart rolled up
an hour or so ago. Soldiers. They took him off somewhere.'

Chapter Nine

According to Galand Dev, it was foolproof. Nothing could possibly go wrong – which was just as well, considering how far behind schedule they were, and how ghastly and terrible the news was from outside. He wouldn't explain the last part of that, but the name Feron Amathy featured prominently in all the rumours; the Amathy house was on the move, had openly declared war on the government, had crossed the bay with an enormous army, had stormed Torcea with horrendous loss of life, was besieging the Emperor in the palace, depending on who you listened to and how long you managed to keep your attention from wandering.

Galand Dev, with Spenno's highly qualified approval, had designed a new furnace. There was a deep pit, in which the mould, properly baked and cured, stood on its end. The pit was lined with two courses of brick, so that the heat from the filled moulds wouldn't dry out the earth and cause a cave-in; the props were thick iron posts, not timber. Over the pit they'd built a tall crane, to lower the moulds and hold them while they were being aligned. Once the moulds were in place, the pit was filled up with handspan-thick layers of slightly damp earth, tamped down with bronze weights (gently heated so the earth wouldn't stick to them) until it was compressed to the point where it was hard work to stick a knife blade into it further than an inch. Each layer was topped off with an inch-depth of potsherds. All this had to be done quickly, so that the damp from the earth wouldn't seep into the bone-dry moulds and spoil them, so everybody took a hand – even Brigadier Muno and his immaculately dressed staff, who made a point of kneeling on sacks to save the knees of their trousers from irreversible ruin.

The furnace itself was a tall brick tower with a ground-level square opening on one side. The firebox, packed with alternating layers of charcoal and cordwood (elm, birch, and beechwood only), was under the furnace floor. Ten double-action bellows, each made from four full hides, blasted up through, forcing the flame through the firehole into the furnace chamber (circular, nine feet across, flat-bottomed), where it played on the carefully proportioned mixture of scrap and virgin bronze – nine parts copper, one part tin – from all sides, to ensure an even, pure melt. To prepare the furnace for the first melt it had been charged and fired and left to burn gently for three days, to dry out the fireclay without risk of cracking. Galand Dev reckoned it would handle ten tons of bronze easily, twelve at a pinch. When the melt was perfect – after three fluxings and skimmings to draw off the slag; when a pine log thrown onto the surface floated, with no bubbles coming up through the glowing yellow pool, until it burned away to cinders, which spat up from the meniscus with no bronze clinging to them (essential, according to Spenno and his book), and when a greenish-white cloud rose off the melt and hung a few inches above the surface – a weir in the furnace wall could be drawn open and the molten bronze allowed to flow down the shallow incline of a brick-and-clay race (carefully heated by a long bed of glowing coals raked out from the furnace) that fed the in-gate of the mould. In theory, according to Galand Dev. Assuming it didn't rain once the furnace was running, in which case the whole thing would probably blow up.

The entire workforce had been toiling day and night to get it built. Now it was finished, dressed, dried, cured, fettled, and for some reason nobody was in any hurry to try it out. Spenno was sitting on a barrel next to the mould pit, staring up at the lead-grey clouds, as if willing it to start raining. Galand Dev was rumoured to be confined to the latrines by a severe case of terror, with Brigadier Muno standing over him demanding to know if he was done yet. Messengers from Falcata and Torcea were arriving practically on the hour with furious demands for progress reports. Fifty tons of new charcoal had come in from the colliers' camp (but there was nowhere to put it, so they'd shovelled it off their carts into a huge pile in the middle of the yard and left it there). Scouts sent out at dawn rode in at noon to say it was raining at Ang Chirra but sunny and warm at Tin, and the wind was either northerly, southerly, easterly or westerly, depending on who you chose to believe.

'Pity you aren't fit to be up and about yet,' Chiruwa was saying. 'You'll miss the fun.'

Poldarn looked at him. 'What, you mean when it starts pissing it down once the furnace is at full heat, and the whole lot goes up? I think I'd rather be in here, thanks.'

Chiruwa shrugged. 'They're talking about roofing it over,' he said, 'only they're worried that with all that heat going up, the roof'd catch fire and come down on the pit. Makes you wonder, actually, whose bright idea it was to do all this in the wettest place in the empire, in the rainy season.'

'There'll have been a good reason,' Poldarn replied. 'You've got to have faith, that's all.' And the matter is closed, he thought, and I have no opinion on it.

'Maybe,' Chiruwa said. 'Here, did you ever find out what became of that bloke, the one you pulled out of the cave-in? He was in here with you, and then he left.'

'I was hoping you could tell me,' Poldarn replied.

Chiruwa shook his head. 'Friend of yours, was he?'

'I knew him years ago,' Poldarn said, wondering if he was telling the truth. 'I wouldn't call him a friend, though. Just someone I knew.'

'You risked your neck getting him out of there, though,' Chiruwa said. 'Bloody impressive, that was. I wouldn't have done it. Got more sense.'

'I never said I was intelligent,' Poldarn replied. 'Any idea when I'm likely to be getting out of here? They were supposed to be fetching a doctor from Falcata, but nobody's said anything.'

'Roads are still bad,' Chiruwa told him, 'though all these messengers from the army and the bosses over to Torcea don't seem to be having much trouble getting through. You're looking better, I must say. You were a right bloody mess when they fished you out of there. Mind, if I were you I wouldn't count on winning any beauty contests from now on, and pulling birds is going to be a problem, unless they're blind.'

'I was wondering about that,' Poldarn said mildly. 'They said my face got a bit scorched—'

'Trying not to worry you, I expect,' Chiruwa said. 'Next time I come visiting, I'll fetch along a mirror or something. I mean, a bloke's got a right to know.'

On that cheerful note, he left and went back to work; they were going to dress out the mould one more time, just to be on the safe side. Poldarn lay still for a while, then reached out and felt for his book, *Concerning Various*

Matters. There wasn't really enough light in the shed, so he could only read for a short while before his head began to hurt; even so, he was three-quarters of the way through. It was very hard going, most of it about things that didn't interest him in the least.

He found his place. He'd just finished *reaping machine, to build*; a bizarre contraption involving long, sharp blades attached to the spokes of an enormous wheel, driven through a gear-train by four oxen on a treadmill. He hoped very much that nobody had ever tried to build one; it sounded rather more dangerous than a squadron of attacking cavalry.

Recurrence, eternal. He frowned. Even harder going than the designs for labour-saving devices were the philosophical and religious bits, and he considered skipping ahead to *red spot, on cabbages, to eradicate*. But he had nothing better to do, and there was a reasonable chance that *recurrence, eternal* might send him off to sleep.

Recurrence, eternal, he read. *It is a precept of religion that nothing happens for the first time; that all learning is recollection; that the perfect draw is perfect because it has already taken place*. Oh for pity's sake, Poldarn thought, but he carried on reading anyway. *The argument runs that in religion everything progresses to a state of perfection (q.v.) in which further improvement is impossible, whereas outside of religion everything tends to a state of dissolution, in which no further deterioration or decay is possible, e.g. decomposition of organic material, erosion of rock into dust, reduction by fire of solid material to smoke and ash; the two final states, perfection and dissolution, being parallel and essentially the same in nature, though not in form or quality. Religion predicates that, since the world is over five thousand years old (see* gods, origin of; world, age of; creation, history of*), inevitably both processes – progress and decline – must by now have run their full course and be complete, in which case it necessarily* *follows that the material world as we encounter it is made up of the end products of said processes, namely religion (the perfected state) and that which is outside religion (the declined state, chaos) and that all human experience is therefore merely recollection of incidents that have occurred during the course of one of the two said processes, remembered out of context, as if in a vision, hallucination, prophesy, nightmare or dream. This conclusion is expressed in religion in the form of the divine Poldarn, who will return at the end of all things – which has, of course, already taken place at some unspecified point in the past – to destroy the world and replace it with perfection (namely the state of affairs currently pertaining, i.e. in religion). In applied religion, perfection is expressed in the draw, where constant repetition during training and practice eliminates the act of drawing in the moment at which the intention is formed, so that the sword has already left the scabbard as soon as the hand moves towards it. In observed religion (see* ethics, applied) *the process of dissolution is expressed in the reduction of materials, e.g. by rotting, weathering, burning, and the process of perfection is expressed as surviving that of dissolution in the perfection of reduced materials, e.g. by fire, e.g. sand to glass, wood to charcoal, ore to metal; essential religion is expressed in the salvation of reduced materials, e.g. scrap reshaped into new objects; the latter giving rise to the so-called essential paradox, whereby salvation can only occur where memory is destroyed in salvaged materials (i.e. when they lose their old shape and are given a new one), the paradox being that the superior or religious process of perfection is thus observed to follow and be dependent upon the inferior or secular process of destruction. This paradox is most usually expressed in the image of the burned scavenger.*

Poldarn wasn't quite sure he followed that, but he couldn't be bothered to go back and read it again; if Spenno spent all his time reading this idiotic book, he thought, no wonder he's barking mad. He turned down the corner of the page and put the book where he could reach it again once his head had stopped hurting.

It hadn't done its job, in any case; he'd only bothered with it in the hope that it'd distract his mind from going over once again what Gain Aciava had told him, and the snatches of what he assumed were memories that stayed with him when he woke up from dreams. As for Gain Aciava himself, whisked away in a cart by soldiers – arrested? Recalled? Rescued?

I'd run away, Poldarn thought, if only they'd let me up out of this bed.

The very least of his concerns was missing the inaugural melt and pour of Galand Dev's utterly foolproof new furnace; but Chiruwa came by a certain time later (how long, Poldarn had no idea; days passed, and he'd long since lost track of them) with the latest news. A fifteen-inch crack had appeared in the firebox wall; the prime suspect was non-homogeneous clay, but birchwood charcoal was also under suspicion. Galand Dev and Spenno had almost but not quite come to blows over the question of whether it could be salvaged or whether they'd have to tear the whole thing down and start again.

A certain time after that, Banspati the foreman came to see him.

'What're you doing still in bed?' he demanded. 'You look just fine to me.'

'Oh,' Poldarn replied. 'That's good. Does that mean I can get up?'

Banspati thought for a moment. 'They were supposed to be getting a doctor in from Falcata,' he said, 'but I don't know what became of that idea. Do you feel all right?'

'More or less,' Poldarn replied. 'But I don't really know what's going on under all these bandages. Do you think I could take them off and have a look?'

Banspati seemed unwilling to commit himself. He wasn't a doctor, he pointed out.

'Well,' Poldarn suggested, 'how'd it be if I said it was all right?'

'You aren't a doctor either.'

'I could be,' Poldarn said, 'for all either of us know.'

Banspati didn't seem very impressed with that line of reasoning. 'Maybe you should just stay put till the doctor gets here,' he said. 'I mean, it's been weeks since they were going to send for him, so he could arrive any day now.'

'So he was sent for, then.'

'They were going to send for one,' Banspati replied.

'But you don't actually know whether they ever got round to it?'

Banspati scowled. 'I'm only the bloody foreman,' he protested. 'I can't do every single fucking thing myself, can I? Besides, you're still alive, so what're you cribbing about? If what they say about the doctors up Falcata's right, he'd have killed you for sure.'

In the end they compromised, as men of goodwill always do when their interests coincide; Poldarn was to stay in bed until the next morning, after which he was at liberty to get up, take off his bandages (entirely at his own risk, needless to say) and report for work. If he was still alive at the end of his shift, he could consider himself officially better.

Perhaps it was the effort of arguing the toss with the foreman; Poldarn slept well, without dreaming, and woke up feeling strong and cheerful. His legs felt unsteady, calflike, after so many weeks of disuse, but he refused to indulge them, and walked awkwardly up and down the shed until they began to regain their memory. Once he was fairly confident that he could make it across the yard without falling over, he sat down on an empty barrel and unwrapped the bandages on his hands.

His skin felt cold without them, but it was still there; white and unnaturally smooth in places, extremely sensitive. He flexed his fingers until he could extend them without discomfort. Everything seemed to be in order; business as usual.

It took him a while to find the knot that secured the bandage wrapped round his face; it was at the back of his head, cunningly placed so as to be almost inaccessible (and he was clumsy with knots, he discovered). He picked at it for a while until he noticed a small knife, rusty and neglected, lying on the floor a few yards away. It was blunt too, but sharp enough to saw through the knot, eventually. The bandage was stiff, as though it had been starched. Once again, these was a distinct chill on his skin once it had gone. No matter.

The daylight hurt his eyes, even though the sky was black and grey – still the rainy season, then, and no comfort for Galand Dev, with his potentially self-destructive furnace. But the air smelled wonderfully fresh, and most of all, *different*. Poldarn grinned as he walked slowly across the yard, heading for the small stream that fed off the river, just below the mud-diggings.

He found a place where the stream ran between broad, flat rocks. Ferns had somehow found a footing there, and their shade had attracted moss, deep and soft. Where the stream fell from one rock to another there was a shallow pool about a handspan deep. He knelt down – knees grudging and rusty – and looked at his reflection.

Strange, he thought. It would've been a shock if he'd known the story that went with his old face, which wasn't there any more. Instead there was white shiny skin, smooth as fine clay carefully levelled and worked flawless by the tip of the sculptor's finger; a fine setting for a pair of huge round eyes, and between them a melted, featureless nose. White and flat, almost transparent; wasn't that the way ghosts were supposed to look? It was a human face made by someone who'd never actually seen one, working from a rough sketch and a vague verbal description.

The so-called essential paradox, he thought, expressed in the image of the burned scavenger. Now if only this had happened a while ago, that day when he'd pulled himself out of the mud beside another river, how convenient that would've been; nobody would have recognised him, and the man he'd used to be (Gain Aciava's old fellow-student, Xipho Dorunoxy's despised admirer, Ciartan Torstenson of Haldersness) would have been lost, like unwanted memory bleached out of good salvageable material. Salvage and salvation, the essential paradox, or whatever.

He sat down, made himself comfortable. Somewhere at the back of his mind there was the faint recollection of an old story he'd heard as a child, about the gods' mirror, in which a man can see himself as he truly is, not as he wants to be seen or as others insist on seeing him. A wonderfully useful piece of kit for a god, or a king, or a prosperous man of business: hang it on the wall behind the chair where your guests sit down, and you'll never again be troubled by shape-shifters, goblins and elves disguised as humans, princesses cruelly enchanted to look like dairymaids, improvident bankrupts wearing expensive clothes when they come to borrow money. If only he'd had such a mirror (a mirror such as this) on the day when he'd woken up in the bloody mud, with only dead men for company, he could have looked himself in the eye, seen who he really was, seen something rather like *this*—

(And wouldn't it be fine if men and women could be melted down, when the quality of their raw material had become tainted with a bad memory; if you could melt flesh in Galand Dev's completely and utterly reliable furnace, flux it and rake it and flux it again to draw off the past,

pour it into a carefully cured and fettled mould and turn
out a high-class flawless casting every single time: featureless, pearly white, translucent.)

Would anybody recognise him now, he wondered. He
hadn't been around for a while, and in a place where people
came and went, it was easy to forget a face. He watched
himself grinning, as it occurred to him that if he wanted,
he could simply walk out of his life and into a new one, no
longer tethered to his past by his face—

No, he couldn't, of course; nobody was allowed to leave
the compound without express permission from Brigadier
Muno. He was surprised at how disappointed he felt. And
of course it wouldn't be long before everybody in the place
figured it out, equated the brave Poldarn who'd been horribly burned rescuing a fellow worker with the pearl-faced
creature who'd be so very hard to miss. Talk about your
paradoxes of religion; he'd never been more immediately
recognisable in his life.

'Bloody hell.' He turned round to see who'd spoken. He
knew the face, couldn't put a name to it. 'What the fuck
happened to you?'

Poldarn didn't answer, and he had a feeling it'd be
unkind to smile.

'Oh,' said the man whose name had slipped his mind.
'It's you, isn't it? Only I didn't recognise you there for a
moment. So,' the man went on, taking a deep breath,
'you're up and about, then.'

'Apparently,' Poldarn said.

'You feeling all right, then? In yourself, I mean.'

Poldarn shrugged. 'Never felt better in myself in my life.
That I can remember,' he added.

'Well, that's good.' The poor fool was trying not to stare.
'There was supposed to be a doctor coming up from
Falcata, but I don't suppose he could've done anything.'

'He could've killed me,' Poldarn replied. 'That's what

everybody keeps telling me, anyhow. I imagine it's all for the best, really.'

'Right,' the man said. 'Good attitude. And you know what it's like, sooner or later people'll get used to any bloody thing.'

'I'm sure,' Poldarn said. 'By the way, do you happen to know what became of Gain Aciava?'

'Who?'

'Gain Aciava. The man I rescued.'

The man frowned. 'That wasn't his name,' he said. 'But the bloke you pulled out from under the furnace, when you got – well, anyway, him. They came and picked him up. Soldiers, is what I heard.'

'Proper soldiers?' Poldarn tried to think of the right word. 'Regular troops, from Torcea or wherever?'

The man shrugged. 'Search me,' he said. 'I didn't see them myself, and all I heard was soldiers, in a cart. There's been so many bloody soldiers in and out of here since this Poldarn's Flute thing started, you lose track. Anyhow, that's all I know; bunch of soldiers came in and arrested the bugger, and they took him away.'

'Arrested him,' Poldarn repeated.

The man nodded. 'Or they were taking him for questioning, or he'd been sent for. Nobody tells you anything around here any more. You know what, if I could get out of here I bloody would. It's getting to be a right misery.'

'Thanks, anyway,' Poldarn replied. 'How's the job coming along, by the way? Banspati told me to report for work today, but I don't know what I'm supposed to be doing.'

The man looked vaguely alarmed. 'You don't want to go starting work yet,' he said, 'not when you're only just back up and about. Besides, there's bugger-all to do. They're still faffing about trying to decide if they can fix the crack in the firebox. You heard about that?'

Poldarn nodded. 'So what's everybody else doing?'

'Standing about, mostly. I got pissed off and came on. Waste of time, if you ask me, the whole bloody thing.'

'No desperate panic, all hands on deck, that sort of thing?'

It seemed to take the man a while to figure out what Poldarn was trying to say. 'Don't reckon so,' he replied eventually. 'So if you're not feeling a hundred and ten per cent, I'd not bother going in if I were you. Most like you'd only get in the way.'

'Thanks,' Poldarn said graciously.

That still left him with the problem of finding something to do. He'd had quite enough of reading, given that as far as he was aware the only books in the whole camp were two copies of *Concerning Various Matters*. He wasn't wanted at work, which wasn't happening anyway. He wasn't hungry or tired, and judging by the way the man whose name he couldn't remember had reacted at the sight of him, he could forget about socialising, too. A leisurely walk round the inside of the perimeter fence would take him a quarter of an hour. That didn't really leave much.

He was seriously considering going back to the shed and getting back into bed when someone called out to him. He turned round, bracing himself for a similar reaction to the one he'd just received.

The newcomer was Spenno, the pattern-maker; and if he'd noticed anything different about Poldarn since the last time he'd seen him, he didn't show it. Poldarn had only spoken to him a dozen times since he'd been at Dui Chirra; but Spenno was acting as if he'd been looking for him.

'So you're up and about, then,' Spenno said. 'Feeling better?'

'More or less,' Poldarn replied. 'How's it going?'

'Isn't,' Spenno said. 'I keep telling them, whole lot's got to come down, says so in the book, but will they listen?

Hell as like. And they call themselves engineers. Whole lot of 'em between them couldn't peel a carrot.'

Poldarn shrugged. 'Must be pretty trying for you,' he said.

'You get used to it.' Spenno frowned, as if trying to remember what he'd been meaning to say. 'Anyhow,' he went on, 'I want your opinion about something, if you've got a moment.'

A moment; which doesn't exist in religion. 'Sure,' Poldarn said. 'But I don't imagine I can be much use to you. I'm just unskilled labour around here. Unless,' he said, remembering, 'it's a blacksmithing job.'

But Spenno shook his head. 'Nothing like that,' he said. 'No, it's rather more important than that. I need to know, you see, who's going to win the war.'

Poldarn looked at him. 'What war?' he asked.

Spenno didn't appear to have heard him. 'It's pretty fundamental, really,' he went on. 'I mean, here we are, making these bloody terrible things; once I've managed to get through to that clown Galand Dev, anyhow. But we'll get there in the end, no doubt about it. And then the question arises: once they're made and proved and finished and all, who're they going to get pointed at? Got to look at the whole picture, see. Otherwise I'm simply not doing my job.'

Spenno didn't look like he was drunk, or as if he'd been breathing in the fumes off the etching tank. 'I'm sorry,' Poldarn said cautiously, 'I don't know anything apart from what we were all told. You could ask Brigadier Muno, but I don't imagine—'

But Spenno smiled. 'Of course *you* know,' he said. 'I mean, it's why you're here, isn't it? You know, when you first showed up asking for a job, I couldn't figure for the life of me what you'd be wanting with an outfit that just made bells. Not your line at all. I thought, surely he'd be headed straight for Torcea, or else he'd have stayed out west, in the Bohec valley, where it all seemed to be happening. I couldn't imagine what it had to do with us – I mean eventually, yes, sooner or later it'd be here as well as everywhere else, but not *yet*, if you see what I mean. But anyway, you looked like you'd rather be left alone, and for crying out loud, it's not my place to tell you your job – I reckoned you had your reasons and you'd just get on with doing what you had to do. And then this all started; and so of course I knew, straight away; where else would you be? Which is why,' he went on with a gentle sigh, 'I haven't really bothered about this much before, since in the long run it's all a bit academic anyway. But like I said, you've got to look at the whole picture; and the way I figure it is, surely once it's all over and you've done your thing and everything's – well, you know; surely what a person did, you know, which side he was on in this war, whether he was one of the good guys, it's going to decide who makes it and who doesn't – afterwards, I mean. Assuming there is an afterwards, of course, and I know, everything'll be completely different, not like anything we can understand. But there'll be *something*, there's got to be, and I'm buggered if I'm going to lose out on my chance of that just because these Poldarn's Flute things got pointed at the wrong bunch of people. Now I've been assuming that because we're, well, the government, call it what you like, that we've got to be the good guys and whoever we smash to bits with these flute things must be the enemy, the bad people. But now we're so close, and suddenly it's all about to happen – well, you can't blame me for checking up, can you? It's just common sense, really, and it doesn't hurt to ask, just so as to be sure.'

'I'm very sorry,' Poldarn said quietly, 'I haven't got the faintest idea what you're talking about.'

Spenno grinned. 'I know,' he said. 'You aren't allowed

to say. I appreciate that; I mean, if you go around telling all and sundry, the whole thing falls flat on its face. But it's all right, I don't suppose anybody knows but me – well, maybe Chaplain Cleapho, after all he's head of religion, isn't he? And the monks, the ones you spared at Deymeson, they'd know, of course; and your priestess, her in the cart with you at Cric. But *people* don't know – especially now, when they won't be able to recognise you any more. And obviously, I won't breathe a word to a soul. So there's no harm in telling me, is there, Poldarn?'

It took some time to sink in. Then he replied, 'No, you're wrong. It's not like that at all. It was just a trick, a confidence trick, a scam. To cheat the people in the villages into giving us food. And we only did it the one time, for crying out loud.'

This time Spenno seemed just a little bit offended. 'Don't worry,' he said. 'That's fine. I understand. I suppose you can't go making exceptions, even for people you know. Must be hard enough as it is, in your position. But it's not like I was asking for, well, special treatment when the time comes, anything like that. I just wanted to know what's the right thing to do. No harm in that, surely? I mean, if I'm trying to do the right thing, then aren't we both on the same side?' He grinned weakly. 'Or would that be telling, too?'

For some reason, Poldarn felt it was important that Spenno be made to understand. 'Please,' he said, 'you've got to believe me. It was all just pretending, to get money and food out of those people. And Copis, the priestess, she wasn't even—' He stopped. *Wasn't even a real fraud* didn't sound right, and he couldn't tell the truth about why she'd been sent with him, even assuming that he knew what the truth was. 'She was only pretending,' he said. 'Really, she'd been sent by the sword-monks, on some mission or other—'

'Well, of course,' Spenno said, now distinctly annoyed. 'Of course. They're in charge of religion, it's their responsibility, of course they'd choose the priestess. Look, obviously I've said the wrong thing, but I wasn't to know, was I? All I ask is, you won't hold it against me, right?'

Poldarn shook his head. 'You're all wrong about this,' he said. Then something occurred to him. 'But how did you know that was me?' he asked. 'Did you see us, at Cric?'

'No, of course not, I was here. But I recognised you.'

'How the hell could you do that? I've never been here before—' He stopped. 'At least, I don't think so. Had you seen me before – before I turned up here for work, I mean?'

Now Spenno was looking at him, as if he was the one not making sense. 'I'd never seen you before in my life.'

'But you said you recognised me.'

'Well, of course. I'm not blind, you know.' Spenno was getting angry. 'I've read the book, see. So of course—'

'Book?' Book. *Concerning Various Matters*. 'Where the hell does it say in the book—?'

'Oh, for pity's sake.' Suddenly the book was in Spenno's hand – nobody had ever seen where he kept it, concealed somewhere inside his raggedy old coat. 'Here, book nine, chapter sixty-seven, lines forty-one to ninety-five.' The book was open; Poldarn reached for it but Spenno pulled it away. Of course, nobody was ever allowed to touch the book. And Poldarn's copy was back in the shed.

'You recognised me,' Poldarn said, 'because of something in the book?'

'That's what I said.'

'Fine. Would you mind reading it out for me?'

'Don't be daft,' Spenno replied, as though Poldarn was making fun of him. 'You know as well as I do, naturally; better. Well,' he added, making a show of looking up at the sun, 'I'd better be getting on, we're very busy at the moment, obviously. I'm sorry about saying the wrong thing, but really, I didn't mean anything by it. You do believe me, don't you?'

Spenno was staring hard at him. 'Yes,' Poldarn said, 'of course. And no, I won't hold it against you, it's perfectly all right.'

'Thanks.' Spenno sounded relieved. 'And I just want you to know: if I have got it wrong and the government people, the Empire, they aren't the good guys – well, I was only trying to do what's right, if that counts for anything. Don't suppose it does, it's not how things work. But . . .' A look of pain crossed his face. 'Damn it, how the hell are you supposed to *know*? I mean, it's so important, you'd think there'd be a way you could know for sure. Still.' He seemed to sag a little, as if he was giving up. 'There'll be a good reason. After all, it's all up to you, isn't it?'

Spenno closed the book and vanished it into his coat. Poldarn took a deep breath, then let it go.

'I'm sorry,' he said, not quite sure what he was apologising for.

'That's all right. Not your fault, after all.'

For some reason, Poldarn was pleased to hear Spenno say that. He went back to the shed, found the book and tried to remember the reference Spenno had quoted at him. But he must've remembered it wrong, because all he found was a detailed description of the proper method of refining curing salt from goats' urine, using a simple refractory made from an old bucket.

It was dark: dark as a bag, dark as twelve feet down a well shaft, dark as crows' feathers. 'This is so stupid' – Xipho's voice, a tiny beacon of context in so much darkness. 'If we get caught, they're going to throw us out—'

'Shut up, Xipho, for the gods' sakes.' Cordo: Monachus

Cordomine, his old schoolfriend. 'It's around here some-where, we've just got to— Right. Lamp.'

Short, deadly silence. 'Well, *I* haven't got it.'

'What?'

'I thought you were bringing it.'

'Oh, for fuck's sake—'

A click; familiar sound, flint and steel. A tiny flare of light illuminating a face. Interesting: a face (he realised) that no longer existed, because of the essential paradox. Interesting, because these days he couldn't get a fire lit to save his life.

'It's all right,' he heard himself say, 'I brought one. Knew you three couldn't be trusted.'

'Speak for yourself.' Gain Aciava.

'Will you all *shut up*.' Xipho, extremely tense. He'd got the tinder going, he was lighting the lamp. At least, it was too dark to see himself doing it, but he could remember lighting it—

'*Yes!*' Cordo, excited; and the lamplight suddenly blossomed, revealing his face, and Xipho's, and Gain's, and his own. 'This is it,' Cordo was saying. 'We've cracked it.'

'That'll bloody do,' Gain hissed. 'Just grab the book and let's get out of here.'

The lamp moved, its circle of light impinging on the spines of several books. 'You sure this is the right shelf?' he heard himself say. 'Only—'

'Here!' Cordo, his voice suddenly brittle. 'Look.' The lamplight picked out a certain book and flowed into the embossed lettering on the spine, filling it like molten bronze poured into a mould. *Concerning Various Matters.*

'Brilliant,' Gain muttered. 'It'd bloody well better be worth all this aggravation, is all.'

'Worth it?' His own voice, recklessly loud. 'Are you out of your tiny mind? This is *it*, this is *the book*. Worth it, he says—'

'It's chained.'

Xipho's voice, dull and final as the sound of the arrow that hits you. Absolute silence.

'What do you mean, chained?' Gain said at last.

'I mean it's fucking *chained*,' Xipho replied, suddenly shrill. 'Like there's a stupid great big chain bolted to the shelf, to stop you taking the book away. Look!' Her hand inside the light circle, her fingers lifting a solid-looking brown steel chain that hung from the top of the book's spine.

'Shit.'

'Oh well,' Cordo said, 'that's that, then. Waste of bloody time.'

'Of all the *idiots*,' Xipho hissed. 'How the hell could you not've noticed?'

His own voice, defensive: 'I only saw it for a moment, how was I supposed to know they're so bloody paranoid they chain the books to the wall? Pathetic. I mean—'

'Fine.' Gain's voice, suddenly heavy. 'Screw it, then. Let's get out of here.'

'You can't be serious.' Himself, angry, upset, cheated. 'After all we've been through getting here. We can't just turn round and give up because of a stupid little bit of chain.'

'What're you going to do, then?' Cordo, sarcastic. 'Chew through it with your little pointy teeth?'

'Oh, come on,' he heard himself reply. 'We're supposed to be bloody sword-monks, Deymeson's finest. Little bit of chain's not going to stop us.'

Hesitant silence; the light centred around the book, with only Xipho's hand visible above the lamp. 'Well,' said Cordo eventually, 'we can't cut through it, not without a file.'

'File wouldn't help.' Gain, sounding gloomy. 'Probably hardened steel.'

'That's right, look on the fucking bright side.' Himself, unreasonably angry. 'Look, all that's holding it is this little staple—'

'This big staple,' Xipho corrected him, 'driven into solid oak.'

'All right,' he replied, 'so how about the other end of the chain? Bring that lamp closer, I want to see how it's attached to the book.'

Hesitation again; then the lamplight circle contracting, getting brighter as it got smaller. 'See?' His own voice, cockily triumphant. 'All we've got to do is slit up through the spine and the chain falls off.'

'You can't do that!' Xipho, as if he'd just suggested murder. 'Borrowing it's one thing, but you can't go cutting it up, that'd be—' Obviously she couldn't conceive of how bad it would be. That bad.

'Watch me.' He couldn't see, but could remember himself fishing one-handed in his sleeve for a little bone-handled folding knife; too clumsy with nerves to open it with just his fingernails, had to use both hands. 'Keep the lamp steady, will you? This leather's tough.'

'You *can't*—'

(Now, he remembered, now we're coming to the bad bit. I'd like to wake up now, please. Please? But the big black crow only shook its head: *No, I want you to see this.*)

The little knife blade sliding, sawing through the crumbling, tough leather; suddenly a chink, as the chain falls away and clunks against the shelf. 'Gotcha.' His own hiss of victory: 'Right, *now* let's get out of here, quick—'

He didn't need to watch the dream, because he could remember it perfectly well; so he closed his eyes, but the dream carried on behind them. Now I'm going to grab the book with both hands and pull; but it's wedged in tight between two big fat books, it doesn't want to come and I've just slit down the spine, I've got nothing to pull it out *by.*

So I grab hold as best I can, both forefingers and both thumbs, and I *heave* – and here's the book coming out in a hurry, and me staggering back. Here's me stumbling, bumping into Xipho; here's Xipho dropping the lamp. Here's where the lamp hits the floor, smashes. Here's where burning oil flies everywhere – the book in my hands, the other books on the shelf. Cordo's sleeve.

'You *fucking idiot.*' Gain, still under the impression that this is just a rotten accident, that the worst that can happen is that someone'll come and find us out. 'Now what're we going to do?'

Cordo, batting at his sleeve, but it's too hot for that, burns his skin. He screams, can't help it. Xipho, yelling *'Shut up!'* Gain, trying to beat out the fire running up his friend's arm with his own sleeve drawn down over his hand. Nobody (except me) appreciating the true gravity of the situation; not just Cordo's sleeve, the *whole fucking library* is on fire—

That cold, sensible ability to assess a state of affairs and understand what's still possible, what's no longer possible. No longer possible to put out the fire, save the library or – regrettably – save Cordo; remember, the massive library doors are locked, the key's in the librarian's lodgings on the other side of the Great Cloister – Cordo and the library and Xipho and Gain and me, all smothered and burned to ash before the librarian can get here with it, even if he's running out of his front door now. As for scrambling back up the way they came, in through the skylight, impossible with a burning, screaming Cordo, but just possible without him – and then down the back wall into the deep shadows of the cloister, hidden from sight as everyone comes running with buckets and pails to fight the fire . . . Still possible (if Cordo is dispensed with) to save three out of four lives *and* get out of here, get back to the dormitory *without getting found out.*

Analysis: Cordo good as dead already, library beyond saving, but the three of us still capable of effective salvation.

'Come on,' he remembered himself saying. 'Back the way we came.'

'We can't'; Xipho, panicking. 'We can't get him up—'

'I know. Leave him. *Now*.'

Gain, lashing at Cordo with a burning book. Xipho likewise. Is it now too late to save them, too? Assessment: no, but action needed—

He remembered what he did next. Not the little knife this time; the big one, the one they laughed at him for carrying stuck down the side of his boot. Smooth draw, up, taking care to avoid getting burnt. One thrust into Cordo's side.

'Now leave him,' he heard himself say; and he remembered the looks on their faces—

'You killed him.' Xipho, stunned.

'Yes.' His own voice. 'Now follow me.'

Born leader, me, he remembered thinking; maybe the first time it'd occurred to him that that was what he was born to do, lead others out of mortal peril. Of course, it had been his idea to steal the book in the first place; but the objective had been worthwhile, that stupid chain had just been sheer bad luck.

They'd hesitated, Gain and Xipho. But not for long. And the next day (by some miracle, none of them had telltale burns on their hands or faces and their burned clothes had been dumped over the wall into the cesspit, where self-respecting sword-monks would be too fastidious to think of looking) standing shocked, ashen-faced, gauntly silent, as Father Tutor broke the news to them: their friend Cordo, foolishly tried to break into the library, burned to death; the little Earwig sobbing (he'd refused to come with them, said it'd all end in tears; but at least he had the wit to keep his face shut in front of Father Tutor).

At least, Father Tutor was saying, at least they'd managed to save most of the books. But not (Father Tutor didn't say, but they knew) not *the* book, the one with all the answers in, unique, the only known copy, lost and gone irrecoverably for ever; memory consumed in fire, like the truth about Cordo—

He woke up, and as he stirred the book slid off him and hit the floor. He'd been reading about how to fix files in their handles using powdered rosin, and had fallen asleep. Not the most enthralling book in the world.

Outside – he poked his head round the shed door, wondering how long he'd been asleep. For the first time in days, people were moving about, even running. Curious, he couldn't help thinking; the last he'd heard was that Galand Dev had finally admitted that the crack in the firebox couldn't be mended, and so nothing could be done until the whole furnace was torn down and rebuilt. The furnace was still there, but now there was smoke pouring out of its chimney.

Oh well, he thought. Might as well go to work.

In the yard he ran into one of the old-timers, a small, shrivelled man who'd been hanging round Dui Chirra for decades. 'What's all this in aid of?' he asked, waving in the direction of the furnace.

The old man laughed. 'Where've you been?' he said. 'That short bugger' (Galand Dev, presumably), 'he's only gone and ordered a fire laid in. Spenno's shitting feathers but nobody's listening to him.'

'I thought he reckoned the whole thing'd crack up if they lit a fire,' Poldarn said.

'He was wrong, then,' the old man replied. 'Around about midnight he had the firehouse boys in there slapping cowshit and clay in the crack; laid in a bit of a fire just to cure it, and now they reckon it's good as new. Hasn't blown up yet, so they must've fixed it.'

'Oh,' Poldarn said. 'So, how far've they got?'

'Fire's been in full since dawn,' the old man told him, 'so it can't be far off ready to pour. Moulds are all in, so they can go as soon as he likes.'

Poldarn shrugged. 'So why the hurry-up all of a sudden?'

'Reckon the military's given Muno a boot up the arse,' the old man replied, with a grin. 'This way, if the whole lot goes up, he can say it wasn't his fault, he was only doing what he was told. But Spenno's in there cussing a blue streak, so maybe it'll work, at that.'

'Right,' Poldarn said. 'Suppose I'd better go and see if I can make myself useful.'

By the time he reached the furnace yard, there was a ring of men standing round watching. That they weren't entirely convinced of Galand Dev's success in patching the firebox was evident from the healthy amount of distance they were keeping. Poldarn nudged his way through to the front; he had an idea that even if the furnace blew, he'd probably be all right.

Apparently he'd only just made it in time; because as soon as he reached the front of the crowd, Spenno (directing the operation from on top of a tall pile of scrap bronze) put his fingers in his mouth and whistled, someone pulled a lever, and a dazzlingly white stream started to trickle out of the side of the furnace tower. It crawled like a burning worm down a short clay gutter, and disappeared into the in-gate of the mould. Immediately a large round cloud of steam lifted into the air and hung over the mould pit, but there was no eruption or explosion of airborne white-hot spatter; that aside, it was like watching the fire-stream pouring out of the breach in the volcano above Haldersness.

Everybody seemed to be cheering, as though all their

problems were over. Obviously premature; there were any
number of things that could still go wrong. Even so, and
in spite of the fact that he'd contributed next to nothing to
the project, Poldarn couldn't help feeling relieved, even
strangely proud. Crazy, he thought; or maybe he just liked
seeing things burn.

The actual pour lasted less than a minute. Once the
mould was filled and the leverman had cut off the stream
of liquid metal, there was nothing to do except wait for the
casting to cool down. It'd be hours before the mould could
be chipped off the casting, and until then there was nothing
anybody could usefully do. He sighed, and threaded his
way back through the crowd, who seemed to be in no hurry
to disperse.

So that's that, Poldarn thought; big deal.

That was the moment when he made up his mind to get
out. If there was any connection with what he'd just seen,
he couldn't pin it down: it wasn't as though he'd cared
enough about the project that he'd been waiting to see if
it'd come out all right; he hadn't been hanging on just in
case they needed him for something. But it was as if
someone else, for once, had taken the irrevocable step, so
that now he had the unaccustomed luxury of proceeding
safe in the knowledge that this time it wouldn't be his
fault— And where that came from, he had no idea.

Getting out of Dui Chirra wasn't going to be easy. A very
quick, low-key reconnaissance was enough to tell him that:
a ten-foot-high stockade, sentries on the gate, further
sentries patrolling the perimeter, still others pulling
lookout duty from the surrounding high points. Stowing
away in an outbound cart wasn't a viable option; the sentries seemed to be working out their frustration at being
cooped up in the lousiest posting in the Empire by spearing
every handful of straw or bundle of rags that trundled

through the gateway. The only vulnerable spot in the defences that Poldarn could see was the river, which came in and flowed out under two watergates at either end of the compound. But the idea of taking that route didn't appeal to him; if he could spot it, it was too obvious. There was, he vaguely remembered, a precept of religion on the subject.

It took him a day of nonchalant strolling, admiring the depth and ingenuity of Brigadier Muno's security arrangements, to remember that he had a stone-cold foolproof no-risk way-out buried in the pocket of his other coat – some kind of small badge or brooch, with a pin and a keeper on the back. Poldarn recalled what Muno Silsny had said about it: *combination safe passage and get-out-of-trouble token; show it to a watch sergeant or a guard commander and unless he's got specific orders to the contrary from the Emperor or myself, he'll say sorry for troubling you and forget he ever saw you.* Perfect, just what he needed – assuming that it was still valid, now that Muno Silsny was dead. He found it, stood it up on its pin on the palm of his hand and stared at it for a while. It looked like the sort of thing you could buy in Sansory market for a quarter, if you and your money were easily parted. Even so; only one way to find out.

It didn't take him long to pack: his one change of clothes, hat, blanket, the sword he'd nearly finished making, the book Gain had given him, the little axe he'd brought from Haldersness, an issue water-bottle and as many ration biscuits as he could cram into a medium-sized feed sack. In the other pocket of his good coat was Muno Silsny's other gift, the chunky gold ring that was supposed to be worth a nice, snug little farm. Having thought about it for a while, he decided that the best time of day for his departure would be somewhere around an hour before dawn, when the sentry on the gate would be thinking about being relieved and not getting involved in anything that might keep him from his bed a minute longer than necessary. The approach, he decided, should be as simple as possible—

'Here,' said the sentry. 'Where d'you think you're going?'

'Out,' Poldarn replied, raising his hand and opening his fingers.

'What's that supposed to be, then?'

Look of pained surprise. 'You mean you don't know? All right, then, we'd better go and have a word with your sergeant.'

Bad-tempered sigh from the sentry, who waved to his colleague outside the gate to come and take his place for a moment; then inside the guardhouse to wake up the sergeant, who was asleep under three blankets and a heavy non-regulation coat.

'This one reckons he's got leave to go out,' the sentry said, 'only he hasn't got a pass or anything.'

The sergeant grunted and swung his bare legs to the floor. 'All right,' he said wearily, 'what's the story this time? It'd better be good, because—'

Poldarn held out his hand, opened his fingers once again. The sergeant stared, as if he'd just met his mother in a brothel.

'Fuck me,' he said softly. 'Haven't seen one of them since I was in Torcea.' He frowned. 'How do I know it's genuine?' he asked.

Poldarn clicked his tongue and dropped the brooch into the sergeant's hand. 'Mind you don't stab yourself on the pin,' he said. 'It's sharp.'

The sergeant turned it over a couple of times, then stood up quickly. 'Very sorry to have bothered you, sir,' he said. 'Just doing my job.'

'Fine,' Poldarn grunted, holding out his hand for the brooch. 'No need to tell anybody about this, is there?'

'Understood,' the sergeant snapped. 'Anybody asks, I never seen you in my life.'

And that was that: the gates swung to behind Poldarn, the outside sentry stood aside to let him pass, just as the first red gleam of dawn diluted the sky. Where next? he asked himself, as if it mattered. Falcata, presumably, not that he knew anything about the place. But from what he'd heard it sounded as though it was on the way to some-where, and that was all he needed it to be.

Chapter Ten

'You know her, then?' the driver was asking.

Pulling himself back out of his complicated train of thought, Poldarn shook his head; fat raindrops scattered from the sodden brim of his hat. 'Met her a couple of times on the road, that's all. Crazy old bat, but fairly harmless.'

The driver shrugged. 'She didn't seem to know you.'

'Hadn't seen her since I got myself all burned up,' he replied. 'Don't suppose many people would recognise me after that.'

'That'd be it, then.' The driver was silent for a while, thinking; a slow process but not without a certain grandeur, like the turning of a giant waterwheel. 'So why'd you help her out, then, if she's just some old nutcase you met on the road?'

Good question. Poldarn's turn to think for a moment. 'I have this odd feeling she's good luck,' he replied. 'Like a mascot or something. If I help her out, at some point I'll get a slice of good luck myself when I need it, later on down the line.'

'Fair enough,' said the driver, in the manner of one humouring an armed lunatic. 'Has it worked like that, then?'

It hadn't actually occurred to him to consider the point, so he considered it. First time he'd met the daffy old woman with the little wicker cage, he'd also met Gain Aciava. Second time, he'd taken part in that ghastly botched robbery shortly afterwards, when he'd had to kill the vicious teenager. 'No,' he admitted. 'Quite the opposite, in fact. Only goes to show, intuition's an arsehole.'

That went over the driver's head like a skein of migrating geese, but he didn't seem to mind. The driver was one of those people who seem to treat the intelligent and articulate as speakers of a foreign language; if he understood one word in twenty, he was happy. 'Doesn't seem much point to it, then,' the driver went on. 'I mean, if you get bad luck for helping her out instead of good, why help her out? Anyhow, that's how I see it.'

'You're probably right,' Poldarn sighed. 'But she was headed for Torcea, so I don't suppose I'll ever see her again.'

'Just as well, really.'

'Just as well,' he agreed.

It had happened on his last night in Falcata. He'd been there a whole week, instead of one night and one morning as he'd planned, but some river or other had flooded and washed away the causeway on which the main east road crossed some bog, or at least that was what he'd been told next morning at the stage office; the taproom of the Benevolence Rewarded had been thick with rumours about rebel armies, bandits, the Amathy house on the prowl again, the Mad Monk and all sorts. So he'd wandered up and down the damp grey city's uninspiring main thorough-fare, wondering why half the shops were shut and the other half were empty; he'd spent money he couldn't afford on needled beer he didn't want; he'd stood looking over the parapet of the covered bridge, watching the fat brown river licking the doorsteps and windowsills of the bankside houses; he'd tried to sell Muno Silsny's ring, but the gold-smiths were either closed and shuttered or weren't buying in off the street. Finally, in desperation, he'd taken shelter from the rain in a grim, dusty building that had turned out to be the law courts and, having nothing better to do, had sat down in the back row of the public gallery while the three resident magistrates worked their way through the morning's crop of drunks, debtors, vagrants, lunatics and inept thieves. Sleep was pressing down on him hard and he'd folded his arms and closed his eyes when he'd heard a voice he recognised – her, the mad woman, sounding dreadfully flustered and upset at being described as a vagrant; more concerned about her unidentified pets in their wicker basket than about her own fate as an indicted criminal. (The watch sergeant had taken the cage from her; she'd tried to grab it back and most unfortunately her elbow had gone in the poor man's eye; of course it was an acci-dent and she was most dreadfully sorry, nothing like this had ever happened to her before, and did their worships think she could possibly have the cage back, because her babies would be so dreadfully hungry after missing two feeds—) And, at some point in this wretched performance, he'd realised he was standing on his hind legs exchanging words with the clerk of the court—

'No, sir,' he'd said, 'I'm not a relative, but I do know her.'

The clerk looked mildly disappointed. 'And can you vouch for the truth of her account?'

Poldarn hesitated. 'Well,' he said, 'what she just said is pretty much what she told me the first time I met her, on the carrier's cart out near Tin Chirra.' (He changed the locale at the last moment; saying he'd been near Dui Chirra probably wasn't a good idea.) 'And I can't see why she'd have wanted to lie to me back then; I mean, she wasn't asking for money or anything.'

The magistrates were muttering to each other, and you didn't have to be a lip-reader to make out the gist of it: *if he wants to take responsibility for her, let him.* After that, it was all nice and straightforward. He'd paid her fine (ten quarters for sleeping in a doorway; another ten for assaulting an officer of the watch) and hustled her out of the courthouse into the rain before she did or said anything that'd get them both arrested.

'Thank you so much,' she kept on saying over and over again. 'You've been so kind and I don't know how I can possibly ever repay you, but do you think you could possibly just nip back inside and see if you can find that watch sergeant and ask if he could let me have my poor darlings back? They'll be so dreadfully frightened, not to mention hungry—'

Fuck, Poldarn thought. But she had enough strength of will to tame wild horses, and eventually he'd begged her to stay there, not move an inch, while he went back in and found the sergeant; recognising him wasn't hard, he was the one with the spectacular black eye. The sergeant had been only too glad to give him the cage, which smelled disgustingly of rodent pee and was distinctly moist on the underside.

'Now listen,' he'd said to her over her grateful chirpings. 'I haven't got any money to give you this time—'

('That's quite all right . . . Far too generous already . . .')

'But,' he'd continued, raising his voice a little to make himself heard over her unwanted gratitude, 'I'm going to give you this badge. No, listen please, this is very important. This is an army courier's badge, they're very rare and valuable, and if you ever get in trouble again or run out of money or anything like that, you're to show this badge to a sergeant or an officer – don't for pity's sake try explaining anything, or he'll think you've stolen it or picked it up in the street. Just show it to him, like this, and tell him what you want, and it'll do the trick. Now, do you understand me, or do you want me to explain it again?'

Remarkably, she'd understood straight away; more use-less thanks and not-worth-the-breath-they-were-uttered-with promises of recompense at some indefinite future date, and then he'd marched her over to the stage office and put down seven quarters of good Torcea money to buy her a seat on the carrier's cart to Fort Cheir and the Torcea ferry. Which was why Poldarn was currently sitting out-side on the box of the Tela Ixwa stage in the driving rain, when he could've been sitting inside, in the dry.

Almost as hard to account for as the act itself was the urge to tell the driver all about it. All the driver had done to unstopper this flood of reminiscence was to say it was a pity Poldarn couldn't have paid the extra quarter and a half, since it was pissing it down and there was a perfectly good empty seat inside the stage; but for some reason, Poldarn had been moved to justify himself by telling this story. Maybe he was proud of what he'd done (though he'd left out the really generous bit, the gift of the courier's badge, to save having to invent some tale about how he'd come by it in the first place); or perhaps it was something about barbers and carters that made you tell them stuff you wouldn't normally tell your best friend; or maybe he was just getting chatty in his old age—

'Pretty decent thing to have done, though,' the driver said with less than absolute sincerity, 'looking after a poor old mad woman like that. Just hope you don't catch your death being out here, is all.'

—Or perhaps he'd done it in hopes that the driver would exercise his discretion and let him have the empty seat in the dry as far as the next stop; in which case he'd wasted his time.

'Oh well,' he heard himself say, bravely cheerful, 'she's probably somebody's mother, bless her daft old heart.'

The driver shook his head. 'Doubt it,' he said. 'Like, if she was my old mum I wouldn't let her go wandering about like that, getting herself arrested and all.'

The subject was getting boring very fast. 'Maybe her son died and that's what drove her off her head,' Poldarn said with a yawn. 'Anyway, with any luck that's the last time she'll cross my path. How long before we reach the – what did you say its name was?'

'The Piety & Fortitude,' the driver grunted. 'Maybe three hours, could be four if the ford's up and we got to go round by the bridge. Assuming the bridge isn't down.'

'Fine,' Poldarn said. 'Tell me, why do all these inns have such god-awful self-righteous names?'

The driver frowned. 'How do you mean?' he said.

They arrived at the Piety an hour after dark, by which point Poldarn was so wet it hadn't mattered for hours. Since he had very little money (apart from the magnificent gold-and-gemstone ring purportedly worth twenty times more than the inn and its contents) he had his dinner out of the kitchen stewpot and dossed down in the hayloft directly over a very noisy, flatulent horse. Sleep proving elusive in this context, he lay in the dark staring upwards, wondering if the mad woman was sleeping cosily in the guest quarters of the Fort Cheir prefecture; wondering also why he'd done such a bloody stupid thing.

He must have dropped off at some point, because the next thing he was aware of was a boot nudging him in the ribs. He opened his eyes and saw the head of a spear, mostly out of focus because it was so close to his face. Someone was telling him to get up.

The soldiers took him into the taproom; it was empty, and the fire was dying out. The man sitting behind the table told one of the soldiers to throw a scoop of charcoal on it before taking notice that Poldarn was in the room.

'Bloody hell,' he said. 'You been swimming?'

Poldarn decided that the question didn't need an answer. 'What's going on?' he asked.

'Shut up and sit down,' the man replied, by way of an explanation; then he caught sight of Poldarn's face and shuddered, as though someone had just poured cold water down his neck. 'Turn out your pockets on that table there. Sergeant, have you got his baggage there?'

'Just the blanket roll, sir,' the sergeant said. He put something down with a thump, just out of Poldarn's line of sight. Poldarn did as he was told and emptied his pockets.

The man appeared to have recovered from his nasty turn. 'Right,' he said, with a predatory smile, 'let's see what we've got here. Bring that thing over here, sergeant, I want a good look at it.'

Not good; *that thing* was the nearly finished backsabre, possession of which was going to be very hard to explain away. The man studied it carefully, turning it over in his hands as if reading invisible writing, then laid it down next to him, well out of Poldarn's reach. 'Fine,' he said. 'Now let's see that book.'

Concerning Various Matters didn't interest the man nearly as much as the sword had done; he opened it at random a few times, shrugged and put it down. He also examined the blanket, the water bottle and the rest of Poldarn's meagre kit before signalling to the sergeant to bring him the contents of Poldarn's pockets: a small knife, an insignificant sum of money, and a gold ring.

From the expression on the man's face, he'd been expecting to see the ring from the outset. 'That's all, is it?' he said. 'No, I'm talking to you, not Sergeant Illuta. Is this all of it, or have you got any more, squirrelled away somewhere?'

'I'm sorry,' Poldarn said. 'I don't quite follow.'

The man smirked and shook his head. 'Makes no odds to me,' he said. 'It's not the trinkets I'm after.' He sighed. 'All right,' he said, 'here we go. My name is Lock Xanipolo, colonel, officer commanding Falcata garrison. Day before yesterday I get a report that some scruff with a burnt-off face's been trawling round all the goldsmiths' houses trying to sell an extremely valuable candidature ring with a Faculty of Arms crest. Stage office tells me a man answering the description caught the common stage for Tela Ixwa; so here I am. Now, do you need me to tell you how a tramp like yourself comes to have a ring that used to belong to General Muno Silsny, who was murdered by bandits on this very same road four months ago, or can we cut all that and get on to some of the stuff I don't already know?'

Poldarn looked at him steadily. 'Such as?'

'Ah. Such as, was it also you who murdered Prince Mazentius during the course of a robbery on the Falcata to Ang Chirra road; how the Mad Monk and his motley crew are involved in all this, and when they're planning to attack the foundry at Dui Chirra; and what exactly is your connection with the people who make and use this particular pattern of sword.' The colonel sighed. 'I'm sorry to have to say that if you say the right thing in answer to these questions, you'll at least live long enough for a trip to Torcea. If it was up to me you wouldn't be leaving this room alive, but I have to do what I'm told, more's the pity.'

The driver was right, Poldarn thought; the next old woman I meet on the road can rot in hell. 'I'm sorry,' he said, 'but I don't understand.'

Colonel Lock shook his head sadly. 'Oh, come on,' he said. 'Do we really have to go through the whole sorry pantomime? Go on, then, let's be having you. Name.'

'Actually—' Poldarn hesitated. It's worth a try, he thought; this man's an idiot, just as well he doesn't know it. 'My name's Poldarn,' he said. 'I'm a foundry worker at Dui Chirra.'

'Is that so?' Colonel Lock drummed his fingers on the table. 'And what are you doing here? Last I heard, all leave at the foundry was cancelled.'

Poldarn shrugged. 'I ran away,' he said. 'But if you send me back there, anybody can tell you that's who I am. And they'll tell you I can't have done any murders or robberies, because nobody's been allowed out of the place since the project started. You do know about that, don't you?'

He could see Colonel Lock thinking about it; not quite as monolithic as the stage driver, but very similar. 'So how come you've got the late General Muno's personal candidature ring? Find it in the slack tub, did we?'

Poldarn shook his head. 'He gave it to me,' he replied. 'He came to Dui Chirra specially to see me. Ask Brigadier Muno at the foundry if you like; he's the general's uncle.'

'I know that.' Colonel Lock was obviously the sort of man who gets irritable when he knows he's out of his depth. Weak; easy mark. 'All right, then,' he said. 'Suppose you tell me about the wiggly sword? Or did Muno Silsny give you that as well?'

'No,' Poldarn said patiently, 'I made that myself; you can see, it's not quite finished yet. I'm a blacksmith, I was making it in my spare time. Copy of one I saw once.'

'Really.' The colonel was getting flustered. 'And this book. I suppose it's just some light reading for the long winter evenings.'

'Yes,' Poldarn replied. 'A friend gave it to me.'

'Did he, now. Your friend was a sword-monk, then?'

Poldarn shrugged. 'I don't know,' he said. 'He didn't say where he got it from.'

Apparently he'd said something wrong, because Colonel Lock was smiling. But he didn't seem to be in any hurry to share the joke. 'Well,' he said, 'that's fine. Care to tell me why you left Dui Chirra, when you knew perfectly well you weren't allowed to?'

'I was bored.'

Colonel Lock looked at him for what seemed like a very long time. 'You were bored,' he repeated.

'That's right. There's nothing to do there except sit about waiting for Spenno and Galand Dev to stop arguing. They're sort of in charge,' he explained. 'And they can't make up their minds how to go about things; and while they're yelling at each other, the rest of us just have to hang around. I'd had enough, so I reckoned I might as well move on. I mean, I'm nobody important, they don't need me for anything.'

The colonel raised an eyebrow. 'That's so crass I could believe it,' he said, 'except that I get the feeling there's more to it than that. I heard all about General Muno Silsny finally tracking down his secret rescuer,' he went on. 'It was going to be a big story, and then it was killed dead. And then, shortly afterwards, so was General Muno. And here you are, the mystery hero, with Muno's candidature ring and a raider backsabre, roaming about the country-side making an exhibition of yourself in the Falcata mag-istrates' court.' Suddenly he clapped his hands together. 'Well,' he said, 'the good bit is, I can hand you over to Brigadier Muno and let him deal with you. I've seen your sort before, every officer in the service has; trouble follows you about like flies round a horse's arse. Sergeant,' he called out, 'get our guest a nice room on the top floor. I want two guards outside his door and another two under his window, in case he gets bored again. We want to be on the road at daybreak, back to Falcata and then on to Dui Chirra.'

It was an improvement on the hayloft; in fact, it was the best bed Poldarn could remember having come across, soft yet firm, with clean linen sheets. There was even a basinful of water for washing in, and a decent fire in the hearth.

'Thanks,' he said, as the guard opened the door and gestured him into the room. 'If you get cold standing out there in the passage, feel free to pop in and warm yourself up.'

The guard gave him a look that would've cleaned rust off an abandoned ploughshare, and shut the door behind him. Poldarn kicked off his boots, lay down on the bed and looked up at the roof timbers, which were carved and gilded. He guessed (not that it mattered) that, like most inns, this one had started off as a monastic house, an out-lying priory, and this had once been the prior's or abbot's lodgings. Nice of the government to put him up in the best room in the house.

Such a soft, restful bed; all he had to do was lie down on it, and all the aches, pains and nagging little injuries he was so acutely aware of would vanish, like water splashed on the hearth. Instead, he perched on a wooden stool in the corner. Just as well the colonel had confiscated his book. A man could slip off to sleep so easily reading that. But going to sleep would be a very bad thing, wouldn't it? Sleep into dreams, dreams into memories, finding out the next part of the story. He wriggled about, looking for the most uncomfortable position to sit in. All those times when he'd wanted to go to sleep but hadn't been able to, because of some minor discomfort. It wasn't too much to ask, a few hours of being awake until the soldiers came back and took him away; and nobody could fall asleep in the saddle on the road back to Dui Chirra, all that rain and mud, seeping through into the bone—

He could see quite clearly, but he also knew his eyes were closed; which could only mean—

Old crow sitting in a tall thin tree.

It started up as he rode past, yelling reproachfully at him

as it battled its way into the headwind, which was pulling it in a direction it didn't want to go. For a long moment it hung still in the air, its wings beating hard. Then it was moving sideways, unable to resist; then it gave in and tried to tack a course back onto the line it wanted to follow.

You and me both, Ciartan thought, shifting his reins into his left hand, flexing the fingers of his right, which were beginning to get numb. Ahead, over the shoulder of the rider in front, he could see a small round building that could only be a gatehouse: too small to be practical, too ornate to be a poor man's house. Some rich bastard, someone who took a perverse delight in manipulating his environment, had had it put there as a conspicuous display of wasted money. He'd arrived, then.

From the gatehouse to the house itself, best part of half an hour, along a pointlessly winding road that weaved its way like a drunk between blatantly obvious landscape features: a raised lake, a grove of flowering cherries, a toy vineyard, a bog garden, a larch avenue. All the daintily engineered exhibits had been chosen so they'd look their best, be in flower or fruit or silver leaf during precisely the same two weeks each year; the two weeks, presumably, that Prince Tazencius deigned to spend at this quaint little sixty-bedroom cottage while Court was in recess for the mid-summer half-term. Ciartan found the rest of the ride up to the front door rather annoying. He'd grasped the point quite some time ago, thank you very much, and didn't need it rammed home with a sledgehammer.

So here he was, the Prince's prospective son-in-law, finally dropping by to meet the folks. She'd be there, of course, the beautiful Lysalis, his bride-to-be; he thought about her, wondering what would be passing through her mind right now. Was she excited at the thought of seeing him again? Would she be sitting at the top of that tower over there, watching the drive? He doubted that, unless

Prince Tazencius considered it a necessary detail. If she was excited, it'd be because Daddy had ordered her a special new dress for the occasion. He had an idea that Lysalis's life was mostly a series of short intervals between pretexts for special new dresses. Which was fine, if you liked that sort of thing.

Prince Tazencius's landscape architect hadn't finished with him yet, not by a long way. True, the main house was now only about five hundred yards away as the old black crow flew; but first he had to be forced to admire the carp ponds, the castellated granite dovecote, the belvedere, the ivy garden, the sunken lawn and the peacock enclosure. There had to be a short cut, for when Tazencius was in a hurry to get somewhere. Probably you could be on the main road in five minutes flat if only you knew the way.

Poor Lysalis, he thought; she was just as much an exhibit as the mulberry plantation or the rose garden, and about as necessary. Whatever it was Tazencius wanted him for was undoubtedly some straightforward piece of business, something that could be sorted out in ten minutes of straight talking in the back room of an inn somewhere, without all this tedious and wasteful business of marrying into the family. But that wasn't how things got done around here, apparently. There was probably a perfectly sound reason for it, something to do with the delicate balance of power at Court, which of course he'd never understand no matter how long he studied it in Expediencies. In the end, all the protocols and forms and procedures came down to a three-handed arm-wrestling bout between the main factions inside the royal family, and all these bits and pieces – castles and daughters and lavender-edged south-facing knot gardens – were just rather ornate chess pieces. Back home at Haldersness, of course, none of this would even be possible, and if it was it'd be resolved in an afternoon on the moor with spears and axes. He couldn't help feeling that was a more efficient approach, but it was easy to be all superior when you couldn't see the full picture.

Now then, he told himself, concentrate. You're letting your contempt for all this decadence distract you from your basic preparations, which is probably the purpose of the exercise. Strip away all the junk, and let's have a look at what's going on.

He cleared his mind, until all he could see was two circles, his own and Prince Tazencius's, gradually preparing to coincide.

A while back, Tazencius's daughter visits her brother at school. While she's there, she happens to meet one of his circle of acquaintances, a promising student but as ineligible as it's possible to be – no money, no family, nothing. A few months and several visits later, the promising student finds himself engaged to be married to the Prince's daughter, and now here is the promising student, working his way like a chessboard knight through the Prince's interminable grounds, on his way to find out exactly what it was that the Prince wanted him for in the first place.

(And it only goes to show, Ciartan thought; because I do believe that she is really quite fond of me, insofar as she's capable of liking anything she can't wear. But there; I'll believe anything, me.)

The welcoming tableau was inch-perfect: Tazencius precisely in the centre of the group; his wife, a thin, gaunt-looking woman in an outfit that must've cost almost as much as the house (but unless you'd been taught in Expediencies to notice trivia, you'd quite easily fail to see her there at all); assorted stewards, chamberlains, personnel both functional and decorative, human salad. No sign of Lysalis, because she'd be making her entrance in just a few moments, probably down a long spiral staircase. She'd look stunningly lovely, of course, or heads would roll.

Gradually nearer; and then the moment came, and the circles coincided. Ciartan stood quite still; no sword in his sash today, of course, which was probably just as well, since it'd have taken a tremendous effort not to give in to that hard-gained instinct and draw, the sense of confrontation being so overwhelming.

'Hello, Ciartan.' Prince Tazencius was smiling. Charming smile. 'It's so good to meet you at last. Lysalis has told me so much about you.'

(Has she? What, exactly? Or did she just read out the summary of the reports?)

'It's really kind of you to invite me,' Ciartan replied.

'Not at all. You're practically family already. Come in and have something to eat – you must be starving.'

Amazing dining hall: long oak table, like the ones back at Haldersness, except that it was polished immaculately smooth, like a mirror (no mirrors at Haldersness ever reflected that clearly). Twenty places set: twenty silver plates, cups, knives and napkin rings, and each setting identical to the one next to it, like crows in a flock. Bizarre people, quiet and grave and respectful, all following the Prince's lead (like the household at Haldersness, but they weren't mind-readers, they were obeying orders, orders so fundamental that they didn't need to be spoken out loud; so it was like Haldersness and also its exact opposite, a mirror image). And amazing food, things he'd never eaten before, things he'd never have believed were edible. Actually it tasted horrible, but it was amazing nonetheless.

'Ciartan,' the Prince was saying, from his place at the head of the table, through a mouthful of what Ciartan had an uncomfortable feeling were probably snails. 'Lysatis tells me you aren't from a religious family. Is that right?'

He remembered just in time: specialist vocabulary. What Tazencius meant was, he didn't come from a long line of supposedly celibate career monks. 'Quite right, sir,' he said.

'She tells me,' the prince went on, sounding quietly amused, 'that you really only got into religion because of a chance meeting. Can that really be true? The most promising student in your year?'

Which he wasn't, of course. 'It's true I really only joined up on a whim, yes,' he said. 'I met a boy about my own age, and he told me he was on his way back for the start of the new term. He told me about Deymeson, and it sounded interesting. And that's all there was to it, really.'

'Remarkable.' Tazencius's smile was warm and friendly, like your own fireside after a long day in the winter fields. All lies, of course. 'You must have an exceptional degree of natural aptitude, to have caught up so quickly.'

'I had a lot of help,' Ciartan lied. 'Extra coaching and so on.'

'Even so.' Tazencius had finished his snails; now he was scrabbling about with a long, thin silver hook inside the shell of some revolting-looking crustacean. Did the high nobility only eat armoured food? 'I also gather that you're quite the linguist.'

As he said it, the prince looked him full in the eye, and his expression clearly said, *agree with me*. 'I'm not too bad at languages,' Ciartan said hesitantly. 'I mean, I can pick them up fairly quickly, at a basic level.'

'Excellent. Only,' Tazencius went on, pausing to remove a tiny shard of shell from the tip of his tongue, 'I have some documents in my study which are written in some language that none of us can understand – we don't even know what it is. If you wouldn't mind taking a look at them, perhaps you could cast some light on the mystery.'

'Sure,' Ciartan said.

The next course was soup – soup with shellfish and whole small crabs bobbing up and down in it. The drill was to fish them out with your fingers and use the butt of your knife to smash the shells. It might have made a degree of sense if they weren't three days' ride from the nearest bit of sea. During the soup course, Tazencius ignored Ciartan completely, preferring to talk to a thin bald man on the other side of the table; Lysatis's mother, on the other hand, suddenly seemed to become aware of his existence, and chattered away for the duration of the course about the latest Torcea fashions in soft furnishings. Odd; although she never once appeared to draw breath, she finished her soup (shell-smashing and all) while Ciartan was still struggling to disembowel his second crab. Also, her fingers remained perfectly clean, while his were soon all coated in creamy white slime.

The next course – Poldarn help us, thought Ciartan – was hedgehogs, quills still on, in butter sauce.

Tazencius, on the other hand, was talking to him again. 'Am I right in thinking,' he was saying, 'that when you were a boy you were taught, um, blacksmithing?' He made it sound like a filthy habit.

'That's right, sir,' Ciartan said. 'It's traditional, back home; the head of the household is the smith, you see, so I was brought up to the trade ever since I was little.'

'How very sensible,' Tazencius replied, 'learning a practical skill, and at the same time keeping control of the most essential craft safely in the family. I suppose you could say that we do roughly the same sort of thing, except that instead of metalwork we teach our sons the martial arts. But the principle's very much the same, I dare say.'

'Absolutely,' Ciartan said distractedly. He'd just figured out what the style of eating favoured by these wonderfully refined gentry reminded him of: crows, pecking daintily at carrion with their long, precise beaks. 'We see it as both a privilege and a responsibility; much, I suppose, as you do with the fighting skills.'

And other rubbish like that. Lysatis, he couldn't help noticing, hardly said a word to anyone all through the meal.

As soon as it was over, however, he saw her join her mother in shepherding the guests out of the hall, swift and totally efficient, until the only people left were Tazencius and himself.

He wondered if he ought to say something; but while he was considering the matter, Tazencius spoke first.

'You're him, then.'

Ciartan couldn't think of a reply to that. He tried smiling politely, but he was pretty sure it came out as an idiotic smirk.

Just a moment, he thought. Something strange about the way Tazencius had said it; suddenly he realised what it was. He remembered that disconcerting lie he'd participated in earlier: *I also gather that you're quite the linguist.* Tazencius had been talking to him in his own language, the one he hadn't heard since he'd left Haldersness; the one that nobody on this side of the ocean was supposed to know about.

He had to think quite hard to remember how to say it. 'That's right,' he said. 'How do you know—?'

Tazencius's grin showed that he was genuinely, absurdly pleased about something. 'You make it sound like you hadn't guessed. Hadn't you? It's why you're here, boy. Do you know who I am?'

What a question. He hesitated.

'I know who you are,' Tazencius went on. 'You're Ciartan Torstenson of Haldersness. And I know why you're here. And may I say, I'm delighted to meet you at last.'

'Likewise,' Ciartan replied cautiously. 'Look; excuse me and I'm not meaning to be rude, but . . .' And then it suddenly dropped into focus: a memory, of a conversation he'd had on the ship, shortly before he'd landed on this side of the world—

You wait till they make contact with you. They'll find you, don't worry about that. Just bide your time, there's no hurry.

Who should I be looking out for? he'd asked.

Haven't the faintest idea. Somebody pretty important, that's all we know. When they find you, remember, you're to do exactly what they say: they've got it all worked out.

How will I know it's the right one?

Oh, that's easy. He'll be the only man in the whole Empire who can talk our language.

'Yes,' he said, 'that's me.'

Prince Tazencius was looking at him. The amused contempt was still there, but also a little caution, a little disappointment. He felt the urge to explain, to justify himself, to restore the Prince's faith in him. He had no idea why this should be important to him, since the rest of him reckoned Tazencius was a creep.

'When I was on the boat,' he said, 'coming over here; I came across with a raiding party, and stayed behind—' He hesitated. Tazencius nodded very slightly.

'I know why,' he said. 'No need to embarrass yourself explaining.'

Ciartan could feel himself colouring, but he ignored the sensation. 'On the boat,' he said, 'they explained. Grandfather – that's Halder, he brought me up when my dad died – he made all the arrangements. Since I was going to be living over here permanently, or at least for a good long time, it was only reasonable for me to do something to help. Well, I couldn't argue with that – everybody should have a job to do, otherwise they're just outsiders, offcomers. Anyway, my job was to meet up with some people on this side who'd pass on useful information: stuff about where the garrisons are and how many soldiers are billeted at each camp, the roads, how a raiding party could get from one place to another without being noticed, the defences of the cities, which ones were worth taking out, all that sort of thing. Then, when the raiding parties landed, I'd pass all this on, and they'd find life ever so much easier – after all, it's been a couple of hundred years since our lot were thrown out of the Empire, and we don't have any maps or anything like that, so when we land we're just blundering about.' He paused, feeling nervous about something; but the look on Tazencius's face made him carry on. 'Anyhow,' he said, 'when I arrived I waited around – I suppose I was expecting whoever it was to come and find me. But after a week or so I didn't have any food or anywhere to sleep, no money – I didn't even know about money, because we don't use it back home, I had to figure it out for myself as I went along. Had to learn the language, too, but it turns out our people are pretty good at that sort of thing, because of the mind-reading stuff: if you can see people's thoughts, it's not hard to relate them to the sounds they make with their mouths. Anyway, to cut a long story short, I'd more or less come to the conclusion that the grand plan had gone all wrong and nobody was going to make contact with me, so I'd better start looking out for myself, earn a living, settle down. And that's when I bumped into this other kid, Gain Aciava; and when he said, right out of the blue, why didn't I come along and try out for this school he was at, of course I thought he must be him, the contact, or else why would a perfect stranger suggest something as dumb as that? So I went along, and they gave me a place at Deymeson, but of course I'd got it all wrong, it was nothing to do with spying for raiding parties—' He hesitated. Tazencius was slowly shaking his head. 'It was?'

'Of course,' Tazencius said. 'You don't seriously believe something like that would just happen, out of the blue? The governors of Deymeson aren't in the habit of enrolling street urchins who happen to be able to wave a sword around without cutting off their own toes.'

'Oh,' Ciartán said.

'On the contrary.' Tazencius suddenly grinned; very disconcerting. 'You're right about one thing; we were planning to meet you off the boat, but it didn't make land-fall where it was supposed to, and we missed you. It took us weeks to track you down. Fortunately, you were so crass, you behaved so conspicuously oddly that we managed to pick up your trail. Then young Aciava – his family have worked for my family for generations, I'm sponsoring him through Deymeson – he staged the little comedy you referred to, and to our amazement you appeared to take it at face value. Needless to say, we'd arranged for a place for you at Deymeson. I made out you were some by-blow of our family, a little dark secret who had to be provided for. It's happened often enough over the years, so there was no difficulty there. Since then, we've been keeping our eye on you, helping you along where necessary, getting you ready against the day when it suits us for you to start doing the job you were sent here to do.' He paused, suddenly thoughtful. 'It's just occurred to me,' he said, 'that you don't know about the connection between myself and your people. Correct?'

Ciartan nodded.

'Dear me.' Tazencius sighed. 'Then I suppose I'd better tell you.' He pulled a jug of wine towards him, filled two silver cups and pushed one across the table. 'For reasons that don't concern you, but in which a certain General Cronan features significantly, it suits me for your extremely destructive kinsmen to cause a certain degree of havoc inside the Empire. The problem that faced me when I was framing my long-term plans, however, was that nobody, myself included, had any idea who you people are, where you come from – or, indeed, why you keep picking on us and doing so much damage. I had to find out; and then I had a stroke of luck. Three members of one of your pirate bands somehow managed to get themselves captured, by a junior officer loyal to myself: young lieutenant Muno – I'm telling you his name because you'll be doing business with him sooner or later. Muno had the wit to keep quiet about his prisoners and hand them over directly to me.' Tazencius sipped his wine, then went on: 'It took a year, with the best linguists in Torcea working on the project, to reconstruct your people's language from what we got out of the prisoners. Tough customers, all three; but unfortunately two of them didn't survive the process. The third one, when at last we were able to talk to him in his own language, was absolutely stunned to learn that instead of wanting to find out where he came from so we could send an armada and exterminate the lot of you, we wanted to join forces and actually help your people against our own. A not unreasonable reaction, I suppose; but in any event, we finally managed to get through to him, just in time to reunite him with another raiding party that took him back home. There he eventually passed on my request to your grandfather, who in turn chose you.'

'I see,' Ciartan said.

Tazencius smiled. 'You don't, actually,' he said. 'There's a lot more to it. It was only through my good graces and unstinting support that you ever saw your precious homeland in the first place. You are, of course, only half an Islander. Your mother was born a few miles from Mael Bohec. She was raped by your father, a raider, and she killed him. I found out what had happened as a favour to Halder – he was the overlord or whatever you call it of the man I'd captured: Scaptey, his name was. Halder wanted to know the circumstances of his son's death, and he sent Scaptey back to ask me to investigate, as a mark of good faith. So, as I said, I found out the whole sorry story, found the woman who'd killed his son – your mother, of course – and discovered that in the meantime she'd had you. I let Halder know that you existed; he begged me to find you and send you back, which I duly did. About that time, things over here took a turn that I hadn't predicted, which prompted me to shelve for the medium term my plans for disrupting the Empire. In the end, I had to wait sixteen years – by which time, of course, you'd grown up and contrived to get yourself into mortal trouble (I wasn't in the least surprised, considering how you'd come into the world) and both Halder and I agreed that you'd be ideally suited for the purpose. As indeed,' Tazencius continued, almost fondly, 'you are. As a half-caste, your appearance is sufficiently nondescript that you can pass for a native both over here and over there. You have to a certain limited extent your people's bizarre ability to read other people's thoughts; but it's incomplete, which means you can't read minds well enough to see what I'm thinking right now – which is undoubtedly just as well; in other words, you'll never be a danger to me because of it, only an asset. You can never go back home; you can never be at home here. Accordingly, your loyalties will inevitably lie with the only man who'll ever be on your side, effectively your creator – myself. I'm the only person in the world you'll ever be any use to, and in a short space of time you'll make yourself practically indispensable to me, which is why I'm marrying you to my own daughter – who, I should point out, I love devotedly. I trust that by now you understand,' Tazencius continued, leaning forward a little, 'exactly how close are the bonds that tie us together. Consider the extent to which you are indebted to me. I found you; I saved you from the life of a mad, penniless whore's brat in a stinking little village in the Bohec valley. Because of me, you were reunited with your family, your people, you were brought up in your own country. Through no fault of mine, you chose to shit in your own nest; thanks to me, instead of becoming an offcomer – that's your word for it, isn't it? – and spending the rest of your life as a vagrant day-labourer hated by everybody you came into contact with, you were able to come here and start a new life – as a sword-monk, no less, just as if you were a nobleman's son, receiving the finest education that money can buy anywhere in the world. Now, because of my continuing benevolence, you're about to marry a beautiful girl and join the Imperial family; you're looking forward to a life of wealth, privilege and power, to a degree that your poor grandfather could never begin to understand. You see, don't you, that entirely because of me you're absolutely the darling of heaven, the luckiest, jammiest, most blessed man who ever lived – it's as though I'm God and you're the first-ever human being, created by me in my image for our mutual grace.'

He stopped, and looked at Ciartan, clearly expecting an answer. 'I guess so,' Ciartan said.

'You guess so,' Tazencius repeated. 'How beautifully put. But never mind; now you know who you are, and how you came to be that way. Now it's time for you to be acquainted with the obligations that make up your part of the contract. You do agree, I trust, that you owe me your duty, absolute and wholehearted?'

'I suppose I do,' Ciartan said; then – 'Sorry, that sounds pretty ungracious too. But it's come as rather a shock, all this. I mean, I was always told my dad fell nobly in battle and my mum died of a broken heart—'

Tazencius nodded slowly. 'I'm not completely insensitive,' he said. 'To be honest, I'd always assumed – foolishly – that you'd know at least part of the story already. It never occurred to me – but, of course, it should have, and I apologise.' He grinned again. 'A gentleman always assumes the blame for the shortcomings of his inferiors, always provided that they know as well as he does that in doing so, he's lying.'

That sounded uncomfortably like an Expediencies essay title. Ciartan wondered if Tazencius had been educated at Deymeson too; the best education, hadn't he said, in the whole world? In which case, presumably he had. And as for the rest of the stuff – the obligations, he'd called it, the being a spy, helping his people conquer and murder and burn – well, he hadn't thought twice about agreeing when he'd been asked about it on the boat, because back then he didn't know a damn thing about the Empire: as far as he was concerned they were nothing but malevolent pests to be destroyed where necessary, just like crows on the pea field. He asked himself if anything had really changed since then.

Not really, he decided.

'Right,' he said. 'Please tell me what you'd like me to do.'

He sat up in bed, his eyes suddenly open, his mouth open to shout, yell a warning to himself, no, don't do that—

A bit late, unfortunately; however many years ago it'd been, there was nothing he could do about it now. A pity – assuming, of course, that the Tazencius in his dream had been telling the truth. Having met the flesh-and-blood Tazencius on two occasions, he decided that this was a fairly major assumption; if anybody was capable of telling lies even though he wasn't actually there, it'd be Tazencius. Or himself. Whichever.

He realised that what had woken him up wasn't in fact the dramatic revelations of his dream, but the guard, banging on the door. He remembered: today they'd be going to Falcata, and from there on to Dui Chirra, where he'd have the embarrassing job of explaining his unauthorised holiday to Brigadier Muno (who was, presumably, the same as the Lieutenant Muno who'd been on Tazencius's payroll back when he first got off the boat; was that useful information, or just another potential danger? Past caring . . .) He pulled on his boots, grabbed his hat and called out that he was ready.

The guards must've heard something about him overnight, because they treated him as if he could kill with

a glance, like the character in the fairy tale he couldn't quite
remember; they made a point of staying well outside his
circle, watching his every move in case he took it into his
mind to grab a spear from someone's hand and start slaughtering everyone in sight. Thinking about it, they had a
point; but today his shoulder was playing him up and his
left knee ached, and he felt a bit too fragile to live up to
their dire expectations. Furthermore, it was beginning to
dawn on him, in the light of what memories he'd been able
to salvage from his dreams, that the palisade and sentries
around Dui Chirra weren't just there to keep him in, but
also to keep the rest of the distinctly hostile world out; in
which case, maybe he ought never to have left in the first
place.

Colonel Lock, it turned out, wasn't going with him after
all. No doubt there was some pressing reason, work to be
done, meetings that couldn't be cancelled; instead, he was
handed over to an escort led by a burly middle-aged
sergeant with a deep scar running slantwise across his face,
from just under the right eye to the middle of the top lip.

'You,' he said, as soon as he saw Poldarn. 'Well, bugger
me. It *is* you, isn't it?'

I shouldn't really, Poldarn said to himself, but what the
hell? 'You have no idea how good a question that is,' he
said.

The sergeant didn't know what to make of that. 'It's you,
all right,' he said. 'Wasn't sure just now, not with your face
all fucked up like that, but I never ever forget a voice. So,
they caught up with you at last, did they? Bloody good job,
too.'

Poldarn shrugged. 'I'm a foundryman from Dui Chirra,
I went AWOL and I'm being taken back. As far as I know,
that's all there is to it.'

The sergeant laughed. 'And the bloody rest,' he said.
'Maybe you kidded Tadger Lock and the rest of 'em but

you damn well don't fool me. I know you.'

Oh, for pity's sake, Poldarn thought, as he hauled himself clumsily into a rickety four-wheeled cart. 'Really,' he said. 'I don't know you from a hole in the ground, but there's a good reason for that.'

The sergeant glared at him. 'Don't suppose you do recognise me,' he said. 'Expect you've lost count of the poor bastards you've cut about over the years. But I know you,' he said, pressing a fingertip to his scar. 'Gave me this, didn't you?'

Fuck, Poldarn thought. 'I have no idea,' he replied. 'Truth is, I lost my memory a couple of years ago, and I can't remember a damn thing from before then. So what I'm saying is, if we have met before, me not remembering you is nothing personal—'

'Lost your memory?' The sergeant grinned. 'That'd be right. Dead handy, that'd be.'

'Not really,' Poldarn said mildly. 'In fact, it's a bit of a nuisance.'

Long silence. In front of them, the road was a thin ridge of mud and rock between the deep, water-filled ruts. Behind them, the troopers talked in lowered voices, like people at a funeral.

'Is that right, then?' the sergeant said eventually. 'You lost your memory?'

'Yes,' Poldarn said. 'As far back as a couple of years ago. I found out a few things about myself since, but there's still some pretty huge gaps.'

'That must be – strange,' the sergeant said slowly. 'Not knowing the things you've done. Like being lost in a fog, not knowing if you've come on a way or you're just going round in circles.'

'You get used to it,' Poldarn said. 'But you say I gave you that scar. What happened?'

When he replied, the sergeant sounded thoughtful;

embarrassed, even. 'It was a long time ago, mind,' he said.
'And in this game, well, everything's always right up to the
edge, right? I mean, if you and me's fighting, either I'm
going to get you or the other way about, someone's going
to get hurt. Doesn't really mean anything – like, it doesn't
mean I'm better'n you, or you're better than me. Just luck,
half the time, or one of you's got a headache or a pulled
muscle, gives the other bloke an edge.'

'I fought you,' Poldarn said.

The sergeant nodded. 'General Allectus's rebellion, now,
how long ago would that've been?' he said. 'Must be sixteen years, give or take. I'd just put up my second stripe,
so that's about right. Anyhow, I was posted at Josequin,
over in the Bohec valley. Our outfit was attached to the old
Seventeenth, under Colonel Scaff; and you know how it is
in a civil war, you go with your unit, whichever way your
CO decides. Scaff was one of the first to go over to Allectus.
Not saying that was right,' he added quickly. 'Basically, it
was nothing to do with us, we just did as we were told.
Anyhow, there was only really the one battle, not far from
a poxy little village by the name of Cric; Allectus had got
between the government bloke, General Cronan, and his
supply lines, pretty well forced him to fight, because
Cronan didn't want to, you know, commit himself. Didn't
know which side the others'd drop in on, see; the irregulars, Amathy house and the other free companies. It was
all to do with Tazencius – Prince Tazencius as he was then,
and he was always a tricky bastard: which way was he going
to jump, was he behind Allectus or not? No way of telling,
one minute he was and the next he wasn't. Anyhow,' the
sergeant went on, 'we knew whose side *we* were on, it was
everybody else who was mucking about. Then come the
battle, your lot—' He paused, frowning. 'Your lot was with
the Amathy house, he'd rounded up a whole lot of
freelances, bits-and-pieces men, more bandits than

soldiers. I remember, our lot'd been sent out wide round a bit of a wood, sort of like a pincer movement. But we came in late, or someone else was early; anyhow, it'd all fucked up, and we weren't where we were supposed to be. So we push on into this clearing, find there's nobody there to meet us, and we're stood about like a bunch of arseholes, no idea what we're supposed to be doing; and then your lot show up, and we don't even know at this stage if you're on our side or theirs, because that bastard Feron Amathy, he hadn't made his mind up yet, see? So your lot come on in nice and slow and we're stood there; and we're just thinking, fine, they must be with us, then, when suddenly your lot start yelling like mad and come at us. Hell of a fight; and you were this officer, don't know if you were actually commanding the Amathy house outfit or second in command or what, but you were out front, giving the order to charge; and you came straight at me like an arrow from a bow, like you were crazy or something, and you rode right up and swung at me with this big inside-out curved sword, like I'd never seen before. Next thing I know, I'm sat on my arse in the mud, and there's blood all over me, and you're charging on carving up my mate the standard-bearer. You've got your back to me, right; and I'm thinking, I'll have you, you bastard; and there's a dead bloke lying next to me, one of ours, with his spear under him. So I roll him over, get the spear – and I never could throw a javelin worth shit, but just this once I get it absolutely right, smack between your shoulder blades. Only of course you've got armour on; the spear bounces out, but you lose your balance and fall off. I run over just as you're getting up, and there's a hell of a scrap. Anyway, long story short, I knock that fancy sword of yours out of your hand and give you a smack round the head, and you're out of it. Thought you were dead, and then some other bugger has a go at me; and then some more of the Amathy house comes up out of the wood and suddenly it's all over and we're running like buggery, and that's about it. Anyhow,' the sergeant said, 'that was the battle; and like I told you, I was damned sure I'd killed you, till the next time I ran across you.'

'Next time,' Poldarn repeated.

'That's right,' the sergeant said. 'About eighteen months after, it must've been, because the amnesty wasn't for a year. I got caught, along with most of Allectus's men who weren't killed on the spot or directly afterwards, ended up in prison camp – miserable bloody place, more of us died there than in the war – and then the amnesty came through and we had the option, stay there or join up with the regular army. Well, we couldn't sign up fast enough. Anyhow, practically the first job we're put on doing is clearing out all the free company blokes and bits-and-piecers, the ones who'd come to the Bohec valley with Feron Amathy for the war, then stayed on after to hang around looting and such-like. Easy job it was, our lot weren't front-line, we were on escort duty, fetching prisoners back to Josequin. And bugger me if the second batch of prisoners we took on, there you were. Recognised you at once.'

'Oh,' Poldarn said.

'That's right. Of course,' the sergeant went on, looking past him, over his shoulder, 'it's human nature, really. Getting even, I mean. Like, this scar, it didn't heal up for a long time, went bad on me, had a hell of a time with it. And it's not pretty now; back then it was a right mess. Long and the short of it was, first chance I got, me and some of my lads – if an officer hadn't come by and made us stop, we'd have killed you for sure. I mean,' he added, 'we reckoned you were good as dead anyway, we might as well save the government the price of a rope. The officer said leave you where you were, it'd waste too much time carrying you; and that's the last I saw of you, sat up under a tree, all bloody. Like I said,' he added, 'no hard feelings. I mean,

you were just another bloody bandit; and the stuff you'd
been doing—'

'Quite,' Poldarn said. 'Just doing your duty, I suppose.'

'Exactly. Funny, though,' the sergeant went on. 'I mean,
that first time, I was with the rebels and you – well, whatever way you look at it, you were on the government side.
And then the next time, I'm the government and you're
the outlaw. And both times, I end up leaving you for dead.
Makes you think, really – you know, third time lucky and
all.'

Poldarn smiled bleakly. 'You mean this time you really
are going to kill me?'

The sergeant had the grace to look uncomfortable. 'My
orders are, fetch you back to Dui Chirra. And in one piece.'
He hesitated. 'Got any idea what's going to happen to you
when you get there?'

'Not really. Best guess is, I'll get shouted at for a bit, and
then it'll be back to shovelling mud out of the river bed.
Nothing horrible, at any rate.'

The sergeant seemed relieved. 'Well,' he said, 'that's all
right, then. I can't remember: did you tell me why you went
AWOL in the first place?'

'I got bored,' Poldarn said. 'It's a very boring place.'

The sergeant looked at him. 'You get bored real easy,'
he said.

The road was still a mess; the knee-deep ruts were full of
mud, and the carts bottomed out and stuck fast with
depressing regularity. When it wasn't raining, the sun
shone spitefully hot – typical Tulice summer, someone said,
and Poldarn assumed he knew what he was talking about.
They were taking a short cut, following a road Poldarn
hadn't been on before; it was a colliers' road, bypassing
Falcata to the south, skirting a large patch of forest where
there were several large charcoal camps. By the time they

stopped for the night, he was filthy and shattered. It would've been far less trouble to have walked. At least he was so tired that he slept without dreaming.

They started early next morning, to try and make up some of the time they'd lost the previous day, but most of the day was wasted in trying to haul the carts out of a particularly deep and tenacious mud hole. In the end, the sergeant decided the mission was more important than the hardware, and gave the order to leave the carts behind, sending a rider back to camp for a team of oxen to drag them free and unblock the road, while the rest of them continued on foot. Though nobody said anything, it was painfully obvious that every man in the escort blamed Poldarn for what was turning into a horribly memorable assignment. He could see their point. If only he'd stayed put in Dui Chirra in the first place, they'd all have been spared the unpleasantness.

That evening, they called a halt at the first building they'd seen all day. Farms were few and far between in those parts; this one gave every indication of having been deserted for many years. Quite common, someone said; the smaller farms were failing, being bought up by the big proprietors, who took the land and let the houses fall down. Tulice, apparently, didn't have much of a future. It cost more to get local produce to market than to ship corn and dried food across the bay and float it down the rivers to the larger towns; meanwhile, anybody who had the option was leaving the land, heading for the cities or the colliers' camps. The more trees that were felled for charcoal, the worse (apparently) the flooding became. Pretty soon, Tulice would be nothing but a wilderness of derelict farms and rotting tree stumps, linked by a network of impassable roads. It was all somebody's fault, but nobody seemed to know whose.

They'd just about managed to scrape together enough

dry wood for a fire and were fixing something to eat when the sentry called out: a small party coming in up the road toward them. It turned out to be three men, regular army, by the look of them more dead than alive. They were surprised, and relieved, to meet anybody on the road; they hadn't eaten for two days, and they'd been on the point of leaving the road and trying to find the colliers before they starved to death. The sergeant asked them where they'd come from.

'Falcata,' one of them answered. 'What's left of it.'

The sergeant asked him what that was supposed to mean; by his reckoning Falcata was due north, on the other side of the forest.

The soldier shook his head. Not any more, he said. No Falcata any more; just burned wood and cracked stone. The raiders had finally come to Tulice.

Chapter Eleven

Charcoal, Monach thought: it's all these people think about. Show them a tree or a lump of wood, and they burn it to black, crumbly cinders. Even if it happens to be part of a house.

There was, of course, an alternative explanation. The question was, who could have been bothered to do this to a place like Falcata?

'Normally,' said the man he was talking to, a former sword-monk by the name of Mezentius, nominally a captain of infantry, 'the obvious answer would be us. But we didn't do it. Or did I sleep late that day?'

Monach shook his head. 'Not us,' he replied. 'Besides, there's not enough of us, it'd take a proper army to do this.'

Mezentius nodded. 'Won't stop them blaming us,' he replied. 'So, it's either the Amathy house or—' He frowned. 'That's not a nice thought,' he said. 'The raiders aren't supposed to have reached this far south, surely. They'd have to come across the bay to get here, for one thing.'

'Maybe they did,' Monach said.

'What, right past Torcea?'

'Maybe Torcea isn't there any more.'

Whoever had destroyed Falcata, they'd been thorough. Though the cracked stone was still hot, there were hardly any traces to show that anybody had ever lived there, or that the horrible mess that currently occupied the site had ever been habitable: no dead bodies, hardly anything in the way of human artefacts. The heat from the fire had been hot enough to melt the nails out of the walls. Mezentius reckoned that they must've herded the townspeople inside the walls and barred the gates before setting light to some very scientifically laid fires; it had burned out like a furnace, he said, total combustion, like they'd learned about in sixth-grade metallurgy.

'Which suggests it was the raiders,' Mezentius went on. 'Don't know if you saw Josequin after they'd finished with it, but it looked pretty much like this. And from what I've heard, it's by way of being their trademark. Apparently, it's what they do back home, where they come from; when they have wars or feuds or whatever, they barricade their enemies in their own houses and burn them to death. Probably,' he added, 'a religious thing.'

Monach made an effort and swept his mind clear. 'The problem is,' he said, 'we were planning on picking up supplies in Falcata. In case you hadn't noticed, we're practically out of food.'

After a short but passionate debate, they decided to head east, back the way they'd just come. If the raiders were really on the loose, there was no telling which direction they'd be headed in or where they were planning to strike next; but there was nothing out east large enough to interest them, only Dui and Tin Chirra, the charcoal burners' camps and the foundry. True, they'd run into Amathy house troops out that way, but the outfit they'd encountered were pussycats compared with the kind of people who could do this to a walled city—

('Unless it was the Amathy house who did this, and not the raiders after all,' someone said. 'People reckon it was them who did Josequin.')

More to the point, there was a small but well-supplied outpost at Dui Chirra: too small to interest a city-devouring army, but big enough to have enough food to feed them. Ironic, Monach couldn't help thinking. When he'd wanted to go to Dui Chirra, they'd decided it was too dangerous, too well defended. Now he'd come to terms with not going there, that was where they were headed, the only alternative being starvation. Was there a precept of religion that said you only got what you wanted when you didn't want it any more? If not, there damn well ought to have been.

That night, when they were pitching camp, the pickets came in with a bewildered-looking old man who was, they reckoned, the last surviving resident of Falcata.

'Who was it?' Monach demanded, as they pushed the poor fool down into a chair. 'Who did it? Was it the raiders?'

The old man glared at him. 'Don't know what you're talking about,' he replied, for all the world as if Monach was accusing him of having razed the city single-handed.

'Falcata,' Monach said. 'The city. Who destroyed it?'

The old man looked at him as if he was mad. 'Destroyed?' he repeated.

Oh, Monach thought. 'Falcata – it's been burnt down.'

'Bloody hell.' The old man's face looked as though it had suddenly melted. 'What about—?'

'All dead.'

So; fat lot of use he was, and Monach hadn't the heart to have him thrown out, not after that. Some time later, the old man asked Monach who he was.

'Me?' Good question. 'Well, I'm sort of in charge.' He hadn't put that terribly well, but his mind was on other things.

'You mean you're the general?'

'I guess you could say that.'

'Oh. What's it for, then, your army? Who are you?'

Another good bloody question. 'It's a crusade,' Monach said. 'For religion. To save the Empire.'

'Oh. So what're you doing in these parts, then?'

Haven't been on the sharp end of so many good questions since fourth-grade finals. 'We felt this was where we needed to be,' Monach said awkwardly.

'What, to save the city?'

'Well, no.'

'Because you made a piss-poor job of it.'

Eventually they gave him some money and sent him away. Of course, there was nowhere he could spend it, and nothing he could buy with it. But it was the least they could do, in the circumstances.

The next day, everybody was on edge, as if they expected the Amathy house, *and* the regulars, *and* the raiders, by the hundreds of thousands, to jump out at them from behind every tree stump and drystone wall. As a result they made good time, in spite of the pitiful state of the road; nobody wanted to dawdle or stay in one place long enough to tie up a bootlace. Hardly the right attitude for an army of avenging angels: a loud noise or a sudden ambush by three field mice would have them all drawing and carving each other to pieces. But what could anybody expect from a thousand scared peasants led by a hundred over-trained academics? It'd be different, Monach couldn't help thinking, if only Xipho was here; because, when all was said and done, Xipho had always been the only one who really seemed to know what they were supposed to be doing, or why it was so important that they should do it. And where the hell was she, assuming she was still alive? (But if she'd been captured – by the government, the Amathy house, the raiders, someone else – they'd had the forethought to take the kid as well; Ciartan's son, of course, which put a further bewilderingly unfathomable perspective on it all. The day she'd gone missing, at least he'd had some idea what to do – find her, rescue her; or was he supposed to follow on and meet up at some pre-arranged rendezvous she'd told him about, on some occasion when he hadn't been listening properly? And Cordo – Cordo was still alive, in spite of the fact that he'd died, stabbed to death by Ciartan and left to burn in the Old Library.)

When the attack eventually came, of course, they'd got over their jitters and weren't ready for it. They hadn't even realised how close they were to Dui Chirra, not until their counter-attack smashed a hole in the enemy front line and they burst out the other side, scampered up a slope in order to regroup, and found that they were looking straight down at the front gate. It proved to be a stroke of luck; whoever was commanding the enemy (they had no idea, of course, who they were fighting) was under the impression that the counter-attack was a concerted effort to get to the foundry compound at all costs. In consequence, their unknown opponent drew back on the wings, where Monach's people were on the point of running away, and made a dash for the gates; mistimed it, found himself caught between the counter-attack coming down the hill and the re-formed and newly motivated wings in hot pursuit of an enemy who'd suddenly and without provocation posted their unilateral declaration of defeat . . . After that, it was just a mess, which only ended when the enemy second in command opened the gates in order to lead a sortie just as his superior had managed to force Monach and the advance party back over the brow of the hill. As soon as he saw Monach's flank men brushing the sortie aside and streaming in through the gate, he must've lost it altogether; he ordered a ramshackle, last-hope charge which allowed the back end of Monach's little army to smash into his flank and rear. If fifty of his men managed to escape with him down the Falcata road, that was all.

'What happened?' someone asked, as Monach slumped against the inside of the gate and pulled off his helmet.

'I don't know,' Monach replied. 'We won, but buggered if I know how. Who were those people, anyway?'

'Government,' someone else replied. 'Too well kitted out for Amathy house, and if they'd been raiders we'd all be dead by now. My guess is, they were the garrison here.'

Brigadier Muno, then. Fine, Monach thought, it's always nice to know who you've been fighting. But wasn't Muno supposed to be some sort of tactical genius? Or was that his nephew, the one who'd died? 'Anybody know how we made out?'

'Not so bad,' someone told him. 'It looked worse than it was on the wings – our lads didn't get close enough to 'em to come to much harm. We may've lost a couple of dozen killed, same again injured, but it's no worse than that. For what it's worth,' the speaker added, 'we must've got a couple of hundred of them, maybe more.'

Big deal. 'Well,' Monach said, 'anyhow, we won. Let's just hope there's some food left. That's what we came for, after all.'

Men were starting to peep out at them from doorways and windows. It was years since Monach had been in a foundry, and that hadn't been anything like as big as this one. He looked round, suddenly wondering if the garrison's antics hadn't all been a ruse to lure him into the compound, where he'd be surrounded by five thousand heavily armed foundrymen. There did seem to be an awful lot of them—

'Look up,' someone whispered at him. 'Someone's coming. Probably the foreman, manager, whatever he's called.'

Monach stopped slouching, stood up straight and tried

to look like a ruthless conqueror. At least the man approaching looked to be marginally more scared than he was. 'Right,' he called out, when the man was a dozen or so yards away, 'who're you?'

'My name is Galand Dev,' the man replied. He was short, bald, looked like a giant who'd been squashed down to fit inside a dwarf. 'I'm the Imperial representative here. Who are you?'

It was a question Monach was rapidly coming to dread. 'My name doesn't matter,' he replied. 'I speak for the brothers of the Avenging Angels of Light.' He hoped that Mezentius and the others couldn't hear him; they'd have trouble keeping straight faces. 'We claim this post in the name of religion. Bring us all your food, now.'

'Food?' the man called Galand Dev repeated, as though he'd never heard the word before. 'You want food?'

'You heard me.' Monach was painfully aware of having said the wrong thing. 'I'm requisitioning your supplies on behalf of the Brotherhood.'

But Galand Dev was looking sideways at him. 'Fine,' he said. 'Is there anything else you want?'

It was obviously a trick question. *Why, what else've you got?* was almost certainly the wrong answer. But this was just a foundry; and what possible use could eleven hundred saints militant have for a heap of charcoal and a couple of large bells?

Then he remembered. Not bells. How could he have forgotten, for the gods' sakes?

'The food first,' he said, with the sweet calm that comes when you've suddenly remembered what you're supposed to be doing. 'Then the volcano tubes – Poldarn's Flutes, isn't that what you're calling them?'

Galand Dev nodded grimly. 'My orders are to defend them to the death,' he said, without much conviction.

Monach nodded. 'Then it was nice knowing you, if only

for a short time. Who should I see about getting them loaded up, after you're dead?'

Galand Dev sighed. 'That's all right,' he said. 'I'll see to it. But don't imagine for one moment that you've won. By this time tomorrow, the whole Falcata garrison's going to be banging on the gates.'

Monach shook his head. 'I don't think so,' he said. 'Now, are you going to bring the food or do we have to come and fetch it?'

Poldarn's Flutes, he thought, as Galand Dev walked slowly away, flanked by Tacien and Runting (just to make sure); on balance, I think I'd rather have had bells. Nice irony: according to Xipho, though the gods only know how she knew, it's the most important top-secret project in the Empire; I've got them, and I don't actually want them. On the other hand, there's always trade.

If only I knew what it is we *do* want.

If only Xipho was here.

Gradually the foundrymen came out, wary as cats in long grass, uncertain whether they'd been captured, conquered, liberated or simply transferred to new owners along with the plant, goodwill and stock-in-hand. Monach didn't have a clue what to tell them. He was rapidly coming to the conclusion that he wasn't really suited to leadership.

(If Xipho was here, she'd recruit them; if Elaos was still alive, he'd explain it all so that they understood exactly why the battle and occupation had been necessary; if Cordo was here, he'd terrify them into unquestioning obedience; Gain, on the other hand, would probably sell them something. And Ciartan? He'd either kill every one of them, or find a secret hole in the perimeter fence and sneak out—)

Instead, they'd got him, the Earwig, the born follower. He climbed up on a mounting block next to the door of one of the big sheds and cleared his throat. They looked up at him, like the assembled novices at Commemoration of Benefactors. He could feel his stomach tightening into a small, hard knot.

'First,' he said, 'there's no need for you to worry. Just do as you're told, and everything'll be fine.'

Judging by the expressions on their faces, they weren't impressed. He cleared his throat again, and tried once more. 'This facility is now under the control of the Avenging Angels of Light. If any one of you has a problem with that, keep it to yourself. This is a nice, straightforward military occupation. All you've got to do is carry on with your work and keep out from under our feet. In case anybody's expecting the army to come back and throw us out, that won't be happening in a hurry. Last I saw of them, they were making very good time down the Falcata road – and don't kid yourselves that the Falcata garrison'll be along in a day or so, because they won't, you've got my word on that.'

They were looking at him as though he was drunk or raving mad, but he ignored that. 'You can have one hour to get used to the idea that you're working for us now, and then I want to see you all back at your posts, doing whatever it is you do. Talking of which, who's the foreman around here?'

A man in the front row slowly raised his hand. He didn't look like a foreman; in fact, it was hard to say what he did look like. Somewhere, Monach decided, between a very scrawny sword-monk and a half-dead crane-fly. 'Name,' Monach called out.

'I'm called Spenno,' the crane-fly answered, 'I'm in charge of the project – well, me and Galand Dev.'

'Fine,' Monach said. 'You stay. The rest of you, go away.'

In spite of his bizarre appearance, Spenno immediately endeared himself to Monach by not asking who the

Avenging Angels of Light were, or what they thought they were avenging, or what they were doing there. Instead, he offered him a tour of the foundry. 'It's a complicated place, this,' he explained, 'and there's a lot of places where it's a bad idea to be at certain times. Like, you don't want to be downwind of the furnace when there's a fire in. The furnace,' he added, pointing at one of the sheds, 'is over here. You know anything about foundry work?'

'A bit,' Monach replied. 'We studied it at – when I was at school, but only really in passing.'

Spenno looked at him and blinked a couple of times. 'Deymeson,' he said. 'Sword-monk. Yes?'

Monach nodded. 'How'd you guess?'

Spenno had an unexpectedly warm smile. 'Takes one to know one. Been thirty years since I graduated, but you buggers always look the same. Spenno Perfirius, but my name-in-religion was Foy . . . Course, there won't be any more sword-monks now Deymeson's gone. And that's no great loss,' he added. 'Don't suppose there's all that many who'll be sorry to see the back of them. It was a good life, though, apart from all that getting woken up in the small hours to go practising pulling a sword out of its sheath and then putting it back again. Reckon I'd be there yet, only they didn't want me and my dad was having trouble finding the fees. Good at sciences and Expediencies, they said, but there's more religion in an old rusty nail than in the whole of my body. Weren't far off, at that. Never could see the point of religion, to tell you the truth.'

Nor me, Monach thought; but I always supposed that was because there was something wrong with me. 'A lot of us are from Deymeson,' he said. 'Maybe even one or two of the old-timers are from your year – you might find there's someone you know.'

'Unlikely,' Spenno replied. 'I didn't make friends back then. Seemed daft, when you were all going to be fighting each other come the end of the year. No, it's the other way about that's more likely. I mean, *you* might run into an old classmate or two while you're here. There's two more besides me working right here in the foundry.'

Monach looked up sharply. 'Is that right?' he said.

But Spenno was frowning. 'I say that,' he replied. 'But neither of them's here right now, come to think of it. One of them was took away by the soldiers, and the other one slung his hook. Course, neither of 'em said who he was. But it's like I said, you can spot one of us a mile off in a snowstorm. You can see their circles.'

'You don't happen to know their names?' Monach asked, trying to sound casual. 'Their real names, I mean.'

For some reason, Spenno found that amusing. 'I recognised one of them, for sure; I knew him straight off, soon as I set eyes on him, that's why I hired the bugger. And they said I couldn't do religion,' he added, grinning. 'But I knew him, just like I'd known him all my life. Scared the shit out of me to start with, but then I thought, why not? Where the hell else would you expect him to be, but working in a foundry? And then of course the government man rolls up and tells us we're going to be making Poldarn's Flutes. Laugh? I nearly wet myself.'

It was like that moment when the egg cracks from the inside, as the egg-tooth breaks through the shell. 'Ciartan,' Monach said. 'One of them's called Ciartan, right?'

Spenno shrugged. 'No idea,' he said. 'I said I knew who he was, not his name. Names don't matter worth spit, you can put them on and pull them off like hats. Like the other one,' he added. 'He didn't say his right name either. But he knew his stuff, and I could tell he used to be a monk, so I gave him a job. Why not? After all, it's not like we're all still trying to cut each other's heads off once a year. And any bloody fool can learn how to dig clay.'

'Ciartan was here,' Monach said, mostly to himself. 'But

now he's gone. Do you know where he went to? When did he leave?'

Spenno shook his head slowly. 'Deserted,' he replied. 'So chances are he'll have headed straight for Falcata; it's the one place round here you've got to go to before you can go anywhere else. And besides, he'll have had his reasons for going to Falcata, same as why he went to Josequin.'

Falcata, burned to the ground, just as Josequin was. When the god in the cart had visited Cric, he'd said, *I have business in Josequin*, and a few days later it had been wiped off the face of the earth by the raiders. But how could Spenno have heard about what had happened to Falcata? Or wasn't that what he'd meant?

'You haven't seen a woman from our lot?' he asked. 'About my age, tall and bony, calling herself Copis or Xipho Dorunoxy?'

'Can't say I have,' Spenno answered slowly. 'And any woman'd stick out here like a bare bum at a prayer meeting. But I know who she is – she's that woman going round with the Mad Monk.' He looked at Monach and grinned broadly. 'That'll be you, I take it. I must be getting old, or I've been breathing in too many fumes. So *that's* what you're here for. When I heard there was a bunch of our lot roaming around like a load of hooligans I couldn't figure out what on earth they could be after. Should've been able to figure that one out. But you're too early,' he went on, before Monach could interrupt. 'We poured the first one the day after your mate skipped out on us, but it's nowhere near done yet. It came out all right and it's cooled without cracking, far as I can tell; but next it's got to have all the scale and shit chipped off the outside, and then we got to turn out the bore on the lathe and saw off the sprue. It'll be ten days at the earliest, so I hope you're not in any hurry; and what your army's going to eat while you're waiting I haven't a clue, unless you send 'em all out in the woods looking for truffles. Still, that's your problem. Meanwhile, we'll be pouring another six tonight. I wanted to wait and see how the first one came out, but Galand Dev said no, if it's fucked up somehow we can just break 'em up again and melt them down. How he ever got to be a master engineer beats me.'

That had answered Monach's original question, before he'd even got around to asking it. But he wasn't really inter-ested in Poldarn's Flutes any more. Ciartan had been here; so obviously Xipho had known, and that was why they'd been headed this way. In which case, why would she have gone off like that (unless she'd wanted to get here first; but she hadn't been here, assuming Spenno was telling the truth). And there'd been two of them—

'The other one,' he said. 'You said there were two—'

'That's right. And soldiers came and fetched the other one away. There was an accident.' Spenno shook his head, a sort of I-told-them-but-they-wouldn't-listen gesture that, Monach guessed, came very easily to him. 'That one got burned up, the other one saved his life. Anyhow, while he was laid up getting over the burns, soldiers showed up and took him on.'

A thought occured to Monach. 'When you say soldiers,' he said, 'are you sure they were regulars and not Amathy house or something like that?'

'No idea. Assumed they were regulars, or why'd old Muno let them take the man away? Must've had some kind of warrant or whatever they call it. I didn't see them myself, though, you'd have to ask Muno or his staff. But, of course, you can't do that, can you?'

They were standing outside yet another shed, outwardly no different from the dozen or so they'd already visited; except that someone or something inside it was making the most appalling noise Monach had ever heard in his life. 'Engine shed,' Spenno told him, raising his voice over the screaming, graunching, whining, squealing and juddering.

'Right now, this is the place where it's all happening. Want a look?'

Before Monach could think of a way of refusing politely, Spenno had opened the door.

The roof was high, with open skylights all the way down one side. In the middle was an enormous brown tube, ten feet long, slightly tapered, and two feet thick at the thinner end, supported at each end by an 'H' of thick oak posts that raised it three feet or so off the ground. Monach saw that the tube was in fact rotating slowly, and the unspeakable noise was caused by a short, thick steel flat-drill, which a man in a leather apron was driving into it by means of a turnscrew. At his feet, the beaten clay floor was littered with what looked like golden snowflakes – thin, flat fragments of swarf, roughly the shape of a butterfly's wing, which tumbled slowly out of the hole in the front end of the tube as the drill cut into it. At the back end of the tube, he saw a thick leather drive-belt looped round a cartwheel-sized flywheel; another belt whose end disappeared into a slit in the wall fed a smaller gearwheel that drove it. Another cradle of oak posts about halfway down the tube's length supported a T-shaped iron rest on which another man was leaning a foot-long chisel; as the tube turned, the edge of the chisel scraped more snowflakes off the dull, pitted brown skin of the tube, leaving behind a smooth, shiny golden surface. In the corner of the shed was propped a three-legged crane fitted with pulleys and chains. A bored-looking man was sweeping up the swarf with a birch-twig broom, though it was pretty obvious that he was fighting a losing battle.

'There it is,' Spenno said. 'That's the first one we poured. They've been at it for a day, a night and the next morning so far, they're on their third cutting head for the drill, and last time I looked they were nine inches in.'

Monach thought about that for a moment. 'It's going to be a long job, then.'

'You could say that, yes. We got a dozen mules on the treadmill on the other side of the wall there, in the mill shed; we daren't lay on any more, in case the lathe bed couldn't handle the torque. Got to keep it absolutely dead straight, see, or the hole up the middle's going to get skewed, and the whole thing'll only be fit for scrap.'

'I see,' Monach said, playing fast and loose with the truth. 'And when you've finished in here, it'll be ready?'

'Not likely.' Spenno laughed, though Monach couldn't hear him over the scream of the cutter. 'Next we've got to saw off the sprue – that's the rough old lump sticking out the arse end, where the hot metal was poured in. That's a week's work, running three shifts a day.'

'Right,' Monach said. 'And then it'll be ready?'

'Once the touch-hole's been drilled and the muzzle's been crowned, yes. Leastways, the tube itself'll be ready for testing. But it'll need a wooden carriage to hold it up – we can't just lay it on the ground and set it off; and we can't figure out the measurements for the carriage till we've done boring out the hole down the tube, because until we've fetched out all that waste metal, we won't have any idea how much the bloody thing's going to weigh. No point building a complicated carriage if we make it too flimsy and it just crumples up soon as we put the tube on it. Mind you, we could get everything right, and then at the last minute we could find there's wormholes or pockets in the tube, where there's been air bubbles that got caught while it was cooling. Something like that, and the whole thing'd be useless.'

Fine, Monach thought; any ideas he might have had about loading a dozen or so Poldarn's Flutes onto the backs of a team of mules and putting twenty miles or so between his little army and Dui Chirra before Muno came back with overwhelming reinforcements wilted on the vine and died. Obviously, Muno and the government in Torcea had been terrified about someone stealing the tubes; wasted anxiety. Even when it was eventually finished, assuming it survived that long and passed its test without blowing up, how in the names of all the gods could anybody hope to steal something that big?

(In which case, either Xipho had screwed up in her planning for once, or else her disappearance wasn't part of some ingenious plan for robbing the foundry and making a lightning-quick getaway into the depths of the forest.)

'Some machine you've got there,' he said. 'Did you build it, or did you have it shipped in from Torcea?'

Spenno was contriving to look proud and offended at the same time. 'They haven't got anything like this in Torcea, not as far as I know. Don't suppose there's another like it in the world. Anyhow, that's it, more or less. Now, are you planning on taking the tube with you when you go? Or was it something else you were after?' Monach looked at him; it was like looking in a steamed-up mirror. 'Something that's nothing to do with the tubes?'

Monach nodded slightly. 'Actually,' he said, 'we only came here to get food.'

'Is that so? But I thought you said earlier that you came on past Falcata. Why didn't you take on supplies there?'

For a moment, Monach was sure that Spenno already knew, about Falcata and what had happened there. But how could he possibly know? 'Too well guarded,' he said. 'We didn't fancy tangling with the garrison.'

'Fair enough,' Spenno replied. 'I can see the sense in that. Still, it's a pity you didn't come along just that bit earlier, you'd have been in time to see these two others I've been telling you about, from the old place. And you reckon he was from your year? Talk about coincidences. Anyhow,' Spenno said suddenly, 'that's pretty much it – you've seen it all now, what we got here. Now it's my turn to ask you a few questions, I guess. Like, exactly what is it you and your lot are after? Why're you Angels, and what is it you're avenging?'

Monach sighed. 'That's just a name I thought up,' he said. 'Basically, most of us, we were at what you might call a loose end when Deymeson got destroyed, so we thought we might as well go into business on our own account, if you follow me. A free company, I believe the term is.'

'Ah. Like the Amathy house.'

'You could say that. Except we aren't mercenary soldiers, we only fight when we're attacked. We just – sort of wander about, looking after ourselves.'

'Oh. That's not what I'd heard.' Spenno shrugged. 'Not that I care. I mean, you or the government, who gives a damn, there's only ever predators and quarry. Not even sure which one you are, at that.'

After he'd thought about it for most of the rest of the day, Monach came to the conclusion that that was probably meant to be a compliment. Of a sort.

The dream had been going on for some time before he managed to figure out who he was, and who he was meant to be in the dream.

There was a crow. It was perched on his shoulder, and its wings were on fire – he could hardly breathe for the disgusting smell of burning feathers. He only had himself to blame for that, since he'd been the one who'd swatted the crow out of the air with the hearth-rake and held it down in the fire, while it had screamed at him and glared murderously at him. Now it didn't seem to feel the pain from the burning; it was his decoy, to draw in the other crows so that he could throw stones and kill them. Its name was either Elaos or Gain or Cordo or Xipho, but he couldn't remember which.

Anyhow, the crows kept on coming, high over his left shoulder, coming from wherever it was they were holding, crossing the hedge, banking on the glide, swooping low and beating upwind, only a foot or so off the ground, wing-tips curled upwards, silent. Each time he waited till he could make out the beak and the eye, to be sure he was in range; then, as soon as his circle was compromised, quickly to his feet, throwing his arm back as he moved, and as soon as he was above the top edge of the hide he let go, hurling the flint so hard that it jarred his elbow and shoulder. So far he hadn't missed; some of them sank unwillingly to the ground in a flurry of ineffectual wing-beats, others dropped straight down, beak first, dead in the air. He'd killed so many that they were landing on top of each other, the stone-dead dropping on the backs of the dying, like the slaughtered monks when the raiders burned Deymeson—

And then he realised that he'd only been seeing a small part of the picture; because in the background behind him was a mountain, a volcano, and the black ash and shit it was hurling high up into the air was crows and more crows, every convulsion and spasm at the ruptured peak throwing out another flock; and the slopes and foothills of the volcano were already black with thousands upon thousands of dead crows, which presumably he'd killed too, though he couldn't remember it offhand. But it didn't matter, because any moment now the furnace deep in the volcano's roots would be hot enough for the pour, and the red-golden lava would cascade down into the valley and cover everything – and he had nobody to blame but himself, because who in his right mind would build his farm in the bottom of a mould?

But he still wasn't seeing the whole picture; because when he turned his head and looked down, he saw that the black fluttering wings drifting out of the air and landing at his feet were the swarf from a great drill that was boring into the mountain top, as Spenno and Father Tutor and the rest of the Order turned out the bore of Poldarn's Flute;

and the crow on his shoulder was saying, *It all makes perfect sense, but you're too bloody dim to see it.*

'Don't be so annoying,' he told the crow. 'Besides, if you were half as smart as you seem to think you are, you'd have noticed that you're perched on the wrong shoulder. This isn't even my dream, for pity's sake. You're going to be in so much trouble when they find out you've given the wrong dream to the wrong guy.'

The crow squawked angrily, opened its burning wings and flapped laboriously up into the wind, battling for height until it was able to turn. As it slowly sailed away, he could just hear it saying, *Told him but he wouldn't listen, they never do*, and he realised it'd been Spenno all along. He watched the bird until it was just a black dot in the sky; it dragged itself through the air until it was right over the glowing orange scar in the mountain, but a spurt of yellow flame licked it out of the sky like a lizard catching a fly with its tongue, and it fell, burning, onto the hearth.

My dream after all, then, the Earwig realised. *I wish I knew where Xipho'd got to, though. It'd all make perfect sense if only she was here.* But he knew where she had to be; somewhere down in the valley, driving her cart down the Falcata road (Falcata burning, burnt to charcoal by the fiery garbage from the volcano) and across the Bay straight towards Torcea—

The black feathery swarf from the great drill was up to his ankles as he stood up and threw his stone, hard and fast and straight as a stone ball shot from the lips of Poldarn's Flute. *All right*, he wanted to scream, *I get the point already.* But of course all this wasn't for his benefit, because he was only the Earwig, born follower, eternal subordinate, assistant sidekick. They were putting on the show for someone else. Went without saying.

(Falcata burning; thousands and thousands of houses, doors jammed and wedged shut, and inside were thousands and thousands and thousands of people screaming and fighting to get out, until finally the smoke and the falling rafters and the burning thatch swatted them down like a hearth-rake and pinned them to the hearth until they stopped moving—)

And Spenno was sitting on his shoulder, the book open on his knees, pointing and saying, *Ciartan was here, but you just missed him*; and at that moment, it suddenly occurred to him what Ciartan was calling himself these days; except that it wasn't possible, because—

'Bloody hell, Chief,' Mezentius was saying, 'what was all that about?'

He opened his eyes. 'Sorry,' he mumbled. 'What?'

'You were having a bad dream or something,' someone else said. 'Screaming and yelling like someone was killing a pig with a blunt knife. We've been trying to wake you up, but you wouldn't open your eyes.'

'Oh,' Monach said. The dream was slipping past him, but it was too late to pull it back. 'What time is it?'

'Hour or so after sunup,' Mezentius said. 'We let you lie in – thought we were doing you a favour.'

'Oh.' Monach sighed and swung his legs off the bed. 'Anything been happening since I've been asleep?'

'Not much,' said someone else. 'They're still doing whatever it is they're doing that makes that horrible noise, over in that big shed across the yard. And around midnight, they were up to something over where they've got that enormous oven contraption; they had one hell of a fire brewed up, and that nutcase foreman was cursing and swearing like they'd put hot coals down his trousers. But they reckon that's normal and everything was going just fine.' He shook his head. 'They're a bloody funny lot, if you ask me.'

Monach nodded. 'The foreman told me that they were going to cast another six of the tubes last night, so I guess that's what they were doing. Best leave them to it, they seem to know what they're doing.'

'Fine,' interrupted Runting, the quartermaster. 'Bloody good luck to them, since presumably it's us they're working for now. Talking of which, what in God's name do we want with half a dozen tubular bells? I suppose we could sell them and buy food, if anybody knows who'd be likely to want to buy them—'

'Runting, they're not bells, they're *weapons*,' someone told him. 'It's some top secret thing the government's cooking up to fight the raiders with. It's what we're here for, for the gods' sakes. Don't you ever bother coming to staff meetings?'

'How can you fight the raiders with bells? You planning to ring them to death, or what?'

Monach pushed past them into the fresh, wet air. Even with Falcata in ashes, how long was it going to take for Colonel Muno to raise enough men to come back and kill them all? He'd only come here because they hadn't got any food left, the Flutes hadn't even crossed his mind. Now they had the food (only enough for a day or so), the Flutes weren't ready to take even if he was minded to burden himself with them, Xipho hadn't even been here and it wouldn't be terribly smart to still be here when Muno got back. Time to go. Absolutely no reason to stay.

Had Ciartan really been here? When Spenno had mentioned another sword-monk, he'd assumed without thinking that it had to be Ciartan; now he couldn't even remember what it was Spenno had said that had prompted the assumption. But if he had—

He went to see Galand Dev.

'Paperwork,' he said. 'I'm assuming Colonel Muno was typical army when it came to filing and keeping copies of letters, all that shit?'

Galand Dev seemed more than a little offended by such

an unashamedly blasphemous attitude, but he managed to answer the question without actually bursting apart. 'He didn't use sealed orders to light fires or wipe his bum, if that's what you mean,' he said. 'I imagine you'll find all his papers in the drawing office. I doubt very much he'd have taken them with him into battle.'

'Fine,' Monach said. 'In that case, you can come along with me and help me find what I'm looking for.'

Galand Dev sighed. 'There's nothing in international law that says a prisoner of war's got to help his captors rifle through official government archives,' he said. 'In fact, it'd probably be treason.'

Monach smiled pleasantly. 'Fuck international law,' he said. 'Do as you're told, or I'll have you hung. Coming?'

Galand Dev nodded. 'If you insist,' he said, as they crossed the yard to the drawing office. 'What exactly are you looking for, anyway?'

'A while back,' Monach replied, 'one of your workers – I don't know his name, but he was involved in a nasty accident and got badly burned; anyhow, while he was recovering from that, some soldiers turned up and arrested him.'

'I know who you mean.'

'Excellent. Now,' Monach continued, 'I'm assuming that Colonel Muno wouldn't have released the man to these soldiers without a proper warrant, or some kind of paperwork at the very least. Do you think you could find it for me?'

Muno's files were every bit as meticulously kept as Monach had expected them to be, and it wasn't long before Galand Dev turned up what he wanted. The paper was still rolled up in its neat brass message-tube, the two halves of the broken seal still in place on either side of the cap. Monach twisted the cap off and teased the paper out with his fingers.

He recognised the form of words. In fact, its very

familiarity struck him as disturbing even before he got to the signature at the bottom, which of course he recognised—

> *To Brigadier Muno, commanding the volcano-tube project at Dui Chirra foundry, greetings. You are hereby required to hand over to the bearers hereof the person more particularly described in the schedule hereto, and to afford immediately and without delay to the said bearers all aid and assistance that they may request in the furtherance of these presents.*
>
> *Schedule: the adult male, identity unknown, currently employed at Dui Chirra foundry in the capacity of black-smith and general labourer, formerly a monk of the Order of Poverty and Education established at Deymeson. To be handed over under restraint, dead or alive. This warrant to supersede all powers, orders, facilities and immunities whatsoever.*
>
> *As witness my hand the day and year hereinbefore written:*
> *Cleapho*
> *Imperial Chaplain In Ordinary*

'There you are, then,' Galand Dev was saying. 'Everything perfectly in order.' Monach hadn't noticed, but he'd been standing on tiptoe to read the warrant over his shoulder. 'The gods only know what that joker'd got himself into,' he went on. 'Must've been something pretty drastic if the chaplain's office was involved. Some sort of treason, anyhow, if it came under ecclesiastical jurisdiction.' He stopped; Monach could almost hear the gears grinding inside his head, as it suddenly occurred to him to wonder why the Mad Monk was concerning himself with the validity of an Imperial warrant. 'Friend of yours, or something?' he asked, trying to sound guileless and failing dismally.

'I want to know what happened,' Monach said slowly, 'on the day when this arrived.'

'Sorry.' Galand Dev was having to make an effort not to smirk. 'But it'd have been handled by Muno and his staff; and, of course, they aren't here for you to ask.'

'Nor they are,' Monach said, dangerously pleasant. 'But someone must've seen them come and go, apart from Muno's soldiers. Don't you think?'

'I suppose so. But—'

'Fine. Find them, I've got some questions. You've got till mid-afternoon, so you'd better get a move on. Understood?'

Galand Dev may not have been the most perceptive man in the Empire, but he wasn't blind and deaf. 'Of course,' he said hurriedly. 'I'll get someone on it – I'll see to it myself,' he corrected himself quickly, 'right away.'

'Thanks.' Monach rolled up the paper, slid it back into the tube and stowed the tube in his coat pocket. 'I won't detain you any longer. Thank you for your time.'

If Monach derived any amusement from the sight of Galand Dev scuttling away like a stranded crab, he didn't stop to savour it. Just like the old story about the philosopher and the child's riddle, he thought; *the more I think about it, the harder it gets.* Cleapho, of all people; nominally the third most important man in the Empire, in practice the second (particularly now that Muno Silsny was dead and no new commander-in-chief had been appointed to replace him). Cleapho, defender of the faith, *ex officio* leader of what was left of the Deymeson order. Of course, Monach had never set eyes on him, Cleapho practically never left Torcea—

Monach frowned, remembering something that Xipho had told him, about the time she'd spent going round the Bohec valley in a cart with Ciartan; how they'd run into Cleapho himself at some inn in Sansory, and Cleapho had taken Ciartan off for a private meeting, and there'd been a fight, government soldiers—

Far away at the back of his mind, a little voice Monach hadn't heard for some time was asking an inconvenient question, and it wouldn't shut up. It was asking: if Cleapho was really up to something, some dark plot involving Ciartan of all people, then how come the government soldiers had found out about it, and come hurrying to the scene to arrest the conspirators? For one thing, nobody outside the palace itself had the authority to arrest the Chaplain in Ordinary, certainly nobody who could be fetched by an informer in Sansory at half an hour's notice. And if a plot had been discovered, with strong enough evidence to warrant arresting the chaplain, how come he hadn't been seized and executed the moment he set foot back in Torcea?

And how come – damn that little voice, why couldn't it keep its nasty suspicions to itself? – how come Xipho had recognised Chaplain Cleapho? Because she'd lived for a while in Torcea, she'd said, and had seen him preach at the Great Temple. Except – Monach was fairly certain of this but he could be getting confused – hadn't her time in Torcea all been part of the lie she told Ciartan, to cover up the fact that she was an agent of the Order? In which case, she'd never been to Torcea at all, and couldn't have seen Cleapho there—

Assuming she was telling the truth when she'd told him she'd been lying—

(Or perhaps she had been to Torcea at some point in her service, the same way he'd been to all sorts of places; in which case, she'd only lied about how she'd come to be in the capital and what she'd done while she was there. If only he could remember; if only Xipho was here.)

But if Xipho had lied to *him* – and if Ciartan had been here; and now Monach was here and they weren't, they'd skipped out on him and left him in possession of a deadly

secret but useless unfinished weapon, and the most strategically important facility in the Empire—

Which should have been the most heavily guarded
facility in the Empire, if it was really so confoundedly
important. But, instead, it had been left in the care of
Brigadier Muno and a couple of hundred infantry, a force
so slight and negligible that the Earwig had been able to
put them to flight practically by accident. As if someone
had set up the Poldarn's Flute project and then left it lying
about, where the first passing bandit chief or Mad Monk
who happened to be in the area couldn't help acquiring it.
As if they'd wanted him to have it.

(But in that case, wouldn't the weapon itself, the Flute,
have been finished, ready and waiting for him to collect?
Or maybe that was the bit of the plan that'd gone wrong,
thanks to Spenno and Galand Dev scratching each other's
eyes out over the right way to build a drop-bottom cupola
furnace?)

The more I think about it, the harder it gets; except, why
would Xipho lie to me?

Not that Monach gave a flying fuck about them, but he
hunted down Spenno in his lair and asked after the six
newly cast tubes.

'No idea,' Spenno replied, looking up and marking his
place in his book with a small piece of rag. 'They won't be
cool enough to break out of the moulds until this time
tomorrow, and until then there's no way of knowing. Could
be absolutely fine, could be cracked to buggery and riddled
with air pockets. You need patience if you work in a
foundry.'

'Fine,' Monach grunted. 'So what about the other one?
How's the drilling coming along?'

'Ah,' Spenno said. 'Now there things are looking a bit
more hopeful. They're over two-thirds of the way down,

and so far it all seems to be working out. Course, we won't actually know till we load the thing up with Morevich powder and set fire to it. Then, if it blows up and kills us all, we can probably interpret that as meaning we've still got a few bugs to iron out.'

Monach nodded slowly. 'It's behind schedule, isn't it?' he asked.

Spenno laughed. 'You could say that. According to old Muno, we should've had a dozen Flutes all polished up and ready to ship by now. Which might've been possible, if I hadn't had to fight that arsehole Galand Dev every bloody step of the way.' He frowned. 'Not that that's any of your concern, is it?' he asked. 'I mean, why would you be worried about what the Torcea government wants?'

Not knowing the answer himself, Monach ignored the question. 'I just found out that the order to arrest that sword-monk came from Chaplain Cleapho. Did you know that?'

Spenno shrugged. 'News to me,' he said. 'Talking of which, surely he's one of us. What does he think of your holy war?'

'I don't suppose he even knows we exist,' Monach replied, uncomfortably aware that he was probably lying. 'So what'd it take to pack up the unfinished Flutes and that lathe contraption of yours, and set them up somewhere else?'

Spenno smiled, revealing missing teeth. 'A miracle,' he said. 'Which is your department, not mine. Like I told you, Father Tutor always reckoned I sucked at religion.'

'What if I made that a direct order?' Monach ventured.

'Then I guess I'd be in even more trouble than I am already,' Spenno answered, yawning. 'But it's like they say: when you're drowning, getting spat on isn't such a big deal.'

Which was about as much Spenno as Monach could take

for one day, particularly on an empty stomach. Which reminded him: he had over a thousand people on his hands still, and enough food to feed them for maybe three days. Small administrative details like that.

(Cleapho, he thought, for crying out loud. And Cordo, unaccountably returned from the dead. And Ciartan had been here; but Cleapho had sent orders to arrest the Dui Chirra blacksmith, and they'd taken the other man instead. And where had Xipho got to, when she was most desperately needed?)

Eventually they found Monach in the grain shed, counting the sacks of flour for the fifth time and still not managing to come up with a more reassuring total. There was good news, Mezentius told him, and bad news: which did he want first?

Well, the good news was that the monthly supply train was coming up the west road. It'd been held up, apparently, by the stinking horrible weather – bridges washed away, fords impassable, roads that swallowed carts whole, the usual stuff – but it was definitely on its way and should arrive the day after next.

The bad news, on the other hand, was that there was an Imperial army coming up the east road, which ought to get here at roughly the same time as the supply train. It could quite easily be a dead heat; in which case, Brigadier Muno and his seven thousand men would be able to celebrate their recapture of Dui Chirra with a hearty breakfast.

Chapter Twelve

'Don't ask me,' the sergeant was saying, not for the first time, 'I don't know what to do, I'm not a bloody officer. Far as I'm concerned, I got my orders and I'm going to carry them out. Nothing to do with me, Falcata.'

'But that's so stupid,' someone else broke in. 'You can't just carry on as though nothing's happened. I mean, what if HQ doesn't know about it yet? What if nobody knows? What if the bastards attack somewhere else, and everybody's killed, just because you failed to raise the alarm?'

'Look.' The sergeant was getting angry. 'I don't remember anything in Standing Orders about having a vote every time a decision needs making. For all we know,' he went on, lowering his voice a little, 'getting this prisoner to Dui Chirra's more important to the Empire than saving half a dozen bloody cities. Besides,' he added, with the harsh enthusiasm of someone who'd just picked up on a previously overlooked good point, 'there aren't any more cities left round here they could burn, it's all poxy little villages and coach stops and charcoal burners.'

It wasn't a good enough argument to stay up for, so Poldarn lay down beside the fire and tried to go to sleep. They'd made hardly any progress all that day, what with the sergeant and his council of advisers bickering and the road in an even worse mess than usual; not that he was bothered, since the last place he wanted to go was Dui Chirra. If his people had really come here and destroyed Falcata, and if they knew there was a bronze foundry in the neighborhood, with enough raw material to supply the forges of a hundred farms for a century, he knew exactly where they'd be headed next. He was almost tempted to slip away – he didn't really want to meet a raiding party from home, which might include friends and relations of Eyvind or some other of his victims; or, worse still, relatives of his own, who'd probably want to take him back to Haldersness – but he didn't have the energy to play hide-and-seek in the dark and the mud with a platoon of already bad-tempered soldiers. The plain fact was, he didn't really care where he went, mostly because no matter where he ended up, he'd have no chance, outside of being killed, of getting away from himself, and the seething mess of memories, half-memories and suspicions he'd been collecting in his mind ever since the man calling himself Gain Aciava had turned up on the cart to Dui Chirra. Compared with sharing his own company, nothing that could happen to him on the Tulice levels was worth getting worked up about.

Eventually he did fall asleep, soothed by a lullaby of querulous voices, and by some miracle or merciful dispensation he didn't have a dream or it didn't stay with him when he woke up, cramped and drenched in dew, at first light the next morning.

Either the soldiers had sat up arguing all night or they'd resumed bright and early: the debate was still going on, though he didn't seem to have missed anything in the way of exciting new arguments. The sergeant, though, was now the only proponent of carrying on to Dui Chirra. The opposition was more or less equally divided between turning round and going back to camp, or heading into the forest and finding the nearest colliers' camp, in the hope of scrounging some food.

Mention of the colliers reminded Poldarn of something; and it occurred to him that, if his sense of direction wasn't completely skewed, he wasn't all that far from Basano's camp, where he'd gone to negotiate a supply of charcoal for the foundry. Had that carefree negotiator really been him? It seemed like a thousand years ago, back in the Age of Gold, before the human race lost its innocence, and there was nothing to worry about except deer ticks, stale beer and boredom. He couldn't help remembering what Basano had said, about how colliery workers came and went, how there was always a job for anybody who was prepared to hang around long enough. At the time, he couldn't get away from the place fast enough. Strange, how the world can change so much so quickly and still look pretty much the same on the outside.

That put a different complexion on all the relevant arguments. True, he'd still be whoever he was, as much so at a colliers' camp as on the road or back at Dui Chirra. The difference was that, during the days and weeks it took for a big pile of cordwood to cook itself into charcoal, the colliers' idea of work was to sit on the edge of the stack and drink their revolting home-brewed beer. Getting rid of himself by drowning his conscious mind in booze was an approach that Poldarn couldn't remember having tried; between intoxication and dysentery, he doubted whether he'd have much opportunity to brood. Ideal.

That was that, then. Unfortunately, it was now too late for him to sneak away in the dark without being noticed; another opportunity neglected. On the other hand, nobody showed the slightest interest in getting up and moving on. It looked as if they'd be perfectly capable of staying here arguing all day, until it was dark enough for him to sling his hook without being seen or missed. But that wasn't so good; waking up to find they'd lost their prisoner might just be enough to snap them out of their differences and bring them along after him. He could always join in the debate and add his support to the pro-food faction; much easier to fake his own disappearance once they were at the colliers' camp, whereupon the soldiers would light out into the forest looking for him, and he could stay behind and ask if there was any work going. He decided against that, however; in the mood the sergeant was in, he'd be certain to veto any suggestion coming from his human cargo. Poldarn gave the matter some more thought, and came to the conclusion that the deciding factor in the debate was bound to be the realisation that they had enough food left for one meal, just possibly two.

So he waited until just after noon, when the soldiers had opened the ration sacks and been reminded of how very little they contained; then he wandered over to the fire, waited for the next tense, gloomy silence, and said in as conversational a tone as he could manage that as far as he could recall, there was a large and well-supplied colliers' camp just across the way from where they were, and maybe they could spare a bit of flour and a drop of beer. When the sergeant started to object, Poldarn added that when he'd been here the last time, the colliers had put him on a good worthwhile short cut back to Dui Chirra, which had shaved at least a day off his return journey—

That put paid to any further resistance from the sergeant, and Poldarn found himself promoted from high-security prisoner to navigator-in-chief. That was fine, the only drawback being that he didn't have more than a vague idea of the way to Basano's place, not without the annoying old man to guide him, and his sense of direction seemed to be allergic to trees in quantity. Annoyingly, the first major landmark he recognised was the filthy, muddy swamp that the old man had called Battle Slough; and he only realised he knew where he was once they'd blundered into it up over their knees.

For some reason, the soldiers didn't seem too pleased about that. Probably because of the rains, the swamp was even stickier and more treacherous than it had been the last time Poldarn had been out that way; and he couldn't help recalling the incident from which, according to his guide on that occasion (Corvolo: he dragged the name out of the back of his mind, with roughly the same level of effort as it was costing him to take one step forward), the place had derived its name. Fairly soon, if Corvolo hadn't been embellishing for dramatic effect, they could expect to come across the mildewed skeletons of the soldiers who'd got themselves hopelessly stuck here, and stayed put until they starved to death—

At least it took his mind off brooding over whether Gain Aciava had been telling the truth. Instead, Poldarn forced himself to concentrate on what he could remember of his first visit, with particular reference to such points as which direction the shadows had been pointing, the time of day, whether the slope had been with or against them. In the end he wasn't sure whether he found the way out of Battle Slough or whether it found him; in any event, by nightfall they were on the faint pattern of bent bracken stems and trampled leaf mould that was the best the forest could furnish them with by way of a road, and on their way to Basano's camp – assuming, of course, that it was still there.

As their circles collided, he drew and so did she.

There was a moment during which time was the circular room in which the examination was taking place. In the middle of the room he stood facing her: at his back was the past – Elaos, Cordo, Gain, the Earwig, the rest of his year, Father Tutor and the two external examiners, draped in heavy black robes like a crow's plumage; behind her was the future, but she was standing in the way and he couldn't see it clearly. But he saw her hand slip down onto the sword hilt, saw the blade sliding smoothly out over her sash, rising to meet him, until its bevelled side collided with its mirror image, his own sword, like the reflection of a face in a still, shallow pool.

There are no moments in religion; no present, only past and future waging war over a disputed frontier. As her hand dropped to her waist, he saw both of them draw, and then the blades smacked together, flat on flat.

A voice inside his head was telling him what to do; and he knew it was his own voice, calling to him from across the border, where he'd already watched the fight and knew what had happened. The voice directed his moves as he cut, parried, lunged, sidestepped – *you tried a cut to her right temple but she anticipated and cut to your left knee* – so he moved across and back as he slashed at her head, and when her counter-attack came, his knee wasn't there any more; *and then you tried a draw-cut across the inside of her elbow, but at the last moment you pulled it and turned it into a jab to her throat, but she dodged back and feinted at your chin, you fell for that and she swung at your wrist*, so he dropped his wrist as he jabbed and her cut missed him by the thickness of a leaf. *And then she recovered before you did and tried for a lunge straight at your neck—*

He opened his eyes, but it was still dark. Something was pricking his throat.

'Easy,' said a voice behind and above him, very softly. 'Perfectly still or you'll do yourself a mischief.'

(But that wasn't right; because he'd woken up, so Xipho should've been left behind, in the dream. Or had she stayed behind just a moment too long, and the dream had left without her?)

'Now then,' Copis's voice whispered, 'nice and slow, I want you to stand up. I will kill you if you try anything.'

(But that was wrong too, because he remembered that term-end duel as if it had only finished a minute ago. She'd lunged at his neck, actually pricked him and drawn a single tiny drop of blood; but he'd expected it, that was the bait in his trap, and a split second later he'd kicked her legs out from under her and ended the fight, the first ever blood-less victory in a sixth-grade year-end duel in Deymeson's history—)

He did as he was told. The violation of his circle told him she was shifting, sidestepping carefully round him like a cat walking along the top of a door. The pressure behind whatever it was that was pricking his throat remained per-fectly constant, very nearly hard enough to pierce the skin but not *quite*. You had to admire the control.

'Walk forward,' the voice went on. 'Keep going till I say stop. Then turn sixty degrees left.'

Once he'd performed the manoeuvre, the pressure light-ened a little, enough so that he wouldn't kill himself if he moved his throat muscles sufficiently to speak. 'Are you going to kill me?' he asked. No answer. He carried on walking, one slow step at a time.

Fifteen paces; and then Copis's voice said, 'Not yet. Not unless you make me, like by stopping unexpectedly or turning round. Keep going.'

By his reckoning, another two dozen paces would take him outside the circle of firelight, out of the clearing where they'd pitched tents for the night, and back into the forest. If he tripped along the way – too many tree roots and fallen branches for blind dead reckoning – the sharp thing pressing into his neck would be the death of him. All the more reason, then, to go nice and steady.

His eyes were getting used to the dark, which meant he
could make out the larger obstacles under his feet (a big
brown and grey flint, a fungus-covered tree trunk, a single
deep rut in the path). 'Copis,' he said, statement rather
than question. 'Is that you?'

'Yes.'

At the edge of the clearing, just as he'd anticipated, the
pricking under his chin stopped. But his spy from the
future had either gone off duty or looked the other way,
because he wasn't expecting the bash on the back of his
head with something thick and heavy—

He woke up and opened his eyes.

He wasn't quite sure what he'd been expecting to see,
being uncertain whether the episode where he'd felt a knife
at his throat and thought he'd heard Copis's voice was just
a coda to the dream about some school fencing-match, or
whether it had actually happened. In the event, what he
saw was a man standing over him, holding a spear.

(Another dream? Eyvind had stood over him with a
spear, that time when he turned them all out of
Ciartanstead. And there were crows, two of them, sitting
in the high branches of a rowan tree on his right—)

'Quiet,' the man said, and he definitely wasn't Eyvind.
Who he was Poldarn had no idea, but he looked vaguely
military – boots, long tatty coat over a mail shirt. 'Don't
try shouting for your mates or I'll skewer you.'

They're no friends of mine, I haven't got any friends . . .
He nodded instead. Above the canopy of leaves and
branches he could see the pale blue of dawn. Whoever this
man was, he wasn't alone, and the people with him were
about to kill the sergeant and the rest of Poldarn's escort.
He wished that didn't have to happen, but presumably it
was necessary – for all he knew, the man with the spear and
his colleagues might be the good guys. He wanted to ask

if Copis had really been there, but he decided not to.

After what seemed like a very long time, the snap of a twig told him that someone was coming, someone who didn't care if the man with the spear heard him. 'All right?' the man called out without taking his eyes off Poldarn's face.

'Job done,' someone replied, sounding weary.

'Get them all?' the spearman asked.

'Think so.'

The spearman frowned. 'Did you or didn't you? How many?'

'Fourteen.'

(Poldarn tried to remember how many there'd been in the party, but he'd never counted them. It wasn't something you did when you met new people, count them so you'd know later if they'd all been killed.)

But the spearman seemed relieved. 'Right,' he said. 'You, on your feet. Easy,' he added, quite unnecessarily; Poldarn knew the drill by this stage without having to be told.

His legs felt weak and cramped, and his head (he noticed) was hurting a lot. Men had appeared out of the darkness, scaring the crows away. They were also wearing greatcoats over mail shirts; but they were altogether too scruffy to be regular army, not like the neatly modular units that had made up Brigadier Muno's command at Dui Chirra. So: not government soldiers, definitely not raiders. Of the armed forces he knew to be operating in these parts, that meant they were either the Mad Monk's outfit, or the Amathy house.

Someone he couldn't see grabbed his hands, pulled them behind his back and tied them tightly with rope. A shove in the small of his back suggested that he should start walking; at the same time, the spearman turned his back and moved on ahead, leading the way. Absolutely no point whatsoever asking where they were taking him.

At some point, someone in front of him started to sing – quietly, badly, maybe without even realising that he was doing it. He sang:

Two crows sitting in a tall thin tree
Two crows sitting in a tall thin tree
Two crows sitting in a tall thin tree
Along comes the Dodger, and he makes it three.

When they stopped walking, the sun was directly over-head, call it seven hours at a fairly slow march, so some-thing the order of fifteen miles (but since he had no idea where he'd started from and hadn't recognised any of the places they'd been, meaningless). A hand on his shoulder pushed him down on his knees; the rest of the party sat down. Some of them took off their boots and shook out grit and small stones, or gulped water from canteens (didn't offer him any; hadn't expected them to). It was dry under-foot, soft leaf mould. They'd been following a shallow path, wider than a deer track, narrower than a cart road and not rutted up by the passage of wheels or horses. Someone seemed to know where they were supposed to be going. This time, he made a point of counting them: twenty-eight.

He was probably going to get thumped for asking, but it was worth a try. 'Excuse me,' he said to nobody in par-ticular, 'but who are you?'

Silence, lasting long enough that he was on the point of repeating the question. Then someone said, 'Fuck me, it's true.'

The man who'd spoken shifted round to face him. 'It's true, isn't it?' he said. 'You don't know who we are. Do you?'

'No,' Poldarn said.

'Amazing.' The man grinned. 'He doesn't know.'

'I lost my memory, a year or so back,' Poldarn ventured. 'A few bits and pieces have come back since then, but I'm

afraid I don't remember any of you.' He tried for an educated guess. 'Are you the Amathy house?'

Someone thought that was highly amusing. 'Wouldn't
have credited it,' someone said. 'I mean, you hear about
stuff like that, people get a bash on the head and they can't
remember their own names, but – well, it's a bit bloody
far-fetched.'

'Unless it's just an act,' someone else said.

'On your feet,' the spearman announced abruptly, and
they all stood up. Poldarn did the same, and nobody seemed
to mind. The spearman led the way, as before. It was nearly
dark by the time they stopped again.

At least they had food with them: small round barley
cakes, stale and hard as crab shells, and cheese you could've
used to wedge axe heads. As an afterthought, when they'd
all eaten something and complained about how revolting
it was, someone got up and brought Poldarn two of the
cakes – no cheese, Poldarn rationalised, because if it was
as hard as they said it was, he might've used the edge to
saw through his ropes. The man laid the two cakes on a flat
stone a couple of feet away from where Poldarn was
sitting, then used another stone to smash them into fragments. Then he went back to his place. After sitting for a
while staring at the bits of cake shrapnel, Poldarn shuffled
forward, leaned down from the waist and gobbled up a
mouthful like a dog feeding from a bowl. His escort found
this performance mildly entertaining, which was more than
could be said for the cakes.

'Better give him something to drink as well,' he heard
someone say, as he bent down for another mouthful. 'Don't
want him croaking on us, when all's said and done.'

So someone brought him a canteen and allowed him four
swallows of warm, muddy-tasting water. Poldarn said
thank you very politely; the man didn't seem to hear.

They were talking quietly among themselves now,

keeping their voices down, and Poldarn could only make out a few unenlightening words, though at least one of them mentioned Falcata, Dui Chirra and Brigadier Muno. Then someone said something that the rest appeared to find extremely funny, and one of them got up and sat down next to Poldarn, six inches or so outside his circle.

'Straight up,' he said. 'Is that right, you really can't remember back past a year or so?'

'Yes,' Poldarn replied.

The man turned to smile over his shoulder at his mates; he was medium height, unusually broad across the shoulders, with a grey stubble of hair sprouting on his shaved head. He had burn scars on his left cheek, old and probably as close to being healed as they were ever going to get. 'So,' he went on, 'you're telling me you don't know who *I* am, either.'

Poldarn looked at him. 'We've met before?'

Everyone, the burned man included, burst out laughing. Poldarn waited for them to stop, then said: 'I guess that means you know me.'

'You could say that,' the burned man answered, grinning.

'Don't suppose you'd care to—'

'No.'

Well, he'd expected as much; he'd already got the impression that they didn't seem very well disposed towards him. 'Do you know a man called Gain Aciava?' he asked.

This time the burned man looked blank. He shook his head.

'Xipho Dorunoxy? Copis?'

'Doesn't ring any bells. All right, my turn,' the burned man said. 'How about Dorf Bofor? Recognise the name? Sergeant Dorf Bofor?'

Poldarn shook his head slowly. 'Doesn't mean anything to me, I'm afraid. Sorry, is that your name?'

This time, everyone laughed except the burned man, who looked as if he was about to kick Poldarn in the face. 'No, it bloody well isn't,' he replied. 'But I got this here' – and he pointed to the burn – 'fishing you out of a burning library when you went back in after him, the useless fat bastard; and there's others, good friends of mine, died that day because of you wanting to be a fucking hero. And you don't remember that.'

'No,' Poldarn replied and braced himself for the attack; it was a kick aimed at his chin, but the burned man missed and connected with his collarbone instead. On balance, the chin would've been better. 'I'm very sorry,' he said, as soon as he could speak again. 'But I can't remember anything, not for certain, and that's just a fact. There's no malice in it.'

'Yeah, right,' the burned man said. 'No malice. Coming from you, that's a bloody laugh.'

Going to get kicked again, but that can't be helped. 'What did I do?' he asked.

The laughter had an edge to it this time. 'What did you do?' the burned man repeated. 'You want to know, then.'

'Yes.'

'*Sorry*,' the burned man said with mock contrition, 'but we only got till dawn; what's that, ten hours?' A small ripple of brittle laughter. 'Couldn't tell you the half of it in ten hours.'

'Never mind, then,' Poldarn said. 'Just pick a few bits at random.'

This time the burned man caught him on the elbow. Not quite as painful, but enough to be going on with. 'All right, then,' he said. 'There was Vail Bohec. Mean anything to you?'

Poldarn shook his head.

'Twenty thousand people, all killed in a day. Ackery: fifteen thousand. Berenna Priory – boarded up the monks in the chapter house and burned them all to death. Josequin: you weren't there, but you planned it all out, right down to the last detail. General Allectus: stabbed him in the back, eighteen thousand of his men cut down where they stood. You don't remember that, of course.'

'No, I don't.'

'Course not. How bloody convenient. Weal Huon: thirteen thousand. Morannel. Deymeson. And whose fault is it we've got that arsehole Tazencius sitting in the palace at Torcea pretending he's the Emperor? Or Caen Daras: the river got so blocked with dead bodies it flooded right up through the Rookwood valley. Who'd want to remember something like that if they didn't have to?'

'That's all just names, though,' Poldarn said. 'Why won't you tell me what actually happened? Why it was my fault. I mean, I can't have killed all those people with my own hands.'

Third time lucky, as far as the burned man was concerned; and Poldarn had been wrong, the chin was far worse than the collarbone. 'You want to know who I am?' the burned man was shouting. 'Sergeant Illimo Velzen, that's my name. You think you can remember that, you bastard, or do you need something to help remind you?'

'All right, that's enough,' said a voice that sounded a long way off – the man with the spear who'd been there when Poldarn woke up. 'It's my arse on the line if he's dead on arrival. Sit down and save your strength, we've got a long day ahead of us tomorrow.'

It took the burned man a minute or so to get a grip on himself, with the spearman and various others telling him to calm down, leave it, Poldarn wasn't worth it and so forth; then he turned his back and sat down, leaving Poldarn crumpled up where he'd fallen. It could've been worse, he eventually decided, nothing broken as far as he could tell (though he'd learned one thing about himself: he had exceptionally tough, strong bones). He wriggled about until he was as comfortable as he could make himself, and tried to clear his mind of what he'd heard – which was impossible, of course.

A pity, though. All that information the burned man had given him, and he still didn't know whether they were the Mad Monk or the Amathy house. On balance, he reckoned, probably the latter; but he had to admit he was mostly guessing. He tried closing his eyes, but that just made things worse; without really wanting to, he started on the mental arithmetic: twenty thousand plus fifteen thousand plus eighteen plus thirteen, that made fifty-six thousand, no, *sixty*-six, he'd forgotten to carry the one – ten thousand people, snuffed out of memory by a simple mathematical error. Not that it mattered, because the data was incomplete in any event. And almost certainly the burned man didn't even know about Eyvind, or Egil Colscegson, or the two gods in the cart, or the troopers he'd killed on the way to Cric. He grinned suddenly. A new cure for insomnia: why count sheep when you can count dead people—?

As he stood up, three crows lifted out of a tall tree and beat an undignified retreat, screaming at him as they flew away. The sound alerted them, and they turned round to see who was there.

'Over here,' he said quietly; and he noticed with amusement that he was speaking his own language with a distinct foreign accent. Been away far too long; but whose fault was that?

A moment of tense silence; then a voice he recognised. 'Ciartan?'

'Over here,' he repeated. 'You're late.'

'No, you're early.' Scaptey's voice; it was absurd, hearing it here, on the other side of the world, on this alien continent. 'Where are you, Ciartan? I can't see you.'

He smiled to himself and started to walk towards them. 'Now can you see me, you blind old fool?'

'Not so much of the old.' There was Scaptey, the familiar shape of his head and shoulders, a memory coming together out of the dark. 'Bloody hell, boy, it's good to see you again. How've you been?'

Scaptey's bear-hug crushed most of the breath out of his lungs; still, he managed to say, 'Don't tell me I've grown, or I'll smash your face in. How's the old man? Is he all right?'

Close enough to see his face. 'Halder's just fine,' Scaptey said. 'He sends his love.'

'And the farm?'

'Just how you left it,' Scaptey said; then he grinned as he added, 'Except for the fucking crows. They got in on the winter wheat where it got flattened in the spring rains, hardly worth cutting after they were done with it. We need you back home, I reckon, teach them buggers a lesson.'

'And there was me thinking I'd killed them all.' He laughed. 'Who else is with you? Anyone from the valley?'

Scaptey shook his head. 'Green River folk, mostly,' he said, 'Halder couldn't spare a crew this year. Fences need doing all up the north side, and we're building three new barns. Just Raffen and me this time; Halder reckoned we weren't no good for anything, so we wouldn't be missed. Rannwey sends her love too,' he added. It was the first time he'd ever heard someone from back home tell a deliberate lie. 'And you have grown too, you bugger. Must suit you, over here.'

'Three new barns,' he said. 'That sounds pretty good. Sounds like you were able to manage without me after all.'

Scaptey grinned. 'Well, we're getting along somehow,' he said. 'Except, we need you over at the forge. That kid Asburn, he does his best, but of course he was never bred to it like you were. He's all right for simple things but when it comes to anything a bit clever he hasn't got a clue.'

'Well.' For some reason, what Scaptey had just said made him want to smirk with pride. And there was something else besides: he was jealous. It wasn't right that Asburn the odd-job boy should be working in *his* forge, using his tools, taking his place. 'Maybe I'll be back sooner than you think,' he said, though he had no call to be saying anything of the sort. 'Anyhow, that's enough about home. I think I've got all the information you'll need.' And he launched into his report, like a small child reciting a carefully learned lesson: the location, topography and defences of Caen Daras, the number and disposition of its garrison, the little-known road across the hog's-back ridge that would bring them unseen to within half a mile of the east gate. He explained the plan of campaign, stressing how vital it was that there should be no survivors. He told Scaptey where the carts would be waiting to carry the raiders' share of the plunder back to the ships, and where to leave the gold and silver hidden so that the Prince's men would be able to find it. When he'd been through everything he'd been briefed about, along with all his own observations that were likely to prove useful, and answered questions about various points that Scaptey wasn't sure about, the first red stains were already starting to seep through into the eastern sky. 'Time I wasn't here,' he said. 'Remember what I told you, and good luck. Though it ought to be easy as shelling peas.'

Scaptey nodded. 'With all you've told me,' he said, 'we should be able to get there and do the job with our eyes shut.'

'You could,' he agreed, 'but it'll be easier with 'em open. See you next year, then.'

His horse was where he'd left it, with Sergeant Velzen standing guard, wide awake and obviously terrified. He smiled. As far as Velzen was concerned, the creature he'd just been talking to was as strange and unnatural as a werewolf, and twenty times more dangerous; but Scaptey was just the old dairyman, who'd taught him how to race sticks down the home paddock stream when he was six. 'All done,' he said. 'We can go back now.'

The relief in Velzen's face was comical to see. 'Have to get a move on,' he muttered, 'if you want to be back in camp by reveille.' He pronounced it *rev'lly*, in the approved manner for old sweats. 'You said you'd only be an hour.'

'Time flies when you're having fun,' he replied, and had the pleasure of watching Velzen's skin crawl. They mounted up and made good time, once they were on the post road. As soon as they reached the camp, he went straight to the staff tent and made his report, leaving out a few bits and pieces that weren't important, and some other things that were nobody's business but his own. It was awkward and wearing, always having to be so careful about what he said and didn't say, always needing to remember who he was being at any give time. Still, as Cordo would've said, it was better than drawing swords for a living—

He woke up suddenly, to find that two crows were perched on his knees, taking a professional interest in the raw wounds he'd been left with after his one-sided fight with the burned man, the one who'd called himself Illimo Velzen. He tried to grab them but they were too quick, and drew themselves into the air with their wings like men rowing a boat against the current.

He watched them circle a couple of times before they pitched in a high, spindly ash tree. For some reason, probably the associations of the dream, he found himself thinking about home. No woods and forests like this one there – what wouldn't they give for a few dozen loads of this tall, straight lumber; and how horrified they'd be at the thought of the colliers' camps, where so much precious timber was chopped up into cords and logs and wantonly burned into black cinders. No wonder Asburn had never let him use charcoal to get the forge fire started; it would've been an unspeakable crime, like wasting water in the desert.

He looked across and saw that they were all still asleep: Velzen and the man with the spear, and twenty-six others. Then he noticed something; or rather, a perception that had been troubling his unconscious mind for some time slid into focus, so that he knew what it was. He could smell woodsmoke – not the campfire, because it was cold, must've gone out during the night; so there was another fire nearby, probably a large one if he could smell it further than he could see or hear the men who'd lit it. He cursed impatiently at his rotten sense of direction. They'd just wandered clear of the swamp where the battle had been when he'd been abducted, and after that they'd marched him a whole day, but in which direction he had no idea. Was it possible that the smoke was coming from Basano's charcoal-burning? The wind, what little there was of it, seemed to be drifting in from the north. How far did smoke carry? Probably they taught you useful stuff like that at Deymeson, but of course he couldn't remember. In any event, it wasn't worth thinking about; even if he did manage to sneak away without waking up the soldiers, and even if by some miracle he managed to find his way to Basano's camp, it was idiotic to suppose that the colliers would be prepared to protect him against twenty-eight armed and angry Amathy house men, even if they were capable of it. Besides, he still wasn't sure whether he'd been captured or rescued, though the aches and pains from Velzen's boot inclined him to favour the former. All right, then; from Basano's camp, would he be able to find his way back up to the main road, in time to make a dash for it and get to the safety of Dui Chirra and Brigadier Muno's regulars before the Amathy house caught up with him? Highly unlikely, and it'd depend very much on how far he'd be able to get before Velzen and his lads noticed he'd gone and figured out which way he was headed.

Even so; it was an alternative, an option, and it'd been a while since he'd had the luxury of one of them. And not to forget the adjustment in the odds that stealing a sword or a halberd on his way out would make; it wasn't something he was proud of or liked to dwell on, but he'd confidently back himself against two, three, maybe four of these men at a time, if it came to a running battle in dense cover. Assuming, of course, that he really wanted to go back to Dui Chirra and carry on where he'd left off shovelling wet clay. That was yet another unwarranted assumption. There was the matter of a voice in the darkness, Copis (no, Xipho; Copis had never truly existed). If it really had been her, and she hadn't cut his throat while he slept, as she could so easily have done – another perfectly good option spoiled by indecision and the faint blemish of memory.

Come on, he urged himself, get real: what possible good could come of running into Xipho again? Even if he survived the encounter and it didn't result in a slow and painful death, the best he stood to gain was more slices of his past, maybe confirming what Gain had told him, or the dreams. Dui Chirra, on the other hand, was the only place he knew of where he stood any chance of being safe from further unwanted revelations, at least until the Poldarn's Flute project finished and the gates were opened and the stockade came down. He couldn't help smiling at his own obtuseness; how, when he'd been there, he'd foolishly assumed that the defences and guards were to keep him in, when all the time they'd been put there expressly to keep the other him out— Besides, he told himself, the food's better at Dui Chirra; and if he got into another orgy of reminscences with Sergeant Velzen, one or other of them wasn't going to survive it, so better all round to make sure it didn't happen.

He took another look at the camp and the sleepers. He could see the man who was supposed to be keeping watch; he was sitting apart from the others, on slightly higher ground, with his back to the trunk of an old, fat copper beech. Maybe he wasn't used to marching all day in difficult terrain; he'd fallen asleep at his post, his halberd lying on the ground beside him where it had slipped through his fingers. Getting past him wouldn't be hard, and neither would taking his weapon; but the rest of them'd be waking up any time now – it was well on the way to getting light. If he was going to go, he had to go now.

Well, he thought, why not? If they caught him before he reached Dui Chirra, they had orders not to kill him. And on general principles, it was better to do something, even something that turned out to be bloody stupid, than hold still and allow things to be done to you.

Painfully and cautiously, he stood up. Dui Chirra it was, then. But first, he had to get out of this clearing.

Something else they almost certainly taught at Deymeson: how to walk about in a forest without making an unspeakable noise. Unfortunately, unlike drawing a sword and killing people, he didn't seem to have learned it well enough for it to have become second nature to him. Maybe it had been something you could only do as an extra, outside regular hours, along with pottery and classical Thurmian literature, and he hadn't bothered with it.

But the sentry turned out to be one of those happy people who can sleep through anything, including an escaping prisoner standing on his hand; so, in spite of forgetting to steal the halberd and having to go back for it, Poldarn made the edge of the clearing and set off into the forest, heading (he hoped) north. All he had to guide himself by was a very hazy recollection of the orientation of the stars – assuming the little white cluster he thought was the Chain wasn't in fact the Seven Sleepers – and a faint taste of woodsmoke on the gentle breeze.

Accordingly, he was as surprised as he was pleased when, about three hours after sunrise, he walked out of a thick curtain of holly and found himself standing on the edge of a broad rutted road. It wasn't where he'd expected to find himself, needless to say, since he'd been heading for the colliers' camp. But there was only one road that this could possibly be: the main post road from Falcata to Dui Chirra. Somehow he'd contrived to cut a day's march off his journey.

Amazing, Poldarn thought. I really should get lost more often.

By now, he had the sun to steer by, so he didn't hesitate before turning left, due west, up a gently rising slope. There were no fresh footprints or wheel tracks in the mud, and the ruts were full of dirty brown water, knee-deep. Obviously not the busiest road in the Empire, and that was reassuring; the destroyers of Falcata hadn't come this way, and he wasn't likely to catch them up round the next bend.

That evening, after a thoroughly exhausting day of picking his way between the ruts, he was eventually forced off the road by a shower of heavy rain, which drove him into the shelter of the trees. He didn't want to lose any time, since there was no knowing if Velzen and the soldiers were on his trail or how far behind they were, but blundering into a pothole in the dark and damaging himself would slow him up even more than stopping for a few hours. He found another patch of dense, scrubby holly and crawled into it to shelter from the rain, not that he could get any wetter than he was already. The thought of his dry shack inside the foundry stockade seemed almost unbearably luxurious. All he had to do was get to Dui Chirra and he'd practically be in paradise, because what more could anybody possibly want out of life than food, a change of clothes and a warm fire?

Poldarn must have fallen asleep; it was light again, though the rain was still falling as briskly as it had been when he'd closed his eyes. But there was another sound beside the patter of falling water on leaves and branches: the creak of wheels and the spattering noise of hooves in mud. Cautiously he peered through the holly branches and saw a small cart with an oiled-leather canopy.

Joy. Whoever they were, they must be going to Dui Chirra, or at least passing by it; and they'd have to have hearts of stone to refuse him a lift. He pushed out through the holly, hardly noticing the scatches on his face and hands, and charged across to meet the cart. Through the curtain of rain he could just make out two faces under the canopy.

'Hey,' he shouted, 'wait up. Are you going to Dui Chirra?'

'Yes,' someone called back. 'Want a lift?'

'You bet,' Poldarn yelled, splashing through the mud at a run. The cart stopped, and he hauled himself up onto the box as the two people sitting there budged up to give him room. The driver was a woman, though he couldn't see her face past the shoulder of the man next to her who was all muffled up in a hooded coat and a blanket. 'Thanks,' he added, as he sat down.

'No problem.' The man turned his face towards him, and grinned. 'You've saved us the job of looking for you. Hello, Ciartan.'

Before he could move, the man leaned forward and grabbed his collar. 'It is you, isn't it?' he said. 'Yes, thought so. Well, this is a happy coincidence.'

Looking at the man's face was like looking at his own reflection: the same white, melted, hairless skin. 'Gain,' Poldarn said.

'Like I said,' replied Gain Aciava, 'we were just on our way to look for you. What're you doing out of the camp? You aren't supposed to leave.'

Gain let go of Poldarn's collar. 'I ran away,' Poldarn replied. 'But then I sort of got into trouble, so I'm heading back. But what're you doing here? They said you were arrested by soldiers.'

'That's right.' Gain was smiling. 'Poor buggers,' he said. 'They're dead now, and it wasn't even their mistake. Just unlucky.'

'I don't understand,' Poldarn said. 'What happened?'

'They arrested the wrong man,' Gain said. 'It was you they were after; but that clown Muno gave them me instead. He'll say it was just a case of mistaken identity, but my guess is he was trying to save your life, repaying the family debt. His nephew,' Gain explained, as Poldarn stared at him blankly. 'One good turn deserving another, and all that. But anyway, it's all been sorted out now, and here we are. Good to see you again.'

No, it isn't, Poldarn thought; and then the driver reached up with her left hand and pushed aside the cowl of her hood, so that he could see her face. 'Hello, Ciartan,' she said.

For a moment he couldn't decide what to do. If he tried to jump off the cart, Gain would grab hold of him, and there'd be a fight; he suddenly remembered that he'd left the halberd behind in the holly bushes, not that it'd have done him any good at such close quarters. Besides, he had no idea whether he wanted to escape or not – it was precisely the sort of useful knowledge that he'd been having to do without ever since he'd woken up in the mud beside the Bohec river three years ago.

He took a deep breath and let it go slowly. At the most fundamental level, it was a choice between walking in the rain or riding in a covered cart. No contest.

'Hello, Copis,' he replied.

Chapter Thirteen

'You're getting better,' she said. 'The last two times I've been driving in a cart with a man and met you on the road, you've killed him. And don't call me Copis,' she added. 'My name's Xipho – or had you forgotten?'

'You see,' Gain interrupted, before he could reply, 'she hasn't changed a bit, even after all these years. Next she'll be saying she won't help you with your homework.'

'Shut up, Gain,' Copis said dismissively, like a mother automatically rebuking a difficult child. 'Well,' she went on, 'I'd like to say you're looking good, but that'd be lying. You look ghastly, just like the idiot boy here. Somebody should've told you two not to play with fire.'

It was a moment before Poldarn managed to figure out what she was talking about. She went on: 'It's just as well Gain's with me, I honestly don't think I'd have recognised you; except, of course, I knew I was looking for a man with a horribly burned face. And your voice is the same. I guess I'd know it anywhere. But what the hell are you doing out here? You never did have any consideration. All the trouble we've been to, just so we'd meet you at Dui Chirra, and you weren't even bloody well there.'

So that was it, the question answered. Gain had been telling the truth. Poldarn felt as though he'd walked across a desert, just to find himself back where he'd started from. 'I don't understand,' he said.

For some reason, they both found that highly amusing. 'It's all right,' Gain said, 'you aren't supposed to. And besides, your sensibilities are probably the least important thing in the whole world right now. Isn't that right, Xipho?'

'Yes.' She took one hand off the reins to wipe rainwater out of her eyes. 'A bit like old times, really; except that this time we're the ones who know what's going on, and you aren't. Shall we tell him, Gain, or would it be more fun to let him sweat for a while?'

'Probably,' Gain replied. 'But remember who we've got here – the most slippery boy in the whole school. Got to do something to keep him from running away. Either we bash him over the head and tie him up, or we tell him a story. What do you reckon?'

'Tell him the story,' Copis replied. 'I haven't got the energy to play games.'

While they were talking, Poldarn was figuring out the chances of getting away: a sitting jump off the box into the mud, followed by a frantic sprint for the cover of the trees. If only he could get a few yards into the forest, he felt sure he could lose them, but in order to get that far he'd have to be faster, cleverer for two whole seconds, maybe even three. It'd be like trying to outdraw two sword-monks simultaneously. Might as well try to escape drowning in a river by strangling it with his bare hands.

He turned and looked Gain Aciava in the eye. 'All that stuff you told me,' he said. 'Was it true?'

Gain grinned. 'Would I lie to you? I never have yet. And I've known you since you were seventeen.'

'I've lied to you a *lot*,' Copis put in. 'But Gain's not like me. Painfully straightforward. Did he tell you what he's been doing for a living lately? Selling false teeth?'

Poldarn looked at both of them. He was quick, he had reflexes that could only be explained by reference to religion, fast and accurate enough to knock a flying crow out of the air with a stone. But not quick enough. 'Who are you?' he asked. 'And why were you looking for me?'

In the end, it was a straightforward race: a quarter-mile dash through the mud, carts on one side, horsemen on the other. The carts won, by a whisker; all but two of them made it in through the gate before Brigadier Muno's out-riders could intercept them. The two stragglers were cut off only yards from the stockade, but the defenders had no choice but to slam the gates in their faces, whereupon the riders surged round them like the incoming tide.

Fine, Monach said to himself, as he watched from the picket tower, it'll have to be a siege, then. I've never done a siege before, it'll be a new experience for me.

At least he was off to a good start, thanks to some appallingly bad judgement on the part of the supply-team drivers, who hadn't realised that Muno's people were, like themselves, government troops. The first they'd known of their mistake was when they'd thundered in through the gates and noticed that the armed men cheering them on and grinning were a bit too scruffy for regular soldiers. Then the gates swept shut, and the garrison men were jumping up on the carts, grabbing the drivers, twisting their arms behind their backs, and it was too late to get away. Monach couldn't help feeling just a little bit sorry for them.

And grateful, too; if they hadn't driven that last couple of miles with breathtaking skill and desperate courage, any further resistance on his part would've been out of the question. Even now, he only had enough supplies to last three weeks, four at the very most; but he had a shrewd suspicion that Muno was probably even worse off in that respect than he was. In Tulice in the wet season, a loaf in the stores was worth a bushel in a supply depot fifty miles away down swamped and flooded roads. Back in sixth grade, they'd been taught a reliable mathematical formula for calculating the probabilities of success in a siege. Assuming he'd remembered it correctly and his data was accurate, the odds were fifty-six to forty-four in his favour; so that was all right—

The bad thing about sieges, Monach rapidly discovered, was the overwhelming amount of administration they entailed. Guard shifts, rations, working parties to secure the defences; officers of the day, officers in charge of supply, officers reporting to other officers reporting to him. Proper soldiers, of course, were trained for this sort of thing and took it in their stride; but he wasn't a proper soldier, he was a sword-monk, and all he really knew about was pulling a sword out of a scabbard. If he'd wanted to be a clerk, he'd have stayed home and gone into the dried-fish business.

Fortunately, Monach soon discovered, he had an ally. Exactly how Spenno the pattern-maker had come to hate the government so much, he wasn't quite sure, though as far as he could tell it was mostly to do with the titanic clash of personalities between himself and the admittedly insufferable Galand Dev. In any event, Spenno was if anything even more determined than he was that Brigadier Muno shouldn't recapture the Dui Chirra foundry; and whereas Monach was a mere warlord, Spenno was a foreman – the same degree of difference, he soon realised, as between cast iron and tempered steel. From the moment when Monach found the courage to abdicate responsibility for the defence of Dui Chirra and let Spenno get on with it, everything seemed to flow as smoothly as a coil of tangled rope teased patiently apart by an expert. Within the hour, teams of efficient workers (foundrymen, Monach couldn't help noticing, rather than his somewhat temperamental and unreliable fellow warriors) were stacking flour barrels, carrying planks of wood and buckets of nails, and hauling carts and wheelbarrows through the standing pools of rainwater in the yard. He had no idea what they were doing; but they did, which was all that mattered. Shaking his head, he went back up the picket tower, to watch the antlike scurrying and listen to the distant but clearly audible sound of Spenno's fluent, musical swearing.

On the other side of the stockade, Monach observed with great pleasure, things didn't seem to be going nearly as well. Brigadier Muno – he recognised him at once by his fine full-length blue cloak – stood in the centre of a buzzing cloud of staff officers, like an azure cow-pat surrounded by flies; but not much work seemed to be getting done. His soldiers were either leaning on their spears or sitting on their shields in the mud, not even bothering to try and find shelter from the pelting rain. Best of all, he had a clear view of Muno's store-tents. Unless he'd arranged for a substantial supply train to follow on after him, Muno was only a few days away from starvation – and even if a hundred heavy wagons laden with flour and biscuits were already on their way, their chances of getting through were poor and getting worse with every gallon of water that fell out of the sky. Another thing Muno seemed to have forgotten in his haste to get underway was a sufficiency of tents. Monach looked up at the thick banks of iron-grey clouds piling in from the south and, for the first time he could remember, thanked the gods for rain: so much deadlier, he couldn't help thinking, than a monk's sword, or even a backsabre.

It was still slashing down when a small group of riders squelched up to the gates, one of them holding a stick from which drooped a thoroughly sodden white flag. Muno, it transpired, was prepared to negotiate, in the interests of avoiding unnecessary bloodshed. Big of him, Monach thought cheerfully, and gave the order for them to be allowed in. It was Spenno, clearly far crueller and more adept at mental warfare than he was, who had them shown into the warm, dry charcoal store and given hot soup and dry clothes.

That night, once the heralds had reluctantly gone home to their sodden blankets and two slices of wet bread, Spenno banked up the drawing-office fire with charcoal and poured Monach a mug of beer. 'I remember doing sieges in fourth-grade Tactics,' he said, 'but I never thought it'd be like this. Cosy,' he added, with a grin.

Monach frowned. 'Let's hope Brigadier Muno sees the funny side as much as we do,' he replied. 'I hate to say this, but my men aren't soldiers. If they decide to attack, we haven't got a clue how to go about defending a fortified position.'

'We know that,' Spenno replied. 'He doesn't. Don't get me wrong,' he added. 'Muno's a good soldier. Which means cautious. Which means sitting out there in the mud till his food runs out, then going away.'

Monach nodded. 'Sure,' he said, 'this time. But we've got nowhere else to go. What's going to happen when it stops raining, and he comes back? It was amazing luck, the supply train showing up when it did, but there won't be any more carts coming down the road from now on.'

Spenno drank his beer and wiped his mouth on the back of his hand. 'He'll come back, all right,' he said. 'It's *when* he comes back that's important. They way I've got it figured, it'll be three days before he packs up and leaves then a week to get supplies. He'll be doing really well if he's back again inside of a fortnight. We've got food for three weeks.'

Monach got the feeling he was missing the point. 'Wonderful,' he said. 'So he comes back, we sit here for a week and then surrender. By which time—'

But Spenno was shaking his head. 'Eight days,' he said. 'That's all I need.'

'Oh.' Suddenly, Monach realised what Spenno was talking about.

'Maybe even less,' Spenno went on. 'Drilling out the bore's going quicker than I thought, and we've made a few mods to the rig that ought to save a whole lot of time when we come to do the next batch. Sawing off the sprues, too, I reckon we can halve the time on that. And making the carriages – well, I was reckoning on having to build limbers, for hauling the bloody things cross-country. Fixed carriages, for shooting down from the watchtowers, much easier. By the time old Muno comes back again, we'll have a welcome for him he'll never forget.'

I wouldn't go that far, Monach said to himself: it's amazing what you can forget if you really set your mind to it. 'You're serious, aren't you?' he said. 'You think we can drive off a full battalion of regular Imperial troops with these tubular-bell things.'

Spenno looked hurt. 'And you call yourself a man of the cloth,' he said. 'You've got no bloody faith.' He shook his head. 'Fine visionary leader you turned out to be. I've been asking around,' he added slyly. 'This is all your idea, this Brotherhood of Light or whatever it's called.'

Monach sighed, as a raindrop filtered through a tiny hole in the roof and fell on the back of his hand. 'Hardly,' he said. 'Oh sure, I'm the Mad Monk. After Deymeson got destroyed – well, actually, I was laid up for months after that, I got in a fight—'

Spenno nodded. 'I know,' he said. 'With Feron Amathy. You wanted to kill him or something like that.'

Monach shook his head. 'Not exactly, no,' he said. 'The

man I was sent to kill was General Cronan; Father Tutor reckoned it was a good idea, but he died before he could tell me why. Still, that was no reason not to obey orders. I failed, of course.'

'But he died anyway.'

'People die,' Monach replied, 'even without me killing them. He was caught by the raiders. I was there at the time. But that's beside the point. After Deymeson was trashed and once I was back on my feet again – no, I'm skipping ahead.' He paused. 'Are you sure you want to hear this? It's a long story.'

'Nothing better to do,' Spenno replied equably.

'Thank you so much.' Monach looked away; the expression on Spenno's face was vaguely disconcerting. 'Anyhow, after the battle when the raiders got a bloody nose, I was sort of left behind, I was nobody's business but my own; which would've been fine except I had four broken ribs and a whole lot of other injuries, and I really thought I'd had it that time. But then someone found me, someone I was at school with—'

'Xipho Dorunoxy. Like I said, I asked around. She took you in a cart to some village.'

Monach nodded. 'That's right,' he said. 'Cric, it was called – it was where the God in the Cart had predicted the destruction of Josequin. Only it turned out that she was the priestess, and the god had been another old school friend of ours, by the name of Ciartan; but that's a very long story—'

'Never mind,' Spenno said. 'Go on.'

'If you're sure.' Another raindrop landed on Monach's neck, making him wince. 'For some reason I never did find out about, Xipho was under orders from Father Tutor to play some sort of mind game with this Ciartan – he'd had an accident and lost his memory, hadn't got a clue who he was, let alone who she was, if you can believe it.'

'You'd be amazed what I can believe when I want to. Like I said, I got faith.'

Monach wasn't quite sure what to make of that, but he put it out of his mind. 'That's what Xipho was doing, anyhow: she was going round with this Ciartan, pretending that she hadn't known him since we were all kids together, that he was just somebody she'd met on the road a few months before. The Order wanted him for something; but whatever their grand scheme was, it got lost in the wash when Deymeson was taken out. So there was Xipho, at something of a loose end, and she happened to find me. So she took me back to Cric, where the locals reckoned she was the priestess of the Second Coming, and spun them some yarn about me being the Redeemer out of some old legend or prophesy, and how I'd fought off the God in the Cart and stopped him bringing about the end of the world. Only while I'd been about it I'd taken one hell of a pounding, so it was their religious duty to help her look after me till I was on my feet again.'

Spenno nodded. 'Little white lie, then. Where was this Ciartan while all that was going on?'

'We had no idea – he'd just sort of vanished. Anyway, while I was healing up in Cric, the story Xipho'd told them – all complete bullshit, incidentally, there never was any such prophecy – it got around, and loads of people started showing up to give thanks to the Redeemer, the sort of mass hysteria you get when there's wars and disasters. But in with all the peasants and knuckle-draggers there were a lot of sword-monks, pretty well all of us who'd escaped from Deymeson. It was Xipho's idea to round up all these misfits and turn them into a sort of army. To begin with, I think it was just that she was bored with waiting around to see if I'd die or not, and it was something to do. Anyway, by the time I was out of bed and on my feet again, she'd got them believing I really was some sort of great hero, and basically they refused to go away again. So there we were with an army, not knowing what the hell we wanted it for or what we might find to do with it . . . Like a huge, violent lost puppy that hangs round your door whimpering till you throw a stick for it. I don't know.' Monach cupped his hands over his face. 'I was too stunned by what'd happened, I guess, I didn't really care. And I didn't *do* anything, it was all Xipho, making speeches and leading prayer meetings and all sorts of stuff. And then when the baby was born—'

'Yours?' Spenno interrupted.

Monach grinned. 'Not likely. No, Ciartan was the father, which only goes to show how dedicated Xipho is to the Order, because she can't stand him. But she spun the troops some ridiculous yarn about an immaculate conception or something of the sort, and the poor fools believed her. She's really good at manipulating the weak-minded.'

'Sounds like it.'

Monach nodded. 'I asked for that, didn't I? Anyway, that's about it. Ever since, we've been wandering about the countryside, living hand to mouth out of what we can scare people into giving us. We've had a few skirmishes with government troops, a couple of minor collisions with the Amathy house, and for some reason nobody ever saw fit to explain to me, we sort of ended up here, in Tulice. Probably Xipho had some reason for wanting to be here, because I have an idea she's always got a reason for *everything*. But she's gone – not dead or anything, she just disappeared a short while back. Took the baby, but left me to mind the army. The baby would've been less trouble – I've been landed with a thousand helpless infants to keep fed and changed.'

'I see.' Spenno was sitting with his elbows on his knees, looking at Monach like a painter studying a spider's web before making his preliminary sketches. 'And the troops:

they still think you're the true Redeemer?'

Monach laughed. 'I doubt it very much,' he said. 'About three-quarters of the original mob have quietly deserted since Cric. I think the ones who're still here just don't have anywhere else to go, or they don't like the idea of working for a living. Xipho didn't seem too bothered about the desertions, so long as the sword-monks stayed with us; and most of them have, though don't ask me why. I'm pretty much convinced none of them think I'm the Son of God or whatever; most of them've known me since I was four-teen.' He smiled bleakly. 'I was the little fat kid who hung around with the big tall ones so as not to get bullied. The Earwig, my nickname was. Hardly your ideal solar-hero material.'

'That's interesting,' Spenno said neutrally. 'And now here you are, and you've got hold of the first working proto-type of the Poldarn's Flute project, which is the biggest military secret in the whole Empire. And you reckon it just sort of happened that way, more by luck than judgement.'

Monach yawned. 'It's possible,' he said, 'but so are three-headed chickens. No, I think Xipho planned all this, like she plans everything. I think that she's got a little bit of paper tucked down her front where she's written down every time I'm going to take a shit for the next five years, assuming I'll be allowed to live that long. But I'm used to that – I was brought up to run errands for Father Tutor. It was what I could do for religion.'

Spenno was silent for a while; then he said; 'Do you think she's got another bit of paper headed "Ciartan"?'

'Probably got bits of paper for everybody in the whole world. A bit like a god, really.' He looked up, smiling crookedly. 'You know, maybe I got it wrong, back when I was sent to find the god in the cart. Maybe she was the one I was meant to be tracking.'

'Sorry?' Spenno said. 'You lost me.'

'Doesn't matter. Anyway, I don't believe in gods, only in religion. You know what I'd really like to do? I'd like to wait till it's pitch dark tonight, and then crawl out under the gate and get as far away from here as I possibly can.'

'Wouldn't we all?' Spenno said. 'But where'd you go?'

Monach pursed his lips. 'Oddly enough, I've thought about that. There's other countries, you know, a long way away across the sea. There's the one Ciartan came from, for one. Or the place where the raiders live, though I don't suppose they'd want me. Still, I'm not exactly welcome here, either.'

Spenno looked at him for a while; then he said: 'You know what? For an educated man, you don't think much.'

'Wasn't brought up to think,' Monach replied. 'Thinking blurs the moment, remember? Don't think, just draw, that's the whole point of religion.'

It was Spenno's turn to yawn. 'If you say so. I think I missed that bit, or else I'd left before we got on to it. So what's you going to do?'

'Not sure. I think that when Brigadier Muno shows up, I'm going to point your Poldarn's Flutes at him and hope they don't blow me up when I give the order to set them off. How does that sound? Reasonable?'

'Don't ask me,' Spenno replied. 'I'm just the engineer.'

Monach looked up at him, and something dropped into place in his mind. 'Are you, though?' he said. 'I'm not so sure about that.'

'What do you mean?'

Monach straightened up a little in his chair. 'For one thing,' he said, 'you're sounding different. The folksy turns of phrase, and the Tulice accent you could cut with a knife. They were out of place anyway,' he added, 'for someone who spent – how long were you at Deymeson? Three years?'

'Four.'

'Four years. They'd have kicked that accent out of you

inside a month. All sword-monks talk like they've just
burned the roofs of their mouths drinking hot soup – it's
the rule. And how did you come to be here, anyway? You
never did tell me.'

Spenno grinned. 'Same way as you,' he said. 'There's
some bugger somewhere with a little bit of paper with my
name at the top.'

Monach thought about that for a moment. 'You were
sent here. Posted, like a soldier.'

'Sort of. More like a merchant company or a bank; in
places that aren't important enough to have a regular office,
they have an agent, someone who looks after their interests
there when the need arises. Same with me. What I do for
a living is cast bells, because that's what I'm good at, it's
what I'm *for*; but one day a year every five years or so I
have to do a little job for the Order. It's no big deal.'

For some reason, Monach felt his skin crawl, and at
the back of his mind he thought of how a flock of crows
sends out its scouts to see where it's safe for the main body
to feed: one tiny part of the great group mind, but con-
taining the whole. 'But that doesn't matter any more,' he
said. 'The Order's over and done with, isn't it? Ever since
Deymeson—'

Spenno nodded slowly. 'Of course,' he said. 'I'd forgotten, you're right. Good riddance, too. I never did figure
out what good it was supposed to be to anybody.'

'First,' Copis said, 'I need to know how much you remember. Just so we don't waste time telling you things you
already know.'

The fire was struggling to stay alight on a diet of wet
twigs and sodden leaves. The rain was still falling, and the
best they could do by way of shelter was the canopy of
the cart, rigged as a rather inadequate tent on four ash
poles. Poldarn felt cold through to his bones, even though

he was so close to the fire that his hands were stinging. It occurred to him to ask where the baby was, but he decided against it.

'All right,' he said. 'And the answer is, not very much. I'm pretty sure that my name is Ciartan and that my father was Tursten; he was killed before I was born. When I was about sixteen, I joined the order at Deymeson. You two were in the same class as me; we learned swordfighting, mostly. Also, I think Prince Tazencius had something to do with it. I may have married his daughter, even. Apart from that—'

Gain and Copis looked at each other; then Gain said: 'That's all true. Actually, you know a lot more than that, because I told you myself.'

'You didn't ask what you told me, you asked what I can remember. There's a difference.'

Copis smiled. 'Meaning, Gain might not have been telling the truth. Fair point. After all, I lied to you from the moment I found you, back in the Bohec country. But what you just said: that's what you can actually remember?'

Poldarn shrugged. 'I'm not sure,' he said. 'It's getting hard to know what's memories and what's stuff I've been told. The things that I know are memories aren't particularly helpful – like, I can remember sitting in a hide in a field of peas, killing crows with a bucketful of stones, and I can remember going with my grandfather to see the hot springs on the mountain above our house. They're proper memories, sharp and clear. But a lot of it's just remembering dreams that I've been having lately, and for all I know they're just my mind chewing over stuff that people have told me – like you,' he added, looking at Gain, 'and other people I've run into who reckon they know me. It's hard to believe that everybody's been lying to me – there'd have to be a very good reason. But what if there is a reason that good? I just don't know, is the straight answer.'

Copis poked the fire with a stick, stirring up a little

swarm of sparks. 'You still think like a member of the Order,' she said, 'which is what I'd expect. And you're very suspicious, which is all part and parcel of the scientific method. What I don't understand, and it bothered me when we were going round in the cart together, is how it's like you don't really want to know; like you're aware you've done some terrible thing you're scared to remember so you're tiptoeing round it so you won't wake it up. That's not how we were taught.'

Poldarn looked at her. 'Isn't it?'

'Of course not,' she said briskly. 'The whole purpose of religion is to annihilate doubt; and fear's just a kind of doubt, after all. The reason we learn how to fight with the sword is so that, once we've been trained, there's nothing on this earth that we need to be afraid of, nothing we can't kill. Once we know that – really know it, believe it – that's fear disposed of, and once we've got rid of fear we're free of the biggest restraint on us, we're at liberty to act purely in accordance with religion. That's absolutely basic, essential. Fear and doubt are what stand between the impulse for the draw and the cut itself. Once the draw's so perfect that it no longer exists, there's no longer any room for fear or doubt. It's what religion is for.'

'You've got to excuse Xipho,' Gain interrupted. 'She learned all that by heart for sixth-grade tests, and it sort of got stuck in her mouth, like a fishbone. She pukes it all up once a week, and then she's fine.'

Poldarn ignored him. 'Well,' he said, 'that's not the way I think. Yes, I'm afraid there's something I did that I don't want to know about. In fact, I'm absolutely terrified of it, and when Gain showed up and – well, threatened to tell me, that's what it comes down to: yes, I really didn't want to know. In fact, I only let him say what he did because by then I'd seen enough of him to form the impression that he wasn't to be trusted.'

Gain burst out laughing. 'Screw you, Ciartan,' he said. 'You were always saying things like that. No wonder nobody liked you.'

'Shut up, Gain,' Copis said, like a mother to a fractious child. 'Well, at least I can set your mind at rest on that score – assuming you'll believe me, of course, but that's up to you. Look, I can't tell you about anything you may've got up to before Deymeson, but I do know everything that's happened to you since then. And yes, you've done some pretty severe things, including killing people, and not just soldiers or enemies in a fair fight. But there's nothing you've done that you need to be afraid of. Nothing you can't live with, I mean.'

Poldarn looked at her for a long time. 'You reckon,' he said.

'I know for a fact,' she answered briskly. 'You did things in self-defence, or to protect other people, or to help the cause, religion. You did things that would've been unforgivable without the right motive. But the justification was always there. Nothing you did was – well, evil, for want of a better word. And each time, it's hard to think of what else you could've done, in the circumstances. Now it's true,' she went on, 'what I said to you that time, at Deymeson, when you were with the raiders, attacking *us*.'

'I remember,' Poldarn said quietly. 'You told me I was the most evil man in the world. You wanted to kill me.'

Copis nodded. 'I know,' she said. 'I was wrong.'

Next to her, Gain whistled. 'Did you hear that?' he said. 'I never thought I'd live to—'

'Be *quiet*. I was wrong,' Copis repeated. 'At the time, there were things I didn't know, hadn't been told. They were things I couldn't be allowed to know if I was to do my job as your keeper. Once that job was over, it was necessary that I should be told, so I could do the next job that was lined up for me. So now I understand a whole lot more about you, why you did those things.'

'Those things,' Poldarn repeated. 'What sort of things?'

Copis shivered a little, probably because of the cold. 'Well, for one, taking part in the attack on Deymeson, not warning us or helping us fight back. At the time, I didn't understand; I thought you could've got away from the savages before they launched the attack, come and warned us what they were going to do. I thought you'd betrayed us out of selfishness, because they'd turned out to be your people, where you came from.'

'Copis,' Poldarn broke in angrily, 'I'd just escaped from your fucking Order, they'd been setting me up to believe I was General Cronan himself, or someone else I wasn't; they were playing some horrible trick on me, as part of some grand strategy. I *wanted* to help my people kill every last one of the bastards.'

'I know,' Copis replied calmly. 'At the time I thought that was wrong. But now I know it was right. Deymeson had to be taken out, obliterated. It was in the interests of religion for it to be destroyed. And before you say that wasn't why you helped the savages,' she went on, before he could interrupt, 'actually, it was. The Deymeson Order had to be taken out because it was following the wrong path, and the error it was making was what prompted it to try and use you, the way it did. So yes, you were right and I was wrong. I hope,' she added stiffly, as though proposing a toast at a formal dinner, 'that you can forgive me for that.'

Poldarn decided not to reply to that. 'What else?' he said. 'What other things?'

This time Copis smiled. 'Are you sure you want to know?'

'I think so, yes.'

'Excellent – we're making progress. Well,' she went on, 'first, you betrayed someone who trusted you; someone who'd always shown you nothing but favour, kindness even. Including giving you his own daughter.'

'Tazencius,' Poldarn said.

'Tazencius. He was your sponsor at Deymeson. He got
you a place there, because you were brought up by the
savages and he wanted someone to be a go-between for
him with them. So he got you the best possible education,
and then he bound you to him with a marriage alliance, to
make sure of your loyalty. But you betrayed him: you took
all the advantages he'd given you, the training and the skills
and the contacts, and you sided with his enemies. Not just
a spur-of-the-moment thing, you knew right from the
start, from before you married Lysalis, that that's what you
were going to do. But you did it for the right reason. For
religion.'

Poldarn frowned. 'You mean for the Order,' he said.

'Same thing,' Copis replied, almost casually. 'Father
Abbot and Father Tutor knew what Tazencius had in mind
for you; you told Father Tutor yourself, as soon as you
realised. And he asked you to go along with it until the time
was right, and then you betrayed Tazencius – to the Order.
To us.' She paused, probably for emphasis. 'And when you
did that, you betrayed your wife as well; she loved you, and
I think you probably loved her, in a way; and your son, too,
as a father should. You had to betray both of them, and you
did, because it was the right thing to do.'

'Was it?' Poldarn asked.

'Of course. Tazencius was going to throw the whole
Empire into chaos, because of his ambitions, his lethal feud
with General Cronan, who was the only hope against the
savages. Thanks to you, we stopped him dead in his tracks.
It saved the Empire. It was the right thing.'

Poldarn breathed in slowly, decided not to comment.
'What else?' he said.

Copis nodded. 'You joined the Amathy house,' she said.
'It was Tazencius's idea, and ours as well. We knew that

Feron Amathy was an even bigger danger than Tazencius; he had the same idea, about using the savages to attack the Empire, so that whoever got rid of them would automatically gain power. He and Tazencius were in it together, at least to begin with, though both of them were planning to get rid of the other at the earliest opportunity. It was Tazencius who introduced you to him, you can guess what for. So, while you were with the Amathy house, you helped us with Tazencius. Then, when that was all sorted out, you did the same with Feron Amathy: betrayed him, to us. And the result was that Feron Amathy ceased to be a threat to the Empire, at that time.'

'Just a moment,' Poldarn interrupted. 'Feron Amathy's still very much alive, and Tazencius is the Emperor. Did something go wrong?'

Copis shook her head. 'Not at all,' she said. 'The beauty of Father Tutor's strategic planning was its economy. He had a genius for reusing the same pieces, instead of having to get rid of them and bring on new ones. Both Tazencius and Feron Amathy were – how shall I put it, they were adapted, or put on the right track; we altered them, so they'd be useful rather than harmful. Like taking a broken piece of scrap iron and making a useful tool out of it. Oh, I'm not saying we made them into good people,' she added, with a wry grin. 'Far from it. Feron Amathy really is the most evil man in the world, there's no possible doubt about that; and Tazencius is just plain stupid. But it's like taking a weapon away from an enemy and using it to defend yourself. The weapon remains the same, but the use it's put to changes. They're now weapons for us, rather than against us. Like,' she added, 'the Deymeson Order, which I helped destroy. It'd become a liability rather than an asset.'

Poldarn couldn't help noticing the look of disquiet on Gain's face while she was saying all this; and he's used to her, he thought. 'And me,' he said. 'What am I, right now?'

'Oh, an asset, like you've always been. Isn't that what I've been trying to tell you?'

He decided to ignore that, too. 'I get the impression,' he said, 'from what you've said, and Gain too, that this Father Tutor's dead now. Is that right?'

She nodded. 'He died before Deymeson fell, if that's what you were thinking.'

Poldarn shook his head. 'Couldn't care less,' he said. 'But if he's gone, who's making all the decisions now? Who's in charge—?'

At that, Copis smiled; warmly, for her. 'You'll be meeting him shortly,' she said. 'Of course, you've met him before. You'll know him when you see him.'

'But you can't tell me his name?'

'I could,' Copis replied. 'But then it wouldn't be a surprise.'

'This is it, then,' Monach said doubtfully.

It lay across two sturdy oak trestles in the small shed behind the charcoal store: a seven-foot shiny yellow log with a hole down one end, as though the pith of the tree had rotted out. The other end was rounded, and halfway along its length two pegs stuck out, like the stubs of trimmed branches. Somewhere, Monach decided, between a very long, thin bell and a giant parsnip.

'That's it,' Spenno replied gloomily. 'Course, the bloody thing might blow itself to bits as soon as we touch it off. No way of knowing till we try it.'

Monach knelt down and peered into the mouth of the hole; as he did so, an uncomfortable thought occurred to him. 'It hasn't got anything in it, has it?' he asked, standing up quickly and stepping to one side. 'The volcano dust, or whatever you call it.'

'Not likely.' Spenno grinned. 'We're storing that right over the other side of the compound, well away from the main buildings. Tricky stuff, see: one hot ember from the fire and it'd go up like the Second Coming. They'd have to get the surveyors in from Torcea to redraw the maps.'

Monach didn't like the thought of that. 'So,' he said warily, 'when are you going to try it out?'

'Tomorrow,' Spenno replied gravely, 'first thing. Assuming it's not raining. That's a problem with the bugger, it won't go off in the wet. We're working on that,' he added hopefully.

'Oh,' Monach said. It occurred to him that a mighty superweapon that wouldn't work in the rain was going to be a fat lot of use to anybody in Tulice, where it never seemed to stop.

'The volcano dust's got to be dry, see,' Spenno explained. 'If it gets wet it just turns into a filthy black mess, like mud, and when you stick the match in it, it just sits there.'

Oh well, Monach thought; let's hope Brigadier Muno chooses the one dry day in the whole year to attack. Otherwise we're screwed. 'If it all goes all right tomorrow,' he said, 'how soon will the next batch be ready?'

'Couldn't say,' Spenno replied. 'We've only got the one lathe working at the moment, but we should have three more up and running in a day or so. Slight technical problems with the drill heads,' he explained. 'Clown of a blacksmith made 'em too brittle – they're cracking up like glass. But we'll get there.'

Monach went back to his quarters in the drawing office, splashing through the deep muddy pools in the yard on the way. Why hadn't the stupid bastard mentioned before that the idiot bloody things didn't work in the wet? Did they know about this minor drawback in Torcea, where they were counting on the Flutes to save the Empire from the raiders? Maybe if he sneaked out quietly and went and told Brigadier Muno that the Flutes were effectively useless everywhere except in the heart of the Morevich Desert, he'd realise that they weren't worth having and go away; in which case, Monach thought with a grin, I could stay here and learn how to make bells. Nice cheerful things, bells, and they chime even when it's pissing down.

He hadn't realised how tired he was until he lay down, boots still on, wet shirt still clinging to his back and shoulders. He couldn't find the strength to stand up again and take them off – chances were that Brigadier Muno would get him before pneumonia did, so it was all as broad as it was long. He closed his eyes—

Someone was standing over him, just grazing the edge of his circle. He sat up and said, 'Who's there?'

It was only Runting, the quartermaster. 'Guess what,' he was saying, in a bemused voice. 'You've got a letter.'

'A what?' Monach said, as if Runting had told him there was a dragon waiting for him in the grain store.

'A letter. Addressed to you. Here.' He was holding out a brass tube the size of a medium leek. 'Sentry on the north gate found it a minute or so ago, as he was doing his rounds. Swears blind it wasn't there when he went round earlier.'

'Oh.' Monach was fumbling with the tinderbox; bloody damp, getting into everything. 'Here,' he said, 'you do this. I never could start a fire to save my life.'

Runting gave him the tube and fiddled with the tinderbox, until at last he contrived to get a lamp going. 'Well,' he said, 'aren't you going to open it?'

Monach thought for a moment. 'I can't see why not,' he said cautiously. Strange, he thought, very strange; time was, I used to spend an hour every morning just opening and reading letters. Now I'm handling this thing like I'm expecting it to jump out and bite me. 'All right, thanks.' He hesitated. Runting wasn't showing any signs of going away. 'I'll give you a shout if I need you.'

'Oh. Right.' Runting shrugged and went out. With his

thumbnail, Monach cracked the small blob of hard red wax and fished out a little scrap of paper. He recognised the shape: the flyleaf, torn out of a flat-bound book. The handwriting was thin, spindly. Familiar.

Earwig—
You must be wondering what's going on, but don't worry, I'll explain everything when I see you. In case you've been worrying, Xipho's just fine, and so's the kid; he's with me now, in fact, trying to eat one of my shoes. The woman I've got looking after him reckons he's teething, whatever that means.

I hope I didn't startle you too much the other night. Anyway, as you've probably already figured out for yourself, I'm not nearly as dead as they'd have you believe. Now, to business. If that clown Spenno's finally pulled his finger out, the volcano-bell things should be about ready by now. Whatever happens, I don't *want Muno or anyone else from the government side getting their sticky paws on them. If the worst comes to the worst, get rid of the bloody things, destroy them. This* is *important. Right?*

Can't say any more now; I'll explain everything when I see you.

Take care,
Cordo
PS Don't you dare let Spenno see this letter, or he'll sulk. Hell of an engineer, but a bloody prima donna, just like Fabricius (remember him from sixth grade? Must be something about working with metal, probably the fumes or whatever). Anyhow, you can keep him sweet, I'm sure. You always were a bloody crawler, Wig.

C.

On balance, Monach thought, I'd have preferred a dragon

in the grain sheds. Less disconcerting, less trouble to deal with.

It was Cordo all right; nobody else he'd ever come across could ever achieve that same effortless, cheerful arrogance. Typical. Not content with not being dead after twenty-whatever years, he comes swanning back into the world ordering people about, promising explanations, nonchalantly letting you know he's been running things behind your back for God knows how long . . . Cordo. *Cordo*, for crying out loud. My friend, from the old days, is still alive. And all this time—

All this time, I've hated Ciartan to death for killing him. But he's not killed, he's sitting out there just outside my circle, pulling my strings. With Xipho. With Xipho—

Jealousy? It was all the Order's fault, come to last; what the hell could they possibly have been thinking of, sticking one girl in with a class of nineteen adolescent boys – *monks*, for the gods' sake. Of all the crazy, thoughtless things to do; Spenno's volcano dust had nothing on it for a disaster waiting to happen. Of course he was jealous, of anybody who spoke to her or looked at her, right through grades one to seven, right through to here and now. (Ciartan; his bloody kid, and she even named it Ciartan after him.) He wanted to get a rock and smash Cordo's skull for that, just for being with her, taking her away from him—

Brings back fond memories, Monach thought; of lectures and classes, when he'd sat in the back row gazing at the back of her head, not hearing a word Father Tutor was saying, his whole mind focused on her – and Xipho, totally, absolutely constant, impregnable as the citadel of Torcea, hard as a file blade, never the slightest encouragement, which only made it worse, turned up the heat in the furnace to where it'd have melted stone into glass. And all this time, this last year when he'd finally had her all to himself – nothing doing, of course, still the unattainable

steel goddess, but at least he'd been with her every day,
him and nobody else, none of the others; he'd taken her
away from Ciartan; finally, after all these years, he'd *won* –
And now Cordo was back, inexplicably alive, and she was
off with him like a rat up a culvert.

And on top of that, he has the *nerve*—

Monach unrolled the letter again. *If the worst comes to*
the worst, get rid of the bloody things, destroy them. Oh,
fine. Yes, of course. And how the hell exactly am I supposed to go about destroying a bloody great big bronze tube
weighing the best part of a ton, just like that? Eat it?

(Cordo's alive. I suppose I knew, because he talked to
me, I heard his voice; but it could just have been a dream.
But now he's definitely alive – he's written me a letter, he's
coming. My friend, who I thought was dead and lost, and
so much of me with him. My past. A refugee from the old
days, coming back, coming alive. My *friend*.)

Coming back how, exactly? Monach frowned, furious
with himself for not being able to figure it out. Cordo was
with Xipho, they were coming to meet him, here; he was
minding the store for them, as a good friend should,
holding the fort (very funny, Earwig, you should go round
the villages with a cart, you could earn a living); they could
rely on him, of course, he'd be loyal to the last drop of
blood, because friends matter the way countries and causes
and religion never possibly could. It was like the arm you
had cut off when you were ten years old suddenly growing
back in the night.

(I suppose if we were to cram the tube full of the volcano
dust stuff and stopper up the hole in the end and then set
it off, it'd blow itself to bits; or would it just shoot out the
stopper? Or we could saw it in two with the big recipro-
cating saw they built for trimming off the sprue; but that'd
take days, according to Spenno. Ditto melting it down.
Cordo, you bastard, why me?)

He went to the door of the office and yelled for Runting, who came scurrying up remarkably quickly, almost as if he'd been lurking about, waiting . . . 'Well?' Runting said.

'Listen,' Monach said. 'At some point in the next few days, some friends of mine are going to arrive. I don't know when, and I don't know how many, and God only knows how they're figuring on getting past Muno's patrols, if they're using the roads. I want you to make sure that the officers of the day are looking out for them, and they're to be let in and brought straight to me. There'll be at least one man, and a woman; probably a young kid as well. Do you understand?'

Runting frowned. 'Yes,' he said, 'all right. Was that all?'

Monach nodded. He was overreacting quite appallingly, losing his grip. 'That's all for now,' he snapped, in his best imitation regular-army voice.

'Right you are,' Runting said. 'Are you going to tell me what was in the letter, then?'

'No.'

Runting's face fell, just a very little. 'Please yourself, then,' he said; and a moment later, the rain had closed around him like a curtain.

He woke up out of a dream in which he'd been back in the cart with Copis, rattling along horrible bumpy roads between burned-out cities. A jolt had woken him up, a wheel catching in a deeper-than-usual pothole.

'Mind what you're doing,' Copis snapped. 'You could've broken the axle.'

'Sure, whatever.' Gain didn't sound particularly concerned, but he'd always been reckless-stupid, not really bothered about the consequences of his actions . . . How did I know that, Poldarn wondered? Or was that just the way Gain had been in the dream? 'If you'd rather drive, be my guest.'

'Just be careful, that's all.' Copis sounded too preoccupied to be properly critical. 'Oh. You've woken up, have you?'

Poldarn yawned. 'Apparently,' he said. 'Are we nearly there yet?'

'Yes.'

'How nearly?'

'Nearly.' She was picking at her fingernails. Had she always done that? And if so, had she always done it when they were students together, or had she only always done it when they'd been together in the cart, when she'd been lying (and therefore nothing she did could be relied on to be the truth?)

'I'm hungry,' Poldarn said.

'Tough,' Gain replied. 'So'm I. But there's nothing to eat. Deal with it.'

Poldarn scowled at him. 'Will there be anything to eat where we're going?'

'Yes,' Copis told him. But they were riding together in a cart, so he wasn't sure he could believe her.

He wasn't really hungry at all, just bored, so really it was something of a trick question, to see whether she'd tell the truth or lie to him. Unfortunately, he didn't know what the real answer was, so the experiment was basically a waste of time. Something he had plenty of. He picked at the edge of the box, teasing a splinter out of the grain of the wood.

'Why won't you tell me who we're going to see?' he asked.

'Because,' Copis replied.

'Leave her alone, for pity's sake,' Gain said. 'If you keep on at her she'll get really snotty, and we've got a long way to go.'

Ah, Poldarn said to himself, absurdly pleased, so she was lying. He felt as though he'd just achieved a victory, as if he'd contrived to fool a crow into coming in to the decoys.

But he was deceiving himself, as usual. Just because she was lying about how far they still had to go – all sorts of reasons why she should lie about that; to shut him up, stop him complaining. All parents tell that sort of lie to their children. Or maybe Gain was the one who wasn't telling the truth. Wouldn't be the first time.

'When we get there,' he said, 'what have I got to do?'

'You'll see.'

No, Poldarn wanted to say, that was a genuine question, not a chess move. 'You must have something in mind for me,' he said mildly. 'You didn't go to all this trouble just so that we could have a class reunion.'

She looked at him. 'Really? Don't you think it's just possible that we'd be prepared to put ourselves out a bit to rescue one of our own? You have a very poor opinion of people, Ciartan.'

Rescue? Where did that concept come from, all of a sudden? 'No,' he said. 'You need me for something. Come on, give me a clue. You're both so mad keen to tell me all about my past, when I don't want to know. How about giving me a few clues about my future? I *care* about my future,' he added, grinning. 'Assuming I've got one.'

Copis sighed. 'I lied to you,' she said.

'Oh.' Poldarn looked at her.

'Yes,' she said. 'There *is* a bit of food left; well, biscuits. Thurm corn-dodgers. The traveller's friend – eat 'em or sharpen knives on 'em. Gain, give him a biscuit. Maybe breaking all his teeth'll shut him up.'

Poldarn shook his head. 'I'm not hungry any more,' he said.

'You said—'

'I was lying.'

Shortly after midday they stopped, for no apparent reason. The road had emerged very briefly from the forest, into a wilderness of tree stumps overgrown with bracken, spindly willow saplings and ground elder – typical char-coal burners' devastation, dating back maybe twenty or twenty-five years. The rain had lapsed into a fine drizzle (Tulice's idea of a sunny day, Poldarn reckoned), which obscured the sharp edges of the sawn-off stumps. Through the wet haze, Poldarn could see a shape that could be a small house, a collier's turf cabin.

'We're here,' Copis said quietly.

'Oh.' It wasn't what Poldarn had been expecting. 'Are you sure?'

'Of course I'm bloody sure—' But she sounded almost nervous, too tense to be properly bad-tempered. 'We're here,' she repeated. 'He'll be along in a minute.'

No sound, except the rain pattering on the cart's canopy. The air smelled fresh, of washed leaves. He remembered the smell from somewhere; not home, obviously, because there weren't any trees. Had he been here before?

'Where's he got to?' Gain muttered. He'd been on edge ever since the cart had stopped. 'He should've been here to meet us.'

Poldarn smiled. 'Maybe he's waiting for the rain to stop.'

That seemed to annoy Gain; a worthwhile objective in itself. 'I'm going over to the shack, see if he's there,' he said.

'No, stay still.' That was more like the old Copis. (How would I know that?) 'Keep still and try and be patient for once in your life.'

'Yes, but what if anything's—?' Gain caught sight of the expression on her face and subsided. 'Well, he should've been here to meet us,' he muttered. 'I mean, this is the right place, and—'

'Shut up, Gain,' Copis said softly. Poldarn looked across at the blurry shape that was probably a shack (unless Gain had been lying), but he couldn't see any movement in that direction. But Copis was pointing, like a bird-dog.

'Told you he'd be here,' she said, apparently to herself, and as she spoke a shape pushed through the curtain of fine rain: a big man with broad shoulders, exaggerated by a bulky coat and hood. He wasn't in any hurry; he wasn't walking so much as *processing*, like someone used to having to be dignified in public. Even at that distance, fifty yards or more away, he looked familiar—

'I know him,' Poldarn whispered. 'Copis, he's that man we ran into in Sansory, at that inn, where we got separated. He's the man who—'

She didn't say anything. Poldarn searched his mind, looking for the name, which he'd put in a safe place. It was only when the man walked calmly up to the cart and pulled back his hood that Poldarn remembered it. Cleapho; Chaplain Cleapho. Second most important man in the empire, or something like that—

'Hello, Xipho,' he said, with a benign smile, 'Gain.' The smile didn't change when he shifted his head very slightly and added, 'Hello, Ciartan. Thanks for coming.'

When he'd spoken, Xipho had closed her eyes just for a tiny moment: relief, pure joy at having completed the task and handed over to her superior officer. Then she pulled herself together, tightened back up.

'Hello, Cordo,' she said.

Chapter Fourteen

'And now,' Copis said, 'everything should be blindingly obvious.'

Poldarn didn't even look at her. 'You're Chaplain Cleapho,' he said. 'I met you—'

Cleapho smiled, and Poldarn felt a gentle glow of benediction, as if his sins had been forgiven. Presumably just force of habit. 'That's right,' Cleapho said. 'At the Charity and Diligence at Sansory. You had rather a hard time there. I'm sorry. My fault; back then I didn't know about you losing your memory. Someone,' he added, not looking at Copis, not needing to, 'should've warned me in advance, but there was a breakdown in communications. Still, you handled yourself very well, and there was no harm done.' He paused, then smiled again. 'It's good to see you again,' he said, his voice lowering just the right amount to convey sincere concern. 'Though I can't say you're looking at your best. I heard about – well, what happened, from Gain here. It was a very brave thing to do, we're all grateful to you. We've got to stick together, after all. Particularly now,' he added, looking at Copis.

'What's been happening?' she said quickly. 'We're so out of touch—'

'Not so good,' Cleapho said. 'He's getting quite blatant about it, and that fool Tazencius doesn't seem to give a damn; too upset about his grandson, they reckon, though that doesn't sound like him to me. Anyhow, the latest news I heard was that they're coming. Might save us some trouble if they run into Muno along the way, but apart from that, it's looking a bit grim. Do you think those monks of yours can do any good?'

Copis shook her head. 'I wouldn't rely on them to cook dinner,' she said bitterly. 'And that Spenno character's no better, from what I've heard – either crazy or stupid or both.'

'It doesn't matter,' Cleapho replied calmly. 'Remember, we don't need them ourselves, it's just important that *he* doesn't get hold of them. And the Earwig won't let us down.'

'Yes, but does he understand—?'

'I've written to him, it's all right.' Cleapho shrugged the whole topic aside. 'Well, are you going to make me stand out here in the rain all day, or shall we make a move? I hate this rotten bloody country, it never stops.'

He scrambled up onto the cart, stepping over Gain and settling himself in the back, fussily, like someone's mother. 'Xipho,' he called out, 'your bloody canopy's got a hole in it. There's water all over the floor.'

'Sorry,' Copis replied. 'We'll get it fixed at Dui Chirra.' She stopped short, then looked over her shoulder at him. 'We are going to Dui Chirra, aren't we?'

'Well, of course we are,' Cleapho replied. 'And the sooner we start, the sooner we'll get there.'

'Just a moment,' Gain called out. He stood up, nodded to Poldarn to shift along the bench, and then sat down where he'd been sitting, boxing him in. 'Not that you're

going to jump off and make a run for it, why should you?'
he explained.

Poldarn looked at him. 'Why, then?'

'Oh, I like looking about me on long cart rides.'

It turned out to be a very long cart ride, at least in perceived time: a ford that Xipho had been planning on using
proved to be flooded and impassable; the bridge ten miles
further down had been washed away; the road they went
back up so as to loop round and join up with another road
that led to another bridge had turned into a quagmire they
didn't dare set wheel to; then Gain suggested that when all
else failed, there was no dishonour in looking at the map;
so they fished the map out of the chest under the box, only
to find that the rain had got in it and reduced the map to
porridge; then Gain said that didn't matter, he was pretty
sure he knew how to get to the second bridge . . . Come
nightfall, they were stuck up to the axles in mud, in a high-
walled lane so narrow that the wheel hubs had been striking
sparks before they eventually ground to a soggy, inglorious
halt—

'Fuck,' Xipho announced, peering at the circle of pale
yellow light thrown by her storm lantern. 'We're stuck in
the mud *and* jammed solid against the wall. We're going
to have to knock the wall down, pack the rubble under the
wheels, and try and back up the way we came as far as the
top of the slope.'

'The hell with that,' Gain snapped. The lane had been
his idea, and guilt was making him irascible. 'I'm positive
we can squeeze through, if only we can get a bit of pace—'

'In this swamp? Don't be *ridiculous*.' Xipho was getting
shrill. Cleapho, for his part, was mostly staying out of it,
limiting his participation to the occasional tongue click and
sigh, to remind them both how disappointed he was in
them. 'Wall's got to come down, it's the only way.'

'Well, it's not my fault,' Gain shouted. 'Besides, what

kind of idiot'd build a walled lane right out in the middle of bloody nowhere?'

'The same sort of idiot who'd drive down a walled lane in the middle of a monsoon,' Xipho inevitably replied. 'Right, we'll need the hammer, the crowbar—'

'What hammer?'

'You didn't bring a hammer? Fucking hell. We'll just have to use the axe.'

'What axe?'

'Oh, for—'

Poldarn lifted his head. It was tones of voice, nothing more, the sheer musical pitch of their shouting and bickering that he recognised; but it was as familiar as if he'd last heard it a week ago. Where, though? He closed his eyes, trying to fit a place to the sound—

'And you're no fucking help,' Copis yelled at him. 'Wake up, for crying out loud. This really isn't the time to fall asleep.'

'I'm not asleep, I'm thinking,' he replied.

'Then don't, it always causes trouble. Just get the crowbar, and—'

He grinned, hoping she wouldn't see in the dark. 'What crowbar?' he said.

'Fucking *hell*! Of all the *idiots*!'

And then it dropped into place like the wards of a lock: the same words, the same shrill fury; of all the idiots— It had only been a dream, unreliable evidence that he had been justified in disregarding; and he'd put it carefully to one side, where it wouldn't be in the way. Until now.

Cordo; Cordo in the library, when they'd broken in to steal the book. Cordo, not dead—

'Shut up a minute, both of you,' he said, so firmly and quietly that they were shocked into compliance. Then he shifted round in his seat, awkward because one of the canopy hoops was in the way and he had to crane his neck round it. 'Cordo,' he said. (Strange to hear himself saying the name out loud; it was as alien as a word endlessly repeated.) 'Didn't I kill you, in seventh grade?'

Absolute silence, except for the inevitable drumming of rain. 'No,' Cleapho replied. Pause. 'You tried,' he went on, 'but you cocked it up. Don't obsess about it, though,' he added. 'Nobody's perfect.'

The bitterness lay in the casual delivery, a matter-of-fact drawl spread thin over twenty years of anger. Which was, of course, only reasonable.

'I can't remember very well,' Poldarn said slowly. 'But I stabbed you—'

'That's right,' Cleapho said. 'My sleeve caught fire, and so did a whole lot of books. Actually, it wasn't nearly as bad as it looked, but you panicked, must've thought the whole library was about to take off like a hayrick. I'm guessing here, but I think you reckoned the only way any of you would get out was if you could stop Xipho and Gain trying to save me, so you stuck me in the guts with that big pig-sticker knife of yours. And then all three of you pissed off and left me there in the smoke.'

Grim silence, practically unbearable. Cleapho was making it sound as though he was describing a game of knuckle-bones, or a barn dance. 'That was so like you in those days, Ciartan, you went to bits at the first sign of trouble. I think it's because of your upbringing, those people you grew up with. As I understand it, they don't make decisions like we do, it's sort of like a nationwide referendum every time one of you can't make up his mind whether to stop for a pee. In your case, once you came over here, it sort of worked the other way; you made decisions at the speed of lightning, never stopping to think. Like that night. Soon as my sleeve caught alight, you'd already raced ahead, you were thinking burning building, trapped inside, falling rafters, collapsing walls, coughing to death in the smoke: so you stabbed me. Religion, Father Tutor would have called it, the impulse to act followed by the completed action without the intervening moment. Only, if you'd stopped to think for just one tiny fraction of a second, you might have remembered the trapdoor down into the stacks . . .'

'Oh.' Xipho's voice, horrified.

'Yes, I know,' Cleapho went on, 'you were just as bad as he was, almost; and you, Gain, though I wouldn't have expected you to remember. But you, Xipho – anyhow,' Cleapho went on, 'fortunately, *I* remembered; and I crawled to the trapdoor, pulled it up and dropped through. Then it was just a matter of walking down the corridor – bleeding like a stuck pig, I might add, but it was only a flesh wound, fortunately – and across the yard to the infirmary.'

'But—' Xipho, struggling to understand. 'We thought you'd died. You let us believe—'

'Ah.' Poldarn could practically hear Cleapho's sardonic smile. 'So I did. And that's why I've forgiven you, all three of you. I guess you could say I owe you everything, because of that night. And coincidence, of course, or you could call it serendipity. Is that the word I'm looking for? It'll do. The point is, I staggered into the infirmary, believed dead by all concerned, on the very evening when Father Tutor realised he needed the services of a ghost: someone who didn't exist, someone with no identity. When the nurse called him over to the infirmary – I was yelling blue murder, I wanted to have you three hung, drawn, quartered and then thrown out of Deymeson in disgrace, in that order . . . But Father Tutor explained to me that it was just fine, couldn't have worked out better if he'd planned it that way, and he wanted to offer me a really splendid job opportunity – which, once he'd told me about it, I was delighted to accept.' He yawned. 'Now I won't bore you with all the in-between stuff, or we'd be here for days. Suffice to say, the end result, after many years of hard graft and brilliant planning, was me becoming Chaplain-in-Ordinary, supreme head of religion in the whole wide world, under the amusing name of Cleapho.' He paused. 'A joke that nobody's ever appreciated,' he added, 'or else they've kept it to themselves. Cleapho in Old High Thurmian means "partly dead". And all,' he went on, accentuating the drawl, 'because I remembered a silly old trapdoor and you three forgot about it. I guess it was one of those moments in religion when everything in the universe suddenly changes, but too fast for anybody to notice: one moment we're all facing south, next moment we're all standing on our heads facing north, but everything looks the same because the scenery's been switched round too, and it doesn't occur to anybody to consult a compass.' He sighed, pure affectation. 'And all this while you – and the Earwig too, I dare say – you've had it in for poor old Ciartan here because you blamed him for killing me, when in fact it's because of him that I got to be the most powerful man in the world. Well, nearly the most powerful, but we're working on that, aren't we?'

Poldarn wanted to laugh; because if this was the most powerful man in the world, how could he be marooned on a cart stuck in the mud in a narrow lane in the middle of the wilderness, in the driving rain? 'Is that what we're doing?' he asked mildly.

'No, of course not,' Cleapho said, as though explaining the blindingly obvious to a small child. 'We're fighting for the survival of the Empire, religion and civilisation; making me Emperor is just a side effect, like tanning salt is a by-product of horseshit.' Suddenly his voice changed; it bristled with sincerity, great big raw lumps of it. 'Have you got any idea of what's happening out there? You must have, if you've got half a brain. You've seen the ruins where great cities used to be, where the savages – no offence – burned them to the ground. I expect you know how that all started, a couple of hundred years ago, when the Empire rounded up the Poldarn-worshippers in Morevich and set them adrift on the ocean to die. Only of course they didn't; they floated across the sea to the islands in the west, and spawned like ants, and then they started to come back – because over there, where you grew up, there're so many things they don't have. No metal ores in the ground, so the only iron and steel your people had was what they brought with them in the ships, a few tools, the nails that held the boards together, the anchor chains and the deadeyes. Amazing what they did with what they had; because a hundred and twenty-odd years later, they were ready to cross the ocean and come here – and they knew what they wanted from us, and they were *angry*.' He paused; effect again. All those years of preaching sermons in Torcea Cathedral. 'They didn't want gold or silver or pearls or silks; they wanted wrought iron and brass and hardening steel, *scrap* – and they were prepared, no, they *wanted* to kill in order to get it. Oh, come on, Ciartan, you were there only recently. Didn't you wonder why every barn in the country is crammed full with rusty helmets and broken spear blades, and why the headman of every settlement is the blacksmith? To them, we're a species of domesticated animal, like cows or pigs: they kill our soldiers for their steel skins, and leave the meat for the crows. And when all's said and done, you can't really blame them for it. We started it, after all.'

Poldarn didn't say anything.

'No,' Cleapho resumed, 'they aren't to blame, for doing what they have to do, in order to get what they need. The evil – not too strong a word, I'm sure – the evil came from us. From one man, the man who thought he could use them, your people, as a means of getting what he wanted, and the hell with the consequences. That was when the evil started.

Before that, your people only came here to get steel and iron, and the best and quickest way of getting the finest-quality material was taking it off the dead bodies of soldiers. So they hunted down our coastal garrisons, killed them and went away again. They weren't interested in towns and cities – not till one of us started talking to them, preying on their resentment, persuading them that what they really wanted, more than bits of broken metal, was *revenge*. Then the massacres began, the cities and towns, whole populations slaughtered with no survivors. Not their fault; our fault. The selfish ambitions of one individual.'

'Tazencius,' Poldarn said. Cleapho laughed.

'Not Tazencius, no,' he said. 'Oh, he was happy to take the idea, thought he'd stolen it, imagined he was being wonderfully clever – and so lucky, finding you like that, so that the plan could be put into effect. But he was simply being used, as you were; and as soon as he'd done what was required of him, he was lucky to escape with his life. Come on, Ciartan, you were a damn sight more perceptive than this when we were students together, or have all those bashes on the head jumbled your brains up? You know who I'm talking about.'

A moment of silence; moments in religion, when two absolutes connect. 'Feron Amathy.'

'Ah.' At any other time, Cleapho's condescending tone would've been unbearably offensive. 'You got there in the end, that's something. Exactly so: Feron Amathy, the worst man who ever lived. It was Feron Amathy who taught the savages to exterminate whole cities, who betrayed everyone who ever trusted him, who treats human beings as expendable tools. As far as he's concerned, the Empire is a forest and he's a charcoal burner, he'll cut us all down and burn us just to make a few baskets of coals. Everything that's wrong with the Empire is his fault. Who do you think tricked General Allectus into starting a hopeless rebellion, just so he could sell him to General Cronan?' Cleapho paused, just for a moment, to catch his breath; Poldarn got the impression that the subject had almost run away with him, like a big dog on a long rope. 'Then who gave the savages – his own allies – to Cronan so he could prise the Emperor loose from the throne and put Tazencius there, simply because Tazencius would be easier to replace directly, once he'd finished him off? *Every* betrayal, *every* deception – and what's possibly the worst of all, the miserly parsimony, using the same people over and over again, twisting them backwards and forwards like you do when you're breaking off a green twig. To be the most evil man in the world, it's not enough just to do evil things; plenty of good men, saints, have done evil for the best possible motives, it's the rule rather than the exception when it comes to evildoing. No, it takes someone like Feron Amathy to do the things he's done *in the way he's done them*. That's what makes him such an abomination.'

Poldarn could hear the passion, the righteous fury in Cleapho's voice: quite a spectacle. A shame it was here, in the wrong context. It was meant for a cathedral, and didn't really fit comfortably in a small cart wedged between two stone walls in the rain. He's no better than the rest of them, Poldarn thought, the only difference is in what they've actually done.

'So that's who you're fighting,' he said. 'Feron Amathy.' He shrugged. 'Well, that's fine, and I hope you nail the bastard. But you obviously don't need me.'

Rather surprisingly, none of them said anything to that. The next words came from Gain Aciava, who clicked his tongue and said, 'Screw it, we're just going to have to dump the cart and walk to Dui Chirra.'

'Don't be stupid, Gain,' Xipho said, automatic as a sword-monk's draw.

'What's stupid about it? The bloody thing's stuck solid

– yes, all my fault, I thought I knew the way and I didn't. But there's no way we can get this stupid cart free on our own. We can walk, or two of us can ride the horses.'

'I haven't come all this way just to be fucked over by a muddy road and your stupidity.' This time, Cleapho sounded quite different. 'We haven't got time to walk, we need to get there *quickly*, before that fool of an Earwig screws it all up.'

'Fine,' Gain snapped back. 'You ride one horse; Xipho, I expect you'll insist on having the other. Ciartan and I will just have to walk.'

'Don't be ridiculous—' Was that doubt in Xipho's voice, as though quite suddenly she wasn't sure what to do next? 'You can't – not on your own.'

Can't what? Poldarn wondered, though not for long. *Can't be trusted not to lose the prisoner.* And he'd had to think before figuring that out. Maybe Cleapho had been right about the effects of concussion.

'What's more important?' Gain was saying. 'Which of us has got to get to Dui Chirra first? Cordo, obviously. And—?'

That, apparently, was a very good question, and neither Cleapho nor Xipho knew the answer. They weren't taking it well, either; two people who couldn't keep their balance without certainty. 'This is ridiculous,' Cleapho suddenly exploded. 'You bloody fool, Gain, you and your idiotic short cuts—'

'It wasn't meant to be a short cut,' Gain whined. 'I only tried this way because the proper roads were blocked. You can't blame me for the rain.'

'Fine.' Cleapho had made a decision. 'We'll walk. Just leave the cart, leave everything. Can either of you tell me how far it is, or do we just blunder about in the dark for a bit?'

It was all Poldarn could do not to laugh. And then he

thought, now's as good a time as any: in the dark and the mud, they'd never be able to find me, they don't even know where they are. And staying with them – whoever heard of such a ludicrous idea?

Very well, then. Plan of action – nothing difficult there. One jump from the cart box to the top of the wall, one jump down, then run; no direction required, I'm not running *to* anyplace, just away. Easy as drawing a sword. It would mean he'd never find the moment to ask Copis about the kid, his son, whom he'd never seen. But there were so many things he'd never know about now, if he turned his back on them—

He jumped; felt the wall under his feet, kicked against it, relaxed his knees for the impact of landing (hoping very much that there weren't nasty sharp rocks on the other side; there weren't. Mud, yes; but a year in Tulice gives you a doctorate in mud studies.) He heard them shouting: Cleapho swearing, Xipho yelling at Gain, Gain yelling back. He grinned as he ran; those three had definitely known each other for a very long time. Too long, probably.

Poldarn ran, and he ran. No idea where he was going, not interested; when you'd got nowhere to go, you could go *anywhere*. Well, not Dui Chirra, for sure. But since that was where they'd been trying to get to, and it had defeated the combined intellect of three Deymeson graduates, one of them being the world's most powerful man, quite clearly finding Dui Chirra was impossibly difficult, far beyond his concussion-inhibited abilities, and so there was precious little risk that he'd manage to do it. So that was all right.

Free again, he thought, as he paused for breath, leaning his back against a tree. This was your true wisdom: when in doubt or danger, run away. He grinned; an image had popped into his mind of the past as a big, shaggy dog, standing in the middle of this very wood, sniffing the air in bewilderment because the scent had suddenly failed. It nearly got me that time, and here's the bite marks on my leg to prove it; but I escaped. Free again.

Just to be on the safe side, however, Poldarn kept on going till daybreak; not running, because running through a swamp-floored wood in the dark gives the best odds known to man for breaking a leg or spraining an ankle, and suddenly there's all that wonderful new-found freedom gone up in smoke. A sensible brisk walk, avoiding all unnecessary risks, until dawn watered down the darkness like a dishonest barmaid, taking away his best protection and freedom. On the other hand, it had, miraculously, stopped raining.

In the back of his mind, that damned song was spinning slowly round, unbalanced, like a broken wheel—

> *Two crows sitting in a tall thin tree*
> *Two crows sitting in a tall thin tree*
> *Two crows sitting in a tall thin tree—*

—And he couldn't remember what came after that. He tried not to think about it, for fear it would drive him mad. Instead, he thought—

They can't still be looking for me, they've got more important things to do; and even if they are, it's a moving needle in a soggy haystack. Even so, it'd be wise to stay out of the light for a day or so. In which case: climb a tree.

The nice thing about dense forest was that there were so many trees to choose from, another beguiling variation on the currently fashionable theme of infinite choice, unfettered opportunity. In the end, Poldarn chose a massive forked oak that couldn't have been easier to climb if it had been specially designed by Galand Dev and Spenno. About thirty feet off the ground, above the first layer of canopy, there was a delightful little platform where the main trunk divided four ways. He was able to lie back with his head pillowed on his hands and his feet crossed, and close his eyes for the best-earned snooze of a lifetime—

'Comedy,' said a voice next to him.

He opened his eyes. 'I beg your pardon?'

'Comedy,' the crow repeated. 'Both the low comedy of slapstick and farce – people running about and falling in the mud, the humiliation of dignity and pomposity in a situation intrinsically ludicrous, such as getting stuck in a tight place – and the high comedy of inversion, the world turned topsy-turvy; as in the man who sleeps by day instead of night, up in the air rather than down on the ground, who runs away from his friends to seek sanctuary with his enemy— Actually,' the crow admitted, 'that's stretching it a little; you're the deadly enemy of crowkind, but I'm the individual, not the group, and I don't actually own the tree. Nevertheless, comedy. Also, add the god running away from the priests – that's a good one.'

'Very good,' Poldarn said, yawning; it was broad daylight, and he had cramp in his back and neck. 'I think I'll wake up now.'

'Don't be silly.' The crow pecked at a slight tangle in its wing feathers. 'You aren't asleep, this isn't a dream. You never met a talking crow before?'

Poldarn drew up his knee and massaged it where it was stiff. 'Not that I remember,' he said. 'Except in dreams. Or hallucinations,' he added in fairness, 'caused by injuries and trauma, like getting bashed on the head. Did I fall out of the tree or something?'

The crow turned its beak toward him. 'Obviously not,' it said, 'since we're thirty feet off the ground.'

'In that case,' Poldarn said, yawning again, 'it's a dream. Is there a point to it, or is it just mental indigestion?'

'I don't understand,' said the crow.

'No reason why you should,' Poldarn replied cheerfully.

'Fact is, I get two kinds of dreams. One kind – well, it's like a series of lectures in remedial memory, so I can catch up with the rest of the class.' He paused. 'Actually,' he said, 'that's more comedy; because the only thing I'm afraid of right now is the rest of the class catching up with me. But they won't, because they're stuck in the mud, like you said. Good joke?'

'Laboured,' the crow replied. 'Go on. The second type of dream.'

'Oh, right. Yes, the second kind is where I'm lying in a river bed or some other place where there's running water, and I hear the two parts of me arguing, like an old married couple: there's the new me, who's trying to run away, and the old me, who keeps on tracking me down. That's about it.'

'I see.' The crow was silent for a long while, so long that Poldarn began to wonder if he'd just imagined that it had talked to him at all. Then it laughed.

'Sorry,' it added. 'I was just thinking of the old song. You know:
Two crows sitting in a tall thin tree—'

Poldarn shook his head. 'This is a tall thick tree,' he said. 'And there's only one of you.'

'No,' the crow said, 'two. But it's not important. I suppose I'd better get to the point.'

'Ah,' Poldarn said. 'So it *is* a dream, after all.'

The crow nodded. 'Actually,' it said, 'you were closer when you described it as a lecture. It's important, you see, to help you decide. Too many choices, and you won't know what to do with yourself.'

'I like having too many choices just fine,' Poldarn muttered, but the crow wasn't listening.

'Now then,' it said, 'I want you to pay attention. Look down there, to your left. Can you see?'

'No,' Poldarn said. 'Oh, just a moment, yes. There's

people coming, on horses. Is that what you meant?'

'Look closely,' the crow said. 'Now, I'm going to open up your memory just a little bit – not too far, obviously, so don't worry about things getting out and escaping. Just enough so you'll know—'

At which point, the man on the leading horse glanced up, looked Poldarn in the eye and smiled at him. 'You know who that is?' asked the crow.

'Of course I know him,' Poldarn replied. 'That's Feron Amathy.'

'Watch closely.'

The man rode on, out of sight. Behind him came a troop of cavalry, carrying spears and wearing mail shirts.

'All right so far?' the crow asked. Poldarn nodded.

A moment later, Poldarn saw a column of men on foot, also armed. But they weren't regular soldiers or even irregulars like the Amathy house. They wore old farm clothes, and their only weapons were backsabres.

'And they are?' asked the crow.

'Easy,' Poldarn said. 'My lot. I never did find out what we call ourselves, but in these parts they're called raiders. Or savages,' he added, with a slight frown.

One of them looked up, saw Poldarn, and scowled: Eyvind. Sore loser.

'Still happy?' asked the crow.

'I guess so,' Poldarn said. 'Is there any point to this?'

'Be patient. Now, who's this?'

Prince Tazencius rode under the tree. He didn't look up, though clearly he knew Poldarn was there. Embarrassed; doesn't want to be seen with the likes of me. Fine.

'Nearly there,' the crow said. 'Now, while we're waiting, let's see if you can tell me what the connection is. Well?'

'Too easy,' Poldarn said. 'Evil. These are all bad people.'

The crow shifted an inch or so along the branch. 'Yes. And?'

Poldarn thought for a moment. 'They're all bad people I've been mixed up with over the years.'

'Yes. And?'

Cleapho rode under the tree, lifting one hand off the reins in a gesture of dignified acknowledgement. For some reason, Boarci was walking next to him, holding the horse's bridle. Poldarn frowned. 'They're all people I've betrayed,' he said. 'Or treated badly in some way.'

'Yes. And?'

'And nothing,' Poldarn replied, slightly annoyed. 'They're bad people, and I've treated them badly. Big deal. They had it coming.'

The crow sighed. 'Oh dear,' it said, 'and you were doing so well. Now, then. I want you to look down on your left side.'

Poldarn turned and looked down. 'I know her,' he said. 'That's my wife.'

The crow laughed. 'Which one?'

'First,' Poldarn replied. 'No, second – no, hang on, first. Lysalis. Tazencius's daughter.'

'Very good.' Lysalis smiled up at him and did a little finger-fluttery wave. 'Next.'

Next came Halder, walking, and Elja. 'My second wife,' Poldarn explained. 'Only, I have a bad feeling that she's also my daughter. Who's that boy she's with?'

'Your son,' the crow said, as the ferocious young swordsman Poldarn had killed in the woods strutted past. 'Lysalis's boy, Tazencius's grandson. Theme emerging?'

Poldarn laughed. 'Piece of cake,' he said. 'These are good people I've treated badly; though that boy wasn't so nice, he tried to kill me—'

'Quite,' the crow said. 'He did his best, and that's all you can ask of anybody. Pay attention.'

General Cronan rode by, and General Muno Silsny ('That's not fair, what harm did I do him?') and Carey the fieldhand walking beside them, his hand clamped to his slashed neck; and behind them a long stream of people Poldarn didn't recognise, thousands of them—

'A representative sample,' the crow said. 'After all, the object of the exercise isn't just making you feel bad about yourself. Anyway, they're in reverse order, so it's the Falcata delegation at the front, then Choimera, followed by Josequin— You get the idea.'

Poldarn frowned. 'Where's Choimera?' he asked. 'I never heard of it.'

'You're a busy man,' the crow replied. 'You have people to deal with, that sort of thing.'

'Fine.' Poldarn tried to sit up, but the branch was slippery; the rain had started again. 'Point made. Point sledgehammered into the ground. I haven't just harmed those bad people but all these innocent people too. That's why I don't want to remember any of it.'

'You just want to run away.'

'Exactly. The more I hang around the places I've already been, the more damage I do, on top of everything I've done already. Going back home proved that. Any contact I have with my past leads to more bad things; it's contagious, and I reinfect myself. Which is why I want to run away – really run away this time, get as far away from all of it as I possibly can. I thought I was doing that, coming here; all I wanted to do was get a job and settle down, it's not my fault that they all came chasing after me. But there's got to be some place I can go, somewhere outside the Empire, where nobody will ever find out who I used to be.'

'Fine,' said the crow. 'Look down.'

None of the people passing under the tree were familiar, though some of them looked up, smiled, waved. There were even more of them than before.

'Do you understand?' asked the crow.

'Yes,' Poldarn said. 'So what do you want me to do?

Should I jump out of this tree and break my neck?'

'Look down,' said the crow again.

All strangers once more, and none of them acknowledged him; but the line went on out of sight in both directions.

'Really?' Poldarn said quietly. 'Even if I kill myself right now?'

'Of course,' the crow said. 'My, what a big head we have, assuming we can redeem the world by an act of supreme sacrifice. Look, there you go now.'

Sure enough, Poldarn could make out his own face in the crowd, just briefly, before it passed out of sight. 'One more victim wouldn't make things much worse,' the crow said. 'Wouldn't make it any better, either. Really, what was your tutor thinking of? You ought to have covered all this elementary stuff in second grade.'

'Maybe we did,' Poldarn said irritably. 'I really don't remember.' The branch was getting very slippery now; he was in danger of falling off. 'All right,' he said. 'I'm assuming there's a point to all this, so you tell me. What have I got to do?'

Then he fell out of the tree.

Comedy, he thought, as he opened his eyes; then, Where did that come from?

He was lying in deep mud; just as well, since he'd only a moment ago fallen thirty feet. It was broad daylight. A crow got up out of the branches above him and flapped away, shrieking. Poldarn didn't need to translate; he could remember what it had been saying.

The only difference is in what they've actually done.

And that, presumably, was the answer: find out who'd done most, and deal with him. I need someone I can ask, he thought. I need to speak to Cleapho, or Copis, someone who can tell me what's going on. Assuming, of course, that they'd tell me the truth.

Assuming I can find them again, having made such a spectacularly good job of making sure that they can't find me. Assuming, even, that I can ever get out of this horrible bloody wet forest.

Big assumption.

As if he'd woken out of something bigger and more malevolent than mere sleep, he got to his feet, stretched and flexed to make sure that nothing had got broken or bent in the fall, yawned and looked around. Trees. Lots of more or less interchangeable trees. Absolutely not a clue about where the hell he was. So breathtakingly well hidden that nobody on earth knew where he was, not even Poldarn or Ciartan Torstenson.

He remembered what the colliers had said about the Tulice forests: so dense that a man could walk for days and never realise that the main road was only twenty yards away to his left. And wet, too: full of nasty boggy patches that'd swallow you up before you'd figured out you were in trouble, in which case the best you could hope for was that you'd be sucked down over your head and drown or smother immediately, rather than stay mired up to your armpits until you starved to death, or the wolves or the bears or the wild pigs ate you (browsing off your arms and face like cows nibbling at a hedge; at the time he'd assumed that the colliers were just trying to put the wind up him . . .). Wonderful place to get lost in, the Tulice forest.

Poldarn walked for an hour in one direction, until the closeness of the trees and the depth of the shadows all around him made him feel like he was buried alive; so he turned left, and carried on that way for another hour or so, until that direction became just as unbearable, or more so. Left was obviously a bad idea, so he turned right. Right was worse. The canopy of leaves overhead was as tight as the lid on a jar; he needed light in order to breathe, and the canopy was choking the light, strangling him; and every change in direction led him to taller trees, thicker leaves, darker places. (Allegory, he thought bitterly; I hate fucking allegory.) How long he'd been blundering about he had no idea, but it didn't matter anyway; didn't matter if the sun had gone down, because it couldn't get any darker than this, could it? No trace, needless to say, of human beings here, nothing to suggest that a fellow human had ever been this way before – so much for the idea that all his problems had been caused by other people. Right now, he'd be overjoyed at any hint that there were such things as other people, that he wasn't the only talking biped left in the universe—

Something whistled in his ear, then went *chunk*. After a moment's bemused searching, he found it. It was a strange insect, with green and yellow wings and an absurdly long brown body, and it lived by boring into the bark of trees. No, it bloody well wasn't: it was an arrow. Some bastard was shooting at him.

Feeling rather foolish, because at least three seconds had passed since the arrow had hit the tree, Poldarn threw himself to the ground and crawled on his knees and elbows for the cover of a holly bush. Silly, he thought, holly not arrow-proof; but he curled up tight in a ball and waited, and no more arrows came. Even so.

Then he heard something, quite close. Grunting, snuffling; a fat man with a bad cold running uphill with a heavy weight on his back. The absurdity of it made him want to burst out laughing, because unless this neck of the woods was swarming with people and he'd just been walking blithely past them for the last five hours, it stood to reason that the grunting, snuffling fat man had to be the secret archer. Well, fine; if Gain and Copis and the most powerful man in the world were to be believed (which was by no means certain), Poldarn was a graduate of the Deymeson academy of killing people, and more than a match for a runny-nosed pork chop, even one with a bow and arrows. The noise was getting closer, so all he needed to do was stay perfectly still, and then, when Fatso came waddling past him any second now, just stick out a leg, trip him up and bang his head against a tree until he came up with directions to the nearest inn. Piece of—

It must already have seen him, some time before he saw it; that was what cowering in the bushes would get you, if you were so dumb that you couldn't tell the difference between a human being and a fully grown wild boar. When he lifted his gaze – purely chance that he happened to be looking in that direction at precisely that moment (rather than half a second later, when it'd have been a quarter of a second too late) – he saw a massive grey wedge with two tiny red lights halfway up the taper, growing huger and huger. His legs figured out what the thing was before his brain did, because by the time the words *wild boar* had congealed in his mind, he was already on his feet and trying to push through a thick screen of holly leaves.

The pig squealed, a silly, high-pitched angry noise like a little girl whose brother was pulling her hair. There was a little blood, black and shiny, on its shoulder. The boar flattened the holly bush about a heartbeat after Poldarn got clear of it.

Then Poldarn hit a tree.

Bloody stupid thing to do, run flat out into a stupid great big oak tree. He scrambled back onto his feet just as the boar thrust its ridiculously thick neck out; one handspan-long tusk gashed the bark an inch below his outspread fingers as he ducked round the tree, hide-and-seek fashion. The pig blundered on, skidded to a halt in a spray of leaf mould, and swung round. (But aren't they supposed to carry on charging? Apparently not.) Superior intellience, Poldarn thought, and superior biped mobility: I'll just dance round and round this handy tree until the bugger gets bored and goes away. Annoyingly, though, he discovered that when he'd run into the tree he'd bashed his kneecap, and it didn't seem to be working properly. So much for superior mobility; that just left intelligence. In which case (the pig lowered its head and shot itself towards him like a huge squat arrow), forget it—

He stumbled, tripped over backwards, and sat down, jarring his back painfully against the tree trunk. Good as dead, in that case, and the pig was very close. But right next to him was a fallen branch, and just by way of going through the motions he picked it up, jammed the butt end against the tree and pointed the other end at the pig's chest.

Superior intelligence after all; because the pig charged *straight*, just like an arrow, and by the time its chest met the branch it had picked up an extraordinary amount of speed. The branch was the nail, the boar's body the hammer and also the wood; the first eighteen inches of the branch crumpled up like dried ferns scrunched in a first, but the next foot burst through first skin, then muscle, until it jarred against bone, broke that, went in a bit further, found more bone, and stopped. The branch bent like a bow, but the boar kept on coming, its broad wet nose no more than two feet from Poldarn's left hand where it gripped the branch: the bastard thing was coming up the branch at him, like someone climbing a rope, and the hell with the mess it was making of its own guts in the process— And then the pig must've impaled its own heart, because it stopped and squealed in utter frustration at the injustice of the world, and the light in its vicious little eyes went out, and time stopped.

Not dead yet, Poldarn thought; I'm still alive, that's so totally fucking *wonderful*— Also, he was forced to admit, bitterly unfair on the pig, who had every right to be pissed as hell, because it'd been a wild and unforgivable fluke, sheer luck. He breathed out what he'd been absolutely sure at the time was his last-ever breath, and savoured the taste of its replacement, the sweetest thing he'd had in his mouth at any time.

'Shit,' said a voice from the sky; not from the sky, from the tree above his head. A tree-god, swearing at him. He looked up. 'Shit,' the voice repeated, and he could identify astonishment, admiration and extreme annoyance, all balled up into one repeated word. Then something scrambled down the tree-trunk and landed *flump!* next to him.

'Bastard,' it said.

Poldarn took a moment to notice that the ground he was sitting on was swamped in pig's blood. Then he looked up. Staring down at him was a round face, a long way off the ground; bright grey eyes, a little snub nose, grey hair and a huge shaggy grey moustache.

'What?' Poldarn said. In his right hand the man was holding a spear, blade as broad as the head of a shovel. *But I haven't got a sword right now, and besides, I can't be bothered any more—*

'Bloody amazing,' the man said. 'Never seen the like in all my born days.' He seemed to remember something, and his huge eyes narrowed into a scowl. 'Who the hell are you, anyhow? Have you got any idea how long I've been after that fucking pig?'

Poldarn looked at him. 'No,' he said.

'All my bloody *life*,' the man yelled suddenly. 'That's how long, ever since I was a *kid*. Thirty years it took me, to find a trophy boar good as this one. And you just jump up out of nowhere and down the fucking thing with a *bit of old stick*—' Quite suddenly, the man seemed to notice the burn scars that covered Poldarn's face. He opened his eyes wide, took a step back, then (with a visible effort; even so, Poldarn was impressed) dismissed them as irrelevant.

Poldarn couldn't help grinning, because it was so delightfully funny. 'You're a *hunter*,' he said, as if he was accusing the grey-haired man of being a unicorn.

'Well, of course I am,' the man said. 'You think I sit up trees in the middle of the woods in rainy season to cure my piles? What did you think I was, a flower fairy?'

Poldarn burst out laughing. 'So it was you,' he said. 'You shot that arrow.'

'Me? No, definitely not.' Now the hunter was offended, on top of everything else. 'You take me for some kind of bloody hooligan? Besides, I haven't got a bow. I was sitting up waiting – and then *you* come along, from the *south-east* . . .' He made it sound like some particularly pernicious heresy. 'What're you grinning at, anyhow?' he added angrily.

'Sorry,' Poldarn said. 'It's just that I haven't got a clue what you're talking about.'

The man scowled horribly at him, then began to laugh too. 'I do apologise,' he said, sticking out a hand – it took Poldarn a second or so to realise that the hunter was offering to help him up off the ground. He noticed that the man was left-handed. 'It's just, I was all keyed up waiting for the pig, and then you happened. Weirder than a barrelful of ferrets,' he added. 'Never seen anything like it. That was amazing, felling a pig that size practically with your bare hands.'

'Sorry,' Poldarn said. 'I didn't realise it was a private pig.'

The man laughed at that. 'Not your fault,' he said. 'Bugger was going to kill you, you did bloody well. Pig that size, it'd have ripped you open like a letter. No, what fazed me was, I was expecting it to come from the north-west, I was actually facing the *other* way; first I knew about it was you hitting the tree – and by the time I'd wriggled my bum round on the branch, I was thinking, what the hell was that, a deer maybe, and there *you* were, and the pig was running up your bit of stick like a fucking squirrel. Talk about nerves of steel, you must piss ice.'

Poldarn wasn't quite sure he followed that, but he reckoned he'd got the general idea. 'Well,' he said, 'I didn't do it on purpose. The fact is, I'm completely lost; and then the arrow—'

'Gare Brasson,' the man growled; Poldarn guessed it was a name rather than abstruse swearing. 'Careless bloody idiot, I'll kick his spine out his ear for that, shooting where he can't see. He might've shot you,' he added, red-faced with rage. 'I'm most terribly sorry about that,' he went on, 'only really, you shouldn't be here. You see, it's not actually very clever, wandering about in the middle of a boar hunt. Well,' he added, with a grin, 'I guess you've figured that out for yourself.'

'Yes,' Poldarn said. 'But I didn't know that that was what I was doing. Like I said, I'm lost.'

The hunter thought for a moment. 'Well,' he said, smiling brilliantly, 'no harm done. And it looks like we're done here for today, so we might as well pack it in and go home. Where was it you said you wanted to go to? My name's Ciana Jetat, by the way.'

'Pleased to meet you,' Poldarn replied. He realised he was shivering, and the knees and seat of his trousers were soaked in blood. 'Would it be all right if—?'

'Wash and a change of clothes? Of course,' Ciana Jetat replied. 'And if you're not in too much of a rush, perhaps you'd care to stay for dinner. We're only a mile or so over the way. Done your ankle?'

'Knee, actually.' Poldarn realised he was leaning against the tree, one foot off the ground. 'I think so,' he said. 'It's not serious, I don't think, but—'

'Amil will be here with the horses directly,' Ciana Jetat said. 'If you don't mind riding on the game cart.' Poldarn assured him that that would be fine. 'Splendid, then,' Ciana said. 'Didn't catch your name, sorry.'

'Poldarn,' Poldarn said.

'Really?' Ciana laughed. 'There's a coincidence.' Then he turned his head away, listened for a moment, stuck his fingers in his mouth and whistled so loud that it hurt. 'Amil and the cart,' he explained. 'Can you put your weight on your knee as far as the track?'

'What track?' Poldarn replied. Ciana took that for a joke, and laughed. The track, as it turned out, was no more than forty yards away, and wide enough for two carts to pass each other without scraping wheels. He'd probably been walking parallel to it for hours, and had never realised that it was there.

'We're just camping out in the lodge,' Ciana said apologetically, 'roughing it. We're only stopping there the one night, so there didn't seem to be any point tarting the place up or dragging the household staff out here in the middle of nowhere. Still, if you don't mind basic campfire hospitality—'

Poldarn smiled; he knew what that meant, of course. When a rich sportsman talks about roughing it, he means honey-roast peacock in creamed artichoke sauce served on the ancestral silver in the Great Hall, by the light of a thousand scented candles. 'Don't worry about it,' he said. 'Really, it's very kind of you to share with me, especially after I mucked up your hunt.'

'Oh, well.' Ciana shrugged, like a man slipping off a very heavy fur cloak, then picked up his hunting bag, which he'd put down for a moment, and slung it over his right shoulder, using his left hand. Poldarn noticed that he hardly used his right hand for anything; the fingers were bent inwards, like a crow's foot, presumably because of some accident. 'It's not every day you come across a three-hundred-pounder with nine-ounce ivories and all his rights, but what the hell. After all,' he added, rather gloomily, 'it's only sport. Talking of which, I suppose, properly speaking, the tusks belong to you. I'll have Cano cut them out for you.'

'No, really,' Poldarn said quickly. 'You keep them. I think I saw quite enough of them when I was back under that tree.'

'You sure?' Ciana brightened up almost instantaneously. 'Well, that's very generous of you, very kind indeed.' He thought for a moment. 'You're absolutely sure? I mean—'

'Really,' Poldarn said.

Ciana's lodge proved to be a lopsided pole-and-brush lean-to tucked under the lee of a small hill. The fire smoked, the food had been better at the colliers' camp, and the beer was only marginally less disgusting. Ciana and his people (there were about thirty of them, packed into a hut that would just about have housed a dozen dwarves) seemed to think it was all a great treat and tremendous fun.

'I mean,' Ciana explained, as another jug of revolting beer appeared out of nowhere, 'this is what it's all about – I mean, life. *Real* life. Bugger being cooped up in a poxy little counting house or joggling up and down in a cart till your pee froths or chucking your guts up over the rail of some horrible little ship. The hunt, the campfire, eating what you kill, a few good friends under the open sky. That's what it's supposed to be like, you know? That's what we were put on this earth to do.'

'Absolutely,' Poldarn replied, managing to give the impression that his beer-horn was still mostly full, and therefore not in need of a top-up. 'I feel sorry for those other poor devils,' he added cautiously.

'Damn straight.' Ciana carefully wiped ash off his chunk of burnt ham, and tore half of it off with his teeth, like a dog. 'There's times when I'm stuck in bloody Torcea, at some bloody stupid Guild meeting or whatever, I think I'll go crazy if I don't get out, breathe some fresh air, feel some *space* around me.' He sighed. 'Got to head back there tomorrow, worse bloody luck. Got fifty thousand jars of salt fish and nineteen thousand gallons of walnut oil due in from Thurm the first of the month, wouldn't do at all if I'm not there to check the bills personally. Not saying the clerks couldn't handle it, actually they're a great bunch of lads, but really, you can't delegate stuff like that, the really important things, you wouldn't last a week. Still, we've had a good break, bloody good time all round, apart from not getting the big pig, of course. But otherwise—' He fell silent and stared into the fire, as if there might be prize boar lying hidden among the clinker.

Poldarn didn't look at him. 'You're heading for Torcea, then,' he said.

'Miserable bloody place,' Ciana said. 'But yes, that's right.'

'Do you think you could give me a lift there?'

If Ciana hesitated for a moment, it was probably only the thought of being responsible for a fellow human being ending up in the unspeakably horrible city. 'Sure,' he said. 'What'd you want to go *there* for?'

'Oh, just a spot of business,' Poldarn answered, as lightly as he could. 'Thing is,' he went on, 'I'm in rather a hurry; but getting lost in the forest has set me back a day, and I'm pretty sure that by the time I get to the coast, I'll have missed the boat I was supposed to be on.' His hand was in his pocket; he fingered Mino Silsny's valuable ring. 'I'll gladly pay you, of course, whatever it costs—'

Ciana waved the offer away as if it was a moth he was trying to swat. 'Wouldn't hear of it,' he replied, 'don't be daft. We've got our own ship sat there waiting for us at Far Beacon, loads of spare room, no bother at all. Glad of the company,' he added, as someone behind him jostled his arm, making him spill beer all over his own feet.

'Thank you,' Poldarn said, hoping that it was a big boat.

Chapter Fifteen

It was a reasonably big boat; but since it had to hold the entire hunting party, their weapons, equipment, camping-out gear, leftover beer, trophies (several sacks full of deer skulls, boar skulls, hares' feet, foxtails, wolf pelts, and bits and pieces of various animals that Poldarn couldn't identify and didn't really want to), as well as Ciana himself, it could have been twice the size and still uncomfortable. It sat alarmingly low in the water, and since the jolly huntsmen were also the crew, Poldarn had severe misgivings about the whole enterprise. On the other hand, it was a free ride to Torcea, always assuming that they didn't sink halfway across the bay.

They didn't. The storm that had been threatening to burst ever since they'd embarked managed to wait until they were unloading at Torcea dock before letting rip. Consequently, Poldarn's first impression of the big city was a stinging curtain of rain that cut visibility down to less than fifteen yards, with a backdrop of forked lightning.

'Looks like we brought the weather with us,' Ciana said, yelling to make himself heard over the drumming of the rain. He was soaked to the skin, his grey hair plastered down over his forehead, even his vast moustache limp and soggy, but the cold and the wet didn't seem capable of damping down his infuriating good humour. 'It's not usually like this until mid-autumn, but obviously the wet season's set in early. No bad thing, it washes the stink off the streets.'

Poldarn tried to say goodbye as soon as they'd finished hauling the gear across to Ciana's warehouse, but the hunter wasn't so easily shaken off. 'Don't be silly,' he roared, when Poldarn suggested looking for an inn for the night. 'You won't find anywhere round here at this time of year – you'll end up dossing down under the viaduct arches. You come on home with me, I'll show you my trophy collection.'

The hammering of raindrops on the warehouse roof drowned out Poldarn's response, which was probably just as well. He had no money, no clothes other than those he stood up in, and his left boot had sprung a leak. Also, he had no idea where to go, or how to set about accomplishing what he'd come here to do. 'Thanks,' he replied, 'that's really very kind of you.'

Ciana's house was slightly smaller than Falcata, but not by much. Once they'd passed under the gate in the outer wall (twenty feet high and six feet thick at the base) they crossed a courtyard big enough to corral a couple of hundred head of cattle, passing a small town of outbuildings, sheds and storehouses, until they reached another gate in another vast defensive wall, which Ciana opened with a small silver key.

'I'm home,' he bawled, as he led the way into a lobby that reminded Poldarn of a fairy story he must've heard when he was young, about the prince who climbed up the magic pepper-vine to the giant's castle. A giant would've been perfectly comfortable in Ciana's house, provided that he had plenty of furniture to fill up the open spaces.

Doors flew open, and men and women streamed out and started grabbing luggage, bustling it away out of sight, all with the same horrible cheerfulness that Poldarn had got so tired of over the last two days on the boat. In the time it took them to walk from the front entrance to the next set of doors, Poldarn and Ciana were stripped of their wet clothes, towelled dry, and dressed in long, warm wool gowns that made a soft huffing noise as they dragged over the shiny marble floor; while behind them, three tall, gaunt men with mops wiped away their wet, muddy footprints.

'That you?' screeched a woman's voice as the second set of doors were opened for them. Now they were in a dining hall half as long and high again as the Charity & Diligence in Sansory, where Poldarn had first met Cleapho. A high gallery, its turned wooden balustrades painted and gilded in an overwhelming variety of colours, ran round three sides of it. Dead centre of the gallery on the far side stood a woman – at least, Poldarn assumed there was a human being somewhere inside the vast billow of fabrics from which the loud voice appeared to be coming. 'That you?' she repeated. 'Have a good trip?'

'Fine,' Ciana replied, as if he'd just stepped out to buy anchovies. 'This is Poldarn, he'll be staying a few days. Where's the mail?'

'Study,' replied the voice among the draperies. 'Dinner's cooking.' Poldarn's newly acquired instinct helped him judge the distance between the woman on the balcony and himself; too far away for her to see his burned, melted face. 'Tell your friend he can have the Oak Suite.'

She disappeared backwards through a pair of enormous panelled doors. 'My wife,' Ciana explained. 'Come on, I'll show you to your room.'

Up the gallery stairs, down one side, down a long corridor hung with dark tapestries that stank of dust, left down another corridor, carpeted and lined with frescoes of sea battles. Eventually, Ciana stopped outside a door (it looked like it had been planked out of a single tree, except there couldn't possibly ever have been a tree that tall and wide) and pushed it open with his fingertip. 'Hope this'll be all right,' he said. 'We don't entertain much, so we only keep a couple of rooms ready. Still, it keeps the rain off.'

Before Poldarn could say anything, four women pushed past him into the room, carrying a huge laundry basket between them like orderlies bearing the wounded from a battlefield. Once inside, they moved so fast, brandishing sheets and blankets and skinning pillowcases off horse-sized pillows, that it was impossible to see past them and admire the view. 'Someone'll be up with water for a bath,' Ciana was saying, 'and then it'll be time for dinner. Not the same as a simple meal under the trees, but you can't have everything.' Then Poldarn lost sight of him behind the whirling clouds of laundry, though he saw the door close.

The women finished whatever they'd been doing and vanished like elves, leaving Poldarn alone in the Oak Suite. Why it was called that he wasn't quite sure, since as far as the eye could see every surface was either black marble or extravagantly carved and gilded burr walnut. In the far corner was a sort of pavilion affair, inside which he guessed there was a bed. On a broad table (wealthy farmers in Tulice worked smaller acreages) was a tall pile of neatly folded clothes for him to change into. A solid silver bath stood in front of the fireplace like a raider ship dragged home and set up as a trophy of war. He'd just taken off the gown that he'd been manhandled into in the entrance hall and was about to put on the new clothes (thick, soft and surprisingly plain woollen shirt, trousers and socks) when the door opened yet again and a dozen women – different ones, as far as he could tell – burst into the room holding tall copper jugs that filled the air with steam. They took no notice of Poldarn, standing in the middle of the room with a face covered in scar tissue and no clothes on; they filled the bath, laid out a tall pile of white towels, and disappeared.

A bath, Poldarn thought, staring at it. Not a dip in a river or a splash of water out of a pool or dunking your head in the slack-tub: an actual bath, indoors, in hot water. Have I ever had one of these before? Must have, or else the smell of the steam wouldn't seem so familiar, and I wouldn't be looking forward to it so much. Chances are I used to enjoy baths, at some stage in my career.

The water was *hot*; considerably hotter than he'd anticipated when he'd vaulted over the towering side and plunged in. For three or four agonising heartbeats he was convinced he was about to die, but then the pain and shock faded, replaced by a feeling of overwhelming comfort. Wonderful bath, he thought, I've missed this— He frowned but decided not to worry about it. Someone had left a tall, slender bronze jug on a pedestal next to the bath, where he could just manage to reach it from where he lay. It was full of some white, milky liquid, and a little voice at the back of his mind said that the right thing to do was pour this stuff over his head, knead it into his hair, hold his breath and duck under the water for a bit. He wasn't quite sure what this performance was designed to achieve, but the instinct was terribly strong. He tried it, and surfaced a few moments later to find that the bathwater had all turned the same milky white colour. Amazing, he thought.

What in the gods' names am I doing here? he asked himself. Superficially, the answer was perfectly straightforward: he'd had the extreme good fortune to scrape acquaintance with a wealthy, generous eccentric, and in consequence was wallowing in a hot bath full of milky white stuff instead of crouching under a cold stone arch in the wet streets, hoping his boots would still be on his feet when he woke up. No problem with that; and he'd forgotten, assuming he'd ever known, just how extremely nice pleasure could be. A man could easily go out of his way for pleasure; he could do far worse than spend his whole life hunting for it, like Ciana stalking the big pig. True, there wasn't really any need for the furniture and tapestries and life-size marble statues and enough servants to colonise a small continent. A bath was probably enough, and clean clothes whose previous owner hadn't died by violence, and something half decent to eat. A man could be fooled into believing this sort of thing was normal if he hung around here long enough.

Normal as a two-headed dog, Poldarn reminded himself, sticking his toes up out of the water and looking at them as if he'd never seen them before. He was, after all, in Torcea, the capital of the Empire, in the house of a giant. (A short giant, maybe; but if he drew back those enormous shutters and looked out of the window, it was a safe bet he'd see outsize leaves and the tree-thick stem of the giant pepper-vine, and below that a soft white mat of clouds.) None of this was why he was here; he hadn't fought and killed his way from Haldersness to Dui Chirra and slaughtered a giant boar with a tree branch just so that he could have a relaxing bath.

> Two crows sitting in a tall thin tree
> Two crows sitting in a tall thin tree
> Two crows sitting in a tall thin tree—

—Still couldn't think of the last line, damn it. The song spun round in his mind, the jagged edge where the final line was missing grazing all his thoughts, leaving them raw and painful. He decided to think about something else.

He was, he supposed, here to overthrow the Empire, kill the most evil man in history and bring about the end of the world. A brief rest, wash and a brush-up, bite to eat, and then it'd be business as usual. Poldarn remembered washing his face in the fern-fringed pool, on the first day, when Copis had found him; this was better, but otherwise the two experiences were pretty much the same, and he was really no further forward.

Dinner with Ciana and his family (which was huge and excessive, like everything else to do with him) would have been an ordeal, except that the food was very good indeed, and there were no soldiers, sword-monks, bandits, pirates, mysterious women who turned into crows or old school friends anywhere to be seen. Ciana's wife, a large woman with thick red hair down to her waist, had taken one horrified look at Poldarn's face and then made up her mind that he was invisible; her three brothers scowled at him through the forest of silverware; an assortment of thickset, hairy men who were probably cousins tried to make him eat and drink enough to feed a large village, and burst out in raucous laughter whenever he asked someone to pass the mustard. Ciana himself told a succession of improbable hunting stories, which neither Poldarn nor anybody else paid any attention to. There was also a tall, slim woman, with grey eyes and light brown hair that curled where it touched her shoulders, who sat opposite him. He guessed she must be Ciana's baby sister; she didn't talk to anyone, and ate nothing except bread, a carrot and a few thin slices of smoked lamb, and if his appearance bothered her, she gave no sign of it. Miraculously, once the last course had been stripped off the plates and cleared away, Ciana stood up and walked away from the table, promptly followed by the rest of the company. Poldarn, who'd assumed that he'd be stuck there half the night while the household drank itself into a coma, found himself following a severe-faced

manservant back through the panelled corridors to his
room, where someone had lit the lamps and turned down
the coverlet. He pulled off his clothes, dropped on the bed
like a shot deer, and fell asleep.

Soft red light light outlined the edges of the window
frame when he opened his eyes. Three women were
standing over him, holding jugs of water and towels; it took
him some time to persuade them to go away and let him
wash on his own. They'd left him yet another change of
clothes, and a pair of beautifully soft green leather slippers;
his boots, however, had vanished without trace. The impli-
cation was that he wasn't going anywhere, at least for a
while. For a moment he was annoyed; but what the hell,
he thought, will it matter so very much if I destroy the
world tomorrow rather than today?

No sooner had he dressed than the door opened (nobody
ever knocked) and yet more women came in; one of them
was the woman he'd reckoned was Ciana's sister. She smiled
at him.

'I'm Noja,' she said. 'My brother asked me to fetch you
down to breakfast.' More food, Poldarn thought, surely
not; she met his gaze and laughed. 'You've missed him and
the rest of them, I'm afraid,' she went on. 'He thought
you'd probably rather sleep in. But if you're not starving
to death, maybe you'd like some bread and cheese and some
fruit—'

'Thanks,' Poldarn said quickly, 'that'll be fine.'

She nodded. 'Food is a serious hazard in this house,' she
said, as she led him down the stairs. 'It sort of stalks you
like a predator. You have to be very careful or it'll over-
whelm you. Which is why I never leave my room in the
mornings till everyone else is safely out of the house, and
nobody's likely to jump out at me and make me eat roast
pork and sausages.'

Poldarn shrugged. 'I've got nothing against roast pork,'

he said, 'or sausages, even. But I've been, well, travelling for quite a while, and I guess I'm out of practice where competitive eating's concerned.'

'I see,' Noja replied. 'In that case, later on I'll show you some good places where you can hide during mealtimes. You can trust me, I've had years of experience.'

She didn't lead him back to the great hall where they'd eaten the previous evening; apparently she had a small breakfast-room of her own, where she could indulge her perverted taste for not guzzling in polite seclusion. It seemed odd to Poldarn that there could be such a small, plain room in Ciana's house; it was scarcely larger than the shed Spenno and Galand Dev had built to house the master furnace, and only about half a dozen servants stood around and watched while they ate their hot rolls and watermelon.

'You probably think my brother's a clown,' Noja said suddenly, as she washed her fingers in a silver bowl. 'Actually, he's not. Our father was a tenant farmer in Tulice; my brother came here with two shirts and a writing set, and worked day and night for five years as a jobbing clerk until he'd saved the deposit for a loan on his first ship. He sent for me when I was fourteen, saved me from having to marry the boy next door, for which I'll always be grateful. The hunting thing comes from when he was about ten, before I was born. The landlord's sons used to come out to Tulice to hunt, and they used to let him carry the nets and work the dogs, and when they'd had a good day they'd give him a generous tip, five or six quarters; that's how he was able to save up the fare and the price of his ink bottles and writing slope. These days he's doing very well, thanks to a good eye for quality and a fair amount of common sense, but he's never forgotten those hunting trips when he was a kid, he's always trying to get back there, even though he knows he can't – he says there's a hole in time that's just big enough for his mind to slip through, but his body's got too fat. I suppose we've all got one or two special memories that we hold on to, like an anchor or climbing up a rope.'

Poldarn looked at her. 'Not me,' he said.

'Really?' Her look suggested that she didn't believe him.

'Really,' he said. 'Which is probably just as well. If memory's a rope, my guess is that the other end would be round my neck.'

She stared at him, then laughed. 'What an extraordinary thing to say,' she said. 'You make it sound like you've got memories, but you've found out how to avoid them, the way I avoid mealtimes.'

'They haven't caught me yet,' Poldarn said, 'but I have a feeling it's more luck than judgement.'

Noja examined him again, like Spenno assessing the strength of a welded seam, then smiled. 'Well, best of luck, anyhow. What would you like to do today? Jetat said that if this is your first time in Torcea, maybe you'd like me to show you the sights.'

'Actually—' Poldarn hesitated. There was definitely a case to be made for it, probably a whole sheaf of precepts of religion about the importance of thorough reconnaissance; it'd be better than having to ask the way in bakers' shops, and he didn't have any money to buy a map, assuming there were such things as maps of cities. 'That would be very kind of you,' he said, 'if you can spare the time.'

Her smile widened, like a flaw in a casting. 'I'm entirely at your disposal,' she said gravely (Copis, assigned to him by the Faculty of Deymeson). 'I'll tell them to get a carriage ready.'

The Ciana family's second-best carriage certainly made a change from carts. The spokes of its wheels were impossibly slim, and there was a dainty little set of folding steps to preserve passengers' dignity as they got in. Two coachmen sat in front, and two large men in livery sat behind (chaperones or bodyguards, or maybe they were just there to produce food in case a passenger had somehow managed to go an hour without eating something). There were four matched horses, and enough non-functional silverwork was riveted and stitched to the harness to pay for a road across the Tulice marshes. Which was, of course, exactly the degree of style appropriate for the entry of the god in the cart into Torcea—

'That's the Oratory, over there,' Noja was saying, 'and you can just see the spire of the North Star Tower over there – no, you've missed it, that's the Merchant Venturers' Hall, and down from there on the left is the Ordnance Grounds, with the Processional leading to the North Bridge—'

'I see,' Poldarn lied. 'Is that near where the Emperor lives?'

Noja looked at him. 'How do you mean?' she said. 'When he visits, you mean? Well, usually he stays at the Guild House, or the Prefecture . . .'

Poldarn frowned. 'The Emperor doesn't live in Torcea?'

'Good heavens, no.' She laughed. 'The palace is at Gondleve, that's a day's drive north; or there's the summer palace at Ondene, or the autumn lodge at Ducuse. And when the Council's in session, of course, he's at Bolway.'

'Oh,' Poldarn said. 'So where would he be now?'

Noja had to think about that. 'Probably,' she said, 'at Beal, for the honey festival. Tazencius likes to be seen at things like that, so people will start thinking he's really the Emperor.' She smiled. 'You know, I haven't been to the honey festival for years. I don't suppose it's the same as it used to be – we used to go every year, but my brother sold off that side of the business. Would you like to go? It's quite fun.'

Poldarn could feel pressure on the edge of his circle. Nobody had asked what his business in Torcea was; one explanation was that they already knew, and of course there were others, more likely. 'How far is it?' he asked. 'I really don't want to put you to any trouble.'

'Not far,' Noja replied. 'We can stay overnight at the Purity of Soul at Orchat, it's not what it used to be, of course, but people still go out there quite often; and the festival proper doesn't actually start until tomorrow evening.'

He studied her for a heartbeat or so, then said, 'It was an accident.'

She looked puzzled. 'Sorry, what was?'

Slowly Poldarn drew the side of his little finger down his face, from his eyelid to the corner of his mouth. He'd never get used to how the skin felt. 'I used to work in a foundry,' he said. 'Getting splashed with molten brass is something of an occupational hazard. Both you and your brother have been amazingly polite about it, but—'

This time, Noja's laugh sounded different; when Spenno rapped a newly cast bell with a small hammer, you could tell by the ring whether the casting was sound or blemished. 'I'm so sorry,' she said, 'I wasn't laughing at you, it's just – you do know why you're here, don't you?'

Here we go again, Poldarn thought. 'I've got a few bits of business I've got to attend to in Torcea, if that's what you mean,' he said. 'And your brother was kind enough—'

'You don't know.' She was looking at him again. 'Well, it's hardly likely *he*'d tell you, but I thought one of his relatives, or maybe the servants— He brought you home with him for me.' She flushed. 'Other brothers bring back lace shawls or amber brooches for their sisters, Ciana brings me – well, ugly men.' She frowned. 'That didn't come out right,' she said. 'Is it all right if I start at the beginning, or would you prefer to make a scene first?'

Poldarn shook his head. 'Perfectly true,' he said. 'Actually, my friends tell me it's an improvement. Go on.'

'Well.' They were driving past a huge and singularly impressive building, but Noja seemed to have abandoned her tour-guide role for the time being. 'I told you my brother brought me out here when I was fourteen, and I was glad because it meant I didn't have to marry some farmer. Truth is, I didn't want to marry *anybody*; still don't. Which Ciana understands, bless him, he's amazingly good about it. He's also very well aware that I get bored very easily when I'm on my own, and too much female company makes me want to scream.' She looked sideways at him. 'Actually, when I'm in a bad mood, I'm not nice to have about the house; so he's always on the lookout for company for me. Interesting people; or, failing that, people who don't get out of the way fast enough. But he can't quite bring himself to keep me supplied with good-looking men, or even ordinary-looking ones – he's still a *brother*, after all – so wherever he goes, he's perpetually on the lookout for men he can trust me to be alone with—'

Poldarn grinned. 'I see,' he said.

'Well, quite.' Noja grinned back. 'Actually, compared with some of the specimens he's fetched home— There was one poor old devil who'd had his jaw smashed by a wind-lass handle, and the bones set all funny; and three or four with the most spectacular harelips; not forgetting the one-legged hunchback – delightful man, he knew all about flower remedies. So, I knew as soon as I saw you. I hope you don't mind terribly much.'

'Doesn't bother me at all,' Poldarn replied. 'I mean, I think your brother is a very strange man, but I'm not in the least offended or anything like that. Is he right, by the way? That is, does it work?'

'What do you – oh, I see what you mean.' She frowned slightly. 'Yes,' she said. 'At least, he needn't bother, I really do only want someone to keep me company. It's just the way I am, really.'

(Copis again, Poldarn thought.) 'Whatever,' he said. 'But – well, I really do have things I have to see to while I'm here, if that's all right.'

'Of course.' She looked at the back of the coachman's neck. 'But not straight away, I hope.'

Poldarn hesitated; then he said, 'There's nothing that can't wait a day or so. I'm sorry if I embarrassed you.'

Noja shook her head. 'Can't be done,' she replied. 'And believe me, better men than you have tried. But when it comes to being embarrassing, I'm the heavyweight champion. Now, do you want to head out to Beal right away, or would you rather see a bit more of the city first, or what? Like I told you, I don't mind. Anything's better than sitting in a room with a lot of women doing embroidery.'

'Let's go to Beal,' Poldarn said, after pretending to think it over for a while. 'And what exactly *is* a honey festival, anyway? I don't think I've ever heard—'

'It's a festival,' Noja said, 'with honey. People – bee-keepers, presumably – bring in thousands of jars of honey from the country, and you can buy it to take home or just stand there eating it with a spoon until you throw up, and there's a prize for the best honey in the show. We used to go because my brother got landed with a bee farm when one of his customers went bust and his assets were divided up; being Jetat, he made a study of the honey trade, hired a good bailiff, turned the business round in four years and sold it at a thumping great profit. And like I said, the festival was good fun, in a nauseating sort of way.'

Poldarn shrugged. 'Fine,' he said. 'Let's go.' He didn't ask again whether the Emperor would be there; he'd heard her the first time, after all, and he didn't want to be too obvious.

Noja sent one of the footmen back to the house to tell

Ciana Jetat where they'd gone; that left one footman and two coachmen (three to one, in Deymeson terms, assuming Noja classed as a non-combatant). The ride out of town towards the northern hills – Beal lay in the valley on the other side – was slow and dull: Noja embarked on a series of tales of mercantile adventure involving daring purchasing coups and bluffs called and uncalled in jute options and charcoal futures, most of which went over Poldarn's head like teal rising out of a reed-bed. He filtered out the words and half-listened to the patterns and inflections of her voice, which was by no means unpleasant, reminding him of a cheerful but repetitive tune played on a cane-stalk flute. By the time her flow of commercial epics dried up, they were outside the city walls and trundling along a wide, dusty road flanked by tall beech hedges. There were carts and carriages and traps in front and behind, more going the other way. He thought about Falx Roisin, and his short time as a courier in the Bohec valley – terrible, fatal things had tended to happen to people who'd shared wheeled transport with him back then. In fact, a large proportion of what memories he had seemed to involve a combination of carts and unexpected violence.

Night fell faster in the hinterland of Torcea than in Tulice or the Bohec valley. The sunset was spectacular but short, and as soon as the sun had disappeared (like a big chunk of bronze scrap sinking down into the crucible as it melted) Poldarn began to feel uncomfortably cold in the thin shirt and coat he'd been issued with back at Ciana's house. Noja looked like she was cold too; she'd stopped talking and was trying to snuggle down under a thin, coarse travelling rug, which she didn't offer to share. All in all, Poldarn was delighted when they passed under a gallows sign and he read the words *The Purity of Soul*, with *Orchat* underneath in smaller letters.

'Food,' Noja said, as the coachmen unfolded the steps

for her. 'Don't know about you, but this chill in the air's given me an appetite. The leek and artichoke soup here was always fairly good, though I think the old cook quit about eighteen months ago. Still, it's risk it or go hungry.'

'We risk it,' Poldarn said assertively. 'And you said we'd be stopping here for the night.'

She nodded. The gesture reminded Poldarn very strongly of someone he couldn't immediately call to mind.

The leek and artichoke soup was fairly ordinary, but the bacon and wild mushroom casserole was much better, or so Noja reckoned. As far as Poldarn was concerned, it was stew, and as such a profound improvement on nothing at all. In scale and volume it wasn't anything like the catering at the Ciana house – you could see over your plate without a ladder – but Noja didn't seem to mind, and memories of what passed for food at Dui Chirra were still fresh enough in Poldarn's mind to make him grateful for anything he could get that didn't have cinders floating on top of it. They ate in a small private dining room wedged in between the kitchens and the common room. It was warm and quiet, and Noja, for some reason, had started telling stories about her childhood in the country; something about stealing a cake from their well-off neighbours and hiding it under her sister's bed, getting her into all sorts of trouble . . . Once again, Poldarn stepped back from what she was saying and treated her voice as music; just because he had so few memories of his own, he didn't necessarily need to fill up the empty space with other people's. Instead, he tried to reconstruct the geography of the forest where he'd first run into Ciana Jetat; which direction had the light been coming from, how far had he walked since dawn when he ran into the hunting party, and (probably most important of all) how had Cleapho, the most important man in the Empire, arrived at the rendezvous with Copis and Gain Aciava, alone and without getting covered in mud?

'So that was that,' Noja was saying. 'My sister was sent to bed without any supper, while I was allowed to stay up until Daddy came home from the fair. Monstrously unjust, of course, and she never did get any of the cake—'

'Your sister,' Poldarn asked quietly. 'What did you say her name was?'

Noja stopped and stared at him, her eyes suddenly wide. He'd seen that expression before, usually when his opponent had been expecting to be parried with the flat, and got a cut across the forearm instead. 'Well,' she said, 'we always called her Weasel, because—'

'Because of the shape of her nose,' Poldarn said. 'But what was her regular name?'

Noja didn't answer for a while. Then she stood up and carefully slipped the catch of the brooch that held her cloak together. 'I'm tired,' she said flatly, without expression. 'I think I'll go to bed now. You coming?'

Poldarn looked at her. She was allowing the cloak to slip down over her shoulders, revealing the sharp profile of her collarbone. 'You go on,' he said. 'I think I'll just sit up for a while.'

'Fine.' Her eyes were ice cold, like the touch of dead meat. 'Don't stay up too late,' she said. 'We ought to make an early start in the morning.'

Noja waited for a reply, then turned and walked out. The angle of her cheekbone as she moved away was entirely familiar. Mostly, Poldarn realised, he felt disappointed.

After she'd gone he counted up to two hundred, then opened the door cautiously and listened; the coachmen and the footman hadn't struck him as the sort of men who had the knack of breathing quietly. A small, detached part of him regretted missing the honey festival, which had sounded rather pleasant, if you liked that sort of thing. But they hadn't been going there in any case.

Nobody in the corridor, which was pitch dark; but it was

easy enough to locate the kitchens by smell alone. He considered his options. There would be people in the common room, but that was no guarantee of safety, and the shortest route to the stables was out that way, so that was where they'd be expecting him to go. Through the kitchens and round the back was three times as far. Simple mathematics: if she followed the relevant precept of religion (sharpen an arrowhead but make a shield as broad as possible), she'd have assigned two guards – the coachmen, presumably, they seemed to be a matched pair – to the common room, and stuck the footman outside the kitchen door. He was fairly sure he could handle the footman, quietly and without making a disturbance. But there was, of course, a third alternative: the stairs.

The bedrooms at the Purity of Soul were on all four sides of a gallery above the common room; one flight of stairs only, leading up from the end of the corridor he was standing in. It'd be a rather bone-jarring drop from a window down into the courtyard, but that couldn't be helped. The Weasel, he thought (assuming she'd been telling the truth), and the Earwig: a regular pest menagerie. Had they given him a nickname too, he wondered? Not that it mattered; but quite soon, one way or another, he'd be in a position where he'd never be able to ask about that sort of thing again. Whether he liked it or not, between them they had possession of most of his life (his memories their hostages, as it were). Even if everything went as well as it possibly could, he'd lose everything they knew about him for ever; and the loss of memories is the destruction of the past, and what is a human being except the sum of his experiences? Dead either way.

On balance, Poldarn decided, he'd rather be dead and still moving; so he turned his back to the wall and slid along it until the side of his foot bumped against the first stair. If they had to creak, he begged providence, let them creak softly. Up to a point, a creaking stair is your friend, because all stairs creak a little during the night, as the compressed fibres of the wood relax. The sound, being usual, is ignored and therefore inaudible. ('Something seen a hundred times becomes invisible': yet another precept of religion. There was probably a complete list of them, in alphabetical order, at the back of *Concerning Various Matters*, but he hadn't managed to get that far.) It's the sudden loud, complaining creak that gives you away and sets the dogs barking.

At the top of the stairs he paused. The plan had been simple enough – find an empty room, climb out of the window, drop down into the courtyard, steal a horse and escape. It was also, of course, the wrong thing to do.

He faced the door nearest to him, lifted the latch and walked in. There were two people in the bed, a man and a woman. The woman shrieked and tried to hide under the sheets; the man sat up sharply and stretched out his arm towards the sword propped up against the bedside chair. It was probably just as well for him that Poldarn got there first. He didn't draw the sword (an elegant if rather fussy object: moulded silver grip in the form of a leaping dolphin, which'd cut into your hand quite horribly if you ever had occasion to hit something); instead he closed his left hand around the scabbard chape and held it against his waist, ready for a theoretical draw.

'Sorry to burst in,' he said, 'but I need your window, just for a moment. You don't mind, do you?'

The man stared at him but didn't move or make a sound. Close enough for country music. 'Thanks,' Poldarn said; he slipped the shutter catch, pushed the shutters apart and swung his leg over the sill. Then he noticed that he was still holding the silver-hilted sword. 'You weren't using this for anything, were you?' he asked politely. No reply. Fine; he swung the other leg across the sill, relaxed his knees and dropped, hoping he wasn't directly above a pile of bricks or a bucket.

Landing hurt; but nothing seemed to be broken or bent, and he felt it would probably be sensible to get away from the open window. Making sure that the sword was still in its scabbard and hadn't been jarred out when he touched down, he hobbled as quickly as he could move across the yard, in what he hoped was the direction of the stables.

No mistake there; clearly his sense of direction was fit to be relied on, even in unknown territory in the dark. His self-satisfaction was ruined, however, when someone grabbed at his arm as he approached the stable door. As always, he felt the intrusion into his circle before the actual touch of the man's fingers, giving him ample time to side-step, reach out, grab the arm by the wrist and wrench it round a half-turn. Not surprisingly, the voice that yelped with pain belonged to the one remaining footman.

'It's all right,' Poldarn said reassuringly, maintaining his grip. 'Keep your face shut and I won't damage you.'

Then someone hit him across the shoulder with a stick. The pain distracted him, when it should have concentrated his mind (take away five points for that); he let the footman go, and got a fist in his stomach as a reward for careless-ness. Bad, he thought; don't want to draw the sword and start hurting people, don't want to get beaten up either. But the punch wasn't followed up, and neither was the attack with the stick. He waited to see what would happen next.

'Did you get him?' Noja's voice.

'Got him,' said one of the coachmen, behind his shoulder. 'He's got something in his hand – stay back.'

'It's all right,' Poldarn sighed, and he let the sword slip through his fingers. It clattered shrilly on the cobbles; probably some slight damage to that fancy silverwork. 'You can let go, I won't run away.'

'Inside the stable, quick,' Noja said. Someone opened

the door and pushed Poldarn through, closing it after him. Inside, it was dark and smelled of horses. He heard the sword being drawn behind him, and hoped nobody would be stupid enough to wave it about in the dark; he could feel where it was, by some sort of deep-rooted instinct, but he doubted whether anybody else shared that abstruse talent.

'I should've noticed earlier,' he said into the darkness. 'But really, you don't look much like her; only when you move, not when you're sitting still.'

'My own silly fault,' Noja replied. 'If I hadn't started telling stories about her, you'd never have made the connection. Still, it doesn't really matter. It just makes things a bit more complicated, that's all.'

Poldarn thought about that but didn't say anything. 'So what've you got lined up for me tomorrow?' he said. 'Are we going back to the city?'

'No, of course not,' she replied. 'We're going on to Beal, like I said.'

'Because Tazencius is there.'

'That's right.' She sighed. 'It'd all have been so much less trouble if I hadn't been so careless. You know, I was worrying myself frantic about how to get you there, after everything I'd been told about you – the most dangerous man in the Empire, you know, all that stuff. When you said that was where you wanted to go anyway, I nearly burst out laughing.' She hesitated. 'Are you sure you only just figured it out?' she said. 'Or have you been playing us all along ever since you met up with Ciana in the forest?'

'Is that really what they say about me?' Poldarn asked. 'Most dangerous man in the Empire?'

'Well, yes,' Noja said, sounding confused; then, 'It's true, isn't it? You really have lost your memory. You don't know—' She broke off. Maybe one of the coachmen sniggered, or maybe not. 'Well, anyway,' she said, 'that's beside the point. As you've probably guessed, these three aren't just your average coachmen. They're Tazencius's own household guards, on loan. We insisted. The three of them together, even you won't be able to—'

'I told you,' Poldarn interrupted, 'I don't want a fight. I came here to meet Tazencius, and all you're doing is giving me a lift. I'm grateful, even if you have been playing me for a sucker.'

Even though he couldn't see Noja's face, he knew she didn't believe a word of that – a pity, since it was true. 'If you think you can make your peace with Tazencius after everything that's happened, you're more stupid than you look.' She was trying to sound harsh but she didn't have the gift for it – unlike her sister, who had difficulty being anything else. '*She* won't be able to protect you any more, not now. Don't suppose she'll want to, either.'

Poldarn had to think for a moment before he figured out who *she* was. 'I wasn't expecting her to,' he replied. 'Truth is, I don't remember Lysalis at all. I've been told she was fond of me—'

'Fond's putting it mildly.' Noja sounded amused. 'I think, honestly, that's what really made Tazencius hate you the most. He felt really bad about using his darling daughter as bait, to get you, the most evil man in the world; and then she goes and falls in love with you – you, of all people – and of course it's all his own fault.' Noja laughed hoarsely. 'Well, it wasn't so bad when you went missing, and he had the boy, of course; sometimes he could almost kid himself he didn't remember who the boy's father was every time he looked at him. But then you turned up again, not dead after all. Where did you vanish off to, by the way?'

Poldarn smiled in the dark. 'I went home,' he said.

'Home? Oh, I see, back *there*—' He could imagine a look of disgust crossing her face. 'But you didn't stay?'

'Got thrown out,' Poldarn said. 'For making trouble.'

'Well, of course. It's a pity you had to come back, things

had sort of found their own level again: Cronan dead, Tazencius getting his chance, the new man turning out to be helpful after all.' Poldarn didn't know who 'the new man' was supposed to be, but he didn't want to show his ignorance. 'And then Gain found you, and of course you had to be right there on the spot, where the new weapons were being made. You know what? Xipho seems to believe it was just a coincidence; at least, that's what she said in her letters. Is that really true?'

'Yes,' Poldarn said.

Short pause. 'No, I don't believe it,' Noja said. 'I mean, the irony'd be too much, you helping to make the weapons that're going to blast your disgusting relatives out of the water before they can get within a hundred yards of land-fall.'

'Maybe I'd like that,' Poldarn suggested pleasantly.

'Maybe you would,' Noja replied. 'Wouldn't put anything past you. Honestly, I can see why Tazencius took to you, in the beginning. You really do think alike. Which is why,' she added, trying hard to sound threatening (but she didn't have the touch), 'you don't stand a chance of getting round him this time. He's got you figured out, you can rely on that.'

Poldarn shifted slightly; he was starting to get cramp in his knee. 'Never mind,' he said. 'I think I've reached the point where I'm not really bothered any more.'

'Nobody ever goes that far,' she said flatly. 'I should know.'

'Really? I expect you've had an interesting life, if you're anything like your sister.'

He'd intended to provoke her; not this much, though. 'You think I'm like *her*? Oh, please!' Noja's anger was so fierce that he could almost see it, glowing in the dark like hot embers. 'I'm nothing like her, never have been, even when we were kids.'

'You're going to a lot of trouble on her behalf, if you don't even like her.'

'She's my sister.' No, she was concealing something. Whatever she was up to, she wasn't doing it just to help Xipho. Bombarded with so many obscure fragments of data, Poldarn was too confused to know what to do with this one; he tucked it away in his mind, hoping he'd remember it as and when it became relevant.

'And Ciana's your brother.' He let that one hang, but she didn't seem to be reacting. Shot in the dark, anyhow. 'Was this all his idea, or does he just do what his big sisters tell him to?'

Her voice cooled down a little. 'What I told you was the truth. It was Ciana who brought me out here when our parents wanted me to marry some *farmer*.' She made it sound like some sort of nasty, crawling insect. 'I guess you could say he's the white sheep of the family. He genuinely went to Tulice for the hunting.'

'Really.'

'Really.' Now Noja didn't sound quite so tense; maybe because this part of her story was entirely true? Hard to tell, especially in the dark. 'And when his good friend the Chaplain in Ordinary asked if he could give him a lift as far as Falcata, he was only too pleased, naturally: doing favours for Cleapho is good business. So when Cleapho asked him for one other little favour – very much in his line, hunting something down in a forest—'

'Me. That's interesting. How did he know where to look?'

Noja laughed prettily. Nice voice; wasted on her. 'Really, you're too entertaining for words. You don't see it, do you?'

'Enlighten me.'

He heard her take a deep breath. 'Chaplain Cleapho wants to get you to Torcea. But he knows you ever so well, from the old days; and he remembers how you fought your

way past – well, past the Amathy house men at the inn in
Sansory. He knows that you're as slippery as a buttered eel.
The only way to get you here is to make you want to come
here; and the only way to do that is to get you to think that
what you're actually doing is running away – running here,
for safety. Hence the pantomime. That loathsome Gain
Aciava finds you and keeps you at that foundry place—'

'Dui Chirra.'

'Like it matters. He finds you, keeps you in play there
like an angler with a fish that's too big to pull in straight
away. Of course, you would have to be there, of all places,
where they're making the weapons. That imbecile Muno
Silsny hears about you – the brave hero who saved his life.'
Noja sighed. 'Fat lot of good it did him, because as soon
as he'd figured out who you were, he had to go. Terrible
waste of time and effort: Cleapho brought him on, trained
him up, from nonentity to commander-in-chief virtually
overnight, because he needed someone in that position
who'd do as he was told and never think twice. Anyway,
that's all done with; Cleapho got rid of him, and just as
well as it turned out. But all his plans got screwed up
because of it, and by the time General Muno was out of
the way, the weapon thing was far too well advanced.
Simply bursting in there and flushing you out like a rabbit
was out of the question with all those soldiers there. So he
had to be clever about it – and wasn't he ever that. Of
course he had good help – Aciava, and that strange man,
Spen-something—'

'Spenno.'

'Whatever. He flushed you out of Dui Chirra, just in
the nick of time—'

'Really?' Poldarn interrupted. 'Why?'

'You don't need to know why, but what the hell. Because
he didn't want you trapped in there when his other man –
another old school chum of yours, incidentally – captured

it, by force, with some bunch of religious zealots he'd somehow turned into an army. See what I mean about clever? No fool, Cleapho. He wanted you in Torcea, and having the weapons safely kept out of harm's way would be nice too; lo and behold, he's got both. Once you were out of Dui What's-its-name and on the loose, it was child's play to shoo you along to where you had to go. It meant bringing forward the business with Falcata a month or two, but that was no big deal.'

'Falcata?' Poldarn didn't need the explanation, but for some reason he wanted a confession from somebody. 'You mean destroying it.'

'Well, yes. That was part of the plan from way back: make it look like your disgusting compatriots are on the loose again, hence a state of national emergency, and Cleapho can start moving troops to where they need to be, recruiting his strange bedfellows, all the stuff that needs to be done but which is such a bother to justify during peace-time. And thanks to the new man, who's a real treasure by all accounts, it was easy, and you went scampering straight into Cleapho's arms, thinking you were escaping.'

Poldarn scowled, grateful that Noja couldn't see his face. 'But that doesn't make any sense,' he said. 'Because I escaped from him, too.'

'Silly.' She was finding him amusing again. 'That's like saying the ball escapes from the stick when you smash it into the goal. He told you just enough to get you all worked up and determined – to do what he wanted, of course, without knowing that was what you were doing – and then let you slip away, to where Ciana was waiting with his pro-fessional huntsmen and tracker dogs and God only knows what, to bring you in and fetch you across the Bay. And here you are. By rights, right now you should be like an arrow on the string, fully drawn and aimed at Tazencius, and tomorrow we let you fly and, well, job done. But *I* have to go and screw it up, by telling you stories about Xipho as a little girl.'

Poldarn allowed for a moment's silence before speaking. 'I see,' he said. 'You've made rather a mess of things.'

'Yes.' Naturally Noja sounded bitter. 'And now, God only knows what I'm going to do. First thing tomorrow we're supposed to go to Beal, where you're meant to give me the slip, sneak through the guards using all the cunning tricks they taught you at school, and kill the Emperor. Then Cleapho takes the throne, everybody else in the picture gets wiped out, and as soon as the wonderful new weapons have smashed the raider ships into kindling, nobody's going to give a toss about legitimacy of succession, all they'll care about is that the new Emperor just got rid of the raiders once and for all. Years and years of careful planning, and I would appear to have fucked it all up. That's very bad, you know.'

'Yes,' Poldarn said. 'So, what are you going to do now?'

A long sigh. 'I think that's probably up to you,' she said. 'Let's put it this way. If this was a perfect world, and you could do anything you wanted, what would you do tomorrow?'

'Easy,' Poldarn replied. 'I'd go to Beal and murder the Emperor.'

Was it the reply she'd been expecting? Or was she trying to figure out whether *he* was lying? 'Why would you want to do that?'

'Because he's Tazencius,' Poldarn replied smoothly. 'Because he grabbed hold of me when I was still just a kid, and he turned me into something evil; because he sold me his daughter – who loved me, so I'm led to believe, though I can't say as I remember. It's all his fault; and it seems to me that, since I'm probably not going to live long enough to pick any of this season's apples no matter what happens, I might as well go out doing something useful as sit back at Dui Chirra forging brackets and drinking bean-pod soup until someone turns up to kill me. True,' he went on, 'from what you've been saying it's something of a toss-up who's worse, Tazencius or Cleapho – not forgetting Feron Amathy, mind, he's another evil bastard. But I don't know where Cleapho or Feron Amathy are, whereas Tazencius is just down the road; I might be able to get to him, but probably I haven't got time to tackle either of the other two. When you prune it all down, it becomes nice and simple.'

'Oh.' Noja sounded worried. 'And what I just told you about Cleapho, manipulating you just as much as Tazencius ever did—'

'Not as much,' Poldarn interrupted, raising his voice. 'Nowhere near as much. He used me for, what, a few months; and anyhow, the damage had all been done by then. It wasn't Cleapho who shaped my character or chose my path in life for me, he's just a very unpleasant man who'll probably be the next Emperor. Probably a very good Emperor, because he's intelligent and organised and patient and all the other things emperors never are. Bloody good luck to him, in that case.'

(*Yes*, said the little voice in his head, *but how did Cleapho arrange for Falcata to be destroyed? And who's the other man she mentioned?*)

Noja stayed still and quiet for a very long time. 'Why should I believe you?' she said at last. 'What you said, it sounds like the sort of motive someone'd have in a book or a story, not the way a real person actually thinks.'

'Ah.' Poldarn tried to put the wry grin into his voice. 'Shows what you know. Maybe I really do believe I'm the god in the cart, like your sister wanted me to. Because if I did, wouldn't this be just about perfect? After bringing about the destruction of Falcata, I kill the Emperor and throw the Empire into bloody civil war; meanwhile the wonderful new weapon doesn't actually work, the raiders land unharmed and kill everybody who's left. Pretty good definition of the end of the world, don't you think?'

She sounded offended. 'Now you're treating me like I'm stupid,' she said. 'You don't believe that. You know—'

'What do I know? Only what I've seen. I've seen how everywhere I go, cities burn and people die, and all because of me – I don't do the burning and killing, but I'm always the *cause*. I'm the dog with a burning brush tied to its tail – my intentions don't matter, only the effect I have. So it was inevitable I'd come here, to Torcea, and wreck the place. And here I am. That's so perfect it's – well, *religion*.'

'You'd know more about that than me,' Noja replied. 'But you're just making all that up to be annoying – everybody knows there's no such thing as the god in the cart.'

'Do they?'

'Well, of course. It's just an old Morevich story that Cleapho dug out of some book and started putting around so that superstitious people'd panic. It's not even a *genuine* old story; some bunch of monks made it up to boost offertory revenue. Any *intelligent* person knows that.'

Poldarn laughed. 'It may not have been true when Cleapho made it up,' he replied. 'But doesn't it seem to you that it's true *now*? You know, religion, that sort of thing. After all, nobody knows how gods come to be born. Maybe what Cleapho did is how you make a god.' He sighed. 'We probably learned all about making gods in fourth year, but of course *I* don't remember.'

'No.' Noja sounded bored and annoyed. 'No gods, sorry. And the world isn't going to end. And the weapons will work.' Hesitation in her voice. 'Won't they? I mean, you were there, you aren't stupid. Will they work or won't they?'

Poldarn thought for a moment. 'I don't see why not,' he replied. 'Basically, it was Spenno who did it all, and I think if anybody could make a Poldarn's Flute, it'd be him. But that part of it's all a bit sloppy, isn't it? What if the Flutes work just fine, but they only manage to sink two ships out of two hundred? And besides, I don't believe the raiders will turn up at precisely the right moment to get blown out of the water, and I should know, I was there only a year or so ago—' He frowned. 'It's not the raiders he's thinking about, is it? He wants the Flutes to use against someone else.'

Noja didn't reply, and Poldarn saw no advantage in pressing the point: he wasn't interested, he'd just pointed out the discrepancy to keep her in play, like that angler with the heavy fish. 'Anyhow,' he said, when the silence was starting to get awkward, 'you can believe me or not, it's up to you. But how about this: if we go to Beal, if I'm not going there to kill Tazencius, what else would I have in mind? Go on, you tell me. I'm not going there to make my peace with him, we both know that; and the honey festival sounds like fun, but not enough to risk my life for.'

She was a long time in answering. 'You could try and run away.'

'I could've run away tonight,' Poldarn said. 'I could've killed your pathetic excuses for guards out there in the yard, easy as anything. But then I'd have had to steal a horse and ask the way to Beal. Too much like hard work.'

'Assuming Beal was where you wanted to go.' *Assuming Gain Aciava was telling the truth; and Copis, and Cleapho, and Copis's sister who's just admitted she's a liar.*

'All right,' he said, 'I could've killed them and gone any-where. But here I am.'

A long silence, unbroken until Noja sighed. 'Yes,' she said slowly, 'here you are.' She was looking at him as though she'd expected more. 'Did you really love her?' she asked.

'Sorry?' he said. 'Who are we talking about?'

Her face remained the same, but her eyes had taken the cold, like molten bronze setting in the mould, flawless and strong. 'My sister, of course. Did you really love her?'

Poldarn considered his answer. 'I honestly don't know,' he said.

'I see. So the child—'

'I loved her *then*,' he said. 'I suppose; I'm not entirely sure. It was more – well, I guess it was something like signing a formal contract between business partners, or a peace treaty. I know that when I thought she might've come to harm, at Deymeson, when the monks captured me, I was worried sick; it wasn't my main priority, but it was always at the back of my mind. But that was probably mostly because she was, at that point in time, my oldest friend; I mean, I'd met her only a few hours after I woke up in the river, and we'd been together ever since, on and off. That's something, but not *love*—' He frowned. 'Sorry,' he said, 'that probably sounds really bad. But I'm too tired to lie.'

'That's all right,' Noja said, sounding almost relieved. 'And before that, at school and so on. You can't remember?'

He shook his head. 'I've been told all sorts of things,' he said, 'and if it doesn't sound too crazy, I've had dreams about those days, which might be memories of some kind, or maybe not. But if I was in love with her, I don't remember.'

'So,' she went on, as if she hadn't heard him, 'when you married Tazencius's daughter, and she loved you, you don't *remember* if you were really in love with Xipho all the time? Or did you ever feel anything genuine for her – Lysalis, I mean.'

'I have no idea,' Poldarn said. 'The part of me that I'm still on speaking terms with reckons that if the worst thing I've ever done is either marry one girl while still being in love with another, or else ditch one girl because I've met someone I prefer, then it could be a lot worse.'

Noja stared at him for a moment, then shrugged. 'That's fair enough, I suppose,' she said. 'I mean, it wouldn't make you the most evil man in the world, or anything.'

Chapter Sixteen

Rain. Rain, just like bloody always.

Rain, when he really didn't want it; because Runting had just woken him up out of his recurring nightmare, the one he was glad he could never remember when he woke up, and told him to get his trousers on, because the enemy were at the gates—

The enemy, he muttered to himself, at the gates. Which would've been just fine, absolutely no fucking problem, if it wasn't bloody *raining*. Because if only it was dry, the enemy at the gates would be the perfect test medium for the four finished, fettled, furnished, burnished, done and dusted but not actually yet test-fired Poldarn's Flutes sitting comfortably in their wooden cradles like cats on rugs on top of the watchtower. The defence of Dui Chirra would've gone down in history as the day when the world changed for ever; when all the art-of-war manuals and all the precepts of religion had to be rewritten, because a few hundred scruffs with four brass parsnips had beaten off the Empire's best troops led by the Empire's best general in the time it takes to boil a kettle. If only it wasn't raining.

Instead, Monach reflected bitterly, we're all going to be killed; and some other bugger, someone who hasn't had to put up with Spenno and Galand Dev and all the mind-meltingly annoying *politics* they go in for in this horrible place, is going to get all the glory and be a footnote in the appendix at the back of the history of the world. And—

And I wouldn't have let down my friends. That's the worst – no (he decided firmly as he dragged on his wet boots), no, dying's going to be the worst thing, but failing Cordo, and Xipho, when they trusted me – the Earwig, they'll say, give him a simple job to do, and a weapon that sneezes hellfire and lightning to do it with, and he screws up, all because of a little spot of rain. Should've known better than to trust—

'Are you coming or not?' someone was yelling. 'They're coming up the east road. There's bloody *thousands* of them.'

And why are wet boots so much harder to get your feet into than dry ones? That said, a man in charge, commander of the garrison of the most vital strategic point in the world, ought surely to be entitled to more than one pair of fucking boots—

Monach stumbled out of the drawing office, trying to find the right hole in his sword belt by feel alone and failing, and splashed through the puddles on his way to the watch-tower stair. People everywhere, of course; most of them foundrymen, standing about looking miserable, muttering, not showing any inclination to make themselves useful – damn it, better that they should be trying to open the gates and let the enemy in than just standing about getting under hard-working soldiers' feet. If they were actively hostile, we could massacre the whole useless lot of them, and then we'd only have the enemy to put up with—

Wet boots on the wet wooden stairs, squelch. Rain gets in your eyes, makes them blurry, stings. Up to the top of the stairs, up to the rampart – people getting out of his way, that's more like it – and look over, and – never seen so many people all together in one place before in my life. Not a parade in Sansory, or Torcea hiring fair, or Formal Service at the Chapel Royal, when everybody who's anybody piles into the great courtyard, pushing and shoving and trampling each other underfoot to get a seat and hear the Chaplain in Ordinary's sermon (Cordo, shooting his mouth off in front of all those people; must be a sight to make a pig laugh). Yes; you measure scenes like that by the thousand, but this is tens of thousands, a huge army—

The enemy, coming to get us, the defending garrison. Shit.

Never wanted to be a soldier. Not cut out for soldiering, let alone being in charge. Perfectly happy doing research in the library, teaching school, running murderous little errands for Father Tutor, rolling out of bed at three in the morning for the first office of the day. Leading armies, preparing defences, no. We must've done defending small wooden fortresses against overwhelming odds in sixth year, but maybe I was off sick that day, or I had a music lesson.

'Right.' The loudness of his own voice shocked Monach. But 'right' was always a reasonable place to start. 'I want five, seven and eight companies here on the front elevation. Two, three and four on the other three sides. One, six and nine in reserve in the yard, ten's going to be a flying reserve on the walls – I want you to stand by, wherever the action is, get yourselves there soonest. There's a fucking lot of them, but the only way they're getting in is through the gate or over the wall, and it's like my old gran used to say, doesn't matter how big the bottle is if it's only got a little tiny spout. Now, unless they're incredibly stupid, they won't try and burn us out with all this volcano dust on the premises, so that's one less thing to piss ourselves about—'

'Sir,' someone said (someone really insignificant,

because of the half-hearted attempt at respect), 'the Flutes. Aren't we going to use the Flutes?'

Monach rolled his eyes; theatrical gesture, helps relieve the pent-up fury. 'Don't be so stupid,' he growled, 'it's *raining*. The Flutes don't work in the wet, remember? That's why we haven't even tested them yet.'

'Actually.' Another interruption; painfully familiar voice. Meanwhile, the front line of the enemy is now so close, we can see the buckles on their belts. 'Actually,' Spenno whined, 'so long as we take care not to let the wet get into the volcano dust or the touch-holes—'

'Fuck you, Spenno, you told me they wouldn't work.'

The most annoying man in the world shook his supremely irritating head. 'That's not quite what I said. I said we ought to hold off testing till it stopped pissing it down, because they *might* not work in the wet and you really do want optimum conditions for scientific testing of a prototype. They may work. They may not.' You evil bastard, Spenno, I ought to have you stuffed down the throat of a Flute and farted up into the biggest cloud in the sky. 'Got to be worth a try, though, surely.'

'No.' Monach surprised himself by the amount of pleasure he got from just that one word. 'Use your common sense, why can't you? They know we've got the Flutes, they're expecting us to use them. Means they'll be holding back, expecting us to lure them into a trap, with the Flutes as the spring; us not using them'll confuse the hell out of the bastards. We try and set them off and they don't go, we'll lose the only advantage we've got.' Not bad, Monach had to admit, for the spur of the moment, when I'm still three parts asleep, not bad at all. 'We do this the old-fashioned way, like I tell you to, or we might as well open the gates now and have done with it. Now, is anybody else going to waste my time making me *explain* things, or can we get on with the job?'

Moment's embarrassed silence – confidence-inspiring generals don't throw temper tantrums – followed by wholesale scurrying about. Monach paused, standing still while everybody else was moving, and spared a moment to review the dispositions he'd just made. Again, not bad at all. The three best companies, full strength, best morale, haven't yet realised about the hiding-to-nothing aspect or don't care, to maintain the point of maximum impact; three companies in the yard, standing by or holding ready if they burst straight in through the gate. Flying reserve: where did that idea pop up from? Must've read about it in some book. Monach peered out to see if there were battering rams, scaling ladders or siege towers anywhere among the advancing multitudes, but all he could see was rain and more rain. Fucking arsehole-of-the-universe Tulice.

For what seemed like a very long time, they seemed to be moving very slowly – until they were very close, and then it became apparent that they were in fact moving very fast. *I've forgotten something, I've bloody forgotten something* shrieked a voice in Monach's head as the soldiers of five, seven and eight company bunched up against the rampart palings, trying to make themselves as small as possible under helmets, behind stakes. *There must be something I've forgotten to do, because I haven't really done very much, just these men here, those men over there; surely a general ought to be studying maps, sending runners, busy, busy, busy. He shouldn't just be standing here waiting for stuff to happen—*

The enemy had stopped. Monach hadn't seen them stop, he'd been kneeling down trying to get his toes the last three-quarters of an inch into his boots, and when he'd looked up again, there the bastards were, standing still in the rain, getting wet, not moving. *Why're they doing that? What're they up to? Shit, I wish we had something nasty we could throw at them or shoot at them.* He leaned out as far as he dared (not very far) hoping to see something significant, but all he got was two eyefuls of cold water.

Do something, please, don't just stand there. But there was something; the front the-gods-only-knew-how-many ranks were standing still, but behind them there were large, rain-mist-shrouded contingents of men moving about; the enemy taking up his position, skilful chess moves that a competent general ought to have been able to read like a book, but Monach couldn't; all he could see was vague grey shapes shifting about through a curtain of flying wet. Calm down, he told himself, let's think about this. They're out there, we're up here, exactly how much scope is there for tactical genius? Still only got two options, you bastards: through the gate, or over the walls. And they're both covered (assuming I haven't forgotten something).

They're waiting. No sweat, we can wait too. *They're waiting, because they're expecting to be blasted at by the Flutes. Can they see them?* Good point; no, dammit, they can't, because I had the smart idea of masking them with shutters. They don't know where the danger is. *They don't know what to do next.*

Monach could hardly keep from laughing. *Bastards*, he thought. *Call themselves soldiers, don't know what to do. Serve them all right if I suddenly whisked the shutters away and thundered them all into bloody shit. Only I can't, because it's—*

Rain trickled down his forehead, down his face, over his lip into his mouth, as he suddenly realised. *Yes, but it's not raining in the animal-fodder store.* Namely, the long rectangular wooden building whose longest side was directly parallel to the gate, at a distance no greater than thirty yards. Good, weathertight slate roof; of course, we'd have to tear down the lath-and-plaster wall – would that bring the roof down? Fuck, it'd really help if I knew how buildings work, or if there was a book you could look stuff up in. But assuming not: we drag down the shutters and prop them up in front of the Flutes; they force the gates, and when they're pouring in, jammed tight in the gateway like a turd in a constipated bum, we give fire—

Brilliant, Monach thought. *Never learned that at school, can't teach stuff like that, it comes from inside.* Of course, it'd mean having to move the Flutes . . .

'Spenno!' Hadn't meant to yell that loud; but here he was, little black tendrils of sodden hair crawling down onto his forehead. 'The Flutes. Got to get them off the tower, into the fodder shed. Mustn't let the enemy see what we're about. Can you do it?'

Spenno stared at him, swearing silently under his breath. 'Yes,' he said. 'But I'll need—'

Monach grinned like a lunatic. 'Help yourself. Take command. You're in charge, and give me a shout when you're done, or if the fuckers attack in the meantime. Otherwise I'm going to the drawing office for something to eat. All right?'

Spenno nodded. 'Fine,' he said, his mind a long, long way away from inanities such as military hierarchies, chains of command. Then he started calling out names, cursing and swearing aloud, waving his arms. Monach smiled. Someone was in charge at last, and they wouldn't be needing him for quite some time. Fine.

He reached the drawing office unmolested. No food anywhere to be seen, nobody to send out to fetch some; so he lay down on his bed in the corner of the main room, and (just for five minutes) closed his eyes—

'Xipho,' he says. *(And who was he?)* 'You're looking very well. Your condition suits you.' He makes it sound like vampirism or lycanthropy; but she's used to him after all those years, and smiles him down like a man whistling to a boisterous dog.

'Ciartan.' She in turn makes his name sound like a

criticism, a familiar complaint, wantonly unheeded, just this side of nagging. 'Wonderful that you could spare the time.'

(And he, himself, the mere Earwig is there too, sitting in the corner of the room – no, it's high up in a tower, circular, no corners; but anywhere the Earwig happens to sit is a corner, by definition. Strange, to see himself through Ciartan's eyes, even though it's only a dream—)

'Always got time for you, Xipho, you know that.' A reproach, and a point scored. Reckoning back seven years to the start of their duel, that makes the score fifteen thousand, four hundred and ninety-seven to Ciartan, fifteen thousand, four hundred and eighty-one to Xipho. 'So, when's it due?'

So calm, her smile. 'Winter solstice,' she says promptly, 'give or take a day or so. Talking of which,' she goes on, just a hint of mischief showing in the cracks under her voice, 'we were meaning to ask, would you like to be godfather?'

Ciartan can feel the pressure on the perimeter of his circle: a hostile intention, if ever there was one. But he doesn't want to fight on this ground quite yet, so he makes a show of turning to Rethman, as though noticing him for the first time. 'Hello, Rethman, how's tricks?' he asks; a question that expects and requires no answer. Then he turns his face back towards Xipho, drawn like a lodestone. 'I'd be absolutely delighted, of course,' he says. 'Though I've never been a godfather before. What'll I have to do?'

'Oh, nothing much.' Ciartan realises she's got something in her hands – *embroidery*, by God, Xipho Dorunoxy is sitting there with a belly on her like a beached whale, and she's doing embroidery. Ciartan can't help shooting a very swift glance at Rethman; *what in hell's name have you done to her, you bastard?* 'You hold him up while Father Tutor says the magic words, then you say "Yes" or something equally incisive—'

'Father Tutor?' He isn't surprised, or if he is he doesn't

give a damn; but he's trying to make it sound like an enormous issue. 'Since when has Father Tutor lowered himself to doing the births, marriages and deaths stuff?'

Xipho shrugs. 'Since I asked him, actually. He seemed quite pleased to be involved.'

'Bloody hell.' Ciartan can't help being impressed; it's as if she'd just told him that she was paying some god five quarters a week to do her laundry. 'Well, in that case I'd be honoured – thanks.' He needs a moment to adjust his guard and settle himself on his feet after an unexpected backwards jump out of danger. 'So, Rethman, how are things in the charcoal business?'

Insignificant Rethman smiles, as though he's flattered that Ciartan managed to remember how he earns his living. 'Not at all bad, right now,' he says. Xipho's husband has a broad, flat face – blandly pleasant apart from an unfortunate chin – and enormous brown eyes like a sick cow's. She could only have married him as a gesture, making a definitive statement of her unavailability, and no need to guess whose benefit such a statement is for. But Xipho was always more of a man than most men; and if Ciartan could marry a dim, wispy, fragile little mouse with huge eyes, loads of money and no brains, so could she. 'Of course, the charcoal trade's very seasonal, and this is usually a slow time. But we're actually up by a sixteenth on this time last year, mostly on account of some very useful new contacts in the Tulice ironworks—'

Ciartan has to try very hard not to stare. This wetslap got Xipho pregnant? *How?* With what? Instead, he consults his mental library, precepts of religion: the strongest defence is to counter-attack the enemy's attack. Since the only purpose Rethman served was to be used as a weapon against him, this was obviously the place to cut, at the fingers holding the sword. Ignore her, talk to him, like he's more important—

'Ah yes,' he hears himself say, 'Tulice. Fascinating place, with a lot of potential. Lumber growing up out of the ground, iron ore underneath it. Pity that communications are so difficult – bad roads and the incessant rains; otherwise, I'd say the region is wide open for sustained development.'

Rethman's eyes sparkle. And why not? It can't be every day that someone in this house actually listens to a word he says. 'Actually, the consortium I'm in with are working on that right now,' he burbles. 'We're looking into the possibility of using waterways – rivers, of course, and building canals; and half the year the lowlands are flooded anyhow—'

She can see right through the ploy, needless to say. The man of the moment doesn't come trundling halfway across the Empire on treacherous roads just to spend an afternoon chatting about commercial prospects in Tulice to the man who married the woman he loves. She's annoyed, in spite of herself, but she's well back inside her circle, guard up, balance perfect, and just sufficiently pissed off to be extremely dangerous.

Fortunately, some servant or other announces that dinner's ready. Excellent. When facing a tactical stalemate, change the locale.

Dinner is a bizarre experience. If the real Xipho, the one he knew at Deymeson, ever thought about food, it could only ever have been in the context of how much valuable time had to be wasted each day, taking food in at one end of the body, flushing it out the other end once it'd been processed. The real Xipho would never, ever, have participated in anything involving devilled eggs in sour cream, or sea bass with mushrooms on a bed of wild rice. *For pity's sake*, he can hear Real Xipho saying, *is this garbage supposed to be food?* And then she tips a whole jug of vinegar over it to drown out any suggestion of flavour, and loads it into her face like foundrymen stoking a furnace. But this Xipho (married, pregnant; those fingers, that can whisk a sword blade through three tightly rolled reed mats straight from the draw faster than any man in the Empire, now used only for stitching little mauve flowers onto a linen cushion-cover) eats like it's a matter of religion: serious, attentive eating, as if there's going to be a test afterwards. So; either the pathetic Rethman has corrupted her utterly, or this is all an act of war—

The meal lasts for ever; lichen smothers trees and rocks crumble into loam, and still they bring on more food, tiny bits of minced-up fish in silly little pastry fortresses, encompassed about with redoubts of rare, weird vegetable. But eventually it ends; and she gives Rethman a look, and suddenly he's deep in conversation with the Earwig (forgotten he was there; don't you always?) while Xipho walks across the furniture-cluttered floor towards the fireplace, choosing her ground for single combat.

'Well, then,' she says. 'You've been busy.'

Ciartan frowns a little. 'Lots of running about, nothing much actually gets done. That's the military for you.'

Her lip twitches. Ciartan could draw you detailed maps of her lips. 'And how's the family?' she asks – an expected opening attack, but hard to defend nonetheless. *If you ever really loved me, how could you possibly go off and marry that popsy?*

'Fine.'

She steps into his circle, following up remorselessly. 'Lysalis doesn't go with you when you're in the field, then?'

Ciartan makes himself show his teeth in a weak imitation of laughter. 'No,' he says. 'Life under canvas isn't really her thing. She'd come along if I asked her to, but—'

'You spend so much time away, though. Don't you miss her?'

Cruel Xipho: because of course he does, and that's the shameful part of it – insipid, flavourless Lysalis, Lysalis who every day renews her fatal crime of not being Xipho; and yes, he misses her. Because he loves her. In a sense. 'It's something we've had to figure out how to deal with,' he lies (floods of tears each time he leaves. *I can't help it*, she always says, *I know you've got to go, but*—) 'I guess it must be the same for you when Rethman's away on business.'

'Not really.'

He lets the words hang, not prepared to commit to what might be a feint. 'Seen Gain lately? I haven't heard from him in ages.'

'He seems to have vanished off the face of the earth,' she replies. 'Last I heard, he was in Josequin.'

'Josequin.' Fine; why not? 'Doing what?'

'No idea. Some errand for Father Tutor, presumably – assuming he's still in orders, that is. For all I know, he could've quit and gone into trade or something. He never struck me as the contemplative type.'

'He'll turn up again soon enough,' he says. 'He always does. The Earwig still hanging round, then.'

Xipho's face softens. Ploy. 'He gets on very well with Rethman,' she says. 'They go and watch the horse races together.' Fine; so why couldn't he have married Rethman? Then all four of us could be happy. 'It's good having him so close, otherwise I'd be completely out of touch.'

Religion: invite the attack you want to defend against. Religion: disconcert the enemy by doing the expected thing. 'So, do you miss – well, the old days?' There, battle joined at last. Took long enough.

'I don't know.' She's looking over his shoulder. 'I guess it's different for a woman. You start off on something, then marriage comes along, children – I can see why they don't like having women in the Order, it must seem like a terrible waste of resources when we suddenly up and leave.'

'Like me.' Step forward to parry, lean back to cut. 'I left before you did.'

'Ah yes.' Smile. 'But look at you now: captain of your own free company, with a prince for a father-in-law. Half the Order's work is training the likes of you – it's just as important as the contemplative side. You go out there, do the things that need doing in the world, taking religion with you. Every bit as important, maybe more so.'

(Xipho, why in God's name did you marry him? It *wasn't* just me, or any of us. Certainly not just me; it was only the one time, and we made more hate than love, and ever afterwards you treated me like I was the most evil man in the world. But yes, I did leave, and I did marry Lysalis—)

'But you're happy,' he hears himself say. 'You don't regret—'

A smile can be as fast as a draw, a moment that doesn't exist, in religion. She smiles: cold, bitter, vindictive. 'No,' she says. 'I'm happy, this is what I want.' She doesn't move, but the swelling in her body threatens him like a sword in the first or perfect guard. 'This is what I've always wanted.'

A challenge. *You got me into this mess, it's your fault; if it was your brat I'm carrying, it couldn't be more your fault.* And she thinks she's got me beaten, put me where I can't fight back, all out of options. And that, Father Tutor, is why I *am* the best of our year; because there *is* a way . . .

(*Monach, in his dream, on the other side of the room, talking to Rethman, knows what will happen, because Monach, awake, will remember what happened. Three weeks later: Ciartan, angry about something, very drunk, hammered on the door of Rethman's house, demanding to see Xipho. Rethman, half asleep, trying to calm him down, believing he's good at handling drunks and excitable people, telling Ciartan to come back in the morning; something in his voice, or maybe an inadvertent gesture misinterpreted as a threat, breaching Ciartan's circle. The draw happens in a moment so brief that it exists only in religion; but after the draw, when the sword had completed its perfect movement and was back in the scabbard, Rethman dead on the floor, sliced from ear to collarbone. Xipho came down to see what all the shouting was about; having no sword, she attacked with a candlestick, which isn't a proper weapon in the eyes of religion, and therefore not covered anywhere in the syllabus. Ciartan, just managing not to draw, defending himself as best he could: a kick in the stomach, no big deal under normal circumstances – Monach, asleep, has all this locked down in his memory, as he dreams of being Ciartan, on the day that caused the act that finally eliminated all remaining options.)*

'Wake up, for crying out loud.' Someone shouting in his sleep: is that Ciartan at the door, drunk, violent, wanting to see Xipho? 'For God's sake, wake up – they're attacking. You're supposed to be in charge!'

Monach sat up, swung his legs off the bed, opened his eyes. 'Was I asleep?'

'They've got battering rams.' Runting, wide-eyed, shaking. 'Bloody great big trees from the forest. They're—'

Monach yawned and stood up. 'How's Spenno getting on? Finished yet?'

Runting shook his head. 'Technical problems – the crane keeps breaking or something. Look, are you coming, or what?'

'Sorry,' Monach said, 'I was miles away. Right, let's get to it, shall we?'

When the world closes down around you and forms a clamp that seems to be squeezing your brain out past your eyes, there's nothing quite as effective as a temporary palliative than taking it out on strangers with a sharp tool. It was their fault; they'd smashed open the gate and come bursting in before everything was ready for them. For a short while, under the gatehouse arch, Monach's life suddenly became pleasantly, wonderfully simple. It was all disgracefully self-indulgent, but at least, for the most part, they wouldn't have felt anything, and they *were* the enemy. Presumably.

He'd already sliced a dozen necks to the bone before he realised: this was all very well, and his performance of the eight approved cuts would've wrung a nod of approval out of Father Tutor himself, but it wasn't the job he was supposed to be doing. True, he was forging ahead like a scythe through dry grass, but all around him the enemy were streaming past, pushing their way into the yard as if he was somehow *irrelevant*, while his men were either falling back or being killed. All his perfectly executed strokes were doing was putting him in a position where he'd be cut off, surrounded and hacked to death, leaving the garrison without anyone to tell them what to do. He stopped in his tracks, trying to figure out how to retreat – not covered in the syllabus, because sword-monks *don't* – and wondering what in hell's name he could do to rally his people and push the enemy back. No idea, not a clue. Then, while he stood still and helpless over the body of the last man he'd chopped down, something slammed into the back of his head and he found himself sprawling on the ground.

Beautiful irony; because it was Monach's getting knocked silly by a stone that saved the moment, not his supreme skill and grace. Someone in the retreating line of defenders saw him go down, and yelled, *The chief's been hit, they got the chief*; whereupon half a dozen of them pulled up short, faced about and rushed towards him. At least one of them ran straight up an enemy spear; at which, more defenders waded in to try and rescue them, and the general falling-back turned into a reckless but effective counter-attack. By the time they reached Monach he was on his feet again, sword in hand and looking round for the bastard who'd hit him. They surged round and past him, as soon as they realised he was all right; just as the enemy had done, they ignored him, as though he belonged to some other battle that happened to be going on next door. The hell with this, Monach thought; but the sheer ignorant energy of his followers stove in the advancing line and rolled them back under the gatehouse arch. There were plenty of other sword-monks in the garrison besides Monach, and they seemed keen to make the most of their chance to indulge themselves, too.

Right, he thought, and glanced up at the gatehouse tower, hoping to see if Spenno had managed to dismantle the Poldarn's Flutes yet. But the angle was too steep – all he could see were palisades. Not to worry; the job in hand was obvious enough. He needed to rally his men, make sure they didn't pursue the retreating attackers too far, then organise work details to patch up the smashed gates.

Monach tried shouting, but he couldn't make himself heard. His voice had always been soft and quiet, and he'd never had occasion to learn how to project it. As he stood in the yard, feeling unpleasantly foolish, he caught sight of Galand Dev. The short, wide engineer was engaged in a faintly ludicrous duel with two enemy soldiers, both of them a head and a hand taller than him; but he was using their height against them, warding off their blows with a captured shield as they cut down at him, and making them skip backwards as he slashed at their knees with a short-handled adze. A few strides brought him up close enough to join in; one soldier didn't see him coming until it was far too late; the other swung round to face him and forgot about Galand Dev, an omission that cost him his life.

'Thanks,' Galand Dev panted, wiping sweat out of his eyes, 'but I was doing just fine—'

'Listen,' Monach interrupted. 'You can shout louder than me. I want you to call them back before they go chasing off through the gate and get themselves cut off. Then I'll need you back here.'

One thing Galand Dev excelled at was giving orders. Soon the last of the enemy had scuttled away under the gate, and the defenders had regrouped in the yard, with Galand Dev barking out assignments by platoon.

Fixing up the gates didn't take nearly as long as Monach had expected it to. One platoon lifted them up and walked them back into position – they'd been ripped off their hinges, and the locking bar had snapped in two, but the panels themselves were hardly damaged at all. Another platoon fetched heavy poles and bricks; they weren't master masons or joiners, but they knew how to prop and wedge. Besides, Monach reflected, he didn't want the gates to keep the enemy out permanently. Just long enough.

He shuddered, not really understanding why. There was, after all, no difference. He could feel the damp warmth in the cuffs of his shirt, other people's blood, an occupational hazard for those who favour the lateral cut off the front foot. Severed veins spurt; there's a knack to blinking the blood out of your eyes quickly, so you don't lose the plot in the middle of a complex sequence of moves. No difference, not even in religion, between a subtle feint that deceives one swordsman, and the setting up of a fire-spitting monster behind a wicker screen . . .

Inappropriate thoughts: you could maybe just about get away with them as a foot soldier, a follower of orders, but not when you're in charge. Instead, he should be playing chess in his mind, figuring out the move after the move after next. (But Monach hadn't got a clue what he was going to do, let alone what the enemy were planning; he couldn't play chess worth spit, either.)

Still.

'We'll need to reinforce the east wall,' he heard himself telling someone. 'Who's in charge up there, anyhow?'

The man Monach was talking to mentioned a name he didn't recognise; it was as though his memory had been wiped away, like moisture off glass. 'Fine,' he replied. 'Take one man in five off the south wall, they won't try anything there.'

Whoever it was he was talking to didn't seem to agree with that. 'You sure? It's high ground on that side, if I was figuring where to put ladders—'

Monach grinned. 'You've forgotten your precepts,' he said. 'Strength is weakness. East wall's the strongest point, so they'll reckon we won't bother so much with defending it. Same principle as with the gates,' he added, for his own benefit mostly. 'Weakness is strength.'

The man (a sword-monk, Monach remembered) grinned suddenly. 'I remember that one from classes,' he said. 'I thought it was a load of shit back then, too.'

Colonel Muno, or whoever was commanding the enemy, couldn't have read the precepts of religion; or else he shared the sword-monk's low opinion of them. He attacked the east wall, just as Monach had anticipated; he brought up siege ladders – the trunks of fifty-year-old ash trees, taller by a yard than the walls and cut with slots up one side to serve as rungs – and sent his men clambering up them like terrified spiders. Monach had his men push down the first three or four; but the wall was too low for the drop to be fatal or even debilitating, and most of the ladder-climbers picked themselves up after they'd hit the ground and immediately set about righting the ladders for another attempt. So Monach told his people to let the bastards come, and placed sword-monks on the walkway at regular intervals. He denied himself the indulgence of joining them.

The essence of religion is, of course, simplicity; it aims to pare away distractions, on the assumption that the divine is an indivisible perfection. There was something wonderfully simple about sword-monks setting about religion, if you could put out of your mind the (distracting) fact that they were cutting human tissue and bone. A purist – Father

Tutor, say – might have quibbled, pointing out that their choice of cuts was too diverse for perfection; some of them favoured the downwards diagonal into the junction of neck and shoulders, others the rising diagonal across the throat, while others opted for a flamboyant, almost blasphemous celebration of variety, ranging from the minimal thrust to the full sweep of the arms, laterally off the back foot, shearing the head off the neck in a shocking waste of energy. Monach (who had specialised all his adult life in just the one cut, a swift drawn slice across the windpipe) didn't really mind, which in a sense was a failure on his part. His only real concern was to keep the enemy out of the enclosure, and so far his approach seemed to be working.

So efficient were the sword-monks, in spite of their lack of true focus, that the enemy commander abandoned the direct assault with ladders after a few minutes – long enough for the dead bodies to become a nuisance and a hindrance to movement on the narrow walkway, but not nearly as long as Monach would have liked. Since there was no danger of losing at this game, he'd have preferred it to continue for an hour or more, with less mayhem but more time-wasting, so as to give Spenno a chance to get the Flutes down from the tower and into the yard. Instead, the enemy withdrew their ladders and almost immediately resumed their attack on the already mangled gates. It wasn't hard to follow the reasoning behind the switch. Monach could only have so many of these bloodthirsty maniacs at his disposal, and the rest of his sad little army was made up of day-labourers, farm boys, runaway apprentices, thieves and outlaws. It would take minutes to get the sword-monks down off the wall and into the yard. It ought only to take half a minute to bash through the botched-up gates and match regular Imperial troops against the rabble. By the time the sword-monks rejoined the action, there should no longer be any scope for a series of single combats. It'd be back to proper grown-up soldiering, in which the trained unit invariably stamped flat the undisciplined individuals. Good plan.

So good, it was the strength that Monach, devout believer in precepts, was planning to attack. His idea had been to lure the bulk of the enemy force into the gateway in just this fashion, and then open up with the Flutes, charged with leather sacks full of gravel. It was annoying that the sword-monks had thwarted his unimpeachably orthodox planning by doing their job far too well.

Never mind. Yelling at Galand Dev to keep the men on the wall at their posts, Monach led the rest of his forces (even he caught himself thinking of them as 'the rabble') across the yard at a run. Mathematics, he thought, as he threw his weight against the planks of the left-hand gate. Factor: the gateway is wider on the inside than on the out-side. Accordingly, it ought to be possible to get more bodies, therefore more weight, against the gates on our side than they can on theirs. A straightforward shoving match, mere muscle and body mass, and we have the numerical advantage. Simplicity.

He was right, of course, though it was a closer thing than he'd assumed it would be. But they were cheating, using the battering rams (mechanical advantage), which not only increased the force they were able to apply, but also smashed the woodwork up still further, making it harder to push against. As he shoved, his mind elsewhere (clearly they hadn't got archers with them, which was a blessing, but why? Because, stupid, they were expecting to fight light infantry in a forest with visibility restricted to thirty yards, terrain that would turn archers into casualties-in-waiting) Monach felt a slight twinge in his shoulder, which he recognised as minor damage to a tendon. Big deal, except . . .

Cutting it too fine. It was only a minute or so before the battering-ram assault suddenly broke off that Monach managed to figure out what their next move ought to be. The enemy commander, he guessed, either kept cats or had played with one as a boy. He knew about flicking the piece of wool backwards and forwards, making the frantic cat lunge left, then right, wearing itself out. So: the master strategist had timed how long it'd take to get the sword-monks down from the wall into the yard, and then he relaunched the attack on the wall. That much Monach had had the wit to anticipate, hence his orders to Galand Dev; what he hadn't considered until it was very nearly too late was that his opponent was a man whose mind wasn't saturated with the precepts of religion, and who therefore didn't know the importance of attacking strength rather than weakness. Accordingly, entirely at odds with religion, he would see nothing wrong in launching a simultaneous attack on the hitherto unmolested south wall—

Monach peeled himself off the door and tried to push his way through the scrum, but no chance; it was like a nail trying to walk through a hammer. When the rams suddenly didn't slam home, and the gate-side mob promptly lurched forward against the impact of a blow that didn't arrive, he was knocked to the ground. Staring up through a forest of legs, he could just see the tops of scaling ladders poking above the south rampart.

Shit, he thought; but apparently there were smarter men than him inside the compound, for which he felt unreservedly, unselfishly grateful. Someone with a brain had sent the two platoons of mobile reserves to the south wall, in good time to push down the ladders before the enemy could come surging up them. Meanwhile, the butcher noises from the east wall told him all he needed to know about what was going on there. In that respect at least, he was ahead on points. What mattered, of course, was the progress or lack thereof up in the guard tower, and he couldn't see that since he was directly underneath it.

By the time he'd contrived to excavate himself out from under the gatehouse mob, the enemy had once again given up on the scaling-ladder approach. In fact, they didn't seem to be doing anything. That was bad; because, according to the scenario in Monach's mind, they ought now to be pressing home an attack on the gate and the south wall. If they weren't, it had to be because they'd thought of a better idea.

It was a good better idea, too. The master of strategy had been fooling with him. The direct assaults had been nothing more than playing for time (him and me both, Monach thought unhappily), while his pioneers were busy in the woods nearby, felling the tallest, straightest trees they could find and lashing them together with the ropes and chains they'd fortuitously decided to bring with them. They were as quick and efficient about it as you'd expect trained soldiers to be. The result of their efforts was a single massive ram, consisting of a dozen substantial tree trunks bundled up together like the twigs of a broom and hoisted onto the two biggest carts in the baggage train. While one section of their comrades-in-arms had been thumping on the gates, and others had been providing Monach's brothers-in-religion with live cutting practice, the pioneers and the reserve had dragged the super-cart round to the hitherto undisturbed north side, which happened to face a long, gentle slope.

The 'walls' of Dui Chirra were, of course, no such thing. The compound was defended by a stockade – as tall and well-built as a stockade can be, but still nothing more than a row of posts driven into the ground. When the cart-mounted ram rolled down the northen slope and crashed into it, there was an alarming splintering of timber, like a violent gale blowing down tall, spindly trees in a crowded wood. Before Monach could do anything, the enemy started to pour in though the breach.

Impossible, Monach thought; where's the religion in
that? The whole purpose of this dismal affair (he reasoned
as he sprinted across the yard, narrowly missing the corner
of the charcoal store) was to provide a pivotal moment in
history, a day when the world would change; this would be
the day when the full devastating force of the Poldarn's
Flutes was unleashed on unsuspecting flesh and muscle, or
else why were any of them there, why had Cordo, his *friend*,
stranded him here in an impossible situation that he otherwise simply wasn't equipped to handle? If Dui Chirra fell
to a breached stockade, with the Flutes dangling in the air
on ropes, not a solitary charge loosed from a single one of
them, where in Poldarn's name was there any religion in it
at all?

The first man he happened to run into was some kind
of officer; brave, conscientious man, leading by example.
He was wearing a thick waxed-leather breastplate, and
Monach had to tug hard to free his sword blade from it,
where he'd cut into it far too deeply, because he'd been
angry and afraid and had slashed down far too deep. In
doing so, he wrenched that abused tendon a little more.
Very bad; nothing, of course, to an ordinary man, but the
slightest imperfection in religion undermines everything
else. If his shoulder hurt him a little bit as he moved into
the cut, his timing would be very slightly off. If his timing
was off, the cut wouldn't be exactly as it should be and
there would be no perfection. Any deviation from perfection would render him mortal; like the hawk, masterpiece
of economy of design, condemned to death by the loss of
three feathers. The realisation hit Monach hard: he was no
longer in absolute control of his actions in the one tiny area
of existence where he should have been able to rely on a
predictable outcome to anything he did. It was as though
he'd just watched a god being killed in front of his eyes.

It took more than courage to keep him steady in his

ground, or loyalty to his friends or his men, or belief in the cause (whatever it was) or religion itself. The instinct to run away would've overridden any of those, or all of them together. But the thought occurred to him, even as panic smashed through his defences into his mind, that if he ran, or if he didn't maintain the defence and drive the enemy out, then the Flutes wouldn't be discharged and everything would be wrong: history wouldn't turn, the world would stay the same, and it'd all be because of one weak tendon. He couldn't face the *embarrassment*.

He overdid his next cut recklessly, swinging with far too much force and not enough direction. The stroke went home, sure enough, but there hadn't been any need to chop bone, and Monach saw an accusing spark fly up as the hard steel of his sword blade chipped against a steel belt-buckle. The slightest notch in the cutting edge would ruin it for the perfect drawn cut, the stroke in which he'd striven all his life to find religion. Everything had gone completely wrong, and he hadn't even lost a square yard of ground yet—

The best and only chance was to close and seal the breach before the decisive number (a constant easily discovered by simple maths) got through it and into the yard. If the decisive number was sixty and he let through sixty-one, he'd failed. One hell of a time to screw up a tendon.

Even so, he thought; and he swung at the next man to get in his way with everything he had. It was a poor cut, a lousy cut, Father Tutor would have rolled his eyes and clicked his tongue, but the dead man hit the ground with a thump, and his sword clattered against the rim of his shield as it dropped. The next one was slightly better, but the annoying fool of a target stumbled, was in the wrong place, and the edge cut into the ball of his shoulder instead of his neck; Monach had to waste a whole cut finishing him. From there, it was all simply dreadful. Some of them

had time to hit back and he had to parry, something he
hadn't needed to do for ten years. One of them even slipped
past a third back guard and nicked the lobe of his ear before
Monach could deal with him. He was tired, he'd wickedly
abused his shoulder, he was filthy with mud and blood and
he'd knocked a splinter as wide as the nail of his little finger
out of the edge of his sword, a forefinger's length down
from the tip. History and the world owed him badly for all
this.

Fortunately, he'd underestimated his men. Their efforts
were so shabby as to be practically an abomination, but
they did contrive to hustle the enemy back into the breach
without getting themselves wiped out – and, to do them
credit, they took a respectably long time about it, unlike
the haughty sword-monks who couldn't be bothered to
spin out a simple job in a good cause. How much longer
could Spenno need, anyway? Two old women and a three-
legged dog could've shifted those Flutes by now—

Only three men were left from the party of enthusiasts
who'd tumbled in through the breach after the ram. Two
of them promptly vanished, cut to bits by a couple of
sword-monks who'd wandered down from the wall, presumably out of boredom. That left just one for Monach
himself, not that he was really fussed. Still, it'd be no big
deal getting rid of a lone infantryman – a long, thin, spindly
individual with a badly burned face. Monach decided to
start from sword-sheathed and do a proper draw. An act of
religion was just what he needed right now, to soothe his
mind and take it off the pain in his shoulder.

As the back of his hand brushed the sword hilt before
flipping over, the infantryman stepped into his circle and
grinned. 'Hello there, Earwig,' he said.

Monach froze, just managing to check the draw in time.
'Gain?' he said. The infantryman nodded, and drew.

Back in third year, before they'd learned anything worth

knowing, Monach had sparred with Gain in the exercise yard: two-foot hazel sticks wrapped in cloth, with a wicker handguard. After the bout had gone on far too long, Gain had lost his temper and lashed out blindly, allowing Monach to do the two-step sideways shuffle that still gave him problems all these years later, and flick a little cut across Gain's forehead, drawing enough blood to establish victory. Curiously, the thin, straight scar had survived whatever had happened to Gain's face in the meantime.

The tip of Gain's sword nipped the very end of Monach's nose, spurting a few drops of blood into his eyes as he rocked back. He heard Gain swearing, couldn't blame him – *nobody* had reflexes fast enough to get them out of the way of a perfectly executed rising throat-cut straight from the draw; most definitely not the Earwig. Nonplussed, Gain neglected to double his hands and step out with a left downwards diagonal; there was an instant, a full moment in religion, in which time wouldn't exist. If Monach could reconcile himself to killing an old friend, Gain was already as good as dead.

Monach drew.

But you couldn't do religion with a trick shoulder; only the perfect could attain perfection. The hard edge of his sword slithered off the opposing flat of Gain's sword, like a skater losing his balance on the ice. Because the anticipated resistance of bone to steel was missing, Monach stumbled forward, turned over his right ankle and flopped on the ground, while Gain's coaching-manual lateral beheading cut sailed over him, slicing air. As Monach scrambled frantically to his knees, he saw Gain step back and shake his head. 'See you, Earwig,' he called out, then stepped backwards through the splintered palisade like an actor leaving a stage.

Someone else must've given the order to bring up logs and stakes to plug the gap torn by the ram. Monach watched them do it – better carpenters than they were soldiers – then trudged back across the yard, just as the rain began to fall. Perfect, he thought bitterly.

But as he came up to the gate, he heard the now-familiar sound of somebody cursing a blue streak: Spenno, at last. Monach broke into a run, and found himself in front of the fodder store, staring at a large round black hole that seemed to go on for ever, right though to the edge of the world and out the other side into infinity. Instinctively he ducked; a burst of laughter greeted his movement. He glanced up and saw Spenno grinning at him down the length of a Poldarn's Flute. 'We did it!' Spenno was shouting. 'We're all done and dusted and ready to go, just got to load up the charge—'

Spenno's next words were drowned out by the hollow thump of battering rams on the tortured remains of the gate. 'Perfect,' Spenno said. 'Right on time – couldn't be better if we'd all been practising for a week. You, for fuck's sake, where's the goddamned vent pick?'

Monach didn't need to know what a vent pick might be. He skipped out of the way, ducked under the muzzle of the Flute and into the shed. A man he didn't know brushed past him, lugging a leather sack the size of a plump cushion; his knees were bent and he was straining. Behind the knobbly stump end of the Flute – he'd heard Spenno call it the cascabel, the gods only knew where he'd got the word from, but knowing Spenno it was the right one – someone else was blowing gently on a manky little stub of smouldering rope, fetching up a tiny red ember. 'Watch what you're fucking doing with that match,' Spenno's voice rasped, and its malevolence was the most reassuring thing Monach had ever heard. 'Clear away, make ready,' someone else yelled – Galand Dev possibly, but it didn't actually matter. The rest of the exchange was blurred by the cracking of timber; Monach turned round to face the gate, and saw the nose of a four-foot-diameter log poking through shattered boards, like a worm in an apple. They were coming. The slayer was set up, and they were smashing their way towards it, pressing forward in their haste to be the first to crawl into the narrow black tunnel to nowhere. My idea, Monach reflected; and the horror of what he was about to achieve made his stomach lurch. They hadn't tested it on wicker screens or sacks stuffed with straw or even just a wall of soft mud: this would be the first time, against muscle and sinew and bone, but there could only be one possible outcome. A hundredweight of gravel, spat out of a short tube at unimaginable speed; the first man through the gates would simply disintegrate, like a rotten apple thrown up in the air and smacked hard with a stick.

The ram crunched into the gates, a sound like a giant eating celery. Monach saw a man stretch out a hand holding a bit of smouldering rope, then jerk it back as Spenno bawled him out; not yet, apparently, because whoever made those gates had done far too good a job. The noses of the rams were having to chew them slowly away, like a child unwillingly eating up the last of his greens. *We could loose now, blast them through the last of the boards.* Yes, we could, but we'll kill even more of them if we're patient just a little bit longer. Next to him, men were already lugging out the gravel-sacks for the next charge, dipping tin jugs into the tall barrel of volcano dust, wetting the heads of mops in the water pail, as though the first charge had already been loosed (in a moment existing only in religion, like the draw). I think I'll look away now, Monach suggested to himself, I don't think I want to see—

He heard the crack of failing timber, saw an arm stretch out and touch a red glow to a spot on top of the cascabel, watched a small, perfect, round white cloud float up, before a wall of burning hot air hit him in the face like a giant's hammer.

Monach was already toppling backwards when the noise came. He could feel the shock wave of raw black sound ramming air into his ears, the pain unbearable as his brain was squeezed in, just as he hit the ground. Wetness splashed his face and hands, then something heavy fell across him. He could feel every inch of the skin on his face and neck, the sensation of flesh suddenly exposed and raw. People were screaming somewhere, a distant background noise like the constant purring of the sea.

Something had gone wrong.

The first thing that was wrong was his legs; they wouldn't work, and neither would his arms. It was dark, and he couldn't see if the problem lay with the heavy weight that had fallen across him, or whether it was more serious and permanent than that. He tried to think, but thinking through so much pain was like trying to swim in mud. *If things hurt, you can feel them; if you can feel them, you aren't paralysed.* It sounded good, crisply logical like a precept of religion, but he still couldn't move his legs. Something unbearably heavy pressed on the side of his head; weight and pressure consistent with, say, a boot – someone was treading on him, thinking him dead or simply not caring.

Monach felt horribly cold. The pressure eased and with its passing his right leg came free. He kicked out, shifting something very heavy a little way. He blinked, and the darkness broke up; instead, it was a thick coating of something over his eyes. He could smell burnt meat, and cloth, and iron, like the smell of fresh filings, which was also the smell of blood. He pushed with his left arm and shifted something, but that accounted for the last of his strength. Time to rest, no matter what the hell was going on. No choice.

The answer dropped into his mind all clean and perfect, like a gold coin dug up out of the ground. The Flutes had burst; all or just one of them had failed under the pressure of the charge, and all the fire and death and altered history he'd meant to bring down on the heads and bodies of the enemy had spat out in his face instead.

It hadn't worked. The Poldarn's Flutes were a failure. Nice idea, but no dice. Pity about that.

Monach moved his head, and as he did so he felt something sharp slicing into his chin. Whatever it was, he judged from its position that it was lodged deep in his shoulder. Best guess was, a jagged chunk of brass from the wreck of a Flute. It didn't hurt, the same way that you can't hear one voice out of a huge choir. Another problem he didn't need.

That was enough rest for now. Another boot landed an inch from his nose – it seemed like days ago that Gain had nipped him there, a slight cut that didn't actually matter, except that it had sliced him right down to his heart. Assuming that he still had a nose, or ears, or cheeks or a chin, because his whole face was glowing, radiating pain like the stones of a hearth heated red by the fire. Fire, he thought suddenly, that'd do it: the pain and such are burns – fire gushing out from the Flute as it failed, stripping the skin off his face and neck. No fun at all, but probably better than what he'd been doing to human bodies all day.

Monach blinked over and over again, until he scrubbed through the smear into the light, and could see. What he saw confirmed his initial hypothesis.

He saw the remains of the Flute he'd been standing next to, ripped open along one side like a letter. Parts of bodies were scattered around, like clothes flung off by a drunk staggering into bed. Next to him on the ground was an arm and shoulder, and some bits of tube; a torso was spread across the barrel of the tube, opened up as if throughly pecked over by crows (one side of the ribcage was still there, bones picked clean, the other side was missing). Monach wondered if any of the bits had belonged to himself at any point. Remarkably, there were living men moving about through all the mess and ruin; but they were the enemy, which explained it, because surely nobody could have been within twenty yards of the Flutes when they failed, and survived—

(Except me. Apparently.)

Then he must have fallen asleep; and when he woke up, he wasn't lying in the shambles and offal any more. He was on his back, on the ground, and above him he could see the beams of a roof, which he recognised as the charcoal store. There were three people looking down at him, impossibly tall, like long, spindly trees in a forest.

One of them Monach didn't recognise, though context would suggest it was Colonel Muno. The other two were the burned man who sounded like Gain Aciava, and Cordo.

Chapter Seventeen

'Beal?' Noja shrugged. 'It's a nice enough place, I guess. Lots of big villas, for rich city types who like to play at being country gentry without getting mud on their trousers. Plenty of open space, all gardens, not a cow in sight. They cut more grass there mowing lawns than all the haymakers in the Bohec valley.'

Poldarn nodded vaguely. He hadn't asked out of genuine interest. 'How much further?'

'An hour maybe, two if there's traffic on the road. Lots of people come for the honey festival.'

The coach was running smoothly over a good road that was fringed with squared-off hedges. No potholes or ruts here; they'd all been painstakingly filled in with river gravel. 'Fine,' he said. 'So we arrive in Beal, where Tazencius is staying. I take it we don't just cruise round knocking on doors till someone tells us where he is.'

She pulled a face. 'Don't need to, we know exactly where he'll be. That's not the problem.'

Poldarn nodded. 'Getting in to see him.'

'Yes and no.' Noja looked tired; probably hadn't slept

much. 'Needless to say, there'll be enough guards around to garrison a city. However, that's all right, because Cleapho's arranged for someone to let us in at the side door and take us right through to the inner courtyard, where the guards will let us through. That's where I'll be saying goodbye,' she added, 'because from there on, you'll be on your own. Even Cleapho can't get you past the household guards, and it's more than his life is worth to try. You get an open door to walk through, and that's it. Also,' she went on, 'if you're hoping for a map or a briefing on the layout of the rooms, no dice. Cleapho's never been in there, which ought to give you some idea of the security around Tazencius. I hope you know about all that sort of thing.'

Poldarn shook his head. 'I'm a great believer in fool's luck,' he said.

She smiled. 'I heard someone say once that luck is like a door: you push it, and you get to where you want to be. Nonsense in my opinion, but I thought it might cheer you up. Hello,' she said, 'why're we slowing down?'

The coachman turned back and said something about a roadblock. Noja's expression changed.

'Not good,' she said. 'Roadblocks are only when there's someone particularly dangerous on the loose.'

'I'm flattered,' Poldarn said. He had the sword he'd helped himself to the previous evening, but he really didn't want to get into a fight: it'd spoil everything.

The coach stopped, and a moment or so later a soldier walked up and peered in through the vehicle's window. 'Sorry,' he said, 'but you've got to go back.'

Poldarn stayed where he was. Noja leaned across him and said, 'What do you mean? We're going to the honey festival.'

'Cancelled.' The soldier looked grave. 'Sorry, but it's a routine precaution. Quarantine.'

Noja looked as though she didn't know what the word meant. 'What?'

'There's been an outbreak of plague,' the soldier said, 'in Tulice. It's all right,' he went on, 'nobody's saying anything about it having reached this side of the Bay, and all shipping's been stopped, roads in and out of there all sealed, and they're looking for anybody who's known to have arrived from there in the last month. Also, all large public gatherings have been cancelled, and they'll be closing the city gates at midnight tonight; nobody in or out until the risk of infection's over. Apparently it's a nasty strain of plague, but quick; if we can keep it out for a week, we'll be safe. That's it, basically.'

'Wonderful,' Noja said, with a slight wobble in her voice, which the soldier would've put down to fear of the plague. 'So what're we supposed to do?'

'You're from the city, right? Well, best possible thing to do is go straight back there.'

'What, and get stuck there when the plague starts? Not likely.'

The soldier shook his head. 'Safest place in the Empire, it'll be; that's why they're closing it off. You'll be far more at risk if you stay outside.'

There wasn't any point in arguing; the only way through the roadblock was over the dead body of the soldier and the rest of his outfit, and there wouldn't be any point in going to that extreme, since Tazencius obviously wasn't going to be at Beal anyway. Noja pursed her lips, putting on a scornful expression that reminded Poldarn of Copis. 'Wonderful,' she repeated. 'So we're going to be locked up in the city for a week. You know how many ships dock at Torcea every *day*?'

The soldier sighed. Clearly he was under orders to be polite to anybody in a posh carriage, and he didn't like it. 'Like I said,' he replied, 'Torcea's the safest place in the

Empire right now. Like, if there was even the slightest danger, would the Emperor be headed there right now?'

'Ah.' Noja smiled at him. 'That puts a different complexion on it. If it's safe enough for the Emperor, it must be all right.'

The soldier seemed relieved, if confused, at her reaction. 'Exactly,' he said. 'So, if you wouldn't mind moving on; it's just that you're blocking the road.'

Back the way they'd so recently come. 'Did you believe any of that?' Poldarn asked.

She shook her head. 'Too convenient,' she replied. 'There hasn't been plague in the Empire for a hundred years. And starting in Tulice, too. No, someone's worried about something. It's a good excuse for them to close the roads, tell people what to do and have them do it; and really helpful for tracking down new arrivals from Tulice, don't forget. They've *never* had plague in Tulice, as far as I know; it only starts in hot, dry countries and cities, and Tulice is cold, wet and rural.' She sighed again. 'Someone's heard something, and they're looking for you.'

Poldarn nodded. 'That'd make sense, I suppose,' he said. 'And it sounds like Cleapho may have been found out. If they know about me, they may know about him too.'

'I hadn't thought of that,' Noja said quietly. 'Maybe we shouldn't go back to town, then.'

Poldarn shook his head. 'That's where Tazencius is, according to that man,' he replied, 'and there's no reason to think he was lying about that. Only question is, can we make it back to Torcea before they close the gates?'

'Just about,' she replied.

'Just about' was right; they arrived as the gates were closing, after a terrifying gallop in the dark that left Poldarn feeling sick and profoundly unhappy, although Noja didn't seem unduly troubled. But she was nearly frantic at the thought of being marooned out in the *country* for a week with only the money she'd brought with her – hardly enough, Poldarn reckoned, to buy a small farm and a flock of sheep.

'You can't come in,' the gatekeeper told her. 'Quarantine. Sorry.'

'Fuck you,' Noja replied. It was the wrong approach; the gate slammed, and a bolt rasped in its rings. Noja stood staring for quite a long time before Poldarn could snap her out of it.

'Did you see that?' she whispered, awestruck. 'He just shut the gates in our faces.'

'You shouldn't have sworn at him,' Poldarn said.

'Fuck you, too.'

Poldarn smiled, though it was too dark for her to see. 'We'll just have to find another way in,' he said.

'Another way in? Are you out of your mind, or just ignorant? This is *Torcea*: the walls are twenty feet high and ten feet thick. Your friends from the foundry and the Poldarn's Flutes couldn't get us in there.'

'I wasn't thinking of digging a tunnel,' Poldarn replied mildly. 'I was thinking more of getting arrested.'

'Getting – what did you say?' But he'd already walked away, looking for something. In the dark, this took him a little while, but eventually he came back to where Noja was standing, holding something heavy in both hands. 'What've you got there?' she said irritably.

'A large rock,' Poldarn replied, as if it was something no well-dressed man would leave home without. 'I think it's some kind of milestone or boundary marker; took a lot of pushing and shoving to get it out of the ground. Could be a gravestone, but who buries people next to the road?'

'What do you want with a—?' He answered her question by swinging the rock with all his strength at the wicket door in the gate. 'You're crazy,' she said. 'You can't break that down. It's bloody great thick oak planks.'

'I don't need to,' Poldarn grunted, and bashed the door again. Half a dozen bashes later, the door swung inwards, and four soldiers burst out in a blaze of yellow light. 'See you later,' Poldarn called back, as they grabbed him and dragged him inside.

They weren't pleased, particularly when he admitted he'd only been bashing on the gate because he'd missed the curfew and wanted to get inside; they clearly felt he'd abused their good nature by forcing them to arrest him. 'It's a night in the cells for you,' they growled.

Poldarn smiled. 'Fine,' he said.

'Then you can explain yourself to the magistrate in the morning.'

Poldarn shrugged. 'Whatever,' he replied. 'Beats dying of plague, anyway.'

Two crows sitting in a tall thin tree—The song, still there, like an arrowhead that has to be left in the wound because getting it out would be too dangerous. But this didn't look like the sort of place where he could reasonably expect to find lost lines from old songs, so he looked about him instead.

At first, he thought he was alone in the cell; but, as his eyes grew accustomed to the faint light of the oil lamp that they'd been kind enough to leave behind, he saw that there was someone else in there with him, a small bundle sitting in the corner, looking sad. He assumed it was asleep, but it spoke.

'Who's there?' A woman's voice, elderly; an aunt, or the little old lady who lives on her own and keeps cats. Poldarn recognised her at once.

'You again,' he said. 'I thought I told you to stay out of trouble.'

She sighed. 'I did try,' she said. 'And it was all going so well. I found a very nice man who said he'd take me across the Bay, for a very reasonable fare; but it turned out he wasn't going to Torcea after all, he was going to some little place down the coast to deliver his cargo. But that was all right, because I still had most of the money you were kind enough to give me, and I got a seat on a carrier's cart, but it lost a wheel out in the middle of nowhere. But then a very kind man gave me a lift on his wagon, but he could only go terribly slowly—'

'All right,' Poldarn muttered. 'How did you end up in prison?'

She shook her head. 'I have no idea,' she replied. 'I arrived yesterday afternoon, and a nice young man at the gate asked me where I'd just come from, so I told him; and when I said I'd come from Tulice he told me to wait, and he went away and came back with *soldiers*, who brought me here. And I've been here for hours, and nobody's told me what's going on, and they've taken my babies—'

She sounded horribly upset. Babies, Poldarn thought; oh, God, yes, her little wicker cage full of mice. 'It's all right,' he said. 'We'll get you out of here in no time. Have you still got that badge I gave you?'

'Badge?' She looked at him.

'Yes, don't you remember? I gave you a badge. It's special. It was given to me by an army commander. We used it to get you out of trouble in Falcata.' A nasty thought struck him. 'You *have* still got it, haven't you?'

She gave him a worried frown. 'I'm very sorry,' she said, 'I don't know what you're talking about. I'm afraid my memory—'

Poldarn jumped up and grabbed her by the collar. The badge was hidden by a fold of dirty cloth.

'This,' he said, not bothering to keep the relief out of his voice. 'Thank God for that, you've got us both out of trouble. This is exactly what I need.'

'Really?' She beamed at him. 'Is it important?'

'Very.' He grinned. 'It's an army thing, a safe-conduct

token. Show this to the officer in charge, he's under orders to help us any way he can. It's more than important,' he added pensively, 'it's practically a miracle.' He looked at her; she blinked and looked back, still beaming.

'Does it mean they'll give me back my babies?' she asked hopefully.

Oh for pity's sake, Poldarn thought. 'I imagine so,' he said. 'Let's find out, shall we?'

They clearly valued their doors in Beal; shouting and yelling had no effect, but kicking the door energetically brought the guard running. 'Fetch your sergeant,' Poldarn said. 'Quick.'

'Piss off,' said the guard.

'Fine,' Poldarn said, and he kicked the door as hard as he could. Something cracked; he hoped it wasn't a bone in his foot.

'Oh, for crying out loud,' the guard wailed; and a few minutes later, he was back with a short, round-faced sergeant. Poldarn held the badge up in front of the sliding panel in the door; he heard the sergeant swear under his breath, and then bolts shooting back.

'I'm really sorry,' the sergeant was saying, 'we had no idea. If only you'd said sooner—'

'Forget it,' Poldarn said pleasantly. 'Memory's overrated anyhow. Look, this lady had a cage with some mice or something. Where's it got to?'

The sergeant looked blank. 'How should I—?' He caught sight of the look on Poldarn's face. 'I'll find out,' he said quickly. 'Acca, take these – take them up the guardroom and get them some food. And some water to wash in. I'll just go and find out about the mice.'

When the sergeant showed up half an hour later with the cage, and various scratching and scuttling noises from inside it confirmed that its contents were still profoundly alive, the delight on the old woman's face was a wonderful thing to see. Poldarn told the guards to make sure she ate something, and that she got to wherever she wanted to go. Then, on an impulse, he handed over Muno Silsny's incredibly valuable ring to her. After all, he told himself, he was taking back the safe-passage badge, so he ought to give her something in return. Besides, one way or another he wouldn't be needing it himself. 'Take it to a jeweller's in a good part of town,' he told her, 'and whatever they offer you for it first, don't settle for less than twice that. All right?'

She was beaming at him. 'That's so kind of you,' she said. 'Of course, as soon as I find my son, I'll make sure he pays you back every quarter.' A terrible thought seemed to strike her. 'But how will we find you? You do seem to travel about such a lot—'

'Don't worry,' he said, 'it's all right. It was an unwanted gift, it doesn't matter. And you,' he added, turning on the sergeant, 'you make absolutely sure she gets to where she wants to go, understood? Because I'll find out, and if she hasn't—'

The sergeant promised faithfully, terror gleaming behind his eyes. Poldarn nodded. 'That's fine, then,' he said. 'Off you go, and remember, I'll be checking up.'

The sergeant bustled away, escorting the mad woman as though she was fragile royalty. As soon as they'd gone, Poldarn turned to the guard, and grinned.

'Right,' he said. 'Now, I want to see the Emperor.'

For a moment or so, he was almost ready to believe it was going to work. But then the soldier seemed to shake himself awake, and gawped at him.

'Sorry,' he said, 'but I can't. I mean, it's not allowed.'

'Bullshit,' Poldarn said. 'You saw the safe-conduct pass. Want me to show you again?'

'No, that's fine,' the guard said quickly. 'But I still can't.

You need sealed orders. Only the captain of the watch—'

'Then let's find him, shall we?' Poldarn said impatiently; and off they went, down passageways, up stairs, down stairs, up passageways, with the guard leading the way and struggling to keep up, both at the same time. After a long march they crossed a courtyard: more stairs, more passages, another courtyard. 'We're here,' the guard announced, coming to a sudden halt outside a small oak door.

No question but that the watch captain recognised the badge and understood its significance; but, as he explained, it wasn't as simple as that. Yes, he could give the necessary orders for Poldarn to be escorted to the City Prefect's office, but the Prefect himself had to authorise admission to the Emperor's private apartments; and no disrespect, but did Poldarn realise exactly what an important man the Prefect was? He could be at a council meeting, or out to dinner, or— They went to the Prefecture. The Prefect was in the middle of a reception for the senior officers of the Torcea Guild; the badge brought him scuttling to heel like a terrier. Yes, he could get Poldarn into the apartments, but actual admittance to the inner chambers was in the hands of the Chamberlain—

More stairs, passageways, courtyards. The Chamberlain was entertaining friends with a recital of chamber music, given by the most expensive musicians in Torcea. When he was shown the badge he didn't scuttle, but he didn't waste time, either. Yes, he could get Poldarn into the inner chambers, but then he'd have to explain himself to the Household Secretary—

At least this time the passageways and stairwells were attractive places to pass through: paintings, tapestries, fine oak panelling, statues, fountains. The Secretary was in a meeting with the department heads from the Exchequer, but a glimpse of the badge persuaded him that he could spare a few minutes. He looked at Poldarn down a mile of narrow nose; then he said that the badge was all very well, but—

'It's all right,' said a familiar voice. 'He's expected.'

None of them had heard the side door open. The Secretary swung round, swallowed and sort of flattened himself against the wall, as if a heavy load was coming through. Poldarn wasted a moment or so staring before he said, 'Noja?'

She moved her lips but didn't actually smile. 'It's all right,' she reassured the Secretary, the Chamberlain, the Prefect and the various other bits and pieces that had stuck to them along the way. 'You don't need to worry about anything. I'll take him the rest of the way, it'll be fine. As I said, he's expected.'

Not far down the next corridor, he turned to her and said, 'Noja, what the hell—?'

She shushed him, as though he was a small child. 'Normally,' she said, 'the Secretary would've referred you to the Chaplain in Ordinary. But we both know why that'd be a bad idea, don't we?'

'No,' Poldarn said; then; 'Oh, you mean Cleapho—'

Noja stopped by a fine red and black lacquered cabinet, opened it and took out a bundle wrapped in soft grey cloth. It was about three feet long. 'Do your dreams still have crows in them?' she asked.

Poldarn nodded. 'Always,' he said. 'How do you know—?'

'Sometimes you'd call out in your sleep,' she said, pulling the cloth back. Inside it was a sword: a raider backsabre, not quite finished, still rough and unpolished. But, since the last time he'd seen it (in Colonel Lock's office in Falcata), someone had hardened and tempered it, fitted the tang with wooden scales, even ground the edge. 'It's all right,' she said. 'Take it, it won't bite you.'

He hesitated. 'What's this for?' he said. She didn't

answer. 'Is your name really Noja?' he asked.

She sighed. 'No, of course not,' she replied. 'And you don't recognise me, which is fine. I actually thought, a couple of times, that you might know who I was. You were looking at me.'

'You – reminded me of someone,' Poldarn said. 'Things you did, the way you moved. I guessed you reminded me of Xipho.'

Her lips were thin and tight. 'No,' she said. 'I think I reminded you of me. But not enough,' she added. 'Which is a shame, all things considered. Come on, we're nearly there.'

He had to hurry to keep up. 'No, listen,' he said, 'this is getting out of hand. Do I know you? Well enough that you've heard me talk in my sleep?'

'Yes,' she said. 'This way.' She'd turned the handle of a door and opened it enough to let a sliver of yellow light slide through. The central panel of the door was beautifully painted: two crows sitting in a tall, thin tree.

'Welcome home,' she said.

('Welcome home,' she'd said.

He'd smiled, and it was probably the right thing to have done; she'd clearly been to a lot of trouble. There were garlands of flowers on the walls, a friendly blaze in the fireplace, bowls of dried rose petals to scent the air, all the things she'd have liked to welcome her home if she'd been away for four months. Wasted on him, but it was the thought that counted. 'Everything looks wonderful,' he'd said, trying to sound as if he meant it. She'd looked pleased, so that was all right.

'Come and sit down,' she'd said, 'you must be exhausted.' She'd kissed him again, then gone over to the long table in the corner and poured out a glass of wine. It was, inevitably, the sweet fortified muck that she liked and he hated, but he'd drunk it anyway. The result had been to make him feel even more tired, something he wouldn't have believed possible. 'You made very good time,' she'd said. 'We weren't expecting you till this evening.'

'Following winds across the Bay,' he'd replied, yawning. 'So, how've you been? And how's Choizen?' She always liked it when he remembered to ask after their son. 'Did he cut that tooth after all?'

She'd laughed, as if he'd said something endearingly stupid. 'That was weeks ago,' she'd said. 'He's cut another two since then. And he's fine. He said another word yesterday.'

'Really?'

She'd beamed at him. '"Biscuit",' she'd said proudly. 'Well, what he actually said was "iskik", but he was pointing at the plate and smiling, so—'

His cue to laugh, so he'd done that. 'Wonderful,' he'd said, stifling another yawn. 'Where is he?'

'Asleep,' she'd said. 'Talking of which, you look tired out. Maybe you should have a lie-down before dinner.'

Before dinner? What he'd really wanted to do was sleep for a week. 'I'm fine,' he'd said, ransacking his memory for another scrap of domestic trivia to enquire after. She liked to believe that he thought about home when he was away; as if he had nothing better to occupy his mind with in the middle of a campaign than carpet-fitting and endless feuds with tradesmen. 'Did the men come to put up the new trellis?' he'd asked. Apparently they had. Oh, joy.

'They had a dreadful job getting the posts in the ground, though.' She'd sat down next to him, cosy but not actually touching. 'It took them two days, and I'm afraid the lavender got a bit trampled. But yes, it's up, and it looks really nice.'

He'd smiled again, thinking, Thank God for that; I've been worrying myself sick over the trellis in the middle courtyard. Even in the middle of the battle, when they broke through and it looked pretty much as though we weren't going to make it, that fucking trellis was never far from my thoughts— 'Splendid,' he'd said. 'Next year we can grow our own sweet peppers. That'll be nice.'

'Oh.' She'd looked disappointed. 'I thought we were going to put in those climbing roses, from Malerve.'

Roses, peppers, whatever; like it mattered. 'That'd be good,' he'd replied.

'Yes, but if you've set your heart on peppers—'

'Roses will be much better.'

But her face had shown she was still disappointed, probably because she'd guessed that he didn't care. Fine; too tired to fret about stuff like that. 'Have you seen much of your father while I've been away?' he'd asked, trying to sound casual.

She'd nodded. 'We went over for dinner a few times; mum and Turvo like to see Choizen. I . . .' She'd hesitated. 'I asked Dad where you'd gone, but he didn't seem to want to tell me. I suppose he was afraid I'd be worried.' Another pause. 'Was it – dangerous?'

Was it dangerous. Just as well he'd got out of it without a scratch, or there'd have been scars to explain. 'No,' he'd said, 'just routine stuff, all very boring. And I'm home now, so that's all right.'

As he'd said it, he couldn't help wondering how she'd have reacted if he'd told her the truth: that, on her father's orders, he'd just led an army of freelances, Amathy house, in a joint venture with the unspeakable, monstrous raiders, who everyone knew weren't even properly human, to wipe the city of Alson off the face of the earth, taking particular care to make sure there were no survivors at all. Would she be shocked? He'd looked at her. She was his wife, she'd borne him a son, in a remote and unsentimental way he loved her; and he didn't know the answer to that.

Like that mattered, too.

'We'd better go round there tomorrow,' he'd said. 'There's a few things I need to talk over with your father. Not tonight, though.'

'Of course not,' she'd said. 'Now stay there, I've got a surprise for you. Promise not to look.'

'Promise.'

She'd bustled out; he'd managed to keep his eyes open while she was out of the room, knowing that once they closed, they'd stay closed for at least twelve hours. About the only thing she could have brought him that he wanted just then was a bath; but that wouldn't have been a surprise.

'Here you are.' She'd handed him a box. Rosewood, with brass fretwork hinges. Nice box, as boxes go, and you can never have too many of them. 'Go on, then,' she'd said, 'open it.'

Oh, *right*, there's something *inside* the box. Too tired to think straight— He'd opened the box; and inside, he'd found a book.

It's very kind of you, but what the fuck do I want with—? He'd caught sight of the spine. Very old book, the lettering on the vellum binding very brown and faint. *Concerning Various Matters.*

'That's—' He hadn't been able to say anything else. *Concerning Various Matters:* the rarest book in the world, just the one copy known to exist, in the Great Library at Deymeson – until a foolish young student called Cordomine had tried to break in and read it, and set the whole place on fire. Since then, no Cordomine and no book: the sum of all knowledge, the entire memory of the human race, wiped out in one moment of destruction—

'Where on earth did you get this from?' he'd heard himself say.

She'd grinned like a monkey. 'It was the most amazing

stroke of luck. There were these monks – not proper monks, like the Order and everything, they belonged to some funny little religion out in the middle of nowhere, and then the raiders came and burned the place down; and there was only just time to save one thing from the whole monastery before they were all killed, and this was it. And they ended up here in the city, and one of them was finally fed up with being a monk, so he left the others and took this book because he reckoned it might be valuable. He was trying to get in to see Dad when I was over there, and the doorkeepers were telling him to go away, but for some reason I was interested, and asked what was going on; and I know it's a book you're interested in, because I heard you talking about it with some of your school friends, years ago. Anyhow, the upshot was that I bought it from him, for thirty grossquarters. Wasn't that a stroke of luck?'

He'd smiled feebly. Nine hundred and ninety-nine times out of a thousand, unique priceless ancient texts bought from wandering dispossessed monks must be handled with extreme care for fear of smudging the still-wet ink; but this was the thousandth time, because the monastery in question had to be Besvacharma, and it hadn't just been the raiders who'd sacked it; and he'd nearly died in that burning library, trying to rescue some clown of a sergeant—

'Fantastic,' he'd said quietly; and he was thinking, five copies, no, six; this one'll have to go to Deymeson, but I'll make it a condition that they make me six copies – Xipho, me, Gain, the Earwig, Father Tutor and one for the open shelves, just to make sure nobody ever tries breaking into the secure section at night—

(One of these days, I might even find the time to read the bloody thing.)

*   *   *

'Are you all right?' she said. 'You look awful.'

He shook his head. 'I'm sorry,' he replied. 'Only – this is where I live.'

'I just said so, didn't I?'

He stared; at the table, the chairs, the candle-stand. 'I remember this room,' he said. 'Do you realise what that means? I *remembered*—'

She shrugged. 'That's good, surely.'

(And no crows anywhere; not a dream. Not that; or this – unless the crows painted on the door counted, in which case all the years he'd spent here, with her, had been a dream too.) 'I remembered that time,' he said, 'when I came home and you'd found me that book—'

'Ah yes.' She laughed frostily. 'The one you liked so much you gave it away at once. What a thing to remember, after—'

'I *remembered*.' He felt weak in the legs, backed into a chair, and sat down awkwardly. 'Your brother,' he said suddenly, 'the man who found me in the woods. He really *is* your brother, isn't he?'

She smiled. 'Well done,' she said. 'Do you remember his name?'

'Turvo.' Poldarn frowned. 'He's got a crippled hand, I noticed it the first time I saw him. And Turvo—'

She nodded. 'You did that,' she said, 'in a year-end duel. You managed to end the bout without killing him, just crippling his right hand; because,' she added sourly, 'you loved me. We all thought you were wonderful, especially Turvo.'

'So that house he took me to, where I met you—'

'That's right,' she replied, smiling; then she went on, 'I couldn't believe you wouldn't figure it out, even if you had lost your memory. Did you really think someone could afford a house like that just from doing well in the dried-fish business?'

'Turvo – but I thought he'd died. Didn't somebody say—?'

She looked at him again. 'Wrong prince,' she said. 'You must be thinking of Prince Choizen. Name ring a bell?'

He felt as though his throat was being crushed from the inside. 'Choizen,' he said. 'Our son.'

'Killed,' she said. 'A month or so ago.' She closed her eyes. 'I'd sent him to find you. Silly, really,' she went on, 'because he hadn't set eyes on you for twelve years, not since Dad sent him away to school because he didn't want his grandson growing up under *your* influence, so how was he supposed to recognise you if he did find you? But no, I had to write to him, ask him—' She looked up. 'He found you,' she said. 'And of course, you weren't to blame.'

He stared at her. 'I don't understand,' he said.

She was looking over his shoulder, at someone who wasn't there. 'He wrote to me,' she went on, 'said he'd heard something interesting, about Muno Silsny and some unknown saviour; he had an idea, from something they'd found in Father Tutor's papers after he died, before Deymeson was destroyed— He was on his way to find you, but he never got there. Robbers, they said, somewhere between Falcata and that foundry place.' He glanced at her, but there was nothing to see. 'So,' she went on, 'now all I've got left is you.'

The young, loathsome nobleman he'd been forced to kill, on the road, that miserable day with Chiruwa, when everything had gone wrong. Small world. 'Me,' he said.

'That's right.' She was so calm it was frightening. 'Our son's dead, and that's that. I finally stopped crying last week, when Turvo wrote and said he'd found you at last, in the forest. You know, I was ashamed. I caught myself thinking, my baby's been murdered by some disgusting bandit, but Ciartan's coming home, so that's all right . . . I knew, of course: about you losing your memory, all the stuff about Xipho Dorunoxy. That was a horrible trick, don't you think? Typical Deymeson; and now she's got her baby and I've lost mine, but I've got you—' She allowed herself one terrible, dry sob. 'So I guess I've won, in the end. On points – isn't that what the monks say about a duel, when both the fighters die but one of them was carved up a little bit more than the other?' She reached out with her fingertips, violating his circle, touching the melted skin of his face. 'I've got what's left of you,' she said. 'Not your face, and not your memory, because they're both gone for ever, but I've got what's left, at the end. Is that winning, do you think? Winner takes all?'

'I suppose,' he said quietly.

She sighed, as if trying to clear all the air out of her body. 'The one thing I always needed to know,' she said, 'and I never dared ask; because there was always the tiny risk, the million-to-one chance, that you'd give me an honest answer, tell me the truth . . . Now I can ask, and it's all right, because you don't know the bloody answer: did you love me? Really? Or was it always Xipho?'

I killed our son, because I had to, with the axe I found in the ditch in the field where I killed the crows; and she wants to know if I loved her. 'Yes,' he said. 'I loved you very much. I had a dream about it.'

'A dream with crows in?'

'Yes.'

She closed her eyes, nodded. 'That's all right, then,' she said. 'There now, I've asked, and you've given me the answer I wanted to hear.' She opened her eyes and smiled at him; it was like staring down a deep well. 'Because I love you, Ciartan,' she said. 'I always have. I know you only married me because you wanted the connection with Dad, because you needed each other for business. I know what you thought of me – airhead, clothes horse, worthless little rich girl. Didn't matter. It hurt so much that you despised me, because—' She shook her head. 'Doesn't matter,' she said. 'You're here now, and that's the main thing. I rescued you, and I'm going to keep you safe, and you need me just to stay alive and I'm the only one who can protect you now.' His face must have betrayed what he'd been thinking, because she laughed grimly, and said, 'It wasn't easy, mind, rescuing you. It was as though you didn't want to be rescued. As soon as it was confirmed that it really was you at that foundry place, I sent Turvo's best men to fetch you, but that idiotic old man in charge of the garrison – he thought they'd come to take you away to be killed, you see, and so he gave them that horrible Gain Aciava instead. And when he got here and we realised what'd happened, he figured out that I knew where you were, and reported back to his master, Cleapho; and so now we're going to have a civil war, just because Brigadier Muno wanted to repay you for saving his nephew's life. Everything to do with you goes horribly wrong sooner or later, which makes loving you ruinously *expensive*, if you see what I mean. This,' she said, holding out her hand and showing him Muno Silsny's badge. 'When I heard that General Muno'd given this to you, I thought, now it'll be all right, he'll use it to come straight here, safely.' She frowned. 'You do know what this is, don't you? It's Dad's personal warrant, you could've gone *anywhere* with this. I gave it to Muno Silsny specially, just in case it *was* you he was looking for. But no, you have to go and give it away to some beggar in the street . . .' She paused, looked at him. 'How did you get it back, by the way?' she asked.

'I met her again,' Poldarn replied. 'The old mad woman.'

'Oh. How fortuitous. You always did have a habit of giving away expensive presents; like that stupid book, of course. When I think of the trouble I went to—'

Poldarn couldn't help grinning. 'But I got that back, too,' he said. 'Gain Aciava gave it to me, at the foundry.'

'Really?' She didn't sound all that interested. 'Well, they always did say you were lucky, Ciartan. If you got drunk and fell in the sewer you'd find a gold piece. After all, you gave me away when you turned against Dad, and here we are again.'

He looked up. 'Did I?'

'You don't— No, of course, how silly of me. Yes, you were going to, though you never actually got round to it; and then he was too smart for you. He's always been too smart for you, Ciartan, but there, I never did love you for your intelligence. Truth is, everybody's smarter than you are; Dad, Cleapho, the new man, Xipho, Father Tutor. Even Gain Aciava, and he's one notch below the little squirmy things you find in dead trees. Even—' She grinned coldly. 'Even silly little me. You always thought you were one step ahead, and all the time you were always one step behind, and someone else was leading you along like a pig to market. There, I've been meaning to tell you that for I don't know how long, but I never had the nerve to actually come out and say it. But you're mine now, so I can.' She looked into his eyes for a moment, then shrugged. 'The silly thing is,' she said, 'really, this is the crowning moment of my entire life, the one thing I've wanted ever since I was that silly young girl who loved you at first sight; I should be *happy*—' She shuddered. 'And this whole ghastly pantomime, with Turvo, pretending I was that bitch's sister, just because I had to know: had you really lost your memory or was it just another ridiculous game? If you were coming back, was it just because you thought you'd be able to patch things up with Dad and save your miserable neck; had you really loved the bitch all along? But that's all fine now, because when you said you wanted to kill Dad it sounded like you meant it; and of course, you'd know that Xipho Dorunoxy never had a sister. But the main thing is, you don't know; you can't *remember* if you ever really loved me, so that information is lost and gone for ever, and so there's no danger at all that one day you'll look me in the eye and say, *No, I never cared a damn about you, it was all just pretending and lies.* So I'm safe, and I've won. Isn't that *wonderful?*'

Poldarn was thinking: all the cities burned and people killed, and all you can find to care about is love? You stupid bloody woman. But he said, 'So what are we going to do now?'

She laughed. 'Oh, anything you like,' she said. 'Anything at all. Don't listen to them when they tell you Cleapho's the second most powerful person in the Empire. My father's the second most powerful person in the Empire; because there's all sorts of things he can do but daren't, but there's *nothing* he wouldn't do for me.' She looked him over as though he was a new pair of shoes. 'First,' she said, 'I think we'll make your peace with Dad – he'd have had you killed like *that* if he thought I wouldn't find out, but as soon as he realises I know you're still alive and right here with me, that makes you the safest man in the world. Then I think we'll get him to recognise you as the heir to the throne. After all, you're my husband, and Choizen's dead, Turvo's not legitimate issue and the Empire isn't really ready for a woman Emperor, so there isn't actually any choice. Do you know, Turvo really likes you a lot? Reckons he owes you his life, and he always admired you, all through school. He even liked Choizen, which was more than I ever did; oh, I loved him, of course, but he was an obnoxious little monster, bumptious and vicious and so wanting to be Deymeson-trained like his father. He worshipped *you*, of course, which was easy enough for him to do since he'd practically never set eyes on you since he was a baby. Yes, I think that's what we'll do with you, my love: we'll make you into an Emperor. That'll serve you right for being with that bitch, even if you didn't know what you were doing.'

Suddenly she laughed. 'My God, Ciartan,' she said, 'you should see yourself. I've seen happier-looking faces nailed to the city gate.'

'I was just thinking,' he said softly. 'You say you rescued me—'

'I did rescue you.'

'I believe you,' he told her. 'But you thought I was coming here to kill your father. How can you say you love me when—?'

She smiled at him as if he was simple. 'Ciartan, my love,' she said. 'You're my husband, he's my father. What on earth makes you think I'd have a problem with loving men just because they're murderers?' She hesitated, and frowned. 'You said that as if that wasn't what you really came for,' she said. 'You aren't trying to tell me you weren't planning to kill him after all? Because I may be morally bankrupt, but I'm not stupid—'

'It doesn't matter,' he said. 'I've changed my mind. I don't want to kill anyone any more.'

She looked at him quizzically. 'Oh? How come?'

'Because it doesn't seem important now,' he said. 'I thought my life was empty, and suddenly it's not.'

'Because I love you?'

'Because *somebody*— Because of something I did,' he said slowly, 'which I'd rather not tell you about. But now everything's different; I don't have to be the sort of man I used to be. I'd got it into my head that I had to put things right, and the only way someone like me could do that was by another killing, because that's all I am, ever since I was sent here by my grandfather, and the monks and your father got hold of me, and they all wanted to use me as a *weapon*. First I thought I could get by just by running away. But everywhere I went and everything I did, I made trouble, and everything turned to blood and fire, and I had to assume it was me, who I really was. But if only I could escape from that, be someone else: I had the chance, you see – I woke up one day and my memory was gone; and now even my face. I'm trying to tell myself, everything bad I've done is just shadows thrown by the past, because no matter what I tell myself to do, I've always been looking back, trying to see what's there.' He looked at her, then looked away. 'You know me much better than I do,' he said. 'What do you think? What I really came here to do was get rid of myself, and someone else as bad as me while I was at it, but that was really just an excuse. Do you think I can start again, properly this time?'

Her eyes were very wide. 'No,' she said. 'There's no way you could ever change, not so it'd make a difference. If you went away as far as it's possible to go, where nobody knew you, it wouldn't change anything: you'd still be exactly the same. Not even if you lived in an oasis in the desert, you'd be red to the wrists in someone's blood inside a year. Oh, you aren't evil, in the way that some people are. You just carry it around with you; like those people who don't catch the plague themselves but give it to everybody they meet. I'm sorry, but that's exactly who you are, and nothing's ever going to change that.'

Poldarn sighed. He knew all that, but somehow hearing it from someone else, someone who knew him better than he could ever know himself, made it feel like being sentenced to death. 'The most evil man in the world,' he said. 'I've been called that by several people who ought to know. Am I?'

'Not evil,' she said, 'I just told you that. Like you said just now, you're a weapon. Maybe if someone took hold of you and used you for something good, it'd be different. But if you take a step back and consider all the people in your life, you can see that's not going to happen. And you can't make it happen all by yourself. If you jump out of the scabbard, people just trip over you and cut themselves.'

'I see,' he said. 'So, what are you planning to do with me?'

She smiled. Not affectionately. 'I'm going to keep you,' she said.

At some point, they made love, in the huge bedroom of his house. Afterwards, she rolled away and lay with her back to him. He drifted into sleep, and the river mud welled up around his face. He could hear voices above him; familiar, in a way.

'So,' said one of them, 'you're back. Welcome home.'

'You haven't won,' the other voice replied. 'You tricked me.'

'Yes, didn't I just? But the result's the same. Here you are, back with me where you belong. That's all that matters.'

'You're wrong.' The other voice was quiet, determined. 'You've got me here, and maybe you can force me to stay, but you can't stop me hating you. And I always will, now that I've seen what it could be like, out there—'

'Balls. Now you're back, it won't be a week before you slide back into the old routine. We were made for each other, you know that.'

'No.' The voice was almost shouting now. 'You only ever made me do what you wanted by threatening me, and now I'm here, the worst's happened. What are you going to threaten me with now? There's nothing left.'

Laughter. 'You really think so?'

'You're bluffing.'

'You know that's not true. Listen, I still have a few bits and pieces up my sleeve. I could tell you, and then you'd *know*; and once you knew, you could never even try and run away again, because there wouldn't be any point. But I want to be nice, I don't want to tell you if I can help it. After all, the only thing I've ever wanted is for you to be happy.'

'I don't believe you. I think the worst you ever had was what I've already found out. After all, nothing could be worse than that, apart from some of the things I've done *since* I left you. Eyvind and Choizen—'

More laughter. 'Funny you should mention them. You really think you did those things on your own. I was there, you just didn't see me. I'm always with you, wherever you go. You might as well try running away from your shadow.'

Pause; the other voice was choosing its words carefully. 'There's no shadows in the darkness,' it said. 'It takes light to make shadows. I've been in places darker than you, but I didn't *become* you. Because I knew that no matter what I did, at least I was free of you—'

'You burned your best friend to death. You killed your own son.' The voice was mocking. 'What is it they say about imitation?'

'Those things were your fault.'

'No. You killed Eyvind because you thought it was the right thing to do; and maybe it was, in that place, at that time. You killed Choizen in self-defence, because you tried to rob him on the road and he fought back. You were there on the road because you'd been laid off at the foundry, and Chiruwa fooled you into going highway robbing with him, and when you found out what he was really planning to do, you weren't bothered enough by it to walk away. You killed Carey, the fieldhand, mostly just because he was there. I had nothing to do with any of that. And there's all the soldiers, and the Deymeson monks, poor fools who had the bad luck to cross your path at the wrong time.' Dry laughter. 'And the joke is, that's nothing at all compared with what you've set in motion, just because you felt sorry for a crazy old woman in a broad-brimmed hat. But I could still tell you something about us – about me – that'd hurt you very much; you'll survive knowing, but it won't make you like yourself any more. Truth is,' the voice went on, 'I know you better than you do; so it follows that I know what's best for you, and for me too. Trust me.'

'No.'

'Trust me,' the voice said urgently, 'and Xipho and the Earwig won't have to die. Together we can save them. On your own, you wouldn't know how.'

Pause. 'I'd rather let them die than come back with you.'

'There.' Total triumph in that voice. 'You see, I've won. You always were your own worst enemy.'

'Apart from you.'

'Me? You love me—'

'I love you,' he heard her say.

He couldn't help yawning, having just woken up. She laughed.

'I didn't mean to yawn,' he said. 'What time is it?'

'Late,' she replied. 'Come on, get up. You always were useless in the mornings.'

He grunted, rolled off the bed and looked for his clothes, which had vanished. In their place—

'What the hell are these?' he asked.

'Get dressed and don't argue.'

He held up the shirt. 'You must be joking,' he said. 'There's enough brass thread in this to make a Poldarn's Flute.'

She clicked her tongue. 'That's not brass,' she said.

'You mean— Oh.' Explained why the shirt was so heavy. He'd come across lighter mail shirts. The trousers were the same, only more so. Even the shoes—

'Whose clothes are these, anyway?' he asked.

'Yours.'

He was about to argue when he caught the faint smell of cedarwood. Keeps the moths at bay, he'd heard some-where. 'Mine,' he repeated.

She nodded. 'Of course, they're three years out of fashion

– you're going to look like a clown, but that can't be helped. I've ordered you a whole new wardrobe, but these things take time.'

'I used to wear things like this,' he said; and he realised what a stranger he'd become to himself. 'Where are we going, then, if I need to dress up?'

She gave him a long, steady look. 'Dinner,' she said. 'With my father.'

Chapter Eighteen

'Hello, Earwig,' Cleapho said. 'Long time, no see.'
Monach lifted his head. He could still see –
just about – out of his left eye. His right didn't
seem to want to open any more.

'Cordo,' he said. His voice sounded dreadful. 'What're
you doing here?'

Cleapho laughed. 'I won,' he said. 'The battle. Come on,
you must remember the battle. Or have you lost your
memory, like Ciartan?'

That didn't strike Monach as particularly funny, but
Cleapho laughed noisily. 'What happened?' Monach said.
'Last thing I remember—' He paused; he wasn't sure what
the last thing he remembered was. 'The Flutes,' he said.
'They failed—'

Cleapho was nodding sagely. 'Of course,' he said. 'They
were supposed to. It's called sabotage, though that's rather
a feeble term for such an intricate exercise.' He narrowed
his eyes. 'You must've been quite close to one of them,'
he said. 'The doctors tell me it's a miracle you're still
alive.'

Monach could remember the heat of the air as it hit him in the face like a hammer.

'Ironic, really,' Cleapho went on. 'No, don't try to move,' he added, as Monach made an effort to sit up. 'You'll only start the bleeding off again.'

Monach hadn't taken any interest in his surroundings, his entire attention having been focused on Cordo, his old friend. 'I'm on a ship,' he said in surprise.

'That's right,' Cleapho said. 'You're being taken to Torcea. We should be there in a couple of hours. You've been asleep for a very long time.'

Other things were claiming Monach's attention now – pain most of all. He hurt all over. 'How bad is it?' he asked, as calmly as he could.

'Pretty bad,' Cleapho replied. 'You're still basically in one piece— Your left leg's a jigsaw puzzle and I think you lost a couple of fingers on your left hand, but that's all. Your right eye's pretty comprehensively wrecked, you lost all the skin off your face and arms, and you've got a lot of internal damage: broken ribs, that sort of thing.'

Monach was surprised at how calm he felt. 'Am I going to make it?' he asked.

'Well, now.' Cleapho almost smiled. 'We're all going to die sooner or later. But as far as the sawbones can make out, none of it's what they call life-threatening. Are you in a lot of pain?' Monach was about to say 'No, I'm fine,' but this was Cordo he was talking to. 'Yes,' he admitted, 'everything hurts like hell.'

'Sorry about that,' Cleapho replied; and Monach remembered. Sabotage.

'The Flutes were supposed to fail?' he asked.

'That's right,' Cleapho told him, holding a tin cup of water so he could drink from it. 'That was Spenno, doing his bit for religion. He was a better man than any of us thought, I guess. It helped that the man the government sent – Galand something – was a buffoon, and knew it too; when Spenno told him he was wrong, he believed it. So Spenno was able to make the Flutes so that they'd fail.' He shook his head sadly. 'Dangerous things,' he said. 'Rather too powerful for my liking. It simply wouldn't do, politically and strategically, for Tazencius to get his hands on weapons that'd make him immune from attacks by the raiders – or anybody else, for that matter. Stealing or destroying the ones they were making at Dui Chirra wasn't enough, you see; they'd only have set up a foundry somewhere else and made some more. But now the whole idea's discredited, at least for my lifetime, which is all that matters. For what it's worth, it's very old knowledge – as you'd know, if you ever read books. They were invented in Morevich five hundred years ago, hence the name, but when Morevich was added to the Empire, we carefully disposed of all records of them; now they only exist in folk tales, as an attribute of the Divine Poldarn.'

Monach stared a him for a moment. 'But that doesn't make any sense,' he said, finding it hard to think past the headache that was tightening round his temples like a snare. 'I thought it was my job to capture them. For *us*.'

Cleapho smiled gently. 'It was,' he said. 'And you did it very well. I have to confess, I've underestimated you too. I'm afraid I kept thinking of you as you were at school – born follower, not much use without someone telling you what to do. But you coped very well on your own, when it came to it. Almost too well.' He laughed again, though Monach still couldn't see the joke.

'I don't understand,' Monach said.

Cleapho was getting up. 'Maybe that's enough for now,' he said. 'You're still very weak, I ought to let you get some rest.'

'No, please.' Monach tried to move, but his legs, and arms, wouldn't obey. At first he assumed it was his injuries, but then he realised he was tied down to the bed.

'Well,' Cleapho relented, 'since it's all as broad as it's long, I might as well tell you now as later. Yes, you were meant to capture Dui Chirra for us. That was the whole point, of all of it. You see, I had plenty of notice of this Poldarn's Flute project; it was practically the first thing Tazencius did when he became Emperor. He's terrified of the raiders, you see; what with them being his former allies – really, Earwig, you didn't know? Good heavens. Yes, he was the one who made contact with them in the beginning, through Ciartan; his idea was to get them to step up their attacks, start annihilating whole cities, so that the Empire would become ungovernable and he'd have his chance at grabbing the throne.' He sighed. 'But then Ciartan double-crossed him, all of us in fact, and ever since he's been scared sick of what'd happen when he finally became Emperor and Ciartan, or—' Cleapho smiled '—or Feron Amathy used the same tactic against him in turn. He used the raiders as a weapon, if you like, and then he desperately needed something that'd protect him against that weapon in someone else's hands. Hence the Flute project. Which, of course,' he added, 'I couldn't possibly allow. Which is where you came in,' he continued, 'among others.'

'Me,' Monach said.

'You and Xipho,' Cleapho replied. 'She knew the purpose behind it – part of it, anyhow; I'm afraid we decided against telling you. That was probably wrong, I don't know. Anyway, Xipho raised that funny little army of yours, and you took it to Dui Chirra and did the rest. Thank you,' he added.

'My pleasure,' Monach said. 'But if you didn't actually want to get hold of the Flutes for yourself—'

'Well, of course I didn't,' Cleapho said indulgently. 'Don't get me wrong, they're fine weapons. But how many of them did you finally manage to get made? Half a dozen?

We'd have needed hundreds to be any use against any sort of large army. Far better to get shot of them for good – and do useful work at the same time, as an added bonus.'

Monach closed his good eye. 'I don't follow,' he said.

'Don't you? Then maybe I was right after all. Your part in the adventure was a bit like Tazencius and the raiders – I'm not too proud to learn from the enemy, you see. I needed the Flutes to fail. I also needed an enemy to overcome, a terrible threat to save the Empire from. That's why I created you: the Mad Monk. You were a bit out of the loop down there in Tulice, but in the city you're very famous. People have been terrified to death of you, ever since we told them about you. We exaggerated, of course; to hear us talk, you had hundreds of thousands of fanatical supporters, all the malcontents and criminals and crazies in the south. And then when you got hold of Tazencius's secret weapon, the dreaded Poldarn's Flutes . . . I wish you could've seen the riots in the streets, Earwig. I nearly injured myself laughing, listening to them howling curses on the most evil man in the Empire, and knowing all along it was just you.'

And that, Monach realised, would explain why I'm tied to the bed. 'I see,' he said quietly.

'And now you've been defeated, and the weapons have been proved to be useless; and it was me who defeated you and saved the Empire, while Tazencius's Flutes have been turned against him, far more effectively than if we'd lugged them into the Square and pointed them at the palace gates. First, people were furious at him for letting those hellburners fall into the hands of our most dangerous enemy – that's you, I'm afraid; and now they're even more angry at him because the things were never going to work after all. His days are numbered, Earwig, and to a certain extent we've got you to thank. Well, you and Xipho. I think you can reassure yourself that you've done your whack for religion. Father Tutor would've been proud, rest his soul.'

Monach didn't say anything for a moment. Then: 'You killed him, didn't you?'

'Not me personally,' Cleapho replied. 'I didn't kill Elaos Tanwar either. I liked them both,' he added, 'a lot. And Xipho, and you too. Not Ciartan, though. I was never comfortable around him.'

Monach couldn't look at him. 'I'm going to die, then?' he said.

Cleapho sighed. 'I'm afraid so, Earwig. You and Xipho too – after all, she's the Mad Monk's priestess and what have you, so she's got to go as well. She took it well,' he added, 'as I'd have expected of her. I'm proud of her. I hope I'll be able to be proud of you, too.'

There had been many times when Monach had known he was probably going to die; but this was the first time he'd known it for a certainty. The ropes, and the pain all over his body, confirmed it absolutely. 'This is for religion, then,' he said.

'Of course.'

'Fine. Am I allowed to know how it helps?'

'Sorry,' Cleapho replied. 'Just have faith.'

'Like Xipho?'

Cleapho shook his head sadly. 'I've always envied Xipho her faith,' he said. 'I guess it's because she was the only one of our little gang who never actually managed to achieve a moment of religion, not in the draw, like you're supposed to. Yes, she was as fast as any of us, but it was just good reactions and coordination – she never made the moment go away. I think that's why she believes; the rest of us got there and realised it was no big deal. I've always assumed your faith was rather more intellectual, what with you being the only other one of us to carry on in the Order after graduation. You must've seen past the mysticism and so forth quite early.'

'Must I?' Monach said quietly. 'I don't remember that.'

'Oh.' Cleapho frowned. 'Oh, I see. I'm sorry. I hope I haven't – disillusioned you. That'd be a rotten trick to play on a man who's about to—'

But Monach shook his head. 'You couldn't,' he said. 'You see, I believe because I've seen. Because I once drew against a god. And I know it's real, because of that.'

Cleapho couldn't hide the grin. 'A god? Good heavens, Earwig, how fascinating. You never mentioned it to us.'

'I didn't know at the time.' He paused; something had just struck him. 'You still don't know, do you?'

'What's so funny, Earwig? I mean, I'm delighted that you can laugh at a time like this—'

Monach was grinning now, and Cleapho wasn't. 'Ciartan,' he said. 'Ciartan really is the god in the cart, Poldarn, whatever his name is. You see, I found out all about him – when Father Tutor sent me to investigate, and then afterwards, after Deymeson was destroyed and I was finally able to get at the truth that the Order's been suppressing all these years. Everything that Poldarn's supposed to do, Ciartan's done. It really is him, Cordo; and that means religion really is true. All of it.'

Cleapho shook his head. 'Everything except destroy the world,' he said gently. 'He hasn't done that, has he?'

'Yes,' Monach replied. 'He must have – it just hasn't taken effect yet.'

'That's easy to say,' Cleapho replied, rather less gently. 'I'm glad you have your faith, Earwig. I'm glad I haven't taken that away from you, too.'

'I saw it,' Monach insisted. 'There was a moment – when we fought, in the year-end. We both drew at the same time—'

—Because at that moment in time there's only been enough room in the world for one of them, and yet both of them had still been there, illegally sharing it, like a shadow or a mirror

image being soaked up into the body that cast it; two circles superimposed, becoming one—

—Which wasn't supposed to happen. And if it did – nobody had known the details, at the time, but it was widely supposed to mean that something really bad was on the way: the end of the world, Poldarn's second coming—)

'It's true,' Monach said, relaxing back onto the hard ropes of the bed. 'Ever since then, Ciartan and me, we've really been one person, or one man and his shadow, something like that. Which means,' he added, as his head began to swim, 'that— Did you say we're going to Torcea?'

'Yes. So what?'

Monach smiled. 'Then it's happening after all,' he said. 'Like in the prophecies and everything. I'm bringing the end of the world to Torcea. I'm bringing *you*.'

Cleapho sighed. 'Whatever,' he said. 'I'm sorry, Earwig, and I'm grateful, too. And I'm glad if you're – well, resigned, or content, thanks to your faith—'

'Happy,' Monach said. 'Not resigned or content. Happy.'

Tazencius had changed little since the day Poldarn had first met him, on the road in the Bohec valley: an injured stranger he'd stopped to help, back when he'd been a courier for the Falx house. Tazencius still looked young for his age, distinguished without being intimidating, a pleasant man who turned out to be a prince, and was now the Emperor.

'Hello, Daddy,' she'd said, trotting up to him and giving him a peck on the cheek, as though she'd just come in from riding her new pony in the park. He smiled at her, then turned to look at Poldarn.

'Hello,' Tazencius said. 'I must say, I never expected to see you again. I heard you went away.'

Poldarn shrugged. 'I did,' he said. 'But I came back.'

'Evidently.' Tazencius sighed and sat down on a straight-backed wooden chair next to the fire. He'd been limping –

the first time Poldarn had come across him, he'd broken his leg. 'Here you are again, and I suppose we've got to make the best of it.'

'Daddy,' she warned him. He nodded.

'I know,' he said, 'be nice.' He frowned, then looked up. 'You got your memory back yet?' he said, as though asking after an errant falcon or a mislaid book.

'No,' Poldarn said. 'People have been telling me things, but I'm not sure I believe all of them.'

Tazencius looked at his daughter, then folded his hands. 'Doesn't matter,' he said. 'I guess it's time we stopped fighting. Faults on both sides, that sort of thing. Besides,' he went on, 'as your wife's been at great pains to tell me, essentially I was nursing a murderous grudge against someone who doesn't really exist any more.'

'I'm glad you can see it that way,' Poldarn replied slowly. 'I know I did a lot of bad things. I get the impression that a lot of the bad things involved you. What I haven't got straight is how much of them I did with you, and how much to you.'

Tazencius was silent for what felt like a very long time. Then he said, 'Like it matters. The fact is, you're my son-in-law, whether I like it or not, and if anything happens to you, she'll never speak to me again. Silly, isn't it? All my life I've been trying to get – well, this; and in the end, all I care about is whether my daughter likes me. I guess you're the punishment I deserve.'

She scowled at him, but didn't say anything. He seemed not to have noticed.

'Anyway,' he went on, 'we don't have to like each other, just be civil. Will you be wanting your old job back? I hope not. I'd far rather you just hung about the place eating and drinking and sleeping; I don't need you for anything any more.'

'Suits me,' Poldarn replied. 'For what it's worth, I have

a vague idea what my old job was, but I'd really rather you didn't tell me.'

'As you like,' Tazencius said. 'It's a pity about the new man – he did me a good turn. But he's got to go. It's time to kick away the ladder.'

Whatever that meant; asking for explanations was the last thing on Poldarn's mind. Right now, everything was painfully awkward and embarrassing, but it was better than sleeping in a turf shack and being forced to kill strangers all the time. Besides, he kept telling himself, an opportunity *will* crop up, and I *will* be able to run away and get clear of all these people, sooner or later.

'Anyway,' Tazencius was saying, 'tonight it's dinner with the Amathy house. Horrible chore, but we need to be out in the open about that sort of thing.'

Amathy house? Weren't they the enemy? Poldarn decided not to worry about it. People have dinner with their enemies all the time. 'Thank you,' he decided to say.

'What for?'

Poldarn grinned. 'I don't know,' he said. 'You're clearly making a big effort to put a lot of things out of your mind so we can all put the past behind us and get on with our lives. Since I don't know what the things are, I can't gauge exactly how magnanimous you're being. But thank you, anyhow.'

Tazencius looked puzzled; then he laughed. 'I'll take that in the spirit in which I think it was meant,' he said. 'But I still don't see us ever being friends.'

'Unnecessary,' Poldarn replied. 'I just want to keep out of everybody's way.'

As they walked back down a long, high-roofed cloister, she frowned at him. 'You were rude,' she said, 'talking to him like that.'

'I'm sorry,' Poldarn said. 'It's the only way I know how to talk to people.'

'No, it isn't,' she replied. 'But it doesn't matter. I think the best thing would be if you stay out of his way as much as possible.'

'That'd suit me.'

She walked on a little further, then stopped and looked at him. 'Tell me the truth,' she said. 'Did you really come to Torcea in order to murder him?'

Poldarn laughed and shook his head. 'Of course not,' he said. 'Why on earth would I want to do a thing like that?'

She shrugged. 'Because he's a very bad man who's done some appalling things.'

'None of my business,' Poldarn replied promptly. 'Anything he's done to me I've forgotten. And things he's done to other people are nothing to do with me. I may be a lot of bad things myself, but at least I'm not an idealist.'

She laughed, for some reason. 'Nobody could ever accuse you of that,' she said. 'So why did you come?'

He shrugged. 'I got sick to death of blundering about in the dark,' he said. 'People would insist on telling me things, but only because they hoped I'd be useful if I was nudged along, one way or the other. That man Cleapho, who apparently is someone I went to school with: he's the one who wants me to kill your father. All I wanted was to find out the truth – not because I want my past back, I'd have to be crazy to want that; but I figured that if I came here and gave myself up, then either your father would kill me or not, but the chances were that at least he'd tell me the truth.'

'Daddy telling the truth,' she mused. 'No, I don't see that.'

'I do,' Poldarn said. 'Because he knows it'd hurt me more than anything else he could do. The clever trick I'd have played on him is that not knowing, now that I've been told all these things that may be lies or may be true, hurts even more.' He breathed out slowly. 'Perhaps I wanted him to kill me,' he added. 'Put me out of my misery, as they say.

There comes a time when holding still and being caught begins to have a definite appeal.'

'I never figured you for a quitter,' she said.

'Really?' He smiled bleakly. 'Maybe it was just that I couldn't remember ever having been to Torcea, and everybody ought to see the capital once in their lives.'

She thought for a moment. 'Do you want me to tell you?' she said.

'No,' he said firmly. 'I've changed my mind since I've been here.'

Cold look. 'Because of me.'

He nodded. 'And the things that come with you, of course, such as clean clothes and regular meals. The plain fact is, when it comes to whether I live or die, I really don't have particularly strong views one way or the other. I'm – empty,' he said. 'Describes it pretty well. I might as well go on living as not, and that's about it.'

She looked at him, then looked away. 'Well, do that, then,' she said. 'I feel a bit like that right now; but it matters to me that I don't lose. I need to get what I want and then hang on to it, or else I feel I've been beaten by somebody. Pretty poor justification for the things I've had to do, but then, I'm not accountable to anybody.' She looked past him, over his shoulder. 'It feels like it's been a very long day and I'm very tired and just want to fall into bed and go to sleep; so, as long as I can make my unilateral declaration of victory without anybody contradicting me, I'll settle for what I've got and not worry about anything else. Does that make any sense to you?'

'Perfect sense,' he said. 'What did he mean, "the new man"?'

She was still looking away, so he couldn't see her expression. 'The man who took over the job you were doing.'

'You mean, when I lost my memory?'

'Shortly before that.'

Inside the cloister was the usual small garden: a square of green lawn, four formal flower beds, diamond-shaped, with a stone fountain in the middle. A single crow dropped out of the air, its approach masked by the cloister columns, so that it looked as if it had come out of nowhere. It settled on the lip of the fountain and pecked lightly at the surface of the water, as if looking at its reflection. Poldarn, who knew about crows and their behaviour, guessed it was a scout, sent on ahead of the main party, to see if it was safe and if there was anything there worth eating.

The guests are starting to arrive, he thought; the Amathy house, and whoever else is coming to dinner. Possibly, Feron Amathy himself would be there – Feron Amathy, who Cleapho had tried to persuade him was the most evil man in the world. That'll make three of us, then, Poldarn thought. Just like the song, which suddenly he could remember—

Two crows sitting in a tall thin tree
Two crows sitting in a tall thin tree
Two crows sitting in a tall thin tree
And along came the Dodger, and he made up three.

He felt better for remembering that; a half-remembered song is like an itch you can't reach, and its incomplete pattern rattles around in your head, the broken parts spinning round in an infuriating cycle that gradually drives out everything else. He had no idea what it meant, or who the Dodger was supposed to be, or why they sang the same, fairly uninspiring, song both here in the Empire and far away, at Haldersness. Presumably at some distant time, someone had made up the song to commemorate some important event; the reason for the song had long since been forgotten but the song remained behind, like the head of an arrow deep in a wound when the shaft has been broken off. Memory had put the song there, and then been lost, leaving only its barbed and rusty sting behind. (The bee dies when it stings, its guts pulled out; the sting remains in the wound. Probably religion; everything else is.)

'What was that you were humming?' she said.

'Sorry, I didn't realise.' He felt embarrassed, to be caught humming in public. 'Just a song I heard somewhere. You know what it's like when one gets stuck in your mind.'

'Like getting something wedged between your teeth,' she said. 'I know exactly what you mean.'

Poldarn thought for a moment. 'You didn't recognise the tune, then?'

'You hum very badly,' she told him, 'always did. It was endearing when you were very young.'

'It's a song about crows in trees,' he said. 'That's all I know about it.'

'Oh, that song,' she said. 'My mother used to sing it when I was a small child. I never liked it much.'

He grinned. 'I must've liked it a lot,' he said. 'It was practically the only thing I could remember, when I woke up that time.'

'Oh.' She looked at him, face blank. 'That's odd, I don't remember ever hearing you singing or whistling it.'

'I wonder where I picked it up,' he said. 'Not that it matters. It's just that I suddenly remembered the last line, just now. Of all the things to remember—'

'Or you may have heard it since, somewhere,' she said. 'It's a very common song, people sing it all the time.' She sighed. 'Apparently, Cleapho's going to be at this dinner party, assuming he gets back from Tulice in time.'

'Cleapho,' Poldarn said. (*The guests are beginning to arrive.*) 'What do I need to know about him?'

She counted off on her fingers. 'He controls the Treasury and most of the civil service, which is fine because it saves Father a lot of work he doesn't like doing; he also controls the army, now that Muno Silsny's gone – he killed Muno, of course, but we can forgive him that, I suppose; but he doesn't have any support in the Amathy house, which is why they're coming to dinner. I'm not sure *why* he wants to be Emperor; it may sound odd, but you don't make it as far as Father or Cleapho unless you actually have a strong motive. In Father's case it was simply staying alive that bit longer, but Cleapho – deep down, I have a nasty feeling that he believes in something. Not religion per se, gods and stuff; but I think he believes in religion in a sort of abstract sense, which is rather worrying. I think he wants to *do* things with the Empire, rather than just *having* it. He was at school with you, of course, but I think you already know that. He was very close to – well, Feron Amathy, a year or so back, but something went badly wrong and threw out all his plans, which is how Father was able to get his foot in the door. He means to kill us all, probably just because he feels we make the place look untidy. That's about it.'

Poldarn shrugged. 'Most of that went over my head, I'm afraid,' he said. He hesitated, then asked: 'How old is Feron Amathy? He seems to have been around for years.'

She didn't answer.

Why am I here? he asked himself.

It was dark; the curtains were as thick as armour, proof against even the sharpest point of light. He'd hoped to be able to snatch an hour's sleep before the ordeal of the dinner party, but apparently not; instead he lay on his back on the bed and stared at the darkness where the ceiling could be assumed to be.

Why am I here?

That was too complex a question, so he broke it down into smaller pieces, splitting off *How did I come to be here?* since most of that had been other people's doing. What remained was *Why did I leave Dui Chirra and head for*

Torcea? He still couldn't make much headway with it.

He could remember quite clearly what the answer used to be. He'd come to Torcea because he was fairly sure he'd find Tazencius here; and he'd very much wanted to kill him, for some reason that had blurred somewhat in the intervening time. As far as he could recall, the justification was that Tazencius was to blame for everything bad that had happened to him; Tazencius had sent to the far islands for a weapon, and Halder had sent him his own grandson, to be sharpened, burnished and used. Tazencius had put him through school and set him up in business as the most evil man in the world. It was all his fault.

That lie had kept him moving and motivated as far as Falcata; at which point it fell to bits like an old rotten tree stump, though he'd pretended he still believed it. Since leaving Falcata, he'd been more concerned with running away than with arriving anywhere, right up until the moment he'd blundered into Ciana (who was really his old school chum, the prince Turvo) in the woods. Even then, if he was honest with himself, he'd only asked for a lift to Torcea because he needed to specify a destination, and he'd still been kidding himself about what he was planning to do.

Now here he was, in Torcea, in Tazencius's house; and killing Tazencius was no longer even a daydream. Instead, apparently, he'd come home. Maybe that was because, having run out of people to lie to, he'd had a go at lying to himself, and failed; at which point, somehow, inexplicably, the game was over.

So: what am I going to do now?

That was an even harder question. He had no idea what the answer might be. What he wanted to do was escape, yet again; but he'd finally been forced to come to terms with the fact that he was the King of the Snails, that whenever he tried to run away, he had no choice but to take his home with him.

So: eventually, after enduring unspeakable hardships and battling overwhelming odds, here he was, and he had no idea what he wanted to do next. Absurd; because an easier man to please didn't draw breath. How absurdly happy he could've been, digging mud at Dui Chirra or staring into the colliers' fire at the charcoal camp, or mindlessly following the pattern of chores assigned to him before he'd even been born, if only he'd been a fieldhand's son at Haldersness rather than the heir apparent. Instead, here he was: an expensive but obsolete piece of equipment, hung up in the rafters because nobody had any use for it any more. He didn't even have a use for himself. The only person who wanted him, apparently, was his wife, Tazencius's daughter, and she only wanted him as an ornament or curio.

A dog running through a cornfield with a burning torch tied to its tail. Was the dog to blame, or the man who made and attached the torch? Was it really possible that all the false, forged prophecies had actually come true, out of spite, and that he genuinely was Poldarn, the god in the cart? He grinned; he could dismiss that one out of hand, because gods didn't exist. Poldarn, he knew for a fact (because Copis had told him, or someone else), was an unmitigated fraud, invented by greedy monks to boost offertory revenues. Unless, of course, he'd created the god himself without even meaning to, like a careless sorcerer accidentally summoning the wrong demon.

He thought: The crows are beginning to arrive, because someone's set out a convincing pattern of decoys. Now that was fair comment; he'd been tricked and beguiled here just like the thousands of birds he'd drawn into his killing zones, back in the fields at Haldersness. He'd come expecting to kill, and now—

What makes a good decoy? Why, familiarity, which

itself is born of memory. The crows see what look like a mob of their own kind pitched among the pea-vines. But there the comparison ended. Whatever had drawn him down here, it wasn't the search for his own memories. He'd been trying to run away from them all along.

Even so; they were starting to arrive, wheeling and turning in to the wind, gliding and dropping into the killing zone, all the old crows from the song. The question was: had he come here drawn by the decoys, or was he the pathfinding scout, leading the rest of the flock? What if—

(What if there was a traitor in the flock – one crow who deliberately led the rest down onto the decoys, into the killing zone? There never could be such a creature, of course, since all crows shared the same mind, just like the Haldersness people. But what if a crow lost its memory, mislaid its share of the group mind; and, while its mind was empty, was persuaded or tricked into turning traitor? What if one crow led the others down onto the bean field, and it turned out to be the cinder bed of a volcano, or the decoy pattern of the boy with the bucket full of small stones? Would that, he wondered, meet the criteria for a moment of religion?)

What if they were all still lying, he wondered; what if Noja, who apparently was his wife Lysalis, mother of his son, the youth whom he'd killed in ignorance on the road in Tulice while moonlighting as a scavenger; what if she'd decoyed him here to be killed, because Tazencius hated him, or because he was the most evil man in the world?

Like it mattered. The truth was, he'd reached the moment of religion where the outcome is no longer important, only the state preceding it – because what we practise is the draw; the death of the man drawn against is an incidental, because the man is different every time. Only the draw can be perfect, since it's capable of infinite repetition, each time exactly the same. He'd reached just such a perfect

moment, where there was no longer anything he wanted –
not to kill or be killed, not to stay or escape; no material
things had any attraction for him, and all people were now
the same to him, friends and enemies and lovers and family.
In this moment, every individual thing and person had
blended together into a great, undistinguished flock, all
colourless (the black of a crow's wing is the absence of
colour), all sharing the same mind, face, memory. It was
the moment when all the wonderful things made by men's
hands are broken up and loaded into the furnace to be
purged by the fire into a melt. If they killed him, how could
it possibly matter? Nothing unique would die with him,
since he had no memories of his own. The scouts drop in
on the decoys and die, and the rest of the flock takes note
and goes elsewhere to feed. How sensible.

He sat up, walked to the window and drew the curtains;
light flooded the room, scattering the shadows like startled
crows. It was probably about time to leave for the dinner
party.

*I don't have anything I brought with me any more; all my
clothes are new, my boots, everything. I could be anybody at
all. But I'm not.*

At least there was one thing – the backsabre he'd made
with his own hands, the unique mark of his people, unmis-
takable anywhere. She'd given it back to him – the gods
only knew how she'd got her hands on it, but she had a
knack for finding things – and he'd hidden it away under
the bed, just in case. He knelt down and fumbled for it. Of
course, it wasn't there any more.

Not that it mattered.

'Feron Amathy isn't coming,' Poldarn overheard someone
say. 'He got held up, is the official report; but there's a
rumour going around that he's dead. Met with an accident,
so to speak.'

He looked round, but it was hard to match words to speakers in this mob: dozens of people pressed in tight together, wearing identically fashionable clothes, all with the same well-bred voices, all saying more or less the same sorts of thing. Like monks, or soldiers, or black-winged birds gathered on a battlefield to feast.

'Sure,' said another voice. 'That'll be the fifteenth time this year. Listen: you couldn't kill Feron Amathy if you threw him down a well and filled it up with snakes.'

Poldarn wouldn't have minded hearing a bit more of this conversation; but people were moving, shuffling out of the way to make room, and they'd suddenly gone quiet. Tazencius? Poldarn wondered; but it wasn't that sort of silence. More shock, disgust and then pained forbearance. It didn't take much imagination to deduce that the Amathy house had just come to dinner.

They didn't horrify him particularly. Mostly they were just working men dressed in rich men's clothes, and they'd had their hair cut and their fingernails cleaned. They didn't seem in any hurry to mingle with the home side; instead, they hung back in a mob near the huge double doors. Quite likely standard procedure for a peace conference, if that was what this was.

Noja, or Lysalis, arrived, looking older and smaller than before. She smiled thinly at him through the gap between some people, but didn't join him. Apart from her, there was nobody there he knew, and that was more a comfort than otherwise.

After what seemed like a long time, someone opened another pair of huge doors, and the flock headed through them without having to be told (like mealtimes at Haldersness). Poldarn followed them into a long, high-roofed dining hall, where someone he didn't know tapped him discreetly on the arm and led him up the side to the top table, in the middle of which stood a wonderfully lifelike ebony statue of a crow with a ring in its beak. That was odd, because he was quite certain he wasn't dreaming; maybe the crow was a scout that had pitched there earlier to see if it was safe for the rest of the flock to feed. Opposite the statue sat Tazencius, quietly dressed for an emperor; Lysalis was sitting next to him, and on his other side was the broad-shouldered snub-nosed man whom Poldarn thought of as Cleapho, though at school his name had apparently been Cordomine. The table was covered with broad silver dishes and jugs. Poldarn was led to a seat down at the end, between two of the home team, both alarming in red velvet and seed pearls. Neither of them seemed to realise he was there, which was probably a blessing.

Food started to arrive, prodigious in its delicacy, variety and quantity. On the long tables below, Poldarn watched the Amathy house men; they were hardly eating anything, and they kept their hands over their wine-cups to stop them being refilled. Up on the top table, silver dishes were as thick as volcanic ash, and the true nobility was talking very loudly with its mouth full, but not to him. That was fine. He picked off a few bits and pieces from the trays and servers as they cruised by; he had no idea what he was eating, and it didn't taste of anything much, but the colours were amazing.

'And just then,' someone was saying, 'the stable door opened and in walked the sergeant; and he looked at the young officer, and he said, "Actually, what we do is, we use the mule to ride down the mountain to the village."'

It was probably a very funny story; at any rate, everyone but him was laughing, and someone suggested that that called for a drink. Before Poldarn could copy the Amathy contingent, his cup was filled up with red wine; then someone away in the distance called for a toast, and everybody stood up, apart from Tazencius. After the toast ('His majesty') they all sat down again and started drinking in earnest, even the Amathies. He noticed Cleapho laughing, his head thrown back, his mouth wide open, like someone who'd had his throat cut from behind. But the red was spilled wine or crushed velvet, and a moment later he was sitting up straight again, listening attentively to something Tazencius was saying. Poldarn also noticed that from time to time, apparently when they thought nobody was watching, some of the Amathies stared at him and frowned before looking away.

'It's all over Tulice,' the man next to him was saying. 'They reckon they've got it stopped at the border, though; the only ships coming across are the charcoal freighters, and they're being unloaded by tender without actually putting in, *and* they're keeping the dockers segregated, just in case. I did hear they reckon it won't cross the Bay; seems that it only flourishes in warm, wet places.'

'Let's hope,' someone else replied, hidden behind his neighbour's head. 'Do they have any idea where it started?'

'Morevich,' someone else interrupted. 'By all accounts the place is practically deserted, all the survivors are drifting east into the desert or scrambling into ships and launching out into the ocean, heading west.'

'Let's hope they pitch up where the raiders come from,' someone else put in. 'Everything comes in useful sooner or later, as my old grandad used to say.'

'Now then.' Someone a little further off. 'We've all had a nice drink. How about some entertainment?'

It was a popular suggestion, something on which the home side and the Amathy contingent were apparently able to agree. Many of the men and several of the women too were cheering and stamping their feet.

Cleapho looked up at Tazencius. 'Well? How about it?'

Tazencius nodded, and made some sort of signal to someone or other in the background. After a brief interval during which nothing much happened, eight men in overstated livery brought in two large wooden frames (like window frames without glass or parchment). Inside each frame a human being was stretched like a curing hide, hands and feet pulled tight into the corners. One of them was a woman, and she looked familiar, although it was hard to make out the details of her face through the bruises and dried blood. The other was a man, in even worse shape; and on the top edge of his frame someone had written, in neat gilt letters, 'The Mad Monk.' They were both naked and dirty and thin, with raw ulcers and sores on their ribs and shins. Their heads had recently been shaved, and their eyes and mouths were red and swollen.

The men in livery manoeuvred the frames up onto a raised dais on the right-hand side of the room – they dropped the woman, which caused a great deal of mirth, particularly on the top table – and someone passed ropes over hooks in the ceiling beam. From these they hung the frames, securing them at the bottom with more ropes passed through rings set in the floor. The presence of these specialised fixtures suggested that performances of this sort, whatever it might turn out to be, were a regular event.

Once they'd finished fastening the ropes, the servants got out of the way in a great hurry; which turned out to be a sensible move on their part, because the company around the table were busily arming themselves with missiles of every sort, from soft fruit to the chunkily vulgar wine-cups. The barrage they let fly was more vigorous than accurate. Most of their projectiles banged and splatted against the wall rather than the poor devils in the frames; but such was the volume of shot that inevitably a proportion found their mark. Poldarn saw the man's head knocked sideways by a goblet, splattering the wall behind with wine or blood or both. Two of the men in the middle of the table were having a contest, to see who could be the first to land a napkin

ring on one of the woman's breasts. Other diners were
throwing spoons and knives.

It wasn't long before the table was stripped bare. The
ebony crow had been the last missile to fly; it had been
claimed by a tall thin man with a very long beard, who took
a long time over his aim and managed to catch the woman
square in the ribs with considerable force. The thin man
got a good round of applause for that.

After the last missile had been thrown there was a general round of cheering, mixed with shouts for more wine
(and more cups). When these basic needs had been provided for by the impressively efficient table-servants, one
of the men down the far end of the table called out, 'Get
on with it!' Everybody laughed and cheered, and two men
appeared from the direction from which they'd brought the
frames in. They were clearly very serious men indeed; they
were dressed in military uniforms, with gleaming black
boots and white pipeclay belts, immaculate red tunics and
breastplates that hurt the eyes, especially after a drink or
two. One of them was carrying a long stick like a broom
handle, and the other a long knife with a curved thin blade.

The man with the knife stopped, right-wheeled, threw
Tazencius a crisp salute and said, 'By your leave, sir.'

'Carry on, sergeant,' Tazencius replied. If anything, he
looked slightly bored.

The sergeant turned to the man stretched in the frame
and wiped a section of his midriff clean of fruit pulp and
wine dregs. Then he pinched a fold of skin near the solar
plexus and carefully inserted the point of the knife, working
it in with the skill and concentration of a high-class surgeon. Once he'd made his incision he pushed the knife in
an inch or so – he was taking care not to puncture any of
the internal organs – and drew down in a straight line, slit-
ting the skin like a hunter paunching a hare. He tucked the
knife into his belt without looking down, then pushed his

two forefingers into the incision and gently drew the skin apart to reveal the intestines. His skill and delicacy of touch earned him a round of applause from the diners that actually drowned out the noises the man was making; it was hard to see how the sergeant could keep his mind on his work with such a terrible racket going on, but apparently he was used to it, because he didn't seem to be taking any notice. Retrieving his knife from his belt, he hooked a strand of the stretched man's gut round his finger and snipped through it. Then he nodded his head and the other soldier handed him the stick, around which he started to wind the severed gut.

The man was, of course, still alive; and Cleapho, who'd looked away for some reason, suddenly jumped up and called out, 'Fat lot of good your faith's doing you, Earwig. Your god's right here, look, and he's just sitting there. Why don't you ask him—?'

The man turned his head – following the sound of the voice, his eyes were both useless. 'Don't be silly, Cordo,' he said in a weak, pleasant voice, 'he's not that sort of god. You of all people should know that.' Then his face contorted into a shape Poldarn had never seen before, and his chin dropped on his chest. The sergeant had pulled out his heart. He put it down on the nearest table, shaking his fingers to flick off the blood. Cleapho sat down again; his face was white and drawn, his eyes were very wide. He reached for his wine-cup but knocked it over.

The sergeant was standing in front of the woman, his knife in his right hand, his left fingers delicately probing for the right place, like a tentative lover. Copis, Poldarn thought. He knew without having to look that Lysalis's eyes were fixed on him, waiting to see what he was going to do; Tazencius too, inevitably. Even if I wanted to save her, I couldn't, he lied to himself – he knew it was a lie, because a servant, quiet and unobtrusive as light seeping through a crack, had just put something down on the table in front of him, and it wasn't a bowl of soup or a warm flannel – it was a sword, one sword in particular, the only one he could remember having made for himself.

Nicely done, he realised. Lysalis knew that he knew that if he wanted to (Deymeson-trained, top of his year at swordfighting), with a backsabre in his hands he *could* rescue Copis, in spite of the guards and the Amathy house officers; he could carve a way out if he favoured the direct approach, or he could grab Lysalis or maybe even Tazencius himself as a hostage— There were only maybe a dozen people in the Empire who could realistically expect to manage such a feat of arms (a few moments ago there had been thirteen, but one of them had since died) but it was possible. Under other circumstances, it would constitute a justifiable risk. Therefore, since it was possible, everything turned on whether he wanted to do it or not; and he had a fraction of a second, a heartbeat, in which to make his decision – he'd choose on instinct alone, and therefore his choice would be irreproachably honest. She'd have a true answer to her question, after all.

Copis. The sergeant found his place and pinched a little flap of skin.

What the hell, Poldarn thought, and vaulted over the table, scattering silverware and fruit with his heels. He didn't want to kill the sergeant but there was no time not to. The poor fool hit the floor with his head hanging by a thin strap of sinew, by which time two guards were crowding Poldarn's circle and three more men were treading on their heels. Curiously enough, as he executed the manoeuvre (three enemies, north, east and west; back and sideways with the right foot as you draw, cutting East across the face; swivel round for an overhead cut to West's neck; as you do so, begin the forward step into North's circle, an overhead downward cut splitting his skull; the

impetus will bring you round naturally to finish East in
the usual way) he could hear a dry, thin voice in his mind
calling him through each stage – Father Tutor, presumably,
though the voice didn't sound familiar. The other guard,
and the fool of a nobleman who tried to stab him in the
back with a carving knife, were as straightforward as splitting logs; getting Copis out of the frame, on the other hand,
was a bitch.

'You idiot,' she hissed at him. She wasn't pleased. He
must've got it wrong again; but how was he expected to get
things right if nobody told him—?

'It's all right.' Tazencius's voice, loud and slightly
annoyed; maybe Lysalis hadn't thought to mention her
cunning scheme beforehand. 'Leave him alone, for crying
out loud. Get a chair for the woman, somebody, and a
blanket or something.'

No blankets at a royal banquet; so they pulled the cloth
off one of the tables. It had wine stains and streaks of gravy
on it, but nobody seemed to mind.

'So now we know,' Lysalis said. 'Oh well. For some
reason I honestly thought—'

Poldarn wasn't interested; he was looking round at the
faces staring at him, trying to feel where the next attack
was going to come from. But it didn't. The worst he'd committed, to judge by the expression on their faces, was a
rather unseemly breach of etiquette, the sort of thing they
expected from the likes of him but were prepared to over-
look, in the circumstances.

Yes, but what circumstances?

'Screw you, Ciartan.' Cleapho was looking daggers at
him from his seat at Tazencius's side. 'You're doubly
pathetic: once for saving her, once for letting him die. I
don't know why people ever bothered with you.'

Perhaps Cleapho couldn't see the two soldiers who'd
materialised directly behind him; or maybe he knew they'd

be there, so didn't need to turn round and look. He sounded like someone who'd just lost a game to an opponent he knew had been cheating; you'd won, but it didn't count.

'I'm sorry,' Poldarn heard himself reply, 'I haven't got the faintest idea what you're talking about.'

While he was saying that, he could already see what was going to happen next; he could hear that voice again, talking Cleapho (Cordo, his real name) through the sequence. Kick back with both feet as you stand up, so that the back of the chair impedes the man behind you; grab the other man's right hand with your left as you draw his sword with your right and draw its blade across his throat backhanded. Kill the first man, freestyle, in such a way as to get a good position for killing the man sitting on your right. Precepts of religion: you should be thinking about the death after the death after next. But Poldarn saw, as the chair legs scritched on the marble floor, that Cordo wasn't going to do as he'd been told and kill Tazencius. At the moment when Cleapho wrapped his fingers around the sword hilt, Poldarn felt the intrusion into his circle, and turned to face it. The year-end test, he thought, and here's everybody watching.

Here goes nothing.

Nobody tried to stop Cleapho as he strode forward, kicking the table over and stepping across it like a fastidious man in a farmyard. Probably it was because nobody wanted to die just then; but Poldarn could also sense the excitement, enthusiastic sword-fight fans anticipating a unique impromptu fixture. He could see their point: it wasn't every day you got to watch the two best swordsmen in the Empire fighting a grudge match. Even if you weren't a devotee of the art you'd feel bound to watch and pay attention, just so that you could tell your grandchildren about it.

In the event, it was all over and done with before it even started; Poldarn saw, clear as day, the stroke that killed his old school chum, before Cordo even reached his circle

– there was all the time in the world, no time whatsoever. As the cutting edge caught in Cordo's neck and Poldarn felt it pull against his sword arm's aching tendons, his mind was already on other things: now what do I do, when I've just butchered the Chaplain in Ordinary in front of the cream of Torcean society? He remembered to pull back his right foot so Cordo's head wouldn't land on it as he hit the floor. He could feel the frustration among his audience; it'd all been so quick that they'd missed it. If the circumstances had been just a little bit less grand, they'd probably have thrown nuts at him.

He caught Tazencius's eye, saw *Two birds with one stone.* He nodded back very slightly: *Glad to have been of service.* But Tazencius's satisfaction at the death of his inconvenient, over-mighty chaplain was a small side-benefit, not the main issue. That, the Emperor's face told him, was still to be decided. Pity, Poldarn thought, because I've had about enough of this. He stayed where he was: any more for any more, or could he relax his guard a little?

Behind him, someone was muffling a sob. He made the time to glance round: Copis, huddled in her chair with her tablecloth around her, was crying because now there were only three of them left. (And where *was* Gain Aciava? Or did his absence mean that the class of '56 was now down to two?) Poldarn decided that it was just as well he didn't have the memories that were presently filling Copis's mind, quite possibly hers alone now. It must be terrible to be the only one left, he thought, the last crow of the flock, the one suddenly forced to stand for the whole.

'Fine,' Tazencius said suddenly. 'Ciartan, will you please put that horrible thing away? You have my word, nobody's going to bother you now.'

I have your word, do I? Lucky, lucky me. Poldarn righted an overturned chair, pulled it out into the open where he could see most of the room, and sat down, the backsabre across his knees. (It was wet and sticky, but his absurd red velvet trousers didn't show the marks. Functional, after all.)

'Right, then,' Tazencius was saying. 'One last bit of carnage, and then will someone clean up this mess?'

Someone who'd been standing at the back, leaning against the wall since the first course was served, now took five steps forward. He was holding a wide silver tray, on which rested a black cloth bag about the size of a large cabbage. It held a man's head, which the servant held up by the hair. Poldarn had no idea who it was supposed to be, but there was a general mumble of satisfaction from the dinner guests; particularly from the Amathy house contingent.

Tazencius cracked a thin smile. 'Gentlemen,' he said, 'Feron Amathy is dead.' Someone handed him a goblet; he took it without looking round. 'A toast, then,' he went on, suddenly looking straight at Poldarn, 'to our good friend Feron Amathy.'

Poldarn felt an urge to look round, in case there was someone behind him he hadn't seen. But he knew there wasn't. Instead, he stared at Tazencius—

'You, you idiot,' Tazencius explained.

Chapter Nineteen

'Me?' Poldarn said.

Tazencius smiled. 'You,' he said.

Mostly silence; the only sound was Copis's muted sobbing somewhere behind him. Everybody else in the room was either dumbstruck with horror or frozen with embarrassment. Welcome home, he thought.

'You don't look pleased,' Tazencius went on, grinning affably. 'I was sure you'd want your old job back. I was trying to be nice.'

Poldarn doubted that. On the other hand he still had the backsabre, and if he made up his mind to a straightforward, businesslike exchange of lives, he had no doubt at all that he could carve Tazencius from ear to collarbone before anybody could stop him. He was surprised at how little he wanted to do that, all things considered.

'I don't understand,' he said.

Gentle murmuring from the Amathy house contingent, who clearly weren't impressed. Tazencius raised his voice over the sound and went on, 'Years ago the Amathy house realised that its most valuable asset was the prestige – not the right choice of words but you know what I mean – of the name Feron Amathy. For as long as I personally can remember it's been a byword for efficiency, ruthlessness and duplicity. So, when the original Feron Amathy died, they didn't let on; their new leader took the name, made out that the rumours of his death were just wishful thinking, and carried on as before. Easily done, since very few people outside the House had ever seen the great man, and for most of those who did he was the last thing they ever saw. Then, when I was looking round for a suitable wedding present for my future son-in-law and decided to give you power equal to that of the Emperor himself, the replacement was duly replaced by you, and the name came with the job. And,' he went on, 'when everybody was sure that you were dead and I needed to find a substitute to fill your place, he became Feron Amathy in turn. Then the House found out that you were still alive, changed its mind and wanted you back. He's dead,' a curt nod towards the thing lying on its side on the silver tray, 'which serves him right for annoying the rank and file; as I understand it, he had delusions of authenticity, actually started believing he was the commander of an army, not the chief executive of a bunch of thieves.' The Amathy house contingent didn't react to that. 'He was fighting a war, he thought: devising strategies, sending expendable units to die for the sake of the grand design. That's not how the House functions: they kill people, they don't get killed themselves. So they decided he had to go, and now—' He pointed at the object on the tray with his little finger. 'You, on the other hand, were perfect for the House; they only allowed me to replace you because I insisted – it was a condition of the contract. They gave me you, and I gave them Josequin, and a licence to plunder every city in the Bohec valley. A bargain, from my point of view; I got the whole Empire in exchange for a few of its cities.' He frowned. 'Unfortunately, it all went wrong without you, and now we have to clean up the mess.'

Poldarn lifted his head and tried to say something. Fortunately, his input wasn't required, since he appeared to have run out of words.

'You'd like me to begin at the beginning,' Tazencius said. 'Very well.'

He leaned back in his chair. Someone took the silver tray away, out of his sight. Someone else brought him a fresh drink. 'Many years ago,' he said, 'when I was young and foolish, a dimwitted cousin of mine fell out with a promising young army officer by the name of Cronan Suilven. My cousin was a coward; he didn't feel up to attacking the soldier directly, so he persuaded me to pick a fight with him, over some trivial matter. I did as he wanted; the duel was a fiasco, I was humiliated, finished at Court. I was determined to make Cronan pay, but by the time I was in any fit state to take him on, he'd been promoted to commander-in-chief; if I was going to destroy him, I'd have to become Emperor first. So that's what I resolved to do.' He paused and sipped his wine, taking a moment to savour it. Theatre, Poldarn thought contemptuously. 'I knew that in order to get rid of Cronan I'd have to create a threat to the Empire, something so terrifying that anybody who managed to get rid of it would be able to have anything he wanted; also, anybody who tried and failed would be broken, ruined, disgraced. It was about that time that your horrible relations began making serious trouble in the coastal districts; but of course nobody knew who they were or where they came from, nobody knew their language or how to communicate with them. I needed them, of course, as my threat. I needed them to extend their operations from mere seaside vandalism to full-scale acts of war: burning down cities, butchering whole populations. Fortune smiled on me; I found you.'

Poldarn glanced round the room. None of this seemed

to have come as a surprise, either to the Amathy contingent or to the domestic nobility.

'You were my link with the savages,' Tazencius went on. 'I had you trained at Deymeson, and gave you my daughter, to secure you; you were, after all, my key component, the most important single piece in the mechanism. You had to be *perfect*, and you had to be completely, indubitably mine. That's why I gave you everything I ever really cared about – apart from destroying Cronan, of course. I gave you my daughter. All can say is, I've been punished appropriately ever since.'

Lysalis looked up at her father, her face blank, just for a moment. Then she went back to staring at Copis, who wasn't listening at all.

'But that wasn't all I gave you,' Tazencius went on. 'As well as the savages, I needed a strike force, something closer to home and easier to control. I never controlled the savages, you see; all I could do, through you, was make it possible for them to attack deep inland, come and go unharmed and with their terrifying anonymity undamaged. You've seen them, Ciartan, you know what they're like. Ferocious, certainly, and they have this bizarre ability to share each others' thoughts; but they aren't actually superhuman. If they started making raids deep into the Empire, it was only a matter of time before Cronan caught up with them and cut them to ribbons, and then I'd lose everything. But I *needed* them to be superhuman, invulnerable, unbeatable; so I made sure that Cronan and the government troops never got near them, or else I arranged for them to fall into perfectly planned ambushes, so that the savages could wipe them out to the last man.

'So much effort, you see; and there was always the risk that something would go wrong, someone in the government I'd bought would let me down or betray me. I needed a second weapon: one that I could control directly, one that could be trusted on its own without my having to think of every little thing. So I bought the Amathy house, and had you installed as heir presumptive to its leader. Then I got rid of him, and you became Feron Amathy.

'For a while, everything went very well. On my behalf, you led the House on a series of raids, burning and butchering, leaving no survivors, all the blame being laid on the savages. At the same time, you were coordinating operations with the savages – I thought I was being so wonderfully economical, using you for both functions; since I had to trust someone besides myself (which I hated doing, for obvious reasons), at least I only had to trust one man, and I'd done everything humanly possible to make you secure. I trusted you. That was—' He frowned. 'A pity.'

Poldarn nodded slowly. 'What happened?' he said.

'You betrayed me,' Tazencius replied. 'Unfortunately, I'd overlooked a detail or two. I'd underestimated the Deymeson Order, and its self-appointed mission as guardian of the Empire. But one of the Order's senior officers – your former tutor, indeed – worked out what I was up to and resolved to stop me. It was while you were still at school, which only goes to show how perceptive your old tutor was, and how patient, too. It was fortunate for him that you were part of a small clique of friends – almost unheard of at Deymeson, where friendship is understandably fraught with problems – who'd formed one of those unshakeable adolescent bonds of loyalty that tend to last for life. He recruited two of your clique; their devotion to the Order was the only thing that was more important to them, you see. One of them was this woman here, Xipho Dorunoxy. You were in love with her, and would be, for life. The other – wonderful serendipity – was the boy whom everybody else in your gang was sure you'd callously murdered when a prank went wrong: Cordomine. Understandably, he now hated you almost as much as he loved the Order. Your tutor forged him, so to speak, into a weapon to use against me; he was to become the Chaplain in Ordinary, in effective control of the civil administration, just as my other enemy, Cronan, was in charge of the military. Meanwhile, as you were going about my business in an admirably efficient way, Cordomine wrote to you.

'He wasn't dead, he told you, and he was prepared to forgive you for what you'd tried to do when you'd stabbed him in the library. All he asked in return was that you should betray me, wreck my plans, and deliver me into the hands of my enemies.

'You were delighted to oblige, since you were being eaten alive by guilt for what you thought you'd done – and also by the knowledge that you could never have Xipho Dorunoxy because you'd murdered her friend; but if he came back to life and forgave you – well, who knows?'

Poldarn looked round at Copis. She lifted her head and looked back at him. It was like staring down a well.

'Cordomine arranged for you to send the savages – your flesh and blood – into an ambush. Cronan would slaughter them like sheep, and the survivors would confess and incriminate me as the most unspeakable traitor in history. You would also lead the Amathy house into a similar trap, and they'd be wiped out too.'

Tazencius paused, and grinned. 'Betrayal comes easily to you, Ciartan; I'd never fully appreciated how easily. I sincerely believed that once you were mine, you'd be mine for ever. I think that was the worst mistake I ever made; because look at you, my dear boy. I know you can't answer this because you can't remember; but is there anybody in the world you haven't betrayed at some point in your distinguished career? Your dearest friends: when Elaos Tanwar found out that you were passing military secrets to the savages, you killed him. When you were faced with disgrace and expulsion because of your foolish escapade in the library, you stabbed your friend Cordomine. Your own people: you'd have sent them to be wiped out by Cronan. Likewise the Amathy house, who'd followed you with absolute loyalty, done everything you'd asked of them. Me – after I'd given you everything. You've never made a promise you didn't break, been loved by anybody you haven't hurt or been the death of. There are clear definitions of evil; I suppose I meet most of the criteria, in that I've caused the deaths of tens, hundreds of thousands of innocent strangers in furtherance of my ambition and my hatred for Cronan Suilven. I chose my path and followed it single-mindedly, loyally, without any illusions about myself. That, I believe, is why you're worse than me, more dangerous, capable of doing more damage. Because, you see, you hardly fit the criteria of evil as established in dictionaries and textbooks. You sided with me because the Empire was your people's ancient enemy – you were sent here in the first place to spy on them, help your people to punish them, and steal the precious materials your people so desperately need, marooned on an island with no metal and precious little timber. You did your duty cheerfully; and when it became apparent that my interests coincided perfectly with theirs, you joined me. Soldiers do worse things in a war; you were a spy, and spies cause the deaths of thousands. It doesn't matter, because the thousands are the enemy. But then, because of one terrible error of judgement, in the Deymeson library, when you were trying to do the best for your friends whom you'd led into disaster, you were chained by guilt to one man, Cordomine. Guilt never bothers *me*, we evil men are immune to it. Guilt made *you* abandon your people, your followers, your wife, me, without a moment's hesitation.' He smiled, wide and bleak. 'If you'd been an evil man like me, Ciartan, thousands of people who died in pain and fear would still be alive. But you're worse than I am, because you're part evil and part good – as most people are, I suppose. Still, in their cases, it doesn't matter.'

Tazencius shrugged; so much for all that.

'Anyway,' he went on, 'you made the usual arrangements with the savages for the coming season; and then you reported back to Cordomine. The idea was, as I've told you, that you would send them strolling blithely into an ambush. But by this stage, I'd found out, from spies of my own in the Amathy house, that you'd turned traitor on me. I gave orders for my agent in the House to kill you – his reward was to be Feron Amathy in your stead – but he failed. You escaped and turned to Cordomine for protection. He was in an awkward position. Needless to say, he hadn't dared to let Cronan in on the secret; Cronan was far too straightforward to play the game out quietly, he'd have told the Emperor all about me and the Amathy house being in league with the savages, and I'd have been forced to mobilise both of my allies against the government in a straightforward civil war – and together, the House and the savages would probably have won, but not conclusively; we'd have seized the Bohec valley, perhaps, and I'd have set myself up as a rival Emperor, hated as a despicable traitor in the city, and everything would have descended into a chaotic mess. So although Cordomine needed you to deliver the savages and the House into Cronan's hands for execution, he couldn't save you openly from your outraged followers in the House. The best he could do was smuggle you to safety, using the resources of the Order; he sent his bodyguards to escort you from Josequin to Torcea, and Father Tutor sent his best agent, Xipho Dorunoxy, just in case something went wrong.

'Something did go wrong: the House's trackers, who'd been following you, caught up with you and your escort beside the river. There was a fight; the trackers and the escort wiped each other out, you were knocked over the head and lost your memory. Xipho Dorunoxy found you and sent a message to Deymeson for instructions. That was the moment when everything began to fall apart.'

Tazencius stopped talking and took a long drink. Poldarn took the opportunity to study distances and angles, make estimates of time.

'The consequence were as follows,' Tazencius went on. 'You failed to turn up at your rendezvous with the savages, to give them the information they needed to carry out the plans you'd previously outlined for them. They knew they had to attack certain places – Deymeson was one of them, I'd decided to get rid of the Order once and for all – but they didn't even know where these places were, let alone the safe and inconspicuous ways of getting there and getting safely back. They decided to set out anyway, hoping to find you, or that you'd catch up with them along the way. Your people are amazingly stupid, Ciartan.

'The new leader of the Amathy house, meanwhile, had bought acceptance as your replacement by promising them a major prize, namely Josequin. They collected their payment, but the savages didn't show up to give them the support they'd expected. Things weren't right, and they were terrified of being found out. They withdrew in confusion and therefore weren't on hand when I needed them, later.

'Then things got worse, rapidly. Your old tutor changed his mind about what had to be done. I think it was some horrible coincidence, some prophecy accidentally fulfilled; he always was a mystic at heart, with far more faith than is good for a priest. In any event, he was suddenly convinced that you were none other than the God in the Cart, harbinger of the end of the world – I think it was the fact that you'd lost your memory, but I'm just speculating – and that it would be sacrilege to impede your disastrous progress in any way. He sent word to his most faithful servant, Xipho Dorunoxy (who by this time had retrieved you from where you'd got lost), and told her that her duty was henceforth to act as your priestess and acolyte, in accordance with the scriptures that foretell Poldarn's second coming. She coped splendidly, I suppose. She knew that the whole point about the God in the Cart is that He doesn't know who He is; by sheer fluke, she'd been using the cover of the fraudulent god as she followed you around. When you accidentally killed the false Poldarn, she made you take his place – the true god pretending to be Himself in order to cheat rustics out of loose change; no wonder the delicious irony of the whole thing was enough to unhinge your erstwhile tutor's brain. Cordomine had him killed as soon as he could, of course; but not before the old priest had sent his other faithful servant, another classmate of yours whose name escapes me, first to confirm that you really were the god (which apparently he did, to Father Tutor's satisfaction) and then to wreck Cordomine's plans for saving the Empire from you and me by murdering General Cronan.

'He failed, of course, but by then everything had come loose, so to speak. Cordomine found you, purely by chance, at an inn in Sansory, but *he* didn't know that you'd lost your memory; he merely thought you were playing some new game, and before he could find out the truth or take effective action, the Amathy house caught up with you. Cordomine's guards stopped them from catching you and you escaped. In the meantime, the savages were blundering wildly through the countryside. For my part, I had no choice but to use the few resources I had to make an overt bid for the throne. I thought I could rely on the Amathy house. I was wrong. A few government soldiers joined me, but very few; I lost a battle, was captured and sent to Torcea to explain myself and be executed. Quite brilliantly, I managed to elude my guards, steal a horse and escape. But, just when I thought that for once luck was on my side, my horse was startled by a rocketing pheasant in the woods; I was thrown and broke my leg. And who should find me but you.' Tazencius shook his head sadly, as if trying to express his disappointment with Fortune, from whom he'd expected better. 'It was a pretty charade we all played out that night. The members of my escort were under orders to make it seem as though I was a noble prince returning home on state business: the government believed I enjoyed far more support than I actually had, and thought that if I was seen being dragged away in chains, loyal peasants would abandon the plough and the hoe and rescue me. I was desperate not to let my guards find out that I was on speaking terms with the notorious Feron Amathy (they didn't even recognise you in the event, but by then it was too late), and of course I didn't know that you'd lost your memory and didn't have the faintest idea who I was. Finally I managed to escape, though I had to cut your colleague's throat first, and the guards came after me, though I shook them off quite easily. After enormous hardship and suffering I reached the Amathy house camp; and your replacement immediately sent me to General Cronan, as a peace offering.

'Things looked bad for me. True, the savages destroyed Deymeson. But then Cronan caught up with them and cut them to pieces, and I thought I was done for. It was sheer good luck that he blundered into them after the battle, and that they killed him and (thanks to you) allowed me to escape. I suppose I should be grateful to you for that, but I'm not. If it wasn't for Lysalis here, I'd have you hung up in one of those frames and smash every bone in your body with my bare hands. Instead,' and he took a deep breath, 'I'm obliged to forgive you, as your former colleagues in the House have done. We are prepared to trust you, simply because you have nowhere else to go, nobody left to betray us to; and because we still need you, God help us all.'

Poldarn looked at him. 'Why?' he said.

Tazencius sighed, as though he was dealing with a particularly stupid child. 'The savages,' he replied. 'They've been shown the way to the dairy, so to speak. We need to make sure the attacks will cease, for ever, which presumably means buying them off; and, tragically, you're still the only man in the Empire capable of talking to the horrible creatures. It changes one's perspective somewhat,' he continued mildly, 'actually getting one's heart's desire. True, I only wanted the Empire so that I could punish Cronan Suilven; after his death, I needed it because it was the only hope I had of staying alive. But now, here I am; all that blood and burning and *waste* was to get me here. In return, I suppose I have some sort of moral obligation to be a good Emperor, to protect the best interests of the people. One thing I can do is make sure the savages don't come back; also, I can pay off the Amathy house. Creating all the problems makes it easier to solve them. And you,' he added, with resigned distaste. 'You as well. Since I can't kill you, I shall have to pay you off too.'

Poldarn managed to raise a smile. 'How do you plan to do that?' he asked.

Tazencius shrugged. 'Tell me what you want, it's yours.' He waited for a reply. 'There must be something you want,' he added. 'Everybody wants something.'

But Poldarn shook his head. 'Not really,' he replied. 'This man you've been telling me about, this man I was supposed to have been once, I'm sure there must've been something he wanted. You've all been telling me I was in love with Copis – with her,' he amended, not looking round. 'I'll have to take your word for it. Your daughter reckons I may have been in love with *her* – as well as or instead of. You also said that I wanted to be forgiven by that man I just killed. For a while I kidded myself into thinking that what I wanted was a quiet life in a place where nobody knew me, because whatever I might've done in the past, as long as I'm alive and breathing I can change, turn into somebody I could bear to live with. And there was another part of me that reckoned what I really wanted was the truth.' He shook his head. 'I don't think so,' he said. 'There's nothing I want, but my instincts won't let me roll over and die, I'm too well trained for that. I can't go back home, I screwed up too badly for that. I can't go away, and I can't stay here. And I've come to the end of the road now: I've got to do something about *me*, before I make things worse still.' He felt an urge to stand up, but he fought it. 'You don't need to worry about my people,' he added. 'I don't think they'll be back in a hurry. In any case, there's not much I can do about them – they won't listen to me any more.'

Tazencius looked at him. 'Very nicely put,' he said, 'but what do you *want*?'

Poldarn grinned. 'I'd like to go now, please.'

Long, awkward silence; then Tazencius said, 'Fine. Can't say I'll be sorry to see the back of you. Do you want to take that woman with you?' He made a vague gesture in Copis's direction. Poldarn shook his head. 'No, thank you,' he said. 'I suppose I ought to care what becomes of her, but I don't really.' He hesitated, frowned. 'I'll tell you what, though,' he said. 'If you want an intermediary between my people and yours, you could send her and—' He paused, trying to shape the words, like an engineer struggling to work from a vague verbal specification of something he'd never seen and couldn't understand. 'Her and our son,' he said. 'Send them home to my country. The boy's the rightful heir to Haldersness – you don't know where that is, but it doesn't matter, my people will know. You want to know what I want? That's it. The boy's still young enough to be raised as one of them. The thought of the poor little bastard growing up here makes me feel sick. Will you do that for me?'

Tazencius smiled. 'Actually, I will,' he said. 'I have scholars who know your language, I'll find a way. After all, I did it before, when I restored you to your doting grand-father. Is he still alive?'

Poldarn shook his head. 'I haven't got a clue who's in charge there now,' he said. 'But send them to Asburn the smith, in the Haldersness region. He'll see them right.' He frowned, as if making sure that there wasn't anything he'd forgotten; then he realised what he was doing, and smiled at the irony. 'That's all,' he said. Then he turned his head a little. 'Sorry,' he said, to Noja or whatever her name was. 'One thing I can guarantee, you'll be better off without me.'

'I know,' she said. 'But that's no consolation.'

He turned away from her – easily, as if from a stranger – and scanned the Amathy house people for someone who looked like a leader. But they all looked the same, like crows in a flock. 'Sorry,' he repeated. 'You'll have to find someone else. You couldn't have trusted me, in any case. Believe me; I've known myself for over three years now, and I wouldn't trust me further than I can spit.'

Nobody said anything. He got the impression that they were glad he was leaving, though on balance they'd have preferred it if he'd been lying on the floor with his neck cut through. But they were pragmatists – they knew they couldn't always have everything they wanted. One of them did call out, 'Where will you go?' but Poldarn didn't answer. Only because he didn't know. He picked up the backsabre, backflipped it absent-mindedly a couple of times, and walked towards the door. All the way there, across a desert of black and white marble tiles, he waited for the pressure on the perimeter of his circle. But it didn't come. No more guards wanted to die, nobody hated him enough to risk the moment of religion as the curved blade swung. It's a special kind of hate, he told himself, when they don't mind letting you live just so long as you go away for ever, so they can pretend you never existed; so they can cut you out of memory, like a child making dolls from folded paper.

When he got tired of walking the streets (the ludicrous luxury shoes rubbed his toes until he pulled them off and threw them away, leaving him a clown in red velvet and cloth of gold, barefoot on the sharp cobbles) he flopped down under the eaves of a shuttered workshop. Above his head he could see a thin plate sign swinging wearily, a black shadow of an anvil against the dark blue sky; his instincts had led him to a smithy, as befitted a hereditary Master of Haldersness. He laughed and stretched out his sore feet, wishing the smith was there so he could beg leave to soak his poor toes in the black, oily water of the slack tub. He closed his eyes, daydreaming about the morning: the smith finding him there asleep, taking pity; casual conversation between strangers, a chance remark – I used to be a bit of a smith myself back home – leading to an offer of work, at least until after the fair, when the rush dies down; work, a livelihood, a home. He was, after all, a skilled man. Give him a good fire, an anvil and a hammer and there wasn't anything he couldn't make.

Eyes tight shut, he smiled; and in his daydream the fire burst up through the hearth, melting the tue-iron into glowing red slag that gushed onto the floor and filled the city, while the sky clogged with fluttering cinders of black ash, wheeling and screaming to each other as they searched for a place to pitch, a beanfield or a battlefield, somewhere beside a river where the God of Fire and Death was waiting for them, feeder and murderer of crows. He saw himself at the anvil, holding his own shadow down in the fire until it stopped shrieking and struggling, until it glowed cherry red, freed from its memories and ready for the hammer; he saw himself draw it down, jump it up and upset it, flatten and fuller and swage it into shape and then plunge it into the water, a little pool fringed with ferns under a waterfall; he looked down, and saw gripped in the tongs his own reflection, a face melted and cast into a blank; and the blank's mouth opened and said, 'My name is Feron Amathy, among others,' before he let go with the tongs and allowed it to sink.

But the morning came, the sun came up cherry red out of the Bay (which was wrong, since the sea should have quenched it) and the smith arrived for work and told him to get lost before he had the dogs set on him. He doubted very much whether the smith had a dog, but one thing he had learned was when he wasn't welcome.

Instead he wandered down towards the docks; and on the way he saw something lying in the street, a bundle of rags and a distinctive broad-brimmed leather hat, and next to it a squashed wicker cage. Two crows were floating overhead. They circled a couple of times, turned in to the slight breeze to slow themselves down, opened their wings and glided in to pitch. He came up close; the crows lifted their heads and looked at him, as though they recognised him in spite of his ludicrously long body and lack of wings; then they hauled themselves sadly into the air and flapped away, like tired men sailing home.

The old woman was still alive, though not by much. 'Hello,' she said, trying to smile; but he guessed her face was nearly cold by now, as the metal grows cold and becomes too brittle to be worked.

'What happened?' he asked, kneeling beside her.

'It was all my own silly fault,' she said. 'I was crossing the road and I didn't look, and a cart ran me over. It doesn't hurt much, though.'

For some reason he couldn't begin to understand, he could feel tears on his cheeks; the first time he could remember the sensation since his newly grown skin had become so sensitive. 'Your cage,' he said. 'It's broken.'

'Oh, it's all right,' she said cheerfully, 'it's quite all right. I let them go, you see, as soon as you very kindly got me out of that dreadful prison. And now they're here, and everything's going to be all right.'

Poldarn found it hard to breathe. 'Well,' he said, 'I'm glad to hear it.'

'It's such a relief,' the old woman said. 'I was so worried about them, all the way here from Morevich, such a terrible journey.' With a ferocious effort, like a man drawing an over-heavy bow, she managed to complete the smile. 'I expect you think I'm just a silly old woman, but I won't forget how kind you've been to me. If it wasn't for you, you know, I'd never have made it here, and everything would have been for nothing. But now everything's been put to rights, and that's all that matters.'

He winced; the pain of not being able to do anything— But she reached out her hand and touched his arm, comforting him. 'I'd like you to know about it,' she said. 'It doesn't matter, of course, because nobody will *remember*, but I'd like you to know, because *you*'ll understand. It was my son, you see. My poor boy, Elaos. They took him away to be a priest, and then they killed him. Well, that was never right, no matter what they said. So I knew, they had to be punished, and things had to be put right.'

He wanted to say something; he knew there was something to be said, but he'd forgotten what it was. She went on; 'Of course, the plague isn't nearly as common nowadays as it was when I was a youngster, they've done wonders about keeping it under control down in Morevich, because of course they understand about it there. But up here—' She giggled, like a little girl. 'Up here, they've got no idea, it's been so long since there was a serious outbreak. We know, of course; we've known for hundreds of years – it's the rats that spread it, and once it takes hold it's like lighting a fire in a hayrick: the wind carries it, and birds, and everything. So all I had to do was find them, my darlings, and bring them here, and Poldarn would do the rest.' She sighed. 'Not many people still believe in him, even in Morevich, but that doesn't matter, does it? We know he's real, you and I. Anyway, thanks to you I got them here and set them free, and it'll only be a matter of weeks – apparently it's already started in Tulice, where you very kindly helped me all those times. They do say there's not a soul left alive between Falcata and the sea, thanks to my little loves, and you. It'll all be put right, you see, there's no way of stopping it now. It's such a—'

She ran out of words and breath, and he stood up. He thought of Tazencius, an honest man in his way, dutifully sending Poldarn's priestess and Poldarn's son along with Poldarn's special salvation across the sea to Haldersness, where they would most certainly put everything right there too. Then he looked up and watched the two crows, still circling, waiting for him to go away.